Mar
Marcellas, Diana.
The sea lark's song

$ 27.95

1st ed.

The
Sea
Lark's
Song

Tor Books by Diana Marcellas

Mother Ocean, Daughter Sea
The Sea Lark's Song
Twilight Rising*

*forthcoming

The Sea Lark's Song

DIANA MARCELLAS

TOR®

A TOM DOHERTY ASSOCIATES BOOK
NEW YORK

THE SEA LARK'S SONG

Copyright © 2002 by Diana Marcellas

Edited by Claire Eddy

Map by Ellisa Mitchell

A Tor Book
Published by Tom Doherty Associates, LLC
175 Fifth Avenue
New York, NY 10010

www.tor.com

Tor® is a registered trademark of Tom Doherty Associates, LLC.

ISBN 0-312-87483-9

First Edition: December 2002

Printed in the United States of America

0 9 8 7 6 5 4 3 2 1

To my parents, with my love

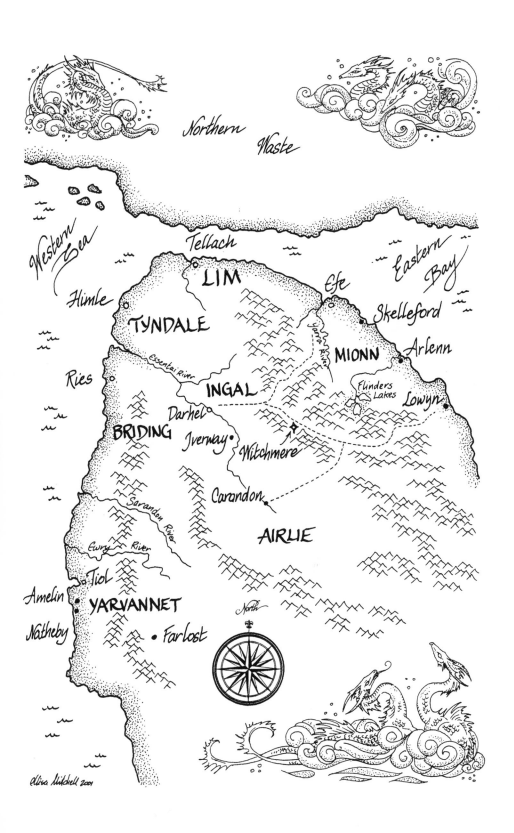

Northern Waste

Western Sea

Eastern Bay

Tellach

LIM

Efe

Skelleford

Himle

TYNDALE

Arlenn

MIONN

Ries

Essentai River

INGAL

Flinders Lakes

Lowyn

Darhel

BRIDING

Iverway

Witchmere

Saranden River

Carandon

Ewry River

AIRLIE

Tiol

Amelin

YARVANNET

Natheby

Farlost

North

Elisa Mitchell 2001

The

Sea

Lark's

Song

s the Daystar set and dusk settled over the land, the Companion, the world's second sun, ruled the short twilight of the cool winter evening, edging every grass blade and tree leaf with a shimmering blue light. Countess Rowena Hamelin rode through a sea of blue shadows and silver, dusky blue under the occasional forest canopy that shadowed the road, brilliant silver in the open meadowlands. For the day's travel, she had dressed warmly in a long woolen riding habit, with a skirt that swept half to the ground, warm underbreeches and tunic, stout riding boots, and a furred cloak with a hood that kept the chill off her ears. The tang of the cold air chilled her face deliciously, and she could smell snow in the air. Beside the road they traveled, the broad Essentai River sparkled in the muted light.

Her heart lifted at the familiar sights of her beloved Airlie, the county that marriage to Ralf had given her and which, over the years, had steadily supplanted in her heart the Tyndale and Yarvannet of her youth. This land she now guarded for her ten-year-old son, for the time when Axel became count in his own right. This land she guarded in all its beauties and its folk, as the counts of Airlie had always guarded their meadowlands. A mere woman, certain High Lords would sniff—a mere woman as regent? Nonsense! But Rowena had defied them all, and dared any to diminish her Airlie in any manner, with any threat.

Two days before, she had resumed her journey home from the duke's capital of Darhel to her own Airlie capital, Carandon, with a small company of her marshal, two lady-maids, and a dozen soldiers. The first day they had advanced a good twenty miles, then had quartered in a village by the river, her folk coming out to meet her and apologizing for the simple lodging they could offer, which was all they had. She had spent a pleasant evening at the headman's house, with her folk craning through windows to watch her as she took the children into her lap and talked to her village folk, at ease with them. As Airlie's regent, Rowena must flatter her Airlie lords to keep their sure loyalty, but among her commoner folk, who had chosen to adore her since she first arrived in Airlie as Ralf's young girl-bride, she had no such purposes. And so she had smiled at them as they shyly told her their news of simple things, fish and grain, a fine foal to drop in the spring. She teased them until they dared to joke with her, and then ate a hearty meal and matched glass for glass of wine with the headman, and so paid with a solid headache the following morning. The village folk had gathered in the road as she left, waving after her, and Rowena had waved back. My Airlie, she had thought happily. My heart and spirit, all in you.

She breathed in the crisp cold air, remembering, and watched a few isolated snowflakes twist down from the sky. A gathering storm over the mountains had threatened snow all day, but the racing icetrails had never thickened as they rode gently along the river road. When the road crested to overlook the long descent into Airlie's southern meadowlands, Rowena saw a herd of winter fawn run leaping across the grass far below, long-legged and graceful. The blue twilight gleamed on their dappled hides. She reined her horse to a stop and watched them run.

"Good hunting, my lady?" her liegeman Stefan suggested, eagerness in his voice. Roger Carlisle, the young captain of her soldiers, turned around in his saddle, adding his own look of sudden interest. Stefan and Roger no doubt found this placid ride through forest and meadow a bit thin in adventures. Roger had that same lean look she liked so much in Stefan, and she felt fond of him, as she felt so often fond of the fine young men now entering her service, one by one.

She eyed both of them reprovingly. "Are you tired of riding guard on me, Roger?" she asked. "I think my soldiers are never bored in my service, whatever I ask of them. Don't you agree, Lord Heider?" She turned to her marcher lord, and saw his grin.

Lord Heider of Arlesby had joined them with a troop of his soldiers near midday a few miles beyond the village, wishing, he said, to guide her through his borderlands as courtesy. Stout and flaxen-haired, Heider had a wicked wit and eyes that saw farther than most. Rowena highly doubted Heider had ridden forth from his comfortable manor into this winter weather, breathless for the sight of herself, and, indeed, he had another purpose, as Heider usually did. During their ride through the afternoon, with grace and not enough to annoy, Heider had steadily probed her with questions about her nephew, Earl Melfallan Courtray, the new earl of Yarvannet. She had warned Melfallan that the more astute of the Allemanii lords were watching him, and Heider's overt interest confirmed her suspicions. When a young falcon rose into sight, the huntsmen below always took special note.

Heider bowed in his saddle. "Of course, my lady," he said smoothly. "How could they dare?"

Perhaps hearing a reproof in Heider's tone, Roger promptly saluted. "I never argue with my countess," he avowed.

"A prudent young man," Rowena said. "Stefan could learn from you." She looked at her liegeman, and earned herself only an impudent grin. She had become too indulgent, it seemed: these pleasant young men rarely feared her now, as was proper. She frowned warningly at Stefan, and only made his smile grow wider. Her lapse was confirmed by Heider's chuckle, but, sadly, one could not glare properly at Airlie's principal marcher lord.

"Winter fawn are good eating, my lady," Roger ventured, then put his hand on his breast, all innocence, when she looked at him. "I dread border rations and cold camps without a fire. Winter fawn have to be cooked, and cooking means a fire and that means warmth." He pretended a shiver and rubbed his arms

briskly. Rowena glared, but Roger was undented, no doubt learning his manners from Stefan: they were close friends.

"Winter is settling in, countess," Stefan chimed in. "I could
freeze my breeches off tonight. And there's this, too: if I froze my
breeches, so might you, and your liegemen must always think of
your comfort and safety." He bowed genially in his saddle. "Don't
you agree, Lord Heider?"

One of the soldiers behind them chuckled, too audibly for
prudence. Rowena turned in her saddle to glare at him, and got
wide grins back from the lot. Yes, she had badly slipped in her
rule. None of her folk feared her: this would not do.

"Good eating," Stefan said.

"Warmth," Roger added fervently.

"What an outrage!" Heider declared, now laughing outright.
"Already your authority is slipping, my lady. Listen to them!"

"I will think of something suitably vile for punishment,"
Rowena promised. She glanced sidewise at Heider. "As I foully
punish all my Airlie lords, usually for nothing important."

Heider grinned. "Oh, I've noticed that, my lady. That's why
all your Airlie lords love you, and would have no other lady to
govern them." He bowed in his saddle, as neatly as Stefan. "Winter fawn is good eating," Heider suggested.

Rowena turned back round in her saddle, and considered the
leaping shapes racing across the meadow. "Hmm."

"It wouldn't take long," Stefan said with sudden hope flaring
in his young face. He obviously hadn't expected her to consider
it.

"Horses can't outrace winter fawn," Rowena countered.

"Neither can shire wolves, but they catch them." Stefan
tapped his blond head. "Strategy, my lady. Sometimes winter
fawn don't out-think a pack."

"And you can go whooping along with your pack, you and
Roger racing your pretty mares at top speed as you love to do—
whether you catch a fawn or not."

"Well—" Stefan grinned, abashed—how incredibly young
they were! He glanced hopefully at Roger, and they traded an

eager look before both young heads swiveled back to her. "But it's for your sake, countess," Stefan said fervently, pressing his hand to his heart. "For good eating and a fire." His eyes danced with laughter, and Rowena smiled fondly at him despite herself, and saw her Airlie in his handsome face.

She snorted. "All right, then. For my sake—but don't take too long. And don't take too many of my soldiers for your pack, Stefan."

"Yes, my lady," Stefan said eagerly. "Walter, toss me your lance. You—you, and you," he said, pointing randomly at three of their soldiers, "come with us. My Destin will leave you all in the dust of her heels, but you can try to keep up, vain as that hope is."

"So you say, Stefan," Roger retorted stoutly.

Stefan laughed, and he plunged off the road and raced down the grassy slope toward the distant herd, the others in instant pursuit.

"Do we ride much farther tonight, my lady?" Lord Heider asked her courteously.

She shrugged. "We probably should," she said. "I wish I had more villages along this stretch of river; I prefer sleeping in a bed, pampered by my lady-maids." She smiled at Tess, whose nose was pinched red with cold, bundled although she was to her eyebrows. Tess was not an outdoors person, never had been, and the new one, Natalie, was obviously even less: both her maids looked miserable, good training for Natalie but not entirely fair to Tess. "Do you believe that lie, Lord Heider?"

"I will believe anything you want me to, countess," he avowed.

"Of that I'm sure," she retorted wryly. Rowena stood in her stirrups to stretch her legs, then sniffed the cold wind blowing up the slope. In the distance on the road ahead, she saw the dark speck of an approaching horseman—but, no, there were two such specks. Somehow her marshal had acquired a companion, and she idly wondered why. She nodded to Heider absently and heeled her gelding forward.

Sir Godric had ridden ahead to find a suitable camping place alongside the river road, for they had no convenient town or manor for tonight. Fifteen miles farther, for tomorrow night's stay, lay Lord Effen's river town, where he guarded the major river ford in central Airlie. Tonight, however, she would sleep beneath the stars and sky, a cold snow camp, surely, but a change she always relished. As a girl in her father's Tyndale castle, Rowena had grown up restless and active, more interested in racing along the river shore and other boys' games than in proper activity for a noble girl. She loved hunting, choosing hound over hawk for its wilder ride through forest and dell. Under the tutelage of her father's castellan, she had learned good skill with the sword, and had been an able horsewoman since the age of eight. Indeed, long after acquiring solemn dignity as awesome countess and ageless mother, she had once astonished Axel, then eight himself, by climbing the courtyard tree to a dizzying height. She smiled to herself at the memory, of which she still felt ridiculously proud, as silly as that was.

To her surprise, and even more so to Heider, Godric's companion was Heider's castellan, Sir Alan Thierry. Another excellent man, Sir Alan had served Count Ralf for years before taking up his post in Arlesby, and he had grown gray-haired in Airlie's service. Alan had been her close friend during the early years of Rowena's marriage, as fond of Rowena as she was of him. Of all her senior servants in that time, Alan alone had truly understood the gaps in Rowena's marriage to Ralf, and had offered his quiet understanding. How blessed I am, she thought suddenly, as she nodded to him with genuine pleasure.

"What brings you away from Arlesby, Alan?" Heider asked brusquely. "Is there trouble?"

"No, my lord," Alan assured him. "I had heard that a courier had arrived from Darhel with a message of some importance. I rode to see that you had received it."

"I did," Heider growled, his displeasure with Alan quite obvious, enough to make Rowena wonder why. She looked at him curiously, then back at Alan.

16

Alan smiled and bowed low in his saddle to Rowena. "Then it's my good excuse, my lady, to see you again."

"How are your wife and family, Sir Alan?" she asked.

Alan grinned broadly. "Six grandchildren now, my lady: they keep my good wife busy. Hmm. Seven, maybe." He squinted. "Yes, I'm sure it's seven."

"Ocean bless you, Alan, you should keep better track."

"I'll hazard you'll have the same problem, countess," Alan said comfortably, "when you're my age and have grandbabies to count. They do swarm so."

"I suppose they do." She grinned at him, then made a show of tsking, to be paid for her effort with another of those wide grins that had been greeting her all day. Alan wasn't afraid of her, either. She sighed.

"Will you be coming to Arlesby in the spring, my lady?" Alan asked. "My wife would love to see you again."

She shook her head, with some regret. "No, I'm afraid not. Melfallan's son will have his Blessing Day next month, and I won't task Sir Godric this year with two grand journeys." On the baby's Blessing Day, Melfallan would acknowledge his new son as his heir to his earldom, continuing that Courtray holding in Yarvannet. It would be a high occasion for the Courtrays, one to strain even Sir Godric's considerable talents at organization. Already a worried line had settled between her marshal's eyebrows, and he sometimes walked into doorjambs in his daze, or so she teased him. In truth, the tease was only half-false, and Godric's preoccupation would worsen as the event approached. She only hoped she could restrain his impulse to empty Carandon Castle for a sufficiently large party to match the occasion; they should leave behind at least a few soldiers for defense, should Duke Tejar use the lapse to invade her county. "In fact—"

"Shall we ride on?" Heider prompted impatiently. "I presume you found a campsite, Sir Godric?"

"Yes, Lord Heider," Godric replied and turned to point along the road. "Another mile or so, in a stand of trees." Rowena could see the shadow of the everpine grove ahead, barely visible in the growing darkness.

"Then shall we continue, my lady?" Heider asked. Rowena nodded, nudged her horse into motion, and they rode on.

"So you've definitely decided you'll go to Yarvannet?" Heider asked.

"Yes, Baby Audric is my grand-nephew, and my presence at his Blessing is important politically. I should take Axel, too, although I worry about the hazards on the road." She grimaced. "These are uncertain times, Heider, and I dislike lessening his protection. In Duke Tejar's mind, I'm too obviously Melfallan's ally, and a blow against me would be a telling blow against him." She scowled, likely showing more worry than she should. "And this duke remembers too well that his Kobus grandfather overthrew a Hamelin duke, and so sees plots where none lie."

"You think he'd strike at Axel?" Heider asked, affecting surprise. She gave him a sharp look: Heider was not obtuse about Tejar, and she wondered why he now pretended otherwise.

"Tejar would strike at anyone," she said, "if he thought it brought him advantage. A ten-year-old is a tempting victim when a full half-dozen claimants would clamor to be Airlie's count if Axel dies. Airlie in contention would be weakened, with opportunity for a duke to meddle to his gain." She shrugged. "Yarvannet isn't the only Allemanii land that hangs on the slender life of a child. At least Melfallan can have more children to protect his succession. A widow cannot, at least not without great scandal." She winked at him. "No, I must wait until Axel is safely married and producing heirs of his own. Then I will feel easy for my county, Lord Heider."

She clucked to her horse and eased him into a slow trot. The others heeled their own horses, and the troop, both Heider's and her own, fell in behind them with a jingling of reins and the quick scattered rhythm of horses' hooves.

The wind was cold, plucking with icy fingers at cloak edges and exposed skin. In the spring, when all was green and new, she liked riding about her lands, stopping at the manors of her

Airlie lords to stay a week or two for feasting and hunting, for parties, and fine banquets, with each of her Airlie lords determined to do her the highest honor. In the beginning of her regency, a few of the older lords, Heider chief among them, had grumbled about being ruled by a woman. After eight years of good governance, her Airlie lords now accepted her as their countess, genuinely so, not with a false smile and mutters behind the hand, but with appreciation, a liking she returned. It was something she had earned in her own right, not given her by her father's rank or her accident of beauty, nor by fact of marriage or motherhood. It was something she had accomplished herself, and so she greatly enjoyed her lords' flattery, perhaps more than she should. As Melfallan had warned her, vanity was too easy a fault.

He always was perceptive, she thought fondly, even as a boy. She easily remembered Melfallan in his youth, quick, active, ready for any challenge, always the leader of the pack of boys who ran with him. Melfallan's inventive mind had lent vigor to his boy's pranks, to her frequent dismay when she discovered the risks he'd taken—breakneck horse races over the meadows, climbing on the roofs of Carandon's tallest tower, swinging from trees. She had not berated him for his madcap adventures during his boyhood summers in Airlie, when for a brief few months Melfallan was free of his grandfather's stern eye. Indeed, Melfallan thought she had never known of his escapades, an illusion she had not corrected.

Her father, Earl Audric, had been overcareful with Melfallan after plague had taken both of Rowena's brothers, all too conscious of the single frail life that ensured the Courtrays' future holding of Yarvannet's earldom. He had restrained Melfallan, lecturing him against unnecessary risk, weighing him down with too early an awareness of his duty as heir, checking impulsive fun that Audric disapproved. And so Melfallan had become solemn too early, and too prone to doubt himself when measured against Audric's high standards, standards that Audric himself did not always meet. It had complicated Melfallan's character, a useful gift for any High Lord enmeshed in Allemanii politics, but had made Melfallan too complaisant in Audric's choosing of his wife. Rowena had played her own role in that, one she now regretted.

Her father had chosen Saray of Mionn more for alliances than any thought of Melfallan's happiness—not that Earl Audric considered happiness a higher good than a deft move against the new duke he despised. In hindsight, Rowena now believed Melfallan's happiness had been more important than her father had realized, for happiness in his marriage would have encouraged Melfallan's personal gifts as a High Lord, lessened his doubts, given him purpose.

Most of the Allemanii High Lords quested for power and, once they had achieved it, often used their power to rule well, as had her father and Earl Giles of Mionn. Other lords, more rarely, drew their strength of rule from other sources—a sense of commitment, of duty accepted, of love for one's folk as sufficient in itself, for commoner and noble alike. Melfallan was one of those others. She suspected that Earl Audric had little understood his grandson, and so had never seen the inner boy and the man he would become.

Perhaps Brierley Mefell, the young midwife Melfallan had chosen to champion against Tejar's accusations of witchery, might change that now, although she did not wish Melfallan the risks. After a duke's man had accused Brierley of witchery, Melfallan had been forced to take her to Darhel for trial. Although Melfallan had only hoped that a trial could clear Brierley's name, if Melfallan could arrange certain High Lords as her judges rather than others, the duke had imagined another gambit in Melfallan's obedience to his summons, and so had ordered his justiciar to murder Brierley in secret. The young woman had defended herself, killing Gammel Hagan in turn, and then had fled into the mountains east of Darhel.

Two nights before, Melfallan had stood before the fireplace in her bedroom at the lodge, still cold from his long ride down from the mountains where he had left Brierley in the safety of a wayfarer cabin. The shifting light of the fire had illuminated the clean line of his jaw as he stared down into the flames. Perhaps he saw there a face, with large gray eyes, gentle curves to the cheeks, long hair curling to frame that face. Rowena, too, had loved a shari'a witch twenty years before, but had failed to save her. Perhaps now Mother Ocean offered a second chance. At times, their Allemanii goddess seemed indifferent to one heart's ardent hopes, choosing instead Her wider vision of all lives, all times. But not always: at other times, even solitary hopes might be answered, sometimes unexpectedly.

When Rowena had risen from her chair to join him at the fire, Melfallan had started slightly as she touched his sleeve. "Where did you go?" she asked him. "Have you fallen into fire-staring, to the loss of your wits?"

"Probably," he said, turning to smile at her.

"You need to practice not thinking about her," Rowena said, and saw his mild surprise. "Soon you'll be home with your wife and son, Melfallan. And Brierley is supposedly dead, not safe in hiding, and pining is not grief." She eyed him. "Stefan and Niall will watch over her. So shall I."

"You shouldn't go up there," he warned. "I know you want to meet her, but you are certainly watched."

"I wanted to meet her in Darhel, but she acted too quickly in escaping Tejar's dungeon."

"Aunt—"

Rowena waved her hand dismissingly. "I have sense. I won't try. But, I, too, have my wistful moments. I do wish I had met her before you hid her away."

"Someday you'll meet her," he promised. "Sir Niall says she resembles Jonalyn, 'enough to be noticed,' in his words. They might have been related."

"As the child is related? Megan—is that her name?"

Melfallan nodded. "Her niece, Brierley thinks. She talks about dream castles and Everlights as the reason she thinks so, but she's probably right. She told me she had waited years to find another shari'a like herself, aching years. I can't imagine that kind of loneliness, having only yourself and no others. She was convinced that if we High Lords ever discovered her, she'd be killed." He snapped his fingers. "Just like that we burn her, because she dared to exist. No matter what healing she had given to others, no matter

21

what lack of blame for being born shari'a. Duke Rahorsum's law is a vile thing. Do you think any other shari'a survive?"

"If so, how do we find them? They have reason to hide."

"True. But I wonder where to look."

"There are none in Airlie, Melfallan. I *have* looked. Twenty years ago I made myself Jonalyn's champion for all to see, and I had hoped it might encourage one of the others to make themselves known to me. But in twenty years I've found not one other shari'a. We Allemanii have been very good at killing witches." She grimaced.

When the Allemanii had come to these shores three centuries before, they had lived in peace for a time with the native people, the shari'a. During the third Karlsson duke's rule, however, Duke Rahorsum had suddenly attacked Witchmere, the shari'a capital, with a great army, and had murdered all he found there. The duke had then enacted the shari'a laws, proclaiming all shari'a witchery as foul and evil, and had condemned to death any surviving shari'a witch, should she be found anywhere in the Allemanii lands. Although no High Lord had found and burned a witch in nearly two centuries, those laws still existed.

Melfallan sighed. "Brierley says there are none in Yarvannet, either. But surely Megan and Brierley aren't the last two—only two, Aunt. I won't believe she has that slender of a hope. How do you rebuild a craft with only yourself and a six-year-old child?"

"Is that what she intends? What craft?"

"I'm not sure she really knows. What is this Everlight she keeps talking about? She says Thora Jodann's spirit lives inside it and sends her dreams, as if a woman who lived three centuries ago somehow can take new life. How does an Everlight, whatever that is, send dreams?" He shook his head and laughed softly at himself. "I mean, what is the procedure? How is it done? And how can a ghost live inside it? How is that explained? I mean, aren't there supposed to be rules?"

"It depends on whose rules," Rowena replied with a smile.

"That really helps," he snorted. "Rules are rules, dear aunt: we don't have separate sets, please, one for us and one for them.

Otherwise the world is chaos, right? But why are there four kinds of witches? And—"

"Four kinds?" Rowena asked, startled.

"We found a book—"

"A book?" Rowena said eagerly, pressing his arm hard with her fingers.

"I'm here for the night," Melfallan said irritably, "and you'll hear the whole tale, Aunt—if you'll let me tell it." Rowena tossed her chin, but gestured for him to continue. "She talked about dragon-spirits that the shari'a revered. In the library in Witchmere, there were mosaic panels of—" He stopped as Rowena opened her mouth with another question, then chuckled as she firmly shut it again. "Ocean, how to tell it in order? Theirs is an entirely different world, Aunt, hidden away, that might now flicker out of existence—and we never even knew it was there." He paused, gazing at the flames for several moments, then shook himself slightly. "I wonder if the Founders had that same puzzle when they met the shari'a after the Landing, and if any of those Allemanii ever really understood the shari'a before they tried to destroy them."

"As they nearly did, nephew, and Tejar might attempt again—not for fear of the witches, but of you. To change the shari'a laws, you must become duke. Don't shake your head, but listen to me. In that goal I support you, and I would have urged it even if you had not found Brierley. Tejar is an evil man in an evil house, and I don't say that merely because his grandfather overthrew a Hamelin duke. Our Allemanii politics are difficult enough without wise rule, and Tejar's sons will be no better than he."

"To become duke, I'd have to kill Tejar, and I haven't accepted that I must." He scowled down at her. "Or his sons."

"Tejar has no such difficulty about killing you, nephew. Accept at least that. Tejar scents the wind changing, as we all do. That's why he struck imprudently at Brierley—and at you. It is time for the coronet to change heads again: all the High Lords feel it, and most are looking to Yarvannet. You must accept that, too.

23

It is expected, now that your contention with Tejar is out in the open."

Melfallan tightened his lips. "I appreciate your advice, Aunt—"

"—but you have a wider issue. I know. I am my father's daughter, dear one, enmeshed in my political plottings, my devious considerations of whom to manipulate, whom to kill, whom to let live. Believe me, I know exactly what I am. Your grandfather never saw an issue beyond politics: to him, that was the highest of all affairs. But I knew Jonalyn, as you now know Brierley, and I, too, wonder about your other shari'a world we've nearly extinguished. It seems it was a gentler world than ours, one of grace and lightness, of marvelous powers, where ghosts could walk in dreams, and a mere touch could heal. I wonder what other wonders they worked with their magicks, and what they thought about themselves, and how deeply we earned their hatred by our butchery at Witchmere. I, too, think of many things besides ambition."

Melfallan smiled. "I love you, Aunt, however bloody-minded you are."

"If I am such, you can be less of it. True?" She smiled back at him, then waggled a finger. "But not too much less, Melfallan. Savagery of thought will keep you alive. Ask Duke Tejar. Ask any of the other High Lords."

"I will do as I choose, savage or not. I don't accept murder of whole families."

"But you must consider its necessity. That is all I ask."

"I think Brierley would hate it," he said slowly, "that I would do such a thing to save her. She's a healer, and healers never accept death as a necessity."

"She lives in a different world, dearest, her shari'a world where all that matters is healing with a touch, and the gentleness of a quiet day, and the care of her child. You must live in your world, to protect hers."

"Perhaps," he said stubbornly. "Must you meddle in everything?" he asked and tried playfully to disengage her arm from his. She resisted, tugging at him until he staggered. "Meddler," he accused.

"Yes, I must meddle. It's a fact of your being, Melfallan. Live with it." She smiled, then disengaged her arm and seated herself in a chair, beckoning to him. Melfallan sat down at her feet and leaned back against her knees. Rowena caressed his hair, as she had done when he was a boy and he had sat at her knees in her chamber, comfortable like this. The wind sighed down the chimney, raising a shower of sparks. "Your face is still cold," she murmured, touching his cheeks. "My Airlie winters can be too harsh."

He rubbed his face against her hand. "I'm warmer now. Don't worry about me." And she had bent to kiss his hair.

Yes, perhaps in Brierley, Rowena now thought as she rode through the crisp winter air, Melfallan has now found his purpose as High Lord—and his happiness as well. His defense of the shari'a witches, for Brierley's sake, would turn Allemanii politics on its ear, and perhaps ultimately give the lands a new duke, a different kind of duke, one who ruled for more than power, as the Kobus dukes had always ruled. Perhaps. She knew she had not convinced Melfallan of the necessity—not yet.

They had entered the long wood, deeply shadowed. Many of the trees had dropped their leaves, but everpine and thorntrees grew thick beside the road, their needles gleaming in the Companion's blue light. Rowena heard the soft hooting of a mock owl in a nearby tree, then the howl of a shire wolf, miles away. Its fellows joined in its wavering cry, beginning a hunt of their own. A cool wind shivered the needles of the everpine, surrounding them with a sibilant murmur. Down the slope, the voice of the forest rose and fell, a sound similar to the surf that had dominated Rowena's girlhood in Yarvannet. She narrowed her eyes and listened, remembering the sea. Yes, perhaps she would stay in Yarvannet for a little more time than needed, if only to hear the sea again, murmuring in all of Mother Ocean's quiet voices.

The Companion now neared the crest of the distant coastal

mountains, and its twilight had deepened into lavenders and deep blues. They might ride another two hours in the twilight, but Rowena felt the fatigue of the day's cold ride seep into her muscles, and the wind had seemed to grow colder. She welcomed Godric's choice of an earlier camp, this pleasant glade beside the road with overarching branches to keep away the snow.

As the soldiers unsaddled the horses, Rowena climbed a small rise beside the road and watched the twilight deepen over the grasslands. Far below, Stefan and his companions were dark specks racing over the grasses in pursuit of the herd of winter fawn. Rowena smiled as the prey easily eluded the pursuit, and eventually both fawn and riders disappeared over a low hill. She turned back to the camp and settled herself near the small fire, then accepted a cup of hot soup from Tess. Tess sat down beside her with a sigh and pulled the edge of the blanket over her head, then shivered for effect, knowing that Rowena would see it. Rowena patted her knee in sympathy.

"Cold," Tess said with a chatter of her teeth, then sipped at her own mug.

"Yes, it is. You've been very good today, Tess."

"Thank you, my lady."

"Does Natalie give you trouble?" Rowena asked.

"Not that I can't handle, my lady," Tess said confidently.

Rowena sighed. She mildly regretted taking Saray's lady-maid into her service, despite Melfallan's pleading. Already she disliked the girl, and not only for the bit of byplay she had seen at a distance between Natalie and Brierley on the Darhel docks. Rowena knew Natalie's type well. First came careful deference to the high lady, until she was wheedled sufficiently into an indulgent good humor, then a bit of overreaching, taking a bit more than one deserved, then presumption, waxing ever greater as time passed, and perhaps, near the end, outright contempt, even if kept safely out of earshot of its target. Rowena had no doubt that Natalie had passed through all four stages with Saray, lending an edge of desperation to Melfallan's hinting, and so she had relented. After thirty years of dealing with lady-maids in her service, first as favored daughter to an earl, then as countess, Rowena was quite familiar with Natalie's tactics. She also knew what to do about them. For now, however, Tess could cope.

Rowena reached for an extra blanket and gave it to Tess, who accepted it gratefully.

"Cold," Tess repeated. "I far prefer our castle with its roaring fireplaces. Even a headman's cottage would be better. You have a hard service, countess."

"In a moment I'll be pitying you. That won't do." Tess laughed softly.

The soldiers cut branches from the nearby everpine and built rough mattresses on the ground, and three of her Airlie troop had sat down on their own beds to eat a trailside meal and drink from their water bottles. They noticed her watching and smiled, then might have got up from their comfort if she had not waved them off. Other soldiers, both Heider's and her own, were tall shadows in the nearby trees, keeping the watch, and two had stationed themselves at the edge of the forest to watch the meadows below. Eventually, Roger's sergeant appeared before her and saluted. "My lady, Lord Heider asked me to report that the watch is set."

"Thank you," she said with a nod. He marched off to his own station.

Rowena looked toward the road. "And where are my eager young men?" she asked, annoyed. "Hasn't it been enough time for their futile chasing?"

She got to her feet and walked over to the road's vantage again, then looked down into the meadows below, then along the river road behind then. The twilight filled the meadows with blue shadows. In the far distance, the dark shapes of winter fawn were leaping across the grasses as they raced up a broad hill, but she did not see any horsemen in pursuit.

"I should not have let them go," Rowena said as Sir Alan joined her. She tightened her lips with irritation. "Why do I indulge them?"

"There's likely some cause," Alan said soothingly. "A lame horse, a throw—or even a winter fawn caught. It would take time to gut the carcass."

"I suppose you're right." She bit her lip, then turned back to the fire. "Sometimes, my dear Alan, I find life annoying, and I worry like a silly old woman."

He smiled. "You, old? Not yet, my lady."

"It will come in time, I'm afraid," she said with a sigh, "and sooner for me than others. I envy Stefan and Roger their youth. I even resent it. Ah, to be twenty-four again! I can hardly remember how it felt. And that in itself shows me turning old." As she settled herself on her bed of soft bracken, Sir Alan stooped to spread a blanket across her shoulders. Tess had curled up under her own blanket, already asleep. Natalie was nowhere to be seen. Likely she had wandered away into the trees to flirt with one of the soldiers. Rowena frowned, then let it go.

Across the glade, Lord Heider emerged from the shadow of the far trees, sword in hand, and walked toward her, smiling. She smiled in response, then something about his stance, the edge to his smile, made her pause. Two other soldiers in Heider's livery appeared behind him, then three more, all with swords drawn. The soft metallic sound of Alan's sword being drawn brought Rowena quickly to her feet, and in that same instant Heider made his charge.

"*Alarm!*" she shouted as Alan lunged in front of her, his sword raised in her defense. "Alarm! To Airlie! To Airlie!" Heider slashed out at Alan, his face convulsed with rage, and steel rang in the glade as Alan's blade met it in midstroke. "Step aside, Alan!" Heider roared.

"Never!" The marcher lord struck again at Alan, shouting curses when the man would not yield way.

Alan's quick defense had won her time. Rowena ran to a nearby horse, where a sword scabbard hung on the saddle. She drew the sword with a shivering clang, and turned just as one of Heider's soldiers reached her at a dead run.

She hadn't time to set her feet, nor even raise her blade, and so she dodged his swinging blow. The blade whistled past her and sank deeply into the horse's haunch behind her, and it screamed in shock, then reared, striking out with its hooves at its attacker. Blood spurted from its flank, a mortal wound, and its hind leg collapsed beneath it, but not before strong teeth had ripped into the soldier's shoulder, dragging him upward as the horse tried to rear again, staggering as it screamed. Rowena thrust upward with her sword, striking for the heart, then skipped backward as both soldier and horse fell heavily to the cold ground.

"To Airlie!" she shouted. "To Airlie!" Rowena ran around the kicking horse and retreated toward the trees as two more of Heider's soldiers menaced her, trying to box her in as one circled to the left. She raised her blade and dropped into a sword-fighter crouch, watching ahead and behind. She heard a piercing woman's scream among the trees, then shouts and the angry metallic clash of swords, but all her Airlie soldiers were still too distant to give her aid. His teeth bared, one of Heider's men swung his sword, and she parried neatly, then met his next blow with ringing force, enough to force him backward. Off balance, his sword swinging wildly, the soldier staggered and Rowena put her sword into his throat. He gasped, his eyes bulging, and threw his hands to his throat to stop the blood that gushed from him. As he staggered and fell, Rowena whirled to meet the other man who swiftly pounced on her, and fought fiercely against the other's longer reach.

"You would murder your liege lady?" she demanded. The man's mouth twisted but he said nothing, and only strengthened his attack. This soldier was not as careless as the other, and nearly outpointed her in his furious assault. She prudently retreated, matching blow for blow.

Her own soldiers had almost reached her when Rowena's foot, hampered by her riding skirt, misstepped on a buried root and she stumbled, falling backward. Knowing her danger, she twisted as she tried to rise, and an instant later felt steel pierce her right shoulder, striking agony as it bit deep and through. With a cry of triumph, Heider's soldier ripped back his blade, tearing open the wound still wider, and raised the sword high over his head. Rowena flinched, seeing her death in that coming stroke.

"To Airlie!" an Airlie soldier cried, and the next moment he plunged his sword into the man's chest. He pushed Rowena roughly to the ground and straddled her, his blade raised against other men who rushed down on them. Another Airlie soldier joined him, then three others, making a ring around her. A moment later, she heard the hammering of horses' hooves on the road, and Stefan burst into view at full gallop, the others at his mare's heels. There was a shout and suddenly the battle turned as Heider's men fled into the trees before Stefan's furious assault.

As their safety was rewon, Rowena pushed away her soldiers' hands and staggered to her feet, then moaned from the pain in his shoulder, nearly falling again at the sheeting of it, the slicing edge of it. She grabbed at her arm and staggered. No spurting of bright blood, she noted, with far more detachment than she expected. I've more than a few minutes to live. It seemed a distant question, hardly important. Odd.

And then Stefan was there beside her, lifting her up in his arms. As Stefan turned toward the fire, she saw Sir Alan, panting heavily, standing over Heider's body. "Rowena!" Alan cried as he saw her wound, shock in his face.

"She's taken a blade in her shoulder," Stefan shouted and carried her to the fire. Then Tess was there, bending over her, and then Sir Godric, her marshal, and the others crowding around her. Rowena's head swam and blackness picked at the edges of her mind.

"I'm all right," she insisted, and struggled to sit up.

"No, you're not," Stefan said and pushed her back again. "Will you not listen to me? Lie down!"

Rowena hesitated and then relaxed against him. Dear Stefan, sweet youth on the morning. But then Sir Alan had pushed Stefan aside, and ripped her sleeve from her gown and put a cloth to the wound. "It's deep," he muttered. "Can you move your fingers, my lady?"

"With some trouble," Rowena said faintly, and then closed

her eyes against the agony that it caused when she tried. "Hurts," she whispered, and blinked furiously as the world shimmered with tears. The blade had passed cleanly through her shoulder, penetrating the seam of her sleeve: a lucky thrust combining the soldier's sword skill and Rowena's own stumble. I should have worn mail like Melfallan does, she thought dazedly. Wise Melfallan, wiser than me. Oh, Ocean, keep him safe! Keep my Axel safe! Blood now gushed from the cut, cascading down her arm and soaking through the cloth in Alan's hand.

"Hurts," she murmured again and her face twisted as Alan's fingers probed her wound in the inadequate firelight. She struggled against her own daze, to do what must be done, to protect— "How many are dead?" she asked faintly.

"Five of our soldiers," Sir Alan answered, "six of theirs, and your other lady-maid, countess. Apparently she and one of the soldiers were in the trees—" He shook his head impatiently. "The rest of the Arlesby men have fled."

"And Heider? He's dead?" She hardly recognized her own voice, so weak it sounded.

"Yes, and rightly so," Sir Alan growled. He pressed her hand urgently. "Countess, you must know about the message that came from Darhel yesterday. The courier would not put it in my hand, only in Lord Heider's. He seemed too lofty a man for a mere courier, and Heider was ill-tempered and silent after he left. Then, suddenly, this decision today to join you. I was worried, my lady." He bared his teeth. "Ocean bless me that I chose this time to act. I served the Hamelins before I served Arlesby—and I still serve you."

Rowena squeezed his fingers. "My thanks that you did, Alan. Dear friend, dear—" Rowena's voice failed her as the world began a slow turning, bringing down the blackness from the night sky.

"She's bleeding badly," Stefan exclaimed from a far distance. "How far to Effen's town?"

"A good fifteen miles," Alan's voice answered far above her. "A hard hour's ride, too rough for the wound, Stefan."

"Then we'll ride at less speed." Rowena felt Stefan's lips press against her forehead, and then felt herself being lifted gently in his arms. As he carried her to his horse, her head sagged weakly against his shoulder. The darkness of the night shimmered in black waves, pressing down on Rowena, merging with the pain. Her head spun, and her breath seemed harder to draw. She could no longer move her fingers in that hand, however she tried, and she felt the blood slowly pumping from her shoulder. *To end like this—* It wasn't right. *It wasn't right, to die by a traitor's murdering, although she'd faced its possibility all her rule. Axel, my son—*

Melfallan, guard my Airlie— Rowena yielded at last to the darkness.

Stefan lifted his countess onto his horse and swung into the saddle behind her; then, muttering an anguished curse, he heeled his horse forward into the night.

"Break camp!" he bellowed. "Leave the bodies where they lay! We ride!"

2

 new gust of wind rattled the window-
panes of the small wayfarer cabin, chat-
tering snow hard against the glass. The
temperature outside had dropped steadily
as another snowstorm settled over Witch-
mere's valley. Despite a lusty fire in the stone fireplace and a
second blaze in the cooking stove nearby, Brierley Mefell shivered
as the wind stole another breath of icy air into the room, teasing
the bare skin of her face and chilling her fingers. She pulled her
shawl closer around her shoulders, making a nest of its woolen
folds, then stared at nothing for a few moments, listening to the
wind.

Sir Niall Larson had gone off to hunt at midday. Melfallan
had bid his aunt's liegeman guard Brierley during this winter's
stay in the cabin, and Niall had taken his charge much to heart,
calling Brierley "lady witch" and "liege lady," however little he
listened to her wishes. Brierley had objected to his leaving, pointing to the storm gathering over the eastern peaks, but Niall had
been determined to restock their larder today with a few hares,
perhaps a teal or partridge.

"Don't worry about me, lady witch," he had said cheerfully.

"But there's no need, Sir Niall," Brierley had protested. "We
have more than enough for days." But Niall had smiled confidently, brushed off her protests, and left. Now, several hours after

33

both suns had set, bringing the True Night, Niall still had not returned.

Brierley crossed her arms and scowled. So much for liege lady, she thought irritably. She highly doubted Niall had ever shrugged away Countess Rowena's wishes. No, indeed.

And so she and Megan had spent a long lonely day in the cabin, watching the storm gather over the mountains and then descend with a howl and chattering of snow. She had often looked anxiously out the windows, worried for him, but all her wishing for Niall's quick return had yielded nothing. She rose from her chair and walked to the window to peer out again, but now saw only her reflection in the glass against the blackness outside. She cast her witch sense for Niall into the storm, but could not hear him. He must be miles away, might even camp out all night if the storm had caught him too quickly.

Have pity on me, Sir Niall, she thought, biting her lip. Have pity on a witch who worries.

She walked the few steps to Megan's narrow bed set under the other window and checked that the child was warmly covered. At her touch, Megan sighed contentedly in her sleep, and Brierley bent to kiss her. She looked down at Megan's small face, the tight black curls of her long hair, the determined focus of her sleeping. My child, Brierley thought with quiet joy.

For years Brierley had longed for a witch-child to be her companion, daughter, and apprentice, but had not truly believed she would find such a child anywhere in the Allemanii lands, not truly. Not quite six years old, Megan had been harried by the tumult of mental voices all around her in Duke Tejar's castle, and now lived half in a world real only to Megan. A kitchen's child suffered a harsh life, and Megan had battled fiercely against her foes, as a drowning child might fight the heavy waters closing over her head. Another year, perhaps two, and Megan would have lost her valiant battle for sanity, as Megan's mother, Brierley's twin, had lost hers. Lana had been a kitchen girl unremarked in her passing, raped at eleven and dying in childbirth nine months later, and afterward little remembered except by a few kind souls who loved all children, even a kitchen's child. Lana's madness and eventual death had been the loss of a precious gift, gone from the world forever, and Megan's would have been another.

As she leaned over the bed, Brierley caught a drifting sense of Megan's dream, of river weeds and a white-stoned castle, where Megan sat at her ease on a sunlit balcony. The wind blew softly over the river, rustling the reeds, and brought the fresh scents of moving water and growing things. A flock of gulls swept bright arrows across the sky above, and all was warm and bright and safe.

To admit the truth, Brierley envied Megan her lovely dream world, to which Megan retreated when the real world grew too harsh. At times when they slept together in the narrow bed, Brierley joined Megan there to share the dream, and sat at ease in the sunlight with Megan, listening to the river. Although she worried that Megan's dream castle might ensnare the child's mind in dreams that forgot reality, she could not yet bring herself to try to wean Megan from it, for love of the child and the beauty Megan had created within herself.

Within her castle, Megan kept memories, nearly all of them not her own. On the second floor of her white castle were rooms, each filled with love or despair, grief or rage or delight, desperate needs, quiet joys—all held within the essential child. A shari'a fire witch had the gift of protection and memory, to guard and preserve in passionate defense all things of value and purpose. How much of Megan's castle was her special gift as fire witch, and how much the child's desperate escape to safety? Brierley was not sure, and so she would not intervene, not yet.

And how, truly, could a sea witch ever understand the fire gift? Until she and Melfallan had discovered Witchmere's ancient library, she had not known other witch gifts even existed. Valena's ancient book had identified four kinds: alchemist, healer, stormcaller, and guardian. *The forest witch, beloved of Amina, she had written, is given the gift of alchemy, that is, knowledge of the substance of things and their sympathies, and of the ways of beasts and plants, and of the patterning of life.*

35

The sea witch, beloved of Basoul, is given the gift of healing, that is, the power of touch to ease injuries and pain, and knowledge of the inner heart, and of the peace that abides between people. The air witch, beloved of Soren, is given the gift of weather, that is, knowledge of storms and winds, of clouds and rain and mists, and of the ether between the stars.

Finally, rarest of all, is the fire witch, beloved of Jain, who is given the gift of memory, that is, knowledge of the people of the past, and the power to preserve, and the control of the guardians of Witchmere.

Four gifts, when Brierley had known of only one, her own healing gift. Did shari'a with the forest and air gifts still survive somewhere in the Allemanii lands, hidden away as Brierley had tried to hide herself in Yarvannet? The ancient books in Witchmere's library, three centuries old, could not say.

Brierley sighed and caressed Megan's small face again, and resettled the warm coverlet, tucking in the ends. She put another log on the fire, slowly paced the small room, listening to the wind, then reseated herself at the cabin table.

She and Melfallan had brought out a dozen books from Witchmere, several written in Allemanii, two in the cursive script of the shari'a, and, most prized of all, a dictionary. Four of the Allemanii books were histories, the first a dry accounting of the resources of Briding County written several decades after the Allemanii invasion. It had long lists of wheat measures for several years of harvest, longer lists of the fishermen's netfuls of fish for those same seasons, the suitable poundage of iron for the smithies, a tedious charting of the herds and game in each town, with careful lists of people who lived in each fishing and river hamlet, each head of family ranked by occupation, family size, and age. Somehow this steward's book, with its preoccupation with tithes and measures and endless numbering, had made its way to Witchmere's library, to sit dusty on a shelf for three hundred years.

More to her interest, two of the other histories were accounts of the Founding, telling of the two noble brothers, Aidan and Farrar, who had led the Allemanii across a thousand miles of interim seas and coastlines to a new home in shari'a lands. It was a tale of truly great adventures, of terrible storms that had sunk three ships, of ice blocks taller than a ship's masthead that had groaned and cracked as the Allemanii sailed warily among them, of desperate battles against wild folk who inhabited a few of the islands. Twice the voyagers had stopped on a cold shoreline to careen their ships for repair and enjoy a brief summer season ashore, only to launch again in autumn onto the deep ocean, sailing eastward toward the Daystar's rising, not knowing if any end existed to the frozen wastelands and cold seas they crossed. As they sailed, they fished the rich sea life of the northern seas, and taught their children their arts of seamanship and sword craft and poetry, and had chanted praises to Mother Ocean, their protectress who had launched them on their voyage away from blight and war in the West. It was a magnificent tale, and likely all true.

Do we know we are heroes? Brierley mused. Usually we don't, I think. I wonder if I'm a hero, and if some future daughter will write an admiring history about me. She dimpled at the thought.

Of greatest interest of all, the fourth history dealt with Duke Rahorsum, the third duke of Ingal, that terrible and relentless duke who had destroyed Witchmere and nearly ended all the shari'a. To Brierley's chagrin, the book ended in the duke's middle years before Rahorsum began his war on the witches, and did not say what had caused the Disasters. What had prompted Rahorsum to his butchery? She still had little answer. To her surprise, she read that Rahorsum had been a good duke in his early years, prudent in his rule, fond of his people, often wise in his judgments. To her even greater surprise, she learned that Rahorsum had composed music, and, more astonishing still, had even written poetry, including a long saga about the Founders. The book quoted extensively from Rahorsum's saga, and even Brierley's untutored ear could hear the skill in the duke's art. Until whatever had turned Rahorsum against the shari'a, the duke had been a decent man, a suitable lord.

The other Allemanii books were a collection of prayers to Mother Ocean, a book of quite bad poetry devoted to a lord's love for his lady, an amusing satire about a pompous lord and a simple

---

fisherman that Brierley doubted had pleased its noble sponsor, a book about swordsman's techniques, and a long treatise on fish, all types, with their habits and ranges and food supply and the fishing for them. However these several Allemanii books had made their way into Witchmere's library, they told their own tale of the Allemanii in those times by their range of topics.

The Allemanii wrote of practical things, politics and fishing, swordplay and a county's wealth: these she could understand. The two books written in shari'a script had baffled her completely. She had puzzled for hours over the green book's diagrams, at times consulting the dictionary for words, and had tentatively decided it might be a manual for air witches. At least the word for air witch, *narris,* appeared very frequently and, more to the point, in the title on the spine. Not having the air gift, Brierley would likely make little sense of the explanations, even when she knew more of the words. How did an air witch work her power over storm and winds? Were the diagrams a key to focusing the air gift? Or did they describe some essence of air and weather? Who could tell? She gave the book a mild glare of frustration and then shut it up. The other shari'a book had even less use, for it seemed to discuss shari'a philosophy, and would have probably given her headaches even if written in Allemanii.

No, the true find in Witchmere's library was Valena's journal. She sighed as she took the book again into her lap, then caressed the cover with her fingers. Here was a voice much like the voices in her cave journals, written by women who had lived the shari'a gift and had found purpose in it. Valena had been an air witch in Witchmere thirty years before the Disasters, and had been friend to the Count of Airlie of that time. The book was not long, less than sixty pages written in a graceful hand, and more a bound set of letters than a book. The personalities of Valena and Armadius resonated in Valena's letters to her count, hers alternately playful and solemn, with a scholar's occasional pomposity, a tendency to the abstract, and his an Allemanii lord's voice very familiar to Brierley, restless and intrigued and sometimes rudely abrupt. In their exchange, hers spoken on the page and his voice heard only by her, the Allemanii lord and shari'a witch struggled to understand each other.

Do you not know, good count. Valena had written, *that gifts are given to every folk? Is not one son better at swordplay than another? Is not another son deft at shipbuilding, knowing the nature of the wood beneath his hands. Among your Allemanii there are many crafts, many gifts, and some of your folk, like ours, are more talented in certain crafts than others.*

Among we shari'a witchery is a gift, given in varying degrees to our women. I myself have no talent for music, yet air witches are often musical, and there is no explanation for my lack that suffices. You yourself have a fine singing voice, and they were right to beg you to sing again at the banquet. Do I then envy you your gift in music, and think it unfair that you are able to make melody and I cannot?

I can see that witchery is a strange art to your Allemanii eyes, she had continued, *but to us it is part of being shari'a, as a love for the sea and for battle are part of you. I make no moral judgment of your violence. In your western lands, as you have explained, such violence was necessary to protect your folk from violent neighbors. And so you defended yourselves, and then took this brave journey across the broad ocean to find a new home. And you have found that home with us, liking those part of our lands that we ourselves do not use. Where, then, is the danger between us? There is room for all in our lands, and there can be friendship between us—if we do not fear each other.*

Valena's hopeful words resonated in their irony: Valena and Armadius had no foreknowledge of what would come. In their time, a generation before the Disasters, when Valena had written her letters and visited his castle in Carandon, all was still peaceful, with both peoples interested in the other. Was Valena still alive when Rahorsum brought his army to Witchmere? Worse, had she seen her count with Duke Rahorsum at Witchmere's gates? Brierley hoped not.

If we do not fear one another, Valena had urged. *If.*

Brierley had hoped for much from Valena's book, but its contents were limited by its purpose. Valena had an obvious fondness for her count, and both had been troubled by the occasional antagonism between the Allemanii High Lords and the shari'a of

39

Witchmere, but many of the questions Count Armadius had asked Valena were not the questions Brierley wanted answered: indeed, several of those answers Valena had never known, for their events happened after her time.

How should I choose? she thought fretfully. In her dreams in Yarvannet, she had been often visited by Thora Jodann, a lone survivor of the Disasters who had founded the line of sea witches in Yarvannet. Alternately playful and solemn, Thora's presence in her dreams had brought comfort and encouragement into Brierley's lonely life of hiding. Brierley had lived a solitary existence for years in her sea cave, venturing out to heal the folk of Melfallan's southern shores when there was need, then returning to the cave with its single bed, simple furnishings, and shelves and shelves of books. All that had changed when she was revealed as witch, but in a direction she had never expected. Her books had warned her of the shari'a laws, of the hunt and pyre that followed exposure as a witch, of the certain terror and death. Yet Yarvannet's young earl had defended her against all accounting, and Yarvannet's folk had championed her, ultimately bringing her to this safety for a winter's season in a high mountain cabin. That safety would not last, but for now she and Megan could live days without fear.

But what then? she fretted. Where did she go then? Into Mionn, where she could live again in hiding? To Yarvannet, where she was known as witch? Thora had bid her to refound the craft, but how might that be done? And what of Melfallan? She had not expected to fall in love with him, nor that he would fall in love with her, and that love was peril to them both. Melfallan's politics as High Lord were dangerous, and his lady wife, Saray, was sweet in temper, an innocent who did not deserve to be betrayed. She frowned unhappily.

I can see where our love might lead, she thought, as clearly as a mountain trail winding down to the sea. I can see great peril ahead, with an outcome neither of us wish but might not be able to stop. Yet I want to do what I will, not thinking of the consequences: I want Melfallan. Is it to be attempted? Or do I hide myself away from him, and so choose again the safer path, to live narrowly, to hide and never trust?

How can I know? Of what of Megan? In hiding, her witch-daughter might live a happy life, safe from the dangers of the shari'a laws. However Brierley might choose for herself, how should she choose for Megan? She got up restlessly, and went to the window to peer outside.

Where is Niall? She scowled fiercely, thoroughly put out with him.

The wind howled anew, shaking the glass in the windows and roaring down the fireplace chimney. The storm seemed to pace around the cabin like a prowling leopard, wanting in, loud in its baffled rage, relentless with its probing claws at every crevice, every crack. Brierley threw back her head and glared at the storm beyond the cabin walls, angry that it frightened her.

Ocean, how it howls! She stamped her foot, but that action did not produce Niall, either.

Brierley sighed and wished she knew all things. She turned down the lamp and joined Megan in their narrow bed, pulling the blankets tightly around them. The storm howled onward, shaking at the windows in its rage.

When she slept, Brierley joined her daughter in the dream castle Megan had built by a broad river, in a dream world in which the suns always shined, the weather always moderated into warmth and gentle breezes. At the foot of the broad steps leading up to the castle door, Brierley looked up at the white façade of Megan's castle, then glanced around at the water and reeds, the soaring birds, the bright sunlight of Megan's world.

Everything here was utterly lovely, created by Megan from sunlight, the tickle of the breeze, and the cry of soaring gulls. In her own childhood, Brierley had often played at such pretending games, imagining herself a great lady or a brave knight, sometimes a sea lark aloft on the wind, piping its high song, or a shell-star creeping through the dim light of the ocean bottom, stalking its prey. She had never thought to build a dream castle, not like this. Did all fire witches build such castles?

She climbed the stairs, opened the broad oaken front door, and stepped into the cool alcove beyond. On the right, she saw a library with shelves of books through a half-closed door; on the left, through an arched doorway, she saw a pleasant sitting-room, cool and peaceful, with the enticing smells of food from the kitchen beyond. A broad staircase led upward to other floors. She heard Megan laughing above and mounted the steps to the top floor. There she entered Megan's best room, in which the child spent most of her time. Along one wall stood a narrow bed, soft and inviting, not bare slats and a thin mattress, but a lovely bed piled high with a feather mattress and high pillows. On the other wall stood bookshelves with Megan's animated toys, blocks that tumbled and giggled, a mild-tempered bear holding his toes, and other delights, all Megan's friends. On the far wall opposite the door, wide glass doors led to a balcony overlooking the river, where Megan now sat at ease, her salamander perched on her hand.

Tonight Megan had dressed herself in fine silks and gold jewelry, Lady Megan in all her finery, and sounded quite imperious in her chatter to Jain. The salamander bore it well, cocking his head as he listened. When Brierley appeared in the balcony doorway, Jain made much of a goggling of his eyes, as if Brierley were an amazing sight, a wonder to behold. Well, no, not that, Brierley decided: Jain did not regard her as a wonder, but an oddity, a weirdness in the day, and his gaze was not meant to be flattering. As fire dragon, if he was such, Jain hadn't much use for a sea witch, and had let Brierley know it, as he did again now. Brierley wrinkled her nose at him. As Megan turned her head and saw her, the dark eyes lighting, the small face filling with pleasure, Brierley smiled.

"Megan," Brierley greeted her.

"It's such a good day, Mother," Megan said happily, then turned her attention back to the salamander. She scowled mildly at the creature. "But Jain has been misbehaving, haven't you, Jain?" The dragon shrugged, unconcerned.

"What has Jain done now?" Brierley asked curiously.

"He won't listen to his liege lady," Megan replied severely. "This will not do." She shook her finger at the salamander, then shook her head as well. "No, no, no."

"Oh, dear," Brierley said, hiding a smile. "What a problem!" She knelt down beside Megan, then rearranged her legs into a more comfortable position and leaned back on her hands. The sunlight was warm and bright against her face, and she breathed in the scent of the river and the reeds. All was peace here, despite the minor bother of a salamander's contrary ways.

"And what must you do, Lady Megan," Brierley asked, "when your liegeman is difficult?"

"I'm telling him to behave. That should work." Megan was all confidence. "You just tell them to stop, Mother, and they do it."

Brierley chuckled. "A good plan, child." In Megan's dream world, all problems were solved with little trouble, as transitory as a shift of the warm breeze. Would that all problems were solved as easily in the real world.

Megan shook her head solemnly at Jain. "No, no, no," she repeated. "This will not do." The salamander drooped his head and sighed repentantly—or at least made a show of it. Brierley highly doubted that Jain chose to repent anything, ever, no matter what he did. "No, no, no," the child said, shaking her finger.

Brierley listened to the river for a time, then watched a flock of gulls arrow across the bright daytime sky. The reeds in the river bobbed gently in a drifting breeze, and all was peaceful, all was safe, bright warm in the morning. Beyond the river spread a wide plain of grass, silver with the ripe heavy heads of thyme and barley. The wind swept broad patterns in the ocean of grass, like a giant palm brushing across the grass-heads, caressing the land. Brierley noticed a drifting cloud of smoke rising from the grass, as if someone had kindled a fire. She sat up straighter, then shielded her eyes against the suns' light to see better. Something moved there, she thought, a dark shape half-concealed in the grasses, but then it disappeared, leaving only the distant spiral of smoke rising upward, quickly torn to fragments by the breeze.

"What's that, Megan?" Brierley asked, pointing across the river.

"What?" Megan asked, turning her head.

"There. See it? Is that a fire?"

Megan stood up and leaned on the balcony railing, then craned her head to see. "Where?" she asked, perplexed. "I don't see anything."

"That cloud of smoke."

Megan looked at Brierley, then looked back at the plain. "Where?" she asked anxiously. "It's only the meadowland, Mother. Like it always is."

Brierley hesitated, then shrugged. "Never mind, child. I thought you might be building something new." Megan shook her head solemnly. "Ah, well." Brierley leaned back, lifting her face again to the sky. She breathed, a deep lingering breath that filled her lungs to the very bottom. All was peace here, all was light.

Beside her, Megan lifted a reproving finger to her salamander. "No, no, no," she said, shaking her head.

The dragon yawned.

By dawn Sir Niall still had not returned. Brierley had risen early and now sat waiting again, tired and fretting, as the first gray light of dawn crept through the cabin windows. The wind had finally relented an hour before the Daystar's dawning, and now snow fell silently from the graying sky beyond the cabin windows, a cold white curtain filling the meadow with deeper drifts. Brierley now felt as angry at Niall as she was worried, easily shifting from one emotion to the other as time passed.

"No, no, no," she muttered darkly, and crossed her arms. This would not do.

Despite an hour of her determined willing, Niall did not appear. A witch's gift sometimes did not stretch far enough, Brierley decided, at least not enough to command a liegeman's prompt attendance—but, then, she'd never had a liegeman before. Perhaps it was a matter of practice. "No, no, no," she said, shaking her head.

Finally she rose and put new logs on the fire in the fireplace, then started a fire in the stove for Megan's breakfast. She sat down again in the chair and hugged her shawl around her arms, and watched the snow fall steadily beyond the windowpane. I can't leave Megan alone in the cabin to look for him, she thought, nor do I want to take her out into that snow. I doubt the mare could breast some of those drifts, anyway. That snow must be piled head-high near the trees.

Niall had taken the other horse for his hunting, and at least had that advantage against the weather. He had been born and raised in Airlie, accustomed to travel as Rowena's courier in all kinds of weather: he must know how to care for himself in deep snow. But what if his horse has slipped and fallen? What if he lies injured somewhere, unable to return? she asked herself anxiously. And where would I look? I warned him to hunt down the valley and not go near Witchmere, but he wasn't listening to me all that much yesterday. He might easily have gone in one direction as the other.

Where *is* he? She ground her teeth, shifting again from worry to anger.

Jain popped in view and hovered in front of her, wafting a faint breeze with his wings, his scaled legs tucked neatly beneath him as he fluttered. Small flames of blue, gold, and red sifted over his small body, flickering restlessly, a living sheath of light. Jain hissed at her absently, insolent as always, as he tried to land on the books piled on the table. He made an awkward business of it, tipping the top one off the stack and lifting back into the air.

"Where's Niall?" she asked, deciding that Jain should make himself useful.

Niall who? Jain retorted, and flipped himself in midair to land on the mantelpiece. Brierley glared at him with little favor. *Is this how we begin?* Jain demanded back. *Myself as convenient oracle?*

"Yes," Brierley said firmly.

Jain sniffed, then sourly relented. *Your liegeman was caught out in the storm, but found shelter in a windbreak. He is safe.* He pointed over his shoulder with one forefoot. *About three miles down the valley, just off the mountain trail.*

"Thank you."

I'm not making this a practice, witch, Jain said irritably, rustling his wings. *When a dragon helps a witch too much, the witch gets careless, lazy, and dull. I'd not like to see that happen to you. Not to mention all the aggravation inflicted on me.* He spread his wings and lifted back into the air. *Get your own answers next time.*

Jain popped out, and the next moment Megan sat up, yawning. She tossed back the covers and threw herself out of bed, then ran barefoot to Brierley for a smacking kiss.

"Good morning, Mother," she caroled, and climbed into Brierley's lap.

Brierley hugged her close. "Good morning, Megan. Did you have a good sleep?"

"Yes." Megan put a small fist to her mouth and yawned even more hugely. "I'm hungry," she said.

"Well, I can fix that." Brierley set Megan on the floor and got up to open a cupboard, put a pan on the stove. She listened as Megan went busily around the small cabin room, greeting the window and the door, the bed and the table. It seemed that each was alive to Megan, as if the bed remembered the many people who had slept in it, the door all the persons who had passed in and out over the years. She sensed a flicker in Megan's mind as she *heard* something from each object, but the impressions went too quickly for Brierley to catch. Megan ended up on their bed, her doll in her arms, waiting for breakfast, as she had done each of the several mornings in the cabin. Perhaps Megan thought, in her child's logic, that her pose with her doll caused breakfast to appear—a thought not entirely without sense, Brierley admitted, for each morning one had always followed the other.

"Where's Sir Niall?" Megan asked, finally noticing that something was missing.

"Out hunting. He'll probably be back later today." The answer satisfied Megan, and she returned to her patient waiting.

Did Megan make much distinction between people and chairs, Brierley wondered as she stirred the porridge. Or did both seem equally alive to her? Or equally unreal? Brierley could sense her witch-child's thoughts, as the child could sense hers, and she knew that Megan slipped easily between the real world and her castle, even when awake. One moment Megan would be sitting on her bed in this cabin, and the very next she sat on her castle balcony above the river, not perplexed by the change, nor even much concerned. For all her short life in Darhel, she must have practiced that easy escape from the harsh life in the kitchens, confusing the real and the unreal to protect her mind from the mental assault of other minds.

Was this confusion of worlds a danger to Megan, the first steps of Megan's long slide into inevitable madness? Or did a fire witch always live between shadow worlds? How could Brierley know? She had learned her own healing gift largely through trial and error, with some help from the journals in her cave. Her mother had refused her shari'a perceptions, and had demanded that Brierley also try to live a normal life, uncolored by their shari'a gift. Adamant in her will, harsh in her punishments, Jocater Mefell had tried relentlessly to deny her own nature, for whatever reasons in her past had driven her to that choice. But can the wind stop its blowing? Brierley asked herself sadly. Her mother had suicided when Brierley was twelve, ending everything.

As she knew from experience, Brierley's own gift did not always follow its own rules. How could she divine Megan's rules for her gift, enough to give her guidance? How *does* one train an infant fire witch? Perhaps Jain might help—if the dragon would consent to help. The salamander came and went as he pleased, invisible to all but Brierley and Megan, and spent as much time not answering Brierley's questions as answering. At times he would ignore Brierley as if she weren't there, focused entirely on

Megan and whatever she was doing. Brierley suspected him of being contrary, for Jain took great enjoyment in annoying Brierley to distraction, but sometimes, it seemed, he genuinely did not see her. Did Jain, too, slip between worlds, occasionally emerging into a world in which Brierley was not present? At times Megan also seemed quite unaware of her, although not as often.

She turned from the stove after dishing porridge into Megan's bowl and stopped short. Megan was sitting on the bed, her doll in her lap, staring distractedly at the far wall—no, not Megan. Someone else looked out from her eyes, someone Brierley did not know. Megan's eyes shifted toward Brierley and narrowed, and for a long moment they stared at each other. Not Megan, Brierley sensed: another mind had surfaced within the child, older, more powerful, and filled with rage, with searing grief, an inexorable need for vengeance. The other's emotions roared at Brierley like a blazing fire, wanting to consume all, blacken, crisp, leaving only ashes and oblivion. For her vengeance, this fire witch would burn all the world to flames, and in that terrible retribution find her own ending as well.

Brierley began to tremble, shocked by the sheer force of the other's willing. Megan's lip curled into a mocking sneer, hatred burning at Brierley from Megan's eyes, then abruptly the other was gone and Megan was herself again, looking back at Brierley.

"What?" Megan asked in confusion.

Brierley swallowed uneasily and opened her mouth, then foolishly shut it without saying anything. She tried again. "Here's your porridge, Megan."

"Oh, good!" Megan declared and hopped off the bed. Brierley cleared a place on the table and set the bowl in front of Megan, then watched as Megan happily ate the sweet porridge, offering an occasional spoonful to her doll. Brierley brought her a cup of hot water and several slices of dried fruit, then sat down weakly in the other chair.

In Witchmere, when she and Megan had confronted the guardians, Megan had seem possessed by a stranger, speaking with authority and rage to the machines. They had not fully obeyed, but

Megan had drawn on some memory in the place to deliver her imperious commands that averted the guardians' attack. Could a memory continue to walk in her mind? Could a memory *possess* a child? Brierley felt a rising panic about all she did not know about Megan's gift, but quickly pushed the fear down. Megan would sense her panic—and perhaps that other might sense it, too, and find strength from it.

A fire witch held memories within herself: it was her gift. Perhaps all fire witches built a dream castle like Megan's, with rooms filled with the past, and all shifted regularly between worlds, one real, one not. But what if a memory seized a witch? What then became real?

As the morning passed, Megan played happily inside the cabin, prattling to her doll, climbing up and down on the chairs, bouncing on the bed, a small bundle of energy careening around the room. She came often to Brierley for a hug and a kiss, and then shot away again, with Jain as her ever-present accomplice. Megan seemed wholly herself, happy and energetic and laughing, with no apparent trace of the stranger who had seized her.

Did I imagine it? Brierley wondered, watching her.

After lunch, Megan demanded they visit Friend, their mare, in the small side stable affixed to the cabin. Brierley dressed Megan warmly, bundling her to the eyebrows, then broke a foot-trail through the new snow along the outside cabin wall, Megan stamping in her wake. Inside the stable, Brierley refilled the mare's grain bin and made sure she had fresh water, then lifted Megan onto the mare's back for a pretend ride. Friend flipped her ears mildly and snorted, a contented beast who liked them both and felt inclined to continue that pleasure.

As she patted the mare's neck, Brierley's vision blurred oddly, and suddenly she seemed to see through Megan's eyes as another woman stood by a different horse. The woman was dressed in green riding leathers, her black hair tucked into a cap, and, oddly, a small furred beast rode her shoulder. It swiveled its sharp-tipped ears in interest as she spoke to the horse. *I know it's been a long ride, Star,* the woman said, *but we'll be comfortable here.* The ferret made a pretend nip at her ear, wanting attention, and the woman absently reached up her hand to stroke its sleek fur. *Perhaps we'll find answers,* she told them both, and turned toward the stable door.

Then abruptly Brierley stood again next to Friend in the warm stable, looking dazedly up at Megan.

The child put her thumb in her mouth and looked around vaguely at the stable walls. Brierley sensed the flickering again in Megan's perception, as other shadows moved and were quickly gone. Then Megan suddenly exclaimed in delight.

"Look, Mother, it's a bird!" she cried, pointing off to the left.

Brierley looked obediently, but saw only a coil of rope on a peg. "Is it, Megan?"

"Oh, look, Mother!" Megan pointed excitedly at the saddle and tack hung on a peg on the other wall. "It's a waterfall!"

"Is it?" Brierley asked, confused. What was Megan doing now?

Pretending, Jain replied into her ear. *What do you think?* Brierley looked around for him, but he was invisible somewhere.

And the woman in green? she asked curiously.

A visitor here, long ago. Megan remembers: so do I. Jain swooped into view and flew a leisurely circuit of the stable, then fluttered to a perch on a box. *It is Megan's gift to shift worlds and remember what once was,* he added casually. *This cabin is very old, and many have slept here.*

"Oh, look, Mother!" Megan exclaimed, pointing again. "It's a tree!"

"Is it?" Brierley asked, bemused. Would she ever understand this child?

Megan looked down at Brierley from her lofty height on the mare's back, Lady Megan in every line of her disapproval. "It is if I say so," Megan asserted imperiously. "You're supposed to pretend, too, Mother."

Brierley wrinkled her nose. "No, no, no," she said.

Megan giggled, and Brierley lifted up her arms. "Come, child, let Friend eat her grain. Let's go back inside the cabin where it's warmer." Megan threw her arms with great enthusiasm around Brierley's neck, and Brierley lifted her down to the stable floor. She took Megan's small hand in hers.

"Oh, good," Megan exclaimed at nothing particular, and allowed Brierley to lead her out of the stable.

That afternoon, as Megan played with Jain, Brierley sat down again with her dictionary. In these books were answers, she hoped, answers for herself, answers for Megan.

Through her study in the dictionary she had learned nearly a hundred shari'a words, for whatever use that might lend. The grammar still largely escaped her, but she was making progress with the words. A sea witch, a healer like herself, was called *dayi*. A forest witch was *shajar*, Megan's fire witch *anshan'ia*. Witchery of any kind was *ish'ar*. The four dragon-spirits of the shari'a were called the *Hirdaun*, and the Beast who tormented Brierley's healings had the dread name of *Masikh*.

The dictionary had also confirmed the names of the Four on the library's mosaic panels: Amina the forest dragon, a drifting emerald shadow in the trees; Soren the golden air dragon striking from the sky with lightning in his claws; Jain the fiery salamander who guarded all shari'a with passionate ferocity and had made himself Megan's constant friend; and, lastly, her own guardian spirit, Basoul, the blue sea dragon with her shimmering scales and a healer's cup clasped in her talons. The shari'a named them the Four, the benevolent spirits who guarded all the shari'a, and to whom they might appear from time to time.

Brierley watched Jain flip through the air, an agile teasing friend who made Megan happy. For that joy, Brierley would forgive the salamander almost anything, a weakness she hoped Jain never discovered. He seemed determined to provoke Brierley to distraction, for reasons he never explained. During their several days in the cabin, he had tried to prod her into answering him in front of Niall, tossing outrageous comments or insulting slurs, then had snickered happily as she struggled to ignore him. Once he had swooped down straight at Brierley, no doubt to make her fling herself aside shrieking, but Brierley had stubbornly stood her ground. For an instant, Jain's body had whispered through hers, bringing a brief wash of heat, fierce in its tenderness, exultant in its joy.

When Jain began moving pots, she had told him furiously to *stop it!* Niall had looked up from the leather strap he had been mending at the table, badly startled.

"Stop what?" he blurted, then looked down at the strap, then at her, and became totally confounded.

Jain rested a paw on a pot lid and grinned, showing his tiny white fangs. *Yes, what? I'm anxious to hear.*

"Nothing, Niall," Brierley said firmly to her liegeman. "I'm sorry I startled you. I, uh, dropped the spoon into the stew." Which in fact she had.

Poor Niall, she thought. Her mouth twitched. Poor Brierley.

The sea witches of her Yarvannet cave had nearly forgotten the ancient dragon-spirits of the shari'a, giving them only a casual mention from time to time, as if the Hirdaun were another fanciful tale, not history, merely legend. The catlings of lore, those dire creatures of the night coast who stalked the unwary, received more mention, along with other tales. And not one of her cave journals mentioned a fire salamander who teased and snickered and made her drop spoons into her stew. Although Jain had desisted from rattling the crockery, she sensed a frantic need behind his wild activity, as if Jain were—running out of time? Why had she thought that?

She watched the salamander zip through the air, flickering, bright motion, a tumbling leaf of flame, with Megan in hot pursuit. Megan could see him; so did Brierley—more than she wished to, to admit the truth. Niall could not, nor had Melfallan and Stefan. By Jain's choice? Or were the dragons visible only to shari'a eyes?

Why? Was Jain truly a shari'a dragon-spirit, as he claimed? Were the Hirdaun truly real? How could she know?

She looked down with frustration at her list of shari'a words. How would single words and dragon names answer such a question? However she tried, Brierley could not read the shari'a books, although she had tried and tried until her head ached. She might do months of trying and fare no better, and she now glared at the two shari'a books more than coveted them. She felt like tossing them out into the next storm, to be ripped apart, page by page, and sent fluttering all over the valley. Let someone else collect the scattered pages and put them together again. Let someone else care about the nature of the Real and nonsensical air spells. There were hundreds of shari'a books in Witchmere's library, likely filled with any answer Brierley might desire, and she couldn't read them.

Patience, she told herself and rubbed her tired eyes. Do you think this should be easy? Well, yes, she answered herself wryly, and quirked her mouth. With a sigh, she bent over the dictionary and hunted another word for her list.

3

t nightfall, after Megan had laid down to sleep, Jain curled by her side, a lusty stamping on the porch finally heralded Sir Niall's return. A moment later the cabin door swung open, bringing in a blast of cold air that ruffled the book pages on the table and sent the flames in the fireplace roaring up the chimney. Sir Niall appeared in the doorway with a large load of wood in his arms; snow dusted across his shoulders, and a brace of quail hung from his belt. He flashed a grin at Brierley and tried awkwardly to shut the door with his shoulder. Brierley jumped up from her chair, relieved to see him at last, and ran to push the door shut.

"Ocean, that wind is cold," Sir Niall swore and stomped heavily toward the wood bin by the stove.

"After that blast through the door," Brierley suggested, "it will take all that wood to warm up the cabin again."

"Likely so," Niall said cheerfully. "But I must come in and out sometimes, true? And we'll be glad of the warmth toward morning. New storm is gathering." He bent to drop his wood on the pile near the fireplace.

"Megan," Brierley warned, nodding toward Megan's narrow bed.

Niall nodded and eased the logs to the floor, trying not to clunk, then looked over his shoulder. The child slept onward, undisturbed. "In truth, lady witch," Niall said, "I think Megan could sleep through a pitched battle."

"Likely so," Brierley said, amused. Megan could box and sell determination, and she slept like a rooted stone. "You're not hurt?" She looked him over anxiously.

"Got caught out in the storm, and I'm sorry to worry you, my lady," he said, but not sounding all that regretful about the worrying. A confident man, her Sir Niall. "No, I'm fine, if a bit iced on the edges. I caught these this morning." He unhooked the quail from his belt. "There's precious little game out in such weather." He tsked absently to himself, then unwrapped the woolen scarf from his neck and eased off his gloves, and stood for a few moments before the fire, warming his cold hands. Brierley sat down in her chair and watched him, a bit put out by his casual air.

Sir Niall Larson was a sturdy-bodied man in his early thirties, with brownish hair and a short dark beard, deft in his skills and cheerful in his service. For many years he had been Countess Rowena's confidential courier to Mionn. Niall may have named himself Brierley's liegeman, although she disclaimed any rank as lady, and truly treated her with great courtesy—if not a matching respect for her wishes.

Well, she supposed, a storm is a storm, and I could forgive him this time. It appeared Niall saw no reason for repentance, quite in tune with Jain, that was obvious. Niall turned to smile at her, his face still reddened by the cold, then nodded pleasantly as he set to the rest of his tasks. He tramped out again onto the porch, allowing a new blast of cold air into the cabin, then brought in his saddlebags, which he placed by the door. With a great stamping of his feet and swinging of his arms, he put another log on the fire, hung the two birds near the stove, and shifted his saddlebags to their peg on the wall. Brierley watched him from her chair as he settled things, relieved that he was back safely.

As Niall sat down heavily in the other chair to pull off his boots, however, she sensed another mood beneath his cheerfulness. "What's wrong?" she asked. From his mind she caught quick images of the forested slopes of the valley, the chill of the falling snow, and a half-seen guardian shadowing him for hours.

Niall shrugged. "One of those Witchmere guardians stalked me yesterday." He grimaced as he pulled off a boot, clunking it to the floor. "You were right about going up the valley. Not enjoyable."

"So long as you can keep a good distance, they won't throw fire at you."

"So far." He grunted. "This valley has a reputation with travelers of being haunted, and now I know why. This one was hunting me, not just watching. I spent most of yesterday putting distance between me and it." He pulled off his other boot and dropped it. "What did you do while I was gone? Read your books?"

"As much as that has gained me." She scowled.

Niall's blue eyes twinkled. "I can drill you in the words. Have you begun a list?"

"On what?" she said in frustration. "I've only your twenty sheets of paper, and I don't want to write in the books. Learning word lists won't help, anyway."

"On the contrary, the words are the key, and nothing but," Niall said confidently. "It's merely a matter of application to your triumphal success." He chuckled at the look she gave him, then reached to shuffle among the papers on the table, moving three of the books to the floor, and found the list she had started. "Here it is. All right. What's the shari'a word for tree?"

"I don't remember," she said contrarily. Niall gave her the courtesy of naming her "lady witch," but she sensed that Niall did not truly believe in witchery or witches or any such fancy. He was a practical man, his feet thoroughly rooted to the earth, and he prided himself on a proper attitude toward nonsense. And so she couldn't compare ideas with him, as she might have with Melfallan, nor even begin to explain the facts of her witchery. A fire ghost that could seize her child? An invisible dragon who teased and flipped himself through the air? She crossed her arms across her breasts, irked that Niall had now decided to tutor her in her own craft, as if he were master and she the student. *No, no, no,* she thought.

"Hmm. Mountain valley?"

Brierley dramatically bunched her brows with hard thinking, then shrugged and looked away.

"River?"

"I haven't a clue," she said promptly.

Sir Niall eyed her in reproach. "I can see you really tried that time. I think you've developed a poor attitude, mistress, though perhaps I am wrong. I've been wrong before, I'll admit. These words are not your enemy, Brierley."

For a fleeting moment, she wanted to throw a book at him. "So you say," she retorted.

He tsked, and shook his head. "You must repair your attitude, lady witch. Think of these words as interesting clues, fascinating details, with hundreds—"

"Thousands—" she amended in despair.

"—to learn, one by one, each a delight, each a treasure, a joy to own."

"So you say."

He eyed her a moment. "I have heard some attitudes are be-yond remedy," he noted.

"I agree." She scowled at him. "It is a truth, indeed."

"Mountain valley."

"It's no use, Niall. I've always had trouble with lists. Ocean knows I've tried, and I'm already tired of trying. I'm tired of this cabin and snowstorms and listening to the wind howl. I'm tired of those guardians stalking you. I'm tired of—"

"Me, perhaps?" he asked with a smile, and put up the list in the papers on the table.

She sighed, and relented her irritation with him. "I was wor-ried for you," she admitted. "I'm Yarvannet-bred and used to mild winters: I've never seen such storms."

Niall grimaced again. "Earl Melfallan meant well, Brierley, but this cabin was not his best of ideas. We're too high in the mountains. We could be easily snowed in, with drifts to the eaves, and then be snowbound until spring. While the weather permits, Stefan can pack in more supplies from Carandon, but the storms this far east are unpredictable. And we're far too close to Witch-mere. That guardian hunted me yesterday: I even imagined I could feel it wishing me dead." He shuddered. "It hates well."

"Is it too dangerous to leave? To travel to Mionn now?"

Niall considered, frowning. "It would be difficult. If Stefan can send up more supplies, we can make it through the winter. That is probably still the best plan, despite my doubts." He smiled benignly at her. "I, too, can sometimes worry beyond reason."

Brierley narrowed her eyes. That comment had just a touch too large of condescension, just a mite too much of utterly irritating male complacence. It hinted, too, how manly measurings of the world outpointed the silly frettings of women, her own included. "So you say, Sir Niall."

"I believe I did say," he observed mildly, then winked at her.

Brierley vastly doubted that Sir Niall had ever winked at Countess Rowena, and wondered what that noble lady would do to him if he dared. Something dire, no doubt, and utterly suitable. "I didn't say the list was a total loss," she said stubbornly. "I only said I was tired of words."

"Tired of words?" Niall exclaimed. "What a heresy! Words are the key to knowledge, the enlightenment of the mind. Try again, and you'll see."

"Tired," she insisted and dared him with a fierce look to say more.

Niall chuckled, stretched his arms over his head, then looked pointedly at the stove. "Long day hunting," he said casually and waited a few moments, expecting his immediate dinner, that being the lot of women to provide to men.

When Brierley remained seated in her chair, he looked back at her more sharply, an eyebrow rising. Yes, a competent man, she thought as she contrarily eyed him back, and well used to his male privileges—but not, she realized, overly accustomed to women. Niall had never married, content with his travels for his countess over the choice of any settled life, and she sensed no sisters in his family. In some marriages a wife might defer too much to her husband, but sisters rarely omitted a brother's necessary education on one's rightful ease in life. And so the eyebrow and the expectant pause, the slightly puzzled look when Brierley delayed in jumping eagerly to the stove.

But after all, she conceded, Niall had spent two long cold days in the snow, determined to provide for her and Megan. It was a petty point. She hesitated a moment longer, then rose from her chair. At the stove, she reached for a pan.

No, no, no, Jain's voice whispered mischievously in her ear.

Be quiet.

Three days later Brierley sat on the porch step of the forest cabin, Valena's book in her lap, and watched Megan play with Jain in the snow. The day had dawned brilliant and clear, bringing a break in the weather, the first in two weeks. Today the clouds did not swirl across the sky, gray and ominous; nor did the wind send snow blowing into high drifts, frozen and cold. Instead the snow glittered brilliant white under the Daystar's warmth, dazzling the eyes, and a thin coating of ice on everpine needles sparkled, filling the trees with a thousand winking stars. The air was cold, but neither Megan nor Brierley could have stayed inside this morning.

Megan ran after Jain as he flipped and teased, exalted with the rush of her own movement and the brilliant sunlight of the morning. She seemed tireless, enthralled with the ever-new novelty of snow. After an hour of wild careening, her footprints and blasted snowdrifts now covered most of the meadow in front of the cabin. Jain had egged her on, and the child had kept warm through her running and shouting. Everything was an adventure for Megan, and Brierley sensed the child's ecstatic delight in the day, in the movement, in the mad abandon of flinging oneself into the snowdrift, then to thrash in the coolness, and then get up to run again. She and Jain were having so much fun that Brierley felt tempted to get up to join them, but she stayed virtuously on the porch, continuing her study despite the distraction. She looked down at the book.

You ask if any shari'a man can be a witch, Valena had written, *but it seems only our women are true witches, for reasons we do not wholly understand. Occasionally a male child may show signs of the gift, particularly if twinned with a sister, but he rarely develops a full talent. Rather, the gift in a male child torments more than comforts, and those of our sons often live unhappy lives. Instead, our men are our craftsmen, our builders, our scholars, often our leaders in the Councils. We love them truly, Armadius, as you love your wives, for is not love common to us both, as is our joy in children, and in the pleasant turning of the seasons from Pass to Pass?*

My husband and I have been married twelve years—I cannot imagine where the time has gone, although I can mark this year and that year and count the twelve to my present hour. I feel no older than when I first loved him, but surely I have become so, and it is indeed twelve years. I will bring him to Carandon on my next visit, and I think you will like each other. He is already disposed to like you, based on my accounts of you, but, like your lady wife, he is mildly jealous and does not like my teasing that he is. May our troubles, dear count, be ever that mild and nothing worse.

Life was thus simple for Valena; Brierley doubted that she really envisioned the Disasters. Rather, Valena seemed to equate the disputes with the Allemanii to the scholarly squabbles in which she involved herself at Witchmere: important matters, true, as were all politics, scholarly or otherwise, but never anything that threatened continued living. That possibility had never seemed to cross her mind: Brierley wondered if Armadius had shared her confidence.

At the time of the Allemanii invasion of the shari'a lands, Valena told her count, the shari'a had entered a time of new intellectual awakening, with new schools of thought and artistry that had produced the Everlights and other devices of amazing design, with new advances in all areas of the gift and the studies they engendered. Valena did not entirely approve of the new schools, for some reformers had suggested rather extreme ideas, to Valena's thinking. *An idea does not create a reality,* she sniffed, *and truly, Armadius, I hesitate to tell you what some have suggested, lest you think the shari'a a wild and abandoned race.* Still, it had been a time of great change, a flowering of the shari'a after centuries of quiet living and careful thought, and a resurgence resisted by the conservative leaders of Witchmere, recklessly urged by the reformers. The conflict with the Allemanii had interrupted the renewal and, as Brierley knew, ultimately ended it, leaving the shari'a a scattered people.

In other letters, Valena wrote about her studies, the pattern of her days in Witchmere, the personalities of the various Witchmere leaders, the pranks of her two daughters. Nearly all of the air witches lived in Witchmere, not in hill or seaside villages like the other adepts, and apparently acted as the general leaders of the shari'a. Most of her Witchmere acquaintances shared her own air gift, and Valena felt more comfortable with her own kind, as if the four gifts subtly divided the shari'a adepts, air from fire, forest from sea. Indeed, Valena had never personally met a fire witch, for they were few in number and rarely came to Witchmere. In turn, she seldom traveled abroad, preferring her mountain fortress and its internal concerns until a chance meeting with Armadius had interested her in the Allemanii. In turn, Armadius seemed intensely intrigued by everything she chose to say, although he often scoffed about her witchery, to Valena's considerable irritation.

Who, then, is the expert here, Armadius? Valena exclaimed. *I think a High Lord should have better manners, barbarian or not, and until you improve yours, I shall not write you again.*

Apparently a quick apology had followed, and Valena had resumed their letters, mollified into a candid half-apology of her own.

My dear count, each of our gifts is distinct from one another, she wrote, *and I admit we witches do not have full understanding of the other gifts. How does a fire witch remember the past? She calls it shifting worlds, but what worlds? Why does each sea witch envision a monster after she heals? Why a monster, I wonder, when healing is a gentle gift, a goodness for the world? In truth, the others think my air gift is just as unlikely, and look at me with puzzled eyes, as I look back at them, and we are all puzzled together. Only the forest witches care not, and say simply that all belongs to the Pattern—a comment which annoys us all.*

It was a fascinating dialogue, and Brierley dearly wished Valena had preserved the count's letters in her book, not merely her own. His was a voice she might easily recognize, for Melfallan had felt as skeptical. Valena and Armadius had lived in a different time, an earlier time, before the troubles worsened, when lord and witch could talk to each other, puzzling together, and find what bonds they could. Did Time truly turn on a wheel, bringing a lost hope into new possibility? Could she and Melfallan resume a dialogue long suspended?

Behind her Niall stepped from the cabin onto the porch, and stopped beside her, an ax in his hand. He shaded his eyes with his other hand as he watched Megan run.

"Busy little thing, isn't she?" he commented in his pleasant rumble of a baritone. "Nice that she has an invisible friend." Brierley looked up at him as she heard the question in his voice. "The one she talks to," he explained uncomfortably, then avoided her eyes by examining his ax handle.

Each morning Sir Niall had watched Megan go through her ritual of greeting the furniture, making the doll bring breakfast, then chattering away to Jain or her doll as she ate, occasionally offering the empty air a spoonful of her cereal. Megan prattled to Jain and sometimes to the table and stove as much as she talked to Brierley and Niall. Niall was as unaccustomed to children as he was to women, and he wasn't quite sure what he thought of Megan's odd behavior, nor if he should follow Brierley's lead in accepting the whole of it as normal. She had been wondering when he'd finally ask.

"Oh, you mean Jain," Brierley said casually, and had to look down at her book to hide a smile. "Yes, it is."

"I suppose little ones her age often have invisible friends," Niall said doubtfully.

"They usually do."

"Hmm," Niall said, and shuffled his feet. "I was wondering, uh," he fumbled, then rushed on. "Does any of it have to do with her being a witch? You said that she is one." He watched Megan fling herself happily into the snow, then grab at the empty air before flinging herself off in hot pursuit of nothing at all. "I mean, *you* don't talk to the empty air. At least I haven't seen you do it—" Brierley dimpled, but Niall was busy watching Megan.

"Megan is indeed a witch, Sir Niall," she answered soberly. "What do you think a witch is?"

"Uh—" His eyes shifted to her. He hesitated badly, then decided he didn't want to know. He liked his opinion of Brierley as someone rather sensible, and preferred not to lose it. "Bless Ocean if I know, lady witch," he said cheerfully. "So long as you're not worried about it."

"I'm not."

"Well, good," Niall said, then returned to the practical with open relief. "I'll go chop some wood, be gone maybe an hour. Our supply is low." He clumped past her down the porch stairs, and set off down-valley. She watched him until he vanished behind the trees.

Brierley flinched as Jain plopped into the snowdrift by the porch and sent snow flying everywhere. Megan lunged to catch him, shrieking with laughter, then slipped and sprawled at Brierley's feet. Jain popped out of the snow a few feet away, easily eluded Megan's grab, and zipped off into the air. Megan ran after him, and then, when Jain abruptly reversed course, ran back again.

The salamander fluttered to the porch railing and sneered. *Can't catch me,* he bragged.

Megan hung on the railing, panting heavily, but was obviously ready for more. She was covered with snow, all clinging wetly, and her face was flushed bright pink. Brierley put aside her book and tugged Megan over to stand in front of her. Megan's dark eyes sparkled with excitement, but she allowed Brierley to brush and tuck her into better order.

"You're all out of breath, child," Brierley said.

"He's fast!"

I'm fast, Jain echoed smugly. And, then, before Brierley had scarcely settled Megan's clothing, they were off again.

It was unbearable.

Brierley jumped to her feet, then ran to join them in their play, but she was no better at catching Jain than her daughter. After ten minutes of taunting calls and wing-twisting display, Jain landed on a nearby bush and jeered triumphantly. *Can't catch me!*

Brierley stopped, hands on her hips, her lungs heaving, then swayed as Megan limply propped herself against Brierley and leaned. They clung to each other weakly as Jain enticingly bobbed his branch, daring them to try again.

"I think you're a *baby* dragon," Brierley declared, "the silly way you act."

Jain sniffed. *You think so?*

"You say you're a fire dragon, but I see only a salamander."

To see a salamander is remarkable enough, is it not? Jain replied archly, and Megan giggled. Jain bared his needle-sharp fangs. *But as you will, witch.*

There was a blur of motion, the snapping sound of hot flame and a rush of heated air as Jain abruptly expanded in size. Brierley gasped and recoiled, slipped, then sprawled onto the snow, taking Megan down with her. Dazed, she propped herself up with her hands and gaped at the enormous scaled head twenty feet above her own, and then gaped at the rest of him, a good fifty feet from scaled snout to tapering massive tail. Flames sifted gold and blue over his reddish hide, melting the snow near him and palpable as heat against Brierley's face, and his laughter was a low rumbling sound from deep within his scaled chest, like rolling echoes in a dark enormous cavern, a muted thunder.

Megan shrieked in high approval, clapping her hands. The fire dragon rolled an indulgent huge eye at the child, then flicked his tongue in and out over his muzzle. *I am Jain, the fire dragon,* he told Brierley smugly. *Do you believe me now?*

"I believe you," Brierley gasped. Then, in a twinkling, Jain was a salamander again, a few hand-spans in length, leathery-winged and agile. He hovered in midair until Megan scrambled to her feet, then landed neatly on her shoulder.

"Do it again!" Megan demanded.

Another time, dear one, Jain said casually. He busily cleaned one claw, then cocked his triangular head at Brierley. *I made my point. Didn't I, witch?*

"Very funny, Jain."

"Funny!" Megan laughed and stroked Jain's scaled hide, the flames flickering harmlessly over her fingers. "Mother's funny, too." She inspected Brierley for a moment, then pursed her lips. "Won't you get wet sitting in the snow, Mother?"

"Yes, child, I will. Why don't you help me up?" She held out her hand and Megan seized on her gloved hand and tugged Brierley to her feet. Brierley began to brush the snow from her clothes.

"What are the dragons, Jain?" she asked. "Are you real? Or my imagining?"

Part of our essence is mystery, little witch. True or imagined, I am Jain.

"That informs me greatly."

Jain snorted. *If I told you everything, what kind of life would you have? No challenges left, nothing new in the day to surprise. All you'd do is sit and feel bored, a sad life, truly.*

"An easier life, for sure," Brierley retorted. "It *would* be helpful if you'd tell me a few things." Jain shrugged delicately and flicked his tongue. "For example, what exactly *are* you?"

I told you that. I am the fire dragon. You have books, Brierley. Read them. Jain's tone was disdainful, as if books were an idiot's wasted time when one had other means to know. Well, from his point of view, Brierley thought sourly, it had sense. But she wasn't a dragon-spirit, snatching answers from the air or another plane, as he well knew. She put her hands on her hips. "Valena's book doesn't say anything about fire dragons."

Valena was an air witch, and knew little of me. Fire is mystery, he then intoned solemnly, quoting from Ocean knew what, *changeable yet eternal. Water is the lesser element, changing form to insubstantial vapor upon the application of fire.*

"Or puts the fire out," she menaced him. "All I need is a bucket."

Megan looked from Jain to Brierley and back again. "What are we talking about?" she asked plaintively.

"Never mind, Megan."

Never mind, Megan, Jain echoed mockingly. *Something is nothing, and nothing something, when you aren't real. Are you real, Brierley? Are you really sure?* He snickered.

"You do *know* things, don't you?" Brierley persisted.

What things?

"All things!" Megan exclaimed happily, ending it. She patted Jain's scaly side, then firmly changed the subject. "Mother's wet."

"Yes, Mother's wet," Brierley agreed, and tried vainly to skirt more snow from her clothes before the rest melted in to chill more of her flesh. "You're wet, too, child. And it's getting cold. Let's go inside now."

Megan hesitated, not wholly replete with the fun of snow, then agreed with a poignant sigh. Hand in hand, she and Brierley struggled through the deep snow toward the porch, while Jain flipped to and fro in the air above their heads.

As they neared the cabin, Stefan Quinby rode into view at the turning of the trail, leading a packhorse through the heavy snow, and Niall tramped along behind him. Megan cried aloud in delight and ran to meet him. Brierley followed at a more unsteady pace in the snow, then nearly tripped in midstride as she caught the men's emotions. "What has happened?" she called in alarm.

Stefan dismounted and lifted Megan high in the air, then kissed her as he set her down. "Treachery," he said heavily to Brierley, and gave her a tormented and bleak look, baffled, angry, and grieved. "The countess has been wounded and is very ill."

"How was she wounded?" Brierley demanded, seizing his arm. As Stefan hesitated, struggling to arrange his answer, she caught images from his mind of a pleasant ride through the Airlie countryside, the sudden campside attack, and Stefan's wild and desperate ride to a nearby town with the injured Rowena in his arms. Stefan blamed himself for her wound, for he had arrived too late, and that guilt had haunted him during the days he had hovered in Rowena's bedchamber, desperately afraid his lady would die. (*My fault*), Stefan keened silently, and hated himself.

Brierley pressed gently on his arm, offering mute sympathy. Stefan's self-blame was not fair, but the others had not convinced him. Stefan looked down at her blankly for another moment, then grimaced.

"Lord Heider, her marcher lord," he said heavily, "tried to kill her while we traveled back to Carandon. One of his soldiers put a sword through her shoulder, and she nearly bled to death before we could get her to safety. Now fever has set into the wound, and everyone is frightened for her." He ran his fingers through his blond hair, pushing back his hood, and stared at her in distracted despair. "She says you're not to come to Carandon, Brierley. It's too dangerous, however you could help."

"I most certainly will go!" Brierley exclaimed. "We can leave tomorrow."

Stefan and Niall both shook their heads. "She said *no*," Niall insisted. "She's right. Carandon isn't safe for you: you'll surely be seen and recognized, and word carried to the duke. If that's not enough, Arlesby is in disarray with Heider dead, and she has no secure forces on the border: Tejar would overpower any resistance when he invaded Airlie to get you." He gripped both her shoulders hard. "She told Stefan to convince you. Ocean alive, whatever you could do, mistress, I'd welcome with a shout of joy, but she's right about the danger."

"She said she won't lose you, too," Stefan said wearily, "no matter what the consequences, and told me to convince you. She *ordered* me to convince you." Megan put her arms around Stefan's waist, clinging to him as she responded to his despair with her own distress, even if she didn't understand the reason. Stefan sagged under her small weight, then sank back helplessly in the snow, unmindful of the cold. "It's all right," he murmured as Megan let out a choked wail, and pulled her into his lap to hug her. "I'm just unhappy, sweet child. Don't cry now."

Brierley knelt beside him and pressed his shoulder, then bit her lip as Stefan struggled against tears of his own. Stefan desperately feared for his countess, she sensed, as if a prop necessary for life itself had weakened and might fall. The long ride upward through the snow, with too much time to think and worry, had only deepened his fear. Was Rowena truly that ill?

"Come, get up," she encouraged him, and helped him and Megan to their feet. By pushing and cajolery, she got Stefan into the cabin and seated in a chair by the fire, then went out with Niall to lead Stefan's horses into the shed. Niall could unpack them later, but they eased the harnesses and made sure both horses had fresh grain and water, then hurried back into the cabin. Stefan had not moved from where he sat, his head still bowed.

As Niall helped Stefan out of his heavy cloak, Brierley bent over him and cupped her hand under his chin. He looked at her dazedly, and with a caress, she used her witch's touch to ease his fear, to bring calm where none had existed, peace where despair had driven him to distraction. "Rest easy, my friend," she said softly, and saw some of the distress ease from his young careworn face. "Rest easy. Ocean has all in her care, especially your lady."

Stefan closed his eyes and shuddered, then tried a weak smile. "It was a long ride up and I didn't stop to camp last night. The snow got deeper as I climbed, and it was very cold." He managed to straighten slightly. "I brought what supplies I could, not much. I'll bring a wagon next time, when the snows have eased."

"Thank you," Brierley said. "Here is warmth, Stefan, and a bed to rest in. You've pushed yourself too hard." She saw the quick flash of anger in his eyes, as if she urged him to fail his countess by taking his ease, and she shook her head at him. "Rest." She and Niall helped him remove his shirt and boots, then put him to bed. Afterward, Niall sat down heavily in a chair and bowed his head low over his knees.

"What's wrong with Stefan?" Megan asked anxiously.

"He has had a great grief. The lady he serves, Countess Rowena, is very sick, and he's worried for her."

"Is she going to die?"

"I don't know, child." Slowly Brierley straightened out Stefan's cloak and hung it on a peg by the door, then put his wet boots beneath it.

"You could make her not die," Megan said. "It's what you do." Niall raised his head and stared at Megan.

"She doesn't want me to come," Brierley said to Megan.

"Why not?" Megan demanded.

Brierley made a helpless gesture. Why not, indeed? A host of reasons why not, and all of them ignored Rowena. She sat down in her chair by the table and held out her arms, then helped Megan into her lap. "It's hard to explain, child. It's so very hard."

Niall shifted his dazed stare to Brierley. "What does she mean, 'make her not die'?" he demanded, but Brierley shook her head at him wearily.

"Will they burn us?" Megan asked in a low voice.

Brierley looked down at her small face in shock. Had Megan shared Brierley's dream on some night, as Brierley often shared hers, and found the nightmare of Brierley's own childhood? Jocater had warned Brierley too vividly of that hunt and horrible fire, trying to frighten her daughter into obedience, and had troubled her dreams for years afterward. She would not have Megan haunted by that same nightmare, and shook her head forcibly.

"Not while I have the saying, Megan," she promised fiercely, and let the child feel her determination, her fixed will. Megan relaxed slightly, reassured, and then laid her head on Brierley's shoulder. Gently Brierley rocked Megan, her thoughts in a tumult that quite undid some of her care, but Megan only tightened her fingers on Brierley's arm.

"What does she mean, 'make her not die'?" Niall persisted hoarsely.

Brierley looked at him and sighed. "You asked what a witch might be, Niall. What did you think Jonalyn was?"

"The countess said she was shari'a." He paused. "I confess I don't know what that means. All those tales—stupid tales."

"But you wondered?"

70

"Wondered? She was beautiful and graceful, and fair to see. I liked to hear her laugh, and once she smiled at me as she passed me in the courtyard. The countess liked her greatly, and she was her great favorite. But I didn't see anything more than that." He looked away, then ran his fingers over his chin, his face baffled and bereft, for Rowena, perhaps for Jonalyn. "I didn't understand why the duke wanted Jonalyn dead, why *others* wanted her dead, even the Airlie folk. I've wondered who wielded the noose, Jonalyn or someone else: there was that much fear loosed because of her—but why? Legends, crazy tales? Old wrongs *centuries* ago?" He stood up in agitation. "I don't *understand*."

"We witches have powers, Niall," Brierley said. "Megan's is to remember and protect. Mine is to heal with my touch and focused will, even a mortal wound. In Yarvannet I healed the local folk. They thought me a midwife who healed by ordinary means, and sometimes I did. But other times I healed with my shari'a gift. I saved Saray and Melfallan's son when both would have died. I healed Melfallan's burns after the guardian attacked him. It is my craft. Whatever Rowena's wound might be, if she is still living when I come there, I could save her, too."

Niall stared at her, openly skeptical. He wanted to believe, for he liked Brierley, and had greater reason now to believe, for Rowena's sake. She felt him struggle and fail. (*There are no witches*), he thought angrily. (*Stupid fancy, nonsense tales: no one could do such things!*) All the tales that Niall had heard about witches flickered through his mind, both marvelous and evil. To his eyes, Brierley was a simple commoner girl, prettier than most and too stubborn for her own good, his charge to protect. Brierley sighed.

"But you can't go to her, anyway," Niall said bitterly. "She's right that you can't. If the duke knows you're alive and finds you in Airlie, it's her life for his knowing—and maybe Earl Melfallan's, too. It would start a war, be the duke's excuse for it, and Airlie has no defense now on its borders. Who knows what evil would come then?"

"I know." Brierley looked at him sadly. "If Countess Rowena dies, Sir Niall, will you hate me?" she asked.

Niall stared at her for several moments, clenching and un-clenching his fists, then slumped his shoulders. "No, I won't hate you," he said quietly. "There are no such powers as you claim, Brierley. Believe in your shari'a tales as you wish, but it doesn't make them true." He started toward the door. "I'll unpack the horses," he muttered as he passed behind her chair, and went outside. Brierley put down Megan to play quietly with her doll in front of the fire, then sat dejectedly in her chair, her arms huddled within her shawl.

Melfallan would suspect Duke Tejar of Heider's plot, no mat-ter how the proof failed. She suspected the duke, too. But why strike at Rowena now? Why?

Because of me, she realized. He must guess that I'm alive, and blamed Rowena for hiding me. Melfallan has loosed a witch into their politics again, and as fate follows fate, the murdering begins. Now the countess was wounded, with treachery loose in Airlie, and the duke is hunting me.

Brierley rose and began to pace the room restlessly, imagining tall shadows stalking the cabin, phantoms in every direction. For centuries, the shari'a witches had lived in these eastern mountains, working their arts. In the upper end of this valley, the ruins of Witchmere had been long lost behind concealed doorways, but the Airlie folk still called this narrow pass haunted, Niall had said, and avoided it, and whispered that in this place, in this valley, bidden by ancient witchery, light and air might combine to drive a man mad, thieving his soul. Madness stalked the air here and filled the wind's voice. Madness—

How I long for home, she thought. How I wish for Yarvannet. She ached with the yearning. But would I be any safer there? Would anyone be safe with me?

In Yarvannet's winters, the sea storms sometimes battered the coastline for a few days, raising a pounding surf and a cold mist that scattered a light dusting of snow on streets and houses in the towns, and rimed the harvest stubble in the fields with glittering ice. The folk walked briskly when outside their houses, muffled to the eyebrows in warm wools, laughing and joking, then returned to their homes, stamping their cold feet, and piled more wood high in their fireplaces and stoked the flames to roar up the chimneys with a blaze of noise and light. In Yarvannet, the winter winds were feared for the plague they brought ashore some winters, but not for themselves, not like these harder winds, cold and vicious, were feared in the east.

I want to leave this valley, she decided suddenly. But to where? To Rowena? She knew the countess was right about the peril if Brierley appeared in Airlie. Both Stefan and Niall solidly believed so, and not just because it was their countess's bidding. Rowena had measured her life against the peril to others, perhaps knowing what she gave up in keeping Brierley away, and that was true bravery. Brierley had sensed that particular strength in Melfallan's aunt, in her one distant glimpse of the countess on the Darhel docks. But where should they go? To Mionn? Through this weather? To Yarvannet?

Oh, how I long for Yarvannet, Megan! I miss the sea. Or is it witchery, that I feel the future descending, moving toward us with malice and threat, to extinguish both our lives? Is it witchery? Why do I feel we must move now, not sit still, and act before whatever shadow moving toward us comes to pounce?

She glanced briefly at her child playing by the fire, and sighed. I wish I were a hero, my Megan, or even a fine lady, the Lady Brierley Mefell, an amazement to all the folk. People would stare at me with awe, and salute me with their plumed hats, and never dare to challenge my will. And if I were such a powerful lady, if I were perfect for you, I would be certain of your safety, Megan. If I were woman enough to be Rowena, we would both be safe—

She started slightly as Megan touched her skirt, then looked down into the child's puzzled eyes. "I love you, Mother," Megan told her solemnly. "Please don't worry so hard."

Ocean, how much had Megan heard? Brierley bit her lip, furious at herself for fretting while Megan was awake. "Megan—"

"I don't understand much of it, but I can try harder," Megan said earnestly, and tightened her fingers on Brierley's skirt. "I know there's danger, but there's me and you and the new one, and maybe we'll meet the girl in green."

"Who?" Brierley asked, perplexed. "What girl in green?"

Megan looked away, her eyes unfocusing. "No, maybe not her. That was years ago, lots of years, when she came here." She pointed at her narrow bed beneath the window, then looked up trustingly into Brierley's eyes. "She slept in my bed, and I remember her. She was looking for people like her—like us. Maybe she's still looking, and we can look, too, and we will find each other. And then you won't have to worry so hard."

Brierley bit back a sudden groan, fighting against the hope that had suddenly flared bright-hot within her. Megan dreamed things, she reminded herself, things not real. Children's blocks that giggled, a castle of white stone, a river that existed only in her own mind. Not real.

"Not this time," Megan said softly, shaking her head.

Brierley stared down at her daughter, wanting to believe Megan, wanting so desperately to believe this child's dreams. "And who's 'the new one'?" she whispered.

Megan laid her palm on Brierley's abdomen. "The one in here." She looked up again and smiled. "My sister. She's barely started and still dreams of the stars and large spaces, but she's in there." Megan spoke with total confidence.

Brierley swayed, abruptly dizzy, and wisely decided to sit down in the chair by the table. Megan climbed into her lap and wrapped her arms around her neck. "See?" she piped in delight, stroking Brierley's hair. "Already you're worrying less. I can help, Mother—really I can. See?"

"Oh, Megan." Brierley buried her face in Megan's curls, then wrapped her arms around her tightly. Megan sighed, and laid her head on Brierley's shoulder, content to be held. Brierley slowly rocked her witch-daughter, this lovely enchanting child who had fulfilled all her hopes for a daughter, those desperate wistful hopes for a companion, a witch-apprentice, a child to love, during the long lonely years in Yarvannet. Knowing her mother's anguish within her marriage to Alarson, Brierley had prudently decided against marriage for herself, and thus against any hope of children she might bear, and had instead focused all her wishes on the witch-child she might meet someday. She had never truly believed she would find another of her own kind, despite her hoping, but against all accounting, all prudent expectation, Mother Ocean had given her Megan.

And now had given—Brierley closed her eyes and choked back a sob, then felt Megan's hands tighten on her arms. *It's all right, Mother.* Megan's mental voice was barely a whisper in Brierley's mind. *Truly it is.*

Yes, child. She sensed again Megan's total certainty about the baby, and felt that certainty echo within her own knowing, although how she knew she could not say.

A baby. My baby. She marveled at the wonder of it. As one of Amelin's midwives, she had helped dozens of women bring their children into the world. Through her witch-sense, Brierley had shared the mother's joy when she felt the child first move in her womb, her amused resignation about an awkward and unwieldy body as the pregnancy advanced. She had shared the mother's pain during labor, her joy after the baby was born, small and perfect, to be placed proudly in the father's arms. But that witch's sharing, she always knew, would be all she ever had, never her own child, always another's.

She had so convinced herself she would never bear a child that she had quite forgotten the idea when she bedded with Melfallan. Nor had he thought of it, either, forgetting because he wanted her. Blithely, passionately, they had both deliberately forgotten a fact they both knew, unwilling to remember lest they be prudent. She smiled impishly. Ah, how we can be willfully blind, we two. She should not have bedded Melfallan, she knew, and he had known it, too, another fact they had ignored. And from this great error in their judgment, Ocean had given them the wonder of a child.

Will he want a child with me? she wondered happily, and thought he would. A by-blow child was not respectable, and her baby would badly complicate his marriage and his politics, but still— She shook her head and sighed, caught again in the dilemma of her love for a High Lord. If Melfallan were not a High Lord, matters would be simple. If she were not witch, simpler still. These facts were not as easily ignored, nor were they facts, to be admitted, either would wish changed, not truly. But whatever now happened between them, whatever future they might have together, if they had a future at all, this child would be always theirs together. The loss, if there were loss, would not be total, for either of them.

A baby. Brierley laughed softly, and felt the answering chuckle of Megan's laughter between her sleeves. *See?* Megan sent triumphantly.

Yes, sweet child. I see. She kissed Megan's hair.

That night Brierley dreamed of a glittering golden ship sailing the stars. Fine crystal gems studded the lines that stretched from deck to the masts, sparkling in the starlight. Broad near-transparent sails billowed gossamer above her head, nearly invisible against the dark sky, like spun spiderweb or thin haze of icy cloud, yet moving and alive. The ship plunged forward with reckless speed down a shimmering silver wave of starlight, descending the stars. Brierley stood on the high stern deck of the ship near a tiller-wheel as tall as she, and balanced easily with the motion of the ship.

In every direction, stars burned against the infinite darkness, gold, blue, red, green, each linked by delicate veils of silver light. Was there music? Their sound swept through her body, resonating with her every fiber, and drew her onward. She threw back her head and yielded to their music, and the ship plunged madly, borne ever faster upon the shimmering light.

When she opened her eyes, she noticed a small child standing on the deck below. She could be no more than two years old, her chubby legs short and solid, her waist-length hair bright gold. The child raised her hands against the starwind, feeling its push, and laughed, a musical lovely laugh that spun itself into the distance. Then she turned and looked up at Brierley, her eyes depthless and filled with stars.

Feel the wind, Mother. Her mental voice spoke clearly into Brierley's mind, resonating with the chime of crystals touching, as if their souls touched. *The wind is alive.*

Yes. I feel it.

The child gestured at the stars all around them. *They sing, Mother. Can you hear them?*

Oh, yes.

They live! They know me, and they know you. The child clasped her hands together ecstatically. *They are everything,* she said in awe, looking around her at the blaze of suns. *They are ours.*

The child raised her hands again, and their golden ship fell alongside a burning golden star, spinning downward like a falling leaf tossed on the storm. The child laughed merrily and gestured greeting to the star as it filled half the sky, then pointed to another star, blazing blue, to their left. Obediently, the golden ship swerved and plunged onward. The brilliant blue star swelled, leaping huge in its size, and the child sent the ship deep into its fires. Brierley gasped and held tightly to the railing as all flared into a dazzling blue twilight.

All is possible here, said a deep voice, as if it rolled beneath endless ocean waves. *All is possible, when we remember what we were.*

Brierley fell ecstatically from the sky, a sea lark blown far inland and tumbling in dizzying spirals on the wind. She cried aloud in her piping voice and swept downward, rising quickly over the white towers of Carandon Castle, then plunged down again toward a lead-paned window on an upper floor. Like a whisper of wind, she sighed through the panes and swept a circuit of the bedroom where Rowena lay. Rowena's eyes, bright with fever, flew open and she looked around distractedly, oblivious to the healer bending over her bed, to the servants gathered in the room corners and watching anxiously.

Rowena, Brierley called, and brushed her face with her wings as she passed, the lightest of touches. *Rowena,* she crooned.

"Jonalyn!" Rowena cried out, thrusting out her hand, then struggled as the healer caught her flailing arm and forced it downward. "No!" Rowena protested, and fought him, exhausting herself.

"My lady," the healer said desperately. "Stop this! My lady, don't fight me!"

"Jonalyn—" Rowena moaned, and still struggled against him.

I am here, Brierley sent, comforting her. *I am with you.* She swept quick circuits of the room, beating strongly with her wings, and dipped again to caress Rowena's face. *I am here, beloved lady.*

But Rowena could not hear her, lost beyond the miles between them, lost in her growing fever and guilt that now threatened to drown her. Brierley rose on flashing wings and swept out of Carandon Castle, crying defiance in her piping voice.

Brierley woke quietly in the narrow bed she shared with Megan, and listened to Stefan's soft breathing from the other bed, to Niall's snores from the rough bed he had made on the floor. All was quiet around the cabin, and not even the wind stirred. The fire popped slowly in the fireplace, dying away into embers. Brierley took a deep breath, and wondered if her dreaming were fancy, or if she had truly dreamed tonight of Carandon Castle.

Why had Rowena called her Jonalyn? And why with such wild anguish, a raging emotion that slipped her hold only in delirium? After twenty years? What strength she has, Brierley thought, marveling. To carry such a grief within her, yet act with such firmness, such courage! She knew Melfallan deeply loved his aunt, but she doubted he knew about this. It was like Rowena to hide it away, even if she punished herself unfairly, to grieve alone and uncomforted.

It was not right, that grieving. It was not right that Rowena, brave Rowena, should die.

She laid her hand lightly on her abdomen. *Can you hear me, Megan's sister?* she asked wistfully, and sensed no one at first, then a drifting sense of stars and—what had Megan said? Large spaces. Oh, yes, very large spaces, she thought, bemused, remembering the starship and the void the child had sailed. How lovely you are, my little one. How very lovely. Should I teach you my mother's fear, the fear that made her abandon Jonalyn and so make new tragedy? That made her abandon Lana and eventually me? Or do we follow Rowena's choice—to find the courage to forge one's way?

If we do not fear each other, Valena had written. If we do not fear life itself, Brierley amended. If we do not fear. Thora had bid her to refound the craft, to raise up the shari'a to a new flowering: *believe!* she had urged.

Believe: one needs courage to believe, Rowena's style of courage. I think you have answered me, sweet child, in the sea lark you made tonight.

Believe. But belief is a choice—and courage the will to act.

ountess Rowena sat by the lead-paned window that
looked over a courtyard of her castle, a furred lap robe
covering her knees, a warm shawl around her shoulders. Her head felt dazed with fever, but she had
improved during the night, enough to sit up in a chair
for most of the day. A huge fire burned in the fireplace, and her
servants came in and out of the room, asking if she needed anything, suggesting some trifle when she declined. A book, a glass
of water, a shawl for her shoulders: how kind they were. She
should stir herself and show her appreciation, she thought restlessly, but instead she merely sat, useless and hot.

She watched the drifting snowflakes fall lazily through the air
beyond the window, to settle cold and motionless on the courtyard
stones below. A faint breath of air stole through the grille holding
the lead panes, cooling her face. Without intending, she leaned
closer, watching that cool touch. Hot: it drove her thoughts to
distraction, muddling everything, and made her feel so utterly
sick.

As she sat, she cradled her injured arm against her body, and
bit her lip against the lancing pain that sheeted from shoulder to
fingers, a pain that waxed and waned and would not be eased,
no matter how she moved her arm or held it still. She could move
her arm, but sometimes dropped whatever she tried to hold. She
could shift her arm from position to position, making the pain
move about, but she could not escape it. The soldier's blade had

struck deep, permanently injuring the nerve, and she had woken in Effen's house to a sheeting fire in her arm, a fire that had never stopped in the fortnight since the attack. It was impossible to write, and for the first time in her life she had to rely on a scribe.

She had written to Melfallan as soon as she was able, reassuring him with words more likely falsehood than truth—no, *she* had not written, Tess had, and likely Melfallan would wonder at the different hand in the script. A few more weeks, perhaps a few months, a passage of two or three more letters, and Melfallan would know the truth, as her healer knew, as all would know in time.

By Allemanii law, a High Lord must be physically whole, capable of military defense and sword service to his liege lord. Her skill with the sword was well known: even Earl Giles of Mionn had grumpily accepted that technical ability to rule. But the blade had passed through her right shoulder, her sword arm, and sheeting pain was a symptom well known to any healer who tended soldiers, and to any swordsman who learned the risks of his trade along with its skills. Such pain meant permanent crippling of the arm. Once the passage of time confirmed to all the world the permanence of her injury, Duke Tejar would demand another regent for Airlie, triumphantly citing the Charter and ancient Allemanii right.

Who then will protect Airlie? she asked herself in anguish. One of Tejar's kept men, who would wax ambitious, thinking his own son the better heir to Airlie, and so plot against Axel's life? Axel! How can I defend Axel now? She stirred restlessly in her chair, then grimaced as the pain moved again, throbbing into her fingers.

Another servant maid bustled quietly across the small chamber, dusting and straightening, then bobbed a curtsey and left the room. Rowena hardly noticed her absence, as she had hardly noticed her presence. Instead, she watched the snow sift down in silent shadowed flakes against the darkness of the descending night, whispering against the panes, floating in their myriads to settle cold and still on the stones below. A faint chill seeped through the glass, touching the air of the room with the continuing winter.

This can't happen to me, she thought irritably. I'm Rowena of Airlie. I can't spend the rest of my life like this, yet my servants look at each other worriedly and tell me nothing, thinking I cannot read their eyes and faces, that I cannot see what is plain. Shall I complain about fairness? What in life is truly fair? Who determines fates such as this? Is it Mother Ocean, who has leveled some grievance at me, blighting me? What grievance? What fault? How have I offended Her?

What of Airlie? The fire rippled through her arm, lancing at her fingers, cramping them, and she flexed them restlessly, then closed the fingers of her other hand over them, pressing hard.

Below her in the courtyard she saw her son Axel ride through the gate, then dismount from his tall colt, coming home from an evening ride. At ten, Axel was already a fine horseman, and quickly learning his own skill with arms at her castellan's tutelage. He was a happy boy, quick to give loyalty, quick to laugh, growing more handsome with every year. He had his father's height and calmness, Ralf's wheat-blond hair, his mother's eyes. He was the pride of her heart, the joy of her life, and only the firmest of self-discipline had prevented her from spoiling him to excess. After three other children buried from plague, gone into the ground, as Ralf had later gone, Mother Ocean had given her this beautiful boy, this shining hope for Airlie.

How can I protect him now? she asked herself again. Dear Ocean, how? Will you not listen to me, divine Mother? How abjectly must I plead to you? Tell me how deeply I should humble myself, and I will.

Axel passed the reins to the hostler as he talked animatedly to his two companions, noble sons his own age who went everywhere Axel did, and would likely follow him everywhere all their lives. He was a popular boy, easy with his friends, forever into everything. At times, he reminded her of Melfallan at that same age, with the same restless intelligence, the same pranks and mischief and horde of boys in his wake, the same winning smile.

Axel had taken those qualities from herself, from the Courtrays and not the Hamelins, and was as much Earl Audric's grandson as Melfallan in all the important ways. In six years, Axel would come of age and take Airlie as his rightful own to rule. Will he be given those years?

I fear for you, my beloved son, my darling. I sit and fret and feel sorry for myself, and I watch you, my bright youth on the morning, and see my entire heart confined in your smile. Why had she not dodged the blade more deftly? One *practiced* for that peril, among the others of battle, during endless hours on the quadrangle under the tutelage of older knights. Why had all her training failed her at the crux? What punishment had she earned, to be so afflicted? What fault?

She sighed and bent her head, then plucked at the fabric of her skirt, feeling wholly and utterly useless. She had always led an active life, accustomed to ease of movement and physical strength. She could outpoint half her own soldiers in swordplay, and more if she ever practiced as much as they did. She could ride the most tempestuous stallion, bringing him in firm control by bit and rein, and loved the power of a difficult animal, the spirit that simmered as it bent to her will. Let other ladies sit primly in their chambers, stitching endlessly at yards of fabric, chattering inanities like birds. I am Rowena, Countess of Airlie. I live my own life as I choose—well, at least most of the time—or had lived it. Not now. When she looked out the window again, Axel had disappeared from sight.

When Rowena was seventeen, Tejar had offered himself to Rowena as an awkward suitor, confident of his success. And, I, Rowena thought wistfully, I was the belle of the lands, the most eligible bride of all the high ladies, with suitors flocking as if I were some treasure to be won. Perhaps I was a treasure; certainly Father thought me so. With my hand came Earl Audric's influence and favor, and he was close friends and ally with Duke Selwyn. But my father did not wish me married to Tejar, whom he disliked, and I did not wish to marry Tejar, an ugly boy at that age. I was cruel in my rejection, invulnerable in my youth and beauty, and not yet aware of how one mistake can lead to later peril. For that error of my vanity, twenty years afterward, the duke had struck hard at her, wanting to steal her life, as perhaps he had.

She had no certain proof of Tejar's involvement. A duke's message had arrived in Arlesby, and Lord Heider had ridden out with murder in his heart. Melfallan had no better proof of Sadon's hand in her father's poisoning, nor of what sly ducal promises had lain behind the count's malice. Even if we had our certain proof, she thought, to whom would we lay our complaint? The duke? She smiled ironically. When Roland Lutke created his duke's council and then attached the High Lords' rights to that appeal, he had crafted a great void into Allemanii politics. He had assumed the dukes who followed him would be just, as he himself had been just. Poor deluded man.

She leaned her head on her hand, cradling the other close to her as the pain moved again. Oh, for an hour without this pain! Only an hour, one small hour, and the hope it would bear. What would I give? Every day the price grows more steep—if only I knew to whom I should pay it!

Dear Ocean—

She had forbidden Brierley to come to her. Healers had a stubbornness about their craft, wanting to lend their personal aid to the injured. Perhaps Brierley could take this pain from her shoulder, as she had healed Saray, and restore her whole to Airlie. It was a wild hope that teased and tormented, but she would not put another witch in peril, for love of Melfallan and perhaps Brierley herself. She would not repeat her old mistake that had cost Jonalyn her life.

Jonalyn—

Sometimes, Jonalyn, I want to shout against this darkness that might swallow me. I want to rail and rant against this drifting snow that falls so silently, so inexorably, to shroud me and freeze me to death, stealing all warmth, stealing my soul away, leaving me nothing. Nothing. Did that same dark despair drive you to your mad act, Jonalyn?

Jonalyn—

She thought suddenly of sea larks, exploding against the bright sky of the morning. Odd, she wondered: why would she think of such a thing?

Then the pain struck again, scattering her thought. She shifted in her chair, moving her arm against the pain, and ground her teeth. I *will* feel sorry for myself today, Rowena thought, that is obvious, but surely I should have a time limit. Another ten minutes and I'll be done with it for today. But then what? Then what do I use to fill the remaining hours of this day and all the day tomorrow?

She heard a quick step outside her chamber door and turned her head as Axel burst into the room. He had taken time to change his clothes, dressing in an embroidered tunic that had been new in the spring but had already grown too tight in the shoulders, hitching up the hem. "Mother!" he exclaimed. "How are you feeling?"

"Better," Rowena lied. She made herself smile and tried hard to appear as she formerly did, a careful task of posture and smile and carriage of the head. Axel crossed the room with a few swift strides and bent to kiss her cheek. "And what did you do today, my son?"

"Went riding." Axel perched on the windowsill and crossed one leg comfortably over the other, his hands holding his knee. "We went fast."

"You always go fast," she noted dryly.

"Sir Mark says I'm just like you, especially when he thinks I've gone too fast, and he scowls when he says it. I think you were a trouble for him when you were younger. Hard to believe, but a hint." Axel grinned.

Rowena leaned her head back against her chairback and twitched her mouth in response. "I'm still a trouble, trouble for everyone. I take pride in that, but don't you copy me. I won't have it, young man."

Axel looked at her for a moment, then bit his lip. "It's hurting this evening, isn't it, Mother? Is your fever rising again?"

"I—" She looked away.

"I know when you worry," Axel said earnestly. "You don't think I do, but I always know. You think I'm too young to know. And I know when you're hurting, Mother, and I know you try to hide that, too. Why?"

Rowena opened her mouth, then shut it uselessly. Recently Axel had begun to ask questions she couldn't answer, a sign of coming maturity, she supposed, however uncomfortable for any parent with that dilemma.

"Do you think I would love you less?" Axel asked curiously. "Do I think I love you only because you're Rowena, Countess of Airlie, undaunted and beautiful, perfect in every way? And if you failed to be any of those things, my love would guggle away like water down a drain? Poor Rowena, I'd sniff. Poor Mother."

"Axel!" Rowena exclaimed in surprise. "I think no such thing."

"Don't you, Mother? I don't claim to be a man, not yet." He flexed his arms, then puffed out his thin chest, posing for her. "I'm still a boy, and I accept that. But that doesn't mean I don't know things, especially about you." He cocked his blond head and studied her again with a frankness of gaze she found mildly daunting. A boy still, she thought, but at times she saw a glimpse of the man to come in his bearing, in the expression of his eyes, as now.

"I know lots of things about you, Mother," Axel said. "I know you won't admit when you're hurting, even though Master Nigel could give you relief with his herbs and potions. I know you're worrying, probably about me and probably Airlie, as you always worry, but you hide that, too. You won't ask for anything, even when you need it—and won't ask even me," he concluded sadly.

"My dear boy—" Rowena looked at her son helplessly, and then clenched her teeth as tears stung her eyes. She blinked rapidly. No self-pity, she swore silently to herself. No weakness, not in front of Axel—but a tear rolled down her cheek, despite all her willing, and suddenly Axel was kneeling by her chair. He gently brushed away the tear with his palm, then took her good hand into his, pressing her fingers tightly.

"You need tending, countess," he said in a low voice, his eyes intent on her face. "Why won't you take the potion Nigel prepares for you?"

"Why, has he spoken to you about it?"

"No, I'm just a boy; you know that. They don't consult me. But I listen shamelessly around wall corners when they whisper to each other."

"When they whisper—" Rowena said, and felt her face heat with the shame. She stirred restlessly in her chair, making the pain shift uneasily, but did not draw away her hand from her son.

"You can pretend to be perfect for them all you want, Mother," Axel said, "but not for me. And I don't think you need to be perfect even for them. You are much loved in Airlie, Countess Rowena."

"A High Lord must have strength in arms, Axel," she said unhappily. "If I can't defend Airlie with the sword, even technically, the duke could challenge my rule. And my arm won't— You're only ten, Axel. We need six more years, and then you can take Airlie as your own, defend her as your own. Six years—"

"Let the duke make his challenge," Axel said confidently. "Cousin Melfallan would never allow it."

"Melfallan has constraints you don't understand, my son."

Axel studied her face earnestly for several moments. "Then explain his constraints to me, Mother, so that I can help you defend our land. It's early, I admit, but I think we have the need."

He smiled then with a simple grace far beyond his years, and for a moment Rowena saw Ralf in his youth as he might have been, before the disappointments, before the grief and the final long debilitating illness. And she saw herself there, too, with her father's strength, her mother's insight into hearts, the fine heritage of the Courtrays. Did Axel know her as well as he claimed? Per-

haps her deceits failed with other persons, too, with only Rowena
cherishing the illusion.

"You will be a fine count, my son," she said softly. "We will
talk later, but now I think Master Nigel should bring his potion."

Axel spread a delighted smile across his face, then leapt to his
feet with a whoop. He laughed at his own display, spread his
arms and whirled in place, and she laughed with him, looking
up at her fine shining son, the hope of Airlie, the hope of her
heart.

"Yes!" Axel declared in triumph, and he was off, skipping
lightly across the room. The door slammed emphatically behind
him, and she heard his footsteps quick on the stairs. Dear Ocean,
Rowena thought gratefully, and closed her eyes. Blessed Ocean,
keep him safe—

Outside her window, the snow drifted to a few last snowflakes, each spiraling lazily to settle on the courtyard stones, then
ceased.

Rowena's fever rose still higher that evening, and she went to bed
early, telling herself she felt better the next morning. Axel found
reason to spend most of the day in her room, chattering away,
stretching for jokes to amuse her, but by evening even his good
cheer flagged as he saw the fever rise in her flushed face. By then
she had stopped pretending about the pain, despite the worry it
caused her son, and clutched weakly at his hand. In alarm, Axel
sent for Nigel, and her healer brought another of his potions. For
Axel's sake, for she had promised him, she drank it obediently
and sank into a doze.

They thought her asleep, but some time later she heard Nigel
talking to Axel, soberly, plainly, trying to prepare him. *Fever this
severe often kills, Axel,* Nigel said, his voice hushed. *Even if she
survives her fever, her mind may be damaged, for high fever can strike
at the brain. She would be twice inflicted, Axel, always in pain, perhaps
demented*— Nigel paused, then forced himself to continue, for

Axel's sake. All things considered, it might be more merciful if—

But Axel would have none of it and flounced out of her bedroom, as if violent movement might erase words he could not bear to hear. After a time, he had crept back to sit by her bed, and held her slack hand as he wept.

Rowena heard the bedroom door open quietly, and light footsteps cross the bedroom floor. A hand settled gently on her wounded shoulder, a quiet touch that brought easement, not pain: her eyes fluttered open in surprise and she looked up into Jonalyn's face.

She had not aged, not a single year: what a wonder! Sober gray eyes, the palest of complexions, the pale brown hair that framed the face: yes, it was she! And Jonalyn's eyes did not hate her, did not pronounce the judgment Rowena had inflicted on herself for twenty years. She saw the girl's lips turn up in a gentle smile, and it was Jonalyn's smile, the very same.

Is this how it ends? Rowena wondered dazedly. With one last chance to see Jonalyn? Alive, in good health, not tormented, not dead! It was one prayer answered—only one, but still an answer. Rowena's heart swelled with gratitude. "Jonalyn," she murmured happily, looked up at the familiar face.

"Dear lady," the girl replied, taking her good hand into her own, "your Jonalyn died years ago, for your sake. I am Brierley Mefell, and I have come to heal your wounds, both old and new, with my strength. It is a strength particular to me and perhaps not equal to your own, for that is formidable, but it will suffice."

She bent over Rowena's bedside, her slender fingers pressing harder on Rowena's shoulder, probing through the heavy bandage.

"But—" Rowena gasped. Then she saw Stefan standing by the door and understood. "But I forbade you—" she began indignantly, lifting herself up, then gasped with the agony that coursed into her fingers.

"No arguments," Brierley said briskly, and gently pushed Rowena back down on the pillows. "Maybe later if you must, but in the sickroom healers rule, my lady." She looked across the bed at Axel and smiled at him, a lovely gracious smile that could tip the heart, then looked around at Nigel. "The blade cut deeply: she has sheeting pain into her fingers?"

"Yes, she does," Nigel replied, his eyes darting from Brierley to Rowena and back again. He scowled pompously, not at all welcoming to this invasion of his lady's sickroom. Brierley gazed at him calmly, waiting, and Nigel relented. "It's too soon to know if the injury is permanent, but her fever—" He stopped and eyed Brierley another moment. "Um, who exactly *are* you, mistress?"

Brierley's smile broadened to a grin. "Oh, yes, who? Well, we'll leave that where it sits for now, Master Nigel. I'm going to remove the dressing. Have you given her elecampane for the fever?"

Nigel glanced uncertainly at Rowena. "Yes, and fennel root for the pain. Fennel works best for injury to the nerve."

"Or sea dittany—but you haven't dittany here, have you? As I remember, it's strictly a Yarvannet herb." She lifted Rowena to unwind the rest of the bandage covering Rowena's shoulder.

"Yarvannet?" Nigel asked in confusion.

"No!" Rowena protested. "Don't betray yourself again—" Brierley placed her palm firmly on Rowena's bare shoulder.

"Be at peace, good lady—" she said, and took Rowena to another place, another time.

The world grayed, then steadied. Brierley knelt by Rowena on a distant beach, the sky turbulent above them, the sea rude and restless. A cold wind blew steadily off the water, disturbing the waves, and shifted a spray of sand grains higher on the beach, as if a fine brush swept upward, then upward again, allowing no peace.

Brierley felt Rowena clutch at her. "I let you die," Rowena cried hoarsely. "Oh, Jonalyn, I let you die. Forgive me!"

Brierley heard raw anguish in Rowena's voice. What was this? she wondered again in dismay. More afflicted Rowena than a sword wound: this wound pierced her innermost depths. Can a soul bleed internally for twenty years, enough to sap the will for living when there came greatest need?

"Don't grieve," she soothed, and kissed Rowena's brow. "It wasn't your fault, dear Rowena. It wasn't. You mustn't think so."

In the surf beyond the beach, the Beast lifted his head above the waves, menacing her charge. Brierley tensed, readying herself, but the Beast roared in surprise as dozens of sea larks exploded through the sky, bright wings in dizzying flight. They plunged down at the Beast, crying their defiance, and buffeted its head with their iridescent wings. Roaring, the Beast retreated from their assault into the water, and hated them as it yielded.

Again and again, the sea larks plunged, driving away the death of both body and spirit, and together rose with glad song, a song of triumph and hope in the future, a hope Jonalyn had despaired. As the Beast sank from sight beneath the water, defeated by their assault, Brierley heard the star-child laugh. The sound of her laughter lifted above the rushing noise of the ocean and the movement of the air, chimed behind the sunlight and the wide bright sky. With wonder, Brierley looked around her but saw nothing but the beach and sky and suns.

Rowena laid her proud blond head on Brierley's shoulder, as gently as a lover might, then sighed with blissful contentment, her fingers pressing into Brierley's sleeve. "I have missed you, Jonalyn," she whispered. "Don't leave me again. Oh, please." All the yearning of the world was in her whisper.

Brierley stroked Rowena's hair and blinked back tears, wishing earnestly that she could grant that whispered request, that one wish when nearly all others had been long surrendered, one by one. But she could not bring back the dead, could not undo a desperate act that had only one ending, and that forever. Rowena began to sob quietly in her arms, knowing the answer Brierley had not spoken. "It's all right, dear lady," Brierley murmured, holding her tightly. "All will be better in the morning."

It was a healer's promise, when sleep was fretful and pain would not retreat, but this pain was one of the soul. Brierley probed deeper with her gift, hunting the source, and found a day

Rowena had replayed nearly daily in her memory for twenty years.

~〇

"I don't care," Rowena had said, stamping her foot on the stone cell floor, and saw the girl seated on the cot smile at her, the smile that lit the eyes. "I will defend you," Rowena insisted, "whatever you deny yourself. I don't care."

"You don't care?" Jonalyn clasped her fingers on one knee and tipped her head. "A strange claim for the new countess of Airlie, whom the folk already love, this sour-faced, cold, nasty person that you are." Jonalyn stirred restlessly on the cot and looked around at the walls of the cell, and her expression sobered. "My time has run out, Rowena," she said sadly. "The Everlight is broken and my only remaining kin has fled into hiding, and now the duke's heir seeks my life. You cannot defend me, dear lady. You must think of your own folk."

"I will defend you—and them," Rowena vowed. "Here, I've brought you a cloak and some food. You can escape into the forest and hide there. When Count Tejar comes here with his army, if he does, my dungeon will be empty and no one will know where you've gone. Please, Jonalyn." Rowena took her hand and knelt by the cot, pleading without pride. "Please. Let me save you."

"But—" the girl began.

"Please," Rowena pleaded desperately. "I can save you. Don't say these horrible words of fate and ending, as if all things are fixed. They don't have to be. We can change what is, and find your safety. I know we can."

Jonalyn hesitated, then smiled and patted Rowena's hand. "Such faith in living, dear friend: where did you acquire it? I envy you for your bright hopes, your belief in future days. Is it an Allemanii gift? My people are murdered and scattered, and I am abandoned. Rumor now gathers like an angry swarm of bees, aloft and ready to descend." She looked beyond Rowena at the blank cell wall, her eyes unfocusing, as if she looked within as well. "The Beast rises again from the sea," she murmured, "and takes us all in our time, however we struggle, however we fight. It wins in every end, bringing the long and bitter defeat."

"Beast?" Rowena asked, confused.

Jonalyn's eyes shifted back to Rowena's face, and the smile tipped up again. Then she laughed softly and shook her head. "I told you not to mind my fancies. I speak nonsense."

"Here, put on the cloak," Rowena urged. "Believe because I do, even if you can't. There doesn't have to be defeat."

"No?" the girl had asked faintly.

And Jonalyn had gently consented, for Rowena's sake, not her own.

Two days later a forester had found Jonalyn's body hanging from a tree. Had she died by her own hand, or had she been found by enemies? No one was sure: the only certainty was her death, with its inexorable proof the cold stiff body that Rowena had buried. The spirit was gone, the movement, the smile, the light in the eyes, gone beyond Rowena's reaching, gone into emptiness. And with Jonalyn something had died within Rowena, too, leaving behind a bleeding wound of regret and guilt.

If I hadn't sent her into the forest, Rowena mourned— Jonalyn—

"I'm sorry, Jonalyn," Rowena murmured as she clutched at Brierley. "I'm sorry, so bitterly sorry." She began to sob again, deep racking sobs that she had taught herself to control by hard effort, but now could not. Rowena's despair shook them both, a despair that had tormented Rowena for twenty years, never yielding, never diminishing.

Why does a memory hurt this much? Brierley wondered in dismay. Why does Rowena blame herself so bitterly? Countess Rowena was strong and capable, a woman of sense: she had no fault for Jonalyn's death, and should know that. Brierley probed deeper and so found the bond between Jonalyn and Rowena, a witch-bond unwisely made, crafted from laughter and sunlight in the meadow, the quick liking between the two young women when they met, Jonalyn's shy love for Rowena, Rowena's admiration, their mutual loneliness. Now only loneliness sighed through the bond, resonating in unending grief, in the lack of connection, in emptiness.

Can a bond run so deeply it links two souls? Does one soul then sense the death of its other half, and grieve forever? She suspected so. This bond was witch-made: she recognized it from her own recent experience, for she had made a similar bond with Melfallan when she healed him in Witchmere. If Brierley died, would Melfallan know this same bitter grief? Her throat closed at the thought. And if Melfallan died, how could she bear such emptiness?

Sadly, Brierley suspected that Jonalyn had not even known what she had done. She would never have left Rowena this bereft, to mourn for years, had she known. She raised her head.

The beach was empty now of Beast and skylarks, leaving only the gray sands and a sighing sea. Gray-white foam ran quickly up the shoals, dying in broad fans as the water receded. Gently, Brierley broke the bond and let Jonalyn go. Then, with Mother Ocean's own tenderness, she willed Rowena into sleep and a new morning, when all would be better, the healer's promise, a healer's truth.

Rowena looked up dazedly at Brierley's face. Like warm water flowing through her arm, out her fingers, the pain flowed away, flowed and flowed, running away to a bare trickle, then—vanished. She watched the pain flow into Brierley's face, aging it subtly, as if the girl now bore the heavy fire, as indeed she did. Rowena had collected every book, every tale, about the shari'a, and had hunted throughout Airlie for any of Jonalyn's kin. Others scoffed at the tales, but this one about healing, rarely mentioned, was true.

Brierley sighed deeply, then moved a step backward, swaying off balance before she caught herself with a jerk. "Sleep now," the girl said, her voice faint. "All will be better in the morning."

Despite her willing, Rowena's eyes closed, plunging her into a comforting darkness. She stretched lazily and smiled, blessedly at ease, so wonderfully at ease. She felt Axel take her hand again and pressed back on his fingers, then slept.

~)

Axel looked up from his grip on his mother's hand. "Who *are* you?" the boy demanded, his quick eyes bright with suspicion. He looked back at his mother, now sleeping peacefully, and then at Brierley, demanding with his look, the set of his young jaw, the anguish in his face.

"I am a healer, young count," Brierley answered. "All will be better now."

"Just like that?" He snorted in disbelief, and cradled his mother's hand against his chest, as if that hand were his only anchor in a stormy sea. Brierley sensed the boy's impatience with his youth, his eagerness, his bright intelligence: Melfallan might have been such a boy. Rowena thought so.

"Yes, like that," she said. "It is my craft."

She held his eyes for a long moment. Nigel had told him tonight Rowena might die, an impossible event, not to be borne, but Axel had struggled valiantly to accept it—only now to find it ripped away, replaced with this wild and incredulous hope, a stupid hope that only stupid boys would keep. Skeptically, Axel looked Brierley up and down, and found her wanting: no great lady here, only a simple commoner in a homespun dress. Axel saw a dozen such girls every day. Brierley dimpled, reading his thought. Axel suddenly grinned in response.

"You're Melfallan's witch," he declared exultantly. "I mean, *really* a witch." He looked down at his mother with wondering eyes. "She's healed? Of everything? The sword wound? She won't cry that way anymore, the horrible broken sobbing?" His young eyes looked back at her, half-fearful that his hope might be in any way diminished.

"I have trouble with fever—" Brierley answered him faintly. "But the rest, I think yes." She nodded, reassuring him further.

"She is healed, young count, of many wounds. You needn't worry now."

"Healed?" Nigel asked, demanding at her, too. Brierley sighed with the burden of his demanding, and now sensed the Beast moving deep under the ocean water, approaching the shore. She hadn't much time. "What did you do to her?" Nigel asked impatiently. "What nonsense is this? Stefan! What have you done, bringing this woman here?"

In his haste, Nigel rudely pushed Brierley aside and probed anxiously at Rowena's shoulder with his fingers, but the gash had shrunk to an angry red line, nothing more. Nigel exclaimed in surprise, then bent even closer over the wound, marveling. Brierley staggered aside, and might have fallen had Stefan not caught her arm, steadying her. She leaned against him, Melfallan's friend, and felt the comfort of his presence, and sensed the joy that sang within him. Even Stefan, for all his trust in his countess and Melfallan, had not really believed, as he did now. She leaned against him, and let his joy suffuse into her like a delicious warmth.

"I need a place to rest, Stefan," she murmured.

"I'll help you." Stefan slipped his arm around her waist for better support. Gently, as if she were fine-spun crystal, he led her out of the room, supporting her when she stumbled. He found her a chamber nearby, a lady-maid's bed perhaps, and now empty of an occupant. "You can rest here. Do you need anything else?" he asked anxiously.

"No. Only rest." Brierley sank down on the mattress, and felt Stefan cover her with the blanket, then reach under to remove her boots, one, then the other. The Beast roared in the distance, rushing closer. There was the creak of a chair as Stefan sat to watch by her bedside, and then only the Beast.

Brierley awoke to find Rowena seated in Stefan's chair, and gave the countess a mild glare of disgust. "Back to bed," she ordered, pointing at the door.

"In a while," Rowena countered stubbornly. "I want to talk to you."

Brierley set her mouth. "No doubt we'll share several wars of will in our lifetime, countess, but this one I win. Nigel will tell you: fever is a warning to be obeyed." She pointed even more imperiously at the door. "Back to bed."

Rowena tipped her head to the side. "Now, how do you know I have a fever?" she asked impishly. "I do have a fever, true, but not much of one. Even Nigel has to admit that," she added, then looked amused. "You have badly disconcerted that good man. He keeps poking at my shoulder, exclaiming and muttering to himself, and stalks around in circles, tearing at his hair as he rants."

Brierley struggled to hide a smile. "Oh, surely it's not that bad."

"Perhaps I exaggerate—just a little." Rowena paused. "And the grief is gone, too—" she said in a low voice, hushed with its question.

"Witch-bond," Brierley answered, just as softly. "I don't think Jonalyn even knew. She would never have left you that bereft."

Rowena nodded slowly. "No, she would not. You saved my county, Brierley."

"I don't think in those terms," Brierley demurred, shaking her head. "I'm no highborn lady, concerned with Allemanii politics and great affairs. I saved you, for your sake and for those who love you. It is my craft." She hesitated, then shyly offered her hand. "Mostly for your sake," she said, "for how you loved Jonalyn, for all that you are, Countess Rowena."

Rowena took Brierley's hand into her own, then smiled down at their joined fingers. "For twenty years I have longed for a witch's touch again," she mused, "and I admit I wondered at myself. Surely this isn't natural, I thought; surely I risk madness in such fancies." She tightened her grip on Brierley's hand. "You understand, Brierley, that I am your champion, too. I can be fierce, but I am constant."

"Yes, I know. I know all about you." Brierley smiled, then

gently detached her hand to point emphatically at the door. "Back to bed!"

Rowena laughed. Then, to Brierley's surprise, she rose obediently from her chair with a rustling of her skirts, but paused at the door. "I'll go back to bed, but only if you share breakfast with me later," she suggested.

"No bargains."

Rowena laughed low in her throat, and shook her head, still laughing. "We shall see, lady witch," she warned. "We shall see."

Brierley listened to Rowena's footsteps recede, then stretched her arms over her head and let them lie there on the pillow, limp and comfortable. She blinked sleepily at the ceiling, and spent a time studying the grain of its wooden planks, fine-cured and deftly laid. That study led to tracing the wainscoting with her eyes around two walls and a corner, a pretty pattern of cornflowers and gold beads of thyme. The whitewashed walls of the small chamber were largely bare, but even a lady-maid in Rowena's castle was given a fine tapestry to hang on one wall, a pretty scene of musicians and dancers. A water jug stood on a stand; a wardrobe stood closed in the far corner. For a brief hour or two, this lovely room was hers, too. She stretched again and sank back blissfully into the comfortable mattress.

Rowena was safe: although the fever still lingered, she had sensed Rowena's return to health both in mind and body, and that finding pleased her profoundly. Brierley had always treasured her healing gift, but with certain souls, those certain persons in whom she found great value, she counted herself especially blessed. Such value of person did not align with noble rank or other mark of importance, but with the value Brierley found within them. Yanna, the Amelin girl with the infected foot, was one; Jared had been another. And Melfallan—she sighed and spent a time thinking about Melfallan.

What is he thinking now? Is he thinking of me? I hope so. She dimpled. Well away, Brierley, be as foolish about love as any girl might be. It's such a happy, lingering fog. My, it's lovely to feel this way, to have this feeling for myself, my very own. She had often sensed such joy in others newly in love, but had never believed it could be hers, not if she would be prudent, not if she wished to be safe.

For weeks now, since her arrest in Amelin, she had greatly feared for the future, first for herself, then for Megan, then for Melfallan, who risked himself in his politics in his determination to protect her. When had there been time simply to lie abed and think of Melfallan, happy and content with the thinking, needing nothing else? Whatever strength she had given to Rowena in the healing, something had also been returned, a new confidence in living, a hope in a life lived openly, without fear, without eluding and loneliness. She understood now why Jonalyn had loved the countess, as Rowena must have been in her youth, before the disappointments, before the compromises of the heart forced upon her. Likely Jonalyn had wistfully envied Rowena's confidence in the future as much as Brierley had envied the happy lovers in Amelin and Natheby, and had felt just as convinced that it could never be hers, not truly.

But courage is the will to act—and to be. *Believe,* Thora had urged her. *Believe in the future, my daughter.* Perhaps Thora and Rowena shared much, in the essentials. Yes, perhaps they did.

I think I'll relent about breakfast, Brierley decided. She had left Megan with Sir Niall in the wayfarer cabin, unwilling to risk her daughter on this dangerous visit into Airlie. She and Stefan had traveled quickly down from the hills, avoiding contact with others on the road, then slipped into the city through a little-used gate. Only a few servants had seen her enter the castle this night, and that hooded, her face concealed. For Rowena's safety, and her own, she must leave today and vanish back into Airlie's hills.

And she must leave as early as possible, and just as secretly. As Melfallan had explained to her, the High Lords regularly used spies against their fellow lords, suborning a trusted servant whenever possible, perhaps even a conveniently restless vassal lord. Duke Tejar had likely corrupted Lord Heider, prompting his treachery, and had certainly placed a spy, perhaps more than one, in Carandon. So far only Rowena's healer, Nigel, had seen her, and she had sensed the man's true devotion to his lady, enough to feel confident that Nigel was safe. But Nigel might mention her to others with less friendly ears, or a lady-maid abroad in the hallway outside her bedroom might have heard Brierley's voice and grown curious. Every additional hour that she lingered in Carandon risked exposure, with the news to the duke hindered only by the lazy speed of castle gossip and the passage of a horseman to Darhel.

In Yarvannet she had feared only her own death if she were ever known for what she was, but now exposure threatened others, too, not only Rowena and her Airlie, but Melfallan. She sighed. However she wished otherwise, a witch was loose again in the High Lords' deadly politics, and that fact could not be safely ignored. Duke Tejar had already tried to use her against Melfallan; given opportunity, the duke would certainly try again.

But a breakfast, to sit and talk a while longer with this re-markable lady whom Melfallan loved—yes, she would delay for that, and hope its careless and self-indulgent extra half-hour would have no consequences. She sighed again and closed her eyes, drift-ing another few moments of lazy ease, then pushed back the bed-covers.

5

Lady Saray watched the sea from the battlements of Yarvannet Castle, hoping for some sign of Melfallan's ship. She knew her wish was a futile hope: a courier would bring word of *Southwind*'s approach long before the ship rounded the harbor point, but still she had watched for a while every morning, awaiting her husband's return. In their nearly six years of marriage, they had never been parted for more than a few days, and she missed him deeply.

The Daystar had risen three hours before, and the faint blue glow of the Companion's rising now tinted the eastern mountains. The wind was cold, whipping briskly through the chill air, bringing the scents of the sea and winter-dry fields. She wrinkled her nose happily. In Mionn, where she had been born, the wind blew much colder, sharp with ice and the promise of heavy storms. Yarvannet's winters were milder, sometimes quite pleasant, and even a high lady could stand on the battlements, watching the sea, and not feel assaulted by the air.

At the harborside, the fishermen had already returned from their morning catch, and now unloaded fish and furled sails and coiled their huge nets. She saw several women and girls helping with the tasks, laughing and calling to each other, as small children ran shrieking up and down the wharfs. She smiled, watching her Yarvannet folk, and felt the familiar tug of a wistful envy. The fisherwomen seemed so very happy, there with their men on their ships, busy and comfortable with each other, laughing and calling. Sometimes when she watched from the castle, as she did now, she wished she could join them on the wharves, to laugh and tease as they did.

When she was very young, Saray had begged her mother to go out with the fishing ships, as she had begged for many other things her mother always denied. A noble girl's list of things she could *not* do, she learned, far outnumbered the list of things she *could* do. High on the "not" list was almost anything to do with the townfolk. Later, when she was twelve, she had asked to visit a shopgirl she had met in the town, a dark-haired girl her own age who had smiled and chatted happily with Saray, as if they were instant friends.

"She seemed so very nice, Mother," Saray had pleaded. "I really want—"

"Saray, a high lady must remember her rank," her mother had replied severely, visibly surprised that Saray would even ask such a thing.

"But, Mother—"

Lady Mionn shook her head briskly and rose from her chair. "We won't discuss it further," she had said, and then had walked out of the room, as she always ended her talks with her younger daughter.

Through her girlhood, Saray had often failed her mother's high standards by thinking and wanting such things a high lady must never think or want. Eventually she had stopped asking, but even that did not win her mother's approval. Her mother favored Daris, her older sister, and after Saray had grown into her beauty as a young woman, outshining plain-faced Daris at her mother's noble entertainments, that, too, had been somehow added to her faults.

"Saray, that dress has too many beads and ruffles. Change to another."

"But, Mother—"

"Saray, you laughed too loudly at dinner last night. When will you learn proper decorum?"

"But—"

"Saray, you are too familiar with your lady-maids. Remember your station!"

Saray sighed softly, remembering how it had been.

Even after she had married and come here to Yarvannet, her mother's strictures seemed a cage she could not escape. Melfallan thought some of her mother's rules were absurd and had told her so, but he never told her what rules should take their place. One must have rules, surely, and unfortunately one of her mother's rules was never arguing with one's husband and lord. And so she could not discuss the rules with him, only offend him again and again as she painfully discovered, one by one, what rules he did not like.

Saray rested one hand on the battlement wall, the stone rough beneath her fingers, and bowed her head. I try so very hard, she thought sadly. Ocean, how I've tried. Why can't I understand him?

And a thought barely above a mental whisper: why can't he understand me?

Melfallan was kind to her, with a sweet smile that she treasured, and he gave her courtesy as his lady wife and open praise for her beauty. He had visibly rejoiced with her at the birth of their son, and she had hoped Audric could erase the divisions between them. Perhaps he still might, and she clung to the hope desperately. Sometimes, when they lay in bed together, she watched him sleeping and might lightly caress his hair, carefully so that she would not wake him, and lean close to listen to him breathe. At such times, she could not imagine anyone more precious, more necessary to her own breathing.

She believed that Melfallan loved her—at least he said so— but he did not seem to love her as much as she loved him. Did he truly love her? How could she know? Even when they quarreled, he always returned to her in time, often with apologies Saray admitted he did not wholly owe. In turn, she had made her husband the center of her life, as one's lord and husband should be, and had bent her will on pleasing him, only to fail again and again.

Was it the rules? What am I doing wrong? What is the answer?

She shook her head, determined not to fret today. Melfallan would soon return home, and all might be better. She breathed in the sea wind and watched the dockside for a while longer, and then retreated to the castle stairs. The guard by the doorway saluted her, and she nodded absently to him, then descended to the family suites two floors below.

As she had every morning since her return from Darhel, she went to the nursery to see the baby. The wet nurse, Leila, sat in the broad rocking chair, giving Audric his morning meal. Saray paused in the doorway of the nursery and watched the girl enviously. Saray had wanted to nurse her baby, something her mother had taught her a high lady must never do, but she had hesitated too long. As was her duty, Saray had accompanied Melfallan to Darhel when the duke had summoned him, and by the time she returned her milk had ceased its flow. She had not known that milk could stop—no one had told her that such a thing might happen—and now she could not nurse her own baby. Another woman had that role, that intimacy with her child.

Saray felt the familiar roil of jealousy as she watched the young servant girl nurse Audric. Saray might tell herself that her next child could be different, but she might not have a next child, given the trouble with her pregnancies, and so might have lost this chance forever. Sometimes Saray could not bear the watching as Leila cuddled Audric to her breast.

It's not fair, she thought resentfully. *Leila has her own baby. Why does she have mine, too? Why is that a rule?*

Leila finally noticed her standing at the doorway, and Saray gestured curtly as the girl began to rise. "Don't disturb his meal, Leila," she said.

"Yes, my lady." Leila reseated herself.

Saray walked to the twin cradles by the window, where Leila's infant girl now slept. She had heard that a baby might take fever from another, and had worried several days now about Simone's presence in the nursery. Her mother had never allowed other children into Saray's nursery, fearing such fevers: it had made Saray's childhood lonely but safe. As she looked down at Leila's baby, she nodded and made her decision. "I think it best that Simone stay in the kitchens, Leila."

"My lady?" Leila asked in surprise.

"The other women can watch her during the day. She'll be quite all right. Don't you think so?" She turned and looked at the girl.

"If—if you say so, my lady," Leila stammered in distress. "But—"

Saray firmed her chin. "I do say so."

Leila ducked her head. "Yes, my lady," she murmured.

Something in the girl's meek voice made Saray hesitate. If I were a nurse, she thought, and the high lady ordered my baby away— Is this truly for Audric, or am I taking my petty revenge on a servant who can't fight back? Saray suspected she would not like the truthful answer. As she looked down at the bowed head she had so easily conquered, she nearly changed her mind. "Leila—"

"Yes, my lady?"

But a child could take a fever, Saray thought frantically, and Audric must be protected. Nothing must happen to her precious baby, nothing. Surely Melfallan would understand; surely he would agree.

"Never mind." Saray swept out of the nursery, nodded distractedly to Audric's two manservants in the anteroom as they bowed to her, and then hurried away.

In eastern Yarvannet, Count Sadon of Farlost paced his bedchamber, his robe flapping as he walked up and down the room. Twice his servant had opened the chamber door, ready to help the count dress for the day, and twice Sadon had chased him out with a snarl. Sadon's head throbbed with a headache, and his bad knee twinged with every step, adding to his fury. He hated growing old, growing bald, with twinges in every joint, the sagging flesh, the wrinkled skin, the pounding headaches that had worsened with the years. His healer could do nothing to cure the headaches, and the pompous man chose to blame his patient, not himself, when each new potion failed.

"If my lord will only control his temper, the headaches would—"

"Get out!"

How could a man think when his head might split apart with the pain? He paced restlessly, cursing the headaches, cursing the world, then finally sat down in the chair by his bed. He tried the deep breaths, then the slow rubbing of the temples, five circles forward, five back, stand up, sit down, bend. The vise eased slightly, enough to encourage him, and he repeated the exercise again, and again. He sank back limply in his chair, gasping, as the pounding finally receded to a dull ache. He could live with that ache, he told himself, however much he hated it, as he had hated every compromise forced on him by Audric Courtray.

A dutiful son in his youth, Count Sadon had married as his father had bid, and had sworn fealty to Earl Pullen, a lord he despised. When Pullen rebelled, Sadon had supported the duke's man, Audric Courtray, only to be disdained afterward by both earl and his duke, when Audric and Selwyn bothered to notice him at all. *Traitor,* the rumors had whispered, and the new Yarvannet lords had looked down their noses at Sadon, following Audric's lead. Earl Audric had mocked him in front of the gentry, had refused even minor requests solely to vex him, had isolated and scorned him, calling him "marsh rat" and "bogfern" behind his back. For thirty years Sadon had endured Audric's contempt, knowing the other lords laughed at him behind their sleeves. Even a merchant's son, once elevated to the nobility by a new earl, could appreciate Sadon's stupidity in trusting.

Once Sadon had believed in the feof oath, of the loyalty between lords, the mutual trust. Although he had disliked Pullen, a vain and arrogant lord, he had submitted and had tried to overlook Pullen's faults as liege lord. Earl Pullen had owed that same feof duty to the duke, but had imagined grievances and rebelled, betraying his oath. The other Yarvannet lords had followed him, although several shared Sadon's opinion of their rash earl. Unlike the others, Sadon had supported the High Lord he thought in the right, and so had offered his loyal troops to Audric when Pullen had rebelled. And what had it gained him? Sadon felt his temples throb anew and closed his eyes, breathing deeply.

What had it gained him? Thirty years of contempt, and a wastrel son who saw how his father was treated, who no longer tried to trust in his father, to admire him, to look to him. Instead, Landreth had chased women and other lusts of the flesh, and dressed himself in foppish clothing that looked grotesque on his fat body, imagining himself a gracious and admired lord high in the earl's counsels. In recent years, Landreth had even copied Audric's scorn, speaking to his father with contempt. Always the mimic. Always the fop. In a small secret place within him, one he now rarely visited, Sadon grieved for the beautiful boy he had loved like his own breath, his own right hand, bright youth on the morning.

And now the Courtrays had destroyed Landreth, too. Oh, the appeal still pended in Darhel, where Landreth now sat in Tejar's dungeon, accused of rape by the new Courtray earl. And likely Tejar would pardon his son, as he had hinted in recent letters, but not for Landreth's sake, no, not for him. Tejar would use Landreth to vex Melfallan, and count him no more useful than that. As Sadon had been one Kobus duke's tool, his son would now be another. Sadon ground his teeth and again began to pace.

He had longed for Earl Audric's death, thinking the removal of his liege would bring new opportunity, a new chance for Farlost and especially for Landreth—there might still be time to salvage his son—but Melfallan apparently hated Sadon as much as his grandfather had. Why else strike at Landreth scarcely six months into his rule? Why else take Landreth to Darhel in chains, to hold up his son's failures before all the High Lords, pronouncing his young contempt for both the son and his father?

I swore fealty to him, Sadon thought bitterly. I knelt before him and placed my hands between his, and swore my oath, like all the others. And for my promises, which I meant, he destroyed my son. What else did Melfallan now plan against Farlost, what other indignities, what other contempts? And what would they matter? If Landreth were truly lost, what did anything matter now?

He stopped pacing and eyed his private chest in the corner, then crossed the floor and opened a drawer, taking out again the duke's letter. A subtle duke, this Tejar, never quite promising the glitter but always hinting, never quite pledging support but always pretending it might come. Sadon had trusted the father: did Tejar think him stupid enough to trust the son? *Find out for me, good count, who poisoned Earl Audric. That man will be greatly rewarded.*

Now what does that mean? Sadon asked himself, glaring down at the duke's rough scrawl. Tejar had written this letter himself, as he had written several others over the years, each delivered by personal courier to be put in the count's own hand. Such a letter, one that suborned another High Lord's vassal, could not be trusted to a mere scribe. Tejar had known of his hatred for Earl Audric— as everyone knew—and had seen an opportunity, cajoling, flattering, promising. Once the duke had even hinted at the earldom itself for Sadon and his heir, a stupid promise. Sadon had shown Landreth the letter, in those days when he had still tried to teach Landreth the subtleties of his future rule as Farlost's count, but the boy had not understood the deceit behind the promise, as Landreth understood so little else. *Betray your earl,* the promises hinted. *The reward will be great.*

And Sadon had felt tempted, but some stubborn part of himself had resisted. In time, Sadon had gotten his hope and Earl Audric had finally died. The rumors had run wildly after his death, hinting at poison, but nothing had been proved. And nothing had changed. Audric's heir treated him with the same contempt and suspicion, and now had struck at his son. Sadon ground his teeth with rage, and felt his head throb anew.

Why does the duke think I know who poisoned him? he fretted. Did Melfallan think the same? He had hated Earl Audric, true, and had not bothered to hide his hatred. He had cause for hatred; all the High Lords knew he had cause. Did they *all* assume his guilt? Did they all snigger behind their hands, nodding sagely, painting Sadon with the blame? Did Melfallan?

Where is the proof? he fretted. When was my trial?

His spy in Tiol Castle had told him nothing, although he saw Melfallan every day. Not once had Melfallan voiced such suspicions aloud, at least not in his spy's hearing. Not once had Melfallan confirmed his hatred for Sadon and his son, blaming Farlost for his grandfather's death. But why strike at my son? Why *now*? Sadon began to pace again, the duke's letter clutched in his hand.

Is hatred such a mortal crime?

Betray your earl.

I should, oh, I should. I have cause, if different cause than thirty years ago, when I still believed in stupid loyalties. I have thirty years of cause, but it would not save my son, not now. And if Landreth were not saved, what use for anything?

Betray your earl.

With a curse, Sadon thrust Tejar's letter into the candle flame and let it burn.

After dawn, Duke Tejar Kobus stood on the battlements of his castle in Darhel, and looked down on the river. At this hour of the morning, little ever moved below, and Tejar often came here to watch his city when it still slept and he could not. Two weeks ago Melfallan's sloop, *Southwind*, had still lain at anchor at one of his principal river docks, waiting for her earl's return from Airlie. That morning Tejar had watched *Southwind* turn slowly on her ropes, bending with the push of the river current, and he had seen a sailor ascend a mast as the watch changed.

He should have watched longer, he told himself bitterly now, or set a soldier to watch those sailors, that ship. He might then have known when Melfallan slipped like a thief aboard *Southwind* and calmly sailed onto the river. Better yet, Tejar could have ringed an entire troop of his soldiers around that ship, and thus forced Melfallan to attend the duke's council Lord Dail had suggested. At that council, using Dail's clever ideas and Tejar's own deft touch at manipulating the anger of a troublesome lord, Tejar might have bested his enemy, as he had now bested Rowena. But, no, he had trusted in his authority as duke, had trusted that Melfallan would give the required courtesy of a vassal to his liege by asking Tejar's formal permission to return to his lands. Acid rose from his stomach as Duke Tejar indulged in a few moments of boiling hatred for *Southwind*'s owner, and then he turned away.

Too late now. His dilemma still dangled in tatters, unresolved and dangerous. His men had searched the town and nearby countryside for Tejar's vanished justiciar, Gammel Hagan, without result. Tejar had given the witch Brierley Mefell to his torturer to gain the confession that proved Melfallan a foul traitor, but the man had mysteriously disappeared—as had his prisoner. How? Why? By whose hand? Tejar had menaced Count Toral of Lim, Hagan's former employer, in case Hagan had fled to Lim, but Toral had professed ignorance of his former justiciar's fate, with enough panic in his eyes to convince Tejar of his innocence in the plot.

Where was Hagan? Tejar fumed. Why had he fled? Melfallan had brought his witch to Darhel for trial, playing a gambit against his own duke, and Tejar had countered that ploy with firm instructions to Hagan. A secret interrogation, a written confession that revealed the woman's evil, and Melfallan would be damned as the traitor he was. Afterward, Hagan was to dispose of the body, to be found weeks later, or never found at all: Tejar had cared little. But instead both torturer and witch had vanished and now could not be found.

Where was Hagan? Where was Melfallan's witch? And who had arranged it? Who? In the days since the girl's disappearance, he had pondered that question and believed he now knew his answer.

Item: his meeting with Hagan had been late at night and unobserved—of that he was certain.

Item: Melfallan had been in bed with his wife the entire

night—Tejar's servants had confirmed that fact. One had even listened at the bedroom door, thinking to please his duke with his initiative, as he had, and had heard the sounds of coupling. Later the servant had slipped open the chamber door to see them sleeping, and had checked twice more during the night. As much as Tejar preferred to suspect Melfallan, it seemed the Yarvannet earl's protest of ignorance had been accurate.

Item: Hagan had taken the witch from her tower cell, but had been seen by a soldier in the courtyard, one of Countess Rowena's soldiers. Who then had received that soldier's report? Melfallan, busy sporting with his beautiful wife in bed? Or Countess Rowena of Airlie?

Tejar began to pace beside the battlement wall, his hands twisting behind him, as if the hard pressure on his own flesh could yield a sure answer.

What if Rowena had intervened, he had asked himself, and her soldiers had overpowered Hagan, then stolen the witch away? When Hagan later woke with a pounding head and found the witch gone, what would Hagan do? Flee for his life, of course. He would have reason to flee, Tejar thought viciously, infuriated at Hagan for his failure. It fit: it all fit. And that meant Melfallan's witch was alive, not dead, and likely hiding in Airlie.

The situation was unbearable. He had protested to his High Lords that he knew nothing, but they didn't believe him. Instead they talked behind their hands and eyed him suspiciously, their own duke, then whispered their malices, began their plottings. Count Parlie of Briding was the worst, finally revealing himself as the sly manipulator he was. For years Parlie had pretended neutrality in Tejar's open contention with Earl Audric of Yarvannet, and had courted Tejar's favor, had paid him compliments, all the while laughing behind that smug fat face. And Rowena! She had laughed at him, too, when he ordered his soldiers to search her Darhel compartments, as she always laughed, always mocked him. He clenched his fists, his head throbbing with his rage at that contrary, idiotic, contemptible woman.

For twenty years Rowena Hamelin had defied Tejar, ruling

her county with an unseemly independence. For twenty years, ten as heir, ten as duke, Tejar had endured her insolence, her unwomanly behavior, her taunts and disdainful smiles and speeches against him behind his back. Had he acted against her as she deserved, Earl Giles of Mionn would not have objected, for the earl shared Tejar's sour opinion of her unnatural womanhood. But Rowena was daughter to Earl Audric of Yarvannet, and that simple fact had forced Tejar to stay his hand. In the eight years since Count Ralf's death, Rowena had not given him much opportunity to strike at her, true, for she was deft, truly her father's daughter. Likely she had thought him ignorant of her newest treachery. Likely she had thought herself safe, and the witch safe with her. But Rowena did not know all, and that ignorance had been her undoing.

Early in Rowena's regency, Lord Heider, her northern marcher lord, had secretly approached Tejar, unhappy with her woman's rule and all too conscious that his marcher lands would be the first invaded from Ingal. Tejar had encouraged the contact, flattering the older Airlie lord, as he encouraged all such contacts. In recent years, Heider had become more reluctant to court the duke against his countess, but no matter: in the passion of his early complaints against Rowena, Heider had written several letters to Tejar, most unwise letters, letters that would get him disenfeoffed and then hanged, for he had intimated the murder of his liege. Three years ago, one of Tejar's spies had quoted excerpts from those letters to Heider, and had delivered Tejar's firm threat. In time, the spy had told the marcher lord, he might receive a brief note from the duke, seven innocuous words that bore a hidden order, and Heider would obey that order or pay with his life.

Heider had agreed, of course, whatever his show of bluff, his lord's hauteur. What else could he do? Through his own idiocy in writing such letters, Heider had given Tejar a death grip on his throat, one Tejar had finally used.

But Heider had fumbled it, curse him to the Hells where he had surely gone. Tejar had hoped that Rowena would suffer before she died. He had hoped her blood would drip into pools, freezing on the hard earth, had hoped that Heider's blade would gut her, cut her arms from her body, set her mutilated body to jerking obscenely as she screamed her throat raw. His breath quickened as the images now ran through his head, blood and pain and ending. If Heider had succeeded in his task, Rowena would never again have defied him before the High Lords. But, he reminded himself, there was still the hope she might die: Arlesby's men had reported a sword wound, and Tejar's spy in Carandon Castle had sent a vague report about high fever. Tejar paced the battlements restlessly, wishing for sure word from Airlie, word that might come soon.

Once Rowena was dead, he mused, he'd appoint a new regent for Airlie, wait a suitable time and then dispose of Rowena's son by a convenient accident and put Airlie into another's hands. But whose? Not Heider's, Tejar gloated. That sorry lord had suffered his rightful punishment for his ineptitude. Tejar stopped for a moment, considering the possibilities among his Ingal lords. Bartol, Charlotte's bastard nephew? Bartol was clever enough, and had fastened his sailor's star firmly to his duke's cause. Had fortunes turned differently, Bartol's gambit of accusing a Yarvannet witch might have proven more useful. At different times Tejar had promised noble rank and several of the Allemanii lands to Bartol, including Yarvannet. The captain still waited patiently for Tejar's ultimate choice. Who else? Tejar scowled and resumed his pacing, then stopped abruptly as another possibility, a most startling possibility, occurred to him. He smiled, then laughed aloud. Well, of course not, but that didn't mean he couldn't dangle the bait.

He turned and strode toward the stair, clattered down the stairs to the floor below, then detoured to fulfill a duty on the way, one he faithfully kept each morning. On an upper gallery near his own chambers, Duke Tejar walked into his wife's suite of graceful rooms, each decorated with flowers and the glitter of crystal. His duchess reclined wearily in a lounge chair near the window that overlooked a fragrant garden, watching the early sunlight of the dawn; two of her ladies sat nearby with stitchery in their laps. Both lady-maids rose as he entered, and gave him a respectful curtsey. Charlotte did not notice him at first, but then turned her head. She smiled wanly.

"Good morning, Charlotte," Tejar said gruffly.

"Sire," she responded.

Theirs was a formal marriage, based on respect and never love, but Charlotte had never failed him in their twenty years of marriage, giving him two strong sons, unquestioning support, and the grace of her great dignity to his court. She had served him well, and he now regretted her slow decline, the inevitability of her death. Deep lines carved her face, deathly pale in her illness, and her body had grown desperately thin. Each day she seemed to die a little more, as if death were a creeping shadow steadily eclipsing her life, and soon the shadow would consume all of her. The healers could do nothing: the wasting sickness had no cure. All that remained now was the waiting.

"Are you feeling better today?" Tejar asked, as he asked every morning.

"Yes, I think so," she lied, as she always did. For months Charlotte had lied to him each morning, pretending she grew stronger.

He bent and kissed her cheek because it would please her, and received another vague smile as she looked up at him. Then he saw the light fade from her eyes as she forgot he was there, and watched grimly as she turned her head to look down into the garden, her face smoothed and blank. In its final stages, the healers had told him, the wasting disease settled into the brain, killing the personality before it killed the body. Already Charlotte seemed to live in another place, her spirit slowly fading and leaving a dry husk behind.

No cure. No hope.

Duke Tejar gestured curtly to the lady-maids to reseat themselves, then left the room with quick strides. Guards snapped to smart attention as he passed through the palace hallways, but he ignored them. Servants scuttled as he walked briskly down a broad hallway, but he waved them away. Another corridor, another stair, and he reached the staircase to the palace dungeon. The dungeon guard on duty was seated at the small battered table against a wall, and sprang to his feet as Tejar walked into his view.

"Sire!" he exclaimed.

"I want to see Landreth of Farlost," Tejar growled. "Take me to his cell."

"Yes, sire." The guard fumbled nervously with his keys, then took a torch from the wall bracket and led the way into the narrow tunnel with its rank of cells. Halfway down the row of oaken doors, each pierced by a narrow slit at eye-level and floor, the guard stopped and inserted his heavy iron key into the lock. "He hasn't shouted much the last few days," the guard said, "but he's not eating all his meals." He toed the half-empty plate on the floor with its half-crust of bread and congealed stew.

"Hmm," the duke said noncommittally, and gestured for the guard to open the door. The door creaked open, revealing a dank and ill-lighted cell within. "Leave the door open and stand nearby," he commanded. "I'll call you if I need you."

"Yes, sire." The guard stepped back and Tejar entered Lord Landreth's cell.

An unkempt young man in rumpled clothes, and not as fleshy as he had been, sat on the cot against the far wall. As Tejar entered the cell, he looked up with dull eyes. Tejar saw the recognition spark in Landreth's eyes, but his prisoner stayed seated and did not bother to rise. It was a calculated disrespect, a sign Landreth still had some spirit in him, despite his misfortunes at Earl Melfallan's hands. Interesting, Tejar thought. He knew little of Count Sadon's heir except by rumor, and that had been mixed. Was the son as sly as the father? And as contrary? For years Tejar had tried to subvert Sadon against Yarvannet's earl, but Sadon had stubbornly refused to respond to his letters. The duke leaned back against the wall by the door and crossed his arms across his chest. "I hear you're not eating much," he said.

Landreth shifted slightly on his cot but said nothing, and his gaze did not intensify into much of a glare. Well, not much spirit left, Tejar amended, but perhaps sufficient for his purposes. Landreth was a beaten man, outdone by Earl Melfallan, and Landreth knew it. Count Sadon should have done better in raising his son, Tejar thought coldly, but Sadon's lacks had marked all that sour lord's life.

"You were too fleshy, anyway," Tejar commented, and finally saw some fury fill Landreth's face. Better, but still the young Yarvannet lord did not stir—although he now sat as if coiled for the strike, waiting only for the prey to come a foot nearer. Tejar did not oblige him. "Accused of rape, I hear, four kitchen maids and Melfallan's witch," he said indifferently, as if neither Landreth nor maids mattered at all. "I heard one of the girls was barely thirteen. And I heard you failed in your lust with the witch. Nearly stabbed you with your own knife."

"I already gave my statement to your justiciar," Landreth growled, barely managing his rage. "The girls were willing, and it wasn't rape."

"Was the *witch* willing?" Tejar sneered. "Or was Earl Melfallan the better match there, too? She lets *him* mount her, but not you? How do you measure a man, Lord Landreth? By the size and boasts, or the doing of it and the girl's moans? Or do you care about the girl liking it at all? I think not."

"They like it well enough," Landreth threw back, then dared to smirk at him.

Tejar studied him, considering that smirk. Past a certain point, a man no longer feared his fate, as Landreth now little cared how he insulted his duke despite Tejar's power to hang him on a whim. Melfallan had produced the evidence and so Tejar had more than a whim, and, in truth, Landreth had his lord's entitlements to a formal trial before Tejar hanged him, but they both knew who had the power. Tejar could kill him or pardon him, or choose a range of options between. Gammel Hagan had suggested castration: Tejar idly toyed with the idea, if only to watch Landreth's face when he was told *that* fate, but saw better uses for his new tool.

"Why am I graced by your visit, sire?" Landreth asked at last, defiance in his eyes.

"Why?" Tejar pretended to ponder the question for a moment. "Earl Melfallan has demanded your immediate trial, but I chose to delay. I'm busy with other things, I told him, come back perhaps later in the summer." He waved his hand negligently. "Until then, Lord Landreth, you will be my guest. My guest to please as I will. Your freedom, Landreth—if you please me."

Landreth's eyes widened and he surged violently to his feet, to do what perhaps even Landreth didn't know. The dungeon guard slapped his hand to his sword hilt and warningly took a step into the cell. Landreth stopped himself, his jaws working, then made himself sit down again, as if nothing had happened, nothing of moment, nothing at all. Tejar nodded with approval, then gestured the guard out of the cell.

"Excellent," Tejar drawled, and saw the rage flare again in Landreth's eyes. A very angry young man, his Landreth.

"I've had enough of your promises," Landreth growled, his fists clenched. "You can promise whatever you want, and the blight still falls on Farlost. I don't believe you, Duke Tejar."

"You refuse my pardon?" Tejar asked, amused.

"I refuse you, Duke Tejar," Landreth shot back, lifting his chin.

"And whom do you hate more, Landreth, me or Earl Melfallan?" Landreth did not reply, but the hatred in his eyes flared again. "However did Melfallan catch you?" Tejar asked curiously. "With the witch's help?"

"A woman?" Landreth retorted with contempt. "Hardly."

"Oh, I see," Tejar said blandly, reading Landreth's discomfort for the truth it held. "It was the *witch* who overmatched you, not the earl. A remarkable woman."

Landreth looked away, his jaw muscles working again.

"Did you get any easement at all?" Tejar asked crudely. "Did you get her down and spread, then manage even a little pleasure?" Landreth flushed, his eyes flicking to the dagger on Tejar's belt, but he had the sense to stay put. "I think not," Tejar said. "I doubt you even got her skirts lifted. Well, no matter. She's dead now." Tejar lounged back against the wall, enjoying himself. A beaten man, this young lord, but a man with potential: Tejar could use that hate, use it well. "Women are plentiful, and most are more buxom and lusty than she was. Shall I send a woman to you tonight, Lord Landreth?"

Landreth took in a deep breath, then leaned back on his cot, copying the duke's own ease, but his eyes gleamed. At the news of the witch's death, or the prospect of another woman for the rutting? Tejar didn't care, so long as the hawk came to his fist.

Landreth made a show of considering, then waved his hand negligently. "As you wish, sire."

"Better still." Tejar paused, staring at him for a moment. "Who poisoned Earl Audric?" he asked suddenly.

"I don't know," Landreth replied just as quickly, and so betrayed himself. What? Tejar thought ironically. No protest that I ask him such a question? More to the point, no shocked surprise, no claim that Audric had died of a stomach complaint, as was officially reported? By his very omission, Landreth had just confirmed Audric's poisoning by Farlost.

Tejar eyed his captive speculatively. Had Landreth taken a role in that deft slipping of poison into a dish? he wondered. Or had a servant been paid? By his father's order? Or by Landreth's own initiative? Did it matter?

Not really, Tejar decided. What mattered was that Earl Audric was dead, and that Melfallan's own vassal—or his son—had arranged his murder. Did Melfallan know? Tejar likely saw the proof of it in the prisoner sitting before him.

"You should consider your choice carefully, young Farlost," he said. "Allow me to help your considering." Tejar called out to the guard standing outside the cell. "Have Lord Landreth taken to the Yarvannet suites. In fact, put him in Earl Melfallan's usual rooms. When he's bathed and dressed, bring him to me."

He heard Landreth take in breath sharply, and thought about playing with that startled hope, snuffing it and then blowing it to life again, but he hadn't time this morning for more play.

"Sire?" the guard asked, confused.

"Do it!" Tejar barked at the dungeon guard, then nodded to

Landreth. "In an hour, then, Lord Landreth," he said courteously.

With a smile of satisfaction, Tejar left the cell. A little more courting, a few subtle promises, and Tejar would have another kept man, one who would do his bidding—and, if Tejar played his gambit well, become a knife at Melfallan's throat.

And, until then, there were other knives—smaller blades, true, but enough to prick a vein and begin the bleeding. A liege lord had many weapons in the law, especially in the duties Melfallan owed him as vassal. Lord Dail had already suggested several ideas for the council Melfallan had avoided, but the Yarvannet earl's elusiveness had won him only a short space of time, not a victory. The duke ascended the stairs and sent a servant for Lord Dail, then settled in his study.

Yes, he thought, greatly pleased, and nodded to himself as he waited for his counselor. Yes, Landreth would do.

6

*E*arl Melfallan Courtray leaned on the wooden railing of his ship, and watched the suns' light sparkle on the ocean water. The wind lifted his blond hair, teasing it, and the brisk sea wind pleasantly chilled his skin. Above his head, the Daystar and its Companion shone near the zenith, casting short double shadows at mast and rail. The suns tinged the sea waves with gold and blue light, a shifting pattern of sparkling color he loved whenever abroad on the sea. On the eastern horizon spread the long green shadow of the Yarvannet coastland. In all other directions, he saw only moving, restless ocean. Melfallan drew in a deep breath of the sea wind and smiled.

Praise Ocean, he thought, this day is beautiful. He squinted happily against the brightness of the water and breathed in the air of home.

At Darhel he had slipped aboard *Southwind* by night, unannounced and unseen, and had given the order to sail. In the cover of darkness, the ship had poled away from its docking at Darhel and drifted effortlessly into the river current, gathering speed. His departure had been unremarked for half an hour, and by then *Southwind* had passed a mile downriver. His ocean-faring ship could outsail any pursuit by Darhel's river craft, and he doubted Tejar had even tried.

A vassal owed courtesy to his liege when departing, as he owed courtesy on his arrival, but for once Melfallan had not complimented the duke. That first day as his ship had descended the river, a Darhel horseman had raced along the riverbank, shouting and waving a paper overhead, but Melfallan had happily ignored him. At Ries, Count Parlie's capital near the mouth of the Essentai, a boat with the duke's banner had put out from port, with more wild waving as *Southwind* calmly outsailed the smaller boat and left it far behind.

What was in the duke's paper, to be waved so frantically? Sir Micay thought it likely a summons to a duke's council, another of Melfallan's vassal duties. At that council, Tejar would pretend he hadn't ordered Brierley's murder, protesting such accusation with great noise and indignation, and then try to turn the accusation on Melfallan, as he had already tried. At council, Tejar had the advantage of his position as Melfallan's liege lord, a superiority he would use to provoke Melfallan's anger, in the hope of imprudent defiance or even—oh, wild hope of Ocean's fortune!—a damning admission of harboring witchery that could disenfeoff Melfallan as rebel and incompetent lord. Tejar had twenty years of experience in such manipulations at his councils: it was not an advantage Melfallan chose to yield, not now, and not ever.

That summons to council might still arrive in Yarvannet, provoking further problem, but probably not. The Allemanii High Lords often practiced the high art of excuses, avoiding Darhel by claiming the burden of rule or other necessity at home. Aside from sending a ship to seize him bodily, Duke Tejar could not force Melfallan back to Darhel, nor elevate Melfallan's stalling into a charge of rebellion, not for a mere summons to council. The burden of rule was, after all, the burden of rule: all the High Lords would agree, nodding their heads and tsking. Under the Lutke Charter, a High Lord had the legal right to disenfeoff any vassal based on one of several listed causes, but, practically speaking, to disenfeoff an earl Tejar would need the consent of the other High Lords, especially the other earl. And Earl Giles of Mionn was Melfallan's father-in-law.

And so Melfallan had calmly sailed for home, without courtesy, and greatly enjoyed that he had.

Two days ago they had passed the river mouth of the Saran-
don, Yarvannet's northernmost river that divided Yarvannet and
Briding, then yesterday had passed the Ewry, and now sailed past
more rocky coast as they neared Tiol. Here high sea bluffs fronted
the sandy beach, with deep forest climbing the hills beyond, shadowing into purple and dark green on the coastland mountains. In
places farmers made a different pattern with cleared fields, now
dusty gold and white with winter frost. At times he could glimpse
the coast road, a tiny brown ribbon clinging to bluff tops and
curves, and imagined he could see carts on the road.

Southwind sailed onward bravely, the brisk wind in her sails,
sprays of white-tipped foam tossed back from her prow whenever
she plunged into the trough of a swell. His principal ship was
one of Yarvannet's newer craft, with the slim grace of a well-
wrought ship, good-set sails that caught every available speed from
the constant wind along the coast, and a trim that rode the ocean
currents with ease. At today's speed, they should make Tiol by
morning.

Several ship-lengths away, a sea lark plummeted into the
waves and emerged an instant later with a tiny fish in its talons.
It climbed with swift sure beats of its dark wings, rising toward
the sky, an iridescent flash of color against the blue sky. It reminded him of Brierley, as swift, as elusive, as precious—but
everything had reminded him of Brierley since he had left her.
His thoughts were constantly colored with his longing for her,
and by the vain temptation to turn his ship around, re-ascend the
coast and Tejar's river, and ride again into the mountains to see
her again, however briefly, however uselessly.

We stood here by this rail, he remembered, Brierley and I,
when she was still shy with me. No, not shy: careful. She had
reason to be careful. He remembered her elusiveness, and smiled.

How long until they met again? His heart ached at the probable answer. They had been given so little time together in the
cabin, not enough to make matters certain between them. What if
this single handspan of days was all the time given? Did their
parting divide his life into two irrevocable paths, one lost into

another Melfallan's life that would never be his, the other chosen for duty? He was the Allemanii earl of Yarvannet, with the charge of his lands and his people; he had a wife and son. Brierley was shari'a witch, forced into hiding by Allemanii laws that had condemned her kind for three centuries. Was it better for her that she vanished again into obscurity, to be safe even from him, the High Lord who hoped to protect her? He might be fallible, as he had already proved himself to be, and in his failure end her life. Was it better for her a dividing forever? he thought in anguish.

Tomorrow he would be home, and there find his own safety, such as it was for any High Lord in the tumultuous politics of Duke Tejar's rule. He had thought much about safety in recent days—for himself, for his newborn son, for Brierley Mefell. But safety did not come easily in troubled times, and could not be guaranteed by complacence or a blind trust in continued living. True safety was often won by risk, even desperate risk. Through that risk a lord might win security that might last a time for all he loved, that might allow a little carelessness that would not unbind, a little ease in the day that would not unravel fortune. But not now, he reminded himself. And not soon.

He listened to the water and wind, the padding of a sailor's soft tread on the deck, the snap of the sails. The sea moved in majestic slow motion, lifting the ship in a rhythmic rise and fall. She was altogether alive, Mother Ocean, not indifferent to men's affairs but complete in Herself, the foundation of life, with purposes greater than Melfallan's petty doings. She lived forever, and such a Being thought in different terms, a wider scale. She had the care of all things, but never thought casually of death for any of Her children. Rather, death was her measured choice as Daughter, come in its true time, inexorable but just.

Mother Ocean,
Daughter Sea,
Living forever,
Strengthen me.

Had he the strength for what he must do? For Brierley's safety, he must abolish the shari'a laws that decreed her death, but those

laws belonged solely to the duke. And Melfallan was not duke—
yet.

He had never had such ambition for himself: he was fully
content with Yarvannet. Other High Lords could scheme and plot
for higher rank, for greater wealth and influence, for the power
over still greater lands and the folk who lived within them. Some
lords wished for war to make opportunities, but he did not, and
knew his attempt at the coronet would surely bring war. Power
was now exquisitely balanced: this war would not confine itself
to a border war between Yarvannet and Ingal, as had Pullen's
rebellion thirty years before, but would engulf all the High Lords,
one by one. And what if Melfallan failed? What if he were not
lord enough, not ruthless enough, not deft enough? And what if
the outcome had nothing to do with his qualities as earl, but ended
only by chance on the battlefield, when the sword that pierced
his heart might have easily pierced any other? He would lose
everything, for himself and Saray, for his baby son, for Brierley.
Everything. Soberly, he measured the possible cost and shuddered.

But what other choice than war? He took a deep breath, and
did not know his answer. With an effort, he shook off his worry
and breathed in another deep breath of the fresh clear sea air.

What is she feeling today? he wondered and looked up at the
cloudless sky, wishing for the sound of her voice. Is she well? Is
she happy? He leaned comfortably on the rail and watched the
sea, content with the day, thinking of her.

He had often envied other men obviously in love with their
wives. Such men sometimes seemed almost ensorceled, as if they
could not draw full breath in her presence, as if her voice, her
smile, made living even possible. Some men, especially when very
young, grew foolish in their adoration, and older men smiled
sagely, shaking their heads at his loss of sense. Other men seemed
unaware of their lady's enchantment, content that their wives keep
their house and bear their sons, with the true purpose of living
elsewhere, in one's craft, in one's rule. It seemed an infinite variation, how a man regarded his lady, and of them all, Melfallan
had most envied those who seemed to find their completion only

with her. He had watched such couples, Sir James with his Maire, Lord Garth and his lady, and had wondered, with a wistful yearning, how it felt.

He had expected to love his wife, whenever he married and whomever she was, but he had not loved Saray when they wed, not yet. Nor had he known, not yet, that love can be intended and then stifled by a wife's docility, by her vanity and pretending, by quarrels neither truly ever meant to happen. Troubles in a marriage also had their infinite variation, it seemed, and he had finally accepted his own, or so he had thought.

And so he had not expected to fall in love with Brierley, but somehow had found himself in the midst of it before he could think of prudence, of his duty to Saray, to Yarvannet. He had thought only of defending one of his folk, this slender girl who had saved the lives of his wife and child. He had not believed in her witchery, not then. Of course not! Old tales! Nonsense! When Captain Bartol, Tejar's latest spy in Yarvannet, had seized upon Brierley to work the duke's plots, Melfallan had charged valiantly to the defense, believing it his duty as High Lord. *To defend the right:* it was part of a High Lord's obligation to his folk, to his lands.

But, in his rush to her defense, his heart had unaccountably betrayed him. He had not expected to fall in love, as those other men loved, not this way. He had not expected it could happen so quickly, and practically without his noticing, yet so it was.

But what of Saray? he asked himself sadly. What of her?

He sighed and leaned on the rail, watching the sea lark spin through the air, aloft on the cool wind. *Ocean, what do I do now?*

The High Lords often arranged marriages of state, and such marriages had no guarantee of happiness. Yet he was often happy with Saray, despite their troubled marriage. He knew his wife genuinely loved him, however little she understood him. And for that love she gave him, he owed her much, quite aside from the proprieties that many lords overlooked. *Can a man love two women, but in different ways?* Brierley had thought so. Saray tried so very hard to be a good wife, and honestly did not understand why she failed. He had tried to be a good husband, but had failed also, and had now failed Saray profoundly with a woman who touched not only his physical passion but his heart.

He cringed from the thought of wounding Saray, after all she had given to him, after how hard she had tried for him.

What *should* I do? I know what I should do, but, Ocean, I can't bear the thought of it. He had accepted the lacks in his marriage, and had counted greater love as not his lot in life. Mother Ocean gave as She will, and many men endured having less. He had accepted that, and had given up looking for something more, as he had looked occasionally in earlier years. He had learned to live with it, and could live with it again.

If he were prudent, he knew, and knew as solidly as the planking beneath his feet, he should give up any future with Brierley. He knew all the other reasons, all of them prudent and wise and obvious. He could still act to protect her: their love was not necessary to that rightful choice. Yet his heart twisted within him at the thought, a nearly physical pain, and a chasm seemed to open at his feet, empty and cold. If he thought first of his lands and his obligation to his lady wife, as he should, his choice should be clear. Any drowning man might make such a choice, refusing the rope cast to him, refusing the rock within reach, if he knew it was his duty.

The sea lark plunged itself into the waves, a bright-feathered arrow, and emerged again triumphantly, a tiny fish in its claws.

I see her in everything, Melfallan thought.

A boot trod nearby on the ship's planking, and a young soldier stopped by the railing a few yards away. He was a stocky young man in Revil's green livery, fair-haired, standing easily against the swell. He seemed oblivious to Melfallan's presence, as if he looked only inward, locked in some misery. Melfallan watched him for several minutes, until his gaze belatedly caught the soldier's attention. The young man's head snapped around and he straightened with a jerk, then made a shambles of a salute.

"Your grace!" he blurted. "I'm—I'm sorry I disturbed you. I'll stand by the other rail."

"No mind. What's your name?" He looked familiar, enough that Melfallan should have known him.

"Jared Cheney, your grace, from Amelin." The salute was better this time.

Melfallan smiled, and leaned his elbow on the railing. "Ah, the young soldier who besieged Sir Micay about Mistress Mefell. Made quite a pest of himself, too."

Jared's face turned pink and he began to edge away. "Yes, that's me, your grace. If you'll excuse me for bothering you—"

"I'm not going to berate you, Jared. I approve of such sieges."

Jared's face twisted. "Not that it did any good," he said bitterly. "She's dead now." He looked out at the sea again, his jaw muscles working, and his hands gripped the rail so tightly that his knuckles were white. Jared seemed to retreat into himself again, quite forgetting Melfallan standing nearby. So many people love her, Melfallan thought wistfully: you'll face this problem over and over again, and each time you put her in greater risk if you tell. Be prudent at least in this, he reminded himself, but Jared's palpable grief touched him. "Perhaps," he said impulsively.

Jared's head turned, and his eyes flashed with sudden anger, for all he spoke to his earl. " 'Perhaps'? Are you joking? The duke's justiciar killed her: all Darhel said so. That's why Hagan ran away."

"Perhaps," Melfallan repeated firmly, wishing to give Jared some hope, however elusive, that might ease his ragged pain.

Jared's mouth worked soundlessly as he visibly wanted to believe, then settled into a scowl. "She's dead," Jared said in a flat voice. "Everyone says so."

"How did you know her?" Melfallan asked curiously.

"We were friends as children," Jared answered sullenly, and would not look at him. "I've known her all my life. She and I— Well, I ended up with the duty to arrest her. I arrested her, and handed her over to you." Jared turned to face him squarely, his feet planted firmly on the planking. "It was wrong what you did, taking her to Darhel and into danger. It was wrong to put her in a cell and accuse her of vile things, and then let that justiciar get hold of her. She's *not* vile. She's—" Jared stopped himself with an effort and glowered. "There! Now you can lock *me* up."

"Why would I lock you up?" Melfallan asked.

"Because I'm angry at you." Jared flushed again, but stood his ground.

"That's hardly a crime. If I locked up everybody that—"

"Because I'm *furious* at you," Jared interrupted. "And don't you laugh at me! Brierley was special. There was no one like her, and you threw her away, like she didn't mean anything. But she meant *everything*, and you High Lords don't care—"

"Jared—"

"Why should you care? You don't have to care." Jared's voice had risen to nearly a shout, attracting attention from the sergeant at the other end of the ship. "You can keep your jewels and your rank and your pride—and the way you *use* people. Just keep it and take it away!"

The sergeant stamped up and raked Jared with a reproving glance. "Cheney," he said harshly, "back to your station!"

"I'm not on duty," Jared said defiantly, effortlessly switching his anger to his sergeant.

"Then go below!" the sergeant barked. "Now!"

As Jared opened his mouth for some further retort, no doubt hot-spoken and utterly insubordinate, Melfallan raised his hand. "Never mind, sergeant. I wish to speak with him further. Pray return to your duty."

The sergeant gave Melfallan a startled look, then decided saluting was the safest course, which he did. "As you will, your grace." The man stalked away.

Melfallan turned back to Jared. "See?" he asked. "I'm an earl, and I can do things like that—make sergeants shut up. You were saying?"

"I won't be your mock." The sergeant's attention had not dented Jared's anger in the slightest.

"I'm not mocking you, Jared. Will you listen?"

"Why should you care that I listen?" he demanded, then stared at Melfallan for a moment. "Listen to what?" he asked eagerly, his expression changing to blazing hope. "You said 'perhaps.' Do you know something, your grace? Have you seen her?"

"Um," Melfallan said, taken aback as Jared neatly boxed him. The High Lords made an art of lies, but now, faced with Jared's honest question, Melfallan found the art had suddenly eluded him. "Um—" he said again, and looked around for help, at the sea, the sails overhead, the distant shore on the horizon. I could jump overboard, he thought wildly, a quick hand on the rail and a fast plunge into the water. The drama of the rescue might divert Jared. He looked back at Jared's face, and decided sadly not. Then lie to him, Melfallan, he thought desperately. Make yourself lie. It's her safety at sake.

But he knew, without knowing how he knew, that Jared would never forgive him the lie, not ever.

"You said 'perhaps,' " Jared insisted, his eyes intent on Melfallan's face.

"Jared—"

"*Is* she dead?" Jared demanded.

Melfallan sighed, then slumped his shoulders. "No," he admitted. "That news must be kept secret from the duke, Jared, for her safety, but you have no reason to grieve." Melfallan touched his breast. "Aren't I the High Lord you truly blame? And I would be to blame, although I thought I had no choice in my High Lord's politics, to do anything else but what I did. Believe me, during those several hours when I thought her dead, I cursed myself more bitterly than you have now."

"But she's truly alive?" Jared asked, too loudly. Melfallan glanced quickly around the deck. When he looked back at Jared's face, he saw confusion there, then Jared's eyes, too, make a quick survey of the deck.

"Safe, in hiding. So will you give up your anger, Jared? I won't lock you up for shouting at your earl, but that sergeant might."

Jared flushed. "I'm sorry. I—"

"As I said, I called myself every name you've thought, and likely more. But she *is* safe."

"Where is she?" Jared asked eagerly. "Does she have someone to protect her?"

"She has someone."

"I want to go, too," Jared said simply.

Melfallan glared, thoroughly irritated with his earnest young soldier. "And leave your service with Count Revil?" he asked pointedly. As Jared promptly opened his mouth to argue, Melfallan raised his hand, stopping him: he had erred enough this day, and this artless young man apparently had an art in trapping him. No more, at least not today. He scowled even more ferociously at the young soldier, with no visible effect on Jared, none at all. "We'll talk about it. I might need a courier; and perhaps you might suit—"

"Oh, your grace!" Jared wore every emotion on his face, it seemed, plain as the Daystar. Yes, Melfallan thought, Brierley would love someone like him, then felt a small jab of jealousy. For an instant, Melfallan was tempted to find out details, but let it go. She hadn't mentioned other lovers: had there been others, perhaps this earnest young man who obviously still loved her? Melfallan suddenly doubted his wisdom in telling Jared, for reasons less noble than Brierley's safety. Whatever Jared saw flicker across his face had immediate effect: his joy erased into stillness, and a calmness settled into the eyes, as if a cloth had wiped a table. "I'm discreet, your grace," Jared said in a low voice. "I have control—I can for her sake." He smiled, his eyes lighting again. "And for your sake, Earl Melfallan. I'm glad you're nothing like Duke Tejar," he added ingenuously.

Melfallan suppressed a laugh at Jared's earnestness, then made himself nod gravely. "We'll talk later," he promised.

Jared nodded, then gave him a most excellent salute. For another moment he lingered by the rail, and they both looked out at the sea.

The Daystar had spread its golds and reds in the west behind them, tinting the waves with brilliant color. As its light faded, the Companion shed its twilight of brilliant blues, becoming a shimmering silver on the sea that shifted with the slow surge of the waves. In the gathering twilight, a sea lark plunged, bright blue and silver.

"I see her in everything," Jared whispered.

"Yes, I know," Melfallan answered.

That evening Melfallan dined in his cabin with Sir Micay and Master Cronin Atwell, the ship's pilot, a pleasant meal with two men he had always liked. Master Cronin, a bluff and hearty man who had known Melfallan all his life, had taught Melfallan to sail and had once taken him as a boy out with the fishing fleet for the winter season. Sir Micay, Tiol's castellan, had taught Melfallan the sword as a boy, and still practiced with him regularly in the castle quadrangle. Now in his sixties, Sir Micay was grizzled and leather-faced but still hale, a master swordsman who had chosen to give his absolute loyalty to the Courtrays, and had never failed in that trust.

As Micay and Cronin chatted with each other over the wine, trading stories that dated back before Melfallan was even born, Melfallan wondered what they would think of him, when they knew of his plan. Would Micay see only ambition in a young upstart lord who thus failed his lands by plunging Yarvannet into war? Would Cronin shake his head and wonder, deeply disappointed in the young man he had taught to love the sea and all its life? Micay would never betray him, nor Cronin, another surety of Melfallan's life, but at what cost to each man? Yet how could he explain? Micay had met Brierley, and Cronin had seen her on the ship as they sailed to Darhel. Would they see only a young man foolishly besotted with a woman, all judgment lost in his passion? He sighed and stared down into his wineglass.

Micay noticed his silence and raised an eyebrow. "Have we

left you years away, your grace?" he asked affably. "Old stories among old men can be a trial for the young."

"Not at all," Melfallan replied, making himself smile. "I like to hear your stories. It's part of my continuing education." He offered the wine bottle to Cronin, received a nod, and refilled the pilot's glass.

"I've another story for you, of more recent vintage," Micay said. "I had a talk with Count Parlie while you were abroad in Airlie, and he's asked me to take one of his soldiers into Yarvannet's service."

"So?" Melfallan asked, mildly perplexed. Micay had full charge of such decisions, and didn't have to ask. "Whatever your best judgment, Micay, as always."

"This case is a little different. Her name is Evayne Ibelin—"

"*Her?*" Melfallan blinked.

"That's the difference." Micay grimaced. "Women often make good swordsmen, your grace, if they have the aptitude—quick, lighter on their feet, a suitable ferocity. Your aunt's a fine example, and Margaret of Tyndale was almost as good in her youth. I taught both of them, and since then I've often wanted to accept the occasional local girl who wished a soldier's craft, but your grandfather always said no."

"Why not?" Melfallan asked, frowning. "If they're good—"

Micay's smile broadened, and he looked openly pleased. "I do swear, Melfallan, that serving you can be a simple joy." He sniffed reflectively. "I argued the point with your grandfather many times, but he never relented. He indulged Rowena when she insisted on sword-training—she would have done it, anyway, no matter what he said and he knew it—but women soldiers were not suitable in his eyes."

"Women do lots of things well," Melfallan objected mildly, "and sometimes better than their husbands." He glanced at Cronin. "Haven't you always told me your wife is the better fisherman?"

"That's a truth, your grace." Cronin's blue eyes twinkled. "And my middle daughter outmatched me some years ago—she

has a true sense for the currents and how fish might be found."
Cronin spoke with open pride.

"So why not?" Melfallan said firmly to Micay. "Did Parlie
say his reasons?"

"She had some trouble with a local Briding lord—no, actually, it was Tejar's rivermaster in Ries—or the son? I forget now."
Micay thought a moment, then shook his head as the fact eluded
him. "I do remember it wasn't her fault. He presumed his own
irresistible charm, and she blackened his eye when he tried, and
the father complained to the duke, and the expected order came
back, demanding she be punished. The duke's clark suggested loss
of her rank and three years in Parlie's dungeon."

"Is there a trial anywhere in there?" Melfallan asked dryly.

"Well, of course. You ought to have the formalities." Micay's
smile was grim. "So Parlie wants to shrug and say the girl has
vanished, his small but pointed comment on Tejar's recent debacle
with Mistress Mefell, I think. But mostly he thinks the girl is
falsely accused and deserves a better start elsewhere. I agree." Micay took a long swallow from his wineglass.

"I see," Melfallan said. "So why are we asking me now?"

"Your earl's dignity, of course," Micay replied with a twinkle.
"I can't have you fainting when you see a woman standing guard
somewhere in the castle." Cronin laughed, and Melfallan pretended to glare at him. "I'll write to the count," Micay prompted,
and Melfallan nodded.

After dinner, Melfallan went up on deck again, to lean on the
railing and watch the sea, now shrouded in darkness. The stars
blazed brilliantly overhead, and were caught in the shimmer of
the water, flickering randomly from crest to crest, a thousand sparkles. The distant land was invisible in the darkness, a shadow
lost within a shadow, and only the sea surrounded him. Above
his head, the sails snapped smartly in the rigging, and the timbers
of the slender ship groaned faintly as she plowed the waters. On
the raised deck aft, Master Cronin stood at the wheel, his hands
shifting gracefully as he controlled the pull of the water on the
rudder. A half-dozen sailors worked quietly around the deck, mov-

ing from here to there and back again, then standing still, more shadows in the darkness. One sailor saluted respectfully as he passed Melfallan on some errand, and Melfallan nodded in response.

The ship slid swiftly through the water, making a chuckling sound over the quiet rushing of the ocean waters. The wind had risen with nightfall, pushing *Southwind*'s sails into great billows overhead. His ship flew across the water, almost like a bird sailing the air, and he loved the speed and the push of the air on his face. He closed his eyes and relished the coolness, the swift movement. Some moments a man might wish could last forever.

The Allemanii had always been a sea people, and the love of the sea came with the blood, however land-bound a lord made himself. At sea everything was pristine and clear, all truths seemed known, and clarity was grasped as easily as a wineglass in the hand. *Am I lord enough?* he asked himself again. *For her sake, I could be, if I can find the way.*

Since his accession the previous spring, Melfallan had worried greatly about his ability as earl, probably unfairly to himself, but had worried nonetheless. His grandfather's sudden death had taken Melfallan by surprise, plunging him from his pleasant heir's life into the cold bath of an earl's reality. At first, in the heavy pall of his grief, Melfallan had drifted, his mind clouded to distraction, and sometimes even moving from his bed to a chair seemed beyond possibility. He scarcely remembered his accession a few days after the funeral, when each of his Yarvannet vassals had sworn fealty to their new earl. He had a vague memory of bright banners, of a glittering throng in the Great Hall, himself seated stiffly in the high seat as each lord kneeled before him, each head bowed in proud submission, and placed his hands between his to swear his oath. Of all the Yarvannet lords he remembered Revil best, when his cousin knelt before his chair and recited the old words of binding and faith, his voice husky with numbed grief but fervent in its promises, ringing into the hall. But the rest was a blur, and afterward he had hated the manner in which life resumed its normal pace. In time, even Melfallan had betrayed his grandfather's memory, for as the weeks passed the distractions of rule and castle affairs, and particularly Saray's new pregnancy, had dulled his shocked grief and brought him back to the living.

And so he had resumed his pleasant lord's life, with enter-tainments and hawking, a dutiful attention to the monthly assizes that gave his folk their justice, his isolated hours in his tower study puzzling over the reality of being an earl. Twice a week he practiced his sword skills in the castle's quadrangle, and tried to think it more than a thoroughly enjoyable contest with his soldiers. A High Lord's life in battle could depend upon his per-sonal skills, he reminded himself, but battle seemed remote, a tale in the history books, nothing more. Nearly every morning he and Sir James, his justiciar, consulted with each other, and they often discussed Yarvannet's politics, measuring one choice against an-other, but even that sober exercise seemed a game. High Lords did certain things as the pattern of their lives, as did all the nobility. Melfallan was a High Lord, so he did them, too, playing his role, day after day. See Melfallan prance.

He grimaced. If Brierley had heard that comment, she would chide him for its harshness. She said he worried too much, and was probably right about that, too. She had a midwife's good sense, an insight into persons that forgave much. And he wanted to be a good earl, a good husband, now a good father: some men, commoner or noble, didn't bother. But he had grown up among the noble folk in his grandfather's castle, surrounded by their self-love and vanities, their occasional ambitions beyond their already high station, their love for fine clothes and posing and frivolous pastimes. In truth, Melfallan greatly preferred the commoners, the fisherfolk and farmers of Yarvannet's shores, who, to be fair in turn, sometimes suffered from the same faults, but not as—uni-versally? He smiled ruefully. Well, not all noble folk: the rule of frivolity did not apply to Revil or Sir James or certain other re-sponsible lords. Perhaps it hadn't applied to himself, either, not truly.

But then Brierley had entered his life, pale and elusive and brave, and everything had changed. He hadn't noticed the difference at first, but it had grown upon him in the weeks since he had known her. It was more than love, he decided after some thought, and sent a vague apology to Brierley that he so diminished her. It was more than love: it was purpose, a reason that might focus his life, something larger than himself, something to guide. Brierley had spoken of refounding her craft, and seemed to find a similar purpose in that. Perhaps they were the same purpose, he decided, this righting of an ancient wrong, of finding peace between two peoples that had failed before—and need not have failed. Perhaps. It could be.

His peers among the High Lords would see only ambition, a willingness for war, envy, hatred, grasping for power. Tejar would understand Melfallan's rebellion as nothing else. He must not forget that fact, and must include it in his plans. The other High Lords would react based on their assumptions, and likely disbelieve any other explanation Melfallan might offer. The Allemanii High Lords often lied to each other, another fact of Melfallan's politics, and so always prudently suspected their peers of hidden intentions.

How could he change the pattern of Allemanii politics that had endured for three centuries? In the West, the Allemanii had battled frequently against their violent neighbors, defending their lands against genuine foes. Here, once Rahorsum had murdered the local shari'a, the Allemanii lords had battled each other, with the coronet as the glittering prize for the victor. Three times the coronet had changed houses, each time bringing war and desolation to the folk, and no duke ever felt secure. Ambition underlaid every plot, every betrayal, eroding even the vassal's oath.

Could purpose become the strength he needed? He leaned on the rail and stared down into the dark waters surging beside the ship.

Beneath the rail, waves surged, dark and flickering with starlight. A larger wave moved, lapping hard against the side of the ship. Then, scarcely a hundred yards away, a great sinuous body slid into view, coiling upon itself, turn upon turn, churning the waves. Melfallan forgot to breathe as a massive serpent's head lifted from the water, large jeweled eyes gleaming with an inner light. The gomphrey opened its jaws, showing long rows of sharp teeth, acres of teeth, all long and white and sharp. It snapped its jaws shut with a hollow boom and dived.

A sailor gave a startled cry as the beast surfaced on the other side of the ship and lifted itself from the water, rising higher and higher, until it reached nearly as tall as the mastheads. Melfallan clung to the railing in shock, his mouth agape, as the gomphrey fleetingly inspected the sailor in the crow's nest with an impassive eye, then flipped itself gracefully backward, plunging back into the sea. As it dove, a great wave lifted over the railing into the ship, setting the deck awash, upending barrels, splashing high against the masts, and nearly sweeping Melfallan off his feet. He clung to the railing, drenched nearly to the waist, and watched a sailor lose his balance and fall with a startled cry. The man quickly found his feet again, unhurt. A moment later the ship timbers trembled with a resonating croon, deep and penetrating, deep enough to rattle the ears, even shift the ocean itself, and then the gomphrey was gone.

The sailors on deck babbled in their surprise, then called out mockingly to the man clinging weakly to the crow's nest above. That earned them a solid cursing, quickly cut off as the sailor belatedly remembered the loftiness of his earl standing below. The others turned toward Melfallan sheepishly and touched their foreheads, then glanced nervously at the pilot as he scowled down at them from the wheel-deck.

"Mind your mouths!" Master Cronin shouted in rage.

"Sorry, your grace," a sailor said, mumbling. "We were startled."

"I understand completely," Melfallan said, finding his voice. He tried to keep his voice in normal range, without complete success. "That was a gomphrey?"

"Yes, your grace," another sailor replied, vastly tolerant of his earl's idiot question. Of course it was a gomphrey, Melfallan thought dazedly, but the man merely grinned at him. "Big one,

too," he said. "The bigger ones like to measure themselves against
the masthead, Ocean knows why. Shortens the nestman's life, for
sure." He threw a glance upward at the man in the crow's nest
and grinned, and got an inarticulate curse back. "They never hurt
us at sea. The juveniles in the rivers sometimes get playful and a
barge can be sunk when they do, but the big ones are more
careful."

"This happens often?" Melfallan put his hand on his chest to
quiet his pounding heart, then took a deep breath, and saw the
grins widen in the darkness. No help for that, he supposed: even
an earl was only a man.

"Not often, your grace, but from time to time. It's like they
keep watch over us. It's lucky for any voyage when a gomphrey
measures the ship." The sailors all promptly nodded in agreement.

"Back to work," Cronin shouted. "Stop gaggling around!"

"The earl asked me," the sailor retorted, shouting back. "Just
steer the ship and find us another gomphrey, Master Cronin, and
we'll be thankful to you."

"Five silver coins, that's your fine," Cronin called from his
high deck at the stern. "Rudeness to the pilot."

"Where's that rule?" the sailor demanded in outrage. "Making
things up now, are you?"

"Paid directly to me, mind you," Master Cronin said with
relish. "And five coins from the mast," he continued happily, "for
that despicable language in the earl's hearing."

"Over my dead arse, Cronin!" came caroling from above. A
wave of laughter ran through the deck as a shadowed face looked
down from the crow's-nest railing. Melfallan saw the flash of the
nestman's white teeth. "Sorry, your grace. I'm a horrible man. I
can't help it."

"Rudeness to his grace," Cronin called. "Ten coins."

Melfallan threw up his hands and laughed. "Enough, Master
Cronin! You'll get the whole crew's profit with your fines."

Cronin grinned, another flash of white teeth in the darkness.
"That's the idea, your grace, excepting your share, of course.

Gomphrey's always an opportunity, if a man is quick with his wits." He nodded, his hands steady on the wheel. "Back to work, men. The beast has gone back to its business."

The sailors laughed and padded back to their chores of coiling lines and the other dozen constant tasks of a ship at sail.

Melfallan vainly watched the sea for another hour, but saw nothing but waves and the starlight sparkling on the water. Why would a gomphrey want to measure the mast? he wondered, in awe now that he had truly seen one, and far closer than he ever expected, amazingly closer. Close enough to be inhaled, if the gomphrey had been inclined, and it was an earl's fortune that gomphreys could be careful. As he turned from the rail to go below to his bed, he thought he heard a distant deep rumble under the sea far to the north, and he laughed softly. Yes, indeed.

he Daystar dawned bright and clear the next morning, with a chill wind from the north chasing the ship as it neared Tiol. Near noon, *Southwind* rounded the northern point into the harbor, and Melfallan saw the gleaming white stone of his castle rising on the far headland, bright-washed in the suns' light. A ridge road led from the port town across the rocky point to the castle gates; even at this distance, the tiny figures of wagons, horses, and persons on foot could be seen passing to and fro on the road. Beneath the castle, descending the steep slope to the water, the homes and stables of Yarvannet's nobility and principal merchants created a bright array. Several ships stood in the harbor at the wharves, including Count Revil's small sloop, *Star Dolphin*. His cousin was in port, to be expected as part of the welcome for his earl's return. As *Southwind* tacked into the bay, Melfallan saw an immediate bustling on the wharves, then the measured descent of a large party from the castle to meet him.

He stood on the pilot's deck by Master Cronin and Sir Micay, and watched the ship glide smoothly to the wharf. A sailor deftly threw a rope to a wharfman waiting on the dock, and *Southwind* was quickly snugged tight. The sailors rigged the gangplank, and Sir Micay marched stolidly down the uncertain footing, followed by a small troop of his soldiers. Melfallan hesitated a moment longer, as if he could delay this arrival by his own willing, then sighed and followed his castellan onto the wharf.

Melfallan gave a hand to his bluff portmaster, Ennis, then greeted Revil and his family. His cousin was grinning so widely, so overtly joyous to see him that Melfallan had to swallow hard. Revil's affection could be counted as one of the certainties in Melfallan's life, a mainstay for living.

"Revil," he said, embracing him.

"Welcome home, Yarvannet," Revil replied, all a-grin. Melfallan kissed dark-haired Solange, Revil's pretty wife, and then boosted little Calla into the air, making her shriek in delight, while Revil's elder daughter, Semaire, now six, shyly clung to Solange's skirts. And then, behind Revil, waiting patiently at the end of the wharf among her lady-maids, was Saray.

Melfallan's wife stood smiling in a lovely silver gown, with bright slashes of blue and green at the sleeves, the sparkle of tiny crystal beads descending her wide silvery skirts in subtle patterns of flowers and surf. Jewels winked at her wrist and neck, with more jewels in her upswept red hair, held in graceful order by silver combs. She looked like an earl's wife, a great lady between the more subdued dress of her lady-maids: if nothing else, Saray's mother, Lady Mionn, had taught her the skills of looking magnificent, as became Lady Yarvannet. Saray's gentle temper and grace had won her the affection of Yarvannet's people, not the fine display, but she did look lovely.

Saray's green eyes sparkled with excitement: she, too, was glad to see him, as she was always glad. Saray laughed up at him as he reached her, and he kissed her in front of everyone. He felt her hands tighten on his arms for a moment, but she quickly disengaged herself, glancing aside at the other noble folk, a slight flush coloring her cheeks. "You have no manners, Melfallan," she chided. "In front of all the folk. Really!"

"Oh, I think they know I kiss you from time to time." He put his arm around her waist and would have kissed her again, but she firmly pushed him off, then stood back a step, smiling up at him, exquisitely lovely in her fine gown and jewels, with the gladness in her eyes. For a brief moment his breath stopped, looking at her loveliness—but Saray was turning away now, collecting her lady-maids to depart. He repressed a sigh and had no better answer for his dilemma, then followed Saray as she gracefully swayed down the wharf decking.

Melfallan nodded to the formidable Lady Tolland and her indolent son Lord Valery, to Lord Garth Souvain and his sweet-faced wife, Joanna, then to old Lord Eldon Grosmont leaning weakly on his cane, his pop-eyed son and ugly daughters at his side, each magnificently dressed in blue velvet and gold. Next came fierce-eyed Sir Justin Halliwell, the armorer, then Lord Tauler Guiscard from his marcher lands in northeastern Farlost, Tauler's young gangling son at his side, and stout Jens Nielsen, the jewel merchant, and a few of the other principal Tiol merchants with their wives.

Melfallan nodded to them all, exchanged a few words with Master Nielsen, a pompous greedy man whose jewels were in fact excellent, then nodded in response to Lord Tauler's bow. Now nearing his fifties, Lord Tauler of Penafeld was in his prime, physically fit, experienced, self-assured in his rule. He was certainly the most intelligent of the Yarvannet lords, and Melfallan had always thought his grandfather underestimated Tauler. Ever prudent, Tauler usually found good excuse to avoid both his earl in Tiol and his count in Farlost, a habit both liege lords had noticed but chosen to ignore. Why was he here now? Melfallan wondered, but saw little answer in Tauler's careful gaze. A gesture of support? Coincidence? As a spy for Count Sadon? From what Melfallan knew of this careful marcher lord, Tauler rarely did anything by chance.

"My son, Estes," Tauler said, gesturing proudly toward his son. Tauler might be wary in his politics, but never scanted in his open approval of his only son, now thirteen.

"Yes, I remember," Melfallan said with a smile for the boy. "Will you be sending him to my court soon, Lord Tauler?" he asked. Estes actually blushed, and still wore every emotion on his sleeve, it seemed. Melfallan had seen him only twice before, each time after a doubling in the boy's height.

Tauler glanced at his son fondly. "Soon enough. I think he

needs more polishing, your grace, before I loose him on Yarvannet Castle."

"Father!" Estes said, blushing even more hotly.

"Send him soon, my lord," Melfallan said, smiling. "I'm certain he will grace Yarvannet's court." Tauler bowed again and Melfallan moved on.

The other gentry bowed genially to Melfallan, greeting him with smiles, and he smiled pleasantly in return. It seemed the Yarvannet gentry had turned out in force, presenting at least half their number for this simple welcome off his ship. He wondered about their various reasons behind the smiles and bows, matching a few particular facts to each face. Most he could probably trust, although Sir Micay had always insisted on certain security: the Yarvannet gentry, especially those of Tyndale origin, had prospered under Earl Audric's long rule and seemed inclined to extend a similar affability to Audric's heir, despite Count Sadon's mutterings. Even so, no High Lord, if he were wise, ever completely trusted his lords. An Allemanii duke had twice lost his coronet by trusting, and a wise earl, especially a young earl like himself, paid attention to such lessons from the High Lords' troubled political history.

That's too sober a thought for such a bright morning, Melfallan told himself, and deliberately shook off his mood. Yarvannet had come out to welcome him home. Here still was Revil and his pretty teasing wife and little daughters, grinning wide as a ship's beam to see him again, and grinning for only that. Here were his faithful stewards, Ennis and Micay and the others, each trusty as the sea air he breathed, who had served his grandfather nearly all their lives, and now served him with the same skill and unswerving loyalty. Here were his soldiers, proud and straight, and more merchants hurrying down from the town, and there the castle servants waiting above on the road to cheer his welcome, all the people in his life who made life worth living. All except Brierley. All except her.

I'll bring her home, he swore fiercely to himself. I'll find the way.

He and Saray moved on and climbed the stair to the road, where the townfolk waved to him as they passed to and fro from the castle. Another group of soldiers tramped by out on patrol, and saluted him smartly. He walked, arm in arm with Saray, and glanced occasionally at her happy face. She always liked the cheers and waved happily back, not for her own vanity's sake as Lady Yarvannet, but for the simple joy and pleasure in the greeting. Saray's sweet temper was her particular gift, however she chose to ignore unpleasant realities and so damaged their marriage. Many men were content with their wives, he knew, and he envied them more than they ever guessed: young Lord Garth had his fair Joanna, Revil his laughing Solange. Sir James had lived content-edly with his Maire for forty years, and he knew many such lucky men.

May I never hurt Saray, he wished desperately, knowing that his heart had already betrayed Saray and that he could wound her deeply. He felt as if a distant swell had gathered on the sea's horizon and now rushed toward the beach where he stood, slowly gathering height as it swept inward to the land, building steadily to crush him when it fell.

Saray squeezed his hand and smiled up at him. This home-coming should have been a simple happy time, with cheers and smiles as Yarvannet's earl returned home to his castle. But not simple, Melfallan thought, making himself smile back at her. Not simple at all.

At the bridge into the castle, more servants waited, gathered in the courtyard beyond the gate, and Melfallan stopped to return their greetings. His chief steward, Sir Bertrand, bowed low, and then Marina was there with the baby, her careworn face open in its joy to see him. Marina gave the baby into his arms, and little Audric kicked vigorously against the blanket. He smiled down at his son.

My sweet boy, Melfallan thought as he cradled the baby, and for a moment forgot all the crowd around him, even Saray standing proudly at his side, as he focused his attention on his son's small person. All the world in one small bundle, everything of value symbolized by two tiny hands, a small face, a toothless smile: all. Melfallan lifted his eyes to the assembled people, cherishing their welcome, but aware of his prick of fear for his son. A High Lord cannot trust, he reminded himself. His son represented much to others, too, a way to unmend, to throw down, to seize. A wise lord did not trust, and Audric's life could depend upon that rule of living.

It was not safe to bring the baby out in public, he thought, whatever the occasion of Melfallan's own arrival. Why had Saray allowed it? She knows nothing of the danger, he realized, none of it. Unconsciously, he held Audric closer to his chest, shielding him with his arms.

"He seems healthy," Melfallan said to Marina, struggling fiercely to control his inward emotions. He apparently managed a good semblance: at least Marina's expression did not change.

"The bloom of health, your grace," the midwife replied, and then held out her arms to take back the baby.

Melfallan raised an eyebrow and refused to give him up, and instead walked forward through the crowd, his son sheltered in his arms, and passed into his castle and home. They crossed the inner courtyard, the small party of himself and the gentry dividing the castle servants like a ship prow cutting the waves, and entering the Great Hall a half-level above. By managing a few thanks, a half-bow, he left the gentry behind chatting in the hall, and mounted the steps to the family suites.

The baby's nursery was guarded by two antechambers, one in which the baby's manservants slept every night, the outer one guarded by soldiers. Audric had further protection of his parents' own rooms nearby, each with their own soldiers at guard in the hallway. Only the most trusted of servants were allowed past the first nursery antechamber, and even fewer into the nursery itself. Each morning Audric's principal manservant, Norris, checked the baby's rooms for poisonous insects or other dangers to the baby, and he unwrapped every bundle or box brought into the nursery. Even the baby's clothes and bedding were kept in locked chests, to protect against poison. Melfallan remembered similar close protections for himself in his childhood, once when tempers had flared between Audric and the duke early in Tejar's rule, another when Audric had been taken ill with a winter fever and the midwife had feared it was plague.

But Earl Audric had possessed another grandson in Revil, a second heir of his body Tejar could not challenge, and Melfallan's childhood had been easier because of it, even after Melfallan's father died and Melfallan became Audric's direct heir. Physical isolation was an unnatural life for a child, and Melfallan remembered too keenly his own pleading against the restrictions. As Melfallan grew older and no one attempted his death, his grandfather had reluctantly allowed him companions besides Revil, then a steadily expanding physical freedom. A growing boy needed to run, to climb trees, to explore. And a lord needed to meet his folk, even in his youth. For now, however, Melfallan would protect Audric as he could.

At the doorway to the baby's nursery, he finally gave Audric back to the hovering Marina, then watched her carry him into the light airiness of the room beyond. The nursery was a pretty room, with wide windows and white-washed walls, a bright splash of color in the tapestries, the warm browns of wooden furniture. Audric's wet nurse, Leila, gave him an awkward curtsey as she saw him, her broad plain face filled with a smile. A soldier stood outside the door, and two lean young men watched from the corners as two nursery maids, one very young, hurried to help Marina put Audric in his cradle. Melfallan leaned back against the doorjamb and watched the activity, wondering if his own nursery had bustled as importantly whenever the baby, the precious all-important bundle, was put to bed.

He turned as someone touched his shoulder, and saw Sir James behind him. "What is it?" Melfallan asked instantly as he saw his justiciar's expression.

"A courier from Airlie, your grace," Sir James murmured, keeping his voice low. "I must speak to you privately."

"Of course." Melfallan followed Sir James out into the corridor, then drew him along far enough to pass from earshot of the soldier standing guard nearby. "What is it?" he asked.

"Rowena's marcher lord tried to murder her as she rode to Carandon," Sir James said, obviously struggling for control.

"*Tried?*" Melfallan asked sharply. "He did fail?"

"Yes, praise Ocean."

Melfallan took in breath again, then looked dazedly around him. "I have to tell Revil," he said distractedly. He saw his cousin in the nursery anteroom, laughing with Saray, and beckoned to him. "Was she injured?"

"A sword thrust through the right shoulder, with fever in the wound." Melfallan bit back a groan and would have torn at his hair, were eyes not watching—the guard at the baby's doorway, the few servants who had turned to watch Revil leave, curious as always about anything the noble folk might do.

"Sweet Ocean!" he breathed. He shook his head at Sir James as the justiciar opened his mouth for the caution, and they turned their backs on the guard. "You said there was a courier?"

"Yes. The first one arrived three days ago, but feared to tell anyone except me. No one else here knows." Revil had now joined them, a question in his eyes. "When he left Carandon a week ago," Sir James continued, "she was still delirious with fever."

"Who's delirious?" Revil demanded.

"Aunt Rowena," Melfallan told him, and saw shock wash across Revil's face. "A sword wound. Her marcher lord tried to kill her—Heider, isn't it?"

"Lord Heider died in the assault," Sir James said with cold satisfaction. "The courier didn't know any more, but another Airlie courier arrived this morning." He took a letter from inside his tunic. "For your hands only, he said."

The hand addressing the letter was unfamiliar, and Melfallan felt a sudden dread. He broke the seal and unfolded the single sheet of paper. *Dear nephew,* he read and sighed. *I trust you are now arrived safely home. My journey was more eventful, and I seem to have lost several days in a fevered dream. It was Heider, prompted by the duke, but do not act on that yet. Do not let your anger mislead you. I*

*have asked Tess to write this for me, and will send more news when I
am better. My darling, my love I send to you.* At the end, Tess had
added an anguished postscript. *She is in much pain, your grace, and
the healer is worried about her fever. I worry for her, too.*

"It's from Rowena." Sir James sighed softly in relief, as if he
had feared different news, as he likely had. Melfallan handed the
letter to Revil to read, and then tried hard to think clearly. "The
courier told no one?"

"Her castellan's instructions. Even so, it won't remain secret
long."

"Lord Tauler's lands lie closest to Airlie," Melfallan said
bleakly, "and he would hear first. I wondered why he was here
in Tiol."

Sir James shook his head. "Tauler has always kept his own
counsel, Melfallan. Don't assume he's Count Sadon's tool."

Melfallan nodded grimly. "Nor should I assume he's not. I
want the guard doubled on Audric, and every precaution taken.
He's not to be brought out in public again until his Blessing." Sir
James nodded. "And tell Sir Micay I want the castle guard put on
alert—no, better, find him for me and bring him to my tower
study—"

"Melfallan!" He broke off as Saray emerged from the nursery,
her face happy and glowing. She hurried over to him, swaying
gracefully across the stone floor on light feet. "Why look so grim,
my lord?" she exclaimed, taking his arm. "I've prepared a wonderful entertainment for you tonight, with all the lords and ladies
to be here. There will be dancing and music, and fine gowns and
a wonderful meal, all to welcome you home!" She hesitated, looking up at his face. "What's wrong?" she asked, then looked con-
fusedly at Sir James and Revil.

"That sounds lovely, Saray," Melfallan managed, and shook
his head slightly at Revil. Ocean save him, he simply could not
take from Saray her joy this day. Saray so loved her entertainments, and had probably planned this one for a week, each detail
decided with high anticipation, with hours of discussion and
laughter with her maids. She might be angry later, but he couldn't

tell her about Rowena, not now. Luckily, Revil distracted Saray
by putting on a hearty air, all smiles.

"You must choose his finery, Saray," his cousin suggested
drolly. "Melfallan never knows what to wear. It's not one of his
arts." Revil tsked. "If he had his way, he'd dress in a fisherman's
smock and think nothing of it!" Melfallan gave Revil a pained
look. His clothes weren't *that* bad, nor his taste in them, thank
you, but it made Saray laugh.

She nodded happily. "I'll do that, cousin," she said, smiling
at them all. "Come, gentlemen! My lord is safely home, and we
must celebrate!" Saray tugged at Melfallan's arm and drew him
away, then shooed off Sir James as he began to follow. "Not now!
No solemn advice or matters of rule, Sir James! He's mine for
tonight. You can't have him." She smiled up at Melfallan, so very
lovely that his heart turned over. "For once *I* rule!" Saray said
boldly, and then blushed crimson at her own effrontery.

Melfallan lifted her hand to his lips and smiled. "As my lady
bids. How can I deny such loveliness?" he added gallantly.

And Saray gave him such a look of joy and love that his mask
nearly slipped, exposing his anguish that she loved him this much.
He fought hard to recover his composure as he bent over her hand,
and then straightened, tucked her arm firmly to his side, and managed another smile for her. "Lead on, Lady Yarvannet," he said.
"Entertain me. I'm braced for it now."

Saray laughed and shook her head at him.

That evening the crowd returned for Saray's formal dinner and
gathered in the castle's Great Hall. Servants hovered in the doorways, watching the noble folk eat, then talk and dance. The pleasant sound of many voices echoed in the hall. Near the middle of
the evening, Melfallan found himself sitting alone at the high table.
As he sipped at a glass of wine, he watched his wife enjoy her
party.

Saray loved such high affairs, for they reminded her of the

glittering Mionn court she had known in her girlhood. There she had been ignored by her haughty mother and unpleasant older sister, pecked on as the youngest of a brood is often pecked, but Saray had adored the finery and laughter and bright lamplight of the constant social balls in her mother's court, however she herself was depreciated. Saray loved the soft conversation, the fine clothes, the elegant dining, the dancing, the grace of lords and ladies in their courtesies to each other. To her, it was a glittering perfect world, with every move a dance step, every word genteel and soft and gallant. All was best; all was perfect. Reality did not intrude, and pain or loss could not exist: all was loveliness. After Saray had grown into her exquisite beauty as a young woman, that fantasy had become even easier to keep, for her mirror confirmed her own perfection, and her beauty drew her constant compliments and deference.

Tonight Saray had dressed in one of her finest gowns with silver embroidery and rich green satin, her red hair stylishly arranged with jeweled clips. He watched her walk gracefully toward a group of ladies near the far corner and join in their conversation. Two merchant's wives bobbed a curtsey as Saray approached and moved back a step, mildly uneasy among such higher-ranked ladies but determined to hear whatever they said to each other. Saray nodded pleasantly to Lady Joanna Souvain, whom she had always liked, then nodded to Lady Alice Tolland.

For generations Lady Alice Tolland's family had owned extensive farmlands and a small fishing harbor in southern Yarvannet, and Alice had been her father's sole heir. Lady Alice rarely visited her lands, preferring the earl's court in Tiol and her own interests in spending money and indulging her son, Valery. A husband had come and gone years before, but Alice had hardly noticed him during their marriage and little mourned him after his death. She had been born to wealth and later gained a much-prized noble title from Earl Audric, and most of her thought focused on that one glittering fact, always had, always would, even as the years slowly leached at her face and body. Saray and Joanna were bright firebirds next to Lady Tolland's marsh hen in dark brocade, despite the older lady's richer jewels.

As the earl's wife, Saray should have been preeminent in Tiol's female society, but Lady Alice had never surrendered the position she'd achieved in Earl Audric's court in her younger years, and Saray had let her keep it, deferring to the older woman as Saray had deferred to her mother and sister in Mionn. That surrender irritated Melfallan, although he knew better than to interfere in ladies' affairs: noble ladies might note a man floundering in their midst, but then ignored him and went right back to arranging themselves as they chose.

And so the Yarvannet ladies bullied Saray, casually turning their backs on her or interrupting her conversation, bending their heads together to exclude her from the most delicious of gossip tidbits, none of it malicious or meaning her ill, just—inadvertent, as a careless tailor might drop a spool of thread and not notice it roll under a table. They made sly comments that diminished her, careless that she might overhear, and giggled together about Melfallan's fine person, their glances at him sometimes dangerously bold and edging on invitation, even when Saray stood nearby, but Saray always smiled sweetly and ignored it all.

Is any of them her friend? Melfallan wondered sadly. A real friend? Or do they all talk behind their hands, giggling their contempt? For years Lady Tolland had led the sly gossip about Saray's miscarriages, waggling her headfeathers about Saray's profound failure as wife, lifting her hands in pretend horror, tsk-tsking about weaker northerner blood. Now that Saray had produced a living son, Melfallan got the credit for it, not Saray, and the gossip rolled on unchecked among the haughty peahens who surrounded her. He sipped at his wine, watching his wife smile and enjoy herself in their company, and felt his stomach churn sourly.

Can't she see it? he thought in frustration. Can't she see how little they think of her? Only Lady Joanna, Garth's wife, was truly gracious to Saray, without the spiteful comments, the careless inattention.

With an effort, he turned his attention away from Saray, and focused on the lords seated at his table. The last remnants of dinner lay on their plates, and a wineglass was in every hand as Melfallan's Yarvannet lords caught up their own version of male gossip. In some ways, Melfallan thought wryly, the worlds of men and ladies were not that different.

At the end of the table, old Lord Eldon Grosmont half-dozed in his chair, his stolid son loyally at his side. Eldon governed the river town at the mouth of the Ewry, as much a portmaster as a lord in his duty to collect the earl's fees and tolls for the harbor, and pocketing a hefty percentage for himself as he did. Eldon had been already rich from his wheat merchant's trade when Earl Audric elevated him to a lordship, and had grown still richer in the thirty years of Audric's rule. Years ago, however, plague had wrecked the older lord's health: he had survived the illness, but it had left him weak and emaciated, bent over a cane, and only half the vigorous lord he used to be. Across the table from Lord Eldon, Merchant Nielsen sat with Valery Tolland, with the fat merchant doing his best to ignore the young fop's chatter. Valery lounged in his chair, his elegant person dressed as richly as his mother, but Valery chose to squander his gifts of wealth and physical grace in self-indulgent dissipation. Despite the middle hour of the evening, Valery was already drunk: Melfallan had rarely seen him otherwise.

Several chairs down, Justin Halliwell, the armorer, and Lord Jarvis Marchand were in close conversation about sword-work, and Revil and Lord Garth discussed similar fine points about horses. Lord Garth, like Tauler, rarely came to Tiol, but Melfallan had always liked him whenever he did. As Yarvannet's other marcher lord, Garth ruled the rolling hills between the rivers that abutted Briding. In his midthirties, Garth was nearer Melfallan's age than Tauler, and liked to talk most about his fine horses, his passion for horseflesh only slightly second to his adoration of his pretty wife, a daughter of a Farlost knight. Melfallan watched as Joanna, quite inattentive to Lady Tolland's topic of conversation, whatever it was, wiggled her fingers at her husband from across the room, and Garth instantly smiled back, his face lighting. Revil had to nudge him hard to regain his attention.

Melfallan sipped at his winecup and hid a smile: Lord Garth and his Joanna were a delight to watch, even though they had been married longer than he and Saray. How did they do it, being that much in love? He felt a tug of envy, and deliberately shifted his attention again.

Are any of these lords *my* friend? Melfallan wondered. Revil openly loved him, of course, but whom among the others could he trust? Valery and Garth were near his own age, but Valery was cruel and useless, and Garth probably friendly but rarely at court. Lord Eldon was a broken man, lost in his pain and weakness, and his son was well-meaning but stupid. Lord Jarvis, a former Tyndale knight elevated to a lordship by Earl Audric, liked to talk, and talked far too much, almost always unwisely. And Lord Tauler of Farlost trod a careful path between his earl and his sullen count, perhaps too carefully.

Even after thirty years, the Yarvannet nobility still divided into two parts, one the native merchants whom Audric had elevated to the gentry, the other the Tyndale veterans whom Audric had rewarded with a noble title. Lord Garth's father and Lord Eldon had replaced local lords who had supported Pullen, but Farlost's lords had remained the same, Lord Tauler preeminent among them. During his rule, his grandfather had openly preferred his Tyndale lords, never quite shutting out the local gentry but treating them with wariness, as if the taint of rebellion clung.

His grandfather had conquered Yarvannet by the sword, however benign and forgiving his rule thereafter: the steel within the glove was always assumed. These lords had feared Audric as well as loved him, those that did love him, but these lords did not fear Melfallan. And even fear of Audric had not deterred Count Sadon from arranging his grandfather's murder, if he had, and that impulse to the earl's destruction, however natural and well nursed these thirty years in Sadon's breast, was a resentment likely encouraged by the duke to its murderous conclusion. A High Lord's

death was a crashing solution to a duke's political ailments, as if
a divine hand swept a chessboard, shattering all the pieces to the
floor, making all things new—and all things possible. A High
Lord made sure he had sons to succeed him, or the temptation to
sweep the board sometimes waxed uncontrollable in restless
lords—but even sons did not protect in certainty.

But he would need all his lords in the coming struggle with
Tejar: who was reliable? Melfallan again quietly studied the various faces at the table, wondering where their loyalties would lie
in the test. Yarvannet's lords had accepted him as Audric's heir,
but he had not yet won their personal loyalty. To be fair, he
hadn't yet tried, being too preoccupied with his grief for Audric
and his worries about his lack of a son, then the crisis about
Brierley. Who among the lords would support him? And if not
now, how to win their support? Each man might require a different approach, a different wooing—and might still not be trusted,
not if Melfallan were wise. He stared gloomily down into his
glass.

He heard a chair scrape across the table and looked up, then
nodded in mild surprise to Lord Tauler. Tauler sat down, glanced
around for a servant, then reached himself for the wine carafe and
filled a glass. Hawk-nosed, with a weathered and rugged face, his
straight blond hair cut below his jawline, Lord Tauler had a
swordfighter's long-limbed muscles and grace. As usual, as he had
all the other times Melfallan had seen him, Tauler had dressed
simply this evening in a gray tunic piped with silver embroidery,
with no other ostentatious showing of his rank.

Tauler took a sip of the wine, gave a slight nod of appreciation
for Melfallan's cellar, and leaned back in his chair, quite at ease.
He looked steadily at Melfallan for several moments, perhaps considering *his* approach to Yarvannet's new earl.

Melfallan matched his pose, leaning back to his own ease, then
smiled lazily. "Shall I match the artificiality of this party," he
asked, "and speak of inconsequentials? The threat of snow perhaps? Or the latest tale of Duke Tejar's court?" Amusement flickered deep in Lord Tauler's eyes, and his polite smile broadened,

just for a moment. "Or shall I ask why you just sat down with me? You've been avoiding me, Lord Tauler, since I acceded last spring."

"I greeted you at the dock," Tauler said in mild protest, "and I spoke pleasantly, your grace. I even introduced you to my son."

"I think the boy liked that," Melfallan commented with a smile, and saw the answering flash of pride in Tauler's eyes. Melfallan reached for the carafe and refilled his own glass. "It's not an easy position for you, Lord Tauler. I know that. My arrest of Landreth must have infuriated Count Sadon." Melfallan took a long sip of his wine.

"Count Sadon *is* furious," Tauler agreed, "or so I've heard. I haven't been recently to his court." He turned the wineglass in his hands, then took his own sip. "In truth, I avoid Farlost as much as I avoid Tiol these days. A sword on the anvil grows anxious when his two blacksmiths hold their hammers high."

Melfallan chuckled. "I'd never punish you for whatever Sadon does, so long as you don't league with him in the treachery."

"Your grandfather was not as careful in making such divisions," Tauler said bluntly. "Some of the lords he killed were guilty of only honoring their oath."

"Not all."

"But some. I agree security can require a sweep of the local nobility, if one wishes a new earl's house to be secure. I also agree the murder of whole families has its precedents—by our current Kobus dukes, for instance. Earls tend to model themselves after the higher nobility, not the lower." Tauler shrugged.

"You have a long memory, my lord. My grandfather conquered Yarvannet thirty years ago."

"Some things cannot be forgotten, your grace." Tauler quirked his lips. "Not that I ever mentioned it to Earl Audric. Your grandfather did not invite such topics." Tauler waved his hand. "He was a goodly lord, wise in his rule, but shall we say—confident in his own opinions?

"Whatever anyone else thought," Melfallan finished for him.

Tauler's mouth twitched. "Nobody could change him. I always considered it his strength."

"Or his flaw," Tauler said quietly, his eyes intent on Melfallan's face.

Melfallan studied him a moment. "Why test me now?" he asked curiously. "We've seen each other, what, twice since my accession? And all the times before, of course, when my grandfather was still alive. You saw me grow up, Lord Tauler, and a prudent lord watches the heir as much as the lord."

"That was before you acted against Lord Landreth." He grimaced. "And went to Darhel in defense of a witch. An interesting start to your rule, your grace."

"The charges were true against Landreth," Melfallan countered, "and not proved against Mistress Mefell. Sir James has four witnesses who came forward. And you know Landreth's reputation enough to think the charges likely. Tell me, Lord Tauler: which aggravates Sadon more? That I arrested his son, or that I arrested him for rape?"

"Women were created by Mother Ocean for the pleasure of men," Tauler drawled, his voice shifting to an unpleasant mocking tenor. "Servant girls have little other value, except the menial tasks they do in the castle. Somebody has to empty the swill to the pigs, or chop the vegetables." Melfallan raised an eyebrow, and Tauler shrugged. "Or so I've heard my lord Count Sadon say, when defending his son's habits."

"And are you teaching this same truth to *your* son?"

"Never." Tauler's mouth tightened into a thin line. "Aside from a general rejection of such self-indulgence, I married a commoner."

"Ah, I didn't know that."

"We don't remind the gentry too much of it. Estes's mother is still beautiful in my eyes, and, more importantly, beautiful in Estes's eyes. To diminish other women diminishes her. I differ there: many lords don't think rape is a crime. I'm glad you disagree."

"Are you?" Melfallan challenged.

Tauler took in a deep breath and grimaced. "How did we ever stray into the truth, young earl? Lords so infrequently share it. Why not keep our truth behind our hands, or make promises we don't intend to keep? Or perhaps we could flatter each other, and eye the women at this most excellent ball?"

"We could do all that," Melfallan agreed.

Tauler grunted. "You forget, your grace, that I've been contemplating Landreth as my future count, whenever Count Sadon is shuffled off by Daughter Sea. Landreth sometimes comes to visit me, when his father makes him. All I can do was warn my stewards to hide the more innocent among the girls until he leaves." Tauler raised his glass and took a long swallow. "Do you expect the duke to pardon him?"

"Probably: it's the obvious countermove. And if Landreth dares to return to Yarvannet, I'll hang him." Tauler's eyes widened in shock. "You might perhaps counsel Count Sadon to leave his son safely in the north."

"Oh, I think I might defer that to you, your grace. Count Sadon has a habit of punishing his messengers." He shook his head slowly, probably contemplating his anvil again, then blew out a breath. "This will cause trouble."

"The trouble has been there for quite some time, my lord. The duke looks to Sadon as an ally, and Sadon has already proven himself untrustworthy to his earl. Farlost's army might have turned Pullen's battle to a different outcome."

Tauler shrugged. "Perhaps. You underestimate your grandfather and his Tyndale soldiers. The truly faithless lord was the Earl of Mionn, who likely promised Pullen support and then failed to send it."

Melfallan coughed in surprise and nearly upended his wine on his lap. "Oh, I doubt that. Earl Giles had no interest in Yarvannet. The Mionn earls are content with their own lands."

"Really? Are you so little versed in your history?" Tauler smiled sardonically. "Look only to yourself. Why did he marry your lady to you, if he had no interest in Yarvannet?"

Melfallan grinned, suddenly at ease with this older lord, a lord who had little reason to love the Courtrays. "Now, please," he drawled, "don't give up all flattery, Lord Tauler. Yes, I know Mionn meddles, but I've never heard that Earl Giles prompted Pullen into rebellion."

"Why assume it didn't happen?" Tauler persisted.

"Why assume it did?"

"Because Mionn is Mionn, that's why. Think about it, young earl, and remember your history. It's the earls acting together that can unseat a duke." And with *that,* he rose gracefully from his chair and lifted his wineglass in salute, then drained the glass.

"Now, surely," Melfallan said dryly, "you're not going to leave now."

"Yes, I am. I want to think over what I've heard from you," Tauler said, "and then decide if I've made a mistake—or not. We'll talk again, your grace." He bowed, then strolled away.

Bemused, Melfallan watched Lord Tauler circle the room, talking briefly to Sir James, flattering Saray, exchanging pleasantries with Lady Alice, who looked sour for some reason. Tauler then gallantly invited Saray to dance, which Saray accepted with a dazzling smile. While they danced, Revil casually strolled down the table and sat down across from him. It started a general slide among the lords, for Garth followed him, then Jarvis and Justin, and even Valery poured himself down the table to court his earl. Melfallan chatted with them pleasantly, then let Saray wheedle him in leading the next dance. By the time the noble folk had finished their party and retired to their beds, True Night had long since fallen.

After he had seen all the lords and ladies depart, some to their guest rooms in the castle, others to their houses in the town, Melfallan climbed the inner stairs to the upper floor, then walked through the interconnected rooms to the bedroom he shared with Saray. He found his wife at her toilette in front of her mirror, brushing her long red hair, a lady-maid in anxious attendance. The girl bobbed a curtsey as he entered the room, and Melfallan nodded, then began untying the laces of his tunic. After a moment he stopped himself, realizing that he had undressed in front of Saray's ladies as habit for years, falling too easily into his wife's practice of ignoring the servants. He looked at the girl again and didn't recognize her.

"Is she new?" he asked Saray.

"Who?" Saray asked, turning her head toward him. "Oh, Berthe. Yes." Saray smiled at Berthe and received a shy smile in return. "Aunt Rowena lent her to me. She has a great skill in beadwork and stitchery, and the countess would like her trained by me in other arts as a lady-maid." She gave another gracious smile to the girl. "You can go, Berthe."

"Thank you, my lady." Berthe gave another bobbing curtsey to Melfallan, then bobbed neatly to Saray, and scurried out.

"Aunt Rowena told me," Saray said, "that Mionn lady-maids are the finest of all, and she thinks Berthe has promise, and so gave her to me for the proper teaching. I agree. I am very pleased with her."

Knowing Rowena's actual opinion of Mionn's courtly pretensions, Melfallan suspected deliberate flattery in Rowena's request about Berthe, to which Saray was happily oblivious. It was a kindness by his aunt, to so flatter Saray, and he smiled at his wife's obvious pleasure in it. Saray was so very easy to please, so very sweet-tempered, lovely, grateful for the slightest attention. He had the power to wound her horribly. If he did, Saray would try to accept the wounding, struggle to hide it, then try to set it aside and fail in the effort. Melfallan had no doubt of his wife's love, how little she might understand him. He caressed her hair, letting his hand glide down its silky length, and then bent to kiss her.

Saray came immediately and dutifully into his arms, smiling up at him. He had expected difficulty in returning to his wife's bed, but now found himself caught up in her perfume, her loveliness, her sweetness, and likely his own sifting guilt about Brier-

ley. What that said about him as a man, he couldn't say, but
suspected it wasn't flattering. That he had now betrayed Brierley
with Saray said still more about him, but he roughly shoved that
thought aside. He couldn't bear thinking of it, wouldn't think of
it. He moved his lips to Saray's neck and shoulder, then swooshed
her up in his arms, sending the silky skirts of her nightdress flying.
Saray gave a little shriek of surprise, then laughed as Melfallan
carried her to their bed.

"At this late hour?" she asked drolly. "I think you've had too
much wine, my lord."

"I've missed you." It was only a little bit of a lie, and mostly
true. "Very much, Saray." Saray laughed again in delight and
pulled him down on the bed with her.

So very easy to please. So very easy to hurt.

Afterward, Saray lay contentedly beside him, pleased to have
pleased him. She never thought of her own pleasure, only of his,
and it restrained her passion in responding to him. A caress deftly
here, a kiss placed there, a careful shifting of position to make
matters easier for him, then the patient waiting beneath him while
he thundered to his release. He thought Saray liked coupling and
found it pleasurable, but she never cried out or moaned wildly or
begged him for more: she thought only of him and his pleasure,
no more, no less. When he was done, panting and sweated, she
shifted slightly beneath him, prompting him to move off, and he
obediently disengaged their bodies. Then, with a sweet smile and
another kiss, she rolled away from him onto her side and sighed
happily, ready for sleep.

"If you persist, my lord," she murmured, "we'll have a second
son for Yarvannet."

"True," Melfallan said awkwardly and bit his lip hard. He
would *not* ask if coupling were reason in itself; she wouldn't
understand what he meant, but would think it only raillery for a
second time. She would keep herself awake until he was ready,
then roll obediently onto her back and move her thighs apart for
him. And so they would couple again, for his pleasure, and when
he was done, she would smile and kiss him, then shift her body

slightly to prompt him to get off. Melfallan lay quietly beside Saray in their bed, careful not to let their bodies touch, and let her fall asleep.

It's not fair to her to think this way, he thought unhappily. It's not fair to want more.

He sighed softly to himself. Can the wind stop its blowing?

ith Stefan in disguise as a farmer, and Brierley plain-dressed enough as his wife, her face concealed within a hood, they had left Carandon early in the morning, leaving the city by a little-used gate. Once out of the sight of the city, anxious to return to Megan, Brierley had urged a faster pace, and then barely kept to her saddle as her horse stretched his legs and ran. After some franctic minutes of clutching at anything possible on the horse, Brierley grew used to the rocking movement, enough to laugh at the rush and the speed and the thunder of his pounding hooves. Her mount neighed in response and pranced a bit, then resumed his swift gallop, flying over the grass. Stefan's mare kept up easily, light and quick on her feet, and tossed her mane in challenge.

"Slow down!" Stefan shouted. "Destin will race him! And he'll race her back!"

"He goes faster than *this?*" Brierley asked incredulously, but her words were whipped away by the wind of their gallop.

"Brierley! Pull up!" Stefan laughed, then waved at her frantically as Destin stretched her legs even more.

Reluctantly Brierley pulled back on the reins, and the horse fought her a moment, then yielded to her pull, dropping into an easy canter. Destin surged ahead, but gave up the race quickly under Stefan's firm hand, and then slowed her pace until they cantered again side by side.

"Thank you," Stefan said wryly, and reproved her with a fierce look.

"You're welcome—I think." She grinned at his expression. "He's fast!"

"That he is," Stefan agreed. "He's bred to it—but my Destin is still faster," he added smugly. Brierley promptly heeled her horse and he took off again, flying over the grass.

"Brierley!" Stefan called in despair. In the next instant, Destin was after them.

The road led down into a grassy valley, spotted here and there with trees now winter-stripped of their leaves. On the slopes ahead, the everpine stood closer together, the groves thickening as the road led upward into the hills. The horses ran onward, happy to run across the grass, leaping strongly, seeming scarcely to touch the ground. It *was* like flying, Brierley thought in delight.

Finally, and again reluctantly, she slowed her horse's wild gallop to a more sedate pace. She wanted to hurry back to the cabin, but, in truth, they had all day for the ride. The horses, eager enough now, would tire badly by the end of the day, more than was fair to a good beast. Brierley eased her horse into a trot, then a walk, and patted his neck happily, nearly as winded as he was. The gelding was a gift from Rowena, brownish-black with a white blaze on his nose, and a finer horse than the packhorse she had ridden down to the city, and—quite impertinent, she sensed. The gelding snorted briskly, his opinion of this sedate walk quite clear, and she smiled in response. He might be obedient, as was proper, but a horse still had a right to his opinions. "Does he have a name?" she asked Stefan.

"Who? Your horse? Not that I know, although the stableboys name them all. But he's yours now, Brierley. You can name him what you want."

"I've never named a horse. What's a good name?"

Stefan shook his head firmly. "Brierley, he's *your* horse. Don't ask me."

"I think I'll call him—" She closed her eyes, trying to catch the essence of the horse. The gelding nodded his head vigorously several times, tugging at the reins, and then pranced sideways a step or two, but pranced back before she could correct him. He then—Brierley opened her eyes. Was that a *snicker?* The horse snorted again, and she sensed more than heard the beast's laughter. Laughing about what? The horse wouldn't say.

"His name is—Gallant," she decided. "He's a very fine horse, isn't he?"

"One of the best in Carandon. He'd bring a few hundred livres at an auction."

She turned her head and stared at Stefan. "What? Are horses *that* valuable?" Many families in Yarvannet counted fifty livres as a whole year's income, and felt graced to have that much.

"Some are. But his value is mostly in his temperament, like my Destin. They have the same sire. Some horses are bred for battle, but others are more suited to the hunt. Destin and your Gallant are hunters, swift and strong and very smart." Stefan patted his mare affectionately. "Aren't you, Destin?" The mare flicked her ears agreeably. Stefan then pretended to inspect Brierley for a moment, looking her up and down from hood to boots. "For your first hard gallop, you did fairly well in keeping in your saddle."

"Was it that obvious?"

"Sad to say, yes, but you're doing better now. Sit back more in the saddle, Brierley. It'll center your weight. And grip him more tightly with your legs. That's right. A good horse deserves a good rider, and that takes practice."

"Hard to do in snow."

"Spring's coming. There will be time," Stefan said comfortably.

"I hope so." Brierley hunched her shoulders, then looked worriedly behind them. No one followed: on this bright morning, they were the only riders in sight for miles.

"I'm sure we got away unseen," Stefan assured her. "It's one advantage of a crowded castle, and of me as your guide. I grew up in Carandon Castle, and I know every crook and cranny. Melfallan and I explored the entire pile when we were boys, and found things that even the countess probably doesn't know about."

"Like what?" she asked curiously. She could easily imagine boys on such an adventure, and Melfallan in particular.

"Oh, there's this tower room, all dusty and filled with broken furniture—from the spiderwebs, it seemed no one had been in the room for years and years. The stairway was cracked and broken, and hidden behind a locked door. It took us two hours with a turnkey pick to undo the lock: Melfallan has a real gift in picking locks—did you know that? Anyway, we decided that the tower room had once been a prison cell, perhaps for a lady fair who wouldn't marry where her father told her, and we, Melfallan and I, broke in to carry her off to the lord she really loved. We both got knighted for that." Stefan grinned.

"You were close friends, weren't you?"

"We still are, although he's now an earl and I'm still a commoner. Not that Melfallan ever cared about those divisions, and that makes him unusual among the High Lords." He shrugged. "My lady countess appreciates us all, commoner or not, but she has her noble ways, being Earl Audric's daughter. The other High Lords are very proud, and I suppose Melfallan is, too. But for him it's—a gift, not a fault, if you can follow my meaning. Pride can be a strength, if it's used right." He smiled at her. "You're the same, you know, prideful that you're a witch."

"You think so?" Brierley asked in surprise.

"Of course you are." Stefan playfully bowed to her from his saddle. "If being a witch is what you showed when you healed my countess," he said, more earnestly, "you have great cause to be proud, Brierley Mefell. Last night, after you fell asleep and I sat the first watch over you, I was thinking about how to thank you for my lady's life. The countess deftly slipped you that horse, knowing you were unaware of its value, but I have no such fine gifts—nor the suitable words, as clever as I am in my courtesy." He paused, thinking a moment about his dilemma, then shrugged humorously. "I'm still working on it."

"It's not necessary, Stefan."

"On the contrary, it is very necessary. But that's the pride speaking, thinking you needn't hear our thanks. You don't need the praise, and rather live above it, isn't that true? I envy you," he added candidly. "My own model of deft courtier is not as admirable, nor as inspiring."

"Now you'll embarrass me. Do give this up."

"No." Stefan stood up in his stirrups to stretch his legs, then settled again. "I'll come up with something. But remember this, lady witch: in some respects, Airlie is now yours, as am I." Another gallant bow, and then a brash, teasing grin.

She wrinkled her nose at him, and he laughed. Oh, yes, she thought, she could see why Melfallan and Stefan were friends, peas in a pod with their flattery.

The suns shone brightly overhead, with only a wisp of cloud in the sky, although the wind was still cold. They rode easily through the long day, climbing steadily into the hills, and then mounted the narrow track into the mountains, heavily shadowed by everpine. Here snow clung to the ground, sometimes piling itself in great drifts, stark white and cold. When Brierley and Stefan finally rode into the cabin clearing, the Daystar had long since set. The clear weather had not lasted through the day, and snow now drifted down from the sky, strangely silent in the absence of any wind. Peculiar shadows moved among the nearby trees as the Companion's light also dimmed, diminished by its own setting and the lowering storm.

Brierley nudged Gallant with her heels, for his steps now dragged with fatigue, however stoutly he still tried. The snow clung as it fell, wetting her clothing with a damp coldness that seeped inward to chill the flesh. She shivered, tired and cold, and half-dozed as Gallant patiently plodded after Stefan into the narrow meadow.

There should have been light from the cabin windows. She noticed that first. Why had Sir Niall let the fire go out? she wondered groggily. And why not light lamps for the night? Her mind moved sluggishly, numbed like the rest of her by the cold, and Brierley puzzled a moment, then instinctively cast her witch-sense toward the cabin, hunting Megan.

Nothing. Where Megan should have been, she sensed—nothing?

Brierley's head snapped up, and for a moment she forgot to breathe. She heeled her horse hard, surprising him into a canter for the last several yards to the porch. Before Gallant had scarcely stopped, she jumped from the saddle and ran onto the porch, then threw open the cabin door. All was dark inside: the fire had faded to dull-red embers when it should be blazing, and the cabin air was now quite cold, enough to ice the interior of the windows. Brierley found a match in the holder and lit the wall-lamp by the door, then looked around wildly. There was no disorder, no sign of violence: her books were neatly stacked on the table, cloaks hung on pegs, the pots of a meal still sitting on the stove. All was peaceful, only—Megan and Niall were not there.

"What is it?" Stefan asked as he joined her, then looked around at the empty cabin, as stunned as she. "Where are they?"

"I don't know," Brierley gasped. "They should be here. Megan!" she called. "Megan!" Brierley knelt and peered under both beds, then scrambled to her feet and yanked open every cabinet, even those too small to hide a child. Then she stopped herself with a hard effort, panting, and tried to find her good sense amid her panic. Calm down, Brierley. There must be a reason. There has to be.

"Would he take her hunting with him?" Stefan suggested.

"No! She's only six years old! He shouldn't have left her at all!" Sir Niall had sought every opportunity to add game to their larder when the weather permitted, and the weather had cleared that day all over Airlie, but surely he knew he could not take Megan with him, if only to avoid the burden of a child while on the stalk. Niall knew little of children, and she could well imagine him asking a six-year-old if he could leave her alone. *Will you be fine for a few hours, Megan?* And Megan would agree cheerfully, *of course,* and Niall would set off, thinking it prudent, thinking it all right. She noticed now that his snares were gone, and his heavy boots and cloak. Stefan's guess might well be true. She rifled through the books and papers on the table, hunting for a note, but found nothing.

Had Niall taken his horse? She dropped the books back on the table and ran onto the porch, then floundered through the snow toward the stable. Were both horses gone? The fool of a man! She slipped on ice and fell sprawling in the snow, and Stefan, close on her heels, helped her to her feet, and together they staggered to the stable doors, then banged them open. Friend, Megan's mare, snorted in alarm at the sudden noise, and swung her head toward them. She blinked at Brierley in the dim twilight, then nickered as she recognized her. At her feet, Megan lay in a huddle, her face hidden in the straw.

"Megan!" Brierley fell her to her knees beside Megan, then carefully gathered her child into her arms. Megan's skin was warm, her breathing nearly imperceptible, but she was alive. Brierley could feel the pulse at her throat, feel the faint push of her breath as she hugged Megan's face close to her own. But of Megan, that lively and vigorous child, she sensed little. Megan seemed emptied of herself, alive but not present, not as she had been, not as Brierley should sense her. Brierley caught back a sob of relief that at least she lived, then shook Megan slightly, trying to rouse her. She cast her thought desperately. *Megan!* There was no response, none at all. Megan's head shifted loosely, falling against Brierley's shoulder as she lifted her.

"Will you start a fire?" she asked Stefan distractedly. "She needs warmth."

"What's wrong with her?" Stefan was still bewildered, his confusion now laced with concern for Megan. Then, demanding: "Where's *Niall?*"

Brierley looked up at him and sudden tears filled her eyes. "I don't know," she said, her voice breaking. "I don't know, Stefan."

Brierley carried Megan's limp body into the cabin and laid her on the narrow bed, then wrapped her warmly in blankets.

Brierley chafed her cold hands, called to her, shook her again. The girl did not respond. Brierley reached out with her witch-sense, but found nothing to heal, no injury, no sickness. Megan was not physically injured at all, although one of her hands appeared slightly burned and—was it soot on her cheek? She leaned closer and touched the blemish, then looked at the gray powder on her fingertip, and lifted her finger to sniff. Ashes. Had Megan fallen into the fireplace? But the fire still burned in embers, too hot for the ash not to leave a burn. Bewildered, Brierley wondered what to do, then got up to get water and a cloth to wipe the ashes away. When she was done, she took Megan's small limp hand in her own.

Megan! she tried again. Her voice seemed to echo into empty places, lost among curtains of sifting smoke.

My child, my child, she keened silently. She had left Megan alone with Niall, a day and a night and another day, only that. What had happened here?

Where have you gone, my Megan? Where can I find you? Where *are* you?

River reeds, rustling in a cold wind. The sky overhead scudded with dark and angry clouds, obscuring the suns. And in the air, a scent of drifting smoke, a reek of death.

Nothing moved in Megan's dream world except the slight stir of reeds, a slow drift of cloud, the sluggish flow of the river. The white stones of her castle were cracked and fire-scored, the windows blackened by soot. The front door gaped open, splintered and charred and broken. Slowly Brierley mounted the steps, every sense alert, and entered the lower floor. Here, more damage—the books in the library upended from their shelves, scattered across the floor, more sign of fire in the parlor. She put her foot on the tread of the broad staircase and looked upward, then grimly began to climb.

On the second floor of her castle Megan kept memories. What

memory had attacked her now? There was the door to grief, with its slow dripping of water. There, the door to joy, bright sunshine and birdsong. And there, the room to rage, with its clashing swords and flame. One by one, she opened the doors, but found nothing she hadn't seen before. Brierley hesitated, her heart pounding with both dread and hope, but could delay it no longer. She ran lightly up the next stair to the third floor.

In Megan's special room, the comfortable bed stood against one wall, piled with soft mattresses and down pillows. On the shelves across the room, Megan's animated toys still moved, but listlessly, dull-eyed and forlorn. On the balcony outside, sun-shadow moved slowly in shifting pattern to the sky, creating creeping shadows that had edged partway into the room. Fire had not touched this room, not yet, had not yet burned the essential child. But where was Megan? And who had invaded here?

Had they waited until Brierley had left Megan alone, vulnerable and undefended? Had Niall's leaving further prompted the attack, an opportunity to be seized, when it came?

Brierley stepped onto the balcony and looked out at the river plain beyond the river, where a thin plume of smoke rose above the grasses. She watched the smoke twist and turn idly in the air, although there was no wind.

Megan, she called desperately. *Where are you? Megan!*

And an answer came, faint but clear, a tickle of laughter, the bright joy on the morning that was her daughter—then silence again.

Is that where you are? Brierley shielded her eyes with her hand, looking across the river at the plume of smoke, then set her mouth.

She descended the stairs in a clatter of movement and burst out of the castle, then ran toward the river. There she found some movement again, with a faint rise of sound. The reeds at river's edge swayed gently in the current, stirred by the paddling of small ducks among their stems. The birds clacked to each other contentedly, suddenly diving from sight and emerging a moment later, then to bob again, as they hunted insects and moss beneath the

water. A ferret skulked nearby, eyeing the ducks hungrily, then
vanished behind a screen of reeds. Beyond the reeds, the river
water moved slowly, but now sparkled in the suns' light as the
clouds thinned. Beyond the river, in the high grasses of the meadowland, smoke still swirled lazily on a light wind.

I'll need a boat, Brierley thought.

She walked along the riverbank, hunting through the reeds,
and came upon a small wooden dock extending into the water,
with a boat tied alongside. She stopped and put her hands on her
hips, looking at the boat. It was her own cockleboat from Yarvannet, the small boat she used to reach her island cave from the
beach. Well, of course, she thought.

And a staff, she decided then with new confidence, and my
hat. She lifted her hands. A moment later she settled the broad-
brimmed hat on her head, then placed the staff in the well of
cockleboat and stepped aboard. Within a dream world, more than
one might dream. With the short paddle, she pushed the boat
away from the dock, and then dipped it into the water.

The river current carried her cockleboat lazily downriver, but
she paddled easily and had drifted only a hundred yards down
the farther bank when she made shore again. She tied the boat to
a clump of reeds, then set off through the high grass. A small hare
sat up on its haunches and looked at her as she passed, its whiskers
working with curiosity, and then hopped away. Another ferret—
or perhaps the same one?—slunk by several yards away, its eyes
suspicious. She clucked to it and held out her hand. It chittered
nervously, then eluded her with great caution, vanishing into the
grass. She heard a thunder of hooves, and a swift herd of winter
fawn raced past, bounding lightly over the grass. And everywhere
the grass sighed in the breeze, stirred in great swirling patterns
by the gentle wind.

She had no path, only the thin spiral of smoke far ahead as
her guide, and she walked toward it, her staff tapping the ground
with each step. The day was warm, the breeze cooling, and everywhere was life—at first. As she advanced, the whisper of the grass
began to still, the wind died, and the first signs of charring ap-

peared in the grasses. The charring spread, blackening the ground in patches, some clumps of grass still smoldering. A mile from the river, she entered a wasteland of dead burnt grass with no life, none at all. She walked up rising ground and then descended into a low dell. At the top of the next low hill, she stopped.

A half-built castle stood there in a small depression, not built in Megan's white stone and blue-flagged casements, but in fire-cracked black stone. The walls now reached well above head-height, tall enough for a first story. Charred timbers stretched black fingers upward for a second floor, but only a pall of smoke served for the roof. The air above the castle danced with heat. All around the castle, flames flickered across the blackened ground in a slow menacing dance. She watched as a curl of flame crept toward her, silently as a ferret on the hunt. As it neared her shoes, she stepped around it and walked forward.

She mounted the riser of steps to the front door, then put her hand on the great metal ring set in its center. The metal flared suddenly hot as she touched it, but she shook her head, denying it, and pulled on the ring.

It was a door into Madness.

Night-deep and hollow, an infinite space opened behind the door, and within that space stood the motionless figure of a woman. She was dressed in fine velvet and gold, but the dress was slashed and rent, its hem in tatters. Her dark hair tumbled waist-length, tangled and smoldering. Terrible wounds gaped on her arms and in her breast, sword wounds that were surely mortal, but the eyes were burning coals, bereft, insane, and implacable. Those eyes fixed now on Brierley, hating with a fury that made Brierley catch her breath. Megan lay huddled at her feet, her face hidden behind her hands.

"Who *are* you?" Brierley demanded.

A smile slowly curved the fire-blackened lips, and the fury did not change. *Your death*— Brierley's staff ignited in her hand and she dropped it with a cry of surprise, then felt her hair, her dress, her hat burst into flame.

"No!" she cried, raising her hands, and willed the flames into nothingness, and then the staff was again firmly in her hand, her clothing untouched. "I do not permit!" She sensed the ghost's start of surprise, as if this one had rarely met anyone her match. How many was she? Only one fire witch of great power who had fought Rahorsum when he came to slaughter Witchmere? Or the combining of many such guardians who had died that day, died in agony and fury, to survive the centuries as a lingering memory?

"What do you want?" Brierley shouted. "Do you want Megan so you can walk in the living world again, to punish those who murdered you?"

I am Death, the woman jeered. *Who are you to question me? A sea witch? What do you understand of battle? Return to your healings, girl, and to your liking for the barbarians. Be the traitor to the shari'a.*

"Rahorsum's war is over!" Brierley answered. "It ended centuries ago!

His war will never be over, for it is my war, and my war will never end. Go away now, silly girl. Give up what doesn't concern you. The woman bent down to Megan, reaching out her hands to seize her, and Megan shrank away with a mewling cry.

Brierley stepped across the lintel of the doorway and lifted her staff. "You will not take her! I will not permit!"

And the Infinite exploded—

The castle door slammed shut with a hollow boom, and Brierley was thrown violently backward down the steps, tumbling over and over. The next moment she found herself on the blackened ground at the base of the stairs, dazed. She shook her head to clear it, and then got to her feet. *My staff,* she thought, and grasped it fiercely as it appeared in her hand. "You will not take her!" she cried.

A high thin mocking laugh spun down around her, plucking with its fingers, licking flame at her clothes. Brierley brushed it away impatiently and put her foot again on the castle step, then looked up as a cold shadow swept down at her.

"Not without Megan!" she screamed, and threw up her staff to shield herself. The shadow gathered force and struck—

The next instant Brierley was plunged into the river water and struggled back to the surface, gasping and spitting. She floundered, upending herself back into the water for a moment, then found her feet on the riverbed. She crawled onto the riverbank, crushing the reeds beneath her, her clothes sodden and dripping.

Then Megan scrambled out of the water beside her, her hair in tangled strings. Her hands slipped on the mud and she fell on her face. "Oof," she said, then sat up scowling, rubbing her nose. "That hurt," she complained. She blinked and looked around at the reeds, the river, then at Brierley. "How did we get *here?*" Megan's voice was filled with astonishment, as well it might be.

Brierley laughed and gathered her very wet daughter into her arms and hugged her. She kissed her and hugged her again, and then carefully inspected her for any injury. Aside from the small burn on her hand, another blotch of soot on her face, easily remedied by a handful of water from the river, Megan seemed unharmed.

"Oh, my child," Brierley said, relieved beyond thinking. "I was worried for you." She got to her feet and helped Megan to hers, then took her small hand. "Come with me."

Together they walked along the riverbank, and Megan stopped short in astonishment as she saw the fire-blackened stone of her castle, the broken door. She broke free from Brierley's hand and ran up the steps, then looked with horror at the dismembered library, the scorched parlor.

"What happened?" Megan cried. She turned to Brierley, her eyes filling with tears, and flung her arms around Brierley's waist. "It's all *burned,* Mother. What—what happened?" Megan buried her face against her, then sobbed into the folds of Brierley's skirt.

"Hush, child," Brierley said, caressing her. "All can be better. Be patient now." Brierley stooped and gathered Megan into her arms, and then carried her up the stairs.

In the top room of Megan's castle, Brierley set her daughter on her comfortable bed, then brought over her bear, who patted Megan's cheek and settled himself firmly in her lap. On the shelf, the animated blocks moved with new vigor, piling themselves into a stack, and then tossing themselves down, giggling. When Megan watched, agog, they did it again, an even higher stack and a huger crash, and this time won a small giggle. Then Jain suddenly flickered into view and landed next to Megan on the bed, crooning anxiously.

"Who is the woman in the other castle?" Brierley demanded.

She also is mine, Jain answered absently as he pressed close to Megan.

"Did you allow her in?" Brierley asked, angry tears starting in her eyes. "Is that how you care for my daughter?"

"Mother?" Megan asked, looking from Brierley to Jain in bewilderment. "What's the matter?"

Brierley took a step forward, balling her fists, not sure at all what she would do, except it might be violent. *Hold!* the salamander commanded in alarm. He lifted into the air and retreated through the balcony door with a quick flutter, then landed on the railing and snapped his wings to his back. As Brierley followed, menacing him, he hissed at her, showing white fangs. *I am bound by my nature, witch, and I cannot choose between those I call to Fire.*

"Who is she?" Brierley demanded.

Jain sighed, then relented with an unhappy shrug. *She is many,* he answered. *When Duke Rahorsum led his army into the passes to attack the shari'a, Witchmere summoned all the an'shania, the fire witches, from the nearby hamlets who could reach Witchmere in time. They fought well, but they died, and their collective rage at their defeat you now see within Megan. When you brought Megan into Witchmere and she invoked the keystone, their rage entered into her. That rage saved you from the guardians, but it now remains within the child.* He rattled his leathery wings in distress. *A fire witch remembers the past, Brierley, and some memories take life and can afflict the witch. It is part of the an'shania gift, as the Beast is of yours. One will prevail, either witch or ghost, and I cannot help one over the other: both are mine to cherish, memory and present child.* He clacked his jaws in emphasis. *I cannot. Your nature is healer: could you kill one patient to cure another? I too, am incapable of such choosing.*

"Then how do I heal her?"

I cannot help you destroy one of mine, Jain said, shaking his head, but neither will I hinder you. That is all I can offer, Brierley, truly, except this: the answers you must find yourself. Go first into Witchmere, to Thora's library.

"The library?" Brierley asked, confused.

The library. Jain's thought was scarcely a whisper. Some of your answers are there.

"Mother?" Megan called plaintively from the inner room. "Why are you arguing with Jain?" Megan's plea made Brierley turn, and she returned to the bed and sat down on its edge, then gathered Megan into her arms again. Megan huddled a moment against her, then looked over her shoulder at her favorite room, and began to sob. "It's all changed," she whispered in despair, although it seemed little different to Brierley.

"But your bear is here, Megan," she said soothingly, "and your blocks, and your sunny room. And—"

Brierley turned back toward Jain, but the balcony was empty.

On the narrow cabin bed, Brierley gathered Megan into her arms and rocked her as she cried, then looked dazedly at Stefan seated at the table. A fire again burned in the fireplace, crackling lustily with the wood Stefan had laid, and another fire burned in the stove. The chill had drifted from the room, the icy traces melting into thin runnels on the windowpanes. Stefan looked utterly bewildered as he sat, not sure if he had seen more witchery, not sure of anything. And he greatly feared for Niall, his friend. As foolish as Sir Niall might be about children, if in fact he had left Megan alone to go hunting today, he would have returned before dark, and Stefan knew it.

"Megan is all right now?" he asked in a low voice. "Truly all right? Did you heal her?"

"I'm not sure." Brierley shook her head wearily. "Some things are still beyond me. Megan's gift as fire witch is different than mine, Stefan, and I don't know enough about her gift to be sure. I can guess, and maybe I'm right." She kissed Megan's forehead.

"But maybe I'm not. I worry greatly about those times that I might not be." She nodded at the cabin window and the valley beyond it, the valley that led upward to a cliffside fortress with a hidden door. "In Witchmere there might be answers, answers I need for Megan. I should go there tomorrow. And maybe Niall will be back by then," she said, although she did not believe it.

"Or maybe not," Stefan countered, sharing her doubts. "Do I mention Witchmere's guardians now?" he asked aggressively. "They might have attacked Niall, and that's why he hasn't come back. And they attacked you, too. You're not immune, witch or not."

"Yes, I know. It doesn't make any difference, Stefan." She smiled ruefully as he sighed, then laid Megan gently on the bed beside her. Megan's sobs had subsided to whimpers, and she clutched at Brierley's hand as hard as she could.

"What happened, Mother?" Megan asked, her dark eyes pleading and afraid. "Why is my castle burned?"

"I'll find out, child. I promise." Brierley caressed her until Megan's eyes fluttered shut, and she sensed her child fall asleep, slipping into dreams, not of a fire-blackened castle, but other dreams more pleasant. Ordinary dreams, as any child might have, safe dreams.

A witch's gift bore dangers as well as blessing: every sea witch in Yarvannet had known that fact of a witch's secret life. The shari'a witches were proscribed by Allemanii law, and condemned whenever found, but the gift itself brought other dangers. Brierley fought the Beast whenever she healed, and a fire witch could remember too much. By taking Megan into Witchmere, by bringing her into range of the memories that lingered there, such a careless and unknowing fault, such a well-meant attempt at safety, Brierley had brought Megan into deep peril. And Megan was too young to defeat this living memory of fire and pain and death, far too young. And Jain could not help.

Brierley set her mouth with quiet determination. I will be your strength, Megan, my child, my darling. I swear it. She laid her hand softly on her abdomen, where her other daughter now grew toward life. We both will, she and I, we healers.

Beyond the cabin windows, the snow fell silently, filling the tree branches with short hats of snow, and laying a deep carpet of white over the meadow. When Megan was fully asleep, Brierley rose and walked to the window, then peered out at the night.

Where was Niall? she wondered. What had happened here?

"B e careful," Stefan said quietly. They stood on the porch of the cabin, Megan clinging with one hand to Brierley's skirt. The Daystar had just lifted above the ridgeline, shining through a haze of cloud that promised more snow by tomorrow, and its light glinted off the heavy drifts of snow that now filled the meadow. She would have a long and tiring walk up the valley, fighting snow all the way.

"I'll be careful," Brierley promised. She lifted Megan up for a last hug, and then gave her to Stefan, who settled her on his hip. Megan had said little since their return the night before, and would not respond to questions about Niall. Brierley had not pressed her. She sensed Megan's fear and a deliberate choice to forget, at least for now, and had decided to trust the child's instincts. Perhaps, as her fright eased, Megan might relent, but perhaps not.

Megan wrapped her arms around Stefan's neck and laid her head on his shoulder, then looked mournfully at Brierley.

"What do I do if—" Stefan began, and looked down at Megan helplessly. "I mean— Hells. I just *watch* witchery; I don't know anything more about it. What if she gets attacked again? And how will I know when she is, and what do I do about it?"

"I do wish I could be two people today," Brierley admitted. She laid her hand on his arm and smiled, then tipped her head to tease him. "I know you don't believe, not really, Stefan, in fire ghosts or dream castles. It takes trust a bit too far."

Stefan shrugged. "You're right about that. Give me a fine sword and a visible enemy, and I'll dash to the defense. I'm very good at that, by the way."

"I have no doubt you are."

"So perhaps I need an invisible sword?" Stefan bunched his eyebrows, thinking about it, then looked at her hopefully. "Where do I find one?"

"Oh, Stefan!" He had been half-serious in his asking, as if she could make such magicks by a mere wish. Well, sometimes I can, she thought, remembering her boat and staff in the strange battle with the fire ghost. But, sadly, only for me. She patted his arm. "I should be back by dark."

He nodded, then looked down at Megan. "Your mother has a new horse, Megan."

Megan brightened. "She *does*?" Megan adored horses, any kind, any style.

"Let's go see him. He's a very nice horse. You'll like him." He winked at Brierley, and then stepped off the porch, bearing Megan away toward the stable.

Brierley watched them for a few moments more, and then took a deep breath. Dear Ocean, she prayed earnestly, please let this not be a mistake. I'm risking Megan by leaving her again, and I risk my baby through the risk to me. She placed her hand on her abdomen for a moment, worried for her child. Witchmere's strange guardians had not recognized Brierley as shari'a, and had attacked her as readily as they had attacked Melfallan. But I have to go, she thought, for the hope of answers for Megan, answers that Jain has promised, answers I need. She closed her eyes, took another breath, then set off.

Brierley slowly retraced the upward climb into the valley of Witchmere, warm enough within her heavy cloak and hood. The path was unmarked, for few travelers found reason to go through this pass with its legends of haunting. The snow was often deep, but walkable when she found stone beneath the snow. She conserved her strength as she walked, often pausing to rest. From time to time, she cast her witch-sense for Sir Niall, hoping to find him still alive in the upper valley, injured and not dead, or trapped by snow, but she did not hear him. After three hours of steady walking, she recognized the waterfall and two tall everpine that faced the porch to Witchmere and looked up at the crumbled yellow stone of the opposite bluff.

The doorway to the shari'a's ancient fortress was invisible from this vantage, concealed from the valley floor by a clever arrangement of stone and brush. The entrance seemed merely part of a broken cliffside. She hunted at the base of rubble for the path upward, and then climbed the dusty track, emerging onto the broad porch with its shadowed open doorway. Here Duke Ra-horsum had stood with his High Lords, and had ordered his army of soldiers into the caverns, there to slay and loot. On that day, the Allemanii had killed every shari'a they could find, and had nearly ended witch-kind.

Brierley hesitated before the doorway, then reached into her skirt pocket and brought out her list of shari'a words, as if they were a talisman against the guardians of this place—as indeed they were, or so she hoped. No shadow moved within the darker shadows of the open doorway, and she peered in cautiously to see the farther corners. Nothing. Taking a deep breath, she walked across the threshold and entered the coolness within. The large entry hall led into greater halls beyond, one a hollow echoing cavern of high ceilings and darkness. Along one side of the large hall stood the shattered remnants, now dusty and corroded, of long banks of machines. Near them were a few tattered piles of rotting fabric and disintegrating bone that had survived the centuries. Silver jewelry glinted in the dim light of the cavern, distant gleams of a lost time. How many had died in this hall? And what had they tried to protect? Cool air sighed through the cavern from high vents in the walls, stirring the emptiness, scented of dust.

As she walked onward, her footsteps echoed hollowly against the stone flagging. She stopped to light the wick of the lantern she had brought with her, and then descended the stairs exiting the cavern, hunting her path downward to Thora's library. She descended stairs, one course after another, trying to walk quietly, and heard no sound except the sigh of air and her muffled footsteps. In the lower levels, her lantern's light was helped by the glowing disk-lights set into the walls, lights that still existed here by some witch's magic for three hundred years. Perhaps the guardians had not yet sensed her presence; perhaps this time, without Melfallan's company, they knew her as witch. Perhaps. She tightened her fingers on her list of words.

Mother Ocean,
Daughter Sea,
In this time of shadows,
Be with me.

Did she tempt the powers of Witchmere by whispering that Allemanii prayer? At what boundary line did a witch abandon her own kind by becoming more Allemanii than witch, and thus be an alien to this place, to be hunted as an enemy? In this place, all Allemanii were enemies: these halls remembered the Disasters and knew no other history. She felt her skin prickle with foreboding and clutched hard at her list, then stubbornly whispered her prayer a second time. Mother Ocean had guarded her since her earliest memories of childhood: she would not give up her protection easily.

Could the guardians hear her thoughts? Had the shari'a built their own witch-gift into these machines? How was such a thing done? How could a machine made of metal and glass think? Yet these guardians did think—and move and threaten and shoot fire. Melfallan had been desperately wounded by that fire and nearly killed, and Megan's hold on the machines had not lasted. Brierley nearly stopped, her thoughts jittering, and felt tempted to hurry back upward, back to safety.

Coward, she told herself angrily. What happens to Megan if you fail today?

Some fears are prudent, she reminded herself anxiously. Prudence—but I must. I must, for Megan's sake. But if I am killed here by the guardians, what of Megan then? Would the fire ghost seize Megan's mind and thus reenter the world—to do what?

What dire destructions could a fire witch deliver on the world, a witch who remembered the full power of the shari'a, a witch powered by overwhelming rage and grief? And how quickly would the Allemanii kill Megan's shell to protect themselves? She shuddered, then set her jaw and forced herself to continue down the next stair.

At the next landing, she hesitated again, not quite sure where she was. She looked to the right and left, hunting some familiarity in the stone walls and gleaming circles of light, but most of the Witchmere corridors looked too much alike. To the left, she thought: they had mainly climbed upward from the left. But had she descended far enough? In their flight upward, she had not paid enough attention, too anxious to escape the guardians that stalked them, too anxious for their return to the upper world. She closed her eyes and listened, hoping her witch-sense would give her the direction she needed.

Did some essence of Thora still linger here, in these halls she had known? In her dreams, Thora had often brought Brierley to her library in Witchmere, and had appeared dressed in a magnificent gown and jewels, her head held high with pride, her movements made with great assurance. In other dreams, Thora had seemed gentler, with a wistful sadness, a tendency to tease and cajole. Here had played out one great chapter of Thora's life, when she lived among the high adepts in Witchmere, and had studied in her library, and perhaps spoken in Witchmere's councils. Some of her words implied she had known the shari'a leaders, had even sat among them despite her youth. Did some part of Thora remain here, as the fire ghost had remained, locked in the dusty stone?

Thora— She suddenly wished for the touch of her dream-friend, although it be fancy and powered only by her own yearning.

She listened to the sigh of air through the corridors, and heard the distant music of moving water, and then, again, as before, she heard faint voices in the depths, voices that spoke without sense, faint murmurings she could not quite catch, like drifts of emotions aloft on the air. The emotions here were not the fear and pain that drove the fire witch, but earlier emotions from earlier times, before Duke Rahorsum brought the Disasters to Witchmere. She heard a trill of delighted laughter of sisters bent on mischief, a wash of joy for a beloved father returned from long travels, a quiet attention as small heads bent over books under their mother's guidance, then a rush of feet as three brothers raced their sister through the halls. One voice rose into a measured chant, spelling the winds; then another sang a few brief notes of a song for festival, and two others made a counterpoint as they discussed some scholarly topic; then all faded again, vanishing back into time.

Brierley opened her eyes and looked left down the hallway. Yes, it was to the left. She raised her lamp and walked onward. The faint drift of voices followed her, speaking again in hushed whispers, oblivious to her presence, as if Brierley were the ghost who walked here, unseen and unremarked, unreal. She reached the end of the hallway and descended another flight of stairs, then recognized the next hallway. Halfway down its length stood the door to Thora's library. She hurried forward, and stepped into a room she knew better from dreams than from her single visit with Melfallan some weeks before.

She saw again the array of ancient shari'a books in their cabinets, the high ceiling disappearing into darkness overhead, the smooth patterning of the flagstoned floor. Some of the library's books stood in open bookcases and were now badly deteriorated, but others had been more protected behind glass. Between the bookcases, spaced regularly around the library walls, were the mosaic panels depicting the four dragon-spirits of the shari'a. Brierley stepped to the mosaic portrait of Basoul, the sea dragon of the healer-adepts, and looked up at the exquisite mosaic. Graceful and slim, blue-scaled, the dragon coiled on a dark sea rock, a healer's cup in her talons. Her scales shimmered bright blue, each touched with a faint shimmer of silver, as if the artisan's skill had caught the essence of the sea in the very stones of his or her creation. The eyes were depthless, deep blue aquamarines, and looked beyond Brierley to some horizon only the dragon could perceive.

All her life she had looked to Mother Ocean as her protector.

She had never met Basoul, that older deity of her true kind. When she had healed Lady Saray in childbed, a blue dragon had fought beside Thora as Brierley suffered the Beast who had come. And when she had healed Melfallan of his burn, unwisely taxing herself beyond her strength, the Beast had seized her. A blue dragon had battled there, too, roaring at the Beast as she struck with silver talons at its noisome flesh, forcing the Beast to release his hold. Hints, drifting memories, a reality behind illusions: if Brierley were sea witch, this dragon was her protector.

Why haven't I ever met you? she asked the panel wistfully. Why? Am I too Allemanii to know you? Will I ever know you? And when?

But this sea dragon made of stones did not see her, did not see anyone, not now. Whatever essence of the dragon-spirits had lived in these panels no longer remained, as Witchmere no longer existed as a living place. She glanced around the library sadly. In another panel between the bookcases, golden-scaled Soren stooped screaming from the sky, lightning blazing in his claws, and in yet another Amina coiled indolently on a branch, half-concealed by leaves. On the final panel, Jain glowed deep-red in a dark cavern, a brilliant diamond sheltered within his claws. But of life within the mosaics, she sensed nothing. The Four were not here, not now. It had been too long.

She heard a sound in the outer hallway and turned around quickly. Had that been a clank on stone? She strained to hear, and heard another muffled sound.

"Kalit!" she shouted. *Stop!* "Il-bajaarin shari'a!" *I am shari'a!* She clutched hard at the list of words still in her hand, not looking at the text: she knew the text. She knew these words. "Kalit!"

And, praise Ocean's breath, the sound stopped! Brierley blinked in surprise. It had worked! She waited, scarcely breathing, as a long silence followed, then heard a stealthy movement. Well, maybe not.

"Kalit!" she raged at the machine, furious that it frightened her now. "Il-ganam illi tidsaq!" *You will obey me!* She clenched her jaws in fury, willing the guardian away with all her strength, enraged that it denied her as witch. How dare it do so? Her heart pounded madly in her chest, with rage or terror she didn't know, joined by a throb in her temples. "*Kalit!*"

"Min kalit," a metallic voice intoned in the outer hallway, and its sounds stopped again.

The silence again lengthened. Was that a refusal? Brierley wondered anxiously. Or an agreement? What did "min" mean? She couldn't remember, and idiotically hadn't thought to look up what the guardian might say *back*. "*Kalit!*" Brierley shouted desperately.

"Min kalit," the guardian muttered, its tone quite irritated, as if a machine could feel irritated—could it?—then she heard the sounds of the guardian's retreat. It did not go far, but it went. She thought of peering around the door lintel to see, but then decided prudently not.

She let out a deep breath, and turned back toward the bookcases. She paused for a moment to listen again, and reminded herself to listen frequently, but for now the machine's sounds did not resume. She doubted it had retreated very far. Well, she'd deal with that problem when she left. If she ended up crisped by the guardian's shooting fire, several books from this library would be crisped with her. But which books? She looked over the hundreds of books on the shelves, easily half too deteriorated to handle, and set her jaw in determination.

The dictionary that she and Melfallan had brought out of Witchmere had its limitations, but it did list words in both Allemanii and shari'a script. Shari'a writing was a graceful flow of loops and whorls, quite different from the regular block-shapes of Allemanii, and she had spent several hours memorizing the letters and their connections. She could write shari'a script neither smoothly nor with any fluency, but she did know their forms. As a test, she compared the names of the Four inscribed at the base of the mosaic panels with her list. The shari'a words matched, and she smiled with a ridiculous sense of relief. Idiot, she told herself, but I'm still glad they match. Now others might.

She studied her list of other words, three slender pages of words that she hoped to find on the bindings of books she might take. The word for fire witch, *anshan'ia*, led the list: if the ancient shari'a had similar problems with fire-witch memories that took too great a life of their own, the healing would surely be discussed in a book about the type of witch afflicted. Or so she hoped. She walked to the nearest bookcase and begin with the top shelf, studying each title carefully before she moved on to the next. Whatever books she found would be written in shari'a, without any helpful translation into Allemanii, and she would need hours of study to translate a single page. But without a book to start, she had nothing to help Megan. With a sigh, she stilted her fingers down the spines, book by book, hunting for answers for Megan.

Dayi. She checked her list. It was the same word: sea witch. Tentatively, she eased the book from the shelf, and felt its cover dent beneath her fingers. For years she had sought answers about herself in the journals and books in her sea cave in Yarvannet. Books had answers—sometimes. Here was an even older predecessor, an author who had known the full strength of witchery before the Disasters had nearly erased the shari'a from the world. What secrets did she tell in her book? What answers had she known? Or would Brierley find the same disconnection she sometimes found in her journals where those other witches had struggled to understand themselves? Had the dayi of Witchmere known themselves truly, being part of a time when the shari'a had created wonders in these caverns?

The shari'a of Witchmere had made the Everlights, and the guardians with their ability to speak and defend with fire, and the odd banks of machines in the upper hall, and the wall-lights that still glowed centuries later, giving light to the darkness. So much had been lost: so much lay here to be regained—and perhaps used more wisely. Melfallan had wanted to return here, and to bring a bookmaster to save these books. Their knowledge might grace both Allemanii and shari'a, perhaps even mold a peace between them that had not existed for three centuries. He had not spoken much of such larger dreams, but she had sensed his hopes when he realized what lay here.

And for herself? Thora had bid her to refound the craft, to

bring the surviving shari'a out of the shadows, to learn all that had been forgotten and begin the rebuilding. When Rahorsum had destroyed Witchmere, the shari'a had hesitated on a new resurgence, a great change after centuries of quiet living, of settled affairs. What new wonders might be made? she asked herself, looking around at the books. What answers might be found, genuine answers that brought clarity, a sudden insight into many other things, a new foundation? She closed her eyes for a moment, grateful to Mother Ocean for this one book about dayi, and then placed it carefully in the leather bag she had brought with her. She resumed her steady progress along the shelves, finishing the first shelf and starting on the second.

In the next bookcase, she found a title with the word "anshan'ia," and then a second book with "dayi," and then— Her fingers stopped suddenly, and she stared at the binding of the next book. She glanced down her list, hardly daring to look. When she was making her list, she had worked out the shari'a letters for Thora's name, and had printed it on her list. She had then traced her own name in shari'a script, and then Megan's, names depicted in the graceful swirls and loops of a language long dead, as if the writing somehow brought an essential back to life in witches now living. Wistfully, Brierley had wondered if Thora had left a scholar's book here, as Valena had left her own writings. Thora had studied in this library: perhaps she had.

She had. Brierley eased the book from the shelf. It was not in too bad a condition, not as fragile as the other three she had found. She sank to the floor and sat cross-legged, cradling the book in her lap, and opened it to the first page. There, on the title page, was Thora's name again. Brierley had not brought the dictionary with her, in a prudent decision that the dictionary would be left for Megan if Brierley did not return, and now she sharply regretted the choice. She wanted to know the words on this page, to know what Thora had named her book, and to know the words on the next page and the next, and she wanted to know them *now*.

Well, you'll have time, she told herself: they were weeks away from any journey into Mionn, weeks of quiet study in the cabin to add to the few weeks already made. Patience, Bri. Patience benefits a prudent witch. Brierley made a rude noise at her own self-counsel. She listened again to the outer hallway, and heard only silence. However long it would last, the guardian still kept its distance.

She ran her fingers over the graceful script and smiled with joy. My dear friend. You left a book here, too. I didn't really believe you might, but you did. *Believe,* you've always told me, and perhaps I should believe in small things as much as great. Thank you for leaving a book here, for me to find. Thank you. Unlike Valena's journal in her cave, recopied several times by the cave inhabitants as the older volume deteriorated, this book was certainly in Thora's own hand. It had to be. In these caverns, where the sea wind and dampness did not penetrate, where books had not been handled for centuries, Thora's own book had survived.

She sat for several minutes with the book in her hands, caressing its pages lightly with her fingers, then reluctantly shut it up and put it in the saddlebag with the others. She continued her search for another hour, working through the volumes in better condition behind glass, then moved to the other cabinets. Most of the books in these bookcases were too deteriorated to handle. After one fell apart in her hands, crumbling to the floor in a shower of broken pages and cracked leather, she gave up her search. She had found eight books, including another anshan'ia book and a third dayi book. The dayi book bore the word after the author's name, not before, perhaps in the style of Valena's own book, who had named herself "scholar and air witch." Another book was partially titled "Basoul," and the final book was named *dasiisa,* the sea-witch word for a Calling. Perhaps another search in the future might find more books with other guide-words, but she would take these for now. If she could find answers, these books gave a good chance of the finding. If there were answers. If.

She looked around the library again, wishing she could save all these books before they were lost. Melfallan had said a bookmaster might know the ways to preserve these volumes, but she dared not bring an Allemanii bookmaster to these caverns, whatever Melfallan's hopes. The guardians would never permit another entry by anyone they considered an enemy, and the High Lords, excepting only Melfallan, did not know about this place. Anything shari'a was proscribed, and other High Lords would come to destroy, not preserve.

She risked much in even possessing the few shari'a books she now owned, these and the others she and Melfallan had brought out of Witchmere. If discovered by a High Lord, far away from Melfallan's protection in Yarvannet, the books would condemn both Megan and herself. It was a risk she was determined to take, for the sake of answers, but she knew full well the danger. In the wayfarer cabin, where she and Megan would stay for the winter, she could study her new books and not worry about discovery, but what about Mionn? In Mionn, where Melfallan had hoped she could find a village, a town, where she and Megan could live again in hiding, she had no Everlight to guard her books, as her Everlight had guarded her sea cave in Yarvannet. But how could she leave the books behind? How?

She looked around at the library one last time, wishing she could take all of these books, those that could still be handled. Perhaps I should look for a book here on book-mending, she thought ironically. Or a book on how to find a book on book-mending, more to the point.

She lifted the leather bag to her shoulder, picked up her lantern, and faced the doorway into the outer hall. She took a deep breath, then stepped through the doorway. A shadowed guardian waited several paces down the hallway, its metal gleaming in the illumination of the wall-lights. It did not move when she appeared, nor speak, but she knew it watched her.

"Il-bajaarin shari'a," she told the machine. *I am shari'a.*

"Bajaarin-illi shari'a," the machine agreed in its hollow voice, but did not retreat. Brierley took one step toward it, and then continued walking steadily, closing the distance between them. The guardian did not lift its arm to point its weapon at her, merely waited. Recklessly, Brierley did not change course around it, but walked straight at the machine. At the last moment, it moved aside and let her pass. As she mounted the stairs, she heard the sounds of its following, and at the landing glanced back quickly, and saw that the guardian had acquired a companion, both following her silently as she continued upward.

The two machines followed her through the dusty silence, never approaching nearer, yet not falling behind. They tracked her relentlessly as she ascended toward the gate, and half a dozen times Brierley thought to repeat her commands, but decided that a confident silence could also serve. At one point, one guardian lifted its arm, as if to attack her, but Brierley ignored the threat, and the arm sank down again to its side. She reached the great hall with its banks of machines, and deliberately fought her impulse to hurry, even to run. Sedately, confidently, she marched through the hall to the entryway, and out onto the porch into the suns' light. The guardians followed her onto the porch, and through half the valley back to the cabin before they finally turned back. When she was sure they had retreated, she sat down on a windswept stone and closed her eyes in relief.

Believe, she told herself mockingly. Which you didn't, not about this—but it wasn't a journey she would easily hazard again. These two guardians had obeyed her voice, but others might be less sane, not at all amenable to confident commands. One had not listened to Megan at all, had even sent its fire against a fire witch who had the charge of the guardians. But in the bag at her feet were more precious books, perhaps with answers. It had been worth the danger, but she shuddered now to think of the risks she had taken.

Mother Ocean. Daughter Sea . . .

Ah, what prayer should she add now? All her life she had looked to Mother Ocean for her protection, and had believed in Ocean's gentle care as much as any Allemanii. The ancient shari'a had worshipped the Four: were there other shari'a deities above the dragons who guarded and taught the shari'a—or only One? And if one, was she Mother Ocean?

She shook her head. *The world turns upside down,* she

thought. She got to her feet and trudged onward, tired to her bones.

By the time she neared the cabin, the Daystar had long since set, and even the Companion's twilight was fading. In the starlight of True Night, the drifts of frozen snow gleamed as pale ghostly forms, stark contrast to the black jagged shapes of the everpine. The forest was silent, with little wind. When still a half-mile from the cabin meadow, Brierley stopped short as she heard a metallic clang behind her, and turned, peering into the darkness. She could see nothing in the dark, but sensed another guardian—off to the left, in the trees. It hovered in the shadows, watching her with an almost palpable malevolence, then oddly faded from her perception.

How did it hide from her sensing? she wondered. Was it still there, hiding behind the darkness?

She cast her witch-sense anxiously, hunting for it, but it seemed able to elude her. When Megan had first seen the guardians in the passes above Witchmere, Brierley had not seen them, nor sensed their thoughts nearby. In Witchmere they heard her but seemed doubtful of her shari'a blood, and now she had heard this one—until it chose otherwise. Were the guardians insane? Or had the centuries diluted Brierley's shari'a blood, enough that they could no longer identify her as shari'a? How could she know?

Defiantly, Brierley lifted her arms wide to the night sky. "Il-bajaarin shari'a!" she shouted. "Il-bajaarin dayi! Il-bajaarin Brierley Mefell!"

Her shout echoed off the trees, the drifted snow, the stones of the valley itself. When the echoes had faded into silence, she lowered her arms, then bared her teeth at the shadows. "Go away," she told the machine with a malevolence to match its own, and willed it away with all her strength.

The guardian did not answer, nor did she hear any further sound of its movement. Brierley waited nearly an hour, listening, although the cold crept inside her cloak and inflicted a long cycle of shivering, but she did not hear the watcher again. Nothing: it had left—she hoped earnestly. She did not want to lead any guardian back to the cabin. Megan's control of the machines was far too uncertain, and, if Jain's warning was right, her control drew partly from the fire ghost who threatened her. She took a shaky breath and looked down-valley toward the cabin meadow, still hidden behind a screen of trees. Stefan would be deeply worried by now: it was long past nightfall.

Ocean protect us, she prayed. Protect us all. She hesitated another moment, then rose from her seat and walked onward, listening with every sense to whatever might still follow. When she reached the meadow in front of the cabin, she hastened toward the cabin's lights and warmth, floundering through the drifts.

When her boots thudded faintly on the wood planking of the porch, she heard quick movement inside and Stefan threw open the front door, his face lighting instantly with relief. "You're late," he growled, then wrapped his arms around her, lifted her quite off her feet, and carried her bodily into the cabin.

"Put me down, Stefan," she protested, then laughed as he contrarily twirled her around, making her skirts and cloak billow. Her bookbag slipped off her shoulder and fell heavily to the floor, and he finally released her, settling her gently down on her feet. With a sigh, Brierley sat down in a chair by the table, then let Stefan take her cloak.

Megan greeted her with almost frantic joy, and climbed into her lap to cling hard. Stefan sat down in the opposite chair and cocked his head at them, then winked at Megan. "I told you, Megan," he boasted. Megan sniffed at him, and buried her face in Brierley's hair.

"No sign of Niall?" Brierley asked.

Stefan sighed. "Maybe. Megan and I went for a walk this afternoon—didn't we, Megan? I found his trail—or I think it was—but the snow had drifted over most of it. It led up-valley." He shook his head and thought to say more, then glanced cautiously at Megan.

"Sir Niall went hunting," Megan piped up unexpectedly, surprising them both. "I wasn't acting crazy, at least not much, and he asked me if I'd be all right for a few hours, and I said yes.

Need to stock the larder," she added, her voice deepening. "Yes, need to do that." Megan sighed gustily. "But he didn't come back, and the cabin got cold, and then——" Megan abruptly broke off, her face filling with slow terror. "I don't remember any more," she said, clutching at Brierley.

"It's all right, Megan," Brierley reassured her. "You're safe now. No need to remember." She rocked Megan slowly, her lips pressed to her forehead, and Megan slowly relaxed. Brierley lifted her head and looked bleakly at Stefan. "Dear Niall. He knew as little about children as he did about women. Leaving a six-year-old alone? Asking her permission, and thinking it all right?" She sighed, tears pricking in her eyes. "Do you think the guardians killed him, Stefan?" she asked.

But she knew his answer before he nodded. Megan began to whimper and Brierley hugged her close.

~9

She dreamed of Yarvannet, of her sea cave and the coast road. Once again she walked the dusty road, greeting the occasional carter, watching the light move on the sea. When the road began to rise on its last ascent toward Amelin, she walked to the bluff edge and looked down at the beach below. The sound of the surf rose up to surround her, part of the movement, the dancing light. She took a deep breath of the sea air, content.

A small hand took hold of her skirt, and she looked down at Megan.

"Is this your home?" Megan asked tentatively, looking wide-eyed around her. "Is all of that water?"

"Yes, it is. It's called the ocean."

"Is it deep?" Megan's hand tightened.

"Yes, very deep, at least out in the middle." She reached and took Megan's hand. "Look, there's a path down to the beach, just over there. Let's go see."

Megan hung back warily a moment, then looked up at Brierley's face. "All right," she said, with great hesitation. They walked along the bluffside to the path, an easy stretch of sand that led down the side of the short bluff to firm sand. A city child from Ingal, Megan had never seen the sea in all her life. A wave ran up the beach and splashed, making her gasp. Brierley tugged at her hand, encouraging her forward, but for now Megan was immovable, standing on this patch of sand by the bluff and no farther.

A sea lark tumbled overhead, piping, then plunged into the sea several cable lengths from the shore. Megan frankly goggled.

"She's catching fish," Brierley told her. "For her dinner."

"Oh."

"Water is fun." Brierley pointed at the gentle waves washing onto the sand, one after another in endless succession. "You can wade in, maybe up to your knees, and the water pulls at you and splashes. I think it wants to play."

Megan gave her a skeptical look, not believing a word.

Brierley hid a smile. "And sometimes you can find shell-stars, Megan. They have six legs and knobbly skin and crawl over the sand. And sometimes a fish will swim by and wave its fins hello."

"You believe all that?" Megan demanded, and Brierley chuckled.

"I used to, when I was your age. Everything knew me then, and all wanted to be my friend, or so I believed." She bent and caressed Megan's cheek. "Later, when I was older and my mother told me not to play with the other children, I used to walk on the beach alone. And I found the cave and its Everlight, and learned about what I was, but I was still alone. And I began to dream about finding another child like me, a witch-child that I could teach and love—you, my Megan." She knelt and tugged Megan's dress into order, then smoothed her curls.

Megan threw her arms around Brierley's neck and clung close, and Brierley stood up, lifting her in her arms. Together they looked out at the waves, where the suns' light danced ceaselessly, an unending pattern of light and sparkles. Far out over the ocean, the sea lark rose triumphantly, calling to the sky.

Megan eyed the water, still dubious. "The water wants to play?" she asked uneasily.

"Shall we go in? We won't go too far, just enough to wet our shoes."

"Do I have to do that to come here?" Megan's eyes glinted with tears, and Brierley kissed her.

"Not at all. So you want to share my dreams now, do you? I think that might be safer, don't you?" Megan nodded. "Then we shall, at least until your castle is safe again. Do you like my dream-home? I liked yours very much."

Megan laid her head on Brierley's shoulder. "You're here, Mother," she murmured. "That's all it needs." Brierley kissed her, and felt Megan's arms tighten.

"Well, shall we go into the water?" Brierley asked a while later. "Or not?"

Megan took a deep shuddering sigh, then raised her head. "Only shoe-deep," she insisted. "No more that that."

"No more," Brierley agreed. At the surf's edge, Megan looked down at the swirling water that slipped over Brierley's shoes, then watched, fascinated, as a taller wave washed up her ankles, splashing into foam.

"Down," she demanded, and, when Brierley had set her down on her feet, Megan promptly knelt to bury her hands in the soft sand, then chuckled as the water splashed her. Quite unmindful of the wet, Brierley sat down beside her and watched her daughter play with the sea. As Megan splashed and exclaimed, Brierley sensed the child relax, as if the sea gave some essential comfort, something to ease the terror and loss.

Brierley looked out at the water that stretched to the far horizon, the ocean she loved, the sea that would be always part of her.

Mother Ocean,
Daughter Sea . . .

Help me, Mother, to save my daughter. Help me keep her safe.

10

$\mathcal{T}$ he next morning Melfallan woke alone in bed and drowsed a while under the covers, thinking of nothing in particular, then got himself up at last. He looked for his clothes, but his manservant had not brought fresh clothing, as he ordinarily did. Rather than stalk naked through the hallways, he dressed in the fine clothes he had worn the night before. As he did, he wondered at Philippe's lapse. He had been gone only three weeks: had the servants forgotten him so easily?

He laughed softly. And you chide Saray, he mocked himself, for taking servants for granted. He drew on his hose, pulled his tunic over his head and settled the hem, slipped the heavy gold necklace over his head, then went to look for his wife.

He found Saray supervising her lady-maids in a nearby room, with the contents of her wardrobes all brought out for airing, and Melfallan saw a similar activity in his own wardrobe room next door. Dresses, tunics, fine stockings, shoes, veils, jeweled clips and heavy necklaces: the rooms were a riot of bright colors, pale laces, and silky fabrics. For some reason, every item of clothing he and Saray owned was out of the wardrobes, laid here and there in great piles. Judging from the state of the sorting, it would take all day to put everything away again, his own clothes included.

"Good morning, Melfallan," Saray said brightly, straightening from her tasks.

"Uh, good morning, Saray."

Curiously, not one of his manservants was in sight, either in the wardrobe rooms or the nearby suites. Not that he actually needed help in changing his clothes, of course, but what he really wanted was a bath. Right now his bathtub held several of his tunics and most of his pairs of hose, a dozen pairs of boots, and a large box of jewelry. Lady-maids were tripping busily in and out, burdened with this or that, and Melfallan had no intention of stripping naked for a bath while they were doing so. He caught Saray's attention again, thought to ask why, and then decided not. He returned her smile and wave, then escaped back into the hall-way.

He walked swiftly back through the family suites and clattered down the stairs to the Great Hall. His disappearing manservants had also disappeared breakfast, and he finally found a steward in a nearby linen pantry and sent him off to the kitchens to bring some food to a hungry earl. Flustered and aghast at the horrible lapse, the man raced off, then brought him back enough for three men. The steward hovered anxiously as Melfallan ate some fruit, a breakfast custard, some bread and cheese. His hovering attracted the attention of other servants passing nearby, and soon a small crowd gathered around Melfallan's table, all eager to help him eat—including one of his vanished manservants.

Tall, gray-haired, and cadaverously thin, Philippe Artois was senior among Melfallan's personal servants. He had served Melfallan since his childhood, arranging Melfallan's clothes and baths, seeing to the neatness of Melfallan's personal rooms, and generally clucking over him like a hen tending a single chick.

"What happened, Philippe?" Melfallan asked dryly.

Philippe fluttered his hands. "She was determined to sort the clothes, your grace," he exclaimed. "We got in the way, she said, and somehow all of us got dismissed to the kitchens. I thought about coming back when you woke up, but if she saw me after telling me to go away—" He stopped short, aghast at the horrible thought.

"Why is she sorting our clothes?"

"I don't know, your grace," Philippe said in despair.

He looked so mournful that Melfallan had to laugh, and then laughed again at the other servants' expressions, as they were visibly torn between the proper solemnity for a high lady's orders and her earl's amusement. Several failed in their effort and grinned back at him.

"It's all right," he assured them all. "I survived. We can only hope she'll finish by nightfall." He smiled and waved his dismissal, then snagged an apple and a slice of cheese for his pocket, a half-loaf of bread for his hand. Lunch might be chancy today, he told himself, considering how the morning had started.

Why *was* she sorting the clothes? Melfallan shook his head wonderingly as he walked out of the hall.

As he had every morning before he left for Darhel, Melfallan next headed for the nursery to see Audric. In the innermost room of the nursery suite, bright with the suns' light through the large windows, Leila sat in a rocking chair, Audric in her arms as the baby nursed at her large breast. Solid and practical, far too stout but still pretty in face, the young wet nurse looked up and smiled as he entered the room.

"Good morning, Leila," he said genially.

"Your grace," she replied in her deep lovely voice.

"And how is your charge this morning?" he asked.

"Lusty and healthy, a fine son," she said, and they smiled at each other. Melfallan walked up to her chair and watched his son nurse greedily.

Melfallan's own mother had been delicate in health and preoccupied with her lady's affairs, and had then died in childbirth when Melfallan was only three. He barely remembered her: a wisp of her perfume, a comforting hand during a childhood fever, a glorious beautiful creature who appeared suddenly in his nursery and smiled at him, then left as suddenly and mysteriously. In her place, the sunlight of his childhood had been his nurse, Mollwen, now long retired and living more in the past than the present in a comfortable suite in the castle. Most days now Mollwen didn't recognize him, but always spoke fondly of her fine young man, the boy Melfallan, as if that boy had just quitted the room and would return on the instant to cheer his old nurse's heart, bright youth on the morning. Melfallan was determined that Audric would have someone like Mollwen, whose only interest was to love him totally, and whom he could love in turn without reservation.

He was pleased with Marina's choice of wet nurse for the baby, despite Leila's youth, and had made sure Leila knew of his approval. Scarcely eighteen, Leila was married to an undercook in the castle kitchens, and had recently birthed her first child, a daughter. For reasons Saray would not say, his wife did not wholly approve of Leila, but had yielded gracefully enough when Melfallan insisted.

He suspected a few of Saray's reasons, which said more about Saray than about Leila. Saray's own childhood had been bleak and cheerless, a forgotten girl put to the side while all the attention went to her brother Robert, the earl's heir. That and Lady Mionn's stern upbringing had shaped his wife's character, likely beyond any changing now—or for any hope of empathy for Melfallan's fond memories of his childhood nurse. And, as taught by her mother, his wife rarely saw great value in any servant, and a wet nurse was nothing but that, and, worse, a servant used for the indelicate work of suckling a baby. Melfallan had noticed that Saray avoided the nursery when Leila fed the baby, and that disturbed him. Saray hadn't seemed to consider nursing Audric herself, just as she had determinedly ignored the embarrassment of her pregnancies: by Lady Mionn's rules, it simply was not done, if one were a high lady.

He repressed a sigh. He doubted Brierley would ever give her baby to another for nursing, nor think any part of her baby's care an embarrassment. He could not avoid the contrasts: they ruled every attitude, every choice.

A son for Yarvannet, he thought then with wonder and pride, as he watched the baby in Leila's arms. A lusty, healthy son who grew larger every day, who suckled greedily and slept profoundly and watched everything with vague blue eyes—and, the more each day passed, a small special person in Melfallan's heart. Leila calmly let Audric take his fill and then laid the baby over her shoulder for patting. As she cuddled him, Leila kissed the top of his head, a caress given almost absently, already familiar and casual.

Audric duly burped. Leila rose from the rocking chair, allowed Melfallan to sit down, then put the baby into his arms, as was already their comfortable practice. Melfallan leaned back and held his son carefully, still not entirely confident with his skills. He watched Audric work his mouth and yawn, put a fist in his eye, and waggle his hands aimlessly. In Audric's first few days of life, Melfallan had been almost afraid to hold him, fearful he would hurt Audric if he held him too tightly, or else drop him if he didn't. There was a trick about supporting his head, Marina had said, the more to Melfallan's anxiety, but the baby had apparently tolerated his father's mishandling well. Babies were stronger than they looked, it seemed.

Melfallan tickled Audric's chin, and the boy kicked vigorously against the blanket, pushing against Melfallan's forearm with rude determination, then stuck a chubby fist in his mouth. He should smile soon, Melfallan reminded himself; he was almost old enough. He had dearly missed holding the baby each morning during his absence in Darhel, more than he had realized: it was an anchor for each day. Audric yawned again, then waved his arms enthusiastically as he and his father began a war of wills about sleeping.

My sweet son, he thought fondly. As he rocked his small child, Melfallan felt a blissful happiness he had rarely known, all too transitory, and too easily lost each day after he left the sanctuary of Audric's nursery. In this brief half-hour with Audric each morning, all matters seemed clear and untroubled, without the frets, the worries, the impatience that usually ruled his waking hours. He knew those habits were faults, and admitted that he might have other faults he never knew. But he did know that he worried too much, and allowed himself to be restless. He lacked patience when he should be patient, with his lords when they were difficult or vain, and especially with Saray.

If my marriage had been different, Melfallan asked himself wistfully, would I have fallen in love with Brierley? Yes, I think so, he decided. Although I'd have different problems. Can a man love two women, but in different ways? Brierley had thought so. And Brierley had a gift with the understanding of persons: it was part of being sea witch, according to the Witchmere book. If anyone knew, she should. *But what can we be to each other?* Brierley had asked him in anguish. What indeed? He had begun their affair and hoped to continue it, once he brought Brierley back to Yarvannet, but what then? What happens when their affair is discovered, as it must be? And what if they have a child?

We might already have one, he realized. It only needed one time, and they had bedded more than once and more than one night. A child by Brierley promised another yawning chasm with Saray, should Melfallan claim the child. Like any Allemanii father, Melfallan could legitimize a by-blow child by acknowledging the child on its Blessing Day. The ceremony was the same for every Allemanii baby, and his claiming gave the child full rights as his heir, to noble rank, to an accepted place among his other children. Saray could not legally stop him. By Lady Mionn's standards, however, which Saray had always adopted as her own, a husband might bed other women, as Earl Giles probably had, and even absent himself too long from his wife's bed, also probable, but should never, ever, claim any child but his lady wife's. It simply wasn't done. That a noble wife must accept a half-commoner child as equal to her own? Admit this public proof of her lord's infidelity, his weakness for the flesh? Never! On such matters, Lady Mionn's voice rolled like thunder.

He grimaced, knowing the trouble that would come, as surely as a wave mounted a beach to crash on the sands. When Bronwyn, a castle servant, had conceived three years ago during their brief affair, he had thought of claiming her child, but Bronwyn's daughter would not have solved his problem of a body heir for Yarvannet. Only a son born to the lord's legal wife could accede without challenge. Any lesser heir, be it daughter or a by-blow son, needed the duke's approval, an approval Tejar would predictably deny. Besides, in truth, he had doubted Bronwyn's baby was truly his, further reason to spare Saray the embarrassment.

What would Saray do? he wondered. He had simply no idea: he so little understood his wife, and that was as much his fault as hers.

A child with Brierley, he mused, as Audric yawned between his sleeves. She said she had been born a twin, and twins ran in families. He tried to imagine two babies at once, growing up like two twigs on the same branch. He tried to imagine more than one child that was his, after five years of yearning for just one. Noble Allemanii children, with the risk of plague and childbed fevers, often died young. His aunt Rowena had lost three children before Axel; Duke Tejar's two older brothers had lived into their late teens but then died of plague, as had both Melfallan's father and uncle in their early twenties. Melfallan had been vaguely aware of the scarcity of children in noble families, and knew the commonfolk shared the same tragedy, but had not fully appreciated the winnowing still caused by plague.

With Audric that would make—three children. What a startling thought! And he might have even more children afterward, by either Saray or Brierley—or by both, he amended wryly. Ocean alive, Melfallan, he chided himself. You may have inherited your other problems, but this one you made all by yourself.

But what will Saray do? He repressed a sigh. What will I do? If you're looking for those faults you haven't noticed, Melfallan, avoiding answers you don't like might be one of them.

But if I had one more child by each— Five children? he marveled. The thought utterly escaped him.

He tried to imagine five children, all of them his, resembling him in face and coloring and thus obviously his engendering, five children lined up in a row from eldest to youngest, each blond head shorter than the next and all smiling at him. He shook his head, amused by his own lack of vision.

Will Brierley want a child with me? he wondered. I hope so.

Audric yawned greatly and finally closed his eyes. Melfallan rocked his son gently.

Leila was bustling around the nursery, putting things to rights. Leila had her own baby to tend, but he noticed the child's cradle was gone, even though Leila spent most of the day and night here. Odd, he thought. Usually a wet nurse had both babies nearby.

"Where's your own baby, Leila?" he asked.

"Down in the kitchens," Leila said cheerfully. "I feed her when I get my own meals and give a kiss to my husband." She turned and smiled.

"You must miss having her with you all day."

"Not to worry, your grace. I can get by." Leila gave him a sidewise glance, and went back to her straightening.

"I could speak to Marina about it," he suggested, wondering if his midwife had decided to be overcautious. A child might take fevers from another child, true, but Marina would not deprive a nurse of her own child for that slender reason. "As long as your baby isn't ill, I think Audric might like the company of another baby—joint wailing, as it were, though that might be harder on you."

Leila flushed slightly and turned to face him. "Please don't, your grace," she said hurriedly. "Your lady wife gave the order. I'm not to be distracted from Audric's care, you see, and—" She stopped and looked down at her shoes.

"A kitchen child might taint the nursery?" Melfallan asked grimly. It was just like Saray, not to think of Leila's need for her own child, as if a servant had no such feelings, existing only to be ordered around as one pleased. Well, of course, Melfallan thought angrily. How else should one think?

"Your grace—" Leila pleaded, and glanced nervously at the nursery door.

"Saray's busy arranging clothes. Don't worry." He eyed Leila for a moment. "I'm considering strategy right now, Leila. Hmm. Let's use Marina. Marina told me once that a male infant does best when he has another baby's company, especially in the first few months. It's a special rule for baby boys."

Leila dimpled. "Did she now, your grace?"

"I'm sure of it. I'll ask Marina to remind me of suitable reasons—she has an inventive mind." He smiled at the young girl. "What's your baby's name? I've forgotten."

"Simone," she answered shyly, averting her eyes. "Our first, and born only two days before your Audric. She looks like her father, very handsome." Leila smiled, then gave him a curtsey. "Thank you, your grace. You're very kind."

"You're welcome, Leila. All I ask, dear girl, is that you love Audric as any good nurse loves her charge."

"That's not so hard," she said, and they smiled at each other, in perfect accord.

Audric was asleep. Melfallan got up cautiously so as not to wake him, laid the baby into his crib, and tucked the blanket. Leila promptly retucked it correctly, unmindful of its comment on an earl's lacks.

"He seems healthy," Melfallan said, looking down at his sleeping son.

"He *is* healthy, your grace. Don't you worry. All is well, and the suns are bright on the morning." She tucked her hands together at her waist, then smiled warmly, completely at ease with him.

Yes, she's the right nurse, Melfallan thought, nodding to her, then left the nursery.

He decided to interrupt Saray in her sorting before he retreated for the rest of the morning to his tower room. Better that Saray knew now about Rowena. Saray loved his aunt dearly, and it seemed a good time to tell her. He promptly learned that it was not.

"You heard this *yesterday*?" Saray exclaimed.

"Yes, Saray. I didn't want to—" Melfallan began.

"And you didn't tell me?" Saray asked indignantly. "You

went to the Great Hall and enjoyed yourself, as if Aunt Rowena meant *nothing?*" Bright spots of color flared in Saray's cheeks. "How *could* you, Melfallan?"

"I didn't want to spoil your party, Saray," Melfallan protested. "You were so happy about——"

"What will the gentry think when they hear of this?" Saray interrupted, her eyes flashing. She threw down the richly embroidered tunic in her hands, then clicked her tongue as Berthe knelt to pick it up. The girl hastily backed away. Melfallan did not want to argue in front of Saray's lady-maids, for an argument it was obviously going to be, but Saray made no move to dismiss them. All of them had retreated to the walls in confusion, their eyes wide. "That you could sit there," Saray raged on, her voice rising still louder, "drinking and laughing and even *dancing,* while Aunt Rowena is perhaps in her deathbed! And they'll think I knew, too, that I didn't care, either!"

"Not in front of your maids, Saray," Melfallan urged, his own anger rising. "You're dismissed," he said to them. "Leave us alone, please."

"You will *not* give orders to *my* servants!" Saray said grandly.

"Fine!" he shot back. "Let's shriek in front of them. I don't care."

"That's obvious, Melfallan." Saray lifted her chin and strode out of the wardrobe rooms, leaving him with half a dozen frightened lady-maids and a tumble of clothing everywhere. One shifted uneasily from one foot to the other; another dabbed at tears. Berthe backed up to the wall and braced herself, trembling.

Melfallan lifted a shaky hand to his forehead, as shocked by Saray's outburst as they were. He and Saray had often quarreled during their marriage, but rarely like this. Saray won their arguments by hurt silences or deliberate misunderstanding, not by rage. Melfallan was the one who eventually shouted, always apologizing later, sometimes abjectly when Saray cried into her pillow.

Jenny Halliwell, Saray's senior lady-maid, knelt to pick up the tunic, then gave it to Berthe. "Put that away, Berthe," she said. "And, you, Margot, carry that jewel chest into the other wardrobe." With deft commands, Jenny sent the other maids out, each with an errand and a gentle word.

"I'm sorry, Jenny." Melfallan said heavily when they had all left. He sat down, not caring that he creased the rich clothing that covered the chair.

She turned. "Y-your grace?" she stammered softly in surprise.

Lords and ladies never apologized to servants, he supposed, another of Saray's rules. "I only meant to——" Melfallan broke off, then gestured helplessly. "She was so happy about the party. I didn't want to ruin it."

"It's not your fault," Jenny declared. "She has been troubled lately," she ventured then, her voice low. "Since the baby came, you see. She quarreled with Leila the other morning, and last week she ordered Margot out of the room after Margot dropped a brush. It happens sometimes after childbirth, your grace. Your lady wife was fine for the first few weeks, but ever since we came home from Darhel, she's not really been herself. I really don't know why, but there *has* been a change."

"But she seemed happy yesterday," Melfallan protested. "So gay and laughing——"

Jenny smiled gently. "I've served your lady for five years, your grace. You and I both know how she hides things, for your sake."

Melfallan grimaced. "Wonderful. You mean she forced herself to go to the party I tried to save for her? That all of that joy was more of the pretending? That last night when we——" He stopped and ground his teeth, then looked away.

"It's not your fault," Jenny repeated firmly. She folded her hands in front of her waist and smiled at him, tipping her head. "How long have we known each other, Melfallan? I think you first came into my father's armory when we were eight. When we got a little older, I had this daydream that Earl Audric might think a knight's daughter would suit you." He looked at her in astonishment, and Jenny chuckled, then winked. "Men are so very blind. I can't imagine what Mother Ocean was thinking when she made only half of us women. But, all things considered, I prefer being your friend, both then and now. And it's not your fault," she repeated, shaking her head vigorously.

"I don't agree, Jenny," he muttered.

"Half at most," she insisted. "If that. And it's not really her fault, either. It just—is, I suppose." She grimaced. "Why don't you try staying away for a while? For once let her apologize first." Her lips tightened into a thin line. "If she does. I expect she'll ignore this even happened, as usual, and then be surprised that you can't. Now don't scowl at me. I'm entitled to my opinions, and to whose side I choose to champion." She tipped her head and smiled. "Aren't I?"

"Hmph."

"And don't grunt, either," she reproved. "It's not becoming to an earl." Jenny shook her head and sighed. "Go along now," she said, waving him out of the room. "I'll care for matters here."

Wearily, Melfallan climbed the stairs to his grandfather's study in the tower. Why can't Saray and I understand each other? he thought in frustration. Why doesn't it ever get better? He closed the door and sat down lumpily in one of his chairs, then looked around the room—another earl's study now, actually, though Melfallan still found it hard to claim it.

For thirty years, the grand old man had kept his own counsel here, planned the future of Yarvannet, decided his decisions, ruled as an earl should rule. As always, Melfallan sat unoccupied, wondering what he was supposed to think about. Jenny was right, he knew: when he saw Saray again, his wife would pretend nothing had happened, and so nothing, as always, would get resolved. If he tried to discuss it, pressed the issue—oh, he knew exactly what she'd do. Avoid, delay, pretend—

Where's your clear thinking, the decisive choices? he asked himself angrily. You can't even solve your wife. He got up to pace.

He never quite understood how it happened. He had meant

to be kind to Saray, to delay the reality she liked to avoid so that she could enjoy her party. She had obviously planned the ball for weeks, a high entertainment to welcome her lord home, as was a noble wife's joy and duty. Yet their quarrels always began this way, in some well-meaning action by himself, some attempt to please her, which she then turned into an affront. He could never foresee what might offend her: it could be literally anything, or nothing. When he expected her to be angry, she was not, only to be taken by surprise when she was.

Now Saray might show her displeasure for days, putting up her chin, deliberately misunderstanding whatever he said, ignoring him as she carelessly chattered to her lady-maids. Apologies were useless—Saray always pretended nothing had happened, and would look at him in feigned astonishment if he persisted. Gifts didn't help—she would smile, accept the present, and then somehow carelessly misplace the gift, under the bed, deep in the closet, buried in some chest. Protests never worked—if his voice rose, she refused to listen and turned her back on him.

Even sex didn't work—abominably didn't work. Twice in their early years he had tried to wheedle her by taking her to bed, hoping that passion might mend the rift between them, but what she had done to their lovemaking had appalled him. Her shudder when he touched her had been delicate, her delay in answering his caresses only slight, but then she had lain utterly inert beneath him, her face turned to the wall, fists clenched at her sides, jawline tightened into an inexorable line. He had unwisely continued, trying desperately to elicit some response from her, only to meet her adamant will that she would *not* respond, would *not* yield.

Afterward, while Melfallan wondered miserably if he had raped his wife, Saray had refused to discuss it in any way whatsoever. It hadn't happened, she pretended, but then emphasized with her flinching from his touch her repulsion for his outrage, his animalistic urges. She had put on a brave smile, despite the slight gleam of tears in her eyes that she failed to hide, and endured the presence of her husband with an uplifted chin, a painful courage. How much was act, how much real? Was *any* of it real? How could he ever know?

Melfallan paced up and down in agitation, his blood pounding in his temples. Oh, he knew how it would be, what awaited him now, from hard experience. Sometimes Saray punished him for days, deliberately confounding him with every answer, every silence. Sometimes her anger vanished by the next morning, or even in the next hour, and she was her sweet-tempered self again. Inevitably, eventually, by rules he never understood, Saray would emerge from her anger, and they would have peace again. And none of it had ever happened, of course.

He ground his teeth, all his happiness in the nursery quite lost.

He thought of another's sweet temper that never faded, of Brierley's quiet smile that always understood. And he had left her in safety elsewhere, far away from him. Oh, he knew the reasons, knew the necessity. He had reconsidered his decision a dozen times, but always reached the same end. As he paced his chamber, Melfallan felt his duty again settle on his shoulders like a crushing weight. If he were not earl, he could go to her now, this very instant, and they could live happily in some remote place, away from the politics, away from the danger. If he were not earl, if he were not bound—

He ran his fingers distractedly through his hair and groaned. What use to think of it?

A quiet knock came at the door, and Melfallan scowled ferociously. Everyone knew he was not to be disturbed in this tower: it was Earl Audric's rule, and his own as well. He crossed the room and opened the door, ready to berate whomever stood there, anything to shout his frustration. Revil had leaned himself casually on the doorjamb.

"It's a rule," Melfallan told him severely.

"Your steward says you have appointments all afternoon, with no time for me." Revil raised an eyebrow. "Says that to a count, mind you, so I'm showing him, rule or no rule. May I come in?"

Melfallan hesitated, then stepped back and gestured him into the room. Revil glanced around at the shelves of books and records, the carefully drawn map on the wall, then walked to the window and looked out. "Can you believe I haven't been in this room for years?" he asked. "You should knock out some stone for a second window, give you something to do like watching the harbor. A lot goes on down there." Revil turned and posed a little. "Now in *my* study, my four windows look out on the garden where I can watch the children play. Sometimes Solange cuts roses from her bushes and waves to me."

Melfallan grunted. "You get a lot done, I'm sure."

Revil leaned back against the window casement and stared at him challengingly. "Can I make a comment?"

"You've already made several," Melfallan said and sat down.

"One more then. An earl—or a count—governs his people best by meeting with them, by riding out and being seen, by holding court, having parties when his wife insists, and *not* by holing himself up in a tower." He shrugged. "Just because Grandfather did it doesn't mean you should."

"It worked for him. And you're meddling, good count."

"Yes, I am, and it won't work for you, and I can give you reasons if you want them. But I have a purpose in my interruption—and a puzzle." He waved his hand airily. "Indulge me, cousin."

"What purpose?"

"To learn whether Mistress Mefell is alive."

Melfallan hesitated. "Why do you think I know?"

Revil's usually cheerful face clouded with hurt. "Why are you blocking me out? Are there new lines drawn now, Melfallan, and I'm on the wrong side of the line?"

"Revil—" Melfallan stopped.

"Thank you for leaping to the chance," Revil said bitterly.

"Revil—"

"I'm the Count of Amelin, her rightful lord. I have a right to know, and I expect my earl to respect my duty to my folk. Others may be deceived, but I know you too well. I've watched your face for any sign of grief—genuine grief, not sad sighs that mean nothing—and I haven't seen it. Nothing for her, yet you turned ashen when the news came about Aunt Rowena. And you've blocked me out, and you're letting my folk of Amelin and Natheby, who loved her, think she's dead." He turned back to the window again, a muscle working tightly in his jaw. "You want to know what I think about you sitting in this tower this morning, keeping your silence?" he asked tightly. "I don't think you do."

Melfallan regarded Revil with astonishment: he had seen Revil truly angry as few times as the fingers on one hand. As Revil was now—with him. He rose to his feet and crossed the space between them, then thought to lay his hand on Revil's shoulder, and thought then Revil might shrug off his touch, as if he were tainted. Revil turned and saw his hesitation, then suddenly smiled.

"One of the advantages of a happy personality," his cousin said, and the smile broadened, "is that my occasional angers have wonderful impact, especially on you. Did you think I'd knock you down?"

"Well—"

"*Is* she alive?"

Melfallan sighed and let his hand fall. "Yes."

"And you thought I'd tell the duke?" Revil's jaw set again, his eyes glinting.

Melfallan glared back in exasperation. "Hells, no, Revil! Be reasonable! But one misstep and I might kill Brierley, just as I almost killed her by taking her to Darhel, thinking I was so clever, so very smart." He started to pace. "The fewer people who know, the better her safety. I shouldn't even have told Aunt Rowena, although I had no choice in that because Stefan knew. But I shouldn't have told anyone else at all, and I already have." He hammered his hand on the other. "This isn't a time for sentiment, for easing hearts who grieve. Her life is at stake, and I can protect only in the ways I have."

"I don't agree," Revil said stubbornly. "You have a duty to your folk."

"I have a duty to *her*."

"I said I *don't* agree. You've told me what you choose to do, which is nicely in keeping with walling yourself up in this tower. What would *she* choose, Melfallan? Have you thought about that? Would she let Amelin grieve?"

Melfallan stopped short in his pacing and glared.

"Of course not," Revil said firmly. "She couldn't bear that any of her beloveds grieve, whatever the danger to her. She accepts the dangers; she's lived with them all her life—and still she went out and healed. Do you think she'd even hesitate? And she'd certainly not let anybody find out later that she never said anything." Revil took a deep breath. "But I forgive you, Melfallan. How *dare* you not tell me?" Revil stalked back to the table, pulled out a chair, and sat down. "You idiot."

"What tact," Melfallan muttered.

"We're past tact. You ever turn arrogant earl on me, Melfallan, and I'll—I'll—Hells, I don't know what I'd do. Hang you by the heels from your own walls, maybe, until you got some sense back." He snorted. "Idiot."

"All right, all right." Melfallan sat down lumpily. "I'm an idiot."

"Actually, no, you're not. What you *aren't* is Grandfather, and I think you should stop trying to be him." He waved his hand at the tower room. "Why do you sit up here every morning? Because he did? And what do you get out of it?"

"He had a good reason."

"What? To sit up here, telling yourself that it's somehow your fault Rowena was attacked? I know you, and the thought of you sitting up here, torturing yourself, isn't bearable. What do you hope to accomplish?"

Melfallan paused, then grimaced. "Surely if I sit up here long enough, I'll find out." Revil started to laugh, and suddenly matters were right again between them.

"You're so earnest about being earl, it's frightening," Revil observed. "Grandfather got hold of you too soon." He pointed an accusing finger at him. "Grandfather would have kept the secret about Brierley and not told a soul, then sit up here plotting what he'd do with it, rubbing his hands with glee." He studied Melfallan's face a moment. "I don't see much glee."

Melfallan grunted. "I'm having trouble finding the glee, I admit, especially when my favorite cousin—"

"By last count, I'm your *only* cousin besides Axel, so that's not so much."

"Stop interrupting, you. I've decided I'm not going to tell you, Revil. I won't." Revil snickered, and Melfallan waved him away. "I won't. I'm determined on it." He added a fierce glare.

"All right, you haven't told me," Revil said affably. "Bend reality as you must, my earl. But for some strange reason, even though you haven't told me, my heart feels eased. If Brierley Mefell were truly gone, a light would have truly gone out of the world." He sat back and folded his hands primly on the table in front of him. "When you decide to tell me, Melfallan, let me know."

"I'll do that."

"But I'm serious about this tower business. I've been waiting to see if you'd give it up on your own, but here we are, fresh back from Darhel and that curious political adventure, and then this desperate news from Airlie, and you're hiding yourself away again. I know you well, Melfallan, certainly more than you'd like. You sit up here and worry about yourself, that you aren't Grandfather's measure. Am I right?"

Melfallan scowled. "Don't nag me, Revil."

"I will nag you. It's my right. It's your fault for trusting me, and I take full liberties." Revil pursed his lips. "Let me propose the issue another way: isn't it to Yarvannet's advantage if you *aren't* like Grandfather?"

"What do you mean?"

"Grandfather was predictable by being contrary, Melfallan. Aunt Rowena's much the same way. Like her, you could always count on Grandfather to oppose anything Tejar wanted, and Tejar has been dealing with that all his rule. Tejar is not Selwyn's measure, and Audric constantly told Tejar so. Do you think Tejar would hate us as much if Grandfather had acted differently? Do you think you would have acceded to the same problems that you have now? How much of those are Grandfather's making? Most of them, I'd say."

"He was a great earl," Melfallan said stubbornly.

"Yes, he was, but he outlived Selwyn, the duke he loved, to Yarvannet's disadvantage. I loved Grandfather, too, you know that. He was a magnificent earl, and his loss is a hollow space in our lives. But Grandfather was too set in his ways, Melfallan—it made him predictable. Grandfather would not have taken Brierley to Darhel, as you did: he would have stalled."

"And that mistake nearly got Brierley killed."

"What mistake? You provoked Tejar into a stupid move, and gave her the chance to escape. How did she escape, anyway? What happened to Gammel Hagan? Is he dead?"

Melfallan hesitated.

"Well, is he?" Revil insisted.

"Yes."

"That wasn't so hard, was it?" Revil asked mockingly.

"I ought to hang *you* from my walls. Don't think I won't." He paused. "I didn't know you thought so poorly of Grandfather."

"Actually, most of these ideas aren't particularly mine, although I've decided I agree with them. I've been talking to Sir James since we got home—about you, mostly, wanting his ideas on how I could help you."

"Sir James?" Melfallan asked incredulously. "He served Grandfather faithfully for forty years."

"A man can love a lord, and still see clearly when he errs. Sir James told me he tried to warn Audric, but he wouldn't listen. Audric *would* dislike Tejar, and continue disliking him, period." Revil gestured expansively. "Would this conversation have gotten past the first few sentences with him? From his lesser grandson, of all people? I don't think so. Yet you sit there, listening to me, however you scowl and fret as you do. You always listen, Melfallan: you listen to everyone. Micay and Ennis know it, and so does Sir James. And he counts you the better earl for it. Ask him."

Melfallan tugged slowly at his ear. "Are you saying I'm better because I let my counselors make my decisions?"

"My dear earl, you've never done that. You never will. As I said, I know you."

"Hmph. Why then do I feel pushed and pulled, tugged and turned, lectured, frowned at, pointed at, with shrieks of dismay, grimaces, hands in the air—"

"I only did half of that." Revil said comfortably. He cocked his head. "I told you I'd help, that you are my earl forever. I told you I will always be at your side. So involve me. Don't treat me like all the other lords do: chatty, pleasant Revil, nothing of depth, but his hat plumes are magnificent."

"It's not that bad, Revil. Count Parlie respects you. More importantly, so does Aunt Rowena."

"Really?" Revil looked skeptical. "Aunt Rowena pays most attention to those that interest her. And I wasn't Audric's heir." Melfallan scowled, and Revil waved his hand. "Aha! A doorway opens. Lo! A light dawns into the room!"

"Oh, shut up," Melfallan said. "I don't believe you're this neglected—or ineffective. I told you about Brierley. I wasn't going to, but you wheedled me."

"Only after I threw a fit."

Melfallan spread his hands. "I'm sorry, Revil, truly. I've got a hundred different issues going at once, and one misstep can cost Yarvannet everything. And I'm *not* saying that you'd tell the duke. I'm just saying I don't know what to do." He crossed his arms and grimaced. "Last night I told Tauler I'd hang Landreth if he comes back to Yarvannet. I'm still trying to figure out why I did that. Here's Count Sadon's principal vassal and my own marcher lord, one of the local lords no doubt with fingers in every net, watching me warily, smiling smooth smiles, and I tell him something like that." He scowled. "I also realized that the Yarvannet lords aren't afraid of me—not like they feared Grandfather."

"Well, of course," Revil said. "He either conquered them or vested them with their lands. Do you want them to fear you?"

"I'd like them to be cautious," Melfallan amended, after thinking about it, "but not afraid. Fearful men think too easily of treachery."

"So do the arrogant." Revil steepled his fingers. "Let me ask you a question, since we're talking about Tauler and our other seawrack of Pullen's rebellion. If you were Count of Airlie, and Toral of Lim rebelled, would you march into Lim at the duke's orders?"

"That involves a little reorganization of geography."

"Still." Revil waved a hand. "Assume you're one of Tejar's counts, and one of the other counts has rebelled. What would you do?"

Melfallan thought a moment. "It's my feof duty, if he ordered it. Probably."

"If the duke were Selwyn?"

"Yes," Melfallan said promptly.

"And so you arrive in Lim and duly defeat the count in battle? What would you do then?"

"You sound like Sir James with his tactical puzzles."

"I sound like Revil who thinks Grandfather murdered a lot of innocent people." Melfallan's eyes widened, and Revil shrugged again. "I'm closer to the commonfolk than you are, Melfallan. I love my Amelin and Natheby folk, and far prefer them to the gentry that afflict me. The older ones remember Pullen's rebellion, and sometimes they talk to me about the terror that came. Grandfather spared the farmers and fishermen, of course, and he didn't kill the soldiers if they disarmed, even if he wasn't that careful to give them time to do so. And he even forgave most of the gentlemen knights. But those farmers and fishermen were loyal to their lords. Their lords weren't perfect. A few were downright vile, but Pullen and his lords were *their* lords. Thirty years is a long time, and our folk in Yarvannet are a practical sort. They adjusted. And Grandfather was a good earl, once the butchery was over."

"You have to remove threat, Revil. Earl Pullen rebelled and was marching north on Ingal."

"So? He was defeated. The threat ended. If I follow you into battle, do you agree I should die if we lose? It wasn't just Grandfather, you know: I'm sure Selwyn was the source. Duke Selwyn was well loved and never had Lionel's troubles, but he was still a Kobus duke. And he and Grandfather were fast friends for a reason. Was it really necessary to kill all the lords who followed Pullen? Could you have done it?"

Melfallan crooked his mouth and thought about it. "No," he admitted.

"Don't ever be another Audric, Melfallan. I will stand with you forever, but past a certain point the wounds might be silent but still bleed."

"I may try to make myself duke," Melfallan warned. "It's the only way I protect Brierley, and maybe Yarvannet, too."

Revil nodded. "I thought so."

"And? Come, Revil. If you're going to suddenly shed all your chatterbird plumage and stand stark naked as what you are, at least commit yourself."

"I already did," Revil said. He smiled and shook his head vigorously. "And I never, ever, want to be earl of Yarvannet, so don't even consider it."

"Most of Yarvannet's current problems lead back to Tejar. If I'm your duke—"

"No."

"Start thinking about it, Revil. You should have some time yet."

"No." Revil bared his teeth in a wolfish smile.

"I won't give up," Melfallan warned him.

"And I won't yield." Revil waved his hand expansively. "Have a second son to be earl—or a daughter you can marry off well. That'll solve everything." Revil grinned at his sour expression. "It's part of the listening, Melfallan," he said. "It's part of why I put up with you."

"I don't know why I put up with *you*."

Revil shrugged. "Ah, well. That's not a problem we'll solve today. Now, will you come out of this hole? Let's go hawking.

I've a new merlin I want to try, and I brought her to Tiol with me, just in the hope of the wheedling."

"And invite whom?" Melfallan asked suspiciously.

"Anyone you want. It's early in the morning: Lord Valery should be still sober enough to stay on his horse. Or maybe Jarvis Marchand: you can hear all his new complaints, if you didn't get enough of them last night. Or Lord Garth, my personal choice. Garth's cheer is good for the spirit, and his lady is truly fair. We can hunt the estuary north of Amelin: the teal are gathering, and your new gyrfalcon could scout some heron. What do you say?"

Melfallan considered, then stood up and stretched. "Actually, I'm fed up with our lords right now. I'd probably say something I'd badly regret, even to Garth. Just bring yourself, Revil. You can tell me more fascinating details about what Sir James really thinks, not just what he feels appropriate to tell me."

"Sir James isn't hiding anything from you, Melfallan."

"I know that. Revil, does Solange ever sort your clothes—I mean, all of them at once?"

"What?" Revil blinked.

"She shouted at me," Melfallan said glumly.

"Who? Saray?" Revil pulled a face. "Melfallan, how can you think clearly if you're worrying about her again? What a time for her to start another fight!" He got up in agitation. "Why can't she—"

"Don't blame Saray."

"I *do* blame her. She never tries to think of the pressures you have as earl. That's your business as lord, she thinks, and her lady's world has nothing to do with it. What's the problem this time?"

"We shouldn't have had the party," Melfallan muttered. "The gentry will think we don't care about Rowena."

Revil threw up his hands. "I don't believe it!"

"Revil—"

"Melfallan—"

They both stopped short, sighed in unison, peas in a pod, and then grinned wryly at each other that they had.

"Never mind," Melfallan said. "Let's go hawking."

"What about your appointments this afternoon?"

"What about them?" Melfallan said aggressively.

"Just asking." Revil gestured toward the door. "After you, my earl."

ut Melfallan was not to avoid his lords that easily, at least not until he rearranged the halls of his castle and installed an escape tunnel. As he and Revil passed through the Great Hall, his movements were marked by dozens of eyes, and word spread quickly. The earl is out and about! they gasped. Where is he going? they whispered behind their hands. Alert the lords! Bustle about now! The earl!

"This isn't going to be easy," Melfallan muttered, glancing behind them.

"Then pick up your feet," Revil advised.

They hurried through the warren of tunnels and small courtyards near the stables by the castle gates. The weather outside was crisp with cold, and Melfallan snagged two cloaks left in a tackroom, completing their disguise, in Revil's amused words, then walked into the mews where Melfallan kept his hawks.

The mews was an airy, pleasant room, with cages along one wall, several tall perches in the corners, and unpaned grilled windows that overlooked the precipitous drop of the northern castle wall. Most of the hawks were still caged at this hour of the morning, waiting to be fed, but a few birds stretched wings on the perches. All the Allemanii High Lords kept hawks, although most preferred the wilder chase of hunting larger game with dogs. Melfallan also kept a kennel of good hounds, but he preferred the other noble sport of hawking, as intrigued by the intelligence and beauty of his falcons as by the difficult intricacy of training them to the lure. He walked to the cage of his favorite merlin, and ran his finger lightly along the grille. Whistle inspected him, first with one large dark eye, then the other. She chimed a few notes of greeting in her soft voice, then ruffled her feathers, happy to see him.

"Good morning, Whistle." Melfallan absently accepted a padded falconer's sleeve from Talbot and pulled it onto his right forearm. "Did you have a good sleep?" he asked the bird. "Would you like to fly today?" Whistle chirped sweet agreement, and Melfallan opened her cage, then offered the sleeve. Whistle calmly stepped aboard, the bells on her jesses tinkling.

The Allemanii hunted three hawks, each with a different temperament and range of prey. The midsized swiftwing and merlin were native to these eastern coastlands, and hunted smaller birds or hares. Like other merlins, Whistle was soft browns in her plumage, her wing primaries edged with black, with a white eye ring and narrow curved beak. The larger gyrfalcon, brought from the West by the Founders, had brilliant black plumage and a splash of bright crimson on its breast feathers and head. Truly a magnificent bird, the gyrfalcon had a wingspread of nearly five feet and a heavy weight to match, and was prized for its strength, if not for its temperament. A gyrfalcon never admitted total defeat, whatever the years of training, and always kept a remaining issue or two with its handler, to be argued at every outing. It was always a stubborn bird, and, sad to say, rather like his wife.

Like most Allemanii falconers, his chief falconer, Talbot Wardell, favored the gyrfalcon as the noblest of birds, an opinion Melfallan did not share. Talbot was a gray-haired wiry man, as alert and contrary as his birds, and today had dressed in his usual forester green. As Talbot uncaged a young female gyrfalcon from a nearby cage, Melfallan eyed the other bird with scant favor.

"No," he said.

"Now, your grace, that's not a good attitude," Talbot reproved. He put on a hurt look. "She's a good bird, ready for her first hunt," he said. "And you might have noble companions this morning, who would expect a gyrfalcon on your wrist." He lifted an eyebrow, to no result. "I think I should win at least half," Talbot complained. "You flew Whistle last time."

Revil had uncaged his own merlin, who rode lightly on his wrist. He grinned at Melfallan's expression. "He does have a point, Melfallan," he suggested.

"Not much of one. Where's that rule, Talbot, half?"

"Just think it fitting, your grace." Talbot patiently proffered the larger hawk, then waited for his earl to see better reason.

"*You* fly her," Melfallan said stubbornly. Two can be obstinate, he decided, as well as three and four. He eyed Talbot back without pleasure.

"You start with her, and I'll carry Whistle," Talbot countered, and again proffered the gyrfalcon. Melfallan hesitated another moment, then, with a sigh, he yielded and traded birds with Talbot, to the gyrfalcon's vigorous protest. She squawked and flapped her wings, and shrieked a harsh arpeggio, up and down, up and down, enough to damage the ears. The noise echoed around the mews, bouncing off every stone wall, and startled the rest of the birds into their own loud flapping protests. Hastily, Melfallan took a firm grip on the hawk's jesses before she launched herself to freedom, and retreated to the courtyard outside. Her chaotic purpose accomplished, the gyrfalcon promptly stopped her squawking. Melfallan eyed her with distaste.

Talbot offered him the small leather hood, but the gyrfalcon protested that handling as well, bobbing her head to the right and left to avoid Melfallan's hand. He finally got her hooded, and then glared at Talbot. "You say this bird is tamed?"

"She's quiet enough now, your grace," the man said imperturbably. "Training is step by step."

"I admit you know everything about birds, Master Talbot," Melfallan said irritably, "but that's no cause to lecture me like I were still a boy learning my first hawk. I won't have it." Talbot grinned and touched a finger to his forehead, quite undented. "Trade you back," Melfallan suggested, pointing to Whistle.

"No, your grace," Talbot said firmly.

Melfallan settled the heavy gyrfalcon on his left arm, and felt her talons settle firmly into his padded sleeve, pricking his flesh beneath with a strong grip. From experience, he knew that his forearm muscles would ache tomorrow merely from carrying her. "I prefer merlins," he reminded Talbot.

"A bias you must overcome, your grace," Talbot said. "Gyr-falcons suit a High Lord like yourself. Merlins are for ladies and lesser sorts among the lords." Melfallan gave him a sour look, and Talbot shrugged elaborately. "It's tradition, Earl Melfallan. Your grandfather understood."

"My grandfather didn't mind talons put an inch into his flesh. Ouch." From Talbot's arm Whistle hooted soft commiseration. "What's her name?"

"The naming is the earl's privilege."

"So you say, Talbot," Melfallan retorted. "You name all my birds the moment they're out of the shell. What have you called this one?"

Talbot hesitated badly, to Melfallan's surprise. His assertive falconer rarely lacked words to say, and feared Melfallan not at all in saying whatever he chose, and, truth admitted, usually got his "half." But now the man's face was a puzzle. "Well?" Melfallan prompted.

"Hmm, if you must know," Talbot said reluctantly, "I've been calling her Madge." He grimaced. "After my wife's sister, you see. I do fear that I'm not totally admired in this world, your grace, a shocking thought, truly, but Madge and I have never gotten on. She hates me." He shrugged. "I mean, truly—she hates me with a vivid passion. I haven't given her cause, well, not much, but she doesn't like my voice or my look, nor how I talk to her sister, although my wife thinks I'm a fine fellow. But Madge wants to march everybody around, especially me, and she'd march me into the sea to vanish forever if she could. A horrible woman." He gave a mock shudder. "I don't hate Madge as much as she hates me—well, actually, I don't hate her at all. She's not worth the time to work up a suitable emotion." He smiled thinly, and for a moment looked as predatory as his hawks.

"And so when this bird offered the chance—"

Talbot smiled more broadly. "Revenge comes in many sweet guises, your grace, as a High Lord would know. The bird just reminded me of Madge, if you'll forgive me. And, to be truthful, that bird's temperament is as unlikely to change as hers. A strong hawk with a quick strike, but badly willful and never much to be liked."

"Like all gyrfalcons," Melfallan said sourly.

"Not all, your grace," Talbot demurred. "Just most of them."

"Hmph." The gyrfalcon ruffled her feathers, then stabbed viciously at Melfallan's gloved hand. That emotion eased, she finally eased her grip. Taming a gyrfalcon supposedly improved the lord who handled her, Melfallan reminded himself: every High Lord needed an occasional reminder that even a lord's will could meet its match.

A groom brought their horses into the courtyard. Melfallan carried the gyrfalcon to his horse, who fortunately was better trained than Madge, and eased the bird onto the pommel of the saddle. He then put his foot in the stirrup and mounted behind the bird. To his surprise, Madge took the jostling well. He coaxed her back onto his forearm, and took the belled jesses firmly in his right fist. The tiny silver bells chimed faintly, a sound he always associated with his beloved hawks. Although blinded by the hood, the gyrfalcon turned her head back and forth, following the sounds in the courtyard and mews. An alert bird, if only she would relent, he thought. Vain hope.

Unfortunately, the gyrfalcon's temper had delayed them too long in the mews. There was another echoing of hooves in the short tunnel leading to the nearby stables, and Lord Garth and his pretty wife, Joanna, rode into the mews yard a few moments later. Both had merlins riding on their wrists. Melfallan repressed a sigh.

Lord Garth reined his horse to a stop and bowed genially in his saddle. He was a tall man, with a broad chest and powerful hands, and truly a master of horses. Most of Melfallan's best animals, sent periodically as gifts to Tiol, had been bred in Carbrooke's paddocks. Beside him, Lady Joanna smiled brightly, then eyed Melfallan's cloak and fine party clothing. She lifted a surprised eyebrow.

Melfallan repressed another sigh, amazed that a woman so effortlessly put a man in his place with a simple lifted eyebrow. He could explain about clothes-sorting, true, or even explain his wish to escape his own castle, but neither would help. He had met Lady Joanna several times over the years, and knew her to be the daughter of one of Count Sadon's knights, a good mother to their children, a loving wife to Garth. He liked her friendliness to Saray and admired her beauty, but, like Yarvannet's other noble wives, Joanna had her own set of noble rules, the richness and especially propriety of noble clothing chief among them. One did not go hawking in party clothes, the eyebrow said: it just wasn't done.

"Good morning, Lord Garth," Melfallan muttered, sounding petulant even in his own ears. "And to you, my lady," he added, managing a bit more grace.

He noted sourly that Joanna and Garth were impeccably dressed for the occasion, as always. She wore a velvet riding dress, sky blue with silver piping, her blond hair smoothed into order under a small sky-blue hat and veil. Garth wore gray and black, his Carbrooke colors, with a woolen surcoat that reached to the knees over his tunic and hose, divided at the hem for riding. And all with only ten minutes warning, too.

Joanna nodded sweetly. Garth gave him a broad smile, as handsome and pleasant as always. "We thought we'd go hawking this morning, your grace," he said, quite unnecessarily, given the birds on their wrists.

"Isn't it marvelous," Revil said cheerily, butting in, "that the earl and I seem to have the same idea? Perhaps you'll join us, my lord, my lady. And before Melfallan can scowl and look ungracious, and thus offend his marcher lord beyond recall—yes, cousin, direct that at me instead, so I can be offended instead of Lord Garth. I'm safer, being used to it. Be warned, my lord, that the earl is escaping this morning."

"Indeed?" Garth asked, glancing at Melfallan. "From what?"

"Well, partly from you," Revil said drolly.

"Revil!" Melfallan exclaimed.

Revil waved him away. "Don't mind him, Garth," he said. "I thought we might hunt my coastland marshes. They lie only a few miles up the coast, and the teal is rising."

"Excellent, good count," Garth said affably. He turned to his wife. "I don't think Joanna has seen that part of Amelin, have you, my love?"

"No, but I look forward to it," his lady replied. For a moment Joanna looked uncertainly at Melfallan's scowl, then at Revil's wide grin, and finally put on a brave smile. A proper earl never, ever escaped his lords, it seemed. It just wasn't done, either. Melfallan had a brief urge to retreat back to his tower, where he could post a guard outside the door, even two or three guards if he wanted, and truly escape all his inconvenient lords. Then Melfallan saw Garth squinting at him, his eyes dancing with silent laughter, and he suddenly grinned back at him. Garth understood, and Melfallan wondered if Garth, too, found occasional reason to escape his lord's duties.

Melfallan reined his horse around, then led the way toward the castle gates. A guard of ten soldiers joined them at the gate, Sir Micay's constant caution whenever Melfallan rode around his own lands. Master Talbot caught up to their party, mounted on his stout black with Whistle riding his pommel, and together they all rode under the gate portico and across the bridge to the headland.

The everwillow had long since dropped their leaves, but the day was bright and clear, with a winter tang in the air. On the road leading south, they passed fields where sheep tumbled ahead of boys and their dogs, and an occasional farmer drove his small herd of cattle from one field to the other. On the other side of the coast road, beyond the beaches and southern bay, fishing boats plied the waters near the sea horizon. It was a lovely day: Melfallan stretched his legs in his saddle and sniffed appreciatively at the crisp air.

This was a good idea, he thought, as his mood began to

lighten, cajoled by the beauty of the forest and sea, the bright suns lifting into the morning.

They rode leisurely along the coast road for a mile, and Garth and his lady seemed as interested in enjoying the day as Melfallan himself. Revil entertained them with conversation, allowing Melfallan to watch the sea and forest, breathing in the clear crisp air. They passed several carts and received a cheerful wave, then began climbing the gentle slope toward Amelin, the sea sparkling an occasional glimpse through the coastside trees.

In time Garth eased his horse to ride abreast of Melfallan, and they chatted pleasantly enough until Garth shifted smoothly to business. Joanna may have arranged the suitable clothes this morning, but Garth had obviously managed its timing.

"It's good to have you back in Yarvannet, your grace," Garth said, "although I hear the duke still has a mystery. Have they found his justiciar?"

"No, and they probably won't. He's hidden himself well."

"Then he killed the girl?" Garth said with distaste. "How did Duke Tejar explain that?" His eyes glinted, and a muscle shifted in his jaw.

"That's not known for certain," Melfallan said cautiously, then stopped as Joanna rode forward to join them. She gave her husband an amused glance. "Is this conversation secret," she asked brightly, "or can I join in?"

Melfallan smiled at her, and managed some grace in doing it. "Of course, Lady Joanna. Your company is always welcome."

"You and Garth share a friendship longer than I could rival, your grace," she replied demurely. "But I thank you for your courtesy. Garth has spoken so often of you to me that I feel I know you well, especially the boy beneath the man's façade." She dimpled.

"I wasn't *that* bad, whatever he has told you," Melfallan protested. "No different than any other boys set on pranks and high adventures. In any event, Lady Joanna, welcome again to Tiol. If you—"

Melfallan suddenly broke off and looked around him. What?

he thought. They were riding by a small beach beneath the bluff of the coast road. Just beyond the beach, a row of eroded sea stones several cable lengths from the shore caught the splash of the waves, and the suns' light sparkled on the small cove they created. The sea stones stood like massive sentinels, each separated from the others by restless water but joined in a common task.

Guarding what? he thought distractedly. He reined up his horse.

"Your grace?" Garth asked. "What is it?"

The sky looked the same, the beach, the waves, the forest trees lining the coast road, as it had all this past hour. Had he heard a voice? *Her* voice? But how? Had she returned home to Yarvannet? His heart leapt at the thought, and he looked distractedly around him, as if Brierley might step from behind a tree, or suddenly appear before him in the road.

He turned his horse and rode through the brush to the edge of the bluff, then looked down at the sea. Forty feet below the small beach fronted the cove and their array of sea stones, the eroded edge of an earlier bluff, he now saw, that had long since fallen into the sea. Some of the sea stones were large enough to be small islands, and numbered a good dozen along this quarter-mile of beach. The waves of the cove rushed up onto the beach, splashing foam nearly to the tumble of rock at the base of the bluff.

He flinched as the Voice spoke again, but it seemed to come from all places at once, echoing from water to sand, from rock to brush, weaving an invisible web around him and his horse, and rooting him to the spot.

What? he thought dazedly. Come where? He looked around again at the beach, the sea stones, the moving water. Where *are* you?

Brierley?

Garth dismounted behind him with a creak of saddle leather, then, cautious of the bluff edge, walked the last several feet to stand beside Melfallan's horse. "Sometimes, your grace," he said assertively, "these bluff edges suddenly tumble down onto the beach."

"Ah," Melfallan said vaguely, then blinked and looked down at Garth. "So they do," he said. "Your pardon, Lord Garth." He clucked to his horse and backed him away from the edge, then turned back toward the road.

"I hope you are more prudent in other respects, your grace," Joanna said crossly when they rejoined her. "Bravery is one thing, rashness another."

"Joanna—" Garth said in quick warning.

"What?" she said, startled, and looked honestly confused. "What did I say?"

Melfallan considered Garth's lady for a moment, then decided he did not like her chiding of his youthful past nor his current rashness, whatever purpose she had in it, if any at all, nor did he care if Joanna saw his displeasure. He smiled tightly, gave her a stiff bow, then nodded to Garth. "Let us ride on, my lady, my lord." Garth remounted his horse, and they continued their ride.

Conversation became subdued after that, with Joanna eyeing him warily as she said little, and Garth speaking mostly to Revil, with an easy manner Melfallan envied. Scarcely a mile further, they heard the distant clatter of fast hoofbeats behind them, and Melfallan slowed his horse to look back. A single rider thundered into view, hunched over his horse's neck for speed, but straightened as he saw them ahead. He slowed his horse to a canter, and trotted the last several yards, then swept off his hat.

"Sir Alan!" Melfallan exclaimed. He had known Rowena's faithful knight from his summers in Airlie. "What brings you here?"

"Your lady aunt sent me as courier, your grace, with further news that she could not trust to a letter." Alan bowed to Garth and his lady, smiled at Revil. "I arrived only this very hour, and they told me you had set out on this road. My news is urgent."

"She's well?" Melfallan demanded.

"Very well," Alan replied firmly, and might have said more, but glanced at Garth and Joanna, a bit overlong. Garth immediately took the hint.

"We'll ride ahead, your grace," he said with a pleasant nod.

"Come, my dear." Joanna gave her husband a sharp look, obviously agog to hear Alan's news, then managed to erase her scowl. Together they rode out of earshot, and waited a hundred yards down the road. Revil motioned to Talbot and the soldiers to join Garth and his lady, and they waited as the others rode by with a clanking of spears and a great creaking of leather.

Melfallan sighed. "That could have been handled better," he muttered. "Not your fault, Sir Alan. I haven't told any of the other Yarvannet gentry about Rowena; perhaps I should have. How is she, truly?"

"Recovered, your grace. A young healer was brought in, I'm not sure from where—the eastern hills, maybe." Melfallan drew in a sharp breath, and heard Revil's matching gasp. "And safely returned, I assure you," Alan added hastily when he saw the alarm on their faces. "The countess forbade she be summoned, and that caution would have cost the countess her life, had the young healer not been determined." Alan firmed his lips. "I assure you she would have died, my lords. There was sheeting pain into the arm and likely permanent injury, for all that cost to Airlie, and the fever had risen to threaten her life."

"How much has she told you about that—young healer?" Melfallan asked cautiously.

"Who? Brierley?" Alan grimaced wryly at his expression. "Ocean's sake, Melfallan, don't worry about me. The countess is my lady, and I met Jonalyn, too, those many years ago, for that further reason. More importantly," he added earnestly, "Mistress Mefell saved my lady's life: there is no doubt of it. For that I now owe my life to defend her, being your aunt's good knight." He looked at Melfallan with a clear and untroubled gaze, and Melfallan relaxed slightly. Rowena trusted this man, he remembered, and he had little choice now but to trust him, too.

Melfallan slowly rubbed his forehead, then grimaced. "Too many people know," he said. "I'm sorry, Sir Alan, but it's too many."

"Two less than needed," Alan replied imperturbably, gesturing slightly at Garth and Joanna waiting down the road. "As I arranged. When have you ever known me to be that ham-handed in maneuvering a lord?" He flashed his white teeth, then winked at Revil. "Be assured, all is well in Airlie. Brierley was brought into the castle secretly, and left just as unremarked. We are certain of that. The countess now lies abed, with her arm in a sling, and takes the fever tonics her healer Nigel brings her, and intends to stay there for a while. She bids you ignore any rumors of renewed illness she might spread as a caution."

Melfallan nodded. "How did the attack happen?"

Alan grimaced, and anger washed over his face. "There was a letter from Darhel before the attack. Lord Heider destroyed it before he rode out, but I heard of it and joined their party near the river, suspecting treachery. Thank Ocean I was there."

"When did the letter arrive?" Melfallan asked, wondering grimly if his so-called cleverness in slipping away from Darhel had prompted Tejar to Rowena's murder.

"The day before the attack," Alan replied. "Likely Duke Tejar hoped Lord Heider would find both of you riding the Airlie countryside with an inadequate guard, as she was." He shrugged. "You were probably his real prey, Earl Melfallan. After all, Tejar has managed to restrain his rage against Rowena for twenty years."

"If Tejar ordered it."

"Yes, if."

Melfallan scowled, then glanced at Revil. "Thank you, Sir Alan. Tell my aunt I feel greatly relieved. Will you be riding back today?"

"She bid me return as soon as possible." Melfallan nodded, and Alan apparently thought it a dismissal. He saluted, then turned his horse and rode off, breaking into a gallop after a few strides. Melfallan blinked, mildly startled by the abruptness of Alan's departure.

"Well, that's that," he said, as Alan galloped out of sight.

"Alan is a loyal and fervent knight," Revil agreed, and squinted at him a moment. "I don't like this, Melfallan. Every castle has spies, and Airlie is likely the most afflicted of Tejar's counties. How can he be certain she wasn't seen?"

"Too many people," Melfallan said. He glanced at the waiting marcher lord and his lady. "How badly am I mangling Garth today?"

"Not too badly. It's the lady who's offended, Ocean knows why. Implying you're still a boy, tsking at you about the bluff—it's not pleasing Garth, that I can tell you. What happened on the bluff, by the way?"

"I thought I heard something."

"Heard something?" Revil asked, confused. "What?"

"I don't know," Melfallan said helplessly, then grimaced. "Prop me up, Revil, if you can. Today isn't my best of days."

"This is news?" Revil retorted. Madge made another of her rude noises, and they both looked at the bird. Melfallan sighed.

"Trade you," he suggested, nodding at Revil's merlin.

"No," Revil said firmly. "Make Talbot give you Whistle back—that'll solve it. Come on. I doubt you've lost Garth's loyalty in a scant hour, and the rest of the afternoon should have as little peril." He reined his horse around, and together they rode to rejoin the others.

After another half-hour, they reached the edge of the marshes, where several streams descended from the coastland forest to enter the sea. In this lowland, the water meandered in small streams and rills, creating a great expanse of seagrass and boggy ground that attracted waterfowl in great numbers. Sea larks spun above the waves on the distant beach, and other birds called to each other in the grasses. Melfallan dismounted and gave the reins of his stallion to one of the soldiers, then walked into the edges of the marsh, his gyrfalcon heavy on his wrist. He unhooded the hawk and let the bird examine the marshes, her proud head turning right and left. The bird tensed as they heard the distant clacking of blue teal, and she gave a low urging cry. With a sharp lunge of his wrist, Melfallan cast the bird into the sky.

The gyrfalcon rose swiftly with strong beats of her wings, a black shadow splashed with crimson. A moment later, four merlins soared in fast pursuit, spiraling upward with dizzying speed.

Melfallan heard the teals' clacking suddenly change as the flock saw the predator hawks mounting above them, and a moment later several teal exploded from the marshes, winging in panic for the safety of the forest eaves a half-mile away.

Her eyes on the birds above, Joanna walked farther down the grassy bank, her expression rapt. Revil followed her, also watching his bird.

"She's a true huntsman," Melfallan commented pleasantly to Garth, trying to mend some of the afternoon. Garth gave him a quick smile.

"Very much so, keener than me, as much as I love hawking. Her father interested her in the birds as a girl, and she's quite taken over the management of our mews at home. Our falconer sometimes sees more of her than I do."

"Oh, I doubt that, Garth," Melfallan said.

Garth shrugged. "Only a mild exaggeration, believe me. Her father also taught her the sword, and she outpoints me half the time."

"Does she?" Melfallan watched as the hawks, the gyrfalcon in the lead, plummeted downward for the strike, and the group of teal swerved in panic, too late. All the birds hit well, taking their prey in a last fatal plunge to the ground. A few moments later, the merlins rose again into sight, struggling with the weight of a blue teal in their talons, and winged heavily back toward the waiting party. Joanna exclaimed praise for her merlin as she brought the teal to her hands, and then rewarded the bird with the head. A few minutes later, she launched the merlin again and it soared again after the escaping flock of teal. Garth's and Revil's merlins also brought back their catch, to be similarly rewarded, and Whistle winged in last, crying her triumph. When the gyrfalcon gave no sign of returning like the others, Melfallan began to scowl. Finally he turned to look accusingly at Talbot.

The falconer shrugged, and looked resigned. "Training, your grace: it takes time."

"If she eats the whole duck, she'll be worth nothing for the rest of the day."

"That's truth, I fear." Talbot shrugged again, obviously embarrassed, then handed him Whistle and stomped forward into the marsh, waving one of the soldiers to follow. Melfallan stroked Whistle's soft wing feathers as she devoured the rest of the head, eating neatly as she always did.

"New bird?" Joanna asked, grinning broadly as she rejoined them.

"Typical gyrfalcon," Melfallan replied. "Yes, a new bird. I told Talbot I'd rather fly my merlin."

"We all have disappointments in life, your grace," Joanna teased. "A wise lord rises above them," she said, even more drolly, "as swift and sure as a hawk's wings." She ignored her husband's warning frown, and Melfallan now wondered about the byplay. Garth may have come hawking with a purpose, but so had his wife. But what?

"Really?" he said. "I'd rather strangle the bird and end my frustration."

"There's a proverb in there, somewhere, I'm sure," Joanna said comfortably, ignoring the jibe, if in fact she had even heard the warning. "With suitability to other aspects of a lord's life, including management of one's vassals. What are you going to do about Lord Landreth?" she asked pertly. "I warn you that Count Sadon is not pleased. My father says—"

"I haven't decided," Melfallan said shortly and turned away to walk a few steps into the marsh grasses. With a practiced flick of his wrist, he launched Whistle and watched her beat upward. With a shrug, Joanna stalked away to await her own hawk.

Garth sighed softly, scarcely a breath, as he looked at his wife, then back at Melfallan. Melfallan felt sympathy for his marcher lord's predicament, for he obviously had one, and their eyes met.

"Not a great day," Melfallan suggested wryly. "For either of us."

"No," Garth agreed. "She's usually not this—well, she's not. You have my support, Melfallan," he added firmly. "In whatever you plan or need to do, you are my liege lord. Please excuse my wife's impertinence."

Melfallan regarded him for a moment, then chose to accept the words as genuine. Perhaps they even were. "I had hoped for that," he said. "Your wife is a gracious lady, but there will be trouble, Garth: her father is enfeoffed to Count Sadon, and Sadon perhaps makes himself my enemy."

"Sir Kaene is a loyal knight."

"But to whom—if there were a choice?"

Garth looked thoughtful, then glanced at his wife. "This could be difficult for her," he admitted, then grimaced. "I just realized I can't merely ask her. She grew up at Sadon's court, and she adores her father. She firmly believes Landreth is innocent. She wouldn't be as ungracious to mention it to you, at least I didn't think so until today," he said with another grimace, "but there's similar opinion among all the Farlost lords. They think you intend vengeance."

"Vengeance? For what? Landreth was a gadfly in my court, but I wished him no ill."

"Well, that's the speculation: they're not sure, but there must have been something to prompt you to arrest a High Lord. Why the Courtrays would wait thirty years for vengeance against Sadon puzzles even the most idle gossiper." Garth raised an eyebrow. "Or perhaps there has been more recent fault?"

"This isn't about vengeance," Melfallan said. So Garth had his own suspicions about Earl Audric's poisoning, he thought. But I don't *know* anything, Melfallan thought with despair. Brierley told me that Landreth knew Audric was poisoned, but how did Landreth know? Had he ordered it? Had his father? Or had he heard only the rumors that had sifted everywhere since Audric's death, rumors everyone had heard. He shook his head.

Garth waited another moment, his eyes sober, then nodded. "I'm glad to hear you say so, your grace."

"Truly, Garth. I did not intend vengeance, only justice." Melfallan held his gaze for a moment, until Garth nodded again.

Talbot then returned with the gyrfalcon, a half-eaten teal in his other hand. The bird arrogantly rode his forearm, appetite sated, head high, as if nothing were untoward, and no fault could

be pressed. Damnable bird, Melfallan thought sourly. Talbot haz-
arded a glance at Melfallan's face, then prudently hooded Madge
and looped her jesses to the horn of Melfallan's saddle. "Perhaps
she needs more training, your grace," he murmured when he was
done.

"Perhaps. Next time I fly Whistle, Master Talbot." Talbot
shrugged his defeat. "And the next time after," Melfallan insisted.
That earned him a scowl, without concession. Ah, well, he
thought. He turned back to Garth, then bowed to his lady as
Joanna rejoined them. "Shall we ride back, my lady, my lords?"

"It grows late, Melfallan," Revil said, nodding at the westering Daystar. "Why not have dinner in Amelin? My lady would
love to see you—and you also, Lord Garth." He bowed graciously.

Joanna looked at her husband. "I think Lady Saray expects us
back," she said. Some signal passed between the two, and Garth
promptly took up her cue, perhaps with hidden relief. He bowed
genially.

"Melfallan?" Revil prompted.

The other merlins had returned. Melfallan looked across the
marshes, where Amelin's roofs were just visible in the distance,
and thought about returning to Saray this night. He would dearly
love an evening in a happier house.

"Yes," he said to Revil. "Lord Garth, will you and Joanna
bear news to Saray that I'm visiting Revil tonight?"

He saw the flash of surprise across Joanna's face, followed by
a small frown of speculation, quickly erased. She and Garth exchanged a look. Melfallan stubbornly ignored their prompting, if
such it was, and divided his soldiers, half to accompany Garth
and his lady back to Tiol, the others to ride the short distance to
Amelin. Talbot shifted the gyrfalcon to his own horse, then accepted Whistle on his sleeve and moved off to follow Garth's
party. As Melfallan mounted his horse, Revil was watching him,
a slight smile on his face.

"What?" Melfallan demanded.

"You're so predictable when you're stubborn," Revil observed, then glanced at the soldiers who waited nearby, all safely out of earshot. "Garth is almost subtle enough to see it, but not quite."

"I don't want—" Melfallan began. "Don't lecture me, Revil."

"I'm not lecturing; I'm observing. In other times and places you would have dutifully ridden home with them, pretending politeness to your smooth-mannered border lord and his lady, as you always do, and then endured Saray's banquet tonight as all the gentry watched her ignore you, talking behind their hands, whispering and giggling. What's changed?"

"I envy you," Melfallan muttered and looked away.

"Whyever for?"

"Never mind. Let's go visit your lady."

"I'm happy to visit my lady, but you're not getting off that easily, I warn you." Revil coaxed his merlin onto his saddle pommel, then climbed aboard his own horse and nudged his sides, and together they picked their way out of the soft ground back to the road. The half-dozen soldiers fell in behind them, smart and efficient as always. Melfallan glanced back, knowing an array of soldiers would mark the rest of his life. He sighed, and then wondered why he minded it.

The Daystar now sank toward the distant ocean horizon, with the Companion low in the sky above, scarcely a few hours behind in its setting. The suns now moved closer together and would soon Pass, bringing storms and wild weather to all the Allemanii lands. In Yarvannet, as in all matters of weather, the storms were milder, often no more than a heavy surf that kept ships in port and battered the piersides. In Mionn, he had heard, the Pass storms sank ships and lifted roofs off houses. He sniffed the crisp cold air, then caught Revil watching him again.

"Stop that," he said crossly.

"I'm trying to decide the difference," Revil said. "You aren't totally gloomy, as you should be, chewing yourself up about your fault in making her angry. I see a certain peace beneath your frenzy. It hasn't been there before."

Melfallan shrugged. "Leave off, cousin. Don't plague me."

"As you will," Revil said affably.

They rode into the outskirts of Amelin, passing small neat houses high on the slope overlooking Amelin's seaside, then clattered on cobbled streets. Revil's townfolk greeted him cheerily, waving their hats, then bowed just as friendly to Melfallan. He had an advantage in his pleasant cousin: Amelin's love for its count seemed to wash over onto its earl. They passed a baker's shop, then the inn where Bartol's soldiers had pursued Brierley in the streets—was it only eight weeks ago? Had her presence in his life counted such a small span in time?

They dismounted in front of Revil's mansion, and grooms took the horses away, the soldiers following to find their own quarters. Solange awaited them on the porch, beaming in surprise to see Melfallan. Revil's pretty wife made him welcome, and Melfallan spent dinner with Revil's youngest on his knee while the other daughter swung on his neck, watching Revil and Solange with a happy but mild envy. Both his cousin and his lady noticed his silences, but kindly failed to ask. Officials from the town—the armorer, the major merchants, a blacksmith—quickly heard of Melfallan's presence, and found excuse to drop by the manse later in the evening. And all the while Saray no doubt held her banquet, entertaining all the Yarvannet lords.

I don't care, he told himself, and tried to make himself believe it.

⌒ 12 ⌒

*I*n the late evening, after the girls and Solange had gone to bed and the house grew quiet, Revil and Melfallan sat in Revil's study overlooking his garden. No flowers bloomed there now, but the shadows made a gentle pattern on the night, and the wind sighed through an open window. Revil got up to close the window, and then refilled Melfallan's wineglass.

Melfallan rose and took the poker from its stand beside the fire, then stirred the flames to greater brilliance, to revel a moment in the warmth. He looked down at the leaping flames and thought he saw in their movement a face. Was she warm? he wished. Was she thinking of him now?

He started slightly as Revil touched his sleeve. He had not heard him approach.

"You're home with your wife and son, Melfallan," Revil said softly. "And Brierley is supposedly dead, not safe in hiding, and pining is not grief." Melfallan turned and eyed Revil with astonishment.

"I don't know what you mean—" He stopped, then set his mouth. "Hells."

Revil's smile spread slowly across his face. "Ah, Melfallan." He shook his head affectionately, then propped one hip on the table, letting his foot swing. "I can surprise even you. If I were less pleasant, men would call me devious. Dangerous, even. But I have an advantage: I have Solange, and so I can see that you've finally found someone. I've always wondered if you would."

"I suppose I could pretend ignorance of what you're talking about."

"There's that," Revil agreed, and sipped at his glass.

"But you'd get offended and shout at me."

"I didn't shout," Revil protested. "I merely objected."

"Saray would call it shouting," he said unhappily and averted his eyes back to the fire.

Revil sighed. "I don't envy you the comparisons, but I wouldn't encourage them. They'll only make you unhappy. I was fortunate, Melfallan. I wasn't Grandfather's heir, and so I could choose the lady of my heart. No one arranged my marriage for Yarvannet's advantage. No one went to Mionn to bring home a Mionn lady to be my beautiful wife. Saray will never change, you know."

"I know. I've had six years of learning that. Why can't we understand each other?"

"You want to do that. She doesn't. It's that simple. Saray wants her perfect world, and you like facts. You want to deal with reality, because you must. She doesn't have to. One major comparison there: a healer faces facts or her patient suffers. And if Brierley is truly shari'a——"

"She is."

Revil nodded, accepting it. "Then she has facts which have shaped her whole life. Is that why you're even considering an attack on Tejar's coronet? To change the shari'a laws?"

"Yes. You and I have never seen war, but we know what it's like—or think we do. And it's not glory on the field, like the books say, but blood and murder and burning. If power is too evenly balanced, as we both know it is, I would devastate all the Allemanii lands. All might lose. The other lords would see only ambition, but how do I explain my real cause?" Melfallan began to pace up and down the small room. "I don't even know whom to tell. I can imagine Sir James's reaction. You say I like facts: Sir James will have nothing else. Healing by a touch, knowing things

246

she can't possibly know, dream castles and Everlights and shari'a legends: he'd think I've gone mad." He touched his shoulder. "I was burned badly in Witchmere by one of its guardians, and she healed me, as if it had never happened, Revil. And Saray would have died from her fall, but she stopped that, too. She battles a Beast—and I saw it seize her after she healed me, only there was nothing I could touch, only the open air. And Megan—the child heard it roaring." He shook his head. "Sir James will never accept such nonsense. It just can't be. And for him to understand my new ambitions, I have to tell him all of it."

Revil had crossed his arms over his chest and watched him as he paced. "A worthy objective, to right an old wrong," he observed. "Perhaps you underestimate Sir James?"

"You really think so?"

"Probably not," Revil conceded. "He tutored us both, after all, and objective reality rules." He frowned. "I'll help you think about it, Melfallan." He spread his hands. "A lord protects his folk, and Brierley Mefell is Amelin-born, in a way mine before she was ever yours."

"What do you know about her?"

"Not much. I've asked Kaisa, but apparently Brierley avoided my midwife and everyone in my mansion, a prudent rule by her terms, I'd say. Harmon Jacoby might know more." He unleaned himself from the table and emptied his glass, then cradled the glass in his hands. "Or—hmm." Revil walked to the door and opened it, then left briefly. After a minute or two, Revil returned, shutting the door behind him.

"More wine?" Revil suggested, picking up the bottle.

"I don't want to get drunk."

"I'm not suggesting that, and a third glass isn't drunk. Cider if you wish, or I can send for something hot. No?" Revil sat down in one of his comfortable chairs after pouring himself another glass of wine. Melfallan sat down in the chair opposite his, and a few moments later a light knock came at the door.

"Come in!" The door opened and Jared Cheney stepped into the room, then stopped short as he saw Melfallan.

"So Jared told you," Melfallan objected mildly. "You knew all along."

"No, he didn't tell me," Revil countered. "As I told you, I guessed. Come in, Jared. Sit down."

"My lord?" Jared asked uncertainly, then moved as Revil again gestured him into the room.

"Sit."

Jared eased himself into another chair, his eyes moving from Revil to Melfallan.

"Have you told anybody about Brierley?" Melfallan demanded.

Jared flushed, then lifted his chin. "No. I said I wouldn't. But some ought to know, because of the way they're grieving for her. They loved her best, and would know the danger if they spread it about. But you said no." He set his jaw stubbornly. "*She'd* tell them." His eyes flicked an appeal to Revil.

Melfallan smiled. "My cousin lectured me today that Brierley would spare her friends. I know she'd hazard the risk, Jared, but I still fear the danger, and I won't be as careless as she might choose to be. Do you understand?"

"I suppose," Jared said, but didn't exactly yield the point. "Actually, if I could, I'd tell only three, your grace. Harmon and Clara Jacoby, of course—they're closest to her—and I'd tell a forester in Amelin. Brierley healed his daughter's foot wound, you see, and when she came back to Amelin to check the wound—it was how we knew where to arrest her." Jared set his jaw even more tightly. "And it was a good thing I was there when we did. That man you sent from Tiol, Shay, might have killed her there on the docks when the folk started following, wanting our reasons for taking her. Brierley and I go way back. It was wrong arresting her."

Melfallan ran his fingers through his hair. How to explain a High Lord's restrictions to this earnest young man?

"He had good reasons," Revil said, trying to help.

"I don't see them," Jared declared. "A High Lord protects his folk."

"Are you always this outspoken, Jared?" Melfallan asked.

"When there's need." Then he suddenly smiled, his face lighting engagingly. "And to the proper lords." His glance flicked again shyly to Revil. "And you did try to give her parole, and Harmon likes you as earl."

"Master Harmon seems to be a weather vane for many," Melfallan said dryly. "Brierley accused me of being jealous of him, to her amusement."

"Can't I tell at least Harmon?" Jared pleaded. "For Clara's sake more than his, your grace. Clara is painfully shy, and Bri was her only real friend."

Melfallan looked his own appeal at Revil, but his cousin only grinned. "Don't look at me for help," Revil said.

"My lord?" Jared asked, baffled. "Help with what?"

"With you." Melfallan took a deep breath, then stretched out his legs in front of him. "I've explained the dangers, Jared," he said, trying hard for patience. "I'm sorry for Mistress Clara, but Brierley's *life* might be at stake. You talk about what Brierley would choose, but how would Harmon and Clara choose, if they understood the danger? Wouldn't they gladly give these extra months of grief, for her sake?"

Jared looked stubborn for another moment, then shrugged. "I suppose," he muttered, thought about it, then finally conceded the point with another shrug. "She's really safe?" he asked.

"I think so. I left her in a cabin above Airlie with one of Countess Rowena's liegemen. It's not safe to bring her back to Yarvannet, although I keep wishing I could. If she were seen here, word would go back to Darhel and I'd have my witch problem all over again. Do you understand any of the reasons I took her to Darhel?"

"Count Revil has tried to explain. I think your lordly affairs are beyond me." Jared looked down at his clasped hands. "It was wrong to arrest her," he muttered.

Revil chuckled. "Melfallan, that's not a point you're going to win."

"So I see. Tell me about her, Jared."

Jared raised his head and blinked. "What do you want to know?"

"Anything. She told me that she lives in a sea cave, and has books there."

Jared's eyes widened in astonishment. "A cave? Ocean, that explains it. Nobody knows where she lives, and I never thought to look for a cave. You see, I thought if I could get her alone, away from the townfolk who might be watching, that maybe—" He stopped, then grimaced. "We were friends as children, but something happened and she stopped talking to me, I don't know why, then I got into that fight with Rob and then her stepfather got involved, and that was the end of that. I'd see her sometimes in town, and once I tried to follow her home, but nobody follows Brierley when she doesn't want it." He frowned reflectively. "I think Jocater told her to stay away from me. She never allowed Bri to play with us. It's one of the reasons I decided to be her friend."

"Jocater?"

"Her mother. You don't know anything about her, do you?"

"Not about her life here in Amelin. I know some other things."

"Hmm," Jared said. When Revil offered him a glass of wine, he took it absently. "Well, her mother's name was Jocater Mefell, and she married a shipwright here named Alarson. Jocater wasn't friendly to anyone, and there was talk about her keeping so much to herself. They thought her strange, and so they weren't that surprised when she threw herself off a sea cliff. Bri was twelve then. Alarson drowned at sea two years later, and Bri started up her midwifery around then, although she was still only a girl. Some of the folk invited her in, trying to be kind by giving her a few coins to keep herself, but she was good at her healing."

"More than you know," Melfallan said wryly.

"Your grace?"

"One of the things I know and you don't. She'd told me that she was shari'a before I took her to Darhel, but I didn't really believe it." Jared's mouth dropped open. "I wish I had believed her or I would never have taken her into that kind of danger."

"She's not a witch!" Jared sputtered.

"Not the way the legends define them. Calm down, Jared. What if witchery is real, not the way the legends say, but a gift for healing at a touch, and Brierley's grace, her elusiveness, what Brierley is? She told me herself," he insisted as Jared continued to scowl in outrage. "She told me it was true. And I have proofs to believe her." He stood up and pulled his tunic over his head. "See that scar? It's barely visible, but my entire shoulder and arm were burned, charring that would have disabled me for life—if the burn didn't kill me, the more likely outcome. But she touched me, and it went away." He flexed his arm, making the muscle ripple, and then pulled his tunic back on. "It's how she saved Saray and the baby. Saray's skull was crushed by her fall and she was minutes away from death. But Brierley saved her, too, and my son. And the groom in the stableyard, another mortal wound. She battles a Beast when she heals, and risks her own death when she does. *That* is what her witchery is, not what the old tales say." He sat down, and studied Jared's face. "Ocean's breath, Revil," he said despairingly, looking at his cousin, "if I can't convince Jared, how will I ever convince Sir James?"

"Why do you have to convince Sir James?" Jared asked curiously.

"It's complicated. I wouldn't know where to begin." Melfallan stared gloomily at his feet. "What else do you know about her, Jared?"

"Not as much as I thought," Jared answered slowly, turning his glass in his hands as he thought. "But if you're right, it explains a lot of things, even why she— Her mother made her send me away, so I wouldn't find out. That's why she couldn't play with the children and why Jocater kept herself apart. It's why—" He stopped. "Maybe it's why her mother killed herself, and why Alarson was so harsh to them. I wonder if he knew." He thought again, even more furiously, then shook his head. "No, not him.

All Alarson cared about was piling up coins. I never did understand why Jocater married him. Do you know where her sea cave
is?" he asked hopefully.

"I might," Melfallan said, suddenly thinking of the strange
encounter on the bluff. "But don't go there, even if you find it,
Jared. It's her one safe place. If I can bring her back to Yarvannet,
I want that safety for—" But Jared was already nodding.

"I understand. I'm sorry now, Earl Melfallan, that I argued
with you about telling folks. I just thought of their grieving, especially Clara Jacoby."

"Brierley would think that way, too," Melfallan said.

"Yes, she would," Jared agreed absently. He stood up, looking
over Melfallan's head at the garden windows, although likely he
didn't truly see them. "I have to think," he muttered, and then
suddenly looked embarrassed, flushing red again. "I mean—" He
looked despairingly at Revil. "Have I been forward again, my
lord? I mean, you invited me in and even gave me wine—" Jared
sat down lumpily. "Hells," he muttered.

"What's wrong?" Melfallan looked to Revil.

"You forget certain facts, cousin, to your credit," Revil answered, amused. "You're the earl of Yarvannet. Jared just remembered that, didn't you, Jared? I've seen our young man do this
with me, too. He'll rattle along, treating me like one of his young
friends, nothing untoward, and then suddenly remember my lofty
rank and crash in a heap. It's all right, Jared. Mistress Mefell
hadn't much use for lords, either."

"It's not that—" Jared stumbled, and his face went through
the most amazing contortions. "It's just—" He hunched over and
buried his face in his hands. "Hells," he groaned.

Revil laughed, and reached to take Jared's glass before it fell.
"Jared is Sir Micay's nephew, Melfallan. Did you know that?"

"I do now," Melfallan said, fascinated by Jared's behavior.

"Not that Jared takes it excessively. His uncle invited him to
dinner with me on our way to Darhel, several times in fact. It
seems Micay is 'developing' Jared, not always with Jared's cooperation."

"I don't want to live in Tiol," Jared muttered, and would not look up. "I won't."

"Powers are now moving that may overwhelm you, young man," Revil said drolly. "Here, straighten up. Earl Melfallan's more like me than you think."

Jared looked up. "She told you those things about herself?" he asked, again diverted by a new thought. "She must trust you."

"I've asked her to trust me. I hope the trust is worthy."

Jared smiled, his eyes lighting and transforming his face. "She always knows," he said with full confidence. "I wish she had trusted me, but maybe now—" He stopped, thinking. "This Airlie liegeman—"

"A good man. He'll watch over her."

"He'll need help."

"I'm not sending you to Airlie, Jared," Melfallan warned. "Asking for her would attract attention."

Jared's smile deepened. "We'll see," he murmured.

"What did you say?" Melfallan asked in surprise.

Jared grinned and stood up, then stretched his muscles. "Oh, you don't want it repeated, your grace. You might have to do something to me." His grin was brash now. "I wouldn't like that. And before I make all this worse, I think I should leave." He bowed awkwardly to Revil. "Thank you for your courtesy, my lord, your grace." Then, without a by-your-leave, Jared indeed left, shutting the door behind him.

Revil laughed at Melfallan's expression. "Like I said, he does that with me, too, since I've gotten to know him better. It's Micay's bloodline, I think. You should knight him, Melfallan, and that's my idea, not Micay's, if you're wondering."

"Knight him?"

"Why not? It's your prerogative as earl."

"But Grandfather never—"

"Never knighted any Yarvannet man, true. When he replaced Pullen's lords, he elevated wealthy men like Lord Eldon and the Tollands to be his landed gentry. But no new knights. Gentleman knights are counselors, a lord's right hand, men you truly trust.

Grandfather trusted only the men he brought with him from Tyndale, even after thirty years here. Remember what I said about not
copying him?"

"You're a nag, Revil," Melfallan observed. "I've decided it's
a fact."

"And pleased to be so. I'm serious. Why accept Grandfather's
choices? Why not make a few of your own? You can see that I've
been thinking, Melfallan. I have all kinds of ideas about how you
should be earl, once I applied myself to the problem." He grinned,
then spread his hands expressively. "I love Sir James, too, and I
respect his wisdom. And Micay would die to save you, without
hesitation, if there is need. But you need men of your own age,
too, like me, like Jared, who will last the years with you after
those grand old men are gone. Have you even thought about the
years ahead?" he asked skeptically.

"Not exactly," Melfallan admitted. "I've been assuming a
short life, given this and that and those."

Revil snorted. "I intend to live into my nineties, and that
means you must, too, given this and that and those."

"Must I?"

"Please," Revil said, then sobered. "Decades from now, I want
us to sit here peacefully in my study in Amelin, looking out on
the garden. Solange will look up and smile as she's busy cutting
roses, and Yarvannet's rule will be given over to others, our strong
capable children who will defend Yarvannet fiercely and well.
We'll be infirm in body, slowing in mind, you and I, but I'll
still raise my glass to you, cousin, affectionate as always." He
paused. "See? I can worry, too, almost as well as you can."

"I preferred you happy and careless, Revil. I don't want this
burden on you, too."

"Those times have passed," Revil said quietly. "Passed forever—or perhaps not. There's still the hope of our garden when
we're old." He got to his feet. "I'm tired. Sleep well tonight,
cousin, and put off facing Saray until tomorrow. Slip a little, even:
delay returning until the afternoon. Make her wait."

"You *are* angry this time."

"And Saray would be surprised that I am, and wouldn't understand why." He gestured toward the door.

In his bedroom upstairs in Revil's mansion, Melfallan listened to the distant sound of the surf, and the room was dark and cool. In time he drifted to sleep, a dark and empty silence without dreams.

The following afternoon, after a long pleasant morning with Solange and Revil, he rode back to Tiol with his soldiers. He paused at the place on the bluff, listening, but nothing spoke to him again from the sea, if in fact it ever had.

Revil's suggestion of delay was an interesting experiment, and arguably Saray would have continued cold and dismissive even if he'd returned more timely. She ignored him when he entered their suites, busily occupied in sorting their clothes. Her anger was obviously settling into a serious quarrel, one that would last longer than shorter. For once Melfallan decided to skip the anxiety her moods inflicted on him, and went about his day. He met with Sir James in the library to review the upcoming assizes, took Portmaster Ennis's report in the Great Hall, then, in the late afternoon, spent an hour on the battlements, watching the Daystar set into the sea.

He saw a sea lark plummet gracefully over the ocean, then saw another rise swiftly to join its mate, twin flames against the darkening sky. Beneath their soaring ecstatic flight, the sea murmured in its several soft voices, surrounding him with its distant sound like a cloak.

I wish you were here with me now, he thought wistfully. *I don't mean to maunder, or pity myself, or put myself into a daze like a love-struck boy. I just need you here with me, more than I expected. I feel half a man without you, and I haven't the heart for all this, not without you.* He bowed his head and his sudden tears surprised him.

What's this? he thought angrily, and brushed the wetness from his face. But the emptiness rose even harder within him, the emptiness without her. It pained his throat with its hollowness, and he choked back a muffled sob, trying desperately not to give in to the weeping. Stop it, he wished at himself frantically. Stop this. What's wrong with you?

He'd done quite well these past two weeks, riding comfortably through the Ingal countryside, watching the coastlands from his ship, dining with his lords, hawking with Revil. He'd done very well, indeed. Is this the price of a touch that shivers like a cool breeze? Is this the price, beloved?

After a time, he regained control of himself, although the hollowness still remained. When the Daystar sank beneath the horizon, filling the world with the Companion's blue shimmering, he turned away from the sea.

Grimly, he avoided any return to the rooms he shared with Saray, and had Philippe make up a cot for him in his tower study. If Saray saw his grief, she might gloat that she had caused it, and he'd not give her that gift tonight. He was half-asleep when one of Saray's lady-maids came looking for him, and he gave her no reason to bear back to his wife. It was a cold satisfaction, one that half-shamed him, but it was done. He lay on his hard cot, listening to the murmur of the waves in the harbor, and finally found sleep again.

At first his dreams shifted uneasily, moving from place to place, first to the high walls of the castle battlements to watch the morning mist move over the harbor, then to the Great Hall and its glittering throng of Yarvannet ladies and their lords. Next he was riding pleasantly through the forest, his horse moving easily beneath him. Snow clung to the ground and lay heavily on the everpine branches that lined the track, and the wind turned suddenly cold. Melfallan pulled his cloak tight around him and shivered. Snow in Yarvannet? he wondered. Then he was riding along the coast road, Whistle on his wrist and his soldiers following behind him, and he turned his head when a voice called to him from the sea. He strained to hear, but the voice did not sound again.

Next he sat in his tower study, poring over a map of Tiol

harbor. They should lay a storm boom from that rock outward, he decided, before the worst of the winter storms struck at Yarvannet. Snow this early boded trouble. The fishing boats might huddle in Port Tiol's safety, but a choppy sea could maroon the fishing fleet inside the harbor, and threaten starvation for too many folk later in winter. He looked around at Ennis to ask his opinion.

A girl stood quietly near the wall with its large map, watching him. She was dressed in homespun and a broad-brimmed hat, her pale satin complexion and tumbling red hair a stark contrast to the simplicity of her dress. A tall staff was grasped in one slender white hand, and her hat brim half-concealed sober gray eyes. For a flashing moment of incredulous hope, Melfallan thought she was Brierley, then realized she was not. Then, puzzled, he realized he did not recognize her at all. Had Saray acquired still another lady-maid? But this girl was no lady-maid, not in homespun. Saray would never allow her lady-maid to dress in such rough fabric—it simply wasn't done.

Then the girl smiled, with a smile of such exquisite grace that Melfallan's breath caught like a sudden pain. "Earl Melfallan," she said quietly, greeting him. "Fair meeting, lord."

"Who are you?" he blurted and rose from his chair, then quickly stepped back lest he frighten her. This girl must not be frightened. One moved carefully, delicately, near such a woman. One should spend all the world to keep her safe, never counting the cost, that she not be frightened. He closed his eyes and swayed, remembering Brierley as if she suddenly lived inside him, soul to soul, so much a part of him that it made her his next breath, his next thought.

"The resonance does not abide easily," the girl said, startling him into opening his eyes again. She smiled and tipped her head to the side. "A witch's heart chooses as it must, and once twinned, both breathe as one. The sea witches understood the bond they might create and were careful, for a resonance is both gift and peril. But a witch is also a woman, and such bonds were sometimes made during a healing, when souls might touch. You are fortunate, and so is she, but it will not be easy for either of you."

"Resonance?" he asked, confused. She smiled at him, then calmly took off her hat and stepped forward to place it on the table. She leaned her staff against the edge, and looked at him.

"Who *are* you?" he demanded.

"A dream-friend," she answered, amused at his effrontery. "Are you not dreaming now, lord, and do I look dangerous? Hardly. Therefore a friend. One thought leads to the next, like logs chained in a boom, one from another, stretching from this rock to that hidden pier. I am Thora Jodann."

"Thora," Melfallan breathed and found his legs suddenly weak. Brierley had mentioned that name, he remembered. *She left part of herself in my Everlight and advised me in dreams,* she had said. *My dearest friend and guide. As Megan is my child, so I was hers.* Melfallan sat down abruptly in his chair.

Thora scowled delicately, then sighed. "Ah, well. I see she told you about me. I had hoped to spin that out a bit longer, if only for my enjoyment. I have grown used to mystery, and often teased Brierley with it, though the mystery was necessary. Counsel too clearly given can lead to error, for it stifles intuition and better choice. My time was long ago, and answers may differ." She glanced idly around the study, scanning the books on the shelves, then half-turned to look at the map. "Your grandfather's study, I see—but not yet yours. I doubt it ever will be until you decide it is." She seated herself in the other chair.

"Why? Don't you think I'm his measure?"

"That I cannot answer, for I am biased. I find your grandfather no great model. Tell me, young earl, would Earl Audric have defended Brierley? And if he did, what would have been his reason? Protection of a deserving lass, or a political dagger against his old friend's loathsome son, the duke? You went to Darhel to protect her, but Earl Audric would have seen only the political chance. True?"

"My grandfather was—"

"An Allemanii earl." She shrugged. "I know. When he was still Count of Tyndale, your grandfather descended on Yarvannet with his army to punish Earl Pullen, and his sword bit deeply.

Those who resisted died, even though they fought for loyal defense of their lords and land, and with them died their families. There was a noble wife who flung herself shrieking at the soldier who had just impaled her husband with his spear. There was a daughter, who fell weeping on her parents' bodies and looked up accusingly at the soldier standing over her, their blood dripping from his sword. He could not bear the look and killed her, too. There was a son, who hid for a time under the wharves, watching the soldiers as they looted from house to house, planning mad vengeance, and then managed not a single death before the soldiers killed him. There was a baby, left to starve in her cradle after the soldiers marched away, uncaring. And for this, your grandfather was rewarded with Yarvannet." Her gaze was bitter.

"Earl Pullen rebelled, Thora," Melfallan protested, stung by her tone. "He marched north to attack his rightful liege."

"Yes, he did. And I know your Allemanii penalty for rebellion. I've seen it three times in Yarvannet since the Disasters, and each time I wept for the innocent. The first time I could not save my witch-daughter: she was too far from the cave when the soldiers came. The second time my daughter fell from the bluff side in her haste, and died on the sand. The last was more fortunate, but she lived in fear of your grandfather's soldiers the rest of her life, too terrified to hear me, too cold and too alone and too hungry." Thora's eyes blazed. "Shame on you, High Lords. Shame on your butchery."

Melfallan glared back. "And how do I answer you? If swords are raised against me, do I stand there, jaw agape, and let myself be run through? Let them murder my folk?" He rose to his feet, shaking with fury. "How do I defend Brierley," he shouted, "except with blood? *How?*"

Thora sighed, and abruptly her anger was gone. "I don't know, fair lord," she said tiredly. "I'm only an Everlight, and I never understood the hatred that drives such killing. I was made to create bindings, not destructions, and to build the peace between persons that is revered by the sea witches. Other Everlights looked to the other gifts, but I belonged to the dayi from the day of my making. Thora understood that kind of hatred, even if I did not—she saw it grow in Rahorsum, but nothing she did could stop it. She saw it murder her beloved, the Briding lord she had dared to trust. She saw it take her sister into the endless darkness, reaving her soul into tatters, lost forever. Although she understood it, although she knew the reasons, nothing made any difference. As I made no difference the day your grandfather rode into Yarvannet."

"I wasn't there," he said helplessly. "How can you reprove *me*? I wasn't even born."

Thora crossed her arms and looked pensively at the window. "Do you hear the sea, beloved?" she murmured. "The life that flows within it, never changing, always restless, the endless play of movement in Her waters. There is pattern in that movement, in an intricacy beyond our understanding. We sense only that there is pattern, and listen in wonder." Her gray eyes returned to him and made a careful study of his face. Finally, she pursed her lips.

"Yes, I should not reprove you for your grandfather's evil. I had already decided," she continued, nodding to herself, "that I would help you for Brierley's sake, but I think I find more now, a reason in yourself, young earl. The Everlights have no reason to like the Allemanii, but all my Yarvannet daughters have loved you as a folk, as Brierley does still. Even great tragedy fades with the years, binding old wounds and erasing memory. It is, I suppose, an Everlight's work, that binding." She smiled gently. "I am old and often hazy in my thoughts, and not always a reliable guide. Be wary of me at times if I seem vague, lest I fail you."

Melfallan frowned. "You're her Everlight?" he asked hesitantly. "She said Thora lived in her Everlight. Are you her dreamguide?" He blinked and looked around at the familiar contents of his tower, although the cot seemed to be gone, and his sleeping body with it. "I think I'm dreaming."

"Of course you're dreaming," Thora said irritably. "How else could I speak to you? On the beach you heard my voice, but I could not let you find me, not with your lords watching. Even

Brierley had to hunt for days that first time, and she was witch-born, the greatest of my many daughters since Thora herself. I am no longer young. And so I must be a 'dream-guide,' as you call me."

"Brierley called you that," he corrected. "Not I."

"Then it must be so." She looked aside distractedly and curled her hair around a finger, then focused on him again with difficulty. "Sometimes I don't know where my thoughts go," she complained, "scattering this way and that like sparks from a flame, and I have trouble gathering them together. Once I was better and did not tire this easily. Forgive me. It is hard to reach into your dreams, Melfallan, for you are not witch-born, not even in part, and the resonance is not yet settled. It might still divide." She looked around herself vaguely again. "Perhaps I came too soon. Do you think so?"

Melfallan reached out his hand, but hesitated to touch her sleeve. If he did, he feared, she might vanish and leave him bereft. "I will never fault you for anything," he said. "I told Brierley that grace can excuse any error."

"Did you say that?" Thora said, raising an eyebrow. "I commend you. You have sensibility of feeling I didn't expect. Perhaps I am too biased against you Allemanii; yes, that must be it. And, whatever you imagine, I don't know everything you know. Even your pattern can escape me, and often will. I am neither dragon-spirit nor deity." She shook a finger at him. "Be warned: the part of me that is Thora will blaze at you for the wrongs long past that were never your doing, but you must believe in that flame, young earl. Thora's love is in the flame, however it scorches. And Brierley is there, too, the last hope of the shari'a. Believe in that one last flame, fair lord, for Brierley's sake, and I will assist you."

"How?" he asked bluntly. "In dreams? How can I know you're real?"

"Brierley often accused me of unreality, but Thora's library still exists in Witchmere, waiting there for centuries to surprise her about her own foolishness. Having seen that library yourself, you should be more polite than she was." The girl sniffed.

"You're like her," Melfallan said in delight. "She talks that way, and tips her head like you do, and smiles— Does Brierley live in you, too, Everlight?" he asked eagerly. "I have been longing to—" He caught himself and swallowed hard. This was only a dream, different from the others, and he wanted more than a dream.

"I am like her, as you say, because Thora taught her and comforted her, and because Thora lives in me. The rest is mostly your wishing."

"Forgive me," Melfallan said dryly and wrinkled his nose at her. "I'm only mortal."

"Even mortals can improve," the girl said and laughed at him. She stood and gathered up her staff. "Fair meeting, young lord. Shall I give you fairer dreams? Dreams can bind what is separated, blending memory and hope for the future. And in that there is comfort." She lifted her pale hand and smiled at him.

Abruptly Melfallan stood on a small beach south of Tiol, looking out on the southern bay. The tallest towers of his castle were just visible over the shadowed headland, and the row of sea stones stood like sentinels against the sea's advance. It was the same cove where the voice had called him, but the Daystar had set. Near the horizon, the Companion shed its brilliant twilight onto stone and water, and made the sand blaze with light.

"There you are!" Brierley cried with delight. He turned and gasped, then swept her up high in his arms, spinning her around full circle. She laughed and sternly bid him put her down, then took his hand. She pointed over the water. "See?" she said eagerly, her face alight. "My cave is there within that sea rock, with my books and Marlenda's dress and the ledge to watch the horizon. I have longed to show it to you, Melfallan. Would you like to see it?"

He smiled down at her and pressed her hand tightly. "Yes, I would, beloved. Very much."

Her face filled with joy as she looked up at him, lighting her eyes with love for him. "Then we shall. Come."

She found a cockleboat among the rocks nearby, then urged

him to enter it. He climbed aboard with some hesitation, for it was an uncertain craft, likely to sink if he jostled it too unhandily. Brierley picked up a paddle from the planking, and then guided them quickly across the cove waves. They rounded the island and waited for the right wave, then plunged into a tunnel to the island's heart. The waves thundered in the enclosed darkness, but after the next turning, he saw a stone landing ahead, with a stanchion for tying the boat. Above the landing was a boxy metal shape affixed to the wall, with a white stone face that flared brightly in welcome. He had seen its mate in Witchmere, darkened and lifeless, and had wondered that Brierley had caressed it sadly.

An Everlight. He goggled at it, his jaw agape, and heard Brierley snicker behind him. "Yes, it is," she said. "Will you never give up your doubting?"

"You mean believe *anything*, just because you say so?" he asked, finding his voice. "Now how can I promise that?"

"Ah, well. I suppose I'll take other promises. Throw the rope onto the landing, and I'll tie up the boat." Melfallan clung again to the sides of the cockleboat as she shifted its weight, leaping quickly to the landing. Seaman by blood that he was, he needed Brierley's help in getting out of the boat, and then nearly took a swim until she caught his other hand and pulled him up. "Umph," she said as he stumbled against her, making her stagger, too, but the next moment they were both upright, standing on solid rock. Brierley took his hand and tugged him toward a nearby doorway.

"Come see. You wanted so much to see my books. Now is the time." She laughed and would have urged him further, but instead he pulled her back close to him, then kissed her soundly, eagerly. Her lips were warm, and moved against his as she smiled. He pulled her still tighter against him and made his kiss more insistent, and felt her arms come around his neck as she fully yielded to his embrace.

"Beloved," she sighed when he was done, and caressed his face.

"Brierley," he whispered, holding her tightly. "Is it really you?"

She smiled sadly. "No, it's not, and you know that." She kissed him, then gently pushed him back. "I'm only a dream. Do you wish such dreams, young earl? To spin from memory what is not yet real, and may never be real?"

"Yes," Melfallan said desperately, reaching for her hand.

She pressed his fingers, looking up into his face. "It will only strengthen the resonance," she warned. "You have no witch's gift, and so no barrier, and some of your Allemanii folk cannot bear its touch. What drove Rahorsum to his madness? A witch's touch that first afflicted his son, and then Rahorsum himself. They tried to steal his soul, Melfallan, and he destroyed them for it, and was then himself destroyed. Thora counseled against the attempt, even tried to warn the duke, but Witchmere did not listen, not even her father who was high in Witchmere's councils." She sighed and shook her head. "Brierley has asked me again and again what caused the Disasters, and I have never told her specifics. Perhaps I should have, and she would not have erred when she healed you of the guardian's wound."

"What error?" Melfallan demanded. "Is love error? Is preserving my lands error? I could never have ruled Yarvannet with such an injury. She saved me from all that, saved Yarvannet."

"You would never have ruled at all," Brierley answered sadly, touching his shoulder. "The wound was fatal. A wiser dayi would have let you die rather than risk a resonance."

"Resonance?" he asked curiously. "Thora said that word, too. What's a resonance?"

Brierley sighed and looked down at their linked hands, then sighed again. "Well, you must be told, and better sooner than later. A sea witch can go too far, young earl, and link souls when she heals. Just as she must guard against rending her own flesh in a healing, she must also guard her soul. If she errs, she and the other are joined for the rest of their lives, one fate tied to the other's. In lesser witches, the resonance can even limit the gift, adding great risk to any later healing. If she fails, the Beast will take them both, a death she will perceive as her beloved torn to pieces before her eyes. That grief can destroy her soul, and it will never rise again into another life, never to bless the world with her special gift." She lifted her eyes to his face, then studied it bleakly. "Does his soul also die when hers is lost? I don't know, nor do the Four. Do they go to a realm the Four do not know? Perhaps. Perhaps there they can find a new beginning, or perhaps they are together yet still divided, without joy, unable to touch. In their wisdom, the Four counseled the sea witches against the resonance, fearful of the lives it could cost."

Melfallan shook his head. "I don't agree it was error—it wasn't error for me, obviously, but it wasn't for her, either. I don't agree," he repeated forcefully. "It brought me closer to her than I thought possible. It shivers in every touch, and makes her precious to me—more precious than I ever thought I could feel about anyone. Being parted from her now, I don't know how I can bear it—" He broke off, then firmed his mouth. "I don't care how we die, Everlight. And I don't understand souls and their fates. All I know is, whatever the cost, it's worth it. So don't tell me it was a mistake. Please."

Brierley smiled and tipped her head, then stepped closer and laid her head on his shoulder. She rubbed her cheek slowly against the fabric of his tunic. "Then prove me wrong, young earl," she murmured. "Prove to me that any love between witch and Alle-manii does not end in tragedy. I have only Thora's memory to guide me, for she lost her beloved and in time lost herself, here in Yarvannet."

Melfallan held her close, then lifted her chin with his fingers and kissed her again. She sighed feelingly, enough to make him smile. "Do we have to talk about error and old tragedies?" he asked softly. "Does everything have to have such dread impor-tance?"

"You are tired of your lords, I see. They and the duke have inflicted you badly."

"Is Lord Garth loyal to me?" he asked curiously, wondering if she would answer.

"I can't tell you that," she said promptly. "No, don't frown at me, and remember my counsel about telling you too much. It's not that I won't, but that I can't. I'm not a witch. I'm an Everlight."

"You can't?" Melfallan asked, more disappointed than he expected.

Brierley shook her head. "As I said, I'm an Everlight, not a witch, and I can't help you with your lords, even if I chose to do so, which I would not. But I doubt I will find any of the Blood among your lords, Melfallan. The shari'a who survived the Disasters would never have wisely loved a lord. Trust a lord to be husband or lover? When that lord had the duty to murder your kind? I think not, and you yourself are a lonely exception. It's in the commonfolk where the Blood survives, and perhaps more than you suspect." Brierley shook her head at him vigorously. "And, no, I won't tell that, either."

"Then what will you tell me?" he teased.

She smiled back at him, then wrinkled her nose, exactly as Brierley did. In manner and face, in voice and smile, she was everything he remembered. The Everlight sniffed. "Well, let's see. How far do you want this dream to go?"

"Meaning what?" he asked suspiciously.

"There are certain other memories of Brierley I could borrow. This cave has a bed, narrow in its width, true, but large enough for two."

"Hmm." He considered it, and saw Brierley's smile broaden, her eyes dancing. "I don't know if Brierley would approve," he said uncomfortably.

"You don't know Brierley as well as you think, although that's not your fault. She has been aware of others' passions nearly all her life, usually more than she wished to. A dayi must learn to guard her mind, lest another's desire influence her into unwise actions. Now, what is that look of horror? Do you think you swept her into bed merely by the wishing? As if she had no will to resist you? You know better." She shook her head. "When will you stop doubting yourself, Melfallan?"

"Perhaps when the wind stops blowing?"

Brierley made a rude sound. "Perhaps. On that we must agree, to our grief. Well?" She stepped back and put her hands on her hips, then posed provocatively by thrusting out her breasts.

"Brierley wouldn't do that," he said instantly.

"Only so that you remember later what was real and what was not. But in all else tonight, beloved, I yield." She spread her arms invitingly. Melfallan hesitated a moment, then stepped into her embrace. She kissed him passionately, then kissed him again, and led him into the cave beyond the landing.

Later he lay at ease beside her in Brierley's narrow bed, warm beneath the coverlet, their bodies sweated against each other. The cave was small, crowded with old but sturdy furniture—a bed, a table and chair, and many shelves of books. He ran his eyes around the shelves, trying to count the books, and recognized one or two titles, but most of the volumes were very old, far older than the books in his own castle library. On the middle shelf across the room stood an array of oversized bound volumes, each covered with bright-colored leather.

"Those are the journals," Brierley murmured. "One of them is hers."

"Journals?"

"Written by the witches who lived here in this cave since the Disasters. Thora was first. Most of her daughters lived alone, as Brierley lived alone here. Here was their retreat from the world, to rest and find peace, and to puzzle about themselves."

"Thank you for showing me this," he said softly, and kissed her hair. "Thank you more than I can say."

"I, too, could not bear your longing for her." Brierley kissed his bare shoulder, and then sighed. "Do not come to this cave in the flesh, I warn you. I cannot allow you in: it is my task to guard this place. If you persist, for her sake I will erase your memory of me and of this cave, and I will not come to you in dreams again."

"All you have to do is say so," he said mildly, pulling her closer. "You needn't threaten."

"Just in case," she murmured and relaxed against him as she fell asleep. Can a dream-guide sleep within its own sleep? he wondered, bemused.

He yawned, his body deliciously relaxed from their lovemaking, and marveled that it had seemed so very real to him. Even the shiver of their touching had been the same. He laughed softly, then stretched his legs against the covers, careful not to disturb the lady beside him, whoever she was, memory or dream-guide or some precious part of Brierley herself, caught in her Everlight. He looked around Brierley's sea cave one more time, and then closed his eyes.

Does Brierley dream of me? he wondered wistfully as his thoughts began to wander and drift into sleep, flotsam bobbing gently on dark water. I hope so.

The sun was bright gold when he woke the next morning in his tower study. He stretched languorously on his cot, unwilling to move much, then lazily watched the suns' light beaming down through the window. As the minutes passed, the light changed subtly, adding more of the Companion's faint dawning lavenders to the strong gold of the Daystar, and the room was filled with light. On such a morning, all things seemed possible, and doubts had no place in it.

With a laugh of pure joy, Melfallan threw aside his bedcovers and rose to meet the day.

~ 13 ~

he Daystar had just lifted above the treetops when
Ashdla Toldane stepped out onto the narrow porch
of her forest house. The railed porch overlooked a
tumbling stream that coursed along the bottom of
the ravine, making its chattering way south toward
the snow-covered meadows and fields that fronted Lake Ellesmere,
the largest of Mionn's Flinders Lakes. Her sanctuary in this witch's
house, as it had been for all the forest witches of her line since
the Disasters, was a place of cool shadows and the flash of bird
wings, the quiet sound of water, and the stealthy movement of
animals coming down to the brook to drink. Now, in this winter
season, snow clung to the ground beneath the trees, chilling the
air, and the birds called sleepily to each other in the cold.

She took in a deep breath of the clear cold air and wished for
spring. In the spring, after the suns had Passed in the sky, the
Companion led the dawn and brought milder weather, welcome
relief after the violent Pass storms. The suns' light then filled the
forest, muted blue and gold dappling on the moving leaves, and
all was movement, all was new life. The greens of the forest were
somehow different in spring, more hesitant and delicate, and she
loved that season above all others. Soon, she thought, and sighed.

She put her hand in her skirt pocket and tickled one of the
tiny shrews who lived there, and heard a high-pitched squeak and
giggle as the shrew batted at her finger and squirmed to escape.
During the nighttime, Nit and Bit and their five children lived in

a nest of sticks and soft bird down on a shelf in Ashdla's bedroom in her father's house, or here on a lintel above the storeroom door. During the day they liked to ride in her pocket, and she indulged their wishing, glad for their company. She felt the nip of tiny teeth, another quick batting of feet at her finger, then all the shrews laughed, high-pitched giggles almost beyond audibility. She laughed softly in response, breathed in another breath of the winter air, and went back into her house.

She looked around her front room with its comforting familiarity. Against one wall stood her small bed, bright with a patchwork quilt made by her mother. Against another wall stood her desk, with the collections of oddments, bits of stone, small twigs and furry moss, the herbs that she and her brother, Will, had gathered. Above the desk on a shelf stood a ranking of books, the books secret to this place that she could never show to anyone else except Will, for it was here that the forest witches of Mionn had kept their innermost thoughts and teachings. On the third wall stood a table and its chairs, where the remains of her morning meal still lay unattended, and beside the table stood a small chest of clothes, with more shelves on the other walls for the collections that filled up her house, some gathered by earlier occupants, others by her mother, the small remainder by herself and Will.

Her mother had died five years before when she and Will were only ten, and with her death her father had seemed to lose half of himself, although he still worked at his smithy, still smiled at his daughter and son. Her father's life had become a life of silences, when he seated himself at the table in their small house, or gentled the horses in the stable with his large hands, or looked out at the wide lake and the forest that surrounded it, regarding all with sober brown eyes. He had found his comfort in small things and tried to teach his children to be content, as much as they could, but, even now, part of her father still waited for a footstep that never came, a voice that never spoke: it was a waiting that would never diminish or end until his own death. If Ashdla had been sea witch, she might have eased part of that grief, but her powers did not run to healing an inner wound. And so part of her father's grief she could not understand, and never would unless Will died first, but she tried to help him as she might, as did Will, and their father had taken cheer from that.

Her brother, like other brothers twinned with a witch, shared her witch senses, although his magic could be erratic, sometimes even hilarious. More often he helped their father in the smithy, running chores as he was bid, a good son. She shook her head absently, wishing Will had come to the cabin today as he had promised. Around their father, and particularly in the company of the townfolk, they kept to their roles of normal Allemanii children, a pretense her father firmly encouraged, even with him, but here at the cabin they could be what they truly were. Her brother had her dark hair, her slender build, her quickness of movement: he was her second self.

As it had been for her mother, and for the forest witches before her, this cabin was her true home: only here did she feel truly secure, only here did she feel complete, here in the long hours of her studies, in the long hours she sat before her window, watching the forest, or sat cross-legged on her porch. Only here did the forest speak to her in its many voices, and brought to her the patterns of its life. Here, safe away from people who did not understand her and in whom she had little interest, she found in herself a truth that was too easily distracted in the town.

She touched the Everlight mounted on the wall beside the door, and it flickered in response. *It is a lovely morning, Everlight,* she thought. *It has been a long winter away from you, but I can't stay long this time, only a few days. Da needs me.*

I am always with you, the Everlight whispered into her mind, its mental tones resonating with its love for her, its quiet understanding. Its square porcelain face flickered in several greens, the mellow green of summer, the dark sharpness of everpine, the lightest of greens for new buds, the transient green in the brook depths as fish moved from shadow to shadow. Although three centuries old, the Everlight still lived and spoke, and guarded the forest witches who lived in this place.

I miss Mother. She sighed.

So do I, daughter. Death comes to all souls in time. It is part of the pattern of living, one you have seen often in the forest. The binding comes with birth and the division with death, and all is renewed.

Yes. I know these things. Everlight, but—I still miss her. I feel very alone sometimes, even with Da and Will and this place and you. I wish—I don't know what I wish sometimes.

Patience, my child.

Patience for what? But the Everlight did not answer. She dropped her hand and watched its flicker for a time, then turned away.

Owree hooted at her softly from his perch in the rafters above her head. She looked up at the mock owl and smiled, and saw him rustle his feathers in pleasure that she noticed him, as he always did, pleased in his fierce way by the simplest of things. She had found the baby mock owl two summers before, hurt by a fall from his nest, perhaps caused by an over-energetic shove by a brother or sister which commonly ended the life of the littlest in the brood. But Owree had been a fighter and had pulled himself several yards into the shrubbery, where she had found him, starving, only half-fledged, and near death. She had taken him home and nursed him, then would have released him back into his forest home, but he would not leave her when he was well, and seemed content to be a companion in this solitary house, as the others who lived with her had chosen.

Slinkfoot slipped through the small hole in the base of the far wall and chittered at her, her black ferret's eyes sly and glittering. The shrews in Ashdla's pocket, sensing the ferret's entry, shrieked in alarm and burrowed deeper, but Slinkfoot had no interest in such a paltry meal as a handful of shrews. Instead, she looked up hungrily at Owree, and the mock owl fluffed his feathers in outrage. Two predators in the same cabin led to inevitable discussions, for both Owree and Slinkfoot considered Ashdla their personal territory, as well as the environs of the forest cabin and the caverns nearby; neither accepted the other's encroachment with any grace.

"You already ate, Slinkfoot," Ashdla scolded the ferret. "Don't plague your brother. He might just eat *you*."

The ferret sniggered at the absurdity, then padded fluidly across the floor to sniff at Ashdla's skirt hem, then lifted her front feet to sit back on her haunches. She squeaked pleadingly for a caress. Ashdla bent to pet her sleek black head, then ran her hands down the ferret's smooth sides and long fluffy tail. The ferret touched her nose to hers, chittered softly, then padded off to her bed in the storeroom for a daytime nap. As the ferret slipped through the half-closed door, Owree hooted a dire insult after her, then fluffed his feathers and blinked happily at Ashdla.

"You aren't any better in your manners," she informed him. "Both of you could improve."

Owree shifted his taloned feet on the rafter, blinked happily once more that she spoke to him, and then settled back to his own nap. One of the shrews squeaked softly its relief at their dire escape, and the family chattered to each other in her pocket as they traded the tale. Ashdla reached into her pocket to tickle again, reassuring them, and then crossed the room to the table. She bent for the small leather bag beneath the table, and then gathered up her herbs, the wand, a small much-worn book of chants, a flask of everholly oil, a glittering stone, and two of Owree's pinfeathers, then left the cabin.

The path leading downward from the porch was steep, but she knew every rock step and quickly reached the wider path that led along the stream. She skipped across the brook on two wide stepstones, and then climbed the opposite slope upward into the forest. At the top, she entered a small meadow ringed by ever-oak and pine. She walked to the middle of the grassy clearing and set down her bag to clear a small circle from the snow, and then laid out the book, the stone, the wand, and her herbs.

The everpine shivered in the slight breeze of the late morning, surrounding her with the sighing, slipping sound of the living forest. Birds called to each other in the distance, and, nearly out of her hearing, the brook water tumbled onward far below. Ash-

dla sat back on her heels and closed her eyes, listening, and felt
the gift stir within her, bringing the patterns. Patterns upon patterns, leaf and bole, feather and fur, the slender wands of grass,
dusky mushrooms in the cool shadows, the movement of life: she
lifted her hands.

"Liin-adani, shari'a shaba'it," she intoned in the old language.
I come now in power for the shari'a, beloved of the Four.

"Li-tiyaad soom, tahad jalid." She lifted her palms to the sky,
and continued her chant in the old words, the ancient words of
power. *I call upon the Four to bless me.*

"Lil-yatin Ashdla sabah tarin, shari'a jan, Hirdaun ba'sar." *I
am Ashdla of the forest gift, and I come to speak for the people, that the
Four might hear.*

She rose to her feet and faced east, toward the distant bay
beyond the coastal mountains, and spread her hands. "I greet the
east," she chanted in the ancient language, "the domain of Soren
and the swift storms of the air." Gravely, she gestured in the air,
forming the graceful whorls of the air dragon's name. "Dragon of
mist and vapor and cloud, stormmaker, the breath of life, welcome."

She turned a quarter-circle toward the lake and raised her
hands again. "I greet the south," she chanted, "the domain of Jain
and the fire of memory. Dragon of the hearth-fire and the rushing
flame, the warmth and passion of life, welcome." Ashdla felt the
forest's patterns began to weave themselves around her, spiderwebs and smoke, ripples on the pond, a trembling of leaves. She
nodded to herself and turned toward the western mountains that
bordered Ingal, raising her hands.

"I greet the west, the domain of Basoul and the healing sea.
Dragon of comfort and wisdom, page of the inner world, renewer
of life, welcome." Again, she sketched the dragon's name on the
air. Finally, she turned north and bowed deeply, then lifted her
hands wide, her voice rising in joy. "I greet the north, the domain
of Amina and the patterns of living. Dragon of the lands, bone
and crystal, ward of the living trees, the beasts and birds, the
stability of life, welcome." The ancient words echoed into the air,

and combined with light and shadow, quiet sound and living thought.

Ashdla spread her hands and smiled happily. "Hirdaun, welcome," she said, slipping into Allemanii. She felt more comfortable in the language she used in her daily life, and Amina had not reproved her for the occasional lapse. "I am yours," she said earnestly, "and I ask wisdom this day. By the light of the shari'a and the old ways, by the light of what is lost and what may be refound, I call on you."

She saw a flicker of shadowed green move through the nearby trees as Amina came to witness her chant, as she always did. The dragon settled on a broad branch in a nearby ever-oak, half-hidden in the green shadows of the branches.

Daughter, crooned a deep and loving voice into her mind, *I greet you.*

I have missed you this winter, Ashdla replied wistfully. *Where do you go when the snow covers the ground?* Amina did not answer, but indicated gently with her chin that Ashdla continue.

Obediently, Ashdla knelt and brought out the stone, oil, and feathers, then arranged them in a star pattern with some blades of withered grass plucked from nearby. She opened her chant-book, although she rarely needed its reference now after long practice, and then sank back on her heels, her hands opened to the suns' light overhead.

"Come to us, your shari'a, your beloveds," she sang in the old tongue. "Rise on the bright morning, Fair Ones, that we might be blessed. Rise!"

The ancient words echoed in the clearing, and for a moment it seemed the trees paused to listen, and the small living things hiding behind leaf and bole turned to look. The suns filled the glade with a shifting green-gold light, moving, moving, and the whisper of the everpine needles rose to encircle her, binding her again into the pattern. She raised her arms and linked her fingers before her face, living pattern of herself, of mind and flesh and power.

What do you ask, daughter? Amina whispered, stirring on the

275

ever-oak branch. The dragon lifted her head and regarded her with depthless emerald eyes.

What do I wish? Ashdla asked herself, thinking carefully. What magic should I work today? She let the question hover in the air before her, never chosen until this moment in the chant. She picked up a small stone, then added a feather, a sprig of grass, and placed them slowly on the snow. "Fire and air," she crooned, "forest and sea, bring us together, one people to be."

You wish again for other shari'a? Amina asked gently. *My daughter, do you believe in such a Finding?*

"Every forest witch has asked for it," Ashdla replied. "You know we have. It is our binding, to bring together the living in the pattern of life. Why have you never answered us?"

How do you know I have not?

Ashdla stared earnestly at the dragon, trying to understand. "There's nothing in the books, Amina. You know how we have waited."

But you have seen.

"Seen what?"

Daughter, you have seen. Amina seemed to fade into deeper shadow, until only the glint of her emerald eyes remained.

"Bring to me other shari'a," Ashdla wished, spreading her hands wide. She cast her plea into the sky and the forest around her. "Gather the shari'a into this forest, and bring us together from our scattering. I, Ashdla, command this." Her words flew away over the trees, as if borne on bird wings or the fluttering of wind-keys, and vanished, without echo.

I cannot promise that—not yet. Amina's voice was firm.

Ashdla tried again, casting her pattern upon pattern. "Gather the shari'a into the forest," she bid, and again her words flew into the distance. Ashdla listened desperately, but all she heard was silence, silence everywhere, from here to the lakes in the south, to the bay in the east, to the inland mountains in the west, and north to Efe itself.

Patience.

For what? But the forest dragon did not answer, and Ashdla

sighed with the familiar edge of her disappointment. For generations, the forest witches in this ravine had called out to other
shari'a, but none had ever answered. A few of the cabin witches
had even traveled to Witchmere and braved the guardians there,
as had her mother in her youth, but had found no one there, no
one anywhere, only Allemanii and more Allemanii. Determinedly,
Ashdla shut her eyes and cast the gift.

"Gather the shari'a—" Her voice echoed hollowly across the
glade and vanished into the earth, probing the caverns, the wind-
ings of tree-roots, the rich loamy soil of the forest, but no one
answered. "Gather the shari'a—" The words lifted above the treetops and flew away on the breeze. "Gather—" Ashdla's voice
broke.

No one had answered. Ashdla took a deep breath and looked
around vaguely. Amina had disappeared from the ever-oak branch.
She wished the dragon had lingered to talk to her, to tell her what
she was doing wrong. Each time Ashdla cast for other shari'a, the
dragon urged patience, but did not promise anything to be patient
for. She shook herself slightly, then slowly packed her bag with
the book and other things, and rose.

On the path back to the cabin, she impulsively detoured onto
the rough stone stairs that led upward to the caverns. She pushed
aside the branches that screened the entrance to the Star Well, and
stepped into coolness.

A wide stone well stood in the center of the circular chamber,
its low walls made of neatly mortared bricks set into the tiled floor
of the chamber. No water stood in the well, and indeed no bottom
had been plumbed by those who had dared to try. Instead, the
well gathered light, not water, in a shifting pattern none had yet
understood.

At Pass and at high autumn, always at noon, the suns' combined light struck down through a circular opening in the chamber
roof, creating a shaft of brilliant light centered on the Well and
the four ghostly figures who stood around it. At that time, the
stones of the chamber seemed to glow with strange power, sending
a tingling through the blood, as if a voice had whispered, barely

heard, or a touch had caressed, barely felt. At other times of the year, the light was more diffused, and but dimly lit the four shades who watched the Well, shifting in subtle patterns across their faces, their clothing, their gesture, that hinted at other meaning— but what meaning, no one knew. Ashdla sat down in the chamber doorway and hugged her knees.

Each shadowy witch was dressed in a cloak and hood; and each faced the stone well, one hand clasping an object particular to her craft, the other held up with upturned palm in silent ges- ture. The figures never moved, never looked up, never had life, only waited in silent immobility, their eyes bent upon the Well. They had no substance, could not be touched. One's hand passed through them as if through smoke, feeling only coolness, a vague prickling to the skin. Ashdla had never dared to touch them, but others had, a very few others.

One of the four figures, the one who stood in the south near the door, was the dimmest of all, scarcely drawn upon the air, nearly faded into shadows. She was young in face, younger than Ashdla herself, and her eyes saw nothing, not even memory. One of the oldest journals in Ashdla's cabin had named her Kaare Jodann, but did not say how that was known. Who had she been, this fire witch, Ashdla wondered, and who had the others been? And why did they leave a part of themselves here?

In the western quadrant of the chamber stood a tall red-haired sea witch, dressed in shadow-blue velvet, Basoul's healing cup in her slender hand. Her expression was stern and marked by recent grief, yet seemed oddly serene, as if a choice had been made, a path chosen. Ashdla had studied her face for hours in the dim light and had noted the resemblance in face to the fire witch. As had others among the cabin witches, she had wondered if they were sisters.

In the north, directly facing the chamber door, stood a forest witch in willow green, dark-haired like Ashdla herself, her lips turned upward in a slight smile, although her other expression was shadowed. She carried an everpine frond in her hand, held gently with reverence. A ferret, enough like Slinkfoot to be her twin, peeped from beneath her skirt hem, and a hawk rode her shoulder, fierce-eyed and proud. Finally, to the east, in the final quarter, stood an air witch in rich golden draperies, her eyes wild and tormented, as if she might burst into action at any moment— to do what? A crystal globe rested on her palm, and some had reported light moving within the globe, although Ashdla had never seen it.

Who had they been? she wondered. And why had they made this Well? The books in Ashdla's cabin had endlessly speculated on the meaning of the shadowed figures, and had faithfully noted the changes in their appearance at each season, and at each config-uration of the suns over the Well. The shifting light also illumi-nated carvings on the walls, moving from line to line in steady advance, touching this curve, then another, patterning Time, and some had tried to pattern those movements of the light with the figures, without success.

Ashdla rose and walked carefully around the circle, then looked into the shadowed face of the forest witch, wondering as all had wondered. Who were you? she asked silently. And why are you still here? Finding no answer, she turned uncertainly to-ward the stone alcove behind the sea witch. It held devices—a crystal wand, an Everlight long since gone dark, a strange box with shifting segments on its sides that could be manipulated, a silver chalice, a perfect glass sphere a handsbreadth wide on a filigree stand, a tangle of golden links and gems that might have once been a necklace. Some of the cabin witches had dared to touch the altar and to handle the objects there, but Ashdla still hesitated, content only to look, as her mother had only looked.

On either side of the shrine with its ancient tools stood two tall narrow cabinets with books long since crumbled to broken leather and disintegrated paper. Although the Well was largely dry, meltwater from Mionn's violent winter storms had sometimes invaded the Well, attacking the books long before Ashdla's time: none had survived the centuries. It was believed that the Star Well dated back to the Disasters, for surely the books and objects in the cavern were that old, and some had argued that these four adepts had brought a purpose here, and had melded their strength to create the Well and its shadowy tableau. But the meaning and the purpose of their willing had long since been lost, lost with the time-shattered books on the shelves, if in fact any of these books had revealed it. Ashdla breathed in the cool and moist air of the Well, and felt comforted for reasons she could not name. In this place was peace, and a long waiting, a waiting for centuries, and here Time held its breath.

She sat down against the stone wall again and watched the play of the suns' light in the Well. Trees had grown on the rock overhead, and their branches varied the light falling into the Well, more so in summer when the branches were fully leafed, shedding their many greens. In certain light, at certain times, an expression on a shadowed face might change, or a figure seem to move slightly, or the well-stones change their cross-hatched shadows, but never much, and likely never at all. But she sat and watched, her chin on her knees, wondering.

After an hour, she felt stiff from the coolness of the cavern, and got to her feet and left the Well. She wandered through the forest for a time, plowing through the drifts, tossing snowballs high into the everpine branches, surprising a pheasant in its brushy burrow. As the Daystar began its descent over the trees, she turned back toward the cabin. There she shared a meal with her animal friends, then watched the sunset over the ravine as the last light of the Daystar disappeared from the sky. A deep peace lay over the ravine, broken only by the soft sound of leaves and the tumbling water of the brook.

She sensed Will's approach on the path before he came into view. When he did, her brother waved at her from across the ravine. "Am I too late?" he called.

Ashdla pointed at the darkening sky. "What do you think?" she called back. "The time for chant is morning, not sunset."

She watched her brother jump nimbly across the rocks in the stream and then climb toward the porch. At the steps, he vaulted over the railing and landed with a thud on the wooden planks, making the shrews in Ashdla's pocket squeak in alarm. "It's only

Will," she murmured, and put her hand in her pocket to reassure them. Will bent to tousle her hair affectionately, then sat down in the other chair. A moment later, Slinkfoot flowed through the cabin door, chittering a welcome. Will lifted her up before his face and chittered back, then draped the ferret around his neck, where she hung blissfully.

"Sorry, Ash," Will said contritely, "but I couldn't get the fishing done until midafternoon. I got here as soon as I could."

"That's all right. The chant didn't work, anyway. I don't know what I do wrong."

"Mother always said it was a matter of practice."

Ashdla shrugged. "Mother never thought she succeeded, either. You know that." She shrugged again, glumly.

"Cheer up," Will bid her. He grinned, handsome and tall and far too noticed by the village girls, not that Will minded, even if she did. "I'm here now." He made that sound as if all cares should be eased, all worries banished.

Ashdla snorted. "I'm vastly comforted. I'm the forest witch here, you know. You're just the twin brother."

"So?" Will retorted aggressively. "I have the gift, too."

"Maybe—if you practiced, which you don't. How was Da today?"

"He's fine." Will stretched out his legs and yawned. "Listen, Ash, you're too hard on yourself. You can't expect every rite to work, whatever you think 'work' means."

"Why not?" Ashdla asked stubbornly.

"Did Amina come?"

"Yes, but she didn't say much beyond the greeting."

"Patience,' again, hmm? Well, if she came to the rite, it worked."

"But Amina *always* comes to the rites," Ashdla protested.

"Then they always work. What's the problem?" He glared at her mildly. "You summoned shari'a, and here I am, a shari'a." He tapped his chest emphatically. "So it worked. Right?"

"I didn't want *you*, Will," she said crossly.

"Thanks a lot, I'm sure." Will made a face at her, and Slinkfoot bared her white teeth beside Will's ear, taking Will's side as she always did, the traitor. "Personally," Will said, "I think all your worrying has put twig-fuzz on your brain."

"Not as much as you have," Ashdla shot back. She crossed her arms and scowled. "It didn't work, I tell you, not the way it should. I don't know why, and I wish I did."

"Then let's go up tomorrow and do it together. Maybe you're mispronouncing some of the words."

"I don't think so," she said doubtfully. "Maybe I'm supposed to say all of it in shari'a, not just the traditional parts. Maybe—"

"You went to the Well again today, didn't you?" he accused. "Why do you do that? It only upsets you."

"No, it doesn't, and it's not that. I want answers, Will. I want to know why the forest won't talk to me, and what the Well means, and why you and I should keep doing the Finding rite, anyway. Mother's gone, and we're probably the last shari'a anywhere. Why say the rite for just you and me? Why keep doing something just because it's tradition?"

"You don't know that we're the last," Will declared, although she knew he shared her uncertainty. "You don't know," Will said more aggressively. "I don't believe it."

"That and a hook might catch a fish," Ashdla shot back snidely, then regretted her retort. It wasn't Will's fault. Aggravating as he could be at times, he was still her twin, the one person who knew her perfectly, as she knew him. Many of the cabin witches had been blessed with a twin, always a brother for some odd reason, never sister. Most of the male twins in the line, despite their gender, had some part of the gift, as Will did. He could sense the patterns, even invoke the voice of the forest, and knew the chants. He was not as diligent in the studies, having a boy's interests elsewhere, but he still shared her secret life, the only one now who did. At least she had Will, she thought gratefully: she couldn't imagine the loneliness without him.

"I'm sorry, Will," she said, shrugging an apology. "I don't mean to fret."

"It's all right." He got up, lofted Slinkfoot high in the air to make her scold, caught her neatly, then set the ferret down on the porch as lightly as thistledown. Slinkfoot chittered excitedly at him to do it again, and so he did, adding a twirl, a few jogs through the air, and a full somersault before landing Slinkfoot a second time. "I'm hungry," Will said. "Feed me."

"You're always hungry."

"So?" Will challenged.

"So come in and eat," she invited, getting to her feet.

They slept curled up in Ashdla's bed, as warm as nested spoons, and near dawn she sensed Will had woken and was listening to the forest. A faint quacking sounded in the distance, quickly gone. "Teal going to the lake," he murmured next to her ear. A splash. "Trout." He yawned.

"Stop showing off, Will."

"Showing off implies a hope to impress."

"That's why I suggested you not waste your time. Ouch!" She elbowed him hard in the ribs, enough to make him gasp, then giggled as he tickled her. "Stop that! Will!" She squirmed away from him, then rose up and slammed him with a pillow, and somehow they were next sitting on the wooden floor by the bed, tangled in the bedcovers. Will looked dazedly around, then at her.

"How'd we get on the floor?" he asked. In the dim gray light coming through the windows, she saw the flash of his grin.

"However we did, I think I bruised something when I landed," she said, fingering her hipbone. "You're getting too rough."

"You started it." He shrugged. "Are you coming home today?"

"Yes. I suppose you'll want to leave early."

"You've supposed right." Will untangled himself from the covers and got up, then reached down his hand, hauling Ashdla to her feet. "I still have chores to do."

"Want some help?" she suggested.

"Sure. That's why I mentioned it. So pick up your feet, Ash."

The walk home to Ellestown took most of the day, but they arrived in the small laketown by midafternoon. As they passed through the last stand of wood near the lake road, Will tucked Slinkfoot inside his tunic, and Ashdla gestured Owree into the branches overhead. She looked up at the mock owl as he settled. "Can you find your way home?" Owree hooted softly. "Good. I'll leave the window open, but not too late. It's winter, you know."

"Come on, Ash," Will said, and Ashdla hurried to catch up with him. Their way home to Michael Toldane's smithy took them through the lakeside marketplace, and she and Will stopped at several stalls, looking but not buying. The proprietors did not mind the looking, so long as one did not linger and block other customers who might buy, and Ashdla listened to the gossip in the marketplace, largely unnoticed as the folk of Ellestown went about their affairs, bustling in the afternoon.

Near a fish-stall, she stopped to look at some fresh bluestripe that her father might like for dinner. It would need a trip home and back again for coins to buy the fish, but they gleamed enticingly in their tray, large and shiny. Will stopped beside her and stared down at the fish, too, sharing her hungry look. *Too expensive,* he sent with some disgust, nodding at the price on the small paper tag by the tray. *Old Grayson cheats everybody.*

It's fresh, Ashdla argued. *And Da loves bluestripe. So do you.*

As do you. If you're going to wheedle, at least be honest about it.

At the next stall, two of their neighbors were talking, their heads close together. "Do you think she really was a witch?" one of the women asked the other. "What do you think happened to her?"

Ashdla paused, exchanged a startled look with Will. She edged closer to the women, although she carefully averted her face. Will drifted off to a bakery stall nearby and looked back. *It's Mistress Sidwell and Sigrid Witt,* he sent, then turned away to inspect the baker's goods. Ashdla edged still closer, trying to hear, as she pretended to inspect more fish.

Mistress Sidwell fluttered her fat hands. "They say that the duke's justiciar killed her, and the duke has put a murder warrant on him."

"For killing a witch?" the other asked incredulously. "What's the harm in that? Witches should be killed, right away, if you ask me, before they can work their evils." Ashdla hunched her shoulders, then fingered one of the fish in the tray before her.

"Are you going to buy or linger all day, Ashdla?" the fish-monger asked impatiently.

"Are you going to be patient, Master Grayson," Ashdla re-torted, "or drive away a good customer? Da likes redfish." The man grunted irritably and moved along to another set of trays, where a young housewife had her money ready. Ashdla turned her head and spotted Will at another stall.

"What if there wasn't proof she was a witch?" Mistress Sid-well argued. "She has a right to a trial, even as a commoner. It's the law."

"Well, then, if there wasn't any proof, why was she ar-rested?" Sigrid countered. "Has to be cause for that."

"So you say," Mistress Sidwell snorted. "Maybe that's why Earl Melfallan was going to defend her, because there wasn't any proof. People can get accused and it not be true." Earl Melfallan? Ashdla wondered. She vaguely remembered a rumor that a new earl had acceded in Yarvannet. But defend whom? She strained her ears to hear.

"Nonsense," Sigrid Witt replied with a snort. "If there isn't any reason, you don't get accused. There must have been some-thing there."

"Just because you're arrested—" her friend began impatiently, but the other woman waved her off.

"Not to matter: it's over now. Brierley Mefell is dead and Earl Melfallan's gone back to his coastland." *Dead.* The word seemed to resonate in Ashdla's ears, over and over, as the woman prattled onward. She felt Will's own shock, then the flash of his sudden grief, also shared. "I do wonder, though, what the duke thought about all that, this witch business coming up again after so long. I can't remember the last time someone found a witch."

Mistress Sidwell shook her head irritably. "Who cares what the duke thinks?" she asked dismissingly. "He's far away and can't bother us. That's Earl Giles's problem and he's welcome to it." She walked around Ashdla and peered short-sightedly at one of the fishmonger's trays. "What's the price of those flatfish, Grayson? I can't read your tiny writing."

"Three coppers a pound," the fishmonger replied. "Fresh today, too."

"That's too much. You're too sharp."

"Price me anywhere else in the market," the man answered indignantly. "You'll see I've set a fair price. Flatfish aren't in season and so——"

"Too sharp," the woman repeated flatly. "And I *will* price you elsewhere, and not come back, I promise you." Mistress Sidwell stomped angrily away, her friend hurrying to keep up. Ashdla eased into the crowd, walking the lanes between the stalls, and then walked onward, her feet dragging.

A witch? Had she truly been a witch, this Brierley Mefell? But dead now, the woman had said. Ashdla felt sad for Mistress Mefell, whoever she was, but told herself to never-mind it more than that. In all the world, at least in the small portion she knew on this lakeshore, Ashdla knew of no other shari'a except Will and herself. To think another shari'a had lived elsewhere in the Allemanii lands, and then had died before Ashdla and Will could meet her—oh, it didn't bear thinking, and she wouldn't.

Will fell into step with her as she left the market, and they walked silently through the several streets to their father's home. They found him in the smithy, stripped to the waist as he hammered, larged-bodied and sweaty with his work. He had the muscles of a blacksmith, and was used to heavy work and the handling of horses. He struck hard at the anvil, setting loose sparks.

"Hullo, Da," she said.

Michael Toldane looked up and blinked, then smiled at them with surprise. A broad-shouldered massive man, he towered over his son and daughter, but his hands were gentle and skilled, his face strong, and now it lit from within as he saw his children. "Ah, here you are again, my girl. I'd been wondering how long you'd stay away this time."

"Not long. Do you want bluestripe for dinner? Master Grayson has a good catch."

"Ah, not tonight, sweetling. How have you been?"

"Fine, Da. And you?"

"Fine, girl," he answered, then grinned. "Everyone's fine throughout the world, I'll hazard, but it's good to have you home again, Ashdla."

"Yes, Da." She leaned against rough wood of the doorjamb "There was talk in the village of a witch in Yarvannet." Michael nodded.

"Yes, sweetling, I heard."

"They said she was killed."

"I heard that, too." Her father brought the hammer down sharply with a new shower of sparks, and then plunged the horseshoe into a nearby barrel of water. He picked up a patch of toweling and rubbed the sweat from his chest and arms, then looked at her, his dark eyes bleak. If anyone knew what such news meant, it was her father. Not a day went by that he didn't think of her mother, not a day passed that he didn't miss her. Two years earlier, at her fervent prompting, he had taken Ashdla downriver by boat to Arlenn. She had walked the streets of the count's town, hand in hand with her father, but had found no one else, no one with witch-blood. She had not asked him to take her again. Until she had traveled down the long river to Mionn's middle bayside town, she had not realized how large the world was. To search it, corner by corner, would be a useless task, and her father had known that, for he had traveled to the bayshore with her mother, too, years ago now, although Ashdla had not learned of that until later.

"Sometimes, Da," Ashdla said in a low voice, "sometimes I

feel so very lonely. Even with you and Will." She glanced an apology at her brother.

Michael stepped forward and rested his large palm on her cheek. "So do I, child. But we have each other, and we have Will, don't we?" He gestured broadly at the town and lake beyond the smithy door. "And we have Ellestown and our pretty lake, and you have your forest house up in the hills, and I think that makes us rich, don't you?"

"Enough for a new dress?" she asked eagerly. She wouldn't think of Brierley Mefell. After this day, she promised herself, she would never think of her again. Will abruptly turned on his heel and walked away.

Michael grunted. "I was speaking in metaphor, my girl. We'll have no real money this winter until I sell the colt the mare has yet to drop, though she's now larger in girth every day."

"Yes, Da. But a new dress then?"

"Maybe. Come along now. Dinner's cooking. Where's Will gone?"

"I don't know, Da."

She shared a pleasant meal with her father, listening to him talk. Will eventually blew back into the house, but her father had kept back some food for him, as he always did. Will made a face at Ashdla when their father's back was turned, wishing at her to jump up and fetch his cup of milk. She grimaced back and stayed put in her chair.

Will glowered at her. "Come on, Ash," he said. "I'm thirsty."

"You're a lazy brute," Ashdla retorted, "and I wish Da would trade you. Anybody would be an improvement."

"Now, girl," their father grumbled, not looking around, "none of that."

"None of that," Will parroted, then held out his empty cup. "Get me some milk, Ashdla. Please?"

"No."

"Please?" Will put on his best pleading face, the one that recently made a few village girls pant heavily, obscenely so: if Will ever got serious about women, he'd break a dozen hearts for sure. Ashdla watched him waggle his eyebrows for a moment, wondering how anyone could think it entrancing, then shook her head firmly.

"No." She folded her arms.

"Give it up, Will," their father advised mildly. "If you want milk, go get it, and bring in the jug while you're doing it." Will rose from the bench and scowled blackly at Ashdla, then stomped outside to the cold box. Michael sat down across the table from Ashdla and dished more stew into her plate, and then into Will's before refilling his own. "Could have gone to get the milk for him, I'm thinking," he commented. "Would have been nice."

Ashdla sniffed. "Once I start *that,* Da, it will never end. If Will wants someone to fetch and carry for him, he can go find a wife. I start doing it, and I'll be fetching for him all day long. You know Will."

"Aye, I do, sweetling, and I'm afraid you're right." Her father chuckled, the sound rumbling up from his chest. "You two have been tussling with each other since the cradle, and I expect it'll last till the end of your lives."

"I expect so, Da." She sighed.

That night, as Ashdla lay in bed in her bedroom, she heard Owree hooting far up the forested slope behind their house, and slipped from beneath the covers to go outside. The air was frosty chill, the snow white shadows beneath the stars, and she stood on the porch for several minutes, looking out at the lake. After taking a warm cloak from the pegs near the door and stuffing her bare feet into some boots, she walked out of the house to the backyard and into the forest behind it. The trees were not as thick here, and the animals had long since fled from the noise of the town, but the forest silence in winter still held, broken only by the creaking of her boots through the thin drifts of snow and the faint shirring of the night wind through everpine needles. A hundred yards into the forest she stopped and breathed in the cold air.

What troubles you, daughter? said a familiar voice into her mind. She turned her head and looked up. Half-hidden by night shadow, the forest dragon regarded her from a long branch overhead.

"They killed a witch," she said sadly. "I heard that in the town today. Was she the only other one, Amina? Are we the last?"

Patience, Ashdla. Haven't I counseled patience?

"But patience for what?" Ashdla said angrily. "You say to wait and be patient, and not to make Da take me to the other towns. I can agree about Da—I know it hurts him to look when all he wants is Mother. But what am I waiting *for?*

Child—

Ashdla heard a creaking in the snow several yards behind her, then the crackle of brush as Will pushed into sight. He was dressed only in tunic and breeches, too thin for the cold night. Shivering violently, Will rubbed his arms vigorously in a vain attempt for warmth as he walked up to join Ashdla. He lifted his eyes to the dragon above their heads.

"Was she shari'a?" he demanded. "And, no, I'm not patient at all, and I don't want to be patient." Amina's eyes glinted in the shadows of the branch. "Answer us, Amina!" Will shouted in anguish. "*Was she shari'a?*"

Yes. Will bent forward and groaned, then shied away as Ashdla reached for him. *But she is not dead,* Amina added softly. Ashdla's hands stopped short in midair, and their two heads swiveled as one toward the dragon above them. Amina smiled benignly at them both. *Patience,* her voice whispered. *There are other shari'a in the Allemanii lands, my children, and we Four will bring them to the Well. Be patient.* The shadows on the branch shifted like swirling smoke, and Amina was gone.

Ashdla and Will looked at each other, eyes wide. Her brother suddenly shuddered convulsively from neck to boots and back up again. "Ocean, I'm freezing," he swore, clutching hard at his elbows.

"Serves you right, stupid, coming out without a cloak." Ashdla threw the edge of her cloak over his shoulders and snugged it tight, then felt her brother's arms come around her. He laughed softly in her ear as he hugged her, and she laughed with him as she hugged him back. Will danced her around in an ecstatic circle as Amina's news sang through them, lilting, amazing, hardly to be believed; then Will went through such a convulsive cycle of new shudders that it set his teeth to rattling.

"The n-next question is 'w-when?'" he stuttered eagerly.

"After all this time to get the patience question answered?" Ashdla retorted. "I don't think so. It's enough to know the Finding is nearly here. Come on, Will. You'll catch your death." Ashdla tugged her brother into motion, and together they stumbled back through the snow to the warmth of the house.

erek Lanvalle rode brazenly into Carandon, confident that none of the Airlie folk would recognize him. His face was not known here, and was rarely seen even in Darhel where Rowena's servants might have met a duke's secret man. Lean-limbed, dark-haired, and dressed in forester green, Derek affably greeted the guard at the city gate, claimed a visit to a sister recently married to a Carandon soldier, and stopped to chat.

He smiled, showing his teeth, and gawked in pretended admiration for Rowena's city and the general good order of her people. He spoke overmuch, exclaiming at his sister's good fortune to live in Carandon and at the wonders of Airlie altogether, and quickly bored the guard nearly beyond bearing. Finally he gave a final gay jest, handed another pleasant smile, and then, to amuse himself, added a heart-stopping pause that he might stop to talk still more, but rode through the gates into Carandon.

Behind him, the guard muttered about enduring such a fool, and Derek smiled behind his moustaches.

He rode slowly through the narrow streets, and saw a soldier taking leave of his wife, then a carter loading wheat into a wagon by an open storage house door. He nodded at a pretty maidservant abroad on an errand, and watched a farmer's stout wife with a basket of eggs on her arm berating a market standman, there for barter and not leaving until she got it. It was a plainday morning like any other, not too cold for late winter, and the suns were shining. It was a day pleasant enough in this pleasant city of white stone and smiling people.

Darhel had seemed such a happy place in his boyhood under Duke Selwyn's rule. His father had served Duke Selwyn for nearly twenty years as castellan of Darhel Castle, and his rank and a knighthood might have passed to Derek's older brother had Daughter Sea not killed both with plague, as that winter's plague had killed many, including Duke Selwyn's two older sons. In memory of his faithful castellan, Duke Selwyn had arranged that Derek be trained as a gentleman knight, to become in time a favored courtier as skilled in the arts of courtly graces as in the sword, and perhaps one day even become castellan in his own right.

Sadly, Selwyn's death had interrupted that pleasant future. Duke Tejar had chosen his principal men differently, and at first Derek had been sent into Briding as a mere spy, to bring the duke tidbits and sniff out intentions. To their mutual surprise, Derek had proven himself a remarkable spy, able to blend into any group of folk and to persuade trusted servants to reveal news their masters would be horrified to overhear. Derek had discovered Count Parlie's secret alliance with Yarvannet, a matter not entirely proven nor fully accepted by the duke when he had told it. He had then trolled through Lim, and had learned that Count Toral's only son and heir often drank himself into a stupor, and would surely kill himself by the way he drunkenly rode his horses. He met Toral's young daughter, a girl barely ten years of age but much younger still in her understanding, dim-eyed, silly, and vain. Last year he had encouraged Toral's marcher lord in his dislike of his count, then slyly interfered in an important trade contract with Mionn. His reports to the duke, always delivered in person and late at night, were spare and to the point, but always useful. And so, over the course of eight years, Derek had become Tejar's most valued spy.

Sometimes he thought wistfully of the opportunity lost as knight, with its gentler life at court, its dignities and interests, and with perhaps more honor than a spy's life. Not that he disliked being a spy, he reminded himself, his dark eyes flicking over the streets and its crowd. Not at all. Any task could be done diligently and with great skill, and Derek Lanvalle was very good at his trade.

Ahead, visible over the rooftops of the gate quarter, he saw the white towers of Carandon Castle, and made his leisurely way through the streets toward it. He arrived at a kitchen gate and dismounted, then told a kitchen boy to water his horse and fetch the understeward, Cullen by name. The boy put his chin in the air, not to be ordered about by a road-grimed stranger, but a copper penny sent him briskly on the errand.

The spy sat down on a bench under a courtyard tree and stretched his legs, stiff from riding all night and half the morning. He had hunted in two of Airlie's minor towns to the north, listening at eaves and doorsills for useful news, but had heard nothing as yet. Perhaps here in Rowena's main town, Ocean might bless him with a whisper, a sly murmur, a slight track to follow. Did the witch hide in Airlie, as Tejar suspected? Did Earl Melfallan plot treachery with his aunt, the regent of Airlie? Were the rumors of Rowena's permanent injury true? The duke wished earnestly to know what now hatched in Airlie, enough to send his chief spy on the errand.

My task is to serve, he reminded himself, and stretched long legs encased in boot leather, then settled his sword more comfortably at his side. He had wondered greatly at the rumors he'd heard about Melfallan's witch. Darhel had been buzzing with wild stories, and every last High Lord had departed indignantly for home, Count Toral among them, after Tejar had sent the High Lords to hunt the witch like common game wardens flushing a pheasant. The pheasant had not been found, if indeed she were even there to be found, and tempers were hasty among the High Lords.

But a witch? Derek snorted to himself. What nonsense. Likely this witch was some dull-witted girl caught up in lords' politics, an innocent tool for Earl Melfallan to attack the duke. And likely dead at Gammel Hagan's hand, as the rumors had it, although Darhel still buzzed and hummed with its rumors. A devious man, this new earl of Yarvannet, Derek thought with disapproval, to use a commoner girl that way for his own ends, and likely Melfallan cared little that he'd killed the girl through the using. Melfallan showed no more loyalty to his local lords, it seemed, with Lord Landreth of Farlost falsely accused of rape to hide Melfallan's true plans, or so the duke had explained. Tejar had spoken much of that matter, too, impressing upon Derek the importance of the treacheries now brewing against him.

"Find out what Rowena's plans are," Tejar had told him. "Listen for what she knows about Earl Melfallan. And find Melfallan's witch."

"But surely the witch is dead, sire."

"Perhaps. If she's alive, she is hiding in Airlie. Find her for me, Derek, and I'll reward you handsomely." Derek stirred uncomfortably on his bench, troubled by the insult that his good service came only upon offer of a bribe. The duke had not thought it an insult, of course, but insult it had been all the same.

The duke had shown him a letter from Lady Joanna, the wife of Melfallan's border lord. The lady spoke most disparagingly of her liege, citing his distracted air and discourtesy to his lords, his estrangement from his wife's bed, his moody retreats to his tower each morning. Of active plots against the duke, she had as yet discovered nothing, but vowed alertness.

"How did you trap her?" Derek had asked curiously.

"I didn't have to," the duke replied, refolding the letter. "She approached me a few years ago, not giving her reasons, nor have I asked. So far she's sent little more than gossip and her active dislike of Earl Audric, which she now extends to the grandson." The duke slipped the letter into a drawer of his desk. "She's daughter to one of Count Sadon's knights; perhaps that's all the reason she needed."

"Does her husband know?"

Tejar had shrugged his indifference. "Does it matter? Through her treachery I own him as well. Let us hope that Garth's service will be more deft than Heider's, when it comes." The duke scowled fiercely, reminded of Heider's failure.

Early in Rowena's regency, Lord Heider, her northern marcher lord, had secretly approached Tejar, unhappy with her woman's rule and all too conscious that his marcher lands would be the first invaded from Ingal. Duke Tejar had encouraged the contact, flattering the older Airlie lord, as he encouraged all such contacts. In recent years, Heider had become more reluctant to court the duke against his countess, but no matter: in the passion of his early complaints against Rowena, Heider had written several foolish letters, letters that would get him disenfeoffed and then hanged, for he had intimated the murder of his liege. Three years before, Tejar said, he had sent a messenger to Arlesby to speak into Heider's private ear, quoting certain excerpts from those letters, then had delivered Tejar's firm threat. A brief note might come in the future, seven innocuous words that bore a hidden order, and Heider would obey that order or pay with his life.

Heider had agreed, of course. What else could he do? Derek shrugged slightly. He knew it was a fact of Allemanii politics that the High Lords often plotted against each other's lives, and that his duke must sometimes counter such threat by striking first. Melfallan's intent on treachery was clear, the duke had told him, and his aunt had begun the disloyalty first, forcing Tejar's countermove in Arlesby. To rule well, a High Lord must be ruthless, or all might be lost. Yes, Derek knew all that, but sometimes he wished for the simplicity of a knight's virtues that ignored such realities. He sighed.

After ten minutes, a sandy-haired man with a scraggly beard appeared in the doorway to the kitchens. He was ill-dressed in a poorly fitted blue tunic and hose, with stains from his meal on both, and too thin for his height. His pale eyes darted around the courtyard and fixed on Derek: he skittered nervously across the pavestones, reluctance and suspicion in every line of his body.

"You asked for me?" he quavered. "Who are you?"

Derek took a sigil from his tunic pocket and showed it to Cullen, half-concealing it by the curve of his hand. "My name is Lanvalle. The duke requests your continued assistance, Master Cullen."

Cullen swallowed hard and blinked, then looked everywhere but at Derek. "So you say," he quavered, and tried to look bold, a paltry attempt. "How do I know it's true?"

Derek pocketed the sigil and stared at him with contempt. This understeward had reported Rowena's affairs to the duke for two years, and had been paid well for his information, such as it was. His respect for the duke's token needed improvement. "Shall I report to the duke that you refused assistance?" he asked coldly.

Cullen's chin jerked. "I have a right to be certain—"

"You saw the sigil. What more certainty do you need? Do you refuse?"

Cullen grimaced. "No." He suddenly looked like a shrew trapped in a mock owl's shadow. Derek repressed a grimace. If this was Duke Tejar's principal spy in Carandon, the duke needed new spies—if only he could find them. Rowena's people were remarkably loyal to her, and Darhel's spymaster had sorted and sifted for months before trapping Cullen. He would have to do.

"Very well," Derek said. "I'm looking for news of Melfallan's witch—"

"I don't know anything about that."

"Shut up." He gestured Cullen to sit down on the bench, then waited until the understeward complied. "Don't look nervous, you fool. You'll attract attention." They both watched a serving-maid carry linens across the cobblestones, then vanish into the kitchens. A groom crossed the courtyard next, a polished bridle in his hand.

"And this doesn't?" Cullen demanded in a near-whisper. "Sitting with you on the bench for all to see?"

"Nobody knows who I am. I'm your brother-in-law or friend or cousin or Ocean cares what, come to visit you in Airlie. Relax." He waited as Cullen made an effort. "What of the countess's injury? Does she recover?"

"Slowly. She's alive, although she keeps to her bedroom and doesn't go out, not yet. The folk are happy she's alive." Cullen's voice had a curious neutrality about the health of his countess, and Derek wondered why. Treachery leached the soul as it progressed, but always began in an impulse toward it. He eyed the thin steward seated beside him, and wondered what motive lay behind those pale eyes. Jealousy? A love of gold? Or simple hatred for everything?

"Which servants are closest to the countess?" Derek asked.

"I don't know," Cullen said, his chin in the air again. "Am I important enough to know her affairs?"

Derek rose abruptly, so menacing in the violence of his movement that Cullen cringed. "I will inform the duke," Derek said coldly, "that you refused assistance."

"All right, all right." Cullen hastily waved him back to his seat, his eyes darting around the courtyard in panic. Derek hesitated, a finger's length from stalking away from this idiot, then made himself sit down again. "She has her counselors, of course," Cullen babbled, "and the Airlie lords—"

"I said servants," Derek interrupted. "Servants know everything, except for you, it seems, and I want more than talk about Airlie's self-important lordlings. Who?"

"Uh, servants? Why do you—" Derek shifted warningly on the bench. "Well," Cullen said hastily, "her favorite liegemen are Stefan Quinby and Roger Carlisle. "They're always around her. Roger is our castellan's middle son and leads one of the castle troops. They say he'll be made a knight next summer."

"Tell me about Stefan."

"He's a younger man, commoner-born, son of a castle steward. Married to a pretty wife, two children already, but you should see his wife—"

"Not that," Derek growled. "What have they been doing lately?"

Cullen shifted uncomfortably on the bench. "Uh, three weeks ago Stefan disappeared, then Roger went off somewhere for a few days." Cullen spoke reluctantly, with many resentful side glances. "I don't know where they went."

"Find out where."

"How can I do that? Ocean knows they don't tell *me* their affairs. I heard a cook talking to a soldier about the gossip, that's all, and nobody knows. Stefan just disappeared. Both of them do that sometimes when they run an errand for the countess. Nobody wonders about it."

Derek frowned, then let it go for now. "What else do you know?" he demanded.

In fits and starts, Cullen revealed his other gossip, nothing of any obvious importance, but a small detail might become important once a spy understood its setting. Lord Chaim had sent his prize bull to Carandon for a rich array of stud fees, a surprise given how Chaim protected his bloodlines to raise his prices. Derek considered that a moment, but saw nothing. Rowena's principal rivermaster had recently worn an expensive silver chain all had admired, apparently a gift from the countess. Derek tightened his lips: nothing. Then: before Lord Heider's attack, Rowena had waited for Melfallan at her northern hunting lodge. He'd ridden in with only Stefan, and Cullen didn't know where he'd gone by himself.

"Alone? Where was his guard?"

"He wasn't alone," Cullen said sullenly. "He had Stefan with him."

"I heard that. Where were his soldiers?"

Cullen didn't know. What did Melfallan and the countess discuss at the lodge? Cullen didn't know. They were closeted together, but Cullen wasn't there. Why had Melfallan slipped aboard his ship and dodged the duke's council? Cullen didn't know.

Ocean save me, Derek thought, but moved on.

He asked about young Count Axel, now ten years old, and heard tales of an ordinary boy with high spirits and open adoration for his mother. Nothing. He asked about Rowena's minor lords, but Cullen knew little about them, whatever his earlier boasting: his duties rarely took him near the other gentlefolk. Cullen apparently gathered his information from others' talk in the kitchens and hallways, often scrambled in the retelling, and only rarely took the initiative to listen at corners. He was a cautious man, he confided to Derek.

There are other descriptions, Derek thought sourly. No wonder the duke had gained so little for his money.

Indeed, the highest of Cullen's contacts were apparently this Stefan and Roger, Rowena's favored liegemen, men who apparently never noticed a mere understeward like Cullen, a fact Cullen greatly resented, among other things. "Oh, they're too high and mighty to notice me," Cullen complained in a nasal whine. "And Stefan born of a kitchen servant, too, for all his airs. Him and his fancy clothes and his pretty wife, and his secrets for the countess. I hate them both." Cullen glowered and put out his lower lip, and Derek was again reminded of a rodent.

He ignored the whine and sifted what Cullen had said, and fixed on two facts. Earl Melfallan had arrived at the lodge without retainers, accompanied only by Stefan. Why? Recently Stefan had disappeared, then Roger, but Roger had returned. Why? Where had they gone? Were the two facts connected? He bit his lip reflectively, then decided this Roger Carlisle should be watched. Derek took a gold coin from the pouch at his waist. "Where's the nearest inn?"

"Uh, the Hawk and Shuttle, four streets east."

"I'll stay there. Watch Roger for me, and if he disappears again, send word to me immediately."

"Roger?" Cullen asked, confused.

"Yes, Roger. Watch him for me." He held out the coin. Cullen glanced quickly around the small courtyard, now temporarily deserted, then took the coin and brightened, as much as his sallow pinched face could manage a happy emotion.

"Do not fail me," Derek warned. The man bobbed his head jerkily, then scuttled off through the doorway, like a rat down his hole.

Derek had the boy bring his horse to him for another bright penny, and rode out of the castle courtyard. Perhaps the inn's taproom might be more productive with its soldiers' and tradesmen's gossip, though Cullen's two facts had promise. If the inn had good quality, perhaps even a nobleman and his servants might stay there rather than take quarters in the castle. Perhaps. Rowena was in her seclusion, healing from her wound: his lordly pickings promised to be few. And men talked more when dissatisfied, and Rowena's folk were not unhappy with her. It was easier to be a spy in Lim, where few were happy.

Still, he had the promise of a decent meal and a soft bed for the night, perhaps even several nights, until Roger's errand took him away again. If Roger had a further errand, if Cullen's paltry news led to anything at all.

Well away, Derek thought, time would tell.

Three days later, Derek and Cullen rode through Carandon's front gate, careful to follow Roger's wagon at a distance. The spate of bad weather had again broken, bringing bright sunshine and the steady drip-drip of melting snow from every eave. Water ran in the streets, inviting small boys to splash small girls and making the girls squeal, and the air was warmer. In the bright morning of Carandon's market-day, the road was newly busy with carter traffic as the local commonfolk bustled into Rowena's capital. Derek passed wagons heavily laden with farm stores for the market, small flocks of sheep tended by herder boys, and women and girls dressed in their brightest colors, faces flushed with excitement at the first real promise of the coming spring. Derek nodded to a forester who passed by on a tall reddish horse and received an affable smile, a touch of the fingers to the cap, then nodded to a farmer who beamed at Derek and Cullen for no reason at all.

Ocean save me, he thought, everyone is too *pleasant*.

In Lim, the commonfolk hurried on their way, shoulders hunched against the cold wind off the strait, as gloomy in face and walk as the harsh moors and rocklands of their sullen count's coast. Their feet dragged through the frequent mud, and even the animals moved more slowly, heads down, feet plodding. There a man might sit in an inn and listen to gossip, turning his ears to the right and then to the left, and gather useful information hour on hour. Here one nodded back to bright smiles and cheerful greetings and learned nothing at all.

Why Roger had loaded a wagon with supplies, Cullen didn't know. Why Roger took this road toward the upper Airlie valleys, Cullen could merely shrug. That Roger had loaded a wagon and drove that wagon on this road ahead of them, Derek could see for himself. Why? Where was Roger taking the supplies? An odd errand, this mere carter's task, for one of Rowena's most trusted liegemen. And Roger had not dressed as a castle servant, but as a common carter in brown tunic, baggy breeches, and heavy boots. Even more odd.

Derek's spirits lifted. Where are you going, Roger, I wonder, I wonder? And why? What were Rowena and Earl Melfallan plotting now? It might be soldiers hidden in the heights. When Duke Lionel had invaded Airlie, the Airlie count had struck back from the mountains. The attack had not worked, but the tactic had its value. Did Rowena again hide soldiers in her upper valleys, preparing a treacherous attack on the duke? Or did she hide a witch?

Where are you going, Roger?

He smiled, and a passing farmer smiled broadly in response. A wave from the farmer's fat wife, another obligatory nod by Derek in response. A spy had to fit in smoothly, he reminded himself, lest he be remarked as strange, and in Airlie that meant—

Nod.

Nod.

Don't the Airlie people ever frown about anything? he wondered.

Nod.

Ocean's breath, he thought, this was a dreary place for a spy.

Except to twit the gate guard, he hadn't acted this pleasantly in months, and then only to impress that innkeeper's daughter in a Lim seatown, quite successfully, he remembered, and to a very satisfactory conclusion. He smiled to himself, remembering her red-gold hair, infectious giggle, and sweet, sweet arms. She hadn't a brain in her head, but no matter. No information, either: her father's small inn catered only to the commonfolk, never the gentry who might have secrets about Count Toral, but no matter. No matter, no matter.

Nod. Derek added a genial wave.

Cullen rode beside him on a dun mare, as ungainly on a horse as he was on his own two legs, shoulders hunched, nose wrinkled in only apparent thought. Alarmed that Roger might recognize him, Cullen had wrapped himself in an enormous cloak and hat, then devised some kind of wig from sheep's wool and added an amazing moustache that kept coming unglued at its corners. Well, perhaps folk would think Cullen always looked odd. Actually, he did: truth was an able tool in a spy's business, but Derek already regretted that he had brought Cullen along. The steward had come twice to Derek's inn, each time with tidbits, and then the sudden news of a wagon being loaded by Roger's orders. Cullen himself, greatly daring, had stolen to the wall of the stable and listened, but had heard nothing specific about Roger's reasons.

Well, we shall see. Derek narrowed his eyes at the cart ahead of them.

The road climbed steadily upward toward the distant hills and the tall peaks beyond. The farm traffic dwindled and ceased: apparently few people farmed these upper hills, though they seemed fertile enough. The grass was dry hay in late winter, but spring must bring vast green to these hills. As the road traffic thinned, he and Cullen became conspicuous as followers, and Derek slowed his horse and once stopped altogether until Roger drove farther ahead. The road began to wind upward through the hills, concealing itself for a time behind a rise of ground and then coming in view as each crest was breached.

The Daystar's light sparkled on a lingering rime of frost on the grasses and everpine, now more frequent as the road climbed toward the mountains. The distant peaks blazed in the sun's light, heavily covered with snow and half-concealed by the angry clouds of another storm. Here in the upper Airlie hills, the land seemed utterly deserted, without a single plume of smoke from a chimney, nor any distant tumble of sheep in a meadow, nor the winding curves of a narrow track branching away to a nearby farm or hamlet. Derek heard the sound of distant bird calls, and saw the occasional spoor of animals frozen into the mud of the road, but of farmer or forester, there seemed little trace except the new-made ruts of Roger's wagon in the half-frozen mud of the road. He leaned forward in his saddle and studied the ground, and finally found the faint traces of an earlier wagon track, appearing and disappearing in the roadbed. Perhaps Roger's track from the earlier trip, he judged, given the infrequent travel on this road: Rowena's liegeman seemed to be going to the same place.

Why? he asked the open air, and again examined the empty hills.

"What is it?" Cullen asked nervously.

"Nothing," Derek growled. "Relax."

At the next crest, Derek sighted the small shape of Roger's wagon just breasting the next hill. When he and Cullen crested that same hill, Derek looked ahead again for Roger's wagon. It wasn't there.

Derek reined his horse to a stop and frowned at the empty road. Stands of everpine bunched along that mile of road ahead, clinging to the bottom of the small valley like a shadow, then spreading upward on the opposite slope, the road visible as a ribbon winding upward through the trees. Unless Roger had galloped his cart horse over the next hill, not likely, he should be in view. He was not.

"Where did he go?" Cullen quavered as he pushed his hat up from his eyes.

Derek loosened his sword in its scabbard and shifted in his saddle, then looked up at the Daystar, now two points past zenith. They had hours of daylight left, with the Companion's short twilight to follow afterward. No reason to pull aside to camp, not yet. "He's noticed us. What's the next town on this road?"

"There aren't any towns. Nobody much lives up here, just a few farms, some old ruins, perhaps a forester station."

"Then where does this road lead to?" Derek asked patiently. Menacing Cullen only earned Derek a cringe and a stammer, as

Derek had proved all too often these last four days. What a waste of a man, this Cullen, he thought with contempt. "The road must go somewhere."

"Up into the mountains," Cullen said, gesturing vaguely at the peaks ahead. Derek glared at him. "It goes over the mountains to Mionn," Cullen added hastily, and gulped, twitching horribly. Well, maybe milder menacing had effect, Derek decided. Perhaps his prior error had been only in degree.

"Then you and I are two travelers going to Mionn. You're my cousin—"

"Nobody goes over the pass in winter," Cullen cried in alarm. "The snow would kill us and—"

"Shut up and listen. When we reach Roger, we tell him that you are my cousin and we are riding to Mionn, there being no next town here in Airlie. Are we clear now?"

"Oh!" Light dawned at last, though it be already full day. "But then what?" Cullen asked in a hushed voice, his eyes flicking worriedly from Derek to the forest ahead. "What if he has a sword? What if he's waiting for us, to jump out and—"

"Hells, man—" Derek bit back a blistering oath. "Of *course* he has a sword. So do you, and so do I. So what? And of course he's waiting for us. He wants to know who we are. We are two cousins—"

"—on the way to Mionn." Cullen brightened. "He'll think we're only travelers like him! A good plan, Lanvalle!" Cullen beamed at him with approval.

"Ocean be praised, he understands," Derek growled. He nudged his horse with his heels. "Are you sure Roger won't recognize you?"

"Of course not," Cullen sniffed. "I'm just an understeward in the kitchens. He hardly ever looks at me, and I'm disguised." Cullen seemed to take a pitiful pride in his awkward disguise. Derek hesitated and thought to leave the man waiting here, but two swords over one, should threat be necessary, were an advantage. I shouldn't, he told himself, looking at Cullen, then shrugged.

"Fine, then," he said. "Just do what I do, Cullen, and don't *say* anything." They rode forward, descending the hill into the valley.

Roger had pulled off the road halfway up the opposite slope and waited, hunched on his wagon seat. Blond and handsome, well muscled beneath his drab clothing, and very alert, Roger eyed Derek and Cullen suspiciously as they rode into view. Derek reined his horse to a halt and smiled affably, then touched his hand to his forehead. "Good day, master! A lonely road for travelers in this season!"

"Well met, traveler," Roger replied, his blue eyes flicking over them both, resting a moment on Cullen, then studying Derek more closely. "Where are you bound?"

"Mionn," Derek replied. "I'm an armorer by trade, and I'm taking my cousin with me to Skelleford."

Cullen bobbed his head. "We're visiting my mother, there in Mionn," he blurted in a high voice. "My mother is his aunt, you see, and she, uh, lives in—" Cullen's voice faded as Roger's eyes flicked back to him and hardened.

"Mother?" Roger demanded. "I know as a fact, Cullen, that your mother died six winters ago. What game is this?" Roger's hand fell to his sword hilt. "Who is this man with you, and why are you following me?"

"Travelers," Derek said hurriedly and tried to hide his fury at Cullen's blunder, but knew instantly he had failed. Roger rose to his feet on the wagon seat and drew his sword, then stood ready on the seat with a swordsman's skilled balance.

Cullen had not described Roger's skills with a sword, but Roger's practiced stance gave Derek all the warning he needed. A skilled swordsman himself, Derek instantly recognized an equal, and would not risk a battle today.

"Back off," Roger ordered.

"I'm only a traveler," Derek said and backed his horse a step, then dropped his own hand to his sword hilt in warning. "Put away your sword, Roger. We're not threatening you."

"You know my name?" Roger demanded.

"Is there point to pretending I don't? I'm not here to attack, only to follow."

"You're not following me anywhere." Roger raised his sword to guard.

Derek shrugged. "Of course not. I am graced with an under-steward named Cullen." He turned his head. "You idiot."

Cullen handed him a sullen glance and fiddled with his belt knife, then looked away sulkily at the nearby trees.

"Who *are* you?" Roger demanded. "And why is Cullen with you?"

"Where are you going?" Derek shot back boldly, given that his deft plan was now fallen into shambles. This kind of adventure never happened in Lim—but then Cullen was likely unique to Airlie, or maybe not. The blunder was Derek's in bringing him along.

"I won't say," Roger said defiantly.

"Then I won't say, either." Derek touched his hat mockingly. "And a good day to you, Roger." He reined his horse around and prepared to ride down the hill. "Come along, Cullen."

Roger snorted. "Yes, go along, Cullen," he said. "And you'll have questions to answer when I return to Carandon! And I can guess what those answers will be, you traitor!"

Derek caught a blur of motion from the corner of his eye and wheeled his horse around. "No, Cullen!" he cried as he saw Cullen pull his belt knife from its scabbard.

It was a coward's maneuver, a desperate gamble by a weakling who had hated secretly and well—and struck luckier than the rest of Cullen's sorry life. Roger tried to dodge the throw, but the sharp edge of Cullen's blade sliced deep into the side of his throat as it whipped by, exploding bright arterial blood from his neck. With a strangled cry, Roger dropped his sword to clutch at his throat. He stared at Cullen in disbelief, then in horror as his blood became a torrent spilling over his hands onto his breast, splashing on the wagon seat and the haunches of his cart horse. Roger turned desperate eyes to Derek.

"Don't hurt her," he croaked from his ravaged throat. "Please. Don't tell the d—"

But then Roger's face slackened and his fingers slipped their grip on his throat. He sagged to one knee, fighting hard not to die, then crumpled slowly downward, a slow terrible motion of weakened legs and loosened flesh.

Derek sat his horse, stunned, as Roger's blood continued to pour onto the ground, a bright crimson stream in the sunlight of the morning, pooling to glisten in the frozen mud. The bright spurting jet dwindled, became a quiet river down the wooden side of the wagon, then trickled to nothing. Beside him, Cullen sat sucking his lip as they watched, then gave a soft obscene giggle.

Convulsively, Derek drew his sword and heeled his horse around, but Cullen reined his horse quickly away, dancing out of range. He flashed a sly grin. "Stupid, am I?" he taunted. "He'll ask me no questions now. No, he won't."

"You didn't have to kill him, you fool!"

"Didn't I?" Cullen laughed, a high hysterical sound. "The countess will need a new favored liegeman, won't she? Maybe she'll choose me. And Roger won't be prancing in front of us, thinking we're mud, not anymore." He gloated at Roger's limp body on the wagon seat. "Roger's the mud now, isn't he? Isn't he, isn't he?" Cullen giggled again, then bared his yellowed teeth.

Derek spurred his horse toward him, sword raised, but Cullen quickly plucked another dagger from inside his tunic and threw it with a practiced flick of his hand. Not waiting to see how it struck, Cullen whirled his horse and galloped away down the hill, racing as if the Daughter's very Hells were after him.

May they be, Derek cursed him silently, clutching at the knife-blade that had buried itself deep into his thigh. With a strangled moan he barely recognized as his, he pulled the knife from his leg and threw it away, but no bright spurting followed. Unlike Roger, he might survive this day. He groaned softly with the agony of the pain, then managed to dismount his horse and tore strips from his undershirt to bind the wound. The cloth quickly stained with his blood.

The sound of galloping hooves faded quickly in the crisp autumn air, followed by glimpses of Cullen's wild ride until he crested the opposite hill and vanished, blessedly taking away all sound and sight of him. The wind stirred softly in the everpine needles, and a quiet murmur of a brook was audible nearby. Derek heard a bird's distant cry near the top of the hill, then another bird far to the left. Roger's cart horse stamped its hoof nervously, then turned its head around, its nostrils widening in alarm at the smell of the blood. It nickered and moved more convulsively, preparing to bolt. Limping hastily forward, Derek caught its halter, then tied its lead-rein to a nearby branch. He stroked the cart horse's face for a few moments, calming it, then looked past it at Roger's crumpled body on the wagon seat, the blond hair shining in the suns' light.

Was any day a good day to die? he thought with regret. I didn't mean your death, Roger. I didn't plan for this.

During his years in Lim, Derek had killed four men, men who came to accost him on the roads or in a dark alley, as bandit or Toral's counterspy or the duke's other enemy, an enemy who had made himself Derek's enemy by drawing sword on him. It was their choice to do so, ending in fatal mistake, but the coin could have turned its face and stolen Derek's life instead. A swordsman understood such odds, and bargained his life against them in every duel, asking only a fair fight.

I misjudged Cullen—as did you, Roger. You should have watched him, not me. We grow too easy in our assumptions, we swordsmen, that the last fight will be fair. Derek took a deep breath and closed his eyes, then blew out the breath, misting the cold air. He shifted his weight to ease the throbbing in his leg, then leaned wearily against Roger's horse.

If he had the Daughter's power, he would take back this useless death, but he did not. And, while he still breathed, Derek Lanvalle still had his duty to his duke, even for a duke who did not understand Derek's reasons for that duty, who thought them different, more mercenary, his spy a bought man. He raised his head and looked up the road leading into the hills.

Where were you going, Roger? Even after this, I must know.

~ 15 ~

"Now, now, now. Remember your station, girl!"

Brierley watched as Megan chattered to her doll on her bed, something about Lady Cornelia and an awkward maid, then glanced at Stefan across the cabin table.

"Who's Lady Cornelia?" she asked curiously, for she'd caught that Stefan knew whomever Megan was copying today.

"Lord Dail's wife." Stefan pretended a shudder. "A horrible woman, simply horrible, and the terror of servants in Darhel. Her voice can bend metal."

"Truly?" Brierley said, amused by the image. Perhaps the Allemanii sometimes had their own brand of witchery, she thought, to amazing effect. She imagined a long table laid for a noble dinner, every fork and spoon bent double by Lady Cornelia's supervision. Yes, indeed. And all the lords and ladies would march in and see— She covered her mouth, and what came out was more a snort than a laugh.

"What?" Stefan grinned. "Megan's caught her perfectly. How does she do that, anyway? I doubt Megan has ever actually heard her voice. Lady Cornelia *never* goes near the kitchens."

Brierley took a deep breath, got control of herself, and firmly put spoons, bent or otherwise, out of mind. "She must have a memory of someone who has," she said. "She gathers memories, Stefan—that's her gift as fire witch."

Stefan looked bemused, but not overly skeptical. Brierley had tried several times to explain Megan's fire ghost to Stefan, for whatever help Stefan might lend in caring for her. Stefan had wrinkled his brow and had understood little of it, but afterward had responded wonderfully, pampering and teasing Megan, calling himself her High Lord Protector, finding games and distractions to keep Megan happy, until the child openly adored him. Brierley sensed that Stefan merely applied what he gave his own children back home in Carandon, one a boy aged five, the other a baby girl just beginning to walk. It was his native gift for fathering, she thought gratefully, as she saw Megan steadily emerge from her fright through Stefan's patient cajolery.

Although he called himself no scholar, Stefan had offered to help in translating the new books from Witchmere, seeking answers for Megan. Stefan had an aptitude for words and made better progress than Brierley, and so Stefan had found the passages that offered some suggestions, partial and elusive. One was to keep Megan from her dream world where the fire ghost held her power. Another was to leave the place the ghost had taken life, for similar reason, but leaving Witchmere's valley wasn't yet possible in the bad weather. Another passage hinted that Jain's absence also helped, although the reason was more obscure.

To Brierley's relief, each day Megan seemed more content to remain in the real world, perhaps lured partly by Stefan's charm, perhaps from fear of the one safe place she now avoided. When asleep, she often entered Brierley's dreams, and seemed happy there. When awake, Megan chattered and bounced and demanded hugs and attention, pretended games with her doll, visited Friend and Gallant each morning, alert and lively and laughing.

There had been no repetition of her staring fit, nor any new assault by the fire ghost on her castle, although Brierley knew that other only bided her time. In Megan's river world, the thin plume of smoke still drifted lazily upward on the plain, smoke that Megan still could not see, the one time she had strayed there. Megan's

only lack was Jain's continued absence, and she missed her salamander deeply. One morning Megan's sighing complaint had led
to further explanation to Stefan, who bore it well and believed
not a word.

Megan berated her doll with one last chastisement, then
climbed down from the bed and came over to Brierley, wanting
into Brierley's lap. Brierley let her climb and get settled, and then
reached for one of the children's books Rowena had sent them.
The daily preoccupation in the cabin with books had led to Megan's demand to be included, and so Brierley had begun the patient process of teaching Megan to read. So far their progress was
fitful, with too easy distraction, but Megan's wide variety of ex-
clamations about the wonders in her book offered encouragement.
Brierley kissed Megan's hair, winked at Stefan, and then opened
the book to a brightly painted page.

"What's that?" she asked, pointing.

"A fish!" Megan exclaimed happily. "They wave hello."

Stefan looked up, but decided prudently not to ask. Sometimes
asking Megan "why" left them both badly adrift, a problem with
questions the child also shared.

"See the word?" Brierley said. "That word names that pic-
ture."

"Why?" Megan wanted to know.

"Um—" Brierley said, and floundered for an answer. "Um,
it just does, Megan," she said inadequately, then heard a low
snicker from somewhere across the table. "See the fish, Megan,"
Brierley said firmly, and gave Stefan a fierce warning in her look.

"I see it."

"Good. Stefan is reading *his* book, just like you're reading
yours. Aren't you, Stefan?" Stefan dutifully bent his eyes back to
his page, although he still grinned.

"Fish!" Megan exclaimed at him.

"Yes, sweetling," Stefan said, "it's a fish." He pretended to
pout, posing for her. "You're lucky, Megan: my book doesn't *have*
pictures."

"Why *not*?" Megan demanded, astonished.

"Um—" Stefan fumbled, and Brierley pointedly sent his snicker back to him. Stefan smiled sweetly. "I don't know. Ask your mother, Megan."

Megan obediently turned to look up into Brierley's face. "Why not, Mother?"

"See the fish, Megan," Brierley said, and loftily ignored Stefan's noises.

"Fish!"

After a time, Megan tired of her book's wonders, and went back to the bed to pounce on her doll. Lady Cornelia again lectured her wayward maid, but soon forgave her freely and tucked the doll beside her for an afternoon nap. Brierley exchanged an amused glance with Stefan.

She watched Stefan fondly as he turned a page in the dictionary, hunting another word. He and Melfallan shared much, and she wondered if she saw in Stefan what Melfallan might have been, had he been born a commoner free of an earl's burdens. Her few days with Melfallan in these mountains now seemed remote in time, almost another woman's memory, not her own. Tentatively, she had asked Stefan about him, and Stefan had happily told her every tale he knew about Melfallan, some of them probably quite imaginary. Seeing her interest, he also described Rowena's court and recounted most of its gossip, until she felt she knew the Airlie folk almost as well as he did. He told her about Earl Audric and his long dispute with Duke Tejar, about Rowena's troubled marriage to Count Ralf, tales of young Axel, and, a bit more shyly, spoke of his wife, Christina. In return, she was prompted to talk of Yarvannet, and shyly to speak of a life she had kept largely hidden from everyone.

Belatedly, she had realized that Stefan was cajoling her with his tales as much as he did Megan, and sometimes sensed that deliberate intent behind his stories. Did she seem that forlorn? she wondered. Perhaps she did. Unlike Sir Niall, who had thought her a helpless female to guard whether she liked it or not, Stefan measured his care of her by other standards, partly from his service to the countess he loved, and partly from his happy relationship with his wife and children. And so they had fallen into an easy friendship, one that had steadily deepened as the days passed, and she valued him greatly.

It was now the height of winter, and nearly every day brought new snow. A good supply of wood in the stable shed and the timely delivery of another packhorse of supplies by Roger Carlisle made them comfortable, at least for the next few weeks. When Stefan had not returned promptly from the cabin, an anxious Rowena had sent Roger to find the reason why. The two young men had taken advantage of a brief break in the weather to hunt up-valley, where they found a recent snow-slide. There they had dug into the snow until they reached the frozen bodies of Niall and his horse. When they explored further on the top of the bluff, they had found odd tracks in the snow that neither could explain, perhaps a guardian, perhaps nothing at all. Grieving, together they had brought Niall's body back to the cabin, then had toiled most of the next day at digging a grave in the frozen ground at the edge of the meadow.

Brierley sometimes walked to stand by Niall's grave when the weather permitted, thinking about him. She had not known Niall long, and now would not know any more about him. It seemed unfair and without good explanation, as Daughter Sea's choices often lacked reason. Life went on, giving her a new liegeman in Stefan, but Niall Larson had been left behind forever. She sighed, wishing it otherwise.

Roger's packs had included more books from Rowena's library, another early history of Airlie that mentioned Armadius, a few romances, and the selection of children's books for Megan. With Rowena's additions, Brierley had accumulated quite a library in the cabin, and she hadn't a clue what she would do when they packed for Mionn in the spring. Once she felt that Megan was no longer in immediate danger, Brierley had begun translating Thora's book into one of the blank journals sent up by Rowena, although it was slow progress. How Rowena had discovered Brierley's love for journaling escaped her, but perhaps Melfallan had told his aunt. Had she told him about her journal? She couldn't remember.

Thora often used words not found in Brierley's dictionary, many of them new words coined by the rebel schools Thora had championed. Her book was a scholar's book, a vigorous intellectual debate of technical concepts Brierley could barely follow, but she persisted, slow page by page.

For the relation of the gifts, Thora had written, *we should consider the nature of the element, but not assume the easiest analogy. Fire and water are contrary elements, unable to exist in combination, but, as is well known, the fire gift most often rises out of the sea gift, as if the pattern of the past lends from patterns of the present. Knowledge of the air includes both storm and wind, but also awareness of the suns and stars, themselves fire. If the fire gift can rise easily from its contrary element, could not a star gift naturally arise from air, taking strength from the fiery part of that element? And if one gift can arise from another, cannot gifts also combine, even divide?*

As with Valena's letters, Brierley could guess the other side of the exchange by what Thora chose to say. That the shari'a gifts might be mutable, capable of breaking into new forms, had challenged scholarly theory accepted for centuries. From that single proposition, the rebels had set about demolishing, one by one, every other certain principle. Perhaps, they suggested, each known gift was actually severable, divisible into new categories, and they had happily speculated on the varieties. Perhaps certain recombinations might create an array of male gifts to match the gifts given to shari'a women, and the well-known limitation was chiefly an illusion. Perhaps, they added, to howls of outrage from their scholarly foes, even the Four were not fixed, and could be reshaped by a common shari'a vision.

The debate had set shari'a religion on its ear, and while the rebels' efforts to create new gifts had largely failed, it hadn't dented their arguments in the slightest. After centuries of calm assumption that all was known, the shari'a had been told they likely did not understand themselves at all, and should change their answers. The air witches, the designated leaders of the shari'a and, not by coincidence, the chief architects of traditional theory, had reacted in fury, lashing out at the sea witches who started it, then howling at the minority of other adepts who decided they agreed.

For decades the argument had raged onward, bringing new ideas, a new flowering of knowledge, until the Disasters had cut all short. Thora and her fellow rebels had thought up questions that Brierley had never even imagined, and seemed quite content to propose answers of any stripe, however improbable. *To question is the key to knowledge,* Thora asserted calmly, *for answers, too, are not fixed.* Where would the debate have ended? Brierley wondered. Where indeed? With a sigh, she shut up the book.

That night Brierley dreamed of dragons seated on thrones, and a white pavilion overlooking the sea. Her dream shifted, and she lay in Melfallan's arms in her sea cave, drowsing comfortably beside him. It was lovely to be beside him, as if nothing else were needed for joy. She reached for him and he kissed her, then he rose to pad naked around her cave, looking at its contents with interest.

"I want to explore," he said, looking around at her. "Do you mind?"

"Explore?"

"Well," he fretted, "maybe not. You might not like it."

"Why not?" She propped her head on her hand and watched him reach for her journal on the shelf, then hesitate as he looked around at her again—

She watched Megan play in the surf, happy to shout and run, and the suns shone overhead with amazing brightness, lighting the world. *Believe,* a Voice said far in the distance: Brierley gasped and lifted her arms in welcome, as sea larks suddenly exploded overhead, rising into dizzying flight—

She dreamed then of a cave she had never seen, and a well surrounded by four silent cloaked figures, shadow upon shade.

The suns' light shed pale greens through an opening in the cave roof, where trees moved quietly in a gentle breeze, and cool air sighed against stone. Brierley slowly paced around the chamber, looking at the shadowed figures and the well, and wondered who they were, and what this place might be. Then the light in the well dimmed, becoming menacing shadow—

Brierley awoke abruptly. Megan was curled tightly against her, and Brierley sensed that the child was awake and trembling. She listened, the child's fear suddenly hers, enough to pound the heart and steal away her breath. A rising wind rattled at the windows, plucking its cold fingers at every chink, every pane, threatening a new storm. Barely audible under the sound of the wind, Stefan snored softly in the other bed, a shadow on shadow under the window on that wall.

"What is it, Megan?" Brierley whispered. The child only trembled harder, then pointed a shaking finger at the window over Stefan's bed. Brierley could gain little from Megan's chaotic thoughts: even a mind could be struck dumb by terror, and Megan was wholly possessed by her fear. Brierley raised herself to an elbow but saw nothing. "Stay here," she said quietly.

She picked up her shawl that covered the foot of the bed, and levered herself over Megan, then gently untwined the small fingers that had seized on a fold of her nightdress. In bare feet, Brierley crossed the room and leaned over Stefan to look through the window.

A shadow moved there, hidden behind the reflected flames in the glass. Brierley waited, hardly breathing, until it moved again. Her hand touched Stefan's shoulder and pressed it. With an interrupted snore, Stefan awoke, but a second pressing of her fingers held him still.

"What?" he asked groggily, though sleep was quickly fading from his mind.

"Ease out of bed," she whispered. "There's a guardian six inches from your face, Stefan." She took a slow step back and Stefan started to comply, shifting himself backward off the mattress.

"No!" Megan hissed suddenly. Both Brierley and Stefan froze, and Brierley slowly turned her head toward the child. Megan was sitting up in bed, her eyes wide and frightened. "It's waiting for him to move so it can see him in the dark."

"It's a not-there thing, Megan? Outside on the porch?"

"Yes," Megan said. "It hates us, Mother, all of us." She pressed her small hands to her cheeks. "It's the sick one, the one who hurt the earl and pushed the snow down on Sir Niall. It's found us!"

Brierley heard a faint whine on the other side of the glass and saw the shadow move a foot to the side, as if it studied her in turn. Likely it did.

"Can you hear its thoughts, Megan?" Brierley asked urgently. "What is it going to do?"

"It hates us," Megan whimpered.

"Will it listen to you?" Brierley insisted.

"I don't know. It wants in."

"Why?"

"It wants Stefan—and then you, Mother!" Megan's voice trembled with panic. "Alert!" she shrieked. "Alert! Intruder!"

"Megan!" Brierley hissed, and Megan shuddered, then blinked.

"I'm going to move," Stefan murmured. "Be ready." A heartbeat, then another, and Stefan lunged to the side, throwing himself off the bed to the floor. The guardian threw itself against the glass, shattering it with a great crash. The wind whipped broken glass into the room and howled in its fierce entry. The guardian lunged at the window again, cracking the frame. Stefan rolled to his feet and seized his sword, then leaped toward it.

"Stefan, no!" Brierley cried.

The machine sheeted fire into the room, narrowly missing him. The flame splashed against the opposite wall, searing the wood, and set fire to the cabinet with its stores. Megan shrieked. Brierley seized the staff she had crafted from a branch, and as one, sword and staff swung through the broken window, striking at the machine. She heard glass shatter, the clang of steel on steel. Fire erupted again, slashing into the room, and Stefan quickly struck a second blow, again shattering glass. Even Brierley, not wholly attuned to the machines, felt the life in it flicker to nothingness. Megan caroled in triumph.

"Stop!" Brierley said as Stefan readied a third blow, catching at his arm. "You killed it, Stefan."

Stefan hesitated, his sword poised, then nodded and ripped a blanket off his bed. He moved quickly to smother the flames across the room.

"Megan?" Brierley went to the child. "Are you all right?"

Megan stared past her at the broken window, her eyes unfocused. "Alert! Alert!" she chanted in a strange singsong. "Attack. Patrol and find." She blinked and her eyes cleared. "Mother, the rest of the not-there things are coming. All of them."

"*More* guardians?" Stefan asked.

"All of them," Megan repeated. "We killed one, and they all attack if one dies, if there's no attack elsewhere. They are coming *now*."

Brierley and Stefan looked at each other. Neither had any doubt about Megan's warning, none at all.

"Into your travel clothes, quickly!" Stefan commanded. "I'll saddle the horses."

"Quickly, Megan!"

The wind from the window whipped Brierley's hair across her face, and sent its cold chill into the room. She shivered, but moved as quickly as she could to find clothes from the bundles on the wall, a tunic and skirt for herself, a cloak, and then helped Megan into dayclothes as well. More clothes into a travel bag, then food. Her hands moved quickly, packing everything in a frenzy. She shoved half her books into safety behind a wallboard, then put the others into another bag. It was dangerous to take the shari'a books, but she would not leave these behind. Last of all she shifted all the bundles to near the door, then added Stefan's saddlebags. Megan stood in the middle of the room, clutching her doll, and watched Brierley with wide eyes.

"How far away are they?" Brierley asked hurriedly as she cast a quick glance around the room. Did she have everything? Could the horses carry this much?

"I don't know," Megan said in panic. "It's dark. They move fast."

"All right," Brierley soothed. She knelt by Megan and gave her a quick hug. "Be brave, child. We'll be safe. It will be all right." Megan sobbed once, and then sniffled. "Help me move the parcels out on the porch. Stefan will bring the horses there."

Megan nodded, and then her face lit as she caught Brierley's flash of pride in her. "I'll be brave," she promised, firming her chin. "I'm a brave person."

"That you are, my darling."

Together they shifted the several parcels onto the porch, where the wind whipped at them, slashing with ice crystals that cut and clung. By the time they had all the bags on the porch, Stefan had appeared at the corner of the cabin, leading the three horses, Gallant and Destin and Brierley's black mare.

Megan ran to the mare and hugged her neck joyfully. "Friend!" she caroled, as if the mare had journeyed a fortnight away and back again, now newly arrived, deeply missed, most beloved. Megan often greeted Friend that way when she saw her, and Friend never tired of the greeting, flicking her ears in pleasure. She nuzzled Megan's face.

"I tried to pack everything," Brierley shouted at Stefan over the howl of the rising wind. The air seemed to rush down at them, a giant's blow that staggered Brierley. Megan squeaked and sat down abruptly on the porch as its push tipped her off balance.

"We'll take what we can," Stefan shouted back. He lifted his saddlebags onto his mare, quickly tied other parcels to Friend's harness, then boosted Megan in front of Gallant's saddle. "Hold on, Megan!"

As Brierley swung into the saddle behind Megan, Stefan ran back into the cabin, and then emerged a few seconds later with blankets. He threw one over Friend, snugging it down tight, then pulled another around Brierley's shoulders and tied its ends to Gallant's harness, using the rest of the blanket to shield the gelding's hindquarters from the bitter wind that tore and bit at them, and then tied another around himself before he mounted. Hastily, they rode out into the darkness, the wind now whipping snow at them, tearing at them with icy fingers.

Stefan heeled his horse into a slow trot, and Brierley copied him, although it jounced them up and down. She grabbed at the saddle horn as the jouncing slipped her to the side, and Megan gave another small squeak of alarm. Then Stefan shifted into a canter, and on his own, Gallant stretched out his legs and galloped after him, Friend running easily on her lead. Brierley could barely see a dozen yards ahead, but True Night had begun to yield to the Daystar now dawning behind the peaks. As the light strengthened, Stefan urged his horse onward with a shout. Brierley clung to the saddle desperately and gritted her teeth as Gallant galloped faster, Megan pinned securely between her arms.

Don't fall off, she told herself fervently.

Gallant now had light enough to see, and flowed smoothly after Stefan's mare, Destin, stretching his young legs. He snorted with spirit, and then neighed loudly, answered by the two mares. *Fun!* Megan agreed, answering some comment from Friend that Brierley had missed. Brierley's answering laugh came out in two segments, broken by the jolt in the middle as Gallant dodged a boulder beside the trail.

Later, Brierley reminded herself firmly, we don't do this. As a midwife, she knew all about the risks of advanced pregnancy, and wild gallops on a horse counted among them. For now, however, she and Gallant could run, and run fast. She smiled into the rush of the cold air on her face, and heard Megan laugh.

Mercifully, after another quarter-mile Stefan eased their pace, dropping into a gentle and effortless canter that the horses could sustain for miles. He looked back, checking that they still followed, and Brierley tried to wave, then quickly clutched at the saddle again. Somehow keeping to Gallant's back had acquired more trouble than she remembered. She saw the flash of Stefan's grin. She had never ridden a horse in Yarvannet, only seen noble ladies abroad on horses, and those riding at a sedate pace, scarves

fluttering in the gentle breeze. She was better at boats, she reminded herself.

"Good for Mother!" Megan cried aloud. "She's still aboard!"

"Hush, child," Brierley reproved.

"Can a horse be a boat?" Megan asked and laughed. Brierley
caught her mental image of a horse afloat in water, bobbing gently
at the pier as Brierley stepped aboard.

"Hush, Megan, and don't tease me." Megan laughed again, all
her fear vanished into the wild wind and the speed of Gallant's
swift pace.

Gallant cantered smoothly onward as the daylight strengthened, leaping the occasional snowdrift in their path, striking down
proudly with his hooves. They rode into the dawning morning,
another mile at a canter, then two more miles at a steady trot. By
midmorning, they were deep into the forest beneath the pass, sheltered partly by the trees from the brisk wind but hampered by
deeper drifts of snow. Friend struggled bravely through the drifts,
helped by Stefan's mare and Gallant who broke the path ahead
of her, but had now tired sooner than the others. She plodded
forward bravely, faithful as ever, but Brierley sensed the wavering
in her muscles, the effort to keep to the trail.

"I want Friend to stop," Megan declared.

"Soon, child."

"That's not good enough." Megan craned her head around to
look at Brierley. "Please, Mother? She's tired."

"Stefan!" Brierley called. "Can we stop awhile?"

Stefan turned himself in his saddle. "It's better travel the lower
we get."

"Friend is tired. Megan asks."

Stefan reined up his horse and let Gallant draw even with his
mare, then watched as Friend stopped a pace behind, blowing
great clouds of vapor into the cold air. After a moment, Friend
lifted her head and snorted happily at Megan, then shifted her
weight comfortably as her head lowered again. All the horses
rested, heads drooping. The Daystar shone brightly off the deep
drifts, bright enough to glare. Brierley squinted at Stefan, then

half-covered her eyes with a hand. "How much farther should we ride?" she asked.

"We should ride all day, I think, to get down off these slopes." He cast his eye at the sky, and even Brierley recognized the high hurtling ice-clouds of another storm. "It's a bad season for beginning travel." He looked behind him. "We've apparently outridden those guardians."

"I worry what Roger will think when he finds those fire-marks on the walls and us gone."

"There wasn't time to leave a note," Stefan pointed out. "And we couldn't, anyway. What could we say? The finder might not be Roger."

"True."

"Maybe you can use your witch-gift," Stefan suggested, "and send the countess a message so she won't worry."

Brierley wrinkled her nose at him. "Sad to say, no, I can't." Stefan shifted his hopeful look to Megan. "No," Brierley said.

"No?"

"No. Not this witch, and as far as I know, it doesn't run in Megan's gift, either. Valena's book has certain claims about air witches sending such messages, but neither Megan nor I is an air witch." She bit her lip and looked up the trail. "I can't go into Airlie again, Stefan, as you've said. It's too dangerous."

Stefan nodded. "It'll have to be Mionn, as Melfallan planned for the spring." He gestured ahead and to the southeast. "This trail divides about ten miles ahead. The western trail goes down into the Airlie hills. The other climbs across the mountains over a saddleback and some low ridges, and then descends into southern Mionn. That stretch of coast has maybe a half-dozen fishing villages, plus some lumberman settlements on the slopes."

Gallant snorted at nothing in particular, then took a playful nip at Stefan's mare. Stefan absently edged his horse out of range, although Destin had better ideas and stamped her foot, glaring.

"Earl Giles is Melfallan's father-in-law, and I suppose would be a champion, too—" Brierley suggested hopefully.

"Perhaps," Stefan said, but she sensed his doubt.

She gave him a curious look. "You don't like Earl Giles. Why not?"

Stefan shrugged. "The countess dislikes him, although her cause is mostly years in the past. A good courtier follows his better's opinion."

"More than that, Stefan," she said impatiently.

Stefan looked startled, then gave a short laugh. "Oh, I keep forgetting." He winked at her. "Hmm, how to explain? It's not that I know anything certain about him, and it's not that I adopt Rowena's attitude without question. I've met him a few times, when the countess has met him, and—I felt uneasy. There are different types of lords, lady witch, as with all men. Tejar's his evil self, the countess can't tolerate fools, and Count Toral of Lim practices his fence-sitting, despite its discomfort to private parts. Earl Giles is— Well, I wouldn't count on him as champion. Not that he wouldn't, but not that he would, either. Earl Giles weighs everything by the advantage to Mionn, and he may decide there's greater advantage in giving you to Tejar."

"But he's Melfallan's father-in-law and ally, isn't he? Wouldn't he protect me if Melfallan asks?"

"Maybe, but I wouldn't count on it. As I said, the *only* consideration is Mionn's advantage. When we travel in Mionn, we should stay in hiding."

Megan brightened. "Can we live in a cave?" she asked.

Stefan chuckled. "We'll see, young mistress. Wouldn't you rather live in a house?"

Megan thought about it carefully. "No."

"I've lived in danger all my life, Stefan," Brierley said sadly. "I know how to hide. And it'll probably be a house, Megan, sad to say."

"*She* has a cave," Megan pouted.

"Who does?" Brierley asked.

"Her." Megan toyed with Gallant's mane, then put her thumb in her mouth and looked around at the trees heavy with snow.

"Megan," Brierley repeated, "who?"

"The girl in green," Megan said carelessly. "The not-there

things chased her away from Witchmere. She didn't want to leave, but she had to."

"What girl in green, Megan?"

"Her." Megan turned to look up at Brierley, her eyes frank and wholly innocent. "The girl in green, Mother."

Stefan cleared his throat, and Brierley shrugged at him. "She remembers things in odd ways, and that's all we'll get from her, I'm afraid. The girl in green. She's mentioned her before, but that's about it." She raised her hand and shaded her eyes to look down the trail. "Ten miles, you say?"

"About that. And we should be getting on." Stefan clucked to his horse and moved forward, and Gallant and Friend followed. Patiently, the horses picked their way through the snow.

The trail wound downward, descending into the upper valleys of Airlie. In a few sheltered places, the wind had blown away the snow, leaving frozen ground for the footing. The height of the snowdrifts diminished as they dropped in elevation, with the spine of the eastern mountains protecting Airlie from the worst of the eastern storms of early winter. Sere yellow grass filled the meadows, and the everwillows stood naked without leaf under the brilliant light of the Daystar. In contrast to the gold of the grass and stark white of the everwillow boles, the dark clinging green of the everpines climbed every slope and tipped the ridge-lines.

At the top of each low ridge, Brierley could see more of the meadowlands of Airlie far below, the glittering vein of a river snaking across the pale greens and yellows of Countess Rowena's inland county. In midafternoon, they paused at the top of another low ridge, with heavy forest on either side, and the plains of Airlie beckoning below. A turn of the road snaked around the next foothill and climbed the next low pass. Brierley pointed to a small black shape toiling up a mild incline far below.

"Look! It's a wagon!"

Stefan frowned. "It might be Roger with more supplies. Our chance to send a message, Brierley."

"I hope so."

"Remember, if it's not Roger, that I'm a forester and you're my daughter."

"I'm too old to be your daughter. You look your true age, Stefan, and you're no man in your late forties to have a daughter my age."

"I started young in generating my progeny. What, you'd rather be wife?"

"Why not?"

Stefan grinned. "I'll leave you to explain that to my Christina. Maybe sister is better. Or you're my niece, and Megan is—" He paused, thinking. "Hells."

"This is absurd, Stefan."

"Better than announcing us as liegeman, witch, and witchling. True?"

"Well, true—"

"Megan is my daughter, I think," Stefan decided, obviously enjoying this remaking of himself. "I'm a widower, and you live with me, I being your only surviving relative after the plague last winter, and you take care of both of us. How's your housewifery, Brierley?"

"Better than yours, Stefan," Brierley retorted with dignity. "Wife is simpler."

"You're probably right." He chuckled. "I've never had a chance to remake my identity: it doesn't appear to be an instant skill. Now, why are we abroad on this trail in early winter?"

"You have business in Mionn, a contract for timber from— what's the nearest Mionn town?"

"Lowyn. But we haven't reached the fork to Mionn, so we're still on the wrong road."

"I really don't think we'd meet anybody except Roger."

"Right. Well, into the fray." He heeled his horse and they moved forward.

They rode downward toward the ascending wagon, and Brierley sent her witch-sense forward, hoping for Roger and news of Melfallan, and the chance to send her own message to Melfallan. Surely the countess could find a safe way. She imagined Melfallan reading her letter—had they brought paper in the packs? And where would he read it? He was likely back in Yarvannet now, enough time for that—and surely safe. Was it Roger?

She brushed across a mind, and her hope died like the curl of a wave on the beach sands. Megan stirred restlessly in her arms as she caught Brierley's dismay.

"Mother—"

Then they both caught the image of Roger from that mind ahead, but Roger lying motionless over the wagon seat dark with spilled blood. Brierley gasped in shock. "Duke's man!" she exclaimed.

"What?" Stefan blurted. Megan whimpered, then began a low soft keening.

"Roger's dead, Stefan." Brierley's eyes filled with tears.

Stefan gave a low sound of anguished denial. "No!"

"It's not certain," she said hastily, grasping for her own small hope. "He *thinks* they killed him. Perhaps he's wrong." But with such images of blood, she thought. She reached for more, and sensed the shadow of the steward, the one who had hated Roger and Stefan, and then Lanvalle's genuine regret at Roger's death. She sensed, too, the lancing agony in his thigh, now edging on infection and fever—Lanvalle had been wounded, too, and by the same hand.

Beside her, Stefan's mind filled a flaring hot wish that blotted out all other need. "You can't fight him, Stefan," she warned. "He's the duke's man, a spy." Stefan drew his sword. "Put that away! He didn't kill him! Cullen did!" She reached out and caught Stefan's wrist, then forced down his arm. "Stefan!"

"Cullen?" Stefan asked, astounded. "The understeward? But—"

Stefan hesitated, then muttered a curse as he resheathed his sword. "We need to get behind these trees." He kicked Destin's sides with his heels and urged her off the trail, and Brierley followed, the other mare on her lead.

They made a wending trail around tree boles and deep brush, descended awkwardly into a ravine, and then came upon a stream at its bottom. Stefan pushed his horse into the water and clattered across the wet rocks, then leaned forward precariously as Destin surged up the other bank. Brierley clung to Gallant's saddle as he followed, holding tight to Megan. Finally, in the depth of a glade several hundred yards off the road and heavy with brush, they stopped to listen.

On the clear mountain air, they heard the distant creaking of the wagon, then a murmur of a voice as the man encouraged the cart horse. They listened intently, their eyes slowly following the sounds of the passing wagon on the trail, and even Megan had stopped her soft sobbing, aware of the danger in any sound.

Brierley sensed doubt in Lanvalle's mind. He had followed wagon tracks on the road, thinking them Roger's from a prior journey, but the tracks had dwindled, then disappeared, as he climbed through the foothills. At the fork in the road to Mionn, he had hesitated, then chose the upper road that still remained within Airlie, the road that led to the winter cabin. As he had climbed onward, seeing little sign of recent travel, he had come to doubt his choice and would soon turn back.

Do it now, she wished earnestly, closing her eyes. After another turning, then a long stretch of trail between heavy trees, he would reach where Stefan had taken them off the road. He would see their horses' tracks, both those leading upward, and those taken to avoid him. And he had the woodsman's skill to know the tracks were fresh.

She looked at Stefan, and he had also realized their mistake. "We should have braved the encounter," he muttered.

"Maybe," she replied, offering a comfort she also disbelieved. Perhaps meeting the spy would have led to greater peril. Perhaps.

"Let's move on," Stefan said. They returned to the road and resumed their descent. When Stefan was sure they were out of earshot, he urged the horses into a floundering canter through the drifted snow on the trail. It would quickly tire the horses, even Destin and Gallant, but would gain them needed distance. At the fork, they turned east, and the snow grew deeper on the road.

"He'll see that someone has been in the cabin," Brierley said an hour later. Their ride had been silent for miles.

331

"Not who it was who stayed there. A wayfarer cabin accepts any traveler. And I doubt he'd continue onward after seeing our tracks." Stefan shrugged. "Too bad for him, if the guardians were still waiting at the cabin. All we can do is try to stay ahead of him. He doesn't *know* you're the witch Tejar is hunting, right?"

"That's true. But Tejar sent him into Airlie to find me, Stefan. The duke knows I'm alive."

Stefan gave a muttered curse. "Then we'll disappear into Mionn, and perhaps find that cave of Megan's and hide there. I'll see you both are safe." Stefan's eyes were grim. "Safe," he said to himself.

Brierley tightened her arms around Megan. "If there is any safety in the world for us."

"If there is, I'll find it for you," Stefan promised.

*I*n Yarvannet, Lady Saray sat by the window of her chambers, her stitchery forgotten in her hands, and looked out the window at the sea. The suns had shone brightly today, their light sparkling on every wave-edge, a shifting moving light that never repeated its pattern. Now the Companion spread its lavender coolness over the sea, promising the True Night, but its beauty brought her no comfort. She frowned delicately, wondering if she should do something about Melfallan's absence from her bed—but what? Melfallan now slept more often in his tower study than with her, and she missed his presence at night. She had relented her anger with him about the soiree, offering sweet words and a pleasant smile, but he had not returned to her as he had always done before. He had always forgiven her angers, willing to admit his fault to please her, but now— What had changed? She bit slowly at her lip, worrying.

How could she ever understand her husband, this restless, vigorous man who expected things of her she couldn't give? Always he seemed to want something more from her, when she had already given him everything she could. When she disappointed him, she racked her brains and found still more to give, yet still— he was disappointed. It wasn't fair, she thought, and felt suddenly tired of trying, this mountain of trying. What did he *want* of her?

Saray bit her lip, dismayed by her own flush of anger at her husband. A lady must be calm, she told herself. A lady must never raise her voice— Such rules had guided all her life, and she would not abandon them. She needed the strength they gave her, the purpose they defined in her life.

But he would not come to her bed. As her mother had taught her, and it was true, a man had need of sex more than a woman, and a wife's duty was to keep him healthy in such matters. Saray had always offered herself whenever he asked, had accepted with good heart what came after. She still found the sexual act somewhat embarrassing, even after nearly six years of bedding with him. However she tried, his unseemly loss of control during coupling dismayed her. When he had vaguely suggested, very early in their marriage, that she behave with similar abandon, she had stared at him in shock. Her cheeks colored slightly as she remembered his answering look, as if he were stricken to the heart. But why? Did he want her to pretend otherwise, and then know she pretended? She liked most to lie next to him afterward, when he relaxed and felt drowsy and smiled at her lazily in a way she adored. Couldn't that be enough? Why not?

Saray felt a sob rise in her throat, and ruthlessly thrust it back into her breast. No crying, she told herself sternly, not in front of the lady-maids. A noble wife did not cry in front of the servants.

A man had needs for bedding, needs he should not deny himself for his good health—was Melfallan satisfying them elsewhere? With whom?

She remembered a similar quarrel three years ago, she forgot now about what, when Melfallan had left her bed for several weeks. Castle gossip had already reached her about the servant Bronwyn, a bosomy girl in the kitchen who freely shared her sexual favors with any man, or so her lady-maids had told her. When that gossip stretched to include Melfallan, Saray had not believed it, not one word, but had grown worried when the rumors continued. One night, unable to resist another day of not knowing, she had followed him down the stairs in her thinnest slippers, anxious of discovery at any noise, and so had seen Melfallan kissing the girl in a hallway. It was not the kiss that had wrenched at her heart, but the girl's low delighted laughter when she looked up at him afterward, and then Melfallan's answering chuckle. His voice was low and tender to her, his caress—a brushing of her hair from her face—almost absently given, for his attention was entirely on Bronwyn's face, and on hers alone. When in all their marriage had Melfallan looked at Saray with such absorption, such complete intent?

In that passing instant, in that space of a single breath, Saray might have done murder—not to Melfallan, but to this interloper, this commoner nothing girl who had dared to entice Melfallan with her sexual poses and allures, playing on his man's weakness, stealing him from Saray, however briefly.

But that night Saray had not murdered. Instead she had waited in the shadows, her hands clenched, her ears straining for every word between them, her back pressed hard against the stone wall to give her strength, until Melfallan led the girl away. Then she had waited mutely on the stairs, knowing that now he kissed her, now he pulled her down to the bed, and now— She had not allowed herself to cry. She had not allowed one tear.

After an hour, when surely it was over, Saray had slowly reclimbed the stairs to their bedroom, her feet leaden. Twice more in the following year, Saray had endured another affair within her tortured silence, waiting for him each night until he chose elsewhere. It was the lot of a noble wife, she told herself, and forgave Melfallan fully. Instead Lady Saray had reserved all her hatred for the girl, however secretly. Bronwyn had married her baker, removing her threat, and Saray had longed to punish the others, but had not. It was a wife's dignity to bear her husband's sexual weakness in silence, and she taught herself that silence, as her mother had learned it, as her sister had learned it, as all noble wives learned it. And always Melfallan had returned to her, as he must.

As his lawful wife, only Saray could give him legitimate heirs for Yarvannet, heirs that could not be challenged by anyone, not even Duke Tejar, Melfallan's liege lord. And her father was earl of Mionn, Melfallan's closest ally, an ally he dare not anger. He had to return to her, however she failed him in his eyes, however he felt tempted elsewhere. A man might have needs, but a woman's rank and alliances protected her even from a husband's failings. Surely Melfallan understood that.

Who, then? Who was it this time? For once, the castle gossip did not aid her. The gossip followed Melfallan wherever he went, be it to hawking or the assizes, to the soldiers' practice yard, or to his daily meetings with Sir James. It reported his good cheer, his interest in his people of any station, how well he ate, when he seemed tired, when he did not. And likely, she knew, it reported his frequent absences from his wife's bed. She felt her face burn with her humiliation. A hundred pairs of eyes watched Melfallan all day long, and they noticed everything. But not once did the gossipers mention another tryst in a hallway, nor too affectionate a touch on a woman not his wife, nor any of the other signs of scandal that the gossipers had so quickly detected before. Not once.

Who then? She ground her teeth.

Her lady-maids sat nearby, occupied with their own quiet tasks, and talked to each other in low voices. She didn't bother to listen, not today, although they glanced at her curiously from time to time, wondering at her silence. Saray frowned, ignoring their looks, and watched the Companion's twilight dance on the water.

Who?

Stefan and Brierley rode late into the Companion's twilight, then sought a camp among the trees before True Night fell. The road still led downward into the foothills, but would soon ascend to cross the southern pass into Mionn. A week's journey, perhaps, Stefan had guessed, a week of cold and snow and tired riding.

Megan sat down and sighed, huddling under her blanket. Brierley sat down next to her and pulled a blanket tighter around their shoulders, then unbuckled one of their saddlebags. Stefan disappeared into the darkness under the nearby trees, hunting wood for the fire.

She brought out cheese and some bread, then a pot to melt snow for water. Megan demanded her doll, and a quick search found it in another bag, to Megan's vast relief. Stefan trod back with an armload of wood, and soon they had the crackling warmth of a large fire. He helped make a campside meal, then began constructing a windbreak to give them some better shelter. She sensed his fatigue and worry, and got up to help, although she knew little about windbreaks.

"Jain!" Megan exclaimed behind her.

Brierley whirled, and had a glimpse of a huge scaled body moving among the trees, then a fluttering shape winging to a branch. There was a hiss like a teakettle, then a scrabbling of small claws, and there was Jain on the branch, flames flickering along his sides, his tail curled neatly in front of his toes. Beside her, Stefan gasped. Brierley sensed Stefan's utter shock, numbing the mind, dropping the jaw.

Greetings, Stefan, Jain said with wicked mischief. He preened a moment, then bowed his head mockingly. *I greet the High Lord Protector.*

Brierley caught Stefan's arm quickly as his knees went unsteady and he almost fell. Stefan made a sound like a croak and nowhere near a word, then abruptly sat down. Brierley sighed. Ocean alive, she thought, he's back, and he's got another damned surprise.

"Jain!" Megan reproved. "That's not nice!"

It's not my fault he didn't believe. Jain launched himself from the branch and winged down to Megan, landing on the blanket in front of her. Megan promptly pulled him into her lap and kissed him with a resounding smack. Jain squirmed as she kissed him again. *Enough kissing, Megan,* he said irritably. He struggled out of her fervent hug onto her shoulder, then rattled his wings as she tried to grab him again. *I said enough.*

"Where did you go, Jain?" Megan demanded. "I've missed you!"

Away for a while. I'm back now. The salamander cocked his

head at Stefan. *I think he believes.* He snickered, enjoying himself thoroughly at poor Stefan's expense.

"So you *can* be visible to Allemanii," Brierley said. "I think a little less on the dramatic pop-in might have been better." Jain shrugged, unimpressed. Brierley knelt beside Stefan and patted his shoulder consolingly. "This is Jain, Stefan, the fire dragon. Life with him is like this, I'm afraid. You might as well get used to it."

"Is he real?" Stefan gasped, his eyes still wide as saucers.

"He says he is," Brierley said dryly, "but asking more on that question usually gets me nowhere." She smiled and patted him again. Stefan blinked, then shuddered violently.

Balancing Jain with one hand, Megan got to her feet and brought the salamander over to Stefan. Without much cooperation from Jain but no particular resistance, she detached Jain from his grip on her shoulder and held him out to Stefan. "He's my friend, Stefan."

Stefan raised his hand slowly, and Jain calmly stepped across the gap onto Stefan's arm. *Greetings, Stefan,* Jain said, his mental voice soft, without any mockery at all. Stefan looked at the salamander with open wonder, then tentatively touched the cool flames flickering along Jain's hide, then moved more boldly to caress one wing. "He *is* real," Stefan said, amazed.

Jain rustled his wings. *What is reality? What is not?*

"Now don't start that," Brierley said crossly.

"Start what?" Stefan asked, looking up at her.

"You'll find out. Can you hear him talk, Stefan?" she asked curiously.

"Yes, but his mouth doesn't seem to move, and, besides, how can a lizard—"

Salamander, Jain fiercely corrected.

"Your pardon, Jain," Stefan said solemnly. Then he watched, agog, as Jain spread his wings and lifted lightly into the air. The next instant, Jain popped out.

"He'll be back," Megan said confidently, and climbed into

Stefan's lap. She patted his face with concern. "Are you all right, Stefan?" she asked anxiously.

"I'm fine, sweet girl—I think." Stefan looked up at Brierley, then began to laugh, shaking his head helplessly.

～⌒

The storm rose to a howl during the night, whipping its snow through the branches overhead. Stefan rose twice to check that the horses were not buried in the clinging drifts, and then returned to the bed they shared for warmth against the storm that now descended. In the cold, Brierley wrapped her arms tightly around Megan, and felt grateful for Stefan's warmth against her back. All that mattered was that nest of warmth they shared as the storm raged over their heads.

By the Daystar's rising, the wind still blew hard, tossing great clouds of white over the forest. Restlessly, Stefan waited an hour past the dawning, then another, and then insisted that they travel before the storm drowned them further in snow. The horses struggled against the new drifts, and twice Stefan lost the trail, forcing them to backtrack up the slopes to the road. Gradually they struggled downward as the wind relented, although both knew the storm merely regathered its forces for another blasting fury.

By the end of the cold day, with the snow slowly sifting around them, they had descended ten miles into Airlie's upland valleys. The Daystar was now westering, removing its warmth from the world, and Brierley shivered steadily from the seeping cold, with Megan even more afflicted. The child huddled miserably within Brierley's arms, her face tucked hard against Brierley's shoulder.

"We should find a place to camp, Stefan," Brierley said at last.

Stefan nodded his ready agreement and pointed at the trail ahead. "There's a suitable place just around the next turning, as I remember. Ruins of an old village, little more than crumbled walls now, but something to break the wind and shield a campfire. We can sleep there."

At the next turning in the road, Brierley saw stone to the left, deep under the trees. Stefan turned his horse and floundered for several feet through the drifts to the lighter snow beneath the grove, then slowly led their way deeper under the trees. Brush grew thickly among the tumbled stone, and the trees now clustered wherever stone had not disturbed seed, creating a windbreak from the weather. Even the wind's voice seemed muted here. Brierley followed Stefan past several taller piles of stone, her gelding's hooves snapping brush in loud echoes.

Near the center of the grove, a ruined wall nearly head-high joined to another to offer a rough shelter. As Brierley made a quick camp from their saddlebags and gathered a pan of snow to heat on the fire, Stefan found wood and built a hot blaze in the stone corner, then hunted other wood nearby, most of it blessedly dry, and brought it to pile high near the blaze. Brierley sat down close enough to the fire to risk a scorching, and let the reflected heat bake the cold out of her bones, then made room for Megan in her lap. As they shared another companionable meal of biscuit and cheese from the saddlebags, the fire popped and swayed in the shifting currents of air coursing through the ruins, its shadows leaping strange shapes across the stones. Brierley looked around curiously.

"It looks very old," she commented.

"Legend says it was shari'a first." Stefan poked at the fire with a long stick.

"Really?" Brierley asked, and looked around again with intense interest.

Stefan waved generally at the forest all around them. "There are several of these ruined villages in the upper hills. The hill folk say they're haunted, but I wouldn't know about that. They have all kinds of tales about the shari'a, ghosts walking in the trees, odd dreams, witches everywhere. Most Airlie folk choose to live elsewhere and leave the ghosts alone." He pointed off to the left. "I think these buildings run several hundred yards under those trees. Maybe four hundred souls must have lived here, but the stone is buried now. Not much left after three centuries."

"Hmm." Brierley sipped at her hot mug, and looked around again at the shadowed stone.

They sat in a companionable silence as the fire crackled between them, giving some warmth against the pervasive chill of the approaching night. The Companion had now set, bringing the darkness of True Night and an icy chill that touched the skin with brushing fingers. The wind had diminished its howl, and the snow began to fall in greater earnest, drifting silently over the forest in slow curtains, building a white blanket over the ground that grew steadily deeper.

"How much farther to Lowyn?" she asked.

"Another forty miles until we reach the lower trail." He nodded at the drifts steadily mounting outside the ring of stones. "Forty miles of *that*. There's a reason folk don't travel this road in winter." Shaking his head, Stefan made a rude sound. Megan promptly mimicked him, then repeated his sound because she enjoyed it.

Brierley kissed Megan's hair. "Ah, well," she sighed. "If we've had to hole up, so has the spy."

"May he freeze to death," Stefan wished darkly. He yawned large enough to crack his jawbones, then began to roll out his bed of blankets. He looked around expectantly for Jain, but the salamander still lingered elsewhere. "I'm tired. Good night."

"Good night."

Brierley watched the fire for a while longer, then made up a bed for herself and Megan on the other side of the fire. After a time, she felt Jain wiggle into Megan's arms, and heard his soft teakettle sigh.

I'm glad you're back, Jain, she sent gratefully, willing to forgive much for the joy he gave Megan.

She is safer away from Witchmere, he answered, yawning. *Enough that I could return.*

Some nuance in his thought prompted a sudden suspicion. The fire witches could control the Witchmere guardians, and perhaps so could a fire dragon. *Did you send that guardian to attack the cabin?*

He missed, didn't he? Jain yawned again.

Not by much. Brierley didn't know whether to feel outraged or relieved, and ended somewhere between. *And Niall?* she thought with sudden horror. *Did you prompt that, too?*

I did not, Jain said firmly. *I can't be in every place at once, my child, and Megan needed me when Niall left her alone.* She sensed his genuine regret about Niall's death, and relaxed. *Nor did I wish to kill the duke's spy,* Jain continued soberly. *Derek Lanvalle may be foolish in his loyalties, but he is not an evil man. Although I am shari'a spirit, I can love the flame within others not my own.*

She smiled. *As you love Stefan?*

Jain's soft mental chuckle sifted like a teasing flame. *There's more to Stefan than you know, witch.*

What? she demanded.

I'm asleep, Jain announced, and made a whistling tiny snore for effect.

Jain!

Go to sleep. Jain sighed, then relented. *Well, consider this, if you must: there is the fire of the soaring spirit, passionate for life and fierce in its defense. That is Megan, as were many of my daughters, including those who now afflict her. But there is another fire, the hearth-fire, mellow and welcoming, the flame that mends and comforts and keeps all beloveds safe. That is Stefan.*

Stefan is shari'a? But I'd know if he was!

Jain made a rude sound. *So you think. Did you hear the witch-blood in Captain Bartol? In Jared? I thought not. Witchery can be a subtle gift, my child, easily mistaken for something else, and it is fitful, rising strongly in certain souls like yourself and Megan, but not in others. It was so even before the Disasters, and became more so after the survivors married Allemanii.* He paused. *I think it would grieve Stefan to know, and telling him would serve no purpose. His gender is against him.* He chuckled softly as he caught her next thought. *I could tease and suggest you find out for yourself, but, no, Melfallan is not shari'a.*

Oh.

Go to sleep. Brierley sighed feelingly. *That's it,* Jain warned, his tone quite firm. *Don't even try for more. I won't tell you.*

You are a vexing creature.

Jain yawned. *Most dragons are. Live with it.* Jain tucked his head under his wing and determinedly went to sleep.

Brierley lay comfortably in their warm bed of blankets, listening to the snow as it whispered onto forest and stone, and considered what Jain had said. *I thought I would know all other shari'a,* she mused, and then tried to remember why she had thought so. Had it been some comment in the journals, that same assumption? Or was it her loneliness for what she had shared with her mother as a small child, before Jocater resolutely denied her gift and so ended it? *What else don't I know,* Brierley thought, *when I think I know? This won't do.*

She wrinkled her nose, then laughed softly at herself. *Yes, what else don't I know? Perhaps a whole world of not knowing.*

Brierley's dream began slowly, more shifting thoughts than true dream, then slid into odd memory of tumbled stone. The shari'a village of Mahel had stood under the eaves of Airlie's upland forest for centuries, quiet and unassuming, its shari'a folk living out their lives from generation to generation. Although scarcely a day's ride from Witchmere, the fire witch who governed the small community avoided Witchmere's politics, looking instead to the needs of her folk and the recording of her memories. Witchmere was now worried greatly about the newcomers, the barbarian sea people named Allemanii who had invaded the western coastlands two decades before, but Linia cared little about Witchmere's anxieties. The Allemanii preferred the seacoasts and riverbanks, not the hills and forests that sheltered most of the shari'a villages, and, in Linia's opinion, there was room enough in shari'a lands for all manner of new folk—not that Witchmere ever asked her opinion, of course.

A dream-shadow within her own dream, Brierley watched as Linia, a tall and slender dark-haired woman, slightly stooped, still more young than old, walked along the main village street, being greeted by the village folk. In this winter season, the wind from the east carried the bite of bitter cold, and Linia had dressed in a long cloak with a warm furred hood, and carried a tall staff in one hand, a small bag in the other. In front of the smithy, she stopped before the open stable door and welcomed the wall of heat issuing from the forge within, then nodded to the smith when he noticed her and straightened from his task.

"A good morning, Linia," the man said, nodding respectfully.

"And to you, Bern. May I share your fiery warmth for a time?"

The smith smiled. "My warmth is freely shared, anshan'ia. You are welcome."

"Thank you." The smith nodded and turned back to his anvil, then pounded vigorously with his hammer on red-hot metal as he shaped a metal strut for a new plow. As Linia watched him, she sensed the echoes of other smiths who had pounded that same anvil in this place: Bern's smithy had stood here for more than two hundred years, and shadows flickered in her mind, of other times, other souls, the gift given to all anshan'ia, the fire witches of the shari'a. Linia smiled contentedly as the past gathered itself around her, misting her in shadows.

She shifted worlds, and a different blacksmith stood at the forge, young and wide-chested, sweaty with his work. The man looked up and smiled as his beloved brought him a cool mug of ale, love laughing in her eyes. Time shifted again, and a lean-limbed boy, dark-haired and intense, watched with fascination as his father hammered steel, sparks flying into the air—

Daydreaming again, Linia?

Linia blinked, abruptly jarred from her gestalt by the sent thought, and she and Brierley turned toward the voice. Dressed in the warm folds of a blue cloak, Gerin joined them in front of the stable door, and stretched out her wrinkled hands to the warmth of the smith's blaze. Now entering old age, gray had changed Gerin's dark hair into near silver, and her youth's beauty had faded from her face with the years, but not from her eyes. Those lovely eyes still saw the world in ways Linia could only guess, despite mind-speech and Linia's memories of other healers, the other dayi, who had tended Mahel during its centuries. Linia smiled at her friend, who shared their common tending of their village, and knew she would be teased now, as Gerin always teased when Gerin caught her trancing.

As a fire adept, Linia knew the people of the past as constant shadows in her mind, but Gerin lived fully in the present, aware of the inner worlds all about her. Was past fundamentally different than present, Linia wondered, with a boundary that could not be breached? Would she ever understand Gerin's own gift as she understood her own? Did Gerin find a similar barrier, or did her dayi's insight into souls understand even Linia's shadows? Well, she supposed, the Four blessed as they would. *Merely enjoying the warmth,* she retorted with dignity. *It's a cold day.*

"You're solemn today," Gerin remarked, changing to spoken word. The old woman pointedly inspected Linia from shoes to hood. "What is troubling you?"

"Am I troubled?" Linia asked mildly.

Gerin chuckled. "Don't you know?"

"That gift I yield to you, my friend. Why? Do I need healing?"

"No more than usual," Gerin teased. Linia wrinkled her nose, refusing to rise to the bait. Still, was this a chance meeting, she wondered, or had Gerin sought her out on this cold frosty morning? Gerin glanced sideways at her, slyly daring her to ask, but Linia chose to be contrary and did not. A Calling for me? she asked herself. Why? With mild anxiety, she listened to her interior. Was she ill?

Then she heard Gerin's soft chuckle. She clucked her tongue in exasperation, and rounded on her friend. "Stop teasing, Gerin," she scolded. "That's not right."

Gerin snorted. "Then stop wrapping yourself in whichness of the why, as you do too much, Linia. I came to see you this morning, that's true, but only to see you." She looked Linia up and down, pretending to inspect her again. "As far as I can tell, you're in excellent health. You worry too much."

"When the suns stop rising, I'll stop my worries." Linia looked around at the village, its houses and central square and

quiet activity, the scudding of snowclouds overhead. "Something's in the air today. I don't know what. Odd." She looked
around again distractedly, now recognizing the vague inner dis-
turbance that had prompted her into the cold street today, away
from her comfortable house and its fire. What was it? What impended today that might threaten Mahel?

The anshan'ia listened to the past and protected the present,
the guardians of the people. Part of her training as fire witch had
involved preparation for violence: she could best a full-grown man
in hand-to-hand combat, and still used swordplay to keep up her
physical training, often seeking out the younger lads in the village
who enjoyed fighting with swords and did not mind losing to a
woman. But preparation for physical defense was more precaution
than need. The fire witches primarily guarded with their witch's
gift, and a few had depths to violence not even the air witches
suspected. To kill with a thought? Linia sometimes wondered
what extremity might force a fire witch to such an effort, and
what effect such killing would then rebound on the witch. She
suspected the effect was fatal. The Four balanced the world, and
death beget death, even for their beloveds, the adepts of the
shari'a. Linia shivered, struck again by a prescience she did not
understand, not yet.

"What is it?" Gerin asked, mildly alarmed. Gerin looked
around at the peaceful village, the smith pounding his anvil with
sure strong blows, the winter clouds moving slowly across the
suns, azure and gold, that bracketed the sky.

"I don't know, Gerin." Linia clutched at her friend's hand.

Then Linia felt the shiver of Jain's voice above the rooftops,
and looked for him, but the fire dragon still concealed himself,
hiding behind the open air, the solidity of the smithy's wooden
walls, the sound of voices in the square. He was here today,
nearby: she could sense his presence, but Jain again played his
irritating games, teasing at her, alerting her to danger by his mad-
dening elusiveness. *Warning of what?* she asked him impatiently,
but he did not answer. *Perhaps you don't know, either,* she thought,
but even such insult did not bring him out. *You are a vexing thing.*

We are all things, Jain rumbled, trembling the wooden planks of the smithy. *You and I, trees and rocks, the air above, the storms that rise.* Suddenly he erupted through the smithy roof and spread his leathery wings wide, flames whipping over his scaled body like a second skin, brilliant and hot. He curved his great neck to look at her; his eyes glowed like huge great coals. *Watch now, beloved. They come.* The dragon-spirit snapped his jaws once, twice, then vanished.

A clamor of hoofbeats echoed far down the street, and Brierley turned with the two women toward the sound. Like a sudden gust of wind rattling the shutters, a party of Allemanii horsemen rounded the corner, clattering on their tall horses, their brightly colored cloaks lifted with the wind of their own passage. High-born Allemanii by their rich clothing and blond hair, Linia guessed, although she had not seen the barbarians often. Why did they ride into Mahel today? she worried. She tested her witch sense, wondering if these strangers were the cause of her morning's disquiet, but did not sense danger in them.

The tall and blond middle-aged lord who led them nodded to Linia and Gerin as he passed by, courteously enough. He was dressed in velvet and fur, with a heavy gold chain around his neck and a silver circlet on his brow, and his eyes moved restlessly, noting everything around him with intense interest. The party of six men dismounted by the well in the village square, and their lord pleasantly asked a villager standing nearby for permission to water their horses. The man gave ready consent, and one of the lord's companions dropped the bucket into the stone well, then began hauling on its rope.

"Who is he, Gerin?" Linia asked. "Tell me."

Gerin narrowed her eyes. "The Allemanii lord Farrar, the duke's brother. He's been summoned to Iverway—and did not like the summons." She sniffed reflectively, her mild gaze fixed on the Allemanii leader. "This one is different than Duke Aidan, I think. Where the other sees only lands to be taken and the towns to be built there, this one sees us."

"He is to be trusted?" Linia asked in surprise.

"No, not yet," Gerin decided, "and perhaps never, but this Allemanii lord still chooses to see where the other will not. There has been contention between these brothers, I've heard, a rivalry that began from boyhood in their western lands, and matters are still uneasy between them, as they likely will always be. Farrar does not like his brother's recent summons to Iverway, neither in its tone nor its manner of delivery, and has willfully delayed on his way. He might have arrived in Iverway days ago by a different route, but now he lingers on the road, making a pleasant journey of it for himself and his companions." She chuckled softly. "I think Duke Aidan will not be pleased."

"As is Farrar's intent," Linia judged.

"Of course. Their quarrel over their High Lords' ranking might be partly mended, but it is not healed. They had no duke's rank in their western lands, and Farrar thinks they need none now, but his brother has persuaded the others. And so both contribute to the delay in that healing, and both still prefer to quarrel. I wonder who will win their struggle."

"Struggle for what?"

"I doubt even they are fully sure. An interesting folk, these Allemanii, vigorous and bright-minded; I rather like them."

Linia gave her friend an affectionate glance. "You like everybody, Gerin. It's a part of your gift."

"Not everybody. There's a few souls I could do without." Gerin sniffed again, then turned and looked up into Brierley's face. Suddenly Brierley was fully in Gerin's world, as if she, too, walked in Farrar's times, three centuries in the past. The old woman blinked in startlement, then smiled with a slow and delighted pleasure, her once-held beauty hers again, lighting the eyes, shaping the smile. "They are much alike, your young earl and Farrar," Gerin said to her. "Remember that, daughter, when you make your choices."

"What did you say, Gerin?" Linia asked, looking around at her friend.

"There is past and present," Gerin replied elliptically, "but also the future." She shook her head at Linia's puzzled frown and

laughed. "Three intersecting yet sometimes one," she added un-
helpfully.

"You make no sense today," Linia retorted, tossing her head.
"I'm tired of you, Gerin. Why don't you leave?"

"I am frequently tiresome, my dear." She gestured at the Allemanii lords. "You should go speak to him," she said. "He wants
the headwoman, and you're closest to that."

In the smithy beside them, the smith's hammer rose and fell
in competent rhythm, and the fire blazed hotly, taming the metal
beneath the smith's skill. Linia hesitated, then sighed and walked
onward toward the well. In the square, Earl Farrar smiled at Linia
and greeted her with courtesy, then bent his head to listen as she
spoke.

Gerin turned back to Brierley, a wicked mocking look in her
old eyes. "Despite his twenty years among us," she said, "Earl
Farrar hasn't quite divined how we govern ourselves, nor why
women seem to be our leaders, odd as that is."

"Is it odd?" Brierley asked, amused, and watched Gerin laugh.
Likely she always teased, she decided, more than Brierley ever
could. Gerin now neared the end of her life in a safer world for
the shari'a, before Duke Rahorsum had ordered the death of all
shari'a, every one.

The gentle mockery in Gerin's face shifted to pain. "Will he?"
Gerin murmured in distress. "Oh, will he?"

The old woman looked around at the village she loved, the
folk she loved and tended. "Mahel is in ruins: I can see it now."
Gerin raised her hands to her face in horror. "The dead lay all
around me—as I am dead, long dead on this horrible day when
Rahorsum burned Mahel. I had no part in that future, to save or
die when the Beast came for us with his sword. I have no part in
your future, my daughter, nor other futures when Death came
again for the survivors, and the hounds wailed in the hunt, the
fire rose, flesh burned, a shari'a died. I had no chance to stop it,
not once. The Beast took them all." Her old voice broke and she
pulled her hood low over her face. "Oh, beloved, time is cruel,"

she said, tears heavy in her voice. "I did not want to know this."
Gerin turned and began to walk away.

"Mother, wait!" Brierley caught her arm, stopping her. "There
is hope——"

Gerin shook her off, but Brierley persisted. "I am the hope,"
she cried, pulling Gerin around to face her. "Don't despair.
Mother, don't——"

Gerin blinked and stood motionless in Brierley's grasp, then
gently raised her hands to Brierley's face, embracing it. In the
future, a white-shrouded figure hurtled off a Yarvannet cliff, ending all fear, all need, and leaving a daughter abandoned. "But all
is lost, my child——"

"No." Brierley choked back a sob. "No. There doesn't have
to be defeat. It needn't be so, if you believe."

Gerin studied her face for a long moment, then nodded sadly.
"I am sorry she failed you, child," she said, shaking her head.
"Fear can drive us to such failure by making us blind." The old
hands lifted again to caress Brierley's face, lingered. "But then you
know that already, my daughter. You understand: it is our gift,
we sea witches, to know the inner heart, and from that knowledge
to restore health through our own strength—as you are strong,
my daughter. As I was strong." Gerin smiled gently. "The Four
bless as they will: listen to them, when the dragons come to you,
and listen to the wisdom of your own heart, which they give. It
is our craft, that listening."

"Please, Mother——" Brierley clung to her. "Please don't leave
me."

Gerin shook her head and gently detached Brierley's hands.
"If you will listen, daughter, I will believe in your hope. I will
believe in you." She looked beyond Brierley, where the Allemanii
lords stood speaking to Linia. "And in him," she added softly.
"There will be a new beginning. Many may die before it comes,
and the first efforts might not succeed, but it will come."

Gerin straightened her shoulders. "Yes," she whispered, and
no longer saw Brierley standing before her, but other times, other
places. "Yes," she repeated to herself, nodding, and turned away.

ℰ ⁓ 17 ⁓ ℰ

elfallan and the Everlight lay together on the narrow bed in Brierley's sea cave, still joined in the flesh, the heat rising from their bodies after his frenzied coupling—in his passion, he had tried to satiate himself in her body, driven to want more of her than ever before. She had responded as passionately, lost in him as he was in her. After his ecstatic release, he felt drained of all strength and lay panting on top of her, his face buried in her hair, unable to move. She shifted her hands slowly down his naked back with a delicious warmth, and he shivered with the touch.

When he could move again, Melfallan lifted himself on an elbow and looked down at Brierley's face, so perfectly hers, so real in every line, every expression.

"This worries you?" the Everlight asked. "I can sense that it does. Why?"

"I sometimes forget you aren't her," he said, and made himself smile. "That worries me, yes." He gently lifted his body off hers, separating them, and lay down beside her on the bed, then entwined their fingers tightly. For a moment he studied their joined hands, then released her hand to cup her breast. Slowly he fondled her, breathing in her scents, nuzzling at her hair. "Everything is perfect: your voice, your touch. When I'm with you, I— Yes, it worries me."

With a sigh, he rolled on his back and took her hand again,

then listened to the surf and the sighing of the cool air through the cave, content to listen, more content that he had ever imagined a man could feel. "This isn't real. Is it natural?"

"Anything that exists must be natural," Brierley said tentatively, her voice puzzled.

"Now you sound like an Everlight."

"Oh? And how does an Everlight sound, Earl Melfallan?"

He smiled at the stone ceiling, amused by her annoyed tone. However the Everlight pretended itself as Brierley to comfort him, or, less frequently, appeared as Thora Jodann, it sometimes slipped and became merely itself, a very special self that he had grown to like. "How does an Everlight sound? Prim, a tad abstract, liking maxims whenever possible," he answered, teasing her. "Did you ever talk to Brierley as yourself in her dreams—I mean, as other than Thora?"

"No. Thora was all that was needed." The Everlight paused. "An Everlight can easily ensorcel a witch if the heart is touched too deeply, and so lure her to prefer dreams over reality. Brierley was very lonely after her mother died: it was a peril I would not risk with her." Another pause. "Perhaps I have erred in offering this," she admitted. "Perhaps you are right to worry."

He turned his head. "I'm not a shari'a witch. You can't ensorcel me, however that is done."

"Oh? Why then are you worried?"

"Not that worried," he said quickly, afraid that the Everlight might stop these lovely dreams, as it might. "Brierley says that I worry about everything—"

"—as you do—"

"—so I'd rather not worry about my feeling worried, if you can follow that particular circle."

Brierley smiled. "With difficulty, but yes."

He smiled back. "In truth, I think you make my life even possible until Brierley comes home again. I can get up each day and go about my earl's affairs with good cheer, confident, easily pleased. I feel—relaxed, more than I used to." He frowned slightly. "I— Well, I can't quite catch it, but this cave is her special place, with her special friend, the Everlight who guarded her and comforted her and gave her peace. I don't know exactly what you are, Everlight, although I know some things you aren't."

"I am many things now," she said comfortably. "Including a part that is you."

"But not Brierley. I must remember that." He grimaced. "You know her best: what will she think about this—affair with her Everlight?"

"You're worrying again." Brierley yawned and then slowly rubbed her face against his shoulder. She trailed her fingers down his chest in light caress.

"Yes, but what will she—?" he persisted, then broke off as her touch tingled against his flesh like a cool sifting breeze. "Please stop that," he said plaintively. "I can't think when you do that." She lifted her hand and put it safely behind her back, smiling impishly, as Brierley would smile. "Will you listen?" he insisted. "This is important." He waited until Brierley gave him polite attention, her eyebrow raised. "We had hardly any time together in the cabin; she can't know me very well, not yet. You need time for that, time we weren't given. What if she won't understand—"

"Won't she?" Now the Everlight sounded amused. "A sea witch?"

Melfallan sighed. "Why do I even expect a straight answer from you?" he said, then sighed more deeply as she brought out her hand and resumed its wandering.

"I haven't a clue," the Everlight said, her eyes dancing. "Shall I stop?" she asked.

"No. Please." He rolled his eyes as she didn't stop and then continued even further, then laughed in sheer delight and turned eagerly toward her, pulling her tightly against him. "Brierley—" he breathed into her hair.

"Not Brierley: remember that, fair lord."

"I will," Melfallan promised.

Later Melfallan again lay curled next to Brierley in her narrow bed in the sea cave, both drowsy and content, nested like spoons. Slowly he caressed the sweet curve of her naked hip, then lightly kissed her shoulder. "Thank you, Everlight," he said softly.

"You're welcome." She chuckled.

The Daystar was now dawning, and its soft light filtered through shafts and cracks in the ceiling, giving enough light to see. After a time Melfallan sat up and dangled his legs off the edge of the bed, then looked around curiously at the contents of the cave. Here was a bed, a table and single chair, shelves and shelves of books, comfortable enough for a single occupant. To the right a lower riser of stairs descended from the central room to a bathing pool and pantry. A doorway in the opposite corner half-concealed a shadowed stair that led upward, and he wondered to what.

"To the door stones above," Brierley said sleepily. "She often watches the sea from there."

"Um. Will you show me?"

"If you wish."

The Everlight sometimes answered questions he hadn't spoken aloud, a habit he still found mildly startling. Well, it did explain how an Everlight could invade his dreams, as it obviously had. Melfallan got to his feet and stretched hugely, then stood a few moments, hands on his hips, his head turning as he looked. Here was Brierley's one safe place in a dangerous world, and he examined everything with intense interest.

He glanced around at the woman on the bed, and saw her watching him, her head propped on one hand. "I want to explore. Do you think she'd mind?"

"Explore?"

"Well," he fretted, "maybe not. She might not like it."

"Why not?"

He hesitated, then walked the few steps to the table, and lightly touched the brass lamp, the curve of an ink bottle with its pen, a small stack of books. He tipped the top book to look at the title. Herb lore, it seemed, by someone named Lorena. Hadn't Brierley said that name in the library? She had been studying this book, he guessed, before she went that last time to Amelin, where

Melfallan's soldiers had awaited her. *I didn't know,* he thought sadly. *I didn't know what I stripped out of her life when I gave my prudent order: how long did she believe she would never see her cave again? Does she still believe that?*

The cave air sifted coolly against his naked skin as he walked to the shelves and looked at the book titles. On a middle shelf in one of the bookcases stood a row of bound journals. He squinted as he read the titles, and lifted down the last volume. With another glance at the woman on the bed, he boldly carried Brierley's journal to the table and sat down. "Hmph," he said an instant later and got up. He stalked over to the bed, and relieved Brierley of one of the blankets. The chair seat had been ice cold.

"Very funny," he growled.

She grinned at him. "I strive to be real, fair lord. It is, after all, winter."

"Hmph." He wrapped the blanket around himself and returned to the table. He opened the book near the middle, then paged onward to the last few entries. She wrote with a graceful hand—he realized he had never seen her handwriting, another new thing to know.

My dear child, he read, *do not despair. I believe that the Blood will continue beyond me, and that I am not the last . . .*

Today I went to Natheby to watch the fishing fleet for a while before my Calling to the herder boy. By the docks I spoke to a northerner captain named Bartol about the lands farther up the coast. He had many strange tales, but no hint of other shari'a—

Or, rather, he had many tales of witches, each shrunken and evil and wishing men into death. In men's minds, we have become creatures of the night, murderers of children, drinkers of men's blood, an evil concealed deep in the earth, within the boles of trees, or in any woman's heart.

My child, be careful. The Disasters still live with us, and none of the Blood can walk openly in the High Lords' lands. Be vigilant, and take great care.

I wish I could meet you, my child. I feel alone. I wish . . . for many things I do not have.

He turned back several pages, then several more. "Did she always write to her apprentice?" he asked softly.

"Usually. After Jocater died, she was quite alone."

Melfallan tipped back the chair and opened the book to its beginning, then began to read. Here the hand was more awkward, less polished. After a few pages, he learned Brierley was then nine, still a young girl. He read about her finding the cave, the Voice on the beach, about Jared and her mother's fears, about her unpleasant stepfather and their unhappy household, her aching grief for her mother after she suicided. He read about a day on the beach, when "Life had called to her," as she phrased it, and she had chosen "the craft." Despite her youth, Brierley had fully understood the dangers of that brave choice. How old was she? he marveled. Ten? Eleven? When he was ten, he had only a boy's trivial concerns, large to him at that age, but easily borne in his easy life, his confident future.

He read about her first attempts to heal, and her speculations and recordings about the experiences. His eyes widened as he learned that Brierley could hear thoughts, like the Everlight did: it seemed to be part of being shari'a, and must be something that Megan and Brierley shared. He thought back to their days in the cabin, and found a few odd instances between Brierley and the child that fit. Not that he'd noticed at the time, of course: elusiveness was Brierley's art, as it must be. But to hear another's thoughts? To know their inner reasons, their true intent? A chill shivered down his spine as he realized the implications. The High Lords depended upon sleight-of-hand in their politics, their hidden purposes, their secret plots.

"You must never use her that way, Melfallan," the Everlight warned.

"But if the other High Lords knew that she can—" he said, turning to her.

"They must never know, or your lands will be plunged into wars such as you have never seen. Fearful men will not chance a witch's restraint in using her gift—nor her lord's."

Melfallan nodded soberly, then had another thought about im-

plications. "Did she always know what I was thinking?" he demanded. "I mean, all the time?"

"When she chose to listen—and she doesn't always. Is this a
problem?"

"I don't know." He frowned slightly. "I'm a High Lord, and
I like to hide purposes, too."

"Even from her?" The Everlight smiled. "Didn't your aunt
tell you that the shari'a live in a different world? This is part of
that world, fair lord. The sharing of thought was the first and
greatest of the Four's gifts to their beloveds: from it all other
witchery flows. For the sea witches, it lends the knowledge of the
inner heart that is a healer's special blessing, and from that knowledge Brierley can renew life and change death. It is part of her,
and she values it profoundly. Will you then impose rules, not this
and never that?"

"No, of course not."

"Then live sometimes in her world, and accept." Melfallan
looked pointedly around at the cave, then heard the Everlight
laugh softly. "But, yes, I chide you unfairly: you are accepting
my dreams quite well."

"You give me good inducements." He winked at her, and she
laughed aloud.

"Yes, I suppose I do," she said, and the smile was back, the
lilting and playful smile that lit the eyes.

Melfallan turned back to Brierley's journal, his fingers caressing the page. Here was Brierley's inner heart, he knew, without
concealment, without eluding, her true self as she struggled to
understand what she was. At first Brierley had felt awkward in
her healings and had greatly feared discovery, he read, but through
practice she learned to hide the gift within her midwife's craft.
After every healing, the Beast appeared, a dread apparition of ten-
tacles and loathsome flesh. Melfallan shuddered: every time? For
lesser healings, the Beast was easily defeated, but when she dealt
with serious injury that might kill, her own life was menaced.
She suspected that several of the cave witches had met their end
in such a healing, and despite the risk, continued her craft.

And on nearly every page echoed her loneliness, this desperate wish for another shari'a who might be her apprentice, her companion, her second self.

He heard a rustle of bedclothes, then felt Brierley's arms slip around his neck. He turned his head to look up at her. "Megan— she's the apprentice, isn't she?"

"Yes, she is—and there's more, fair lord. Later she writes about Clara Jacoby's farmhouse, a house she would dearly love to have as her own, but knew she could not. She had resolved never to hope for such a home, such a beloved." She smiled gently. "She never expected you. After the Disasters, some shari'a dared to love an Allemanii lord, Thora among them. It was dangerous, imprudent—but still they chose." She tipped her head to the side, her lips curving into a wistful smile. "A woman's heart has many dreams."

"I shouldn't have left her in Airlie," he fretted. "I should have brought her home."

"You chose as best you could, with sound reasons, and she thought it the better choice. So do I. Don't doubt yourself. All may be well in time."

He reached and pulled her into his lap, then wrapped his arms around her. He kissed the sweet curve of her neck, then closed his eyes in the wonder of holding her. "You are so much like her," he marveled.

"I am part of her, as she is part of me." She slowly caressed his face, then teased his hair with her fingers. "She would want me to comfort you, to be with you until you are together again. In that I am certain, so do not worry. I have tended the witches of this shore for three centuries, growing old and sometimes scattered in my thoughts. Brierley is the last flame, Thora's own witch-child and apprentice, long-awaited, deeply cherished. How can I not love someone that she herself loves? It is no burden, none at all, fair lord."

Melfallan tightened his arms around her, then pressed his face against her hair, breathing in the scent of it, like heather or the sea wind, like Brierley's.

His dream shifted, and he found himself a dream-shadow within his own dream, watching with two shari'a women as Earl Farrar and his company rode to the village well. Linia gave her friend an affectionate glance. "You like everybody, Gerin. It's a part of your gift."

"Not everybody. There's a few souls I could do without." Gerin sniffed, then turned abruptly and looked up into Melfallan's eyes. The old woman blinked in startlement as she saw him, then smiled with a slow and delighted pleasure, her once-held beauty hers again, lighting the eyes, shaping the smile. It was Brierley's smile, the very same, and for a moment Melfallan's breath caught in his chest. "Farrar was much like you," Gerin said to him. "Remember him, beloved, when you make your choices."

"What did you say, Gerin?" Linia asked, looking around at her friend.

"There is past and present," Gerin replied elliptically, "but also the future." She shook her head at Linia's puzzled frown and laughed. "Three intersecting yet sometimes one," she added.

Linia tossed her head. "I'm tired of you, Gerin. Why don't you leave?"

Gerin laughed at Linia's fierce scowl. Likely she always teased, Melfallan decided, more than Brierley ever could. Gerin now neared the end of her life in a safer world for the shari'a, before Duke Rahorsum ordered the death of all shari'a, every one.

The gentle mockery in Gerin's face shifted abruptly to pain. "Will he?" Gerin murmured in distress. "Oh, will he?" Gerin looked around at the village she loved, the folk she loved and tended. "Oh, beloved, it is all in ruins: I can see it now." She raised her hands to her cheeks. "I have no part in your future, young lord, nor other futures when Death came again for our survivors, and the hounds wailed in the hunt, the fire rose, flesh burned, a shari'a died. I had no chance to stop it, not once. The Beast took them all."

She pulled her hood low over her face. "I did not want to

know this. I did not want to know." Gerin turned and began to walk slowly away.

"Wait!" Melfallan called. He took a step after her, to mend what he had inflicted if he could, but in that same instant the shari'a village vanished, as if it had never existed. Perhaps it never had.

Instead he dreamed now of another woman, slender and pale, in another place and time near Briding's shore. He smiled down at her, and she shyly laid his hand on his arm when he offered it.

"Dram, you are too bold," she protested, shaking her head.

"It's a soldier's lot to be bold," he teased. "I'm called away to Duke Lutke's war against Airlie, and have only this day before I leave. Surely I can ask for your company to stroll through the town."

"And how does one lead to the other, your war and my company?"

"Because I will it, of course." She laughed and he tucked her hand possessively against his side. It was their last day together, although he had not known it then, for he had died in the war, pierced by an Airlie lance, and had never returned to her.

Time shifted and he drowned, a Lim fisherman's young son lost overboard in a sudden storm, never to meet the slender pale-haired girl born the following spring.

Time shifted and a sea witch in Yarvannet failed against the Beast, and never met the young Tyndale lord who visited Tiol two years later.

Time shifted, and the dragons wrought again, but both boy and infant girl died in that winter's plague in Ingal—

Time shifted and Melfallan walked with another young woman, slender and pale, on the high battlements of Efe Castle in Mionn. War now loomed, for a usurper, Lionel Kobus, had seized the duke's coronet through foul murder of his liege, and all was in doubt. His wife turned her head and smiled up at him, lifting his heart, as her smile always lifted his heart, even after five years together.

"Soon he'll be born," she said contentedly, laying a slender hand on her swollen belly. They stopped by the battlement wall, arm in arm, to look down at the bay far below. "A boy, I think. Perhaps he'll be the earl's castellan, like his father."

"Perhaps. I care only that he is healthy, my love." He bent to kiss her, and then kissed her a second time for no particular reason save he wished to, and smiled as she laughed at him.

But that winter, when cold and bitter storms struck from across the eastern bay, the plague had come again and had killed her in childbed, emptying his life into nothingness.

Time shifted and Melfallan dreamed of Brierley in their bed in the cabin, her hands like silk on his body as he hammered into her, possessed by his lust for her, making her his. But then it was Saray beneath him in the cabin bed, as eagerly enjoyed, the two merging into the same woman. In Brierley's cave, on her narrow bed, as the sea sounds surrounded them as cloak for their nakedness, he kissed his wife passionately as he took her yet again, and felt her hands tighten on his body.

"Love me——" Saray pleaded.

Time folded——

In a white pavilion high above the sea, as the waves crashed far below and sea larks cried wildly on the wind, he mounted Mother Ocean herself, young lusty god to her divinity, and gave her his seed in ecstatic release. She shouted and cast him away, and he fell through the air, spinning slowly, and then spread his falcon wings and beat upward, climbing toward the suns.

He fell again, tumbling helplessly, the sea rocks looming beneath him, and struck stone.

He fell a third time, falling into endless darkness.

He fell——

Melfallan awoke with a start and rolled violently to his feet, his blankets scattering, his cot upended, then lurched off balance as he stumbled. He caught himself with one hand on the tower table, his breath coming in great gusts, his blood pounding in his ears and groin.

After a few moments he looked around dazedly, and seemed to see the crumbled stone walls of a ruined shari'a village, its stone covered with shadowed white, beneath the heavy shadow of Airlie's trees. Darkness lay all around him, whispering with the fall of new snow. On the other side of the dying fire, a man snored softly, and nothing remained of his dreams. Nothing. All else was dark shadow, huddled shapes, clinging cold, and the wind was rising again.

Melfallan shook his head, and the next instant he was back in his tower in Yarvannet, where he was supposed to be. He touched the tower table, assuring himself of its reality, and looked at the other familiar contents of his tower study, one by one. The map on the wall, the chairs, the solid walls, the window looking out on Tiol Harbor. All real—were they real? The power of his dreaming still gripped him, and he wasn't entirely sure, not yet.

He listened for a time to the rhythmic sound of the waves in the harbor beyond the window, then looked around once more. He checked everything over a third time, then sat down gingerly on a chair. It held him, solid comfortable support. Real. When his head was better and his groin had stopped its painful throbbing, he bent and picked up his blanket and wrapped it around him tightly. He'd had enough of dreams for tonight, whatever the cost of short sleep for the morrow.

His dream had started pleasantly enough, with the Everlight again wooing him into bed into Brierley's cave, but then had shifted elsewhere. By what means? By the Everlight's sending? Witchly games should go only so far, Everlight or not. I'll talk to her, he promised himself irritably. He frowned then, wondering at what meaning the Everlight had intended.

There is past and present, but also the future, Gerin had said. *Three intersecting, yet sometimes one.* But what past had he dreamed tonight? Or what future?

Why remember Farrar? Melfallan puzzled, and frowned even more deeply.

And who were the other women, the other Melfallans? Or had his dreams any sense at all? How very odd: before the Everlight had invaded his dreams, he had rarely dreamed this vividly, and never of other times, especially not of white pavilions and consorting with a goddess. He looked around at his tower study again, wondering again if a witch's ancient place elsewhere could haunt a man's dreams—and had this night.

(*I love you*), a sweet voice said into Melfallan's mind, resonating like slow ripples through a cool pond. Melfallan sighed deeply and closed his eyes. (*I am with you*), her voice said from the air above, from the frozen ground of Mahel beneath his feet, then whispered away on the rising wind. He stood again in the Airlie hills, yearning for her.

Melfallan strained to hear, but the voice did not come again, only the sound of the sifting snow, falling in its gentle curtains all around him. He raised his face to the snow, feeling its gentle cold touch, its wetness against his skin. The touch was like hers, delicate, gentle, yet adamant in its necessity, with a healer's strength. He took a deep breath of the cold icy air.

"This time, beloved," he whispered, "fate will not divide us." He set his jaw. "I swear it."

"I swear it," Melfallan whispered.

Brierley awoke suddenly in her campside bed in Airlie, thinking she had heard his voice next to her ear. It had seemed Melfallan lay abed with her again, his arms encircling her, his breath warm against her bare shoulder. But no—

Had she spoken to him? He was leagues away in Yarvannet, far beyond her calling! She ached with the wish for his touch, and longed bitterly for him, as if breath itself depended on his presence. Her eyes filled with hot tears, the ache a hollowness within her. Vain wishes, vain dreams.

"Melfallan—" she whispered brokenly, and might have

reached out her hand and touched him, crossing the leagues, if only she knew how. But no—

Not real. It was only a dream, another vain and tormenting dream. Brierley dried her eyes on a corner of the blanket, took a tremulous breath to steady herself, then tried again to sleep.

~◦

In Yarvannet the next day dawned clear and cold, with a light wind stirring up dust on the castle battlements and the ridge road. Melfallan watched the sea for an hour from his tower window, then descended to his chambers to dress for Jared's knighting. He still hadn't shaken off the effect of his vivid dream, and it preoccupied him badly, as if great matters portended this day just beyond his perception. Usually the details of his dreams faded upon waking: even his romps with the Everlight in Brierley's cave bed tended to blur into a happy but unspecific memory. But he could clearly remember the details of Mahel—the smithy, the tempermental Linia, Gerin's ancient but ever-young eyes, the glittering procession with Earl Farrar as they rode to the village well. When the Briding girl shyly took Dram's arm, it had seemed his own arm, and he could remember that touch as a distinct physical memory. When the Mionn castellan had kissed his wife on the battlements, it seemed his own lips had pressed on hers: the memory still tingled, colored by the deep love that had existed between them, as if that love, too, had belonged to him as well. How very strange, he thought. And later in the cave, and then the pavilion—

What did it mean, if anything? Why Farrar? Melfallan shook his head, and determinedly thought of other things.

In the nearby chamber, he could hear the low voices of Saray and her lady-maids as she also dressed, but Saray did not come in to see him. It had been their habit that he would seek her out each morning, one imposed early in their marriage, he wasn't quite sure how, but a habit he had neglected badly of late. He shrugged. Since Saray didn't complain, he'd assume she didn't mind. If she did mind, he'd outwait her pretending. Surely there was some strategy that would work, he thought irritably, so why not try this one? And Revil had a point about cooperating with games.

His manservant Philippe came hastening in, all aghast that he'd missed most of Melfallan's dressing. "Your grace!" he exclaimed. "I didn't know you were ready to dress!" He brushed Melfallan's shoulders of dust that wasn't there, straightened a wrinkle that was, then circled him anxiously, inspecting.

"It's all right," Melfallan said. "I—" Philippe bent to lift his foot to check the fit of his shoe, and Melfallan quickly demurred, lest in his anxious zeal Philippe lift both feet at once, to that catastrophe. "Enough, Philippe."

Philippe took a step back and looked him over again from head to toe. His face flushed with pride. "You look a noble earl indeed, your grace!" he exclaimed.

Melfallan smiled. "It will be a fine day. I should dress the part, don't you think?"

"The whole castle is talking about the knighting," Philippe said excitedly, "and most of Amelin's folk has arrived to witness it. There won't be enough room in the Great Hall!" He looked aghast at the horrible thought.

"We'll fit them in," Melfallan assured him. "Don't worry."

His announcement the week before of Jared Cheney's elevation to gentleman knight had stunned everyone in the castle, especially Jared himself. Melfallan grinned as he remembered that young man's expression when he was told, and the incredulous joy that had followed the surprise. Revil truly had a gift about his people. His cousin often knew best their hearts, sometimes more than they did themselves. Jared had never in his wildest hopes expected a knighthood, and Melfallan found it a surprising pleasure to give it to him, more than he had expected. Nor had Melfallan anticipated the enthusiastic reaction of the Yarvannet commonfolk, who had gladly cheered the elevation of one of their own, and had feted Jared for a solid week, both in Amelin and Tiol. At a single stroke, Melfallan found himself a wildly popular earl, at least with the commonfolk, and at least for today.

Revil's inspiration, he thought fondly as he tied the laces of his tunic. And if his dream of the sea cave were true, this knighting would be a quiet gift to Brierley, too, this honoring of her childhood friend. All the reasons fit, and for once he had no doubt about his decision, not in the slightest.

Philippe clucked his tongue and redid his laces, then fussed over him until Melfallan shooed him away. Melfallan took his silver circlet from its case and settled it on his blond hair, then buckled on his sword with its gold-chased scabbard. Philippe brought a heavy gold necklace with a large jewel, and settled it over Melfallan's shoulders, then stood back for another inspection.

"Wonderful!" he exclaimed. Melfallan took a final look into his mirror and happily decided he agreed, then turned and left his suite.

Melfallan descended the stairs to the Great Hall, where everything was bustling. Most of Amelin seemed to have showed up, as Philippe had said, and half of Natheby, too, a fact Philippe had omitted. With the company of the local Tiol gentry, who never missed any high occasion at the castle, whatever it was, they made quite a crowd. In a far corner he saw Harmon Jacoby and his wife, happily part of a group of Amelin folk clustered around Revil; in mid-room, a similar clustering of Amelin ladies chatted gaily with Solange, all happy and excited. Saray and the other noble ladies had already taken their seats in the ladies' gallery off to the left, their husbands hovering nearby, but Solange still stood with her folk, reluctant to leave them.

When Melfallan entered the room, all heads turned and watched as he walked solemnly toward the dais. They waited until he sat down in his chair, then, with an excited rustling and low murmuring of voices, they drifted toward the walls, creating a lane leading to the opposite door of the Great Hall, now closed.

The chamberlain stepped forward and the room was abruptly silent. "Jared Cheney of Amelin, step forth!" the man cried.

The large doors of the Hall creaked open. Jared walked through the doorway, Sir Micay at his side. Jared was dressed in fine blue and gray velvet, tailored neatly to fit his sturdy body, and a rich chain of gold gleamed on his breast, Melfallan's gift the night before. An empty scabbard hung from his golden belt, and Sir Micay carried Jared's sword on a wide pillow. They solemnly paced the length of the hall floor, with all the crowd watching, then bowed to Melfallan on the dais.

"Your grace," Jared said in greeting, visibly nervous but bearing it well. "Did you summon me, lord?"

"I have," Melfallan replied solemnly, nodding to him. The words of the knighting ceremony dated back to the West itself, as had the institution of a sworn man. "I am inclined, Jared Cheney, to grace you with knighthood. Are you willing?" The crowd seemed to hold its collective breath.

"Lord, I am," Jared said proudly.

Melfallan extended his hands, and Jared knelt on the single step of the dais and put his hands between Melfallan's palms. "I swear fealty to you as my liege lord," Jared said slowly, "to be faithful and true as your man, to give you fair counsel, and to defend you with my life." His voice rose proudly, ringing through the hall. "I will be the shield on your arm and the sword in your hand, lord, as Ocean is my witness." He rose, took a step backward, and knelt again, his head bowed.

Melfallan stood and descended the single riser of the dais, then drew his sword from its scabbard. "I accept your fealty, Jared Cheney," he said, looking down at Jared's blond head, "and I promise to be faithful and true as your liege, to seek your counsel, and to defend your right." Melfallan laid his sword blade lightly on Jared's right shoulder, lifted it with a flourish, then lowered the blade to his other shoulder. "Rise now, Sir Jared," he said with satisfaction, "and join my company of honorable knights."

As Jared got to his feet, Sir Micay proffered the pillow on which lay Jared's sword. Melfallan took the sword and eased it into the scabbard hanging from Jared's belt, then knelt to fit Jared's spurs. When Melfallan straightened again, a happy sigh whispered around the watching crowd, followed by a low hum of voices. For a moment Melfallan and Jared grinned at each other. They had practiced this only once, but neither had stumbled their words, nor tripped over his own feet nor dropped a sword. It was a fine day. Taking Jared's arm, Melfallan turned him to face the crowd.

"Here, my good folk," he said, "is Sir Jared Cheney, my trusted knight. In him I place my confidence."

Jared blushed as the crowd applauded wildly, with the loudest cheers in the back near Harmon and Jared's family. Lord Tauler and Lord Garth had not come to the knighting, although invited, and Count Sadon's presence had been a useless hope, but the Amelin folk now covered that lack with their thorough delight in Jared's honor. Revil and Solange came forward to greet Jared, and then the others of Amelin and Natheby, each pumping Jared's hand, then bowing shyly to Melfallan. The Tiol gentry drifted forward, too, their greetings more subdued but still hearty. Even Saray was gracious in her congratulations to Jared, however little she meant them.

As Jenny had predicted, Saray had overlooked her bad temper and would not discuss it, and instead fluted her hand and sweetly forgave him his faults. For a time, it seemed they had peace again, but then Saray began to forget the small attentions she had always given him, the touch of a hand, the smile across the table, the courteous questions about his health. At times, he caught an odd expression on her face as she watched him, quickly erased when he looked at her. Last week he had overheard her talking to her friends, and had wondered if she had always spoken of him in that belittling, sweet-voiced, poisonous way.

He slept more often on the cot in his tower study than with Saray, not caring what the servants thought or said behind their hands. At times her sweet smiles and feigned passion revolted him, and the scent of her perfume could set his stomach to roiling. He still managed to perform physically, once he lost himself in his lust, but as the days had passed he had bedded Saray less and less. Saray never commented on his absence from her bed, never suggested otherwise. Confined by her lady rules, Saray could not demur when he chose to escape to his tower or merely rolled his back to her in bed. Perhaps she missed it a little; perhaps she felt secretly relieved. Perhaps Melfallan no longer cared.

He might worry about a coming war with Duke Tejar, but he was now aware that a more subtle war was raging with his wife in his own castle, and he hadn't a clue what he'd done now. Saray was settling a score, Ocean knew about what. It had extended their quarrel far too long, and neither of them seemed capable of ending it. He had spoken to no one about it, although surely the strain must be obvious to everyone. And Saray did not even know about Brierley, that was the irony.

I should try to make it right again, he told himself unhappily, as he watched Saray walk back to her ladies. I should try as I've always tried, but, Ocean, I don't want to. He was tired of trying, weary to his bones of trying. He was tired of forcing himself to bed her, tired of listening to her chatter and watching her pose, tired of complimenting her beauty to make her happy. Trying got him nowhere. Years of frustration had finally made itself an unclimbable mountain, and now he stood at its base, looking up, weary beyond counting.

When he had told her about his intention to knight Jared, Melfallan had ignored Saray's hint of disapproval, the lifted eyebrow, the pursed mouth, the half-spoken sentence, and it had become yet another silent issue between them. Finally, two nights ago, Melfallan had flatly warned her against any slighting comment to Jared, or any other posturing in front of the gentry that she might be planning, to Saray's professed hurt and surprise.

"But, Melfallan," she had protested. "I would never—"

"Just don't," he interrupted. "Don't play to the gentry who watch you. This is Jared's day, and I won't have you ruin it."

"But—" she had said, fluttering her hands, pretending and denying and aghast that he would think so, and he had stalked out.

I should try harder, he thought unhappily, and watched Saray smile sweetly at Lady Alice, then give Justin Halliwell her hand. Saray's beauty could still catch at his breath, and he admired her grace, the sweetness of her smile, the gentle attentions she gave to everyone. Women as well as men could fall out of love as easily as into it, and he wondered what he had done to lose Saray's love, as perhaps he had. Had she sensed Brierley within his heart, without even being told, without any clue? Did she understand that one truth, even if she understood nothing else about him?

After nearly everyone had come forward to offer a bow and a few words, the crowd bore Jared away through the wide doors into the dining hall, where Jared was seated at Melfallan's right hand, Saray at his left. Revil rose and made a pleasant speech, followed by other speeches from Jared's folk in the audience, all to Jared's flattering and praise. Near the end, Jared put all his attention on his plate, totally embarrassed by the attention.

Melfallan nudged him with an elbow. "Cheer up, Jared," he said. "It'll be over soon."

"So you say," Jared muttered back. "This has been going on for a week. Am I allowed second thoughts, your grace?"

"No," Melfallan said affably, "you're stuck." Jared sighed.

"Sir Jared," Saray began, then stopped short as Melfallan shot her a warning glance. Her mouth set and she glared back at him a moment, then smoothly reordered her expression. "Has my husband set your income?" she inquired.

"Uh—" Jared said uncertainly, then glanced at Melfallan. "Well, there's a house in the town, and something about port fees." He smiled. "Actually, I'm not sure. It's been a busy week, my lady."

"You should notice such matters of finance," Saray reproved in a sweet but quite poisonous tone. "Although I agree you are unaccustomed to—"

"Saray!" Melfallan warned.

"I was only saying—"

"You've said enough." Saray shot him a resentful glance, then busied herself with the food on her plate. Melfallan reached for the decanter of wine and refilled Jared's glass, then his own. When he offered to Saray, she pointedly turned to Lady Tolland on her other side. Melfallan shrugged and put the decanter back on the table.

Jared leaned closer and spoke in a low voice. "Did I say something wrong, your grace?"

Melfallan shook his head. "Don't worry, Jared. Enjoy your day." Melfallan gestured at the crowded room. "And it *is* your day, and sometimes I can be 'Melfallan,' not 'your grace.' All my knights take that liberty."

"I still don't know why you picked me—" Jared broke off and looked flustered.

The noise of the crowd had created an ocean of sound around them, one in which their own talk would not be easily overheard. Melfallan half-turned in his chair to face Jared. "Many reasons," he said seriously. "Because I need another friend my age, one I can trust." He had Jared's full attention now. "Because you knew *her,* and I will need counsel. Because I need someone who will speak his mind, as you do, and because you are a good man, Jared, a man she trusted. I hope you find some of the same qualities in me, and that you will serve me not just because I'm your earl, but because I merit your friendship. I'll have to earn that, I know, but I'll try."

"But I'm just a common soldier," he said, flushing slightly. He touched the gold chain on his breast. "This chain alone is worth my father's entire smithy, and the house and the revenue—"

"You're not a common soldier, not anymore. You're a gentleman knight of my household." Melfallan smiled when Jared still looked unpersuaded. "It does have its air of unreality, I know. I felt the same way when I became earl, and I still do at times."

"You?" Jared goggled.

"Have you ever learned hawking?"

"Uh, no. That's a—"

"—nobleman's sport, yes. It's time you learned, and I need better practice with sword-work. Sir Micay says you're a fair swordsman. I'll teach you hawking, and you can spar with me in the quadrangle. How's that for a trade?"

Jared hesitated another moment, then seemed to relax at last. His smile was shy. "I'd like that—Melfallan. I'd like that very much."

"So would I." Melfallan grinned. "So we'll do it."

~⌒

"How *dare* you reprove me in front of the gentry!" Saray's eyes flashed angrily. Melfallan wondered if she planned to throw the hairbrush in her hand, just once throw something. He leaned on the doorjamb of her dressing-room, then glanced pointedly at Berthe, who scurried out.

"Nobody else heard," he said tightly, "and I doubt Jared even understood. I warned you, Saray."

"All I was asking was—"

"I know what you were asking, and I know the tone you used. I know he's a blacksmith's son: well, I've just elevated him to the nobility. He's noble now, and you should start thinking of him as that. I intend to make Jared a close friend, as any knight should be to his lord. And you aren't going to use him as someone to scorn. I've tolerated your behavior toward Leila, but it ends there."

"Leila's just a servant! You can't expect me—"

"Leila is our son's nurse, Saray," Melfallan said, struggling for patience. "Audric will see *her* face over his cradle every morning, not yours or mine. He will look to *her* for his comfort and love and care. For these first few years, Leila is the most important person in his life, as Mollwen was for me. She's not 'just a servant,' as you call her."

"Hmmph!" Saray turned around to her mirror and began vigorously brushing her long hair. She muttered something he didn't catch.

"What did you say?" he asked.

Saray slammed down her hairbrush on her mirror table, and turned to face him. "I said you're far too close to servants. I know all about her, Melfallan!"

"Who?" Melfallan asked, startled.

"The castle girl you're bedding. Don't you think I know why you don't sleep in our bed? Don't you think I hear the servants' sniggering? Well, I'm your lady *wife*, Melfallan Courtray, and I insist that it stop!" Saray's cheeks flushed vividly, but her face was adamant.

"I'm not bedding anyone else," he protested. Well, not anyone real, he amended mentally. "I'm not," he stated more firmly, and saw that Saray did not believe him. "If you know all about her, who is she? I'd like to know, since I'm the one supposedly bedding her."

Saray put her chin in the air and turned back to her mirror, then resumed brushing her hair. "Please call Berthe back in," she said. "I need her."

"Saray, I'm *not* having an affair with a castle girl. I just thought you weren't that interested. You certainly hadn't complained." Saray tightened her lips and said nothing, her brush moving briskly. "Do you want me in your bed? Fine: all you have to do is ask." Melfallan pulled off his golden chain and tossed it to the floor, then began unlacing his tunic.

"Don't mock me!" Saray shouted, and Melfallan ducked as the hairbrush came flying across the room. It smashed into the doorjamb a few inches from his head, then shattered into pieces. Saray moaned in dismay, then buried her face in her hands and began to cry. Melfallan clenched his fists angrily and wanted to walk out, but after another moment he made himself go to her. He put his hands on her shoulders and squeezed, then bent to kiss her hair.

"I'm sorry, Saray," he said quietly. "Don't cry." He eased himself onto the bench beside her, then held her as she cried. "I'm sorry I shouted."

"I don't understand you," she sobbed.

He stroked her hair and pulled her closer. "I know, my love," he said sadly, and it was true, one fact Saray would finally admit. "I know you don't." She sniffled and leaned against him, and after a while he kissed her and her arms came shyly around him, and he carried her to their bed.

o you lied to her," the Everlight said.

"I did not," Melfallan objected. "Brierley's not a castle girl, and you're not real."

"That's a quibble to help you dodge. She'll have to know eventually."

Melfallan rolled on his back and sighed, then looked up into Brierley's sweet face, shadowed by the dim light in the cave. Cool air sighed into the cave, chilling the skin, and the waves crashed against stone, a muffled sound like a cocoon, walling away the world. "I always wondered if Saray knew about the other women. I think I just found out." He sighed again.

"You think you and I should stop." Brierley tipped her head and smiled wryly.

"Not the dreams—I'd still like to see you—but the bedding, yes. It was lovely, but now it—distracts me. I'm saying things I've never said to her before, and avoiding her when I shouldn't. I shrug and say I don't care, but I *should* care." He made a face. "Whatever Revil thinks, ignoring her was not a good strategy. We've never quarreled this badly. I mean, she finally threw something at me. I used to wish she would, but now I find I don't like it at all." He grimaced again. "I don't want to be cruel to Saray. It's not her fault."

"Isn't it?"

"Do you think it is?" he asked curiously. "You're Everlight to a sea witch. Do you have the same insight into hearts? Do you

know why we can't—" He made another face. "I try to do the right
things, Everlight. I made Jared a knight: that was right. I'm trying
to understand the dream about Farrar, and that's right. I'm trying to
protect Brierley, and to keep the peace if I can—that's right, too. But
when Saray starts her games, I can't think at all about other things.
I don't know what to do. Nothing I try works." He raised his hand
and traced his finger down her nose, touched her lips. "Listen to me
pity myself. What would Brierley think?"

She smiled. "When she returns to Yarvannet, ask her. Some
problems may have no solution, Melfallan," she offered. "Be
thankful that dilemma exists only within your marriage, and not
the safety of your land."

"I can't find any solution about Tejar, either."

"You've well educated in matters of rule," she said, objecting.
"Sir James saw to that. You've studied history and appreciate its
lessons. You seek truth, not self-flattery. And the Four have sent
you a dream of times past, a vision that holds answers."

"You didn't send the dream about Farrar?" he asked in surprise. "I thought—"

She shook her head solemnly. "Not I. The Four do not often
speak to an Everlight, but I know their voice." She pursed her
lips. "And the Four do not speak to Allemanii, ever: it is outside
their nature. Yet they spoke to you through your bond with Brierley, through the resonance she made in Witchmere when she
healed your shoulder." She shook her head again, wonderingly.
"I am old, fair lord, and have seen much, but I've had little
experience with such bonds. The shari'a of older times avoided
them, in fear of the grief if one soul died untimely, and for their
other dangers. I worry for you both, and I wish it had not been
made. But it exists and can be broken only by death, and perhaps
not even then." She touched his face, then trailed her fingers
slowly along the line of his jaw, returning the caress. "Surely I
could not be this present to you in dreams without the resonance.
I doubt I could have made dreams with you at all."

"But what did Gerin mean?" he asked, hoping she would
know. "Why Farrar?"

"The vision was for you, not me," she said, shaking her head. "But I will help you think about it, if you like. Look to me, but also look to your other counselors. You have delayed talking to Sir James too long."

"Now you sound like Thora," he complained.

"I sound like Brierley," she insisted, "or myself—or you. You can delay telling Saray, wiggle as much as you want, but don't be imprudent with your lands. You are too good an earl for that. And Sir James deserves your confidence, being your good and loyal knight. Is that not so? Isn't that what you told Jared?"

"I suppose."

"More than suppose, please."

He shrugged, conceding the point.

The next afternoon Melfallan found Sir James in the library, and they spent an hour reviewing judicial matters that had piled up during Melfallan's absence from Yarvannet. Most of the petty assizes were handled by Sir James and his clarks—disputes over ownership of a cow, damages for a brawl at the inn, an occasional appeal to the lord for nonpayment for goods. Lord Valery Tolland generated a regular income in fines for the earl's court, to the point that few of the Tiol merchants would sell anything to him except for coin in hand. Sir James kept raising the amercements for Valery's indifference to his accounts, and Valery's indulgent mother, Lady Alice, gladly paid every time.

"How many sets of clothing can he buy, anyway?" Melfallan muttered as he read through the brief. "Or bottles of wine to drink?"

"It's a good thing Valery married an heiress," Sir James agreed equably. "Whatever his other qualities, Lord Valery Tolland is always apt—she's daughter to a wine merchant."

"But his mother pays, not him."

"Lady Tolland has always paid for Valery's comforts. She was an heiress, too, and that's what heiresses do." Sir James shrugged, then smiled tightly. "Lord Valery knows that *you* know his mother pays, and so expects mercy for that good lady's purse—not that he cares if it's offered or not." Sir James sniffed. "A rather useless young lord."

Melfallan frowned, tapping his pen on the brief as he thought. "Set the amercement at twice the bill again, I think. Lady Alice can afford it." He threw the brief on top of the others, and then watched Sir James as he sorted papers.

Lean-bodied and hawk-nosed, Sir James was Melfallan's rudder of practicality and good judgment, a fixture of his life for as long as Melfallan could remember. Knowing his justiciar's solid adherence to the practical and the real, Melfallan had not dared Sir James's opinion on the reality of witches. As much as he loved the man, and however much the Everlight encouraged him, he still felt uncertain about Sir James's reaction. He earnestly wished to keep his justiciar's good opinion, not only for its own sake but because Sir James's counsel was essential to his plans. He needed the older man's wisdom. It was a mainstay of his rule.

Sir James had met Brierley in both Yarvannet and Darhel, and had talked to her at some length, but Melfallan doubted she had confided in him any truths about herself. A shari'a needed great caution, at peril of her life, and Brierley's books had told her dire tales of the High Lords' vengeance, many of them true. Like nearly everyone else, Sir James still believed Brierley was dead and that Duke Tejar's justiciar had murdered her, an injustice that had deeply offended Sir James's sense of the right.

Yet, Melfallan suspected unhappily, if Brierley had been properly tried, with witnesses and oaths and the orderly process of law in the duke's court, Sir James would have watched her burn and think the killing just. An earl might be cold-blooded in his politics, but a justiciar learned another kind of cold-blooded thinking in the assizes. At least Melfallan knew his politics were cruel; he was not entirely sure that Sir James recognized the potential cruelty in his own sphere of proof and judgment. And so he had hesitated at telling Sir James much at all, and thus lost the good advice of his closest advisor. Melfallan hesitated again, then picked up another brief and began to read.

Sir James cleared his throat to regain his attention, then extracted a paper from the pile at his elbow. "You should read this next. The duke's courier is downstairs and waiting for an answer."

"Answer?" Melfallan asked. "To what?"

"To this letter from Duke Tejar. No, it's not about Rowena. He's not that stupid to gloat so soon—after all, she's not dead yet." His craggy face flickered with anger, as much from his love for Rowena as his sense of justice. His long fingers unrolled the parchment. "It says, your grace, that it pleases our august duke to assess an additional tallage for your accession—"

"My accession?" Melfallan frowned, perplexed. The tallages were the feof fees prescribed in the Lutke Charter, paid upon certain events in a vassal's life—his accession, his marriage, the Blessings of his children, and his death. The fees were nominal, more respect to the liege than a real source of income. "We paid that months ago," he objected. "A hundred livres."

"Yes, we did. The duke says, however, for reasons cited herein, that it pleases him to increase your tallage by a thousand livres, for a total of eleven hundred livres by his reckoning. He does acknowledge the one hundred already paid."

"But he can't do that," Melfallan protested. "The accession amount is set in the Lutke Charter, Sir James. It's never been changed." Sir James's lips tightened to a near invisible line. "What reasons?" Melfallan asked suspiciously.

"He says," Sir James said, "that your youth and inexperience as High Lord, the, um, expected fragility of your only heir, given prior miscarriages by your lady wife, and particularly the strong rival claim of Count Sadon to Yarvannet—"

"Rival claim! Sadon doesn't have any claim!"

"The duke suggests he does." He raised a hand as Melfallan sputtered. "It gets worse," he warned. "He's also assessed an amercement for, quote, 'your abandonment' of Brierley Mefell's cause in his court. 'Given that witch trials have high ducal concern for the welfare of all Allemanii lands,' he says, 'and given your default in your duty as High Lord,' he adds, the duke feels a suitable amercement must be made as an example to all the High Lords, and mandates it at three thousand livres."

"Three *thousand*!" Melfallan took a deep breath. "I didn't abandon Brierley's suit. She disappeared while in the custody of the duke's own justiciar—ask the duke about that!"

Sir James sighed. "That's not the point, I'm afraid. *This*, I suspect, is what Tejar intended to spring on you at the council you so deftly avoided. As Mistress Mefell's High Lord, you are responsible for her appearance in court. She has now disappeared, the means and reason unproven. You stand as her champion for the default, at least until the blame is proven to be elsewhere."

"Not proven *yet*." Melfallan got up to pace. The clarks, busy at their various tasks, looked up and watched him. "This is absurd, Sir James."

"Furthermore—"

Melfallan grimaced. "There's *more*?"

Sir James sighed. "Furthermore, the duke graciously warns you that abandonment of your cause against Lord Landreth of Farlost will cost you an additional amercement of two thousand livres."

"*Two*—!" Melfallan set his lips tightly. "It was Sadon's appeal, not mine, and Sadon didn't pay anything close to that to take it."

"Amercements also accrue for default—whether by lord principal or the defendant. The duke begs enlightenment on your intentions."

"That's sweet of him." Melfallan scowled and reseated himself. "If my summing is right, that's six thousand livres."

"In this letter, at least," Sir James said calmly. "I expect this letter might be the first of several. This is written by Lord Dail, I'm sure, one of his more deft advisors. Tejar might launch a murderous attack on a vassal, but Lord Dail is more subtle. He uses the Charter to keep it legal."

"But that's half my annual income from my lands!"

"The duke sets amercements as he pleases, just like you do in your own court. It's a liege lord's right, yours and his."

"I won't pay it!"

"And thereby will put yourself in default of your fealty to the duke, on pain of forfeiture of your lands."

Melfallan glowered at him for several moments. "That's tidy," he remarked.

"Very tidy," Sir James agreed. "Lord Dail has my sincere admiration."

"If I do pay it, the other High Lords will see it as weakness."

"If you don't, they'll think you a rash fool, risking your earldom for a few thousand livres. The sum is quite deliberate, Melfallan, quite deftly chosen. If he asked for enough to drain your lands in a single demand, the other High Lords would protest, if only to preserve themselves from similar ruin. But in smaller sums, several thousand here, several thousand there—in time, he's taken all your income for this year and next, and you'll have to raise the rest of the sums from your capital. Or you could raise your land rents, thereby alienating all your lords and tenants. You could cut down a considerable part of your forests and sell the timber to anyone who would buy, thereby wrecking Earl Giles's trade for *his* timber." He sniffed, then steepled his fingers thoughtfully. "What else? Hmm. You might sell one or two knighthoods to merchants who could pay handsomely, or perhaps offer some largesse to one of Tejar's lords. Enfeoffing Captain Bartol with, say, a manor inside Garth's marcher lands would likely be a useful credit on Tejar's ledger."

"When the seas dry up, will I enfeoff Captain Bartol."

"I doubt Duke Tejar has any real hope that you might." He gave Melfallan a wintry smile. He offered the letter across the table, and Melfallan took it reluctantly, then tossed it down after a glance. "What do you think Tejar expects me to do?"

"Obey and pay the sums. What else without risking your feof? And then Lord Dail will draft up his next letter."

"Asserting what?" Melfallan asked in outrage.

"Oh—" Sir James thought a moment, his eyebrows knotted. "A tallage for the birth of your son in addition to his Blessing fee," he suggested. "That he might be duly enrolled on the duke's records as Yarvannet's heir, you see, and thus officially recognized by your liege lord."

"There's no such record—or tallage."

"Yet. A lapse easily cured. Or he might assess an additional tallage on your marriage to Saray." Melfallan scowled. His grand-father and Earl Giles had paid that tallage years ago, with a hefty sum beyond it to get Tejar's consent. Sir James shrugged. "Upon reconsideration, the duke now opines, the tallage just increased, say by another half. I'm sure his clark can think up suitable rea-sons. Or there's the penalty for knighting Jared without the duke's permission, not that the Charter says you need it, but any prece-dent has to happen a first time or it's not a precedent."

"So what can we do *back?*" Melfallan asked.

"We're somewhat limited, being vassal and not liege. You could restrict our trade with Darhel, but that hurts Yarvannet's merchants as much as Ingal's. You could write letters to the other High Lords, protesting your treatment, and be accused of treachery by spreading disaffection. On the petty side, you could harass his couriers—we have one available downstairs right now. Duke Lio-nel did some novel things to his vassals' couriers when he wished to make a point. Remember, however, that Tejar *is* the duke and your liege lord."

"And I'm earl of Yarvannet," Melfallan retorted. "And I have an army, too."

"A dangerous thought, Melfallan," Sir James said soberly.

"Perhaps a necessary one, Sir James." Sir James fell silent.

"Is he trying to push me into war?" Melfallan asked quietly. "This soon?"

"I honestly don't know," Sir James replied, frowning. "An attack on the Charter is one way it could begin. If the other High Lords feel too comfortable—and thus disinclined to take a stand for you—even the Charter can be violated. After all, what one

High Lord can take in excess, others might, too, and so add to their coffers."

"If I start the war," Melfallan said, and saw Sir James lift his eyebrow at the suggestion, "I might win or I might not. The same applies to Duke Tejar. The power between the earls and duke is too evenly balanced, and our war would necessarily involve all the Allemanii lands. Do you agree?"

"Yes," Sir James said with a slow nod. "As you said, the power is balanced. Have you been considering starting the war, Melfallan?"

Melfallan looked at the several clarks at the other tables, none of who were obviously listening but might be, if he had exceptional ears. He rose and beckoned to Sir James. He led Sir James out into the hallway, then leaned comfortably against the wall, arms crossed, and smiled at Sir James's expression. In many ways, they would always be tutor and restless boy. "Do you absolutely trust every one of your clarks, Sir James?" He nodded toward the library. "I've made that assessment of every vassal and principal servant since I got home. Revil, yourself, Sir Micay, a few others, I would trust with my son's safety, but if that is the measure, I can count no more than a dozen such men in Yarvannet, if that. And Tejar has similar problems with his lords. The count of Briding is our secret friend, Rowena is regent of Airlie, and I'm husband to one of Mionn's daughters. We surrounded Tejar by undermining his counts' loyalties, then added our alliance with Giles to box him."

"Instability creates opportunity," Sir James quoted serenely, as well he might, since he'd been the architect of Tejar's several internal troubles in Ingal. "You haven't answered my question, Melfallan. Are you considering starting the war?"

"Nor have you answered mine—do you trust every set of ears in that room?" Sir James eyed him a moment, then sniffed. "My tower room?" Melfallan suggested.

"Lead the way."

Sir James smiled gently. "She's alive? Why didn't you tell me earlier, Melfallan?"

Melfallan shifted uncomfortably in his chair, then sighed and looked away. "I didn't know who to tell. I want to protect her, and to do that I have to change the shari'a laws."

"And to change the shari'a laws, you must become duke. I see." Sir James nodded to himself, but did not seem overly alarmed. "And that led you to thinking seriously about war against Tejar, not as some future possibility, but as reality. An impossible reality, I agree. The times are too dangerous for war. You are fully Tejar's match, Melfallan, perhaps not quite yet, but soon." Melfallan blinked. He hadn't known Sir James thought so highly of him.

"I doubt Tejar agrees," Melfallan said, "or he wouldn't have pushed the new tallages."

"True. To think you the lesser man pleases his vanity. When a lord surrounds himself with flatterers, it soon affects his judgment." Sir James paused and looked bemused. "So the shari'a still exist. Remarkable. In all my political calculations, I had not considered that event." He narrowed his eyes, thinking.

"Saray's injury was mortal," Melfallan said earnestly, "and so was Rowena's. Brierley healed her, too. Her witchery is real, Sir James. And precious. It's not delusion or fancy—"

Sir James raised his hand, stopping him. "Relax, Melfallan. I believe you." He grimaced. "I've always suspected there was some truth behind the old tales. Witchmere did exist—it's on the older maps. And something happened during Duke Rahorsum's rule, something that changed a relatively good duke into a madman. All the sources attribute it to the shari'a, as they blame the shari'a for the plague that followed. We Allemanii are a practical people, Melfallan, and not given to justify our wars with wild fancies. And there's your aunt, of course. Even if your grandfather wouldn't listen to her about Jonalyn, I did." He smiled. "What? Did you think I would reject the idea out of hand? Pronounce you a fool?"

"And stomp out to get help." Melfallan flushed slightly. "I'm sorry, Sir James. I misjudged you."

"I'm not offended, son. I was your grandfather's counselor. Why shouldn't you think I'd share his opinions?" His smile deepened. "I didn't always, you know."

Melfallan took a deep breath, then spread his hands. "So what do I do, Sir James?"

Sir James considered, frowning. "Let me think about it for a few days, and then we'll talk again. There must be a solution, although I admit I can't see it now. What about the duke's courier?"

"He can wait. I'm not paying this extortion meekly, Sir James. A message goes back with him, a suitable message—I just haven't decided what the message is." He grimaced. "Sir James, you've ruined my day."

"Not I, your grace." Sir James rose from his chair. "I put that fault on Duke Tejar."

Melfallan grinned, and got a flash of a smile back before his justiciar quietly shut the door behind him.

Melfallan rose and walked over to the window, then looked out on the harbor. The suns shone brightly in the sky, casting twin shadows in every crevice, tinting white stone and wavecap alike with blue and gold. The ships below shifted quietly in the swell, their white sails furled. Beyond the harbor and its town, the shadowed forest rose up the slopes of the coastal mountains, tier by tier, a living curtain on Tiol's eastern horizon.

Melfallan stared down gloomily at Tiol's harbor, disturbed that Tejar's counterstroke had come so soon. Where would he find the time he needed? Where was the time to bring Brierley home, to earn his vassals' sure loyalty, to make his choices certain? Tejar would never have dared provoke his grandfather in this manner, nor would the other High Lords have sat by, blandly accepting this erosion of their Charter rights: Earl Audric would never have allowed it. But Melfallan was still a cipher in Allemanii politics, not yet tested, perhaps weak, likely nowhere near his grandfather's match. His youth was against him, and the alliances that

Earl Audric could count as certain might not hold for Melfallan, when the crisis came.

Doesn't Tejar see the danger? Melfallan thought angrily. Is he that confident of his victory?

Why Farrar? he asked himself in frustration. Where is the answer?

~‿৴

Later that afternoon, Melfallan returned to the library seeking an-swers. Located near the Great Hall on the western wall of the castle, Tiol Castle's library numbered nearly two thousand books, for its many earls had tended to be scholars, or in the lack of that interest, careful recordkeepers of their rule. Heavy leatherbound books lined each wall of the long room, rank upon rank, with several large tables in the center occupied by Sir James's clarks. Oblong windows above the bookcases on the western wall gave some light; lampstands and table lamps provided more. When Melfallan walked into the library, the clarks looked up, mildly startled by his unexpected appearance at this hour, then began to rise. He waved them back to their tasks and began walking down the shelves, looking at the titles.

As a boy, Melfallan had spent long hours in this library, for here was where Sir James had chosen to tutor his noble charges. Tucked away in a corner of the castle, the room had few distrac-tions for a restless boy, and its seclusion kept Melfallan and Revil safely from under their grandfather's feet as they studied. Here Melfallan had learned how to write, forming his letters with a schoolboy's scrawl, whispering and giggling with Revil until Sir James firmly put a stop to their nonsense. Here he had learned law and history, first the dramatic tales of the Founders and other heroes that easily catch a boy's interest, and then law and history in their sober progressions. Sir James had been an excellent teacher, patient and steady, and tolerant of practically anything so long as Melfallan tried.

Sir Micay had taught him the other nobleman's arts of sword

and horse, and Master Talbot had taught him hawking, encouraging Melfallan's natural athleticism and liking for the outdoors. When he was fourteen, he had spent a month in Sir Justin Halliwell's armory, watching Sir Justin and his assistants make swords and armor for the castle soldiery. A castle steward had taught Melfallan the art of graceful dancing, and Audric's chief musician had tried to teach him an instrument, one of his many tutors' few failings. No musician was he, although he liked to listen. A High Lord needed many skills, and Melfallan's boyhood had been happily busy with acquiring them.

Melfallan had thoroughly enjoyed his tutoring, and acquired a love for books that he often wished for more time to indulge. Books had answers, if you looked long enough. Most of the books here were older than he was, and he sniffed appreciatively at the faint acrid smell of leather and dusty paper. Why Farrar? he wondered curiously. That question seemed a key, but for the life of him he couldn't see its connection.

He stopped and looked around him at the long tiers of books, the quietly occupied clarks, the mellow daylight that suffused the room, making visible a faint scattering of dust on the air. It reminded him pleasantly of Witchmere's own library, a place of books now buried inside stone. Perhaps Brierley's answers did lie there, guarded by dangerous machines. Perhaps his own answers lay here. He hunted along a top shelf to find a book he remembered, and brought down a much-handled volume about the Founders and the ducal institutions Duke Aidan had created. As Melfallan found a seat at an unoccupied table, a clark glanced at him with mild curiosity, then bent again over his laborious recording with pen and ink.

Melfallan squinted absently at the opposite wall for a few moments, then opened his book. Remember Farrar, Gerin had said. Fanciful dream or not, it was a place to start. Earl Farrar, the first of the Mionn earls, had ruled Mionn for thirty years, dying an old and venerated man in his bed. He, too, had contended with his duke, his brother Aidan: was that the connection?

Farrar had opposed Aidan's new innovation of duke, with its

ordering of the other High Lords into lesser ranks beneath Aidan, a distinction not known in the West. Earl and count, lord and gentleman knight, all bound by laws of liegeship and obligation: it was a pattern that Aidan had deliberately established, and had ruled Allemanii politics ever since. During Farrar's lifetime, only Farrar had been an earl, with the semi-independence enjoyed by the Allemanii earls that continued to the present day. Later the second Karlsson duke had elevated his younger son, then count of Yarvannet, to the more lofty rank, and so created a second earldom to the west of Ingal, as Mionn was earldom to the east.

Melfallan turned to another chapter, skimming through lessons he had studied in detail under Sir James's determined attention. In the West, the gentry and commoners had looked only to their own High Lord, of whom the Allemanii had several, all equal in authority, who combined for the lands' common defense but otherwise managed their own affairs independent of the others. In a time of crisis, one of the High Lords, sometimes two, would assume a temporary leadership until the crisis had passed. The Allemanii had prospered under their High Lords in the West, but the author of this history had assumed Aidan's innovations a necessary improvement. Wider lands required more structured government, or so the historian flattered Aidan's reasons. With a clear ranking of lords, each bound to each other by laws of right, Aidan thought he had built the foundation for peaceful and orderly rule, an expectation that had rarely proved itself in subsequent history.

When the Great Plague killed Duke Rahorsum and his only legitimate heir, Aidan's institutions did not stop the collapse of Allemanii government. Bram the Butcher, Rahorsum's bastard son, had seized the coronet, then began a vengeful hunt for shari'a witches in his dying Ingal towns. When Bram could not find shari'a to burn, he had turned on his own folk, accusing Allemanii women of witchery on trumped-up excuses or the mere suspicion of their sex. In some towns, Bram had left not one woman or girl still alive. Finally the other High Lords had intervened and caught Bram, executed him, then chose Roland Lutke of Briding as their new duke.

A generous and thoughtful leader, Duke Roland had bid a group of learned scholars to write a charter, one that clearly defined liege and vassal rights, established an assizes court in each Allemanii land to systemize justice, and centralized some authority in the duke, although not all. The Lutke Charter, a brilliant document in its logic and clear principles of rule, had stablized Allemanii politics for several generations, but it had not prevented later treachery by a son-in-law, nor still later the duke's murder by a trusted castellan. Nor would it prevent Melfallan from similar rebellion, although it should.

Where is the flaw? Melfallan asked himself soberly. And why?

Was it the division of power between the duke and the earls? What if the Allemanii had only one principal lord instead of three, only one army, one system of courts, with genuine taxes on all the subordinate lands, not just nominal feof dues? One lord, one Allemanii land, not several. Had Aidan not gone far enough in consolidating the duke's power? Or had he secretly hoped for such primacy, only to be blocked by Farrar? The book did not say.

Melfallan frowned thoughtfully. Would the gift of all power to one principal lord have stopped the wars? Or would it have engendered more rebellion and instability, whenever the duke was unworthy of his trust? If the duke were always a good and wise man, the Allemanii lands would prosper, as they had under Roland Lutke and other wise dukes. But if he were not—Melfallan imagined what Duke Tejar could do with that kind of unchallengeable power, and shuddered. No, Farrar was right: such a system trusted too innocently in the goodness of men.

He skimmed through the rest of the book, then went back to the shelves and chose two others, then brought them back to the table. Was it the change in ranking the High Lords, Melfallan wondered, where lesser might aspire to be greater, with the duke's coronet as the highest prize? Each of the major crises in Allemanii history, each involving the fall of a ducal house, had been impelled by a middle-rank lord, first a duke's bastard son, then an ambitious son-in-law, a murderous castellan knight. In other unstable times, a knight might be elevated to a county if he had his liege's favor, as had Melfallan's great-grandfather, or from count to earl, as had happened to Audric when instability sparked into Pullen's rebellion. Any ambitious High Lord, knowing unstability could bring opportunity, might set about to provoke disorder, not avoid it.

Provoke another High Lord's vassal into vaunting ambition, with promises or lies or threats, and a High Lord created instability where he wanted it. A High Lord with unreliable vassals was weak, distracted by internal problems in his own land. Push further, and an ambitious vassal might be prompted to treachery in the hope of reward elsewhere, as Sadon had betrayed Pullen, and may have betrayed Audric. Manipulate the middle lords, both yours and the other lord's, his book coldly advised, and any purpose might be won.

He thought about each of Yarvannet's middle lords, and wondered whom Tejar had approached. Count Sadon was too obvious, too sour and restive and sullen, his son disgraced, although both father and son might still be useful. Garth? Tauler? If he were Duke Tejar, he'd woo Melfallan's marcher lords, as he had subverted Airlie's Heider. Revil was incorruptible, and the Tolland lands in southern Yarvannet irrelevant to any northern attack, as were the minor lords who ruled Yarvannet's river ports. No, it would be Farlost and his marcher lords, the same combination that had ruined Earl Pullen.

Melfallan rose and walked half the room for a book of maps, brought it back to his table, then opened the book to a map of Yarvannet. If Tejar struck at Yarvannet, it would be by sea, or through the northern passes from Briding or Airlie, or perhaps all three. Melfallan frowned. Geography gave the duke an advantage, for Darhel could not be attacked by sea, an advantage of his inland capital Aidan had perhaps deliberately intended. For Yarvannet to move against the duke, its earl also had to use the mountain passes through either Briding or Airlie. In his rebellion thirty years before, Earl Pullen had chosen the Briding route, marching straight north through the coastal mountains, confident that Lord Gainn, Lord Tauler's father, would hold the Airlie passes to the northeast. But Sadon had withheld Gainn's soldiers from that defense, allowing Audric to invade from both the northeast through Airlie and from the sea. With Tiol threatened by Audric's pincer assault, Pullen was forced to march south again, and the two armies had met in Garth's riverlands, where Pullen had lost the battle.

Garth's Carbrooke and Penafeld, Tauler's lands: those were Yarvannet's fences against invasion. Melfallan frowned at the map. Grandfather should have elevated Tauler to count, he thought, and thus detached him from Sadon. It was the obvious prudent move, and he wondered at the lapse. Perhaps his grandfather relied too much on Rowena's control of Airlie, or perhaps, even for thirty years, Audric could not bring himself to favor any of Pullen's lords. Instead, he and Sir James had meddled inside Ingal. They had made a secret friend of Count Parlie, and had then married Audric's only daughter into Airlie, thus subverting two of the duke's counts in the Ingal counties which coincidentally protected Yarvannet's borders.

Why had Duke Selwyn allowed it? Melfallan wondered. Had he felt that indulgent toward his old friend, that confident in Yarvannet's loyalty? After Selwyn's death, Earl Audric had married Melfallan to a Mionn daughter, compromising Tejar's other border to the east. Duke Tejar had to reach into Yarvannet to protect himself, Melfallan conceded grudgingly, encouraging Sadon and perhaps Garth, perhaps Tauler, subverting in turn. Melfallan and Tejar might now whittle away at each other's lords for years, until all loyalties were uncertain. Then, when they smashed their armies together in Airlie, either might win, and then probably by pure accident of battle.

Melfallan rubbed his eyes slowly. If Melfallan lost, he lost everything not only for himself, but for Brierley. But what other way besides war? Every major political change since the Founding had involved war, sometimes a long and bloody struggle, sometimes mercifully abrupt. Noble familes usually died with the defeat of their liege, and other noble families then rose to new prominence, bringing new blood into the nobility—not always to its advantage. Lord Valery's wastrel life, his mother's pompous self-importance, stood in stark contrast to the able and intelligent lord who had ruled the southern Yarvannet lands under Pullen. All of Pullen's principal vassals had been vigorous men, proven in their rule for years, able, intelligent, war-ready, and fierce in their loyalty to Pullen. When Audric had swept them all from life's table, Yarvannet had suffered a loss that Earl Audric had never acknowledged—if he even thought about it at all.

A war at this point, Melfallan realized, with the board pieces arrayed as they were, might kill half the Allemanii High Lords, with Tejar free to replace them with any of his choosing. And Tejar would want toadies and graspers, men whose fortunes were beholden only to him, but such grasping men would not be easy lords to control. There would be more wars, lesser in scope but constant, with Tejar likely the victor in each, and so another toady would be put in place, only to rebel in his turn. Melfallan's failure might destablize Allemanii politics for a generation, ravaging the lands with turmoil and destruction not seen since Bram's day, and with no assurance peace might ever come again.

Yet if Melfallan won, he'd have enemies in every land, perhaps including Mionn itself. The count of Lim would not accept the change easily, nor the other middle lords who favored Tejar, and Earl Giles might feel threatened when Melfallan melded the other earldom to the coronet. More instability, more plots by the middle lords, more rebellion and war.

The times are wrong, Mefallan thought with despair. When he and Brierley had talked of the dangers in the cabin, he had told her, with a casual flip of his hand that now shamed him, that war with Tejar was inevitable. It likely was, but he hadn't fully appreciated its futility.

He shut up the books and took them back to their places, then wearily leaned his forehead on the shelf. Brierley, my beloved, you're worth all the world to me, but must I destroy my world to save yours? And if mine is destroyed, where could you live in safety? Where could anyone? But what other way than war? It had been the Allemanii's ultimate solution for centuries.

Why Farrar? Melfallan ground his teeth in frustration, then stalked out of the library.

19

I n Airlie, Rowena snuggled down under the warm coverlet as a new blast of wind rattled her bedroom windows. Ruling one's county from bed had its advantages, she decided, then kissed Axel's forehead as he leaned against her. This morning her son had suddenly announced that he was joining her in bed for the day. They had made an adventure of it, dining elegantly in bed at noon, rattling Axel's dice and cup onto the coverlet, then reading Rowena's letters together, quickly slipping the letters out of sight under the covers whenever a servant not in the know entered the room. After weeks of pretending a slow recovery from her injury, Rowena looked forward to resuming her usual life again. Still, lying in bed all day was a pleasant luxury, a fact she had not previously known. As she broke the wax on another letter, Axel sighed contentedly next to her.

"I could get used to this, Mother," he said, echoing her thought. He rubbed his face lazily against her shoulder.

"Don't," she advised with mock severity. "The folk expect an active count, not a lazy slug-a-bed." She nudged his ribs to make her point, and Axel promptly went as limp as a sun-basking hound. She chuckled. Her near-fatal injury had badly shaken her young son's confidence, and he was only now showing more of his old self. Although Axel knew she was well and her long "recovery" only a pretense to protect Brierley, he had still haunted her bedchamber every day, hanging on the bedposts, sprawling in a chair, or, today, demanding to share her comfortable bed.

As she unfolded the letter, Axel stirred himself to crane his neck, then sank back blissfully into his limp. "Oh, good," he said. "More gifts."

"My gifts, not yours," Rowena reminded him, and gave him the letter while she opened another.

Airlie had rejoiced at the news that she had survived her fever, and a steady stream of gifts and letters had flowed into Carandon from her lords and commoners alike. Although Nigel permitted few visitors, citing her need for total rest, he gave the town regular reports, and had twice allowed a crowd into the courtyard below, where the entire lot sang a song "to cheer her." She had waved at them from the window, and they had laughed and called up their good wishes, then went away again.

My Airlie, Rowena thought happily. She looked at her son, and felt her heart fill with gladness.

It was all Brierley's gift, truly hers. Nigel still doubted his own eyes, and humphed and wrinkled his nose, but in truth, once the last of the fever had subsided, her wound appeared fully healed. When Brierley had finally consented to breakfast with her that next morning, Rowena had found her shy at first and had enjoyed trying to win her trust. She wasn't sure she had succeeded until Brierley had ventured her tale about Count Armadius and the book from Witchmere. It was a tale that had greatly pleased Rowena. At Rowena's request, Axel had found a history on Armadius in the castle library, and she and Axel had made it a common gift to Brierley. The girl would take nothing else, and Rowena had not pressed richer gifts on her, at least not that Brierley knew. She smiled, feeling quite clever with herself. Stefan would likely tell her about the gelding, but, nicely, far too late.

After all, she mused, what is a county worth? She looked at her son blissfully collapsed beside her. Or my son's safety?

She rearranged the letters on the counterpane into stacks, and Axel stirred himself to help. When they had a fine array, Axel fingered the large letter with the duke's ribbons and seals. They

had avoided opening the letter all morning, happily insulting Airlie's liege lord by the delay.

"Maybe he admits he made Lord Heider do it," Axel thought
aloud, and idly turned the letter over.

"All things are possible, son, but I highly doubt that."

"Maybe he's invited you to Darhel, for a great ball in your
honor. I like that idea."

"Maybe," Rowena said indulgently.

Axel pushed the letter idly along the counterpane with a forefinger. "We could open it tomorrow, Mother," he suggested, "and
not today at all."

"True, although the duke's courier *is* waiting downstairs."

"Or maybe we can open it next week—or maybe never,"
Axel continued. "That courier won't eat too much while he's
waiting the rest of his life, not so much that Airlie can't afford
it."

Rowena stifled a laugh. "Also true. Of course, he might be
fat, with an appetite to match." Axel shrugged, confident of
Airlie's resources. "The world has many choices, my son," Rowena agreed.

Axel smiled, looked up at her face for permission, then broke
the wax seal. He paused before he unfolded the letter. "What do
you guess?" he asked.

"A demand I step down as regent, being unfit to defend my
county."

"Me, too." Axel unfolded the pages, then began to read.
"Well, he says he's sorry you've been injured. That's nice. And
here's the quotation from Duke Roland's charter, and his liege
lord's duty to Airlie. Tsk." He turned to the next page. "With
great regret, with appreciation for your fine service as regent for
eight years, da, da, da."

"Does he propose anybody as regent?" Rowena asked mildly.

"Somebody named Bartol. Who's he?"

"Duchess Charlotte's bastard nephew, one of Tejar's graspers." She clucked her tongue. "Odd. I had heard that the duke
had promised Amelin to Bartol, but perhaps the good captain is

impatient. A duke must shift as he can with current opportunities." She frowned, thinking. "I hadn't appreciated that Bartol had risen that high in the duke's favor, by-blow connection or not—it's a recent shift, one to note."

Axel looked up at her curiously. "What are you going to do, Mother?"

"Do?" She looked down at her son. "What would you do, Count Axel, if you were me?"

"Stall," Axel decided. "Something vague and polite to go back with the fat courier. 'Thank you for concern, dear duke. I'll think about it, and how are you, too?' "

Rowena nodded her approval. "Exactly. And, I think—" She frowned, considering. "I think we'll go to Yarvannet for Audric's Blessing."

Axel sat up in surprise. "I thought we weren't going."

"That was before the duke provoked me. What better way to prove my health than hard travel over mountains?" She smiled. "Yes, indeed. And Earl Giles of Mionn will be there, to see me in my full wonder, and can bear witness to the duke on his way home. Even earls can be useful, my son."

"And then?"

"We stall again. Another few letters back and forth, to the duke's great irritation, and it will be summer. By then I'll be quite recovered. I may even practice my sword in the quadrangle, for whatever spy might watch." She nodded sagely. "Yes, an excellent plan." Axel laughed, then sank back into his hound's ease beside her. She smiled as his giggles tickled her ribs.

Then, reluctantly, Rowena extracted another letter from the stack spilled across her counterpane and gave it to him. "This came last night," she said. She had delayed showing Axel the letter most of the day, giving them this good day together as long as she could. Axel glanced at her curiously, and then opened the letter.

A week ago, the winter weather had unexpectedly cleared again, bringing one of those warm late-winter days that promised the coming spring. Roger Carlisle had loaded a wagon with supplies for the cabin, enough to last the rest of the winter. When he did not return the next day, Rowena had anxiously sent other liegemen to the cabin, which they found deserted and marked with fire. On the porch were deep gouges in the wood, as if something heavy had been dragged away, further mystery. Searching downward, her men had found Roger's wagon concealed among the trees by the trail, its wooden panels dark with dried blood.

Despite a vigorous search, Roger's body still had not been found, and who had murdered him and why Stefan and Brierley had abruptly left the cabin had remained a mystery. Last night a letter from Stefan had arrived at Carandon, brought by an Airlie rider who had ranged farther along the road to Mionn and so come upon their camp in the snow. Cautious of sending any letter, even entrusted to an Airlie man, Stefan had related only the bare news of their safety and Roger's death. And so Stefan's letter had brought confirmation of both comfort and grief.

"Roger?" Axel asked brokenly, raising his head. His eyes filled with tears. She felt her own tears start again in response, and gathered her son into her arms, then rocked him as he wept.

A knock came at the door, and Rowena hastily blotted her son's face with her sleeve, then helped him push all the letters under the coverlet. She took a deep breath, then glanced at her son. "Ready?" she whispered.

"Yes." Axel closed his eyes and pretended to sleep.

"Come in," Rowena called. The door opened, and the understeward, Cullen, came into the room with a tray of glasses and wine. He bobbed nervously into a bow, nearly upsetting the decanter.

"The healer Nigel said you might like wine, my lady," he quavered. He bobbed again, then attempted a simply ghastly smile, something nervous and toothy. Her chief steward had recently promoted Cullen to her personal service, perhaps in the hope of teaching Cullen some graces, of which he had none. He was an ugly young man, thin and gangling and awkward, but seemed desperately anxious to please. Well, Rowena decided reluctantly, a man couldn't help his weasel looks.

"On the table, Cullen," she said casually, then pretended a wince as she shifted her bandaged shoulder. "Thank you."

"Yes, my lady." Cullen put the tray on the nearby table, then awkwardly bowed himself out again.

"I don't like him," Axel murmured.

"Why not, son?" she asked, surprised. Although a handsome boy, Axel had little personal vanity, and so rarely suffered from a vain man's prejudices about beauty. "He can't help being awk-ward. What counts is that he tries."

"I just don't, Mother," Axel said stubbornly.

"Hmm." Rowena opened her mouth, then decided not to press, although it made her wonder. What had Cullen done to earn Axel's displeasure?

Her son sighed and shifted his head restlessly on her shoulder. "Why do people have to die?" he asked in a broken voice. "First Sir Niall, now Roger. Was it a trade, Mother? You don't die, so they do?"

"No, son. Daughter Sea doesn't trade lives, one for another. Don't think that way." She caressed his hair. "There is danger in the world, Axel, and sometimes it catches even a good man un-awares. We can live in fear of Daughter Sea and lock ourselves away in safe rooms, refusing to live, or we can accept Her, know-ing She might come for us when we least expect it."

"As She almost came for you," Axel said aggressively.

"True." She kissed Axel's forehead. "But sometimes we are spared, for reasons quite unlooked for. Sometimes our failure to die might be for a purpose. And perhaps sometimes," she added softly, thinking of Jonalyn, "we die for a purpose. I wonder——" She fell silent, remembering the long years of grief, a grief that had never eased, only tormented and galled, until another witch's hand took it gently away. A woman might build great strength in such grief, she thought, against such a future need.

"Wonder what, Mother?"

Rowena shook her head slightly, scattering her thought, then smiled down at her son. "Nothing. Bounce out of bed now, and go tell Sir Godric I want to see him. Audric's Blessing is only a week away, barely time for our travel to Yarvannet. I'm afraid our poor marshal is about to get a horrible shock."

In Yarvannet, Melfallan lounged against the battlement wall of his castle, watching the harbor below. Only *Southwind* turned slowly at anchor near the end of the wharf. The fishing ships of Tiol had left hours before, sailing far out past the sea horizon to hunt the shoals of fish plentiful shortly before Pass. During the summer, the coastal fishes tended to stay near shore, but as the Pass storms neared the schools moved farther out into the coastland current, joined there by deep-ocean fish on migration. In late winter, most of the fishermen spent several weeks aboard their ships, returning to shore only to unload their catch for salting and to replenish their stores. Their women often went with them, and whole streets in Tiol stood untenanted while they were gone.

As a boy, Melfallan had begged to go with the fishing fleet for the winter catch, and his grandfather had stalled one season after another, thinking Melfallan's interest would fade. But it had not, and finally, when Melfallan was fourteen, he was allowed aboard Cronin Atwell's ship, and had spent the next six weeks at sea. He had learned to haul line and tack a course, to gut fish and dive for shells on the outer reefs, and at night had listened to the fishermen's songs and jokes, many of the latter directed at the earl's young heir to make him blush. Master Cronin's wife and children had sailed with the ship, as they did every year, and his youngest daughter had been Melfallan's age, eager to lose her virginity. Given Bette's determination on seducing him, Melfallan had lost his as well on that one lovely starry night.

Bette was now married to a fisherman and the mother of three, but he sometimes saw her in town. Bette had never presumed nor sought better favor for herself, but she was truly a wicked tease, capable of saying anything at all, however outrageous. Once Bette had accosted him when he and Saray had gone down to a merchant's shop by the docks, and Saray had felt shocked, simply shocked, at "that woman's" presumption. Saray had complained about it all the way back to the castle, and Melfallan had nodded and looked wise and tsked, until finally he had to laugh, to Saray's consternation.

"Well!" she had said indignantly, quite put out with him. And that had made him laugh all the more, until she got upset and flounced off, her lady-maids in tow.

I really shouldn't have laughed, Melfallan thought with a smile, but what else could I do? Saray had always assumed, Ocean knew why, that Melfallan had come to their marriage bed as inexperienced as herself, bent on "saving himself" for his wife, as Saray had saved herself for her husband. She would have been shocked, simply shocked, to hear about Bette and the three or four girls afterward before they married. Worse, she would have felt deeply hurt, even though he hadn't even *met* Saray until years later during his courtship visit to Mionn, long after the other girls had fallen out of his life. And so it had begun in the very beginning of their marriage, this hiding of unpleasant facts that Saray didn't want to hear.

He had never again gone out with the winter fleet, and perhaps he ought to. Saray would be shocked by the idea, an earl on a commoner's fishing ship, but perhaps Brierley would agree to go with him. He imagined Brierley on that voyage, excited by the ship's speed, the tumbling fish, the wind snapping overhead in the sails. Her eyes would sparkle and her long hair whip in the wind, and when she looked at him, her face would be filled with joy.

He shifted his weight uncomfortably. These comparisons aren't fair, he told himself yet again. Whatever his willing, they had continued these past weeks as his marriage continued to unravel. He hoped Audric's Blessing Day, now set for next week, would lift Saray's mood. The Yarvannet nobility was now assembling in Tiol for the first high event in Audric's life. Even Duke Tejar had chimed in, delivering the expected request for the extra Blessing tallage, but this time Melfallan had not even bothered to promise something he wouldn't pay.

Although Rowena likely could not come, Earl Giles would, sailing the long month's voyage from Mionn through the northern strait and down the western coast. Last evening the Ewry outrider had reported Earl Giles's ship rounding the point by the Ewry river mouth. So far, however, although both suns had long since risen, the ship had not appeared. Melfallan sniffed the wind blowing from the sea, not unhappy to have the delay.

Saray adored her father, Earl Giles, who largely ignored her, and adored her mother, who treated Saray with the same cold indifference she gave to everyone. Saray also highly admired her older sister Daris, a pinch-mouthed sour gossip married to a minor Efe lord. Saray's betrothal to Melfallan had surprised and deeply offended Daris, who thought herself the greater lady, and she had taken out her spite on Saray the entire time Melfallan had visited in Efe. Saray had seemed oblivious to Daris's nasty comments, perhaps another fact she deliberately chose to ignore. Only Robert, Saray's brother, truly deserved Saray's adoration. In fact, in these last few hours of peace before Mionn swarmed into Yarvannet, Melfallan privately admitted that Robert was the only member of Saray's family he liked. Robert had a volatile temper like his father and was inclined to be rash, but he was good to Saray.

He had not yet met his father-in-law as earl of Yarvannet. During the courtship in Mionn, Giles had acknowledged Melfallan's presence, even chatted pleasantly on several occasions, but most of his attention had gone to Earl Audric. Giles was an efficient lord in his affairs, and so tended to limit his attention to the important. I wonder if I'm important enough now, Melfallan thought sourly, and felt surprised by his own mild surge of resentment. He thought he hadn't minded being ignored five years ago in Mionn; perhaps he had. He narrowed his eyes.

Mionn is your principal ally, he reminded himself. Be good.

He straightened as an array of white sails appeared over the point, then watched as the Mionn ship surged into view, just beyond the point's breakwater, and turned gracefully to enter the harbor. On cue, a troop of Sir Micay's soldiers marched down a street toward the wharf, and other townfolk began to gather for the display of an earl's arrival. Melfallan straightened the hem of his tunic, adjusted the gold links of his chain on his chest, and ran his fingers through his blond hair, mentally timing his walk down to the harbor against the ship's progress toward the docks. He wondered belatedly if he should wear his earl's circlet—likely Earl Giles would be wearing his. Melfallan grimaced. Only the nobility had such problems, all of them self-inflicted.

Ocean, I'd rather be fishing today, he wished again, and took one last look at the broad ocean.

He turned and walked briskly toward the stairs leading off the battlements, and then clattered down the two tiers of steps. Saray appeared at the doorway of her chambers, right on time, magnificently dressed in green and gold to honor Mionn's own colors. He smiled at her and gave her a compliment, which made her color, then extended his arm. With a nervous giggle, she slipped her hand around his elbow, and then walked proudly with him down to the Great Hall, for once not punishing him with studied indifference or a delicate scowl or whatever else she might inflict today. After all, her parents had arrived, and all must be light and goodness. And so the pretending continued, Melfallan thought sadly, as the assembled gentry and servants watched their earl and his lady begin the procession to the docks.

The welcoming party added to its numbers as they passed out of the castle, with Lord Garth and his lady, Revil and Solange, Lord Eldon, and Lady Alice Tolland dressed in the stiffest brocade, her son Valery looking bored at her side. They all had a pleasant walk down the bluff road and into the town. Melfallan refused to hurry, casting fate to the wind that he arrived at the dock before Earl Giles. As it was, the ship's crew had just cast their wharf-lines when Saray and Melfallan turned the final corner in the street and approached the long wooden wharf. The timbers boomed softly beneath their feet, rising to a hollow cacophony as the others followed them. High on the aft deck of his ship, Earl Giles stood next to the frigid figure of Lady Mionn, and Melfallan paused halfway down the wharf to bow genially to them both. As he straightened, he saw Giles respond with a stiff nod.

Earl Giles Fauconer was a short, square-bodied man, heavily muscled in his limbs, and today magnificently dressed in cloth-of-gold and silver, with a touch of Mionn green and gold in his felt hat. Now in his fifties, the earl's short blond beard and hair were shot with gray. Giles was indeed wearing his silver circlet, Melfallan noted, but he marshaled a smile as he and Saray arrived at the base of the ship's gantry. The earl descended, his wife on his arm.

Behind Earl Giles, Robert courteously offered his arm to Daris, a tall and slender woman who looked pinch-faced, put out, and sour. Melfallan wondered why Daris had not brought her husband, and who had decided that matter, Daris or her long-suffering spouse. He strongly suspected the latter: if Melfallan were Daris's husband, he'd find reason to be elsewhere, too. Oddly, he didn't see Robert's wife, either, although surely Elena had intended to come. Saray and Elena, the eldest daughter of the Count of Arlenn, had known each other since childhood and were close friends. Perhaps she had stayed home with the boys, he guessed, but her absence puzzled him.

Melfallan bowed to Lady Mionn as she stepped off the gantry and kissed the proffered hand, then gently held back Saray from the embrace she was ready to launch on her mother. It gave Lady Elinor a few moments to smile stiffly and extend her cheek, which Saray dutifully pecked. Saray then curtsied to her father, and giggled as Robert gave his usual swashbuckling bow.

"Welcome, Mionn," Melfallan said genially.

"Hmph," Giles responded and stalked past Melfallan onto the dock. Lady Mionn smiled vaguely and followed her husband, swaying in her fine dress as she looked straight ahead, and not once at any of the castle retainers or townfolk who gladly greeted her.

Melfallan shut his mouth as he nearly gawked at the retreating earl, and heard a shocked murmur among the waiting crowd. I don't believe it, he thought angrily. Earl Giles stumped onward, not looking back, the crowd parting to allow him passage.

"Well, I guess we're going back right away," Saray said uncertainly, looking after her father. She embraced Daris, with another peck on the cheek given and received, and the two sisters began to walk away, too, arm in arm, leaving Melfallan behind like a stranded fish. Melfallan's gentry and townfolk looked at each other, not daring to say a word. Lord Eldon took a hesitant step after Earl Giles, and then stopped abruptly, flushing. Lord Garth's face was carefully blank, but Lady Joanna looked openly amazed. She turned to whisper to her husband.

"I'm sorry, Melfallan," Robert said, obviously embarrassed. "It's more about me than you. Father's preoccupied—"

Melfallan stared at him. "The first time in five years that he's seen me, the first time he's seen me as earl, in front of all my *folk.*" His voice had risen, easily heard by the several lords standing nearby, but Melfallan didn't care.

Robert flushed. "You're making it worse," he warned in a low voice.

"It's mine to make worse, just as this is my land and my folk. Sir Bertrand!"

Melfallan's chief steward bowed. "See that the earl and Lady Mionn are shown to their apartments, and that they are comfortable."

"Yes, your grace." Bertrand hurried off. It started the crowd moving off the dock, although they glanced back uncertainly as they left. Saray and Daris had long since vanished into the general medley, but then Melfallan saw Saray hurrying back, flushed with embarrassment at forgetting her husband. The crowd parted courteously for her as she hurried, and Melfallan suffered through her apology, which Saray did not bother to keep hushed.

"Oh, Melfallan, I'm so sorry—" she said a third time.

"Never mind, Saray," he said curtly. Why didn't Saray ever understand? Why did it always have to be *her* way, however she wished it, and never what it truly was? He saw the sudden jab of hurt in Saray's face at his harshness, and forced himself to not care, for once not care.

"But— But—" she said, color washing up her slender neck into her face. Her hands threw themselves to her face, adding to the drama for those who still watched. Melfallan looked away, grinding his teeth. "But——"

Melfallan turned desperately to his brother-in-law. "Robert, would you mind conducting Saray back to the castle? I know you and she have much news to share, and I'm sure it would please Saray to delay it no longer. Isn't that so, my lady?" Saray now had tears starting, her lovely face filled with distress. Melfallan forced himself to look away again, before he gave in to the tears, gave her the pretending she wanted. Don't, he warned himself silently. Don't.

"If— If you say so, Melfallan," Saray quavered. "But would it be more seemly if I walked with you? I mean——"

"Not at all, Saray," Robert intervened. "For once this unworthy husband of yours must yield your loveliness to me." He smiled and gallantly extended his arm. "After all, I had first claim on you as brother, and I insist on enjoying it again." Saray smiled uncertainly at him, glanced again at Melfallan's averted face, and then sighingly allowed herself to be led away.

Melfallan turned to face the harbor, and ignored the interested stares of Giles's ship crew nearby. They had gathered at the railing to watch the gentry, and had seen it all. He heard a whispered comment, then a snigger. Melfallan crossed his arms across his chest and stared out at the bay, and imagined he could see the topmasts of the winter fleet, far out on the ocean.

What a blow it would have been, he told himself, if he had been out fishing when the earl of Mionn arrived—and he had even thought of it, too. Likely he made it worse by standing on the wharf, looking sullen and put out and useless, no doubt deserving Earl Giles's reproof to his worth as earl, for whatever reason it had been offered. Or perhaps the snub, in Earl Giles's wise estimation, was a comment on the man, not the earl, who so little merited his high rank: yes, that's probably what his Yarvannet folk thought.

The earls of Mionn are subtle, Melfallan reminded himself coldly. They make an entire commentary out of a single stare or a casual wave. Mionn had stripped one duke of his coronet, and

granted it to two others. What role had Yarvannet, the lesser earldom, in those high affairs, except to be pressured into agreement
after it was done? When Earl Audric conquered Yarvannet, that
had changed, for Audric had elevated Yarvannet to equal power
with Mionn by the sheer force of his personality. Obviously Giles
thought that situation had reverted, now that Earl Audric was
safely dead.

It's stupid to stand here, he told himself, aware that Giles's
crew continued to gawk and whisper. Probably the townfolk are
watching from the wharf behind him, too. He felt that his feet
were mired in mud, incapable of moving, and so made an even
greater fool of himself by doing nothing.

At the end of the wharf, Master Cronin walked down *Southwind*'s gangway and steered a course for Melfallan, his boots
thumping on the wooden decking. His approach diverted the attention of the Mionn crew, causing a new round of whispers and
gawking, and Melfallan dared to glance behind him. Except for a
half-company of his soldiers waiting at the end of the wharf, everyone had gone.

"I have those reports for you, your grace," Cronin said loudly,
hurrying forward to thrust a sheaf of papers into Melfallan's hand.
"I'm sorry to keep you waiting here, truly sorry." Cronin knuck-
led his forehead, his face creased with embarrassment.

Melfallan looked down at the papers in his hand. Reports?
Cronin had already delivered—My dearest husband, he read on the
top page, the grandchildren are well, and I miss you. He fingered
through the rest of the stack, and all were letters from Mistress
Cronin to her husband, much dog-eared from rereading.

He remembered Cronin's wife from that winter season years
ago, a bluff happy woman who was deft with her fingers, her face
lined from salt water and sea air, and quite aware of what he and
Bette had started. She had said nothing about their bedding, at
least not to Melfallan nor in public, although surely she had told
her husband. At the time, being only a boy, Melfallan had not
appreciated the kindness Bette's parents had given him and Bette,

when they might have interfered loudly with the indignant protest entitled to any parent of a young daughter.

He puzzled why Cronin would give him his wife's letters, then realized his good pilot was intent on rescue. He looked up at Cronin, and saw the laughter hiding in the older man's eyes.

"Reports," Cronin said firmly, loud enough for all of Giles's crew to hear. "Perhaps you should take them with you for further study."

"Perhaps I might do that," Melfallan agreed. "Come along with me, Master Cronin. I may have questions." Cronin touched his forefinger to his head, and then walked beside Melfallan down the wharf. When they had passed out of the crew's earshot, Melfallan gave Cronin a wry glance. "Your wife's own letters? Really, Cronin."

"Not to worry, your grace," Cronin said comfortably. "We've been married long enough there's nothing embarrassing. No, keep them a bit, and put them away. We're putting on a show, remember?"

Melfallan tucked the letters inside his tunic. "Thank you," he said gratefully. "Was it that obvious I needed rescue?"

"Not yet," Cronin said confidently. "I got there in time." The pilot sniffed reflectively as they walked down the wharf. "When I was newly captain of Southwind, your grace, some ten years ago now, my second mate put a pinch of sea-puffer toxin in my ale. I spent the entire next day, the first of my new command, upchucking into the waves. Fortunately Earl Audric had been called away to other business and wasn't aboard that day." At the end of the wharf, Cronin turned left into the town, not right toward the castle, and Melfallan genially followed his lead. The soldiers tramped along behind them, keeping a diligent guard on Melfallan's person, even abroad in his own port town.

"What did you do?" Melfallan asked indulgently.

Cronin smiled. "Well, at the next port I took the rascal into an alley and settled our score with a good pummeling, then sailed off without him. Left him behind to shift as he would." He clucked his tongue. "Too bad neither beating nor sailing is an option for you and your father-in-law."

"I would think not." Melfallan pretended shock.

Cronin chuckled. "That man works a ship in Briding now, and wouldn't dare put his chin-whiskers into Tiol. I've bribed Ennis, you see—happens he's my mother's brother—to arrest him if he ever tries. But mind you don't tell the earl that: bribery's a crime under his laws."

Melfallan nodded and stifled a laugh. "Your trust is safe with me, good master."

As they walked by a small lace-maker's shop, the shopwoman came out of her door and began shaking the dust from a small rug. She stopped short, gawking as she saw Cronin's company. "Your grace!" she exclaimed in surprise.

Cronin affected hurt. "Ah, but you won't notice me, Clarette!" he called out. "And I'm the one who nodded to you, not him, and whose wife buys too much at your shop."

"Get along there, Cronin," she retorted, "and take away your complaining. You don't bother me." The woman gave an awkward curtsey to Melfallan, and then beamed a wide smile. "A good day to you, your grace," she said shyly.

"And to you, Mistress Clarette," Melfallan replied, making her color with pleasure. She curtseyed again.

These are Brierley's folk, Melfallan reminded himself as they walked onward, his soldiers clumping behind them. My folk, too: it is one great treasure that we share. Cronin's kindly rescue somehow made the day brighter, put matters in their rightful place, away from the nobility's frets and poses. He looked up at the suns in the sky and smiled.

They turned a corner into another street. Foot traffic was light in the town with the fleet out at sea, but a few heads craned, and several bowed, their faces lighting with a smile for him. Melfallan had called it a rescue, but it now impinged on kidnapping—not that Melfallan minded, particularly.

Cronin found reason to stop at the baker's next, and took him in to talk to Bronwyn and her fat husband, Geoffrey. Melfallan sniffed appreciatively at the smells of baking bread and pastries, then looked around at the well-ordered shop with its broad counter display of bakery goods, large ovens, wall-shelves laden with flour and spices, and a few chairs for customers in the front to sit while they waited. He smiled as Bronwyn came forward to greet him. As Cronin inspected pastries at the counter with Geoffrey, Melfallan took Bronwyn's hand, then bent to kiss her cheek. Her husband, a bluff and pleasant man, knew about their affair three years ago, as he knew about Bronwyn's other lovers before their marriage, but felt no jealousy.

"Good day, Bronwyn," Melfallan said. "How are you and your family?"

"Very well, your grace," she replied, smiling up at him. "How good to see you again, truly. But what are you doing here, Melfallan? I heard Earl Giles was arriving today."

"He did. For the rest, ask Master Cronin." Melfallan lifted Bronwyn's little dark-haired girl, now nearly three, high into the air to make her squeal, then sat down with the girl in his lap while Cronin finished his purchases. Bronwyn took the chair beside him, then narrowed her eyes as she looked at him.

"You're escaping again," she mildly accused.

"Not by my will this time, dear one. I've been kidnapped by our good pilot, who thought I needed rescue, which I did. My father-in-law snubbed me at the dock."

Bronwyn looked astonished. "Why would he do that?"

"I haven't the faintest idea." Melfallan gave the little girl in his lap a kiss and hug, and then put her down to toddle off toward Geoffrey. "Surely he had some good reason, being an earl."

"Not that you care if he did or not," Bronwyn suggested.

"Probably," Melfallan said with an affable shrug, then grinned at her as she tsked and shook her head at him.

Justin Halliwell's smithy was next on Cronin's tour, but Sir Justin and his wife had gone with the other gentry to the castle. "Ah, I forgot," Cronin declared, slapping a palm to his forehead. They stopped at a fabric shop, where Cronin had Melfallan hold his box of pastries—"would you mind, your grace?"—while he inspected cloth; then they looked in at the cooper's, where Cronin checked on his order for *Southwind*'s water casks. As Cronin and the cooper stomped out briefly to the yard, the cooper's wife came forward shyly to talk with Melfallan, her small sons wide-eyed behind her. The half-made casks inspected, Cronin soon had Melfallan back in the street again, the soldiers marching stolidly in their wake. They turned up one street, then took the corner at the next.

"Cronin," Melfallan asked, "where are we going now?"

"Wherever you like, your grace," Cronin said genially. "I thought you might like a walk into town. Do you good, in case you're thinking your folk think less of you because Earl Giles was rude. I happen to think the folk might be offended. Happen to think they might have watched you left there on the dock, proudly refusing to follow him off the wharf like a rowboat on a tether. Happen to think maybe they might beat up Earl Giles himself for embarrassing you that way." He sniffed. "I hope the earl has a good guard of soldiery while he's here. He might need it."

"No fights, Master Cronin," Melfallan warned. "I won't have it."

"Not even with those twiggy sailors of his?" Cronin's eyes glinted. "My sailors were asking, each one of them."

"Not even them." Melfallan shook his head in emphasis, and saw Cronin shrug away his disappointment. To his amusement, Melfallan realized Cronin had been half-serious in his offer, but the last thing Melfallan needed was brawling between the earls' sailors. Well, he amended, there were a few other last things he'd like to avoid: blight, floods, rebellion in Farlost, invasion by the duke—

"How are Bette and the rest of your family?" he asked in courtesy as they strolled.

"Well, Bette's expecting her fourth now, due any day now. She's up at my house while her husband's out fishing for the season. Your choice whether to go to see her, knowing what she'll do to you if you dare. That's my Bette; she'll say anything, given a chance."

"I remember." Melfallan smiled.

Cronin smiled back. "So do I, your grace. Too bad you were the earl's heir. Life might been different for you and Bette—not that she's unhappy, of course, but a father's always looking out for his children, as you will when your little son gets older, and whatever other little ones might be coming in time. When all is put in its rightful place, there's nothing more important than that." He pointed up the street. "Down that lane and around a corner, and we'll be at my house, with cakes and ale for you and all your soldiers, and the only price the teasing."

Melfallan looked up at the bright sky, and the wind swirled down the streets of Tiol, flapping every banner. "Lead on, pilot," he decided. "It's a good day for kidnapping an earl."

"I thought you might like it," Master Cronin allowed.

Melfallan delayed two hours at Cronin's home, enough for an alarmed Sir Bertrand to send a boy to find him and fetch him back to the castle. Intent on his duty, the boy tried to hurry Melfallan along, but Melfallan hardly walked fast enough to suit him, to his great anxiety. Taking pity on the boy, Melfallan finally sent him running madly off to alert Sir Bertrand of his impending return.

His steward met Melfallan at the castle gate, eyebrows poised halfway between shocked disapproval and incredulity, as he always did when Melfallan escaped his own castle. Bertrand Gallois was a lean-bodied and gray-haired fusspot, loyal and true, and an expert on every ceremonial and rule of court. Like any good steward, he would go to his grave still determined to teach his earl proper behavior. As Bertrand opened his mouth, Melfallan for once dared him with a look to say one word, any word, then strolled past him into the gateway courtyard, not hurrying.

When Melfallan walked into his bedroom suite to change out of his rich clothing, he found Robert waiting for him. Had Robert been waiting all this time? he wondered. From the angry flush in his brother-in-law's face, Melfallan suspected that he had.

He nodded coolly, then opened the wardrobe door. He pulled off his tunic and heard the crackle of paper, then realized he'd forgotten to return the letters to Mistress Cronin. An excuse to go back, he realized, and hid a smile. He slipped the letters into a nearby drawer. As Melfallan reached for a new tunic, Robert was watching him impatiently.

"He won't apologize, you know," Robert blurted. "He just doesn't—ever. And I told you his quarrel is with me, not with you. He forgot how it looked." Melfallan lifted his earl's circlet from its case and put it on. He gave his head a quarter-turn for the profile, jaw properly squared, and Robert snorted in exasperation. "Stop that and talk to me, you oaf. It was my fault, Melfallan, as I'm trying to explain to you if you'll only listen."

"Really?" Melfallan asked. "He forgot how it looked?" Melfallan took off his circlet and put it back in its case. "In front of my folk, Robert."

"Yes, he did forget. Please, Melfallan!"

Melfallan sighed, and relented. Robert charged through life with the fine mettle of a high-blooded stallion: his temper was legendary, in keeping with his fiery-colored hair, but he had a heart to match. Robert had been happily married to Elena for ten years, with two young sons. He was a good count for Efe, would be a good earl for Mionn. And Saray loved him. "So what was the argument about?" Melfallan asked reluctantly.

"He wants me to divorce Elena."

"What?" Melfallan swiveled to face him.

Robert grimaced, visibly unhappy. "We've been arguing about it ever since we ported in Lim for water and Father heard the news."

"Why in the Hells should you divorce Elena?" Melfallan asked, perplexed. Then he registered the rest. "What news in Lim?"

Robert shrugged. "Two weeks ago, well, four now, Count Toral's son was killed when his horse bolted and threw him. Broke his neck. He was Toral's only male heir, and so now there will be a bidding war for Toral's other child, the daughter. Lim will descend through an heiress, with her bridegroom the next count of Lim. And Father wants me to be that count." Robert scowled ferociously, then threw up his hands. "Imagine the glittering prospect, brother: one grandson to take Mionn, and another to take Lim, one of the duke's own counties, and that the marcher county bordering Mionn. What security for our defense! What influence over the duke! What glittering opportunities to gouge Lim trade! I've told Father it's absurd, but he won't listen." Robert got up from the windowsill and began to pace. "He never listens," he muttered.

"You can't be count of Efe *and* Lim," Melfallan protested. "The duke would never agree."

"The duke has suggested he might, for a proper boost in the tallage. The minute Father heard the news, he sent a rider to Darhel suggesting it, and we waited in port two days for the answer."

Melfallan's stared at him, struck speechless at Earl Giles's treachery. Whatever Giles's dynastic motive, it was an incredible signal to send to Tejar, this hint that the earls' alliance might be undermined if Tejar were deft in his bribes.

Robert was pacing up and down, his hands working furiously behind him. "Tejar does have his own candidate, a Captain Bartol. Isn't he the captain who—?"

"Yes," Melfallan replied tightly. "But Bartol's not nobly born. Lord Estin never acknowledged him."

Robert shrugged. "That's easily fixed. Knight him and make him 'Sir Bartol,' then elevate him to count. It's been done before. Didn't the Courtrays get Tyndale that way?"

Melfallan scowled at him, not pleased by the analogy, an idea Robert had probably picked up from his father. "Sir Mourire proved himself in Lionel's service, Robert, and was a knight's legitimate son, not a commoner. And I don't like your comparison of my family to a toady like Bartol."

Robert shrugged. "Don't take it personally, brother. If I had the choice, I'd rather Lim in Bartol's hands than a few others in

Tejar's court. But Father wants me to be Lim's bridegroom. Ocean alive, Melfallan! She's only ten years old! I couldn't bed her decently for a year or two, and then might kill her with a pregnancy at that age. But tell that to Elena! She's convinced that I'll do it, that I'll let Father win." He looked away, his jaw muscles working. "Once she heard Father's new idea, she wouldn't come with us past Lim. She took passage home on another Mionn ship in port. And Father let her go, thinking it would help him win if she was gone." He sighed and spread his hands in appeal. "That's why she's not here. It has nothing to do with you or the baby— just like Father's rudeness has nothing to do with you. Believe me, Melfallan, please."

Melfallan considered it. Maybe the family quarrel did explain Earl Giles's behavior: Robert's quarrels with his father sometimes approached the legendary. On the other hand, Giles's rebuff on the wharf might be mere show for a spy to bear tale back to Tejar, assuring him of Giles's sincerity, if Earl Giles had any. "Did Tejar offer any other terms?" he asked curiously.

"Tejar as regent for my sons," Robert answered with disgust, "both in Mionn *and* Lim if I die untimely."

Melfallan whistled. "That's putting a target on your chest, Robert."

"Tell me about it. Oh, there's a condition. Father is regent first, should I shuffle off. That or Father pays the duke twenty thousand livres in gold for his consent." Robert made a face. "Which do you think the duke will take?"

"Oh, I'd take both. Riches *and* control of Mionn's minor heir. Does Tejar get Mionn's income while he's regent?"

"At least you're thinking past the first few terms." Robert shook his head. "Father's not stupid, Melfallan. I think he really wants the Lim girl married to my younger boy, but he won't admit it. Elmond is only six, and too much can happen before he's old enough. And so he points his finger at me, just to get Mionn's marker on the table." Robert began to pace again. "Father hates trading with Lim, the way Toral hides behind the duke's influence, but that's not cause to set me up for murder. But he says, airily, waving his hand, 'the duke wouldn't dare.' "

"Oh, Tejar would dare. My aunt thinks he prompted Heider to his attack on her."

"She does?" Robert asked with surprise. "Based on what?"

Melfallan shrugged noncommittally. "She feels she has proof."

"Your aunt would think anything vile of Tejar," Robert said, fluting his hand in dismissal. "I wouldn't give it much credence."

"Why?" Melfallan asked, nettled by his tone. "Because she's a woman?"

Robert blinked and sat down again on a clothing chest, looked at him with genuine puzzlement. "Where did *that* come from? I don't understand you, Melfallan. But, since you're asking, Rowena has done well enough as regent, but Airlie will be better off when Axel accedes in his own right. And she's not reasonable about Tejar, never has been. Heider was a traitor. It doesn't take the duke's meddling to make a lord rebel against a woman. I'm surprised it hadn't happened earlier."

"Is that your opinion or your father's?" Melfallan asked.

"Both." Robert rose again from his seat, highly displeased. "Go ahead: scowl at me again. You defend Rowena too much, Melfallan—Earl Audric could be foolish about the daughter he overindulged, but you don't have that excuse. To my mind, you should practice better reason and stop listening to your aunt."

"Have I asked your advice?" Melfallan said coldly.

Robert flushed, his temper rising. "I've told you that Father did not mean you insult," he said tightly, "and I've explained why. But if you want to be insulted, go ahead." Robert stalked angrily out of the room.

Likely he expected Melfallan to call him back, but Melfallan chose to be contrary and let him go. He listened to Robert's footsteps recede down the hall, thought he heard a slight hesitation at the stair's turning, then heard the footsteps resume their descent, angry and emphatic.

So much for careful diplomacy, Melfallan thought with a sigh. He shook his head at himself in the mirror and shut the lid on his circlet case. And I told Cronin not to start fights with Mionn. Tsk.

20

elfallan?" He heard Saray call from an adjoining bedchamber, and he walked into the next room. Saray had her hands full of satin cloth, with more packages still to be unwrapped on the bed. Her sister Daris sat in a chair by the window, watching, and narrowed her eyes as Melfallan came in. She did not quite hide her smirk, but then Daris never really tried. "Were you arguing with Robert?" Saray asked in concern.

"Were you eavesdropping what we said?" he challenged.

Saray shook her head, then fluttered her hands at his tone. "I merely heard your voices rise. Were you arguing with him? Why?"

"Yes, why, Melfallan?" Daris echoed, more snidely. A washed-out and older version of Saray's beauty, Daris had become plainer as she aged, her nose slightly spotted, her mouth a bit too wide. Now she batted her thin eyelashes at Melfallan, and rounded her mouth with coquettish interest. Melfallan looked at her with distaste.

Well, I could make three for three, he thought, and felt tempted. What would most offend Daris? He considered the various possibilities, and then reluctantly decided not to try. Knowing Daris, she'd only take it out on Saray after he'd left.

"It's nothing," he said to his wife, then made himself smile at her reassuringly. Perhaps he erred again in guarding Saray's happiness from unpleasant truths, but he could not bring himself to ruin the joy of this day. For the first time in weeks, they had spoken pleasantly to each other, without the edge, without the war, and Saray honestly had not understood her mistake on the dock, as she so rarely understood anything of his politics. "Are you enjoying your presents?" he asked politely.

"Oh, yes. Here, Daris brought something for you, too." She held up a length of wool felt. "In blue!" Saray smiled happily. "I thought I'd make you a long robe, something you can wear in winter, embroidered in silver for the gray in our colors."

"That sounds wonderful, Saray." He glanced at Daris and caught her looking sour again, then deliberately sat down on the bed to let Saray show him her other presents, one by one. Saray's look of delight rewarded him more than he deserved. Saray's aw-ful family was not her fault, he knew, and perhaps her lady rules had preserved Saray as she grew up, even made living possible. Perhaps those rules were Saray's strength and shield, he thought, not the weakness he had assumed. It was an entirely new thought about Saray, and an idea fully validated by Daris's face right now.

As Saray brought out each gift for display, Melfallan slowly relaxed and enjoyed watching his wife's happiness. She smiled shyly back at him, obviously pleased without any pretending, that he allowed her to show him her gifts. She did so love presents, especially presents from her family, no matter the real purpose behind them. He also watched Daris try to hide her expression as her eyes glittered enviously. For the gifts? Because Saray seemed happy? Or because Saray had married an earl?

Yes, he decided, maybe it is three for three today. With some creative thought, he might find some way to offend Lady Mionn, too, and so complete the task.

My principal ally.

Daris listened to the retreating sound of Melfallan's footsteps, then cocked her head at Saray. "I'm glad he liked the velvet," she said brightly.

"Oh, yes." Saray smiled at her sister, pleased that Melfallan had delayed to see their gifts. For once he had not scowled but had seemed genuinely interested, and it lifted her heart and her hope. She desperately wanted this quarrel to end, as had all their quarrels in time, but Melfallan had prolonged it wilfully, making an unpleasant scene about that blacksmith's son and now shouting at her on the docks when all she meant was— She felt her face flush slightly, then determinedly thought of other things. Her family was here and the baby's Blessing would come in just a few days, and all would be better.

As Daris unpacked three beautiful gowns from a trunk, Saray reseated herself on the bed and watched. The first was a brilliant azure blue spangled with tiny beads; the second was lowcut and sea-green with elaborate laced sleeves and a shimmer to the fabric. Saray thought she should ask the name of Daris's clothmaker, for surely these fabrics were to be prized, enough to justify the expense of transport from Mionn. The third gown was all in silver, with entwined silver chains across the bodice in intricate filigree. Daris brought the silver gown over to Saray and let Saray touch the fine stitching and silky fabric.

"They're beautiful, Daris," Saray said in awe.

"Only my latest," Daris said, with a toss of her head. For a few hopeful moments, Saray had thought Daris might intend the gowns as more presents, but it appeared she wished only to show them off. Saray sighed softly. Ah, well.

Red-haired like Saray, as were all of Lady Mionn's children, Daris wore her hair piled high, netted with silver traceries. Elaborate filigree earrings dangled beneath her ears, and her daygown bore a subtle tracery of gold threads throughout its fabric, a process of hours of work by her seamstress, but, Daris professed, only a simple morning gown. As always, her sister carried herself with self-conscious pride, and had the habit of looking down her nose at people—but that was Daris, Saray thought comfortably. Daris always had a certain refined air about her, and seemed to know everything about the finer things in the world. She certainly had an excellent seamstress.

Saray bent to look more closely at the woven chains that defined the bodice of the silver gown, then ran her fingers lightly
over the lacy sleeves. Before she was done with her inspection,
Daris had whisked the gown out of her grasp and put it back in
the trunk.

"It is so lovely to have you visit," Saray said, folding her
hands in her lap. "I wanted Father to see the baby."

An odd expression twisted across Daris's face, quickly gone,
that puzzled her. "Oh, yes," Daris said with a fluting of her hand,
"your baby. At last you produced a baby, Saray. It was too bad
you failed the three times before."

Saray colored slightly and looked away. "But I do have my
son now," she said quietly.

"And there's hope you might produce another," Daris said
heartily, with a brisk shake of her shoulders. "I advise it most
strongly, Saray. Infants can be very fragile, and it is always better
to have another child in reserve, in case this child fails, too." Daris
walked across the room and busied herself at the boudoir table by
rearranging the jeweled flasks and silver combs. "Merely because
a child survives birth, you know, doesn't mean he'll live much
longer. Children often die in infancy." She tsked, then picked up
a mirror to look at herself.

Saray firmed her mouth. She did not like this talk about dying
children. "Audric is very healthy. Our midwife says so."

"Does she?" Daris asked indifferently, preening before the mirror in her hand. "Be cautious of your wet nurse," Daris advised,
turning back to Saray, her expression now solemn. "Wet nurses
can sometimes be in the pay of a rival High Lord, and Duke Tejar
does not like your Melfallan, I've heard. Robert told me about
their meeting in Darhel—I believe you were there, too, weren't
you?—and Robert feels most concerned about Melfallan's open
defiance to the duke, and the great trouble it could bring Yarvannet. He was talking about it again just the other day."

"Defiance?" Saray asked, bewildered. "When? I didn't see—"

Daris laughed. "Oh, Saray, you're too naïve. Don't you pay
attention to anything? You were there and you must have seen it."

"I don't know what you're talking about, Daris," Saray said, and tried to hide her sudden stab of worry. Sometimes she did miss things somehow obvious to others—was Yarvannet in danger? Perhaps that explained Melfallan's recent moods, his preoccupation and his easy anger. Perhaps it wasn't another affair at all. Had she misjudged him? She shook her head firmly at Daris. "Melfallan is a good earl for Yarvannet. He knows what he is doing," she said loyally.

Daris again rearranged her dressing-table, moving a crystal flask, a jeweled box, then gave Saray a most unpleasant smile. "Does he? I don't think Father agrees."

"Father?" Saray asked with real alarm. "What has Father been saying?"

"Quite a bit, I assure you," Daris said. "Particularly about his foolish championing of that commoner woman."

"You mean Brierley Mefell?"

"Yes, if that was her name."

"She is a healer from Amelin," Saray said. "Captain Bartol falsely accused her of being a witch, an absurd claim." She flipped her hand. "She helped me at Audric's birth, and I believe that he and I owe our lives to her. She was a gifted healer, indeed. I quite liked her," Saray added firmly. "It was such a shame that she died. No one knows quite why, but it seems that justiciar of the duke's was responsible. Melfallan says they're still looking for him."

"Are they?" Daris asked. "I can't imagine why. She would have been condemned and burned, anyway. You know what the witch laws say."

"The shari'a are a myth, Daris. There are no more shari'a."

Daris sniffed. "Well, there once were, and the commonfolk still look out for them. You never know where they will appear, doing their evils. Are you sure you're quite all right, Saray? I've felt most alarmed that you gave yourself into a shari'a's power. There might be horrible consequences."

Saray tightened her mouth. "I don't want to hear about it."

Daris ignored her, as usual. "You've heard the tales. The

witches can control minds and steal souls. I *do* hope your baby is truly all right. It's so hard to tell, at least in the beginning, when a child has been possessed by evil. Eventually the shari'a returns, you know, and takes the child for her rites." Daris shook her head in wonder, then raised one finger in sudden insight. "Perhaps that's why she helped you, so she could steal him later!"

Saray's lips thinned even further. "No one's going to steal Audric," she said with spirit.

"I'm glad you feel alert, sister. That is surely to your son's protection."

"Brierley helped us," Saray declared. "I am very grateful to her."

"That's how they get into your confidence," Daris said, shaking her head. "They make you believe that they're good, but really they're not. And when you least expect it, they strike." She snapped her fingers. "And just like that, your son is lost to you—and perhaps yourself as well."

"How can I lose myself?" Saray felt bewildered now.

"Well, I wouldn't know. I've never met a shari'a, unlike you."

"She wasn't shari'a!"

Daris flipped her hand. "But that's the trick, don't you see? They make you think they aren't, until it's far too late to protect yourself." Daris turned away, casually fluting the lace on her daygown's sleeves to a better arrangement.

Saray frowned, upset. Daris always professed that she said such things for Saray's betterment, a loving elder sister giving good counsel. All of Saray's life, Daris had lectured so, not caring that it upset Saray, and not listening to whatever Saray said back. When she was younger, Saray had valued the attention from Daris when their parents were so often busy with court affairs and Robert was away with his friends. She had valued it, however much it disturbed her, but now she decided she could do quite well without it.

"I don't want to hear it," Saray repeated firmly and looked away.

"As you will. Shall we talk about the ball tomorrow night? And now you have a baby to show off, too, at long last. I am overjoyed, I assure you."

"We won't bring Audric to the ball," Saray said. "He'll stay in the nursery with his nurse."

But somehow that topic, too, turned to Saray's disadvantage. Daris affected surprise. "You won't bring him out to display him to your gentry? How unfortunate. It would be better, sister, to settle any concern they might have that he even exists. After all, you *have* failed three times to produce an heir. If nothing else, since you care nothing about the opinion of your Yarvannet gentry, it would benefit your reputation in Mionn, which had sadly fallen into tatters. Mother was shaking her head just the other day, worrying about it."

"My reputation?" Saray asked reluctantly.

"Ah, but you didn't wish to speak of that." Daris toyed with her hair.

"You never change, Daris. You always think the worst."

"I never change? Think the worst?" Daris affected hurt. "I don't know what you're talking about, sister. I'm only giving you advice out of my love for you."

"So you say." Saray stood up and smoothed the wrinkles from her skirt, then lifted her chin. *I am Lady Yarvannet*, she thought proudly, and for once Saray allowed herself a sniping addition, although not aloud. *And who are you, Daris? Wife to a minor Efe lord, and ugly and getting old.* "I am pleased you are here, sister," she said sweetly. "Welcome to Yarvannet. I hope you enjoy your stay." Saray nodded graciously, then abruptly walked out.

Sadly, it would have spoiled her effect to look back and see her sister's reaction. Perhaps Daris had gaped her mouth, a sight Saray dearly wished she could see, just once. Saray walked firmly through the next chamber into the hallway. Like a fish, she wished then, and nearly giggled. Steal Audric indeed!

She hesitated near the stairway to the uppermost floor, then impulsively climbed the stairs to Melfallan's tower. A soldier stood next to his door, helmeted and dressed in mail, a lance in his hand. Saray stopped short as she saw him, slightly startled to come upon him up here. She so rarely noticed the soldiers on guard.

"Is the earl inside his room?" she asked hesitantly.

"Not at the moment, my lady," he answered, straightening his shoulders even more rigidly.

"Oh." Deflated, Saray turned and walked back down the stairs, a slight drag in her steps. Where might he be? Somewhere with Robert? She hoped so. However Melfallan had tried to reassure her, she had heard quarreling in their voices. People so often quarreled, she fretted. Why can't we be pleasant? Vain wish!

Earlier that afternoon, she had overheard two of her lady-maids talking, and had belatedly realized what had happened on the dock between her father and Melfallan. She had seen only Father behaving as he usually did, preoccupied and gruff, but the Yarvannet folk had seen something quite different. When Daris and Mother had followed Father, Saray had thought everyone was leaving and had walked with them, only to notice that Melfallan had stayed behind with Robert. So she had hurried back to apologize for not waiting for him, and had made things quite worse. Like her father, she had humiliated Melfallan in front of the folk. The lady-maids had felt quite indignant, and had painted the fault equally on both her father and herself, as she deserved.

She stopped on the staircase, and bit her lip hard. I didn't know! she thought in anguish, then shook her head at herself with contempt. So that's your excuse, Saray? she thought. Poor helpless Saray, who doesn't understand anything? Poor, stupid, incompetent Saray.

It was proper for a lady wife to walk with her husband, and she had thought only of that, but should have thought of more. She knew that now. By not thinking, she had helped her father insult Melfallan, and so insult Yarvannet itself. She writhed internally in shame, remembering particularly the stricken look in Melfallan's eyes. But Melfallan had not berated her as she deserved. He had hidden his hurt, and had instead given her courtesy, even a compliment. How hard that must have been! And how often he had made that effort for her, covering up her mistakes, pretending she hadn't failed him! She sat down on the stairs and bowed her head miserably.

Why did Father insult Melfallan? she wondered, bewildered. And Daris! Why did Daris say such poisonous things about the baby, about Mistress Mefell?

But why, Saray, she asked herself angrily, do you always expect them to be kind? They never are, never were. You knew better, but you didn't think.

She firmed her mouth. She had told herself fancies, in her great anticipation of her family's impending visit. She had imagined her mother's quiet pride as Saray showed her Yarvannet Castle, pleased that Saray had done so well as wife and lady. She had thought Daris would give up her sniping, now that Saray was also married and had a child of her own. She had even imagined her father's high approval as he held Baby Audric in his arms, the visible proof of Saray's success as wife. She had rolled herself up in a blanket of her happy illusions, when she could have warned Melfallan about her family. He didn't really know them; he had never seen how it really was. When he had visited Mionn years before, Saray's family had behaved pleasantly, even winningly, quite unlike their usual selves. Saray had told herself at the time they did it for her, in their happy joy that Saray would marry so very well, when it was nothing of the kind. Of course it wasn't. And because she had not warned him, Melfallan had been taken off guard.

She knew how it felt: how thoroughly she knew how it felt! She had allowed it all her life until she married Melfallan, but had then discovered someone in her husband who could be kind, not cold and indifferent, who loved instead of used. She sighed. She could not undo her mistake today, that was sadly accomplished and done, but certainly she could stop helping her family diminish him—and help him instead. But how? Saray wrinkled her brow, thinking hard. What could she do? She had no skills in politics, but she did have skills.

Tomorrow night she planned an entertainment to welcome her

family, and she thought suddenly of Jared Cheney. Jealous of Melfallan's attention to Jared, she had not been kind to him, and had truly angered Melfallan, an issue they still had not resolved. This morning, as Saray and her mother walked to the castle, her mother, unfailingly alert to such things, had noticed Jared among the gentry, and, when Saray had told her about the knighting, had frowned in cold disapproval that a commoner, a mere blacksmith's son, should be so rewarded. And I was the one who told her he was a blacksmith's son, Saray remembered with shame, when I could have said he was our castellan's nephew. I helped Mother play her proud games, because I was jealous.

Saray thought of the shopgirl who might have been her friend, and the fisherwomen on Tiol's docks that she had envied, and suddenly understood why Melfallan had knighted Jared. He's like the shopgirl, she thought in amazement, a friend who might really be a friend, someone without games to play, lands to protect, pride and rank and secret agendas. She had never had such friends herself—although I could, she realized now. I really could—but that's for later. She smiled in ecstatic relief, knowing what she could do for Melfallan, and she knew just as certainly how much it would please him—and answer her mother. Insult my husband, will you? she thought indignantly. Insult his choices? She set her jaw stubbornly.

But first she had to find Melfallan. Where was he? Saray got to her feet and continued her search for her husband.

She finally found him in Sir James's library near the Great Hall, looking through papers. Sir James always had papers to show Melfallan, piles and piles of papers—and books stacked high. Melfallan spent too much time poring over Sir James's papers; he'd no doubt make himself short-sighted. She peeked around the doorjamb, and saw their two heads bent close together as Sir James droned on about something. She wondered what—probably something legal and dull. Does Melfallan ever feel bored with all those papers? she wondered. And would he say if he was? He took his duty so very seriously. She craned her head further, trying to hear what Sir James was saying, and was spotted by a clark across the room at another table. He jumped to his feet and bowed.

"My lady!" he exclaimed. Sir James and Melfallan both looked around, as did every other head in the long room.

"Oh!" Saray said, and nearly leapt back out of sight—but then saw Melfallan's smile—and his surprise. Was there pleasure there, too? It emboldened her and she stepped fully into the room. "What are you reading?" she asked bravely.

Melfallan pulled out the chair beside him. "Why don't you sit down, Saray? I think I need help."

"*Me* help *you?*" Saray scoffed.

"If only in the listening. Have you settled Daris then?"

"Why, yes," Saray said and batted her eyelashes. She sat down beside Melfallan, and felt his hand slip into hers under the table, even though his attention was already back on his papers. She looked at his averted face, blond and handsome, with a strong nose, a firm chin, and could not imagine how she had managed to quarrel with him. She must be wrong about the castle girl, she decided, and regretted the trouble she had made for him. She resolved to do better—*would* do better, for her love of him. "Not really to the benefit of my good character," she murmured as he turned a page.

His head turned to her, and she caught her breath as he smiled, so handsome, so winning. "Oh, did you finally tell Daris off?" he asked, and looked amused.

"Not exactly," she had to admit.

Melfallan grinned. "It's only a matter of practice, Saray. A little today, a little more tomorrow. But I warn you: it takes a while to get as mean as Daris."

"Melfallan!" she scolded, shocked.

Sir James cleared his throat and looked up at them both, his mouth twitching, and Saray suddenly remembered she didn't belong here. She murmured an apology and started to get up, but Melfallan abruptly tossed down his papers and stood up with her.

"Enough for today, Sir James," he said. "I'll look at the other briefs later." He offered his arm gallantly to Saray. "For now I think I'll walk through the castle courtyards with my lady wife,

to the envy of men and the jealousy of women. You'll notice that
flattered us both, Saray."

She slipped her hand into the crook of his elbow. "I'll overlook it, Melfallan," she said demurely, then covered her giggle
with her hand as both Melfallan and Sir James laughed aloud.

Oh, yes, Lady Saray thought earnestly, she would try harder.

~⁌

That evening Earl Giles and Lady Mionn retired early to bed after
dining alone in their guest chambers, claiming fatigue from their
long voyage. The next morning he and his lady finally emerged
from their bedroom, and Giles graciously condescended to attend
a late breakfast with Melfallan and his principal castle guests. Lord
Tauler had not yet arrived from Penafeld, but Lord Garth and
Lady Joanna had, and had brought Lady Tolland with them to the
breakfast. Melfallan had not invited them, nor did he think Saray
had time this morning to mention it, but there they were, seated
in a row near the other end of the table, chatting pleasantly to
Saray as the servants brought the meal.

Although Melfallan seated Earl Giles at his right, the place of
honor, the earl's greeting to Melfallan was the stiffest of nods,
followed by total refusal to notice Melfallan in any way whatsoever. Instead, the earl chatted genially, with great wit and charm,
to his lady wife, his son, Revil and Solange, and even Saray. He
flattered Lady Joanna, joked charmingly with Lord Garth, even
paid Lady Tolland a compliment. Robert shifted uneasily in his
seat several times, visibly upset, his eyes flicking between his
father and Melfallan. Saray's eyes soon gleamed with tears. Lady
Mionn seemed oblivious to it all, eating with small elegant bites
as she listened attentively to her husband, smiled in gracious good
humor at his jokes, nodded courteous agreement whenever appropriate.

"I raise fine horses myself, Lord Garth," Earl Giles was saying
expansively, waving his hand. "My measure of a good steed is
that old truism of any horse's worth."

"And that truism is, your grace?" Garth asked, his face eager in its attention. By his side, Joanna was nearly agog in her fascination, leaning on the earl's every word. Melfallan felt his stomach start to roil.

Giles waved his hand again. "Haven't you heard it? 'A good horse should have six qualities, three from a man, three from a woman.' Earl Giles paused, then recited with relish. " 'From a man, he should be bold, proud, and hardy; from a woman, fair-breasted, fair-haired, and easy to leap upon.' " He grinned, and Garth gave him the expected laugh. Even Lady Mionn smiled.

Then Earl Giles started another horse story, with Garth and Joanna again hanging on every word. Melfallan rose abruptly and left the hall.

Robert caught up with him on the last staircase to Melfallan's tower, nearly stumbling in his haste to catch him. "Melfallan!" he called. "Wait!" Melfallan turned hard on the riser, then angrily shook off Robert's grip. "I told you——" Robert began.

"This isn't about Lim, Robert," Melfallan said coldly. "This isn't about another argument you're having with your father. Your father is deliberately breaking our alliance. Excellent. Yarvannet will survive alone."

"No!" Melfallan turned away. "Listen to me!" Robert demanded.

"Why should I?"

Robert spread his hands, openly pleading now. "Because I'm Robert, not Giles. Because I'm your brother."

Beneath them in the stairwell came the heavy tread of someone climbing toward them—a servant, or a soldier coming on watch. Melfallan seized Robert's arm and pulled him up to the top of the stairs, then half-dragged Robert through the upper hall. At the entrance to the battlements, Melfallan glanced briefly at the soldier standing door-guard outside. "Stay out of earshot," he ordered curtly.

"Yes, your grace." The soldier saluted and quickly moved inside the doorway.

His hold still hard on Robert's sleeve, Melfallan stalked to the middle of the battlement wall, giving them a good twenty feet of open space in both directions. Only then did he release his grip. Robert half-staggered as he caught his balance.

"So I'm listening," Melfallan said.

Robert slowly straightened his sleeves, then took several deep breaths, visibly struggling with his temper.

"Well?" Melfallan prompted.

"Just a minute, will you? I'd deck a man for that kind of handling, Melfallan!"

"Between earls," Melfallan advised coldly, "it can be far more lethal. You might tell your father."

"Ocean alive, Melfallan! I didn't do the insulting! I've tried to help: I didn't fight with him at all yesterday, and he still, still—" Robert shook his head helplessly. "Ocean alive, he treats you as if— And in front of Revil and your marcher lord!" Robert sighed and sagged against the stone wall. "I think he had this planned before we left Mionn. Hells, it might be the only reason we even came. I never thought he'd take it out on you."

"What?" Melfallan demanded. "What have I ever done to Mionn?"

"Not you. He hated Earl Audric, Melfallan, hated him for years, and now he's apparently getting even by insulting you. All those times he had to pretend, all those times he had to suffer Audric's arrogance— He doesn't think you'll strike back. He thinks you'll just roll over and take it, because he's Mionn and you're—"

"I'm what?" Melfallan asked dangerously.

"Like me." Robert sighed again, gestured helplessly. "Young, untested, and mainly not *him*. I'm there to be ordered around, controlled because he's liege lord, outshouted, outmanned, out-ordered. He rags me, goads me, and pushes me until I lose my temper, and then tells me I'm weak because of it. He doesn't like my wife, although *he* chose her for me. He doesn't like how I raise my sons. He uses my inheritance like a whip to keep me in line. 'I'll disenfeoff you, boy.' Sometimes it drives me mad and I could tear apart—Hells, the whole world! You don't really *know* him, Melfallan. When you came to Mionn to court Saray, he wanted the marriage, and so he was pleasant to you. You've never seem him the way he really is; neither did your grandfather." Robert laughed harshly. "Earl Audric thought they were friends."

"But why—"

"Are you joking? A knight's grandson made into an earl, equal to Giles of Mionn? Of course he hated Audric, hated you all. Mionn's earls descend in unbroken line from Farrar himself! What was Mourire? A minor knight in a traitor's household, handed a county by Lionel, and then his son handed an earldom by Selwyn. Hells, Melfallan, Father expected Pullen to *kill* Audric in the battle here. That's why he encouraged Pullen to rebel."

So Tauler was right, Melfallan thought dazedly, stunned by the confirmation. What irony: had Count Sadon not withheld his soldiers in Pullen's last battle, Earl Pullen's war might very likely had ended Audric, as Giles had hoped. Sadon's help might have come merely thirty years too late. "He's a good dissembler," Melfallan said slowly. "Grandfather wasn't easily deceived."

"The best," Robert said in disgust. "You just had an example at breakfast. That was *all* an act, every word of it, and most of it aimed at Garth. After the way Father behaved yesterday on the dock, Melfallan, it was stupid to invite Garth to the breakfast."

"I didn't invite him. He just showed up."

"Then Father sent the invitation, intending to embarrass you. It's just spite, all an act, just to prove he can. He may think you're young and lack brains, but he doesn't hate you, not like he hated your grandfather." Robert seized his sleeve. "Melfallan—"

Melfallan bit his lip and tried to think clearly. If Giles had hated Audric with such venom, how much more had he hated Duke Selwyn, the son of a traitorous knight who had seized the coronet by murder and force of arms? And Duke Tejar, of that same traitorous blood? What *was* behind the Lim marriage?

It's a trap, Melfallan decided suddenly. Tejar's focused on me—he's made that blindingly clear—and Giles is going to ambush him. But how? With a snaking chill up his spine, Melfallan realized that the earl's war Tejar expected may have already begun—not in Yarvannet, but in Mionn.

Melfallan glanced around them to make sure they were truly alone. "You shouldn't have told me about Pullen," he warned grimly. Robert charged through the world, never thinking when he should. "Your father would call it treachery."

"*Treachery?*" Robert exclaimed in outrage, and Melfallan gestured quickly that he lower his voice. Rebelliously, Robert complied, and stood simmering beside him.

Melfallan grasped his sleeve. "Listen, brother, this is what we'll do. You've talked reason to me, as a good son should, and so now we'll go back and I'll apologize."

"You'll *what?*" Robert asked incredulously.

"Robert," Melfallan said, impatient with him, "for once stop thinking with your temper, if only because it's predictable." Robert flushed and might have said more, but stopped when Melfallan gave his arm a small shake. "Your father's right, you know," he said fondly. "Your temper *is* a weakness—your only one, in my opinion. Don't breathe a word to your father that you told me about Pullen," Melfallan warned again, deeply afraid for him, but Robert still looked perplexed. "You have two sons," he explained. "Don't make yourself inconvenient."

Robert stared at him even more blankly. "My sons? What do you mean?"

"Your father has two legitimate heirs the duke can't challenge. He doesn't need you to protect the Mionn accession."

"Don't be absurd! He's my father!"

"He's also earl of Mionn. If you need a precedent, look what he's risking for Saray in an open breach with me. Her fortunes ride with mine." He tightened his hand on Robert's arm. "Robert, don't tempt him," he pleaded earnestly. "He has too much at stake."

"And that is?" Robert demanded, but he was listening now.

"A coronet for Mionn. Don't you think it's about time? After all, the Mionn earls have unmade three dukes." He tugged Robert into motion toward the doorway. "Think about it, brother. Think hard." Robert still looked stunned, but nodded and seemed to hear. Melfallan hoped he had.

When they returned to the hall, Melfallan reseated himself beside Earl Giles. "My apologies," he said pleasantly. "A sudden errand."

Giles gave him a sharp glance, then narrowed his eyes as he watched Robert walk around the table to his own chair. Melfallan caught the gleam of satisfaction, as if a spirited stallion had been brought to rein—himself? Robert? Or both? Earl Giles deigned a stiff nod to Melfallan, then went right back to ignoring him. Saray gave a small sigh of distress, then quickly lowered her eyes to her plate. Daris smirked, Lady Mionn smiled blankly, and Robert's color began to rise again.

What a family, Melfallan thought. He took a deep breath, then picked up his spoon.

Eventually the horrible breakfast ended, and Giles left the hall with Lord Garth, both set on a trip to the stables that Garth had suggested. Melfallan rose courteously from his chair as they walked away, but neither Earl Giles nor Garth gave him a backward glance. Melfallan tried hard to control his expression, for benefit of those who watched as Giles again insulted him, with help from Lord Garth. Was Garth's liking for courtesy to an earl so extreme that it robbed him of good sense? Melfallan wondered. Or did Garth merely follow his wife's fawning lead?

Saray came to him, and he kissed her and sent her off with her sister and Solange. Robert hesitated, then stalked angrily in another direction, his bootheels ringing on the flagstones. With a sigh, Melfallan sat down in his chair, and looked bleakly at Revil.

"What was *that* all about?" Revil demanded, his eyes glinting with anger.

Melfallan shook his head. "I'm not sure, Revil. I think I know, but—" He shook his head again, then crooked a wry smile at his cousin. "And I was trying to persuade you to be an earl. Foolish me."

That evening Earl Giles and Lady Mionn again retired early to bed and declined to attend the entertainment Saray had arranged in their honor. Daris came, to sit and be courted by Yarvannet's ladies, all agog at the presence of another earl's daughter in their midst, and Robert came in determined good humor, his outburst at Melfallan set aside for Saray's sake. But the assembled Yarvannet gentry had expected an exalted banquet, and spoke with much disappointment about Earl Giles's absence. Watching their faces throughout the dinner, Melfallan saw that nearly all had heard about the snub at breakfast, as most had seen the snub at the dock. Apparently Cronin's advice held even for the gentry: by insulting Yarvannet's earl, Giles also insulted Yarvannet. Saray especially felt embarrassed by her father's behavior, and made a great effort as hostess, gracious and flattering to all.

Melfallan tensed slightly as he saw Saray beckon to Jared Cheney, but Saray smiled winningly at the young knight, and laid her hand lightly on his arm. A few moments later, to Melfallan's total astonishment, Jared was leading Saray onto the dance floor. He knew, sure as breathing, it hadn't been Jared's idea. Despite Melfallan's encouragement, Jared still felt awkward among the nobility, disliking his fancy clothes, lurking in corners at every ball. But now Melfallan watched in delight as Saray now took that problem firmly in hand, guiding Jared around the dance floor, talking to him with bright animation, in every way showing her favor. When the dance had ended, Saray took Jared's arm and led him to the nearest group of gentry. Whether Jared liked it or not, it appeared, Jared was about to get socialized.

Lord Tauler of Farlost, who had arrived in the early afternoon, stood with his wife on his arm, chatting genially with Sir James. He turned and bowed with pleasure to Saray, then bowed genially to Jared as she introduced him. It started another of those occasional gentry slides, this time toward Jared, as Saray had deliberately arranged. Melfallan watched as Lady Joanna walked up, Lord Garth in her wake, both stylishly dressed, both graceful and handsome. Joanna smiled prettily at Jared, but then laid her hand on Tauler's arm; he bent to listen. He saw Joanna's gay smile, Garth's quick joke, and then watched as Garth drew Tauler out of the room for a private talk.

Should I read anything into that? Melfallan asked himself sourly. Do I see conspiracy between my marcher lords, or merely a happy social occasion? Lord Tauler still played his careful games, balancing his earl against his sullen count: Melfallan now suspected Garth of games as well. Lady Joanna's father was one of Sadon's principal knights: did that bend Garth's loyalty to Sadon? Or not?

"Why do you scowl, Yarvannet?" Revil asked, and dropped into the chair next to him. Well, at least one Yarvannet lord is safe, Melfallan thought fondly—but I need more than my trusty one or two.

"Oh, general purposes," he answered. "I'm intimidating my lords again, including you." Melfallan leaned back and accepted another glass of wine from a steward. "Solange is very pretty tonight."

"And insists on dancing with other men," Revil complained, pretending to be put out. "You must speak to her, Melfallan. This won't do."

"And say what?" Melfallan asked. He sipped at his wine and watched the armorer Justin Halliwell bow low to a pink-faced Solange. "I hate to tell you this, Revil, but Justin has her now."

Revil sighed as if truly heart-rent, and his foolery made Melfallan smile. His eyes met Revil's, and he saw the mocking humor there, the steadiness, the fierce determination to protect Melfallan at any cost, even from Melfallan himself when there was need. One certain lord—and a few others in his knights. Melfallan wondered how many High Lords could boast that much.

"Perhaps I could make a new law," Melfallan offered, and waved a lofty hand. " 'I decree that Countess Solange of Amelin shall dance only with her husband.' "

"It wouldn't work," Revil objected, shaking his head.

"Why not?"

"She'd make me decree a *count's* law that she can dance with anybody she wants. You'd get angry, she'd forbid me to change my law, and, next I know, I end up in your dungeon."

"Or disenfeoffed," Melfallan said affably.

"That, too," Revil agreed with pretended gloom.

The dance tune ended, and Justin bowed amiably to Solange, then began to conduct her off the floor. Melfallan drained his glass and stood up. "I think I'll ask Solange to dance," he said.

"I knew it," Revil muttered. He shrugged mournfully, added a large sigh.

"Planned it, you mean," Melfallan mildly accused. "What? Does Solange think I'm that much in need of cheering? Enough to send you over?"

"Ask her yourself," Revil retorted. "I think her word for you tonight was 'grim.' Her words about Earl Giles are considerably more colorful. She'll tell you those, too, probably without your asking at all." Revil waved Melfallan toward the couples assembling for the next dance, Jared and Saray again among them. "Go talk to her. Be cheered: it will please my lady, and all your folk tonight."

Melfallan intercepted Lord Jarvis as he bowed to Solange, and neatly took her away into the next dance. Saray wheedled him to dance next, after firmly settling Jared with Lady Tolland, to that matron's startled surprise as Jared twirled her onto the floor. Saray was pink with excitement, her eyes sparkling, and laughed up at him as they danced, and he could have kissed her right then, in front of everyone. But, sadly, Saray had her lady's rule about kisses in front of the gentry and he could not, and felt a real regret that he couldn't. And so the pleasant evening wound onward, ending in the early-morning hours.

Saray looked visibly exhausted as they climbed the stairs to their chambers, and was already asleep when Melfallan joined her in their bedchamber some minutes later. He stood at the foot of the bed, watching her face as she slept. She had surprised him yesterday, seeking him out in the library, oddly shy with him. He had walked with her around the castle, talking pleasantly, being seen, and had once surprised tears in her eyes. And now this gesture toward Jared tonight, gracious and sweet, Saray's personal art, one she had long perfected.

He shook his head sadly. What do we do, my love? Can we truly make it better? And what of Brierley? When do I tell you about her?

$\mathcal{M}$ elfallan started to unlace his tunic, then changed his mind. It was late, but he wasn't particularly tired, and so instead headed for his tower study. He needed distraction, for he hadn't a clue about what to do about Earl Giles. Well away, he wished himself rid of both earl and duke, however that might be done.

He stopped short on the stair and frowned. Something lingered behind that thought, but what? He puzzled for a moment, hunting the connection that eluded him, a connection that led—to what? Duke Tejar and Earl Giles were a fact of his life as earl. He couldn't just wish them away. A fact was a fact. He scowled more fiercely, thinking hard. There was something there, but what? He puzzled for several more moments, but the idea tantalized, just beyond his grasp, and would not take shape. Finally he shook his head, irritated with himself, and walked onward, nodding to the night guard as he passed him.

Since he had decided to stay up, he might as well do some work. He detoured to Sir James's office and picked up a brief, then saw one of the books Sir James had marked and took that, too. It was a complicated appeal, an inheritance contested by the children and a second wife of a knight enfeoffed to the Tollands, with both sides determined to strip the other of all comforts. Lord Valery had casually chosen the stepchildren's side, perhaps by flipping a coin—Melfallan saw no other obvious basis for his decision—and the widow had appealed to Melfallan, Valery's liege lord, to claim the minimum of dower rights that were clearly hers.

Melfallan always took care with the assizes appeals, more than most High Lords likely did. His politics as High Lord might be tumultuous, but the law always assumed an orderliness to men's affairs, a hope that reason and wise principles would prevail. That theory attracted him, even if the presumed order sometimes never existed, and he considered this judicial work as the foundation of his good rule. His grandfather had been as careful with the duty, although perhaps for different reasons. After the chaos of his taking Yarvannet, Earl Audric had established firm order through his courts, and had won his new folk's acceptance by his balanced and reasoned judgments. Melfallan hoped to do the same.

In another life, Melfallan might have been a clark, burying himself in books and precedents. It was a pleasant scholar's life, he thought, built upon writing down facts and hunting through books, with the real decisions made by someone else. A clark could spend years in his toils if he chose, content with his comfortable living, or aspire to greater ambition in the lord's counsels. Any clark could rise to the trusted rank of justiciar, a post often rewarded with a knighthood, as had Sir James. Even now, Melfallan suspected, Sir James still treasured his youth as a Tyndale clark, when the law was still the shining hope of order and peace. The years had tempered Sir James's expectations, but Melfallan knew his old friend still cherished a belief in that great orderliness given by laws, and had never conceded his trust despite the contrary proof.

The night was dark beyond the tower window, emblazoned with stars, and all was quiet nearby. He put the brief and book down on the table in his tower study, then sat down. A moment later, he got up again to find some paper on a shelf, then got up again to get a pen. He sat down again, and waited a moment to see what else he had forgotten, then untied the parcel of the brief and laid out the papers on the table. Revil might chide him for hiding out in his study, but Melfallan was gradually discovering his own purposes for his grandfather's tower. Sitting here now, late at night with a brief, the frets and annoyances of the day subsided, brought him peace of mind. He had no answer to his dilemma about war with Tejar, and significant problems with Earl Giles that he had never expected, but for now he set those frets aside. Yes, he might have done well as a clark.

He opened the book of prior judgments to the markers Sir James had left, and read the accounts of previous appeals, when other inheritances had been settled, then made careful notes as he read. Whatever the claims of the stepchildren, who had hated their father's new wife from the day she stepped across their threshold, she was entitled to a dower third of her husband's estate. It was the law's protection for the widow, a tradition that dated back to the West, and Valery had erred in stripping her of everything save a few jewels and a small farm south of Amelin. He wondered if Valery had rendered the judgment himself or had merely delegated it to a clark, perhaps a clark with some personal motive against the widow. Melfallan shook his head. Valery was truly useless as a lord, wasting his youth and talents by indulging his sensual appetites, all the while encouraged to his lacks by his mother. Melfallan could restore her rightful property to this widow, but the larger trouble of Lord Valery was not as easily solved.

He leaned back in his chair and frowned slightly, considering the problem. The Tollands were directly enfeoffed to Melfallan, as were his marcher lords and Count Sadon. He could expand Revil's feof to include the Tolland lands, thereby putting Valery under Revil's control. His cousin would never tolerate Valery's indifference to the needs of his folk, and would gladly take up the problem to help Melfallan. But if Melfallan expanded Revil's feof, rewarding his favored cousin for no obvious reason, his other lords might eye their earl warily, wondering when Melfallan would rearrange their rankings as well. And Lady Tolland, despite her vanity and airs, had influence in Melfallan's southern lands; her folk liked her, and felt comfortable with her ways. After all, the Tollands had owned lands in southern Yarvannet for nearly two hundred years. After sufficient time, such longevity became immovable.

Better that Lady Alice be the lord, despite her faults, he thought wryly, but some problems were not so easily solved. The

Allemanii still preferred men as their lords, and women like his
aunt battled expectations whenever political chance brought them
to rule. Most of the commoner trades were shared equally by men
and their wives, if only for economy's sake when all hands were
needed to support the family. Wives went to sea with their husbands to fish, and a widow often farmed her husband's lands as
capably as he had, and not always with her sons' help if they
had a family elsewhere. Some trades like smithing required a
man's greater physical strength, and other trades like lacery and
midwifery required a woman's patience, but the commoners did
not have the rigid divisions the gentry chose to impose on themselves. In Melfallan's castle, women tended to be the cooks and
maids, and men the stewards and soldiers, but Sir James had two
female clarks on his staff and Sir Micay had proposed the Briding
girl as Yarvannet's first woman soldier in the castle guard. It was
a flexibility Melfallan favored, but he knew that few of the nobility, including his own in Yarvannet, agreed with him.

He shut up the book of precedents, and then got up from his
chair. Behind his map on the wall, he had hidden some sheets of
paper and now drew them out, then carried them back to his table.
He was trying to write a letter to Brierley, should he find some
way to send it, but found it a frustrating task. Everything he wrote
sounded stupid, either too much for prudence in a courier's hand,
or too little to avoid the stilted and inadequate. The first page was
covered with half-sentences, quickly crossed through, and he still
didn't know how to begin.

Dear Brierley, I miss you— With a snort, he crossed it out. Not a
good start. *Dear Brierley, I hope that you and Megan are well*— Ocean
alive, he swore, scribbling ink over the words. *Dear Brierley*— He
sat and looked at the two words on the paper, chewing his lip. He
couldn't send the letter, anyway: just writing her name put her in
danger if the letter were intercepted. But he might have the means at
hand to try, if he could somehow write an acceptable letter to her.

Perhaps Jared might take it to her, he thought. Jared had not
yielded his pressure on Melfallan, and it was an assault Jared
showed little sign of relenting. Melfallan smiled, thinking of him.

Jared had a dogged earnestness in his petitions, and an attractive openness of face and manner, at first awkward with an earl's magnificence, but falling easily into a comfortable familiarity that neither he nor Melfallan felt odd, even if others might. Melfallan still had to repress a slight jealousy, and absolutely refused to speculate now if Brierley and Jared had ever bedded, but Jared's own manner easily turned the jealousy aside.

They were truly becoming friends, he realized, as friendship sometimes happened between men, who became in time as close as brothers. It was an unlikely friendship with a commoner and far too rare in Melfallan's limited circle of the nobility, but perhaps it might be the beginning of one of those lifelong associations between lord and knight that sometimes graced a lord's rule. Audric had shared a similar friendship with Sir James in their youth, and later with Sir Micay, and both men had remained in Audric's service all his life, as trusted as the ground upon which Audric walked. Jared might likely become such a man to Melfallan. He shook his head bemusedly, then looked down again at his letter.

Perhaps if he addressed the letter to Niall. *Dear Niall*— But he didn't want to write to Niall. He wanted to write to Brierley. *I've met your Everlight*, he wrote, plunging onward. *Or perhaps she is Thora Jodann, your dream-guide. Or perhaps it is all pure fancy, as a way to dream of you, my love. She showed me your cave and the journals, and we*—

He stopped and frowned. Well, he couldn't write about *that* in a letter, although they had now stopped the sex. When the Everlight now visited his dreams, not often but regularly enough, he didn't always get the answers he wished, but he also talked to Thora's shade about the larger things of High Lords and witches, the Disasters and Rahorsum's desperate mistake. At times, the Everlight seemed to fade in its sense, drifting into confusion, but it had pronounced itself very old and so sometimes fumbled in the illusions it created. At other times, Thora's anger flared out at him, reproving him for the Allemanii's cruelties to her shari'a people, and she berated him angrily, her eyes flashing with her passion. At times the rage possessed her so completely that it abruptly banished the dream, waking Melfallan in his bed, his heart pounding in reaction.

The more he met the Everlight in his dreams, the more he recognized Brierley's Everlight as her guardian, not fierce and insane as the strange machines in Witchmere, but a gentler voice, whimsical and affectionate. Brierley had named Thora as her teacher and friend, and had known this Everlight as a constant companion: through its presence in his own dreams, he began to understand how Brierley had survived in Yarvannet isolated from her kind, and why Brierley had chosen to heal despite the risks. Allemanii legend painted the shari'a as vicious women who stole men's souls, but the Everlight carried the essence of their sea witches, the healers, as they had lived in their time before the Disasters and since, as Gerin had lived in her small village in upper Airlie, as Brierley and her predecessors had lived here in Yarvannet.

With the Everlight's permission, he had read further in the journals in Brierley's cave, including the sad and short journal of Marlenda Josay, the knight's daughter driven into hiding by Earl Audric's invasion. Revil had called that campaign a terror for the local folk, when Tyndale's soldiers had ravaged the land, and Marlenda had been one of the victims. Had such fortune befallen Saray, she might have been such a girl, stripped of all she expected and loved, left to grieve alone, bewildered and afraid and bereft. How many such girls would Melfallan harm if he launched a similar war? How many unremarked girls, how many others he would never know?

Another journal, much thumbed and delicate, had been Thora Jodann's own writing. Thora had usually written to her future apprentice, a pattern copied by several of the journals, including Brierley's own. Hers was a comforting voice, clear and tender, strong in its purpose, adamant in its hope. *A great gift can bring great peril,* she had written. *My daughter, have hope, and believe in the future. All is not lost, for a new day will dawn, a new purpose arise.* Sometimes Thora wrote the most amazing words, words that turned the world on its ear, words that thrilled, words of defiance and hope and inspiration. He had returned several times to the journal to read Thora's words, then often thought about them all the next day. Together the cave journals of Thora and her daughters spoke across the years, lending hope, fighting despair. They must have been Brierley's constant comfort.

He looked down at his letter and read his words to Brierley, but did not cross them out. He wondered where Niall would hide her in Mionn. He had assumed Mionn held some safety for Brierley, at least for the interim: had he been too confident in his alliance with Mionn's earl and sent her into danger? He fretted, worrying for her.

He had hoped to ask Earl Giles's help in finding Brierley when he was ready to bring her home: announcements in Mionn's villages should eventually bring them back into contact. He now knew that help would not be forthcoming, not with Giles courting the duke with his dreams of a Lim alliance. How to find her again in Mionn? Without Giles's help, it was likely an impossible task, whatever Jared thought. Or should he send Jared now, before it was safe for Brierley to come home to Yarvannet? Melfallan shook his head and dipped his pen back in the ink, took a deep breath as he looked at the scribbled page, then turned to a clean page.

My love, I miss you, he wrote. *I worry that you might fall out of love with me while we are parted: such matters must be tended carefully, I know, as a farmwife tends her fragile herbs in a box through the winter. Aunt Rowena told me—I hope you aren't angered I spoke with her—that we should let fate carry us to where it will, but I don't accept that. Nor will I tell myself that I should, even if you disagree. I hope you don't disagree.*

Melfallan grimaced and stopped. Now I sound like an old woman worrying, querulous and shrill, he thought, and he nearly abandoned the page, then stopped himself with another scowl. Surely he had some ease with her, and this letter would not doom their love beyond recall. He snorted at himself. What an idiot you are, no different than any other lovesick boy, and Ocean, what a lovely feeling it was. Brierley would laugh if she ever knew, and forgive him more than he forgave himself.

But I have to be perfect, he thought fiercely: that will make it certain. And Brierley would surely laugh at *that,* too, even more than the other. She had more sense than he did, an acre of good sense when he might fill a small garden-patch, if that. He smiled.

I worry that you might hide yourself away, he wrote, *thinking it saves me: you have great skill in your eluding, and I might not be skillful enough to find you. I want you home in Yarvannet, Brierley, and I now doubt our choice that you live elsewhere. You would be safer here—*

He yawned suddenly, a great jaw-cracking yawn that made him blink afterward, then shook his head hard. Damn it to the Hells, he thought irritably, I'm just getting started right—don't go to sleep now. Another yawn followed, and he thought he might lay down his head on the table for a moment—

He dreamed of a road, heavily covered with snow. Tall everpine stretched snow-filled branches toward the sky, where another storm now gathered over Mionn's high peaks. He stood alertly on the snow, breathing in the crisp cold air, and then noticed a light flickering among the nearby trees. The snow creaked beneath his boots as he went to investigate. Who was traveling this winter road so deep into the season?

Several yards into the trees, a man and a woman sat by the shelter of a short bluffside, their fire reflecting heat and light from the towering stone. Both were dressed carefully for the weather, in heavy cloaks and hoods, stout boots, gloves. Each sat on a warm pad of blankets, another blanket drawn warmly around the shoulders. The man bent intently over a harness strap, mending a break in the leather. The woman, her face shadowed by her hood, studied a book in the lap, the pages tilted to the firelight, then picked up another book from beside her and turned its pages. She looked up at a branch overshadowing their camp, her head turned away from him, and the man looked, too, then laughed quietly. Puzzled, Melfallan looked and saw nothing on the branch. He stepped forward into the small glade formed by the encircling trees and the bluffside, then looked again, craning his neck. Nothing.

The woman turned her head and smiled at the man across the

fire, and the fire illuminated her face. It was Brierley, he realized with a shock—and then Melfallan suddenly recognized Stefan as the man seated across the fire, and saw a small huddled form of a child in a nearby rough bed beyond Brierley, the blanket drawn up to cover her face and hands as she slept.

But it's winter, Melfallay thought, bewildered. Brierley and Megan are supposed to be at the cabin, safe with Sir Niall, not traveling on this road to Mionn. And why is Stefan here? Melfallan looked around the small campsite with its fire and packs, and the horses standing nearby in the shadows. Where is Niall?

Brierley said something to Stefan he couldn't hear, and he moved still closer, then sank to his heels beside her, close enough to touch.

"Brierley?" he said, but she showed no sign that she heard him. He reached out to touch her sleeve, suddenly yearning for that touch, but his hand passed through her arm, as if he were a ghost and no longer among the living.

Have I died? he wondered sadly. Is this how we remember life, not as Ocean's pleasant undersea realm, but a reality we cannot touch, cannot hear? He craned to look at the book in her lap, and saw the graceful shari'a script, then strained to listen as she spoke again and Stefan replied. She smiled and his heart turned over in his chest; he saw her shake her finger at Stefan, teasing him, then laugh.

Beloved, he thought yearningly, aching deeply for her touch, her voice. Brierley straightened slightly and looked around herself, but her gaze blindly passed over him. She looked confused, then bit her lip, and tentatively reached out her hand, groping through the empty air, not quite in his direction.

"What is it?" Stefan said, his voice suddenly audible over the popping sound of the fire, the soft movement of the wind through the trees.

"I thought—" she said, and looked again at the trees surrounding them, the slow fall of snow drifting downward "For just for a moment, I thought—" She shook her head. "Another of my witch's fancies, Stefan. Don't mind me."

"Fancies, hmm?" Stefan asked skeptically. "I've noticed that some of your fancies, lady witch, turn out to be quite real. Not that I'm complaining—"

"—much," she finished for him. She chuckled. "There's no help for it, Stefan. Melfallan had the same complaint about witchly affairs." Stefan shrugged with good humor, then wrinkled his nose as she laughed at him again.

Brierley— Melfallan reached again to touch her, but she was not there, not truly.

He heard a faint rustling of skirts near him, and groggily lifted his head from his pillow, then looked dazedly around at the tower room. Dressed in homespun, her red hair tied loosely at her nape, Thora Jodann stood on the other side of his table, and studied the map on his wall.

He sighed and rubbed his face slowly. Had he dreamed of Brierley? Or was it again only the Everlight? "I was thinking about you earlier," he said.

She turned to look at him and smiled. "I have been thinking, too. So Earl Giles was ungracious to you. An incautious lord, and far too complacent in his plans. The future is not set, whatever Mionn's wishing." She sniffed.

"Do you know why he's being rude?" he asked, hoping she might tell him Giles's true reasons, but Thora firmly shook her head.

"Let's remember where the line is, fair lord. I will not help you in your politics, at least not that way. But I might help you in another. As I said, I have been thinking." She turned again to face the map of the Allemanii lands, then took a step forward to trace the Airlie hills with a slender finger. "My sister lived here," she said wistfully, "and my cousins and other family." Her hand moved to a high pass in the mountains, one they both knew. "And my parents lived here in Witchmere. My father was high in its councils." Her hand moved slowly to the high inland valley in

Mionn that held the Flinders Lakes. "And I lived here, near the end. Peladius and I loved here first, one spring night in a forest glade. He was an Allemanii lord, sent by his Briding count to negotiate trade with the count of Arlenn: I met him when I visited the Arlenn court, I forget my reason why. He lived a season with me in Flinders, one season, only one, for a lifetime." Her hand fell away. "Now all the names on this map are Allemanii, and nothing remains of what was."

"Not all is lost, Thora," he said, disturbed by her sadness. "You were the one who believed in the last flame."

"Was I?" She turned and regarded him with sober gray eyes. "So much was lost, to be never regained. So many were lost, to be never reborn. And now your world is threatened with similar loss. How many will die in your war, Melfallan? To what purpose? The future is not set, but one can dream possible truth—or not." She walked to the table, moved the chair, and sat down. "As I said, I have been thinking, dear one. What distinguished Earl Farrar from his fellow High Lords?"

Melfallan scowled. He had been racking his brain for days on that question, as she well knew. "He opposed Aidan's reforms."

"Not exactly. He opposed the creation of a duke, and the ranking of the lords. What if Farrar had prevailed? Would your people have had such terrible wars?"

"Well, there's no one here to fight except ourselves—"

Thora shook her head. "Your folk are better than that. The Allemanii are a warrior people, but not foolish in seeking trouble. In the West, did the High Lords ever war on each other?"

He shrugged. "Occasionally."

"But not often." She turned to look again at the map. "What if there were no duke, as Farrar wished?"

"I can hardly ignore Tejar," he objected. "He's a fact of my life."

"Why? He likely had a role in Earl Audric's death, and he attempted the murder of one of your liegewomen to deny her justice, and then subverted your aunt's marcher lord to attempt murder on her. Under your Charter, doesn't murderous treachery by your liege dissolve your feof bond?"

"Yes," Melfallan said slowly. "If it's proven."

Thora dismissed that with a shrug. "Any proof can be brazenly denied, as your duke likes to do. Do you have any doubt of the truth?"

"No."

"Then deny Tejar as your rightful lord, citing that cause. Make Yarvannet fully independent, and not beholden to him. Make your land a sanctuary for the few shari'a who still live, and then defend their right, as you wish most to do."

"But that invites the war! The duke would never accept it!"

"It is easier to defend than to invade: all your tactical books say so. And a purpose can be hidden for years, can it not? Years to make your marcher lands secure, to disenfeoff Sadon and Valery and give your lands the strong lords you need, as Pullen had. 'Remember Farrar,' Gerin said. Remember what? That he wished to rule his land as he ruled it in the West, equal to the other High Lords, with knights he trusted, and not beholden to a liege." She spread her hands. "Not beholden, you can rule as you see is just. Not beholden, you can rescind the shari'a laws in your own lands." She smiled triumphantly. "What do you think about my thinking?"

"Hmm." Melfallan looked beyond her at the map, narrowing his eyes. With a flush of excitement, he recognized her idea was entirely new, and a new idea meant new possibilities. He had never thought to undo history, at least not in this way. No one had.

"Grunting is not becoming," Thora advised him severely. "Brierley would tell you so."

"I'll grunt as I please, witch." He rose to his feet and circled the table, then stood in front of the map. She turned in her chair to watch him.

Would it work? he wondered.

"You have seen Ingal's inland advantage," she said. "Yarvannet also has advantage as the southernmost land. He can invade only from the north, and you will see him coming."

"It still means war," he said thoughtfully.

"But a war you can win, Melfallan, and one that will not draw in the other Allemanii lands. Because you do not seek the coronet, the other High Lords can remain neutral, even Earl Giles. It will be only Pullen's rebellion again, Ingal against Yarvannet, and you will have the defensive position."

"You *have* been thinking," he said admiringly, and turned to face her.

Thora shrugged. "You had edged on the same idea, in your wishing the duke into oblivion. And what else can I do," she said in mild complaint, "with you reading every military text you can find? I tire of the topic, fair lord. You should find better reading and—"

—and suddenly it was bright daylight shining through the windows, and his study door boomed open. Melfallan jerked up, startled, and gaped stupidly as his father-in-law stalked into the room and sat down heavily in the opposite chair.

"Hmph," Earl Giles said, eyeing him with obvious irritation. "You often sleep at this table, Melfallan?" His tone implied fault in the practice, as if better lords did differently.

Melfallan eased several of the appeal papers over his letter, then made a show of yawning. "I was working late on an appeal. I must have fallen asleep. Good morning, your grace."

"Good morning," Giles mumbled darkly, then looked around at the tower study, inspecting it. "A pleasant room," he decided reluctantly. "I had forgotten how pleasant Yarvannet Castle could be in its accoutrements. My lady wife and I slept well last night."

"I'm pleased to hear it," Melfallan said smoothly. He leaned back in his chair, matching his father-in-law's pose. Giles had taken time to dress well this morning, his hair and beard in neat order, his jewels polished, and he was again wearing his circlet. Perhaps I should tie a string to mine, Melfallan thought irritably.

A quick haul, and the thing would rachet up the stairs, hitting every tread with a resounding clang, and he could pop it on his head and be adorned, just like Earl Giles. Then he imagined his father-in-law's reaction if he ever actually did such a thing, and bit hard on his lip to stop the grin.

"Sorry I missed your banquet." Giles waved a dismissive hand, as if even lords had to accept the unavoidable, and somehow conveyed the impression he wasn't sorry at all, the probable truth.

"I'm sorry, too, Earl Giles," Melfallan said, even more cautiously. Why was Giles here? And so abruptly, banging the door and taking a chair as if he owned it? Did he understand anything at all about this irascible High Lord? "We missed you."

"Hmph," Giles said again, looking around the tower room. "This was Audric's study."

"And is now mine," Melfallan said firmly, suddenly impatient with Giles's stalling, whatever purpose the earl had in this morning invasion of his tower. "Robert told me about the Lim marriage," he said, affecting a casual tone. "Do you really think it wise to anger Elena's father with a divorce? After all, Arlenn is your principal county after Efe." Giles's eyes swiveled back hard, but Melfallan forestalled any reply with a negligent wave of his hand. "I'd think Robert's younger son the better choice. Perhaps that's your true intent, Earl Giles? If so, it might be better to advise Robert rather than distress him this severely." Then Melfallan waited, looking back at Giles with a pleasant, interested gaze. Certain moments could define the future, and Melfallan knew with sudden clarity that this was one of them.

Giles opened his mouth, but stopped himself. His eyes narrowed a moment, then his lips firmed into a thin and unpleasant line. "I haven't asked your advice, Yarvannet," he growled.

"It's offered, anyway," Melfallan replied evenly, giving Giles another chance to accept Melfallan as Yarvannet's earl, as Melfallan was in fact. "If you dangle a Mionn regency in front of Duke Tejar, he'll snap at it. He's already struck at Rowena, and he'll use Lim to strike at Robert and Mionn. Margaret of Tyndale would be next, perhaps even Briding if Tejar can find a suitable pretense, and all the Ingal counties would be roused. That kind of instability can lead to war."

Giles lounged back further in his chair and gazed at Melfallan for several moments, then affected an indulgent amusement. "What do you know of war, boy?" he asked with contempt.

"What do you, your grace?" Melfallan retorted. "Mionn has never suffered invasion, only manipulated in secret. You tempt the duke too much with this proposal, Earl Giles, and that choice could impact on both our earldoms."

Giles chuckled unpleasantly. "Are you threatening *me*?"

"Not at all," Melfallan retorted. "Mionn is your earldom to throw away, not mine."

Giles jerked up in his chair, then flushed with his well-known sudden rage. "You dare to lecture *me*?" he demanded. "An idiot who fumbles that stupid charge against Farlost and then defends a *woman* in Tejar's court?" He snorted. "A mere boy, who takes five years to get a living child on your wife? If the child lives much longer, of course. I've heard he's sickly." Giles waved his hand, unconcerned, and Melfallan wondered for an instant if Giles deliberately provoked him with this pose—or truly didn't care about his own grandson if the benefit lay to Mionn not to care. As always, Mionn came first with the Mionn earls, with no concern for the wider Allemanii lands—it had never changed, never would.

Melfallan took a breath to steady himself. "My lady wife is your younger daughter, Earl Giles," he said evenly, "and you will grant her respect. My son is not sickly, whatever you've heard about Duke Tejar's wishes. And the charges against Landreth are true, but not your concern. These are my lands, and Lord Landreth is subject to my justice." He tightened his lips to a thin line. "And I will defend my commonfolk as I choose."

Giles snorted. "Tejar has outmatched you, boy. He'll bleed you dry with his demands for money, but you just give in. Oh, I've heard about the new amercements. All the High Lords have, and think you a fool."

Melfallan tightened his lips. "I agreed to pay the amercements. That doesn't mean I'm going to."

"Ha!"

"You're making a mistake, Earl Giles, I warn you. Don't dismiss me."

Giles smirked, then rose to his feet. Melfallan watched his
father-in-law walk to the door, then open it and leave. He heard
the soft shuffle of the guard's feet outside as he saluted. Giles's
footsteps clumped down the stairs, not hurrying, quite at ease with
an earl's choices, then faded from his hearing.

My principal ally—

Melfallan closed his eyes and shuddered convulsively, then took
a deep breath. Ocean alive, what have I done? he thought. No, not
I—what Giles has done. There would be war now, he knew—at
Mionn's arranging, or so Earl Giles thought, with Mionn pulling
the strings as always, taking the advantage with little risk, indifferent to even his daughter's ruin. The first pebble had begun the cascade down the mountain, to be followed by a roar of stone.

Melfallan got up to pace. Could I reason with him? he asked
himself carefully. Will he change his attitude after he's had time
to think? He thought not. Giles's behavior toward Melfallan the
past two days had been relentless, and had lasted too long to be
mere spite, as Robert thought. Giles had a concerted plan in this,
although its full objectives still eluded Melfallan.

Do I need him? Where one can coldly measure the value of a
land or a man, so can two.

He had seen Earl Giles in many moods during his courtship
visit in Mionn six years before, but nearly all of them affable. His
grandfather and Giles had sat up many evenings, trading stories
of their youth and Duke Selwyn, laughing at each other's boasts,
wagging their heads as they discussed items of rule. He had seen
Giles clap Audric on the shoulder in apparent affection, and
known his grandfather had returned the liking, very much so. At
times, the two earls had seemed so enchanted with each other's
company that they almost forgot the purpose of their meeting, but
from time to time they would call Melfallan and Saray into the
room, to tease the couple and raise a glass and congratulate each

other on the wedding. He heard the tales of Giles's temper, but had seen it more often in Giles's son, Robert. And he had heard of Giles's reputation for canny dealings, for firm control of his Mionn counts, for confidence in all things. He had personally seen the respect borne for Giles by all the High Lords: even the duke trod carefully when dealing with him.

But he had never seen the contempt, nor the brutality, that Giles had shown him today. Had Giles drawn sword and lunged at him to take his life, he could not have felt more dismayed. He had counted on Mionn's support, counted more than he realized.

Do I need him? Melfallan narrowed his eyes thoughtfully. Certain moments define the future, he reminded himself. Earl Giles had chosen his; perhaps I should chose mine.

He saw his letter to Brierley on the table, then sat down to write a few more hurried lines. *You must come home, and soon.* He folded the page, and lit a new candle to melt the wax—the others in the room had all guttered while he slept—then slipped the other sheets of paper behind the map again, the letter inside his tunic, and stepped into the hallway.

The guard's head snapped toward him as he appeared, and the man straightened with a jerk—no, a woman, Melfallan abruptly realized, despite the visored helmet and hauberk that partly concealed her face and body. "You must be Evayne," he said in surprise.

"Yes, y-your grace," she stammered, then firmed her chin and stood straighter, her lance upright in her hand, sword buckled by her thigh. She was tall for a woman, lithe and leanly muscled. Sir Micay had said her sword skills equaled the best in the entire Tiol guard, and Micay was usually painfully sparse with his praise. "Evayne Ibelin, from Briding," she said in a soft, almost musical voice. "Sir Micay assigned me this post, and said you were not to be disturbed." Her eyes glanced down the stairs, and her face colored slightly below the visor. "By anyone. I'm sorry, your grace. He— He walked right past me, and he seemed to be an earl."

"He *is* an earl," Melfallan said dryly. "Never mind—it was

all right." He took a step toward the stairs, then on impulse turned
back round again. "When did you join our castle guard?" he asked
curiously.

"Um, three weeks ago," Evayne answered. "I came with a
letter from Count Parlie, who recommended me. I had to leave
Ries, you see——" She stopped abruptly and flushed again.

"Why?"

"Not my fault," she said, lifting her chin.

"I wasn't saying it was, Evayne. Relax. Sir Micay has praised
you, and I almost always rely on his opinion. In fact, I can't think
of a time I've gone against it."

Evayne blinked, then quirked her mouth attractively. "I'm
pleased to hear that, your grace."

"Did Earl Giles notice you as he passed?" Melfallan asked. He
had no doubt his conservative father-in-law had noted the female
guard at Melfallan's door. Perhaps that had helped set his mood
for the confrontation, not that Giles had needed much help.

"Definitely." Evayne shrugged a slight apology, and then
looked embarrassed. Melfallan couldn't imagine her problems in
an all-male barracks, but the look she returned him was steady
and unafraid. For a moment, her gaze reminded him of Brierley,
as had the smile, and the two together impulsively decided him.
He knew nothing about her, but Jared might need another swordsman's help in Mionn, especially when that help was not obvious
when dressed in a woman's skirts.

"I'm sorry to add to your troubles, your grace," Evayne said
softly. "It seems my lot in life." Again the tilted quirk of the
mouth, the dark eyes glinting behind the visor.

"Hmm. Since I'm leaving my tower and I don't need a guard
up here, come with me, please."

"Your g-grace?"

"Please." Melfallan turned and clattered down the stairs, then
looked back to see that Evayne was following, then led the way
downward to the main floor of the castle.

He found Sir Micay near the quadrangle barracks, inspecting a bundle of new swords from Halliwell's armory. His castellan bowed pleasantly when Melfallan appeared, then frowned when he saw Evayne behind him. "I told her to come," Melfallan said quickly. "Sir Micay—"

"You may be earl of Yarvannet, your grace," Micay drawled, "but I set the guard in this castle. You'll kindly not interfere with my arrangements." He pretended to scowl fiercely. "Is there a problem?" His eyes flicked back to Evayne.

"Not at all. Sir Micay, will you please find Sir Jared?"

"Jared?" Micay blinked. "What's he done now?"

"Nobody's done anything," Melfallan said impatiently. Evayne's eyes darted from Micay back to Melfallan. "I just want you to find—"

"I heard you," Micay said imperturbably. "No need to repeat. Jared's in the quadrangle, I think."

"Good." Melfallan turned back to Evayne.

"I trust you'll explain before the year is out," Micay drawled. He made his tone long-suffering, a trusted man long put upon, unfairly so, but still loyal to his lord. Melfallan gave him a sour look, got a sniff back. "Slow down a moment, my earl," Micay suggested. "One swing at a time. You there! Kay! Go find Sir Jared for me, and say the earl is asking for him." A soldier set aside the sword he had been polishing, and hurried off. Micay turned back to Melfallan and planted his feet fiercely. "Now explain," he demanded. "Why are we looking for Jared?"

Melfallan glanced around at the soldiers occupied with their tasks. "Not here," he decided, then raised his hand as Micay opened his mouth again. "And if you use that suffering tone with me one more time, Micay—"

"Wouldn't think of it," Micay retorted. Evayne's eyes widened in astonishment at the raillery between them, but Melfallan had heard Briding's guard kept a stricter regime. Melfallan had never known Parlie's castellan to smile, except wolfishly, and the man liked to talk pleasantly of hacked limbs and torrents of blood.

The bloody talk perhaps inspired Parlie's soldiers, but Melfallan had never found it to his taste.

"Never mind his grace, Evayne," Micay advised her as he also noticed Evayne's surprise. "He's been that way since he was a boy, as I know too well in my grief, and I suppose he's past remedy now." He gave Melfallan a sour look and stalked past him toward the inner door. Melfallan beckoned to Evayne.

"I want you to find her. It's urgent," Melfallan said to Jared. "She might have left the cabin." Had last night's dream been more than a dream, but truth? Perhaps. But why would Brierley leave for Mionn in winter when the weather was dangerous? Why not wait for spring? And why was Stefan with her, not Niall? Melfallan shook his head irritably, pushing away the worry, and refocused on Jared. "If she has, she's gone to Mionn. I don't know where you should look, but since you want to try, I'll send you. This is Evayne Ibelin—"

"We've met," Jared said, darting a look at Evayne.

"I want Evayne to go with you—"

"Go where?" Sir Micay interrupted. "If you're going to re-order my guard, your grace—"

"Please, Micay," Melfallan said firmly, raising his hand, and his castellan stopped short, startled by the quiet reproof. "You decide, Jared, what to tell Evayne. I don't have time to make that judgment, but you will. When you find her—if you do—give her this." He pulled the letter from his tunic. "If this letter is intercepted, it—"

Jared nodded. "I understand, your grace." He took the letter and put it inside his own tunic, settling it deep beside his ribs. "I'll keep it safe," he promised.

"Good." Melfallan nodded and felt part of the burden lift from his shoulders. He glanced at Evayne distractedly, then returned to Jared, conscious that Sir Micay now watched him with great intensity. Later, he told himself. Later, good sir. "Bring her home,

Jared. Tell her she must come home, and quickly." Jared nodded again. "Ocean's grace protect you both. Ride out tonight." He offered his hand, and Jared clasped his hand firmly. Evayne's eyebrows rose again, her eyes flicking between Melfallan and Jared.

"I'll find her, Melfallan," Jared said confidently. "I promise." He drew himself up to salute, then beckoned to Evayne. "Let's go, Evayne. I'll explain as we pack."

Evayne looked back at Melfallan, her dark eyes full of questions, but nodded and followed Jared out. Melfallan sat down in a chair and let out a breath, then rubbed his face slowly.

"What has happened, Melfallan?" Micay asked quietly.

"We may lose Mionn as ally, and Brierley Mefell may be somewhere in Earl Giles's lands. I just sent Jared to find her."

Micay pursed his lips and nodded, not surprised. "So she's alive."

"Yes. This morning Giles called me an idiot and a boy, and walked out on me. He's making an alliance with Lim, and is courting Duke Tejar to do it." Micay whistled softly, his eyes widening. "He won't accept me as earl, Micay. Is it because I'm too young?"

"Or he's too old and set in his ways. He's always tended to that fault, even when he was young, if you get my meaning. Even your grandfather had his occasional problems with Mionn, and fooled himself to think your marriage to Saray would solve them." Micay's eyes unfocused as he thought. "This is dangerous, Melfallan. Tejar will see it as a way to divide the earls."

"As I told my father-in-law. He laughed at me. Aunt Rowena warned me about Giles, and she was right. She thinks war is inevitable now. So do I."

Micay nodded slowly. "What are you going to do?"

Melfallan smiled. "Rely on my good knights, of course—and somehow survive the next few days until my father-in-law goes home. If it were possible, I'd postpone the Blessing, but everything would get worse if I did."

Micay nodded again, then sighed. "Lords who like to insult other lords, it's true, hate the insults that come back, however

deserved. Giles would never forgive you, making him come all
this way and not have the baby's ceremony."

Melfallan agreed unhappily. "Well," he said, pretending some
cheer, "all I need now is Count Sadon."

Micay snorted and shook his head. "I received the news an
hour ago. Count Sadon left Farlost with a large party two days
ago. He's on his way here." He shrugged his sympathy at Melfallan's startled dismay. "You did invite him to the Blessing, after
all, as you invited all your Yarvannet lords. Who'd have thought
he'd actually come, when he could better insult you by staying
away? So you're about to get your wish, your grace. Perhaps you
might take it back." He raised a sardonic eyebrow.

"If it were only that easy," Melfallan said glumly.

Evayne resisted Jared's pull on her hand, then finally planted her
feet as they entered the tunnel to the main barracks. "Not so fast,"
she said, and pulled her hand out of his grasp. Jared whirled on her,
his usual easy manner vanished into intense agitation, as if every
moment now counted somehow against some peril. Perhaps it did.
With her witch-sense, she felt his need, his utter *will* to be gone—
wherever they were going. That was the rub: Evayne had lived too
many years in great caution to be tossed off a cliff now.

"Move your feet," Jared barked.

Evayne put her hands on her hips and did nothing of the kind.
She had sensed the witch-blood in Jared on their first meeting, as
she had in a very few others in the castle, painfully few, but, like
Jared, none of them were aware of it. The true witch who knew
herself as shari'a, or such rumor had pronounced her, was no
longer in Yarvannet, murdered by the duke in Darhel. Evayne bit
down on the agony and banished it. She had come too late to
Yarvannet: no use crying on it now.

"Not until you say where we're going," she replied reason-
ably. She could take the reasons from his mind if she willed it,

but she had learned the folly in such self-betrayals, once nearly to her undoing. She practiced better caution now.

"The earl ordered it."

"That's not enough, Sir Jared. Oh, I'll go because he ordered me, but he also said you would explain. So where are we going, and why?"

Jared clenched his fists, and Evayne braced herself, suddenly aware that Jared was poised to attack, to seize and drag her along if necessary. She raised her hands. "All I do is ask," she said softly. "Tell me."

Jared hesitated. "We're going to Airlie, and maybe then to Mionn," he said reluctantly. "To find Brierley Mefell."

Evayne gasped in shock, and hope newly dead flared bright-hot within her, enough to dizzy her. In the distance, Soren snapped his tail in a great clap of thunder and plunged downward through the clouds. Evayne staggered as the air dragon pulled sharply at her, willing her into the air to ride the storms, and there forget all else in his fierce exultation. *Not now!* she cried back at him. *Not—* That next moment Evayne found herself sitting dazedly on the stone floor of the tunnel, with Jared kneeling beside her.

"Are you all right?" he asked, his eyes wide.

Evayne clutched at his arm. "She's alive?" she asked desperately. "Brierley Mefell is alive, not dead?"

"That's what Earl Melfallan says. She's hiding in Airlie, or was the last he knew. We're going there to bring her home." Jared looked quizzically at her, alarmed by her abrupt collapse, and she felt his emotions beating at her mind: shock, puzzlement, concern. And beneath them pulsed the Blood, stronger here than in Briding, far stronger. More had survived in Yarvannet than in the other counties, perhaps because Thora's sea witches had lived here. Thora Jodann, who had built the Star Well in Mionn, who had given the Promise to the exiles. After so many years, so many years, it had come—

Every air witch of Briding had hoped for the Finding, and had ridden the winds in constant search, but all had been frustrated. The Four had not permitted—until now.

Evayne laughed and jumped lightly to her feet. "Then let's go," she exulted. "Now!" Jared hesitated, gaping up at her. "Close your mouth, Sir Jared," she ordered severely, shaking her head at him. "You were in such a hurry—so move your feet!"

"Uh, wait a minute—"

With another laugh, Evayne seized his arm and pulled him up. "All will be explained, brother. Move!"

22

rierley and Stefan arrived in Lowyn shortly after dark, chilled and wet from the steady rain. The snows had stranded them in poor shelter for several days in the mountains, but once the storm relented, they reached the eastern foothills in another few days. There the snow had not fallen as heavily, more often turning into cold rain. Tonight the wind blew gustily from the east, heavily moist with melting ice, and tugged at their cloaks and hoods with persistent cold fingers. Megan shivered within Brierley's arms and had not spoken for hours, as if she, too, drew in her strength against the bitter weather.

The first sign of hope for warmth was the marker-post on the outskirts of the small fishing village, pointing the way down a turning in the road. The main road continued onward, heading north to Arlenn, the capital of Mionn's southern county. There, Stefan said, the road branched to the north and to the west, north to Skelleford and Efe, Giles's other Mionn counties, west to the hamlets high in the mountains near the Flinders Lakes. Stefan turned Destin's head toward the town, and Brierley followed him gratefully.

They passed several small houses with fenced yards, each lit bright golden by lamps through the windows. A dog barked behind a fence, warning the town of a stranger's approach. In the distance, just below audibility and part of the wind's rush came

463

the sound of the pounding sea on the beach. A familiar sound, Brierley thought: how many miles had she traveled away from the sea, only to reach the sea yet again? A different sea, not as heavily salt as the Western Ocean, but almost as vast. The Eastern Bay stretched easily a hundred leagues eastward to another shore, a land rarely explored by the Allemanii and, the legends said, rumored to be haunted by catlings. Few of the ships who had ventured there ever returned, Stefan had told her, adding to the legend.

The lights from the houses gave some illumination for the road, and they followed its twisting lane down a gentle slope toward the town proper. Halfway to the wharves, Stefan turned up another street and, a block beyond, Brierley saw the large square shape and brightly painted sign of an inn. They dismounted at the inn door, and a stableboy promptly appeared to take their horses. Stefan lifted Megan down from Brierley's arms, then unstrapped his saddlebags from Destin's back. Brierley dismounted, her muscles protesting after the long cold ride that day, and she unfastened Gallant's saddlebags, then helped Stefan collect the rest of the packs from Friend. She watched the boy lead the three tired horses toward the stable at one side of the inn.

"This is good lodging for Lowyn, considering the size of the town," Stefan said. "A warm bed for you tonight, Megan," he added, bending down to her level. "Cheer up."

"I'm cold," Megan complained.

"So am I, sweetling." Stefan mounted the broad steps of the inn and opened the front door, then guided Brierley and Megan into the warmth and noise within.

The room was large and high-ceilinged, with a number of plank tables and benches for seating, half-full now with villagers and a few travelers eating their dinner. Two of the local lord's soldiers sat at one table, their helmets on the bench beside them, a sword propped at hand; at another, a group of fishermen were recognizable by their long leather tunics and heavy boots, a few with their wives seated beside them, out for a rare evening at the inn with its good meals. A fire burned lustily on the broad hearth, warming the room to fever-heat: Brierley closed her eyes in relief as the warmth beat at her face.

Stefan led the way to the near corner, where a square table sat with chairs. Brierley seated Megan next to the wall, and sat down beside her as Stefan stored their bags next to him on the opposite side. Within a minute or so, a broad and balding man, wiping his hands on his white apron, came over to them.

"Good evening, master, mistress," he said pleasantly. "How can I help you?"

"We'd like dinner," Stefan answered. "What are you serving tonight, good sir?"

The innkeeper pursed his lips. "Well, we have a tolerable stew, fresh baked bread and ale, and warm milk for the little one. Passing through, are you?" he asked with mild curiosity. "From where, I might ask?"

"From Airlie," Stefan replied easily. "I didn't know if we'd make it through this last storm. The snows have hit the pass hard."

"That's the truth. Few travelers attempt that road this late in winter, but I'm glad you arrived safe in our town. I'm Bart Toresson, proprietor of this inn and hostelry. Will you be staying long in Lowyn?"

"A day or two until the weather clears," Stefan said, and shook Bart's offered hand. "Willson is my name, Nels Willson. My brother's fishing boat burned in Arlenn last month, and he needs help in rebuilding it. This is my wife, Master Toresson, and our daughter."

The innkeeper nodded pleasantly to Brierley. "Sit yourself there and warm yourselves, mistress, young lass," he said kindly. "And call me Bart, good sir. Will be a silver penny for a room. Includes meals."

Stefan nodded genially. "Thank you, Bart."

"Ocean welcome you, traveler," the innkeeper replied, and then glanced distractedly as someone shouted on the other side of the room. "You there, Finley!" he bellowed, loud enough to silence every voice in the room. "That's enough ale for you!"

Brierley looked around, and saw that a young man in fishing

leathers actually had another young man by the throat, his fist cocked back for a blow. At Bart's shout, he quickly released the other's collar, and both young men looked guilty. "No brawling in my inn," Bart shouted in outrage, "or I'll have you dragged in front of the lord's factor himself. You hear me, Finley? None of your trouble tonight in my inn!" The boy scowled, made a sullen shrug, and Bart seemed to swell. "I asked if you heard me!" he bellowed.

"I heard you, uncle," the boy muttered. Then he lifted his chin and put on his bravado, then held out his glass. "Another mug of ale, good man."

"When the seas freeze," Bart retorted. He jerked a thumb at the door. "Get home now. Your mother will be wondering where you are. It's well after dark."

Finley opened his mouth to protest, then thought better of it as Bart took a menacing step toward him. He rose from his chair and sauntered toward the door, taking a careful distance from the innkeeper, who turned in place to watch him go. There was a gust of frigid air from the door and a slam. The murmur of voices rose again in the room as all turned back to their meal.

Brierley wondered if Finley would go home or, more likely, slip back after his uncle's temper had eased. She sensed a history of such quarrels, with Bart worried his nephew would take the path of drink like his sister's husband, and so put himself into an early grave. It made Bart's reproofs too harsh for a proud boy, and too easy assumption of Finley's fault when actually the other boy had started it, to the public embarrassment of the boy in front of all. After a few minutes, she saw Bart go out, thinking he might have spoken too quickly and might be needing the boy's forgiveness, which he did.

At another table, one of the soldiers celebrated his promotion that day, bringing a raise in pay that would allow his wedding to his sweetheart of many years. At still another, a farm family enjoyed an unaccustomed fine meal at the local inn, with the two children properly solemn for the occasion. Across the room, the fishermen laughed together, pleased with the catch of the season, now nearly done after all their hard labor, and let themselves drink too much and grow too loud, with no one else in the room really minding. Brierley listened to the emotions drifting in the room, each bringing its small store of knowledge about the persons there, then sighed softly. They reminded her strongly of her Yarvannet folk, these sturdy Allemanii folk with their practical air, their good sense, their confidence in living. That familiarity brought its comfort, for she did not know how long she would live here in Mionn, far from home.

Brierley opened her cloak and wrapped her arm around Megan's shoulders, who now felt a little warmer. The shivering had subsided to bursts now, and Brierley cuddled her close. After a few minutes, the warmth of the room began to penetrate, and Megan looked up sleepily at Brierley's face.

"Just rest there, child," Brierley said. "We'll eat, and then there'll be a nice comfortable bed upstairs."

Megan yawned and leaned her head on Brierley's shoulder. Stefan winked at Megan and told her again to "cheer up," earning himself a sweet sleepy smile.

"I'm not as cold as I was," she admitted.

"Wonderful!" Stefan exclaimed, determined to cheer her. "Now all you need is—" Stefan stopped short as Jain popped into view and fluttered down to the table. The salamander snaked his neck to croon at Megan, then snapped his wings to his back.

"Never mind," Stefan said dryly. "He's here." He looked around quickly at the other tables, where the folk ate and drank and chatted with each other, but no one had leapt to his feet, shrieking.

"He's invisible," Brierley assured him.

"The question is whether he stays that way," Stefan said, deciding to worry about it. Jain yawned, showing his teeth, quite unconcerned, then turned in place once before curling up in mid-table, tail tucked neatly over his feet.

A few minutes later, a servant girl brought three large bowls of stew on a tray, with a loaf of warm bread, a small block of cheese, and glasses. Jain affably moved himself to Megan's shoulder to make room, and Brierley poured herself and Megan some milk. After Stefan had filled his glass with ale, Jain investigated the pitcher and sneezed mightily as the bubbles went up his nose.

You're alarming Stefan, Brierley reproved. *He's not used to you yet.*

Are you? Jain retorted, but relented his noises.

They spoke little more as they ate hungrily. When they were finished, the servant girl came to collect the dishes, and shortly afterward Bart returned, Finley at his side. The boy swaggered a little, but his uncle allowed it, and Bart soon came over to their table to show them to their room. As they got up to follow him toward the stairs, the inn door boomed open, caught by a gust of wind, and all the lamps flickered. Jain promptly popped out, and Brierley wondered why.

A man in a travel-stained cloak stepped in, his hands swiping the wet from his cloak ends and tunic beneath it. He looked around the room with fever-haunted eyes, passing over herself and Megan and Stefan. With a flash of pain in her own thigh, Brierley sensed the festering cut in his leg, a wound that twinged with every step and now filled his head with fever, impairing his judgment about his own injury. Derek had not stopped to care for the wound properly, although he knew how to do so, and now he kept doggedly to his duty and ignored it angrily, unaware of his danger. Brierley sensed deep infection building in the leg that would soon break into his blood, an infection that might kill him. She felt an impulse to go to him, spy or not, then felt a Calling shape itself in the future, a Calling for Derek.

Heal the duke's own spy? she asked herself, appalled. Have you lost your wits?

Brierley carefully turned her face away, then firmly pulled Megan's face against her skirts as the little girl wanted to crane and look, attracted by Brierley's own interest in the newcomer. With a muttered apology, Bart excused himself to see to the new guest, leaving them standing by the staircase doorway.

Stefan had not noticed Derek's entry with any particular interest: he hadn't seen Derek's face in the pass, and so wouldn't recognize him as Tejar's spy. But Megan knew him, and would have blurted something had Brierley not given her a slight warning shake.

Not now, she sent. *Be silent, Megan.*

But he's the man— Megan protested.

I know. Hush, child. "Stefan," she whispered, "we should get upstairs. Now."

"Why?"

Brierley nodded slightly toward Derek. "It's him. The duke's spy." Stefan stiffened, then carefully turned himself to put his back to Derek.

"Has he noticed us?" he asked in a low voice.

"Not yet. His leg is wounded, and he's dazed with fever."

"We have to wait for Bart," Stefan decided reluctantly, although he wished otherwise. "If we try to go upstairs by ourselves, he'll notice and come hurrying after us, like any good innkeeper would do. He might as well point."

Brierley sighed. "I suppose you're right."

They stood quietly, trying not to attract Derek's attention, as Bart seated Derek at a table and beckoned to the servant girl. Then, after another affable word to his new guest, Bart hurried over to them. "This way, good master, sweet mistress," he said affably. Brierley held Megan's hand firmly as she and the child followed him, Stefan clumping his boots on the stairs in their wake.

Their lodging-room on the second floor was wide and spacious, with a large double bed in the corner, several sitting chairs, a small oaken table, and a bureau against the opposite wall. The innkeeper used his candle to light the lamps on the bureau and table, then lit the wall-lamp mounted by the door. "You'll have light enough, I think?" he asked pleasantly, bowing Brierley into the room.

"Oh, yes," Brierley said. "Thank you, Master Bart." Megan ran past her and leapt onto the bed, which bounced superbly. "This is a very pleasant room," Brierley said, and Bart smiled broadly, pleased. He took great pride in his inn, she sensed, and regarded all the world through that sense of satisfaction and good pleasure. A good man, as bluff and hearty as Harmon, and as trusty.

"I've the best inn in Lowyn, Mistress," Bart allowed with pride. "Be welcome and warm."

"Thank you." The innkeeper nodded to Stefan and left, shutting the door behind him. Brierley stood on the twilled carpet in bright rag colors, and looked around at the walls and furniture, truly admiring the room. She hadn't expected accommodations this pleasant, but admitted she had little experience of sleeping at inns. In fact, this was her first.

"We'll be safe here for the night," Stefan said as he put their bags into a convenient corner. "If we're lucky, we can get away early tomorrow. Megan, you'll break the rushes in that bed."

"Fun!" Megan agreed, and managed a somersault down the mattress, her heels clumping hard on the bedstead. "Whee!" she cried in delight.

"Megan—" Stefan warned again, to as little effect.

"I'm glad she's warm enough to play," Brierley said comfortably. "It was a cold ride today, and she hasn't much flesh to keep out the chill."

"Warm is nice, but I don't want straw-ends sticking in my back all night," Stefan growled. He caught Megan in his arms just as she started another somersault, then tossed her upward, to her shrieked delight. "I think you're a moss lizard, Megan. Torpid the morning until the suns come out, and then it's flickering lightning over the rocks. Right?"

"What's a moss lizard?" Megan asked curiously, having never in her life seen one.

"Sort of like Jain," Brierley answered, and then glanced around the room's air quickly, hoping Jain hadn't heard that comparison, wherever he was.

When Stefan put Megan down again, the child took one look at Stefan's face and curled up sedately on the mattress, then poked at its softness with her fingers. "I like this bed," she announced. "Do we get to sleep on it?"

"Yes, child." Brierley lifted one of her saddlebags onto the bed and unpacked a nightshirt for Megan, then helped her out of her clothes. In a few minutes, Megan was tucked in under the blankets, but then popped out of bed to do the round of the furniture, greeting table and chair, door and windowsill with great solemnity. When she was done, she gave a vast sigh of contentment and smiled up at Brierley. Brierley promptly put her back to bed, where she stayed this time. Brierley bent to kiss her forehead, and felt the child's fingers close on her hair, tugging gently.

"You'll sleep on the bed, too?" Megan asked, with mild worry that Brierley might not.

"Yes, I will. We'll both sleep here, but I'll lie down later."

"Good." Megan closed her eyes and sighed again.

"She seems happier," Stefan observed as he unpacked part of the contents from another saddlebag. "Perhaps she's out of danger now."

"I don't think the fire ghost is that easily defeated," Brierley said. "But yes, she's better. I'm glad that she can be a normal child much of the time, happy and busy. It's what I most want for her, Stefan. I don't think she really quite believes all this is real. Maybe in time she will believe, and can forget unpleasant memories. A kitchen waif has a hard life, and hers was harder than most." She watched Megan's face for a time and sensed the child fall asleep, wind on reeds by a river. Once again, Lady Megan sat on her balcony in his castle, admiring her domain. Much of her fear had subsided, enough for Megan to sit again on her balcony. Perhaps she was better.

She unfocused her eyes and looked with Megan out on the plain. In the distance, beyond the river in the high grasses, smoke still drifted, and something now moved there in busy activity. Brierley concentrated and tried to see more clearly, but the distance defeated her. She had not defeated the fire ghost, who still built steadily at her castle in Megan's dream world, even if today the clouds sailed slowly across the sky, and all basked in the suns' warmth.

She started as Stefan thumped several books onto the table. He sat down in one of the chairs with as sigh and pulled off his wet boots, then sat for a moment, blinking. He was as tired as she, but not yet ready to sleep. "I think you should sit down, too," he said severely.

Brierley wrinkled her nose, but took the chair next to his. Stefan picked up one of the dayi books and opened to his marker, then found his list of words, but then yawned and merely sat comfortably, blinking at the comfortable room.

Brierley sat with her hands in her lap and drifted a while, then listened again to the shifting sea of nearby minds in the common room below. A goodly crowd still remained, sharing their news and enjoying the company, and only a few of the travelers had climbed the stairs to bed. She listened for Derek, but could not sort him from the other minds: she didn't know him well enough, and was not that skilled in sorting minds, to admit a sorry fact. She hoped he would ride on after dinner, although that was unlikely this late in the night with a new storm brewing over the bay.

The last thing she needed was discovery by one of the duke's men. She had no interest in further contact with the duke, and made that wish lifelong, and could guess how her discovery in Mionn would compound Melfallan's politics. He was determined to defend her, and might take action he otherwise might not, for her sake, and she worried for him. Her eyes closed.

"You're falling asleep," Stefan accused.

"Not at all," she answered and opened her eyes.

"I could have sworn—" he teased, then suddenly gave a great yawn of his own.

"A delusion, Stefan. It strikes even the best of us." She gave him a level look and picked up the top book on the stack.

Stefan snorted but decided wisely to study his own book, although he smiled to himself as he did.

That night she dreamed of Melfallan, in great particulars, remembering his caresses and the touch of his mouth the few times they had lain together. She saw the curving rock ceiling of her cave above her, its silky darkness all around them as he moved above her. She raised her hands and caressed his face, felt his warmth, his fire, then gasped with him as passion swept through them, one emotion, one sure flame, rising higher and higher. She sighed within his embrace, then sighed again as he kissed her, and held him fiercely.

As a girl, she had become aware of the passions of coupling, if by secondhand and not at all welcome, and now those other memories invaded her dreams, bringing him to her. Their passion replete, their very souls entwined, he lay lazily within her arms in the cool darkness of the cave, and she caressed him, and then fell asleep beneath him, asleep within her own dreams, pressed next to his nakedness.

When she awoke, she felt Stefan's sturdy back against hers, likely enough reason for dreams of such fervency. He was turned away from her and snored softly, sleeping without dreams. They had not shared a bed in the cabin, there being two such beds and one for him to sleep alone, but Stefan had climbed into the inn bed with her easily enough, said good night, and then turned on his side, asleep within a few breaths.

It isn't the same, Brierley decided judiciously, and then laughed quietly at herself. The man she wanted was leagues away, dozens and dozens of leagues away, sleeping beside his wife, as was rightful. I always hoped for a man to share my bed, she reminded herself, and had doubted that grace would ever be mine, being secret witch, but I never thought on the problem of the wrong man beside me. Do other women have such problems? Well, of course, she thought. The heart is not always obedient, and she had sensed that particular quiet despair from time to time among the Amelin folk. Perhaps the beloved had loved another rather than she, or had died untimely, lost forever, forcing a second choice. Sometimes a woman married for security, not for love, or found herself bound to a man after a casual impulse of bedding had produced a pregnancy. Or, worse, as had afflicted her mother with Alarson, the man she married had proved himself a different

kind of man than expected, harsh and unloving when away from
other eyes, often indifferent, even cruel. On her other side, Megan
snuggled closer and sighed, and Brierley began to stroke the child's
hair softly, light slow movements down the silky curls. She felt
this might be a perfect moment, to be remembered later in life as
one of those few perfect moments that made all things possible,
even a witch's dreams. She smiled.

She sensed Derek emerge from his room into the hallway before she heard any warning sound of his soft movements. He
moved cautiously, as befit a spy, and counted the doors by his
fingers as he crept, trying to be as silent as he could. The need
for caution sent jolts of agony into his leg, but he gritted his teeth
and pressed on. He had a purpose in his counting of the doors,
she sensed: but how had he learned they slept here at the inn,
and behind what number? She reached out, probing; to her surprise, Derek responded easily with the right memory, unaware
that he did so.

"Any other late travelers this night?" Derek had earlier asked
the innkeeper, after nearly all the common room had emptied of
its guests. "I'll not wish my road today on anybody else, believe
me."

Bart had taken a long drink from his mug, content now that
most of the inn guests had gone home or above to his rooms, and
smiled at his last remaining guest. Derek had tipped him liberally
for the meal, and then had bought Bart a mug of the inn's own
ale, and the innkeeper felt most congenial toward the young man
for doing so. Well-spoken he was, and courteous. More than a
fisherman or farmer, perhaps a steward-in-training for the countess
in Airlie, as Derek had hinted.

"Three others," Bart had replied. "Traveling to Arlenn, to fix
a brother's boat, as I remember, him and her and their little girl."

"Were they from Airlie? I might know them."

"Yes, but I don't quite remember the name. Not castlefolk or
townfolk, I'll hazard, although good folk nonetheless. Tired and
cold they were, but my inn will give them a good sleep." Bart

had drained the last of his ale, and nodded genially. "As I hope my inn will give you also, good master."

Derek feigned a yawn. "I could use a good sleep, Master Bart. Lead on." As he followed Bart down the upper hall, he had heard Megan's piping voice behind one of the doors, and had noted its number.

Derek had reached the room two doors from hers. He paused and listened to a soft sound behind him, but the sleeper's bed creaked again and soon the man resumed his snoring. Derek moved his sensitive fingers to the engraved numeral in the wood of the door in front of him, traced the form, then edged onward, his teeth set against the pain in his thigh. A stubborn man, Brierley decided.

Brierley nudged Stefan hard in the ribs, then quickly covered his mouth with her hand. "Stefan!" she whispered in his ear. Stefan stirred sleepily, then came awake with surprise, resisting her hold for a moment. "Stefan, wake up!" she whispered.

Stefan nodded, fully awake now, and she removed her hand. "There's a man stalking our room, out in the hallway," she said.

"The duke's spy?" Stefan asked quickly.

"Yes."

Stefan eased away from her, slipped his legs out from under the coverlet, and slid quietly to the floor. He moved as silently along the room walls, then quickly crossed in front of the door to the other side. The starlight through the window gave the barest of illumination to the room, little more than a recognition of shadows. She saw one of the shadows move, tall and narrow, as the door slowly opened. Stefan allowed Derek to ease himself into the room before he pounced. A sharp blow to the chin and Derek reeled; the second blow put him on the floor, unconscious. Stefan reached down and hauled him toward a chair.

"The lamp," he said quietly, then listened for any sound of alarm in the hallway or neighboring rooms.

Brierley stumbled out of bed and moved her hands blindly for the match, then struck it with a sharp flare to light the lamp on the table. Stefan now had Derek propped in the nearby chair. "A bit of rope," he suggested. Brierley ran to the saddlebags and brought the halter ropes they had used to tether the horses in camp, then closed the room door. Stefan made quick work of tying Derek's hands, and then stooped to his feet, tying his ankles to the chair legs. Then he stood back and waited.

Derek moaned and rolled his head, then stiffened in alarm as he came back to consciousness and felt himself bound. Dazed, he looked up at Stefan and promptly scowled, then gave no prettier a scowl to Brierley. Megan was sitting up in bed, alarmed, and watched with wide eyes.

"Who are you?" Stefan demanded roughly. When Derek did not answer promptly, he raised his hand, but Brierley stopped him.

"None of that," she said.

"A man steals into our bedroom," Stefan demanded, "and I'm not to lay hands on him?"

"I'd say you already have laid hands on him." She looked down at Derek and tried to make her expression severe. "Who are you, man? Why do you steal into our room like a thief?"

"But, Mother!" Megan blurted. "He's the man on the cart! You know that! He was there when Roger died!"

"Hush, Megan!" Brierley said quickly, but the damage was already done. Derek's head jerked toward Megan and his eyes widened.

"You killed him?" Stefan asked, his fist clenched, and was ready on that instant to strike, to pound this man into a bloody ruin.

"He didn't kill Roger," Brierley said quickly, checking him again with a touch. "It was the other one."

"How—How do you know that?" Derek asked, his face ashen white. "How—" His head turned toward Megan again, then back to Brierley. "You were watching?" he guessed wildly. "From the trees? But I searched the trees. I would have seen any sign." He stared up at Brierley and twisted his hands violently within his bonds. "Who *are* you?" he demanded.

476

"What do you mean, 'the other one'?" Stefan asked, ignoring Derek's struggles.

"There were two of them," Brierley said, "as I told you before. The other one, Cullen—do you know him, Stefan?"

Stefan nodded uncertainly. "One of the castle understewards, I think. Thin, looks like a weasel?"

"That's him. Cullen hated Roger and struck at him without warning with a knife, even though Roger was on guard. Derek would have stopped it if he could; he wanted only to know where Roger was going. And after Cullen killed Roger, he wounded Derek, a bad wound that's festering." She pressed Stefan's arm earnestly. "He's Duke Tejar's spy, Stefan, but not an evil man. The duke bids him to find out things, a duty he follows as faithfully as you obey your countess." Brierley sighed, then put her hands on her hips and stared bleakly at Derek. "Unfortunately, he is good at his trade. I haven't the faintest idea what to do with him."

"A man is easily silenced," Stefan growled, only half-believing Derek had not killed his friend. Although Stefan was a fighting man by training, Brierley doubted that he could actually kill a helpless man, however fierce he felt at the moment. If he could find that act within him, it would change him forever.

"And do as the duke and his torturer?" she asked quietly, "Silencing the inconvenient? I have cause against the duke for that evil; I won't repay it with the same, whatever the danger to us."

Derek stared up at her, then gawked with sudden understanding. "You're Brierley Mefell," he breathed. "The witch."

"As you had already half-guessed," Brierley admitted, "however you thought witchery a nonsense idea. A dim-witted commoner girl used by the earl of Yarvannet? That's what he told you? And Earl Melfallan a traitor, devious and evil?" Derek's mouth had slowly sagged open again, fear beginning in his eyes. Derek Lanvalle had not often known genuine fear, dealing with it as a brave man would, but now he feared her. Brierley tightened her mouth. She regarded him for another moment, and then made her choice, responding to the decency she sensed within him. She had killed Gammel Hagan to save herself from death, but she would not begin a pattern of killing all who threatened her. She was a healer, and although this spy threatened her deeply with what he now knew, she would neither kill him nor accept the convenience of letting him die by doing nothing.

"Derek, you have a fair spirit," she said. "You honor your father's memory in that, he who was castellan to Duke Selwyn, and still mourn your elder brother. Both are now lost to you, leaving a hole in the world. You might have been a gentleman knight, abroad in the duke's court as a man of substance, counselor, soldier, perhaps castellan in your own time. Instead, you are a spy, not an ignoble calling, for all High Lords need spies, and one can make it an honorable calling, as you have tried. I don't fault you for that, but you have made yourself inconvenient to me. My liegeman is tempted by that inconvenience, more than I'd like of him."

Derek's eyes widened still further. "How do you know all that?" he croaked.

Brierley smiled at him ironically. "I'm a witch," she said. Despite all her proof, Derek snorted skeptically, and was angered by her lie. Brierley sighed.

In all her imaginings about the revealing of her witch's nature, she had not thought stubborn disbelief would count so largely. All the days in the cabin with Sir Niall had not budged him an inch, and she sensed similar trouble with Derek. No matter. "Among the shari'a," she persisted, "I am called a sea witch. I heal by touch, and know the inner heart, and the peace between persons. Under the duke's laws, I am evil and to be killed in the instant of my discovery. My child is also a witch." She pointed at Megan in the bed who watched with wide eyes, small and vulnerable in her white nightshirt. "She's six years old, Derek. Is she evil now? If not, when is she evil? When she becomes a woman at twelve? An adult at sixteen? When she does her first evil act? When she's condemned? When she burns? Or never? The shari'a laws order her death, once it is known she is witch. Is proof of evil even required?"

478

"You'd say any lie to save your life," Derek declared.

"Would you do the same?" Brierley asked curiously "Are you that kind of man, another of Duke Tejar's toadies who work only for his pay?"

Derek snarled and fought furiously at his bonds, twisting in the chair. Stefan took a warning step forward, but Brierley stopped him again. "He's nowhere close to escaping those ropes. He can feel their tightness. And he's half-faint with his fever."

"Where is Gammel Hagan?" Derek demanded. Stefan tightened his fists and looked despairingly at Brierley, thinking it madness to tell Tejar's spy such things, madness. Brierley shook her head absently, intent on Derek's face.

"I killed him as he was trying to kill me," she replied evenly. "He sought to dispose of me, and was disposed himself. Poor man. The world tips on its ear, and the will of men is confounded. Why does Tejar hunt me, Derek? To bring me to justice for Hagan's death? I doubt it."

"I don't care about High Lord politics," Derek retorted. "I care only that I do my duty to the duke, who is my lord as much as Earl Melfallan is yours."

"No matter," Brierley replied evenly. "Choose as you will."

"What are you going to do with me?" Derek demanded, panting from his struggles against the ropes. "Kill me as this lout wants to do?" he asked defiantly. A determined man, this Derek.

Brierley smiled. "And what is your crime, Derek, to deserve death? That you are trusty to your own lord, that you are deft in your skills as spy?" She pointed ironically to herself. "Is loyalty evil? Is a gift for healing evil? Where is your crime? That you exist as a fact?" She spread her fingers. "Here you sit, within my web, glaring at me, and you are a fact I dislike. You could bear news to the duke that I am alive and set the hounds upon me. If I were Tejar, I would stamp you out in an instant: he allows no such threat to exist long, be it earl or witch or you. But I am not Tejar."

"If I disappear, they'll look for me," Derek said bravely.

"But you're not sure they will, not really," she corrected

mildly. "Spies disappear all the time, don't they, when they mis-step? Twice already you've nearly disappeared, in your duels with Toral's man and later those bandits on the road." She shook her head sadly. "As Roger disappeared when you buried him."

Derek looked wildly around, hunting his escape, then strug-gled madly at the ropes. He winced at the lancing pain in his injured leg, now tied back uncomfortably against the chair leg, and then grimaced again as agony shot up the limb.

"Believe me, dear one," Brierley said softly. "I understand the fear I create." Brierley took a step toward him and Derek cringed backward. He struggled hard as she laid her hand on his shoulder, then jerked his chin away as she moved one hand to his face. As she felt the Calling move into the Now, Brierley bowed her head, and blended her future selves into one, and yielded to her gift.

On a distant beach, the Beast lifted his head from the waves and stared at her coldly, wanting her death, as it wished all into death. Brierley lifted her chin and looked back calmly. I deny you, Beast, she thought. I deny you this man. Cast the future as you will.

She moved her hand to Derek's injured leg and traced the cut beneath the leather of his trousers, sensing the heat from the wound. She felt a throbbing echo in her own thigh, and heard Derek's gasp of surprise as she took the pain from him. Behind her, Stefan shifted uneasily from one foot to the other, tempted to stop her yet suspecting he should not, caught in a net of his di-lemma as thoroughly as Derek.

She eased her hand down the length of the gash, then knitted up the flesh with her own willing, her own thigh throbbing in response. Another touch to his face, where he had been bruised by his fall, and a pass of her other hand down his chest, easing the fever, not all of it, but enough. When she was done, she leaned forward and lightly kissed his forehead, although he flinched again, and then willed him into a healing sleep. Derek fought sleep fiercely, all his emotions in a tumble of awe and fear, won-dering if she killed him now, but her willing won the battle.

With a deep sigh, Derek's chin finally sagged onto his chest and all his body relaxed against the ropes.

Brierley straightened, and took a deep breath, then looked distractedly around the room. "He should sleep the day around, and we can be far away by then. We should carry him back to his own bed."

"But he knows about you now."

"Yes, he knows. We must hide me well, Stefan, against the time he tells the duke." She sighed, then looked up into Stefan's face. "Could you really have killed him as he sat helplessly in that chair? I think not. Nor could I let him die, being a healer."

"You are a remarkable woman," Stefan said quietly, although he shook his head. "Is there anything you don't fear?"

"Oh, Stefan, many things. I fear for Megan. I fear I'll never see Melfallan again, and that is agony to me. I fear for you, good friend." She looked down at Derek sagging in the chair. "I didn't convince him. He sees only his duty, and thought I lied in the crucial points. Well, loyalty is to be admired." She bent to untie the ropes, and Stefan helped her, and together, with care they woke no one, they carried Derek back to his own room and put him into his bed.

Derek woke late in the afternoon, and lay drowsily for several minutes, gazing at the ceiling. A blissful sense of well-being suffused his mind and body, the slothful ease of waking after good dreams, content to lie abed, drifting. He stretched his legs drowsily, then noticed the pain in his thigh was gone. He had carried that pain for days now, with every movement a punishment. He sat up abruptly and looked around the inn room. He was alone.

Outside the window he heard the low hum of voices raised in mild dispute, and below him in the common room came more muted sounds of laughter and a scraping of chairs. The suns' light struck at a low angle through the window; most of the next day had already passed him by.

He fingered his leg under the covers, tracing a slight scarring in the flesh. Yet only last night—had it been only last night?—the gash had gaped, filled with a seeping poison. Have I lain here for days? he wondered in confusion. Yet he saw no sign of a sickroom, no cloths or compresses, or basin of water, only a tray on the table with cheese and bread, the modest breakfast left by the inn maid.

I feel very well, he thought in surprise, and stretched his arms over his head with a spine-cracking pleasure, then looked around his room again. Was it all a dream? he wondered. It might be. He had traveled in a fevered stupor for days, barely managing his rough snow camp each night by a boulder or in a glade of sheltering trees. His thoughts had wandered frequently as he rode, and at times he had conversed at length with companions he now realized had not been there.

Derek frowned, deeply confused. He pushed back the covers and saw that he was dressed in tunic and breeches, not the nightshirt he had worn to bed earlier in the evening. Not wholly a dream then: he distinctly remembered dressing for bed, yet now his nightshirt hung on the chair across the room. Odd. He must have changed clothes after going to bed: that fact implied he had later left his room as he had intended, and so the rest might have followed until she had—

Derek sprang out of bed and violently stripped off his breeches, then propped his injured leg on the bed's mattress. He bent over his thigh and probed the flesh inch by inch with his fingers. A faint scar, no more. And no pain—and no gaping wound, seeping its pus. *I am a sea witch,* she had said, smiling at him with a simple grace that could catch the breath. *I heal by touch, and know the inner heart, and the peace between persons.* As she had healed him, with her witch's touch.

Derek sat down hard on the bed, and again scanned the empty room, utterly bewildered. "Why didn't she kill me?" he asked aloud.

Her liegeman would have killed him, had she permitted—or perhaps not, he amended, remembering the man's hesitation. Had the advantage been reversed, could Derek have killed a helpless bound man? He knew many of his acquaintances in Darhel would have no such compunction, Gammel Hagan the chief among them. Gammel had enjoyed the fear he created in Tejar's court by his menaces. Like others, Derek had heard the drifting rumors about Hagan's dungeon and what transpired there. Indeed, Hagan had attempted a few hinting boasts as he and Derek shared a flagon of wine, perhaps hoping to entice Derek into sharing his pursuits some dark night. But Derek had shrugged Gammel off, not wanting to hear it, and then had rebuffed him more sharply the next time, and Hagan had desisted in his invitations.

While they drank together, Hagan had laughed obscenely about "mistakes," and had waggled his eyebrows and smirked when he hinted at obscene and lingering tortures, especially for the women Tejar gave him to question. Derek had thought his posing no more than Gammel's sick game-playing in Tejar's court, but now he sifted a dozen drifting rumors about the man, including the recent accusation he had murdered Brierley Mefell and fled for his life. Derek shuddered, wondering if Hagan's hints and brags about his dungeon play had been true. Whether true or not, Gammel would never dare kill a prisoner of Mistress Mefell's importance without the duke's permission. That was certain. Yet Brierley said Gammel had tried, and she had killed him instead, saving herself. He shivered again, guessing what Brierley had faced in Hagan's dungeon, in that foul man Duke Tejar had set upon her.

The duke had insisted on Earl Melfallan's treacherous plots against him, that Melfallan had used a dim-witted commoner girl, indifferent to her fate. He had even suggested that Melfallan might have stolen the girl from Tejar's dungeon, perhaps himself murdering the inconvenient once his traitorous plot had failed. The duke had ranted against Melfallan, calling him a devious and evil lord, and called on Derek to help him. "Use your best skills, spy," he had said. "I trust in you."

All the High Lords had suspected Tejar of ordering her death, but Derek had believed Tejar's protests it could not be true. Why?

Because Tejar was the duke, and Derek his trusted man? And he had never met Earl Melfallan, this young lord of whom Brierley had spoken with such quiet trust, more trust than he'd ever felt for his own lord. Who had the truth?

I never cared about truth before, he admitted, only for my duty to Tejar, my damnable duty when I never became a knight. He leaned forward and propped his elbows on his thighs, then sighed wearily.

How long does this go on? he asked himself. How long do you ignore what you see, and make the excuses for your duke? Duke Tejar was a harsh man, frequent in his rages, cruel in his disappointments, but still kind to his duchess, who now had begun a long course of hard dying. He was bluff and hearty with his sons, encouraging the elder, Vande, in his sword training and studies, greatly fond of the younger boy, Holen, who worshipped him. And he had rewarded Derek for his services, praising him for his skill and meaning it, and sometimes offered a rough companionship that nearly bridged the difference in rank between them. Derek had not loved his duke—Tejar was not a lovable man—but even without loving him, he had given his loyalty, done his best.

But Tejar had ordered Brierley Mefell's murder: Derek now knew that fact beyond question. Witch or not, she was still a commoner maid entitled to justice, still an innocent until trial was held. Despite that fact, Duke Tejar had given her to Hagan, without trial, without defense, knowing what the man was. That truth had resonated in her voice, lain in the calm serenity of her gaze. Brierley Mefell could have found her safety without even taking the trouble to kill Derek, this new menace to her life. All she had to do was stand aside and watch him die from his wound—yet she had not. He touched his leg again, marveling. Had their places been reversed, would he have chosen as she did? He did not know, and felt ashamed that he did not.

Find me the witch, Tejar had bid him. Find her before Melfallan uses her against me. Serve me, your rightful lord, as is your duty.

And what will you do with her, my duke? Derek asked himself in anguish. What? Give her again to your torturer, if you can
find another as able as Gammel Hagan? Do you even now seek
such a man who can do such evil? Or in me, do you already own
such a man, that I would tell, knowing what I know?

No doubt Brierley and her liegeman had ridden onward early
this morning, trying to escape him. No doubt they would try to
vanish somewhere into Mionn, although Derek could search and
try to frustrate that eluding. But even if he didn't find her again,
he had news for the duke, news the duke lusted to hear. The
witch is alive, sire, and hiding in Mionn.

What then, my duke? Derek groaned and held his head.

Where is your crime, Derek? she had asked him gently, and in
her eyes he had seen no fault, no blame.

Where is my crime? Do I consider it even now?

23

That night Melfallan dreamed of the Voyage, when storms had ripped men to tatters, and dire beasts had risen from the sea to seize men and women from the decks, and then, when the folk were soul-weary near to death, the day a green shore had risen on the sea's horizon. He stood at the ship's wheel on its high deck above the ship, his frayed boots planted wide on the wooden planking, balancing on the surge of the sea. He shouted in exultation, and pointed ahead.

"There, my lord! Look there!"

All heads turned toward where he pointed, where a green and inviting land beckoned to them. The people began to rise to their feet, giving a great shout, and their cry was echoed by the other ships behind them as their folk, too, saw the land ahead.

"There!" Melfallan cried down to the deck below him, and Lord Farrar turned to look up at him. The years of the Voyage had lined Farrar's young face with care, and put the first streaks of gray into his brown hair, for all he was scarcely thirty. A strong face, one the folk trusted, one that now shone with joy and relief.

"Yes, pilot," Farrar shouted back exultantly. "There!"

And all the Allemanii shouted with him and threw their arms around each other and wept. And Melfallan wept, too, though he kept his strong gnarled hands on the wheel of the ship, as was his duty. It was a pilot's gift to stand tall on an Allemanii long-ship, and be first to see any land ahead. Melfallan's lips moved in silent thanks to Mother Ocean that he had seen first, seen their new home ahead, so long awaited, so many years awaited, and that he had known the long voyage had ended—the first to know.

Melfallan's dream shifted to another time, another place, and Yarvannet's shore now beckoned on the horizon, as green and inviting, as fair. *Southwind* tacked into the broad harbor of Port Tiol, passing near the foot of the broad headland and its glittering white castle, and turned gracefully toward the piers. There on the dock a slight figure dressed in homespun stood waiting, her head covered by a broad-brimmed hat. Brierley lifted her hand in greeting and smiled as the ship drifted forward the last several yards to the pier. The sailors had scarcely tossed their lines when Melfallan leapt the rail, landing with a resounding boom on the timbers of the pier, and swept her into his arms.

And then suddenly the woman in his arms was Saray, her red-gold hair winking with diamonds, her gown fine satin that rustled as he crushed the fabric in his hands.

And then Saray was gone, too, as if neither woman had ever stood there, an aching empty space, a hollowness within his arms, within his heart.

And then Yarvannet was gone, leaving him nothing, nothing at all. He stood on a vast wasteland of a river plain, surrounded by the bodies of his soldiers and the enemy. Dead horses lay bloated in the mud, and blood had half-dried in obscene muddy pools, linking the dead. And only he remained standing, his breath coming in great gasps, his heart pounding painfully, as if it might burst any moment, drowning him in this battlefield of the dead. And then he saw Brierley's crumpled body at his feet, her chest a sheet of blood, and saw the bloodied sword that had killed her in his own gloved hand, and his heart did burst—

Melfallan woke abruptly, his heart hammering in his chest. He looked dazedly around the darkened bedroom, heard Saray's soft breathing beside him, then eased out of bed. He'd had enough of such dreams tonight, of such exultant hope changed to hopeless despair, of a new beginning ending in total disaster—and disliked the fears within himself that the dreams revealed. Perhaps that future on the battlefield might come, but he wished himself well dead before he ever faced it.

His body was bathed with sweat, his nightshirt sodden with it. He stripped it off, then dressed in tunic and hose, and left their bedchamber.

The castle lay silent, shrouded in the darkness of True Night, and only a few soldiers stood at guard in the hallways. He descended the flight of stairs from the upper floors and passed through the Great Hall, now empty and shadowed. The room seemed odd in its silence, and somehow less substantial than Farrar's ship and that deadly battlefield: he wandered onward into the short hallway that led to the chapel.

The castle chapel was a broad and pleasant room on the western wall of the castle, with fine brasswork, whitewashed stone walls, and seating for several dozen on benches and chairs. Tomorrow, in this room, at the Blessing ceremony that marked every Allemanii child's first formal step into life, Melfallan would acknowledge his baby son as his heir, continuing the Courtray line. The gentry would gather as witness, and Melfallan would take the baby into his arms and pronounce the old words, words ever new, and commit Audric to Mother Ocean's care.

If only naming a child, he wished earnestly, ensured that prosperity followed, without care or worry. If only naming a child could prevent a future of horrors that might come, caused by a father's desperate mistake, by a father's frailty in judgment.

Or a grandfather's— Melfallan moved farther into the room, cautious of his movement in the darkness.

Large tapestries hung on the chapel walls, their colors brilliant in the suns' light during daytime, now muted in the illumination of a single altar light. On the left wall, a broad arras depicted Mother Ocean's abundance of life. A star dolphin leaped from the waves, and sea larks spun high overhead. On the nearby shore, a shire wolf lifted its head from the concealment of brush on a bluff, and teal ducks swam comfortably in their marsh ponds. In a stand of everpine, a snow leopard crouched on a branch, watching a herd of winter fawn nearby, although, properly speaking, leopards and fawn were inland animals rarely found in Yarvannet. The tapestry was very old, fraying at its corners despite repeated repairs: castle records dated it to Farrar's time, perhaps an exaggeration to please an earl's vanity, but perhaps not.

On the right wall hung a newer tapestry commissioned by his grandfather: here were the Yarvannet folk in all their guises. Noblemen rode forth on fine horses to the hunt, passing farmers as they threshed the autumn grain, a boy herding sheep, a carter urging his horse up a hill. Beyond a beach, where three boys hunted shells, a fishing ship dipped its seines into the sea, its captain calling the cast. In the town, recognizable as Tiol itself in its array of white-washed houses, a blacksmith hammered bright sparks on his anvil, while his wife, sitting in her workroom, wove new cloth on her loom. On the promontory near the town rose Yarvannet Castle, the sea surging over the rocks far below, and the Daystar shone down upon the castle's white stone and high battlements.

It was a lovely tapestry, Melfallan's favorite, but he knew his grandfather had not commissioned it for sentimentality. After his butchery of Yarvannet's rebel lords, Audric had ruled uneasily for several years, with restiveness among the commoners, seditious talk among the minor gentry Audric had spared, until the Yarvannet folk grew used to their new array of lords, including Audric's Tyndale retainers. During that time, his grandfather had commissioned this tapestry for his castle chapel, and had made it known he had done so. Yarvannet is mine, the tapestry stated, mine to enclose in a new weaving, mine to portray as I direct. In time, that control had become true.

Melfallan skirted around the broad high stone of the altar, then passed through the tall paned doors to the balcony beyond. The chapel balcony overlooked the castle's western quadrangle, the large grassy compound where Sir Micay's soldiers exercised and trained, and where merchants brought their wares to the castle's seasonal fairs. On the balcony was a small garden, with boxed plants and hanging pots, and a few chairs for sitting. Saray liked this balcony and sometimes sat here with her ladies, watching the sea and the activity below.

Along the balcony wall, a series of stone basins recreated a tidal pool, with seawater pumped through pipes by wave action far below. Beneath the surface of the water, sea anemones waved pastel fingers, and several varieties of shellfish hid in rocky crevices from the shell-stars that stalked them. A stiltfinger drifted its knobby legs in the current, fishing for the tiny fish called damios that raced from end to end in the pools, flickering silver in the starlight. Here were Mother Ocean's own small creatures, who lived in the sea that had blessed the Allemanii from their beginning, long ago in times vaguely remembered. Here they lived their tiny lives, lovingly tended by the Allemanii who had placed them here, a microcosm of the great ocean that supported living for all of Her beloveds.

Audric had not built the chapel pools—that innovation dated back a century when a previous earl of Yarvannet had built his new castle on the promontory. The seawater that ran continuously through the balcony pools vanished into pipes, eventually running downward through the stone walls to flush the castle middens into the harbor, another innovation by the remarkable castellan who had built Yarvannet Castle. In older castles, the middens had to be periodically emptied by bucket, a task noisome enough to be assigned as punishment for the castle's miscreants. In Earl Giles's castle in Efe, the oldest of the Allemanii fortresses, the castle air always bore a faint miasma, however often the middens were cleaned, a cloying underscent to the other odors of too many people in too little space. Saray said that she never noticed the smells, and likely most of Giles's castle folk did not after years of enduring it, nor did Saray mind the cramped rooms, the cold floors, the narrow windows with time-distorted panes.

Earl Giles apparently felt the castle's antiquity added authority to his rule, or else found better use for his wealth than rehabilitating his old castle. The Mionn earls had always prized Earl Farrar's ancient castle despite its inconveniences, and flaunted their continuous rule since the Founding, when all other lands had changed houses several times. Such antiquity could tempt a High Lord's arrogance, and find in it a self-created superiority over the other High Lords.

Two castles, each quite different, he mused, each in its odd way representative of its current earl, and perhaps Mionn and Yarvannet as well.

Melfallan sniffed the sea wind and listened to the murmuring of the surf far below. He sat down in the cool darkness to watch the stars, as the sea murmured on the rocks below and the wind rustled the leaves of the garden around him. A peace of sorts settled upon him, crafted of the sounds of the night, the clinging coolness of the darkness, the flickering of silver in the pools as the damios raced each other endlessly. He bowed his head.

I love you, Grandfather, he thought, and felt the familiar flick of his grief. Where are you now? he asked wistfully. Mother Ocean gives life to the world, and Daughter Sea gathers the dead to Herself when that life closes, and all souls are blessed for a time in happiness before their return to the world. Are you happy, wherever you are? Do you remember me? Or do we forget who we were and whom we knew after we pass into Daughter Sea's undersea realm, where all is peace and joy, and we are each part of the rhythm of the world, unbent by life's troubles?

"Why did you fail me, Grandfather?" Melfallan whispered in anguish.

He remembered a portrait now hanging in the Great Hall, of Audric as young count of Tyndale. How old was Audric when he stood for that portrait? Older than Melfallan by several years, most likely, old enough to have fathered two sons and a baby daughter, old enough to be settled in his rule of Tyndale after Count Mourire's death, the trusted confidante of Duke Selwyn, the well-proven soldier, the avid huntsman, the just lord, the able father. Sir James had known that younger Audric in their common youth, and likely remembered the earl best as that young High Lord in his prime. To Melfallan had been given only the older Audric, a man still hale but bent by age, still proud but increasingly aware of his mortality as long-held friends, including his closest friend the duke, grew white-haired and infirm and eventually died, one by one. Now Audric had also died, nearly completing their number.

Audric had been the one sure anchor of Melfallan's life: what more had he been as a younger man when that portrait was painted, when Audric's strength was still assured and decades lay ahead for the living, year by year? What more—before the mistakes?

Melfallan shuddered and felt his heart constrict as the man he had adored proved—fallible.

Audric had mocked Selwyn's third son, a sly ugly boy whom Selwyn himself disliked. Even after Tejar became heir, Audric still disdained him, spurning his suit for Rowena's hand, marrying her instead to a weak and self-indulgent man nearly twice her age. After Selwyn died and Tejar was duke, Audric still challenged Tejar's worth, lecturing his duke contemptuously as if he were a miscreant boy. And then, to provoke Tejar still further, he had married his heir Melfallan to Giles's daughter, flaunting the earls' traditional alliance against their duke. Tejar had fine cause for his hatred of the Courtrays, although Earl Audric had flattered himself to give Tejar the blame.

Then in Yarvannet, Audric had also erred. He had allowed the Tyndale and Yarvannet division to remain among the nobility, never wholly accepting the local lords, vaunting his boyhood friends to new honors and wealth over the others he had conquered. Worst of all, in the error that had perhaps killed him, he had disdained the Yarvannet count who had helped his victory, and so had denied Count Sadon his expected favors, even mocking him as traitor.

And Audric had believed, because it pleased his arrogance to believe, that Earl Giles shared his love for Duke Selwyn, merely because it seemed so. He had trusted Earl Giles, because it flattered Audric to be Mionn's friend, and so allowed himself to forget Mionn's long and subtle history. The two earls could make or unmake a duke: that balance of rule had defined Allemanii politics for three centuries—but the balance played both ways. A weakened earldom tempted more than the duke, and Audric had weakened Yarvannet both within and without through his pride. In an effort lasting half his life, Audric had focused Tejar's violent hatred wholly on Yarvannet, and thus handed Giles an opportunity. Audric had weakened Tejar by blinding him to Mionn.

For months Melfallan had worried that he was not earl enough to rule Yarvannet. That question had now become irrelevant. He had no choice but to be the earl required. Had Robert not been the intemperate and rash man that he was, the good friend to Melfallan, the loving brother to Saray, Melfallan might not have known his true peril—and Duke Tejar's peril as well—until it was far too late. The Mionn earls had previously unseated three dukes; likely those dukes never suspected, either, until all was lost.

Melfallan slowly rubbed his face with his hands, then leaned on the stone wall of the balcony, and listened to the movement of the water of the pools nearby, and to the deeper and softer sound of the surf in the harbor.

Come home, Brierley, he wished earnestly. Come home.

For an instant, he thought he felt the touch of her lilting presence, briefly there, then gone. He sighed deeply and closed his eyes. Was it the Everlight, he wondered, somehow breaching the barrier of dreams, or was it a deeper connection to Brierley across the leagues between them? Or was it nothing at all?

Come home, beloved. Please.

He heard a faint noise behind him and turned, then saw Saray standing hesitantly in the balcony doorway, a short robe pulled over her nightgown, her long red hair tumbling on her shoulders. He spread his hands, beckoning to her, and she came to sit beside him. He put his arm around her waist and pulled her closer, kissed her. "Thank you for helping Jared, dear heart."

"You're welcome," Saray murmured shyly, then boldly pulled his head down for a second kiss. He chuckled as she released him, then felt her relax comfortably against him. "I'm sorry I made the mistake on the dock," she said softly. "I should have warned you about Father instead of thinking stupid wishes." She sighed. "I'm sorry for many things, Melfallan. Do you forgive me?"

"Yes." He pressed his face against her hair for a moment, and suddenly knew it was time to tell her. It wasn't fair that she didn't know. He closed his eyes for a moment, wishing an inarticulate prayer to Mother Ocean for the right words, then took a deep breath. "I need your forgiveness, too, beloved, for more than you know. Mistress Mefell isn't dead. She escaped from Darhel and is hiding in the Airlie mountains."

Saray drew in a surprised breath. "She's alive?"

"Yes, and there's more. I've fallen in love with her, Saray." Saray gave an inarticulate moan. Before she could shrink from him, Melfallan pulled her closer and she looked up at him, bewildered. "But that doesn't mean I stopped loving you. Truly, Saray." He looked down into her eyes, now shining with tears. "I know how hard you have tried, and often I've helped you fail. I've expected you to be perfect, but on my terms. I wasn't that certain of my own rules, so I criticized yours." He closed his eyes a moment, knowing it was all true, and how he had truly failed her. "You gave me all you had, and I made it not enough. I'm sorry, beloved," he said contritely.

"It wasn't all your fault," Saray quavered. "I make mistakes, but I don't know they're mistakes until, well, they obviously are." She looked down at her hands. "But sometimes I know before I do it. I sent Simone out of the nursery because I was jealous of Leila. I can't bear to watch her suckle Audric, Melfallan. I wanted so much to——"

"You wanted to nurse Audric?" he asked, surprised. "I didn't know you even considered it."

"*Mother* doesn't consider it," Saray said tightly. "But I didn't know milk could dry up. By the time we came back from Darhel, it was too late. Oh, Melfallan——" She clung to his hand hard, and he kissed her hair.

"Well, we'll have another baby, my love," he said gently, for she was sobbing now. "Next time we can get it right."

"You want another baby?" she whispered, not looking at him.

"Of course."

Saray shook her head. "That doesn't make sense. You can't love two women at once."

"I admit it's an uncomfortable idea, but why not, when both own part of my heart?"

Saray firmed her mouth. "Because it's not *proper*, Melfallan Courtray. I'm your wife. Don't you think you owe something to me, just because of that?"

"Yes, and not just because of that. You are beautiful, Saray, and have perfected sweetness and grace. You are a wonderful Lady Yarvannet, the mother of my son, a jewel on my breast as earl. Because of your lady rules, you are exquisitely a lady." He lifted her hand to his mouth. "I've always thought that, even when I chose to criticize the pretending that goes along with it."

Saray studied his face anxiously in the darkness. "All I want is you," she said. "I was rude to Jared because he was one more person to take you away from me. Then I helped Father insult you on the dock, just because I wasn't thinking. I was so happy to see my family, at least then. I haven't seen Father and Mother and Daris for nearly six years, and somehow they aren't—aren't what I thought they were. Daris was spiteful about the baby and what everybody is supposedly saying about you. And Father has been simply *beastly*." Saray's cheeks colored at her effrontery, but she stubbornly firmed her chin. "We're supposed to love our families but, Melfallan, I don't think I even *like* them anymore." He chuckled softly, and she had recovered enough spirit to glare at him. "Well, I don't."

"Neither do I," he admitted, "except for Robert, of course, but Mionn is still our principal ally. Maybe we can pretend a little, Saray."

Saray gaped at him a moment, then suddenly giggled, covering her mouth with her hand. Then she sighed and shook her head. "That doesn't solve our problem about Mistress Brierley," she said, her voice sad and resigned.

Melfallan grimaced. "No, it doesn't. I've thought about you every time I thought about her, wanting not to hurt you. I know it's not proper, but——" He looked down at their entwined fingers. "I didn't mean to, but I have. To love her is not right with you, but it is with her."

"A lady wife accepts such things——" Saray began slowly.

"Dear heart, that *is* a stupid rule. I may reconsider your other rules, but not that one."

Saray laid her head on his shoulder, and they listened to the surf far below them. The wind sighed across the balcony, crisp with the chill of winter. "Are you going to divorce me?" Saray asked, her voice barely a whisper.

"No. Never, Saray."

"Are you going to give up Brierley?"

He hesitated. "No." He should, he knew, but it would leave him half a man. Perhaps Melfallan repeated his grandfather's mistakes by going his way as he willed, against all prudence, against the right, but a stubborn part of him rejected that possible truth. Yarvannet would need all of him in the coming crisis, not just part, and he could not be whole without Brierley, not now. His heart ached for Saray, for the injury he inflicted on her. He closed his eyes and pressed his face against Saray's soft hair, then lowered his mouth to her ear, kissed it lightly. "I'm sorry, beloved," he whispered.

Saray sighed deeply. "It seems, Melfallan Courtray, that you indeed have a problem. I could decide to hate her, like I hated the others. I could make your life miserable. I know exactly how," she admitted.

"I'd deserve it," he said grimly. "I'm hoping you won't. I could have kept this a secret, until you found out as wives usually find out."

"Then why did you tell me? It's easier not to tell. You pretend it's not happening, and when I find out and ask you, if I do, you lie. That's what Father did, when he cheated on Mother. I have two half-sisters and a half-brother that Mother won't allow to live in Efe; I don't know how Daris found out with nobody admitting anything, but she told me." Saray snorted softly. "It was part of her advice to the bride, warning me about you and what I could expect." She leaned closer to him in anguish. "Oh, Melfallan, it hurts. It hurts so much."

Saray began to cry again, and Melfallan rocked his wife slowly, holding her tightly against him.

~9

Audric's Blessing Day dawned sunny and clear. Melfallan rose well before dawn and restlessly prowled their bedroom, then finally sat down on the bed beside Saray. Her eyes opened, and at first she didn't smile, but then turned up the corners of her mouth. "That took an effort," she admitted. "This whole day will be an effort."

"I'm sorry, Saray," he said uncomfortably.

"Not that sorry." This time the smile was more genuine, and she reached up her hand to touch his face. "Today is the baby's day. Today is our son's day, our beautiful baby son. Today is a day I show only pride as Lady Yarvannet."

He caught her hand and lifted it to his lips. "Which you are, Lady Saray."

Saray pressed her fingers against his mouth. "Today we will dress in our finest clothes, Earl Melfallan of Yarvannet, and we will make a great procession before the gentry. Today we will forget about Brierley Mefell. We will keep pretending until my family leaves."

"All right," he said slowly.

"And then I'll decide if I'm going to make your life miserable. I still might." Her smile turned wry. "You may earnestly wish, husband, that I had kept to my pretending." Saray sat up and pushed back the covers, then leaned to kiss him. "Worry about it," she said with spirit and added a mild glare, one he deserved, and got out of bed.

Bemused, Melfallan watched Saray walk out of the room, and heard her greet the lady-maid who neatly popped into sight for her ready service, as all lady-maids should do. I should feel surprised, he thought dazedly, and wondered why he wasn't. I should feel miserable, he knew, but strangely his heart had lifted, rising to meet the joy of Audric's day. His dilemma had not changed, and had likely worsened by telling her, yet— Melfallan shook his head, then laughed softly.

Our finest clothes, he thought and nodded, then went to find Philippe to help choose his best.

The gentry assembled in the Great Hall later that morning, and, to Melfallan's pleasure, their number included Countess Rowena and Axel. Melfallan's aunt had arrived scarcely an hour before, travel-stained and tired, and had bathed, dressed, and quarreled with Earl Giles in record speed. It appeared, Melfallan was told, that Giles had started it by commenting too loudly to his wife, and Rowena had replied vigorously. When Melfallan and Saray entered the hall, the baby in Saray's arms, each had arrayed themselves on opposite sides of the crowd, Rowena smiling gently to herself and Giles visibly fuming.

Melfallan sighed softly when he saw his father-in-law's expression, but he and Saray walked forward sedately, nodding pleasantly to the right and then to the left and right again, greeting the assembled gentry as they crossed the hall. They then led the gentry into the nearby chapel, where all had been prepared. The suns' light glanced brilliantly through the broad glass doors leading to the balcony, lighting every color in the great tapestries and glancing off the brasswork. The altar, ordinarily squarely in front of the balcony doors, had been moved to one side and replaced with an elegant stone pedestal, a large porcelain basin filled with seawater set upon it. With a quiet murmuring, all the assembled nobility settled in chairs. Melfallan and Saray walked to the front of the room and turned to face the crowd.

Count Sadon had made himself deliberately late and would not arrive until the late evening, or even tomorrow, but all of Melfallan's other lords and knights were there, Lords Tauler and Garth with their wives, Lady Tolland and her son, Revil and

Solange, Lord Eldon and his family, Lord Jarvis, Sir Justin, all except Jared. Earl Giles sat in the front row with his wife, Robert, and Daris, his frown unpleasant and sour. He saw Rowena bend toward Solange and listen, then nod with a smile, and arrange herself comfortably in her chair, with no feigned discomfort from her arm, none at all. Melfallan nodded pleasantly to them all, then turned to Saray.

"My lady wife," he murmured and bowed to her in courtesy.

"My lord husband," Saray replied proudly. Norris, one of the baby's manservants, stepped forward attentively. Saray gently removed Audric's christening dress of lace and satin, then gave it to Norris. The winter air was crisp through the open balcony doors, and their tiny naked son protested his abrupt exposure to the elements with a wail. Saray smiled and cuddled him for a moment, then lifted her eyes to Melfallan. "I have borne you a son, my lord," Saray said. "Will you claim him as your firstborn and your heir to Yarvannet?"

"I will." A murmur of satisfaction ran through the crowd, and Melfallan extended his arms, took the baby carefully from Saray, and then turned to face the basin pedestal and those who watched.

"My lords and ladies," Melfallan said happily, "today is my son's day, when Mother Ocean welcomes our child into new strength, new blessing, and new hope." He looked down at Audric with pride. The baby kicked against his arm, then giggled. In the past few days, Audric had begun to laugh—at a tickle, at Simone's arm-waving beside him in her crib, at the suns' light streaming through the window, at his father's face. Now the baby smiled up at him, thrust a stubby hand into his mouth, and wiggled vigorously.

"Mother Ocean's blessing on you, sweet child," Melfallan said softly. "May Ocean's favor protect you always, as child, boy, and man, and as husband, father, and lord. May Daughter Sea give you many years of joyful life and honest rule until she gathers you home. This wish comes from your father, who now claims you. Your name is Audric Courtray, and I further name you as Count of Tiol and my body heir to Yarvannet." Melfallan took a single step forward to the basin, and began to lower the baby toward the water.

Fair lord! Startled, Melfallan looked up and hesitated, hunting Brierley's voice, then looked down at the basin in confusion. What? He looked at Norris standing nearby and frowned. "Has this water been tested, Norris?"

"I prepared it myself, your grace," Norris replied, and nodded toward the balcony pool. "Is there a problem?"

"*Tested?*" Earl Giles blared. "Get on with it, Melfallan!"

Melfallan froze, eyes widening in shock at the vicious contempt in Giles's voice. He gaped at his father-in-law for a moment, his jaw sagging, then felt a rush of sheer rage flood into him at this insult to his son. All his hard-won patience, his studied deference, his tolerance for his father-in-law's pride, vanished in that instant. He heard Saray's soft gasp behind him, saw Revil and Lord Tauler rise half to their feet, their faces flushed with fury.

Melfallan glared at his father-in-law. "Get out." His icy command sliced through the room. "Leave Yarvannet, Earl Giles."

"Leave? Are you joking, boy?" Giles scoffed, and sat back in his chair with a smirk, his arms crossed. Lady Mionn fluttered her hands, for once jarred out of her icy calm, and made an inarticulate sound. Giles silenced her with a hard glance.

"Sir Micay," Melfallan said evenly, "summon your soldiers to conduct his grace. Your ship sails within the hour, Earl Giles." The castellan stepped forward, his hand on his sword hilt, and Giles looked at them both in open amazement.

"You wouldn't dare!" Giles protested and surged to his feet. He stamped forward aggressively. "There's nothing wrong with this water, you fool!" Bent on his purpose of humiliating Melfallan yet again, Earl Giles contemptuously thrust his right hand into the basin water.

"No!" Melfallan shouted, but his arms held Audric and Micay was a step too far away. The next instant Earl Giles's piercing shriek of agony split the air. Giles quickly yanked back his hand, his mouth distorted, his eyes bulging, then staggered drunkenly to one side and fell. The room erupted into pandemonium.

Robert leapt forward and knelt at his father's side. "He's fainted!" he exclaimed.

"Don't touch his hand, Robert," Melfallan warned. "It's probably contact poison. Where's Marina?" he shouted over the crowd, then saw the castle midwife hurrying forward, pushing aside the gentry forcibly when they blocked her path. Marina knelt by Earl Giles and peered cautiously at the blisters on his right hand, careful not to touch. Then, briskly, she gave her orders. A flagon of seawater was fetched from the balcony pool to flush Giles's injury, then another. Finally she called upon Sir Micay and Norris standing nearby, and Giles was carried out of the chapel. Lady Mionn hurried after her husband, Daris in her wake, but Robert stayed.

His brother-in-law stared at Melfallan for a moment, then straightened his shoulders. "You haven't finished the ceremony, brother," he said mildly. "Shall we continue?" Calmly, Robert turned and walked to his chair, then seated himself. One by one, the other lords and ladies sat down behind him, in calm and studied indifference to Earl Giles's fate. Melfallan swallowed uneasily, recognizing their profound rebuke to his father-in-law, then nodded, accepting it, and sent for another basin, to be dipped into the balcony pool as all watched.

"Be blessed, my son," he said quietly, as he lowered Audric into the water. "Be blessed and take your strength from Mother Ocean's abiding love."

A small round of applause greeted the baby as Melfallan lifted him from the water. Audric kicked vigorously but chose not to cry, and lay quietly in Melfallan's hands, a chubby fist in his mouth as he stared up at Melfallan in open wonder. Melfallan smiled and pressed his lips briefly to Audric's forehead, then dried him carefully with a towel, dressed him again in the lacy robe, and gave him to Saray. Then, led by Count Robert, the assembled lords and their ladies trooped out to enjoy the fine banquet awaiting them in the Great Hall.

Sea-puffer toxin meant to kill a naked infant, with perhaps the boon of painful injury to his father, could not kill a grown man. Giles's hand had been badly blistered but would heal in time, and Marina's potions quickly eased the earl's nausea and shock. Later in the afternoon, Melfallan went alone to Earl Giles's chambers to visit him. He found his father-in-law propped up in his bed, pale and sweating, his forearm and hand wrapped in a cooling bandage.

Already Sir James had begun his inquiries, sorting which servants had contact with the poisoned basin, and suspicions had fallen immediately on Norris, the manservant who had assured Melfallan of the water's safety. That Norris was caught in the stables, his horse saddled in urgent haste, sealed his fate. Who had paid Norris for his treachery? Was it Count Sadon? Or Duke Tejar himself? This time, Melfallan promised himself fiercely, the truth would be discovered, in every detail, and especially that fact.

Melfallan stopped in the bedroom doorway, and nodded coolly to Lady Mionn sitting by her husband's bedside. He and his father-in-law then regarded each other, until Giles grunted and gestured him into the room.

"Earl Melfallan," he said, for once admitting Melfallan's title in his greeting. Likely little could truly chasten Earl Giles, but his self-inflicted debacle today at the Blessing had apparently come as close as it might.

"Your grace." Melfallan nodded to Lady Mionn sitting by her husband's bedside. "My lady."

"Wife, will you leave us some privacy?" Giles said curtly to Lady Mionn, and she rose, gave Melfallan a cool nod, and left the room. Giles shifted uncomfortably on his pillows, wincing as he moved his bandaged arm. "I suppose you think me an old fool." His voice was gruff.

Melfallan sat down in a chair near his bedside and stretched out his legs. "It was a stupid thing to do, I agree. There are better ways to snub me, several of which you've explored in the last few days. How's your arm?"

"Badly blistered, hurts like blazes. Sea-puffer toxin, your healer tells me. Fortunately, she knows how to care for it. I'll survive, and with only moderate pain, her phrase. It's amazing how a healer can put you in your place with a bare word or two." He paused. "You were right, and I was wrong," he blurted.

Melfallan supposed Giles meant it as an apology, as if stating the obvious, when one was an earl, had some significance. He leaned back and crossed his arms. "That wasn't so hard, was it?" he asked wryly.

"Harder than you know, boy," Giles retorted. "I feel like a damned old fool," he said, more candidly, and a faint flush spread across his face.

"Which you were, Earl Giles."

Earl Giles scowled even more ferociously, then gave a harsh bark of laughter. "No mercy, I see. Well, I suppose I deserved that. You're more than I thought, son."

Melfallan nodded coolly. "I'm glad you think so. Earl Giles, my grandfather is dead, and well beyond your scorn. Don't dismiss me as useless: the times are too dangerous. Whatever you're planning with this Lim marriage could easily plunge our lands into war, and it's too soon."

Giles tightened his jaw a moment, then snorted mildly. "You're telling me not to be an old fool in other ways."

"Essentially."

"I never liked the Courtrays, never will," Giles grumped. "You're all upstarts, you and your grandfather and your aunt."

"Upstarts or not, the two earls restrain the duke: it's in every text."

Giles regarded him a moment longer, then frowned again. He sighed, worked his eyebrows a bit longer, and then reluctantly extended his unbandaged hand. Melfallan took it, pressed. "You'll never trust me, not completely," Earl Giles suggested.

"Of course not. Unlike you, I'm not a fool."

"Peace!" Giles protested gruffly. "I'll stop my insults if you'll stop yours. How's that for a bargain?"

"Workable, your grace." Melfallan smiled thinly, and yielded not an inch.

Earl Giles grunted. "I suppose it'll have to do." He looked down at his bandaged arm and grimaced. "Hells," he muttered irritably.

Melfallan tried to hide his surprise. Earl Giles seemed to think his embarrassment today no more than a slight stumble on the stairs, a wineglass spilled, nothing more. Yet this story would spread like wildfire among the High Lords, and with the tale would travel Robert's actions afterward, and the firm rebuke inflicted by Melfallan's vassal lords. Through one petulant impulse, Giles had damaged Mionn's high influence, yet Giles seemed unaware of his great error. *He really doesn't know,* Melfallan realized. *He truly doesn't know that Duke Tejar will alert like a hound to the hunt, once he hears of what happened here,* and will again apply his malice to both earls, not just one. Weakness in a vassal lord, for a Kobus duke, was a chance to be greedily seized, and never wasted. In Giles's spite, in his attempt to humiliate Melfallan and thus even his old score with Melfallan's grandfather, a rival gone eight months into his grave, Earl Giles had thrown away a coronet.

And, by that same rash act, he had also given Melfallan time, time he had needed desperately—time to bring Brierley home, time to prepare Yarvannet for the conflict to come. *Praise Ocean,* Melfallan thought in relief so profound it almost dizzied him. He took a deep breath, then nodded courteously to Earl Giles and rose from his chair, said a few more pleasant words, and left to rejoin the celebrations in the Great Hall.

～ 24 ～

egan, that's enough bouncing," Brierley had said earlier that morning.

"Not, it's not!"

"Enough for now." She waited as her daughter considered, watched the last somersault on the bed, and heard the reluctant sigh. Megan slid off the mattress and hung on the foot-post, and gave her mother a reproachful look.

"No, it's not," she declared firmly.

"No, it's not," Brierley conceded, "but stop, anyway." Another heartfelt sigh.

Stefan was busy packing the last of the saddlebags when Brierley got quietly sick into the chamberpot. She sat on the floor afterward, her hand on her stomach, and sighed. Well, one thing proven: witches got it, too. And right on schedule.

"Are you all right?" Stefan asked in alarm. He knelt beside her and touched her arm. "What's wrong, Brierley? Are you ill?"

She hesitated. She hadn't yet told Stefan that she and Melfallan had been lovers, still feeling a little shy with him. But Stefan would have to know eventually—and would know in time, if only from the evidence of his own eyes. "I'm all right," she reassured him. "It's only morning heaves."

"Morning—" Stefan gawked at her. "You're *pregnant*? By whom? I mean, when—" Then he made the connection and stopped short, and gawked again.

"It's the new one," Megan informed him brightly. "My sister."

Stefan's head swiveled to Megan, then back to Brierley. "How does she know that?" he demanded.

"She's a witch," Brierley answered wryly. "Megan *knows* things, don't you, Megan?"

"I know *lots* of things," Megan agreed.

Stefan gawked another moment, then suddenly sat down hard on the floor, truly astonished, then laughed at himself because he was. "Well!" he said. "You hadn't mentioned that part. Does Melfallan know?"

"Now, how would he know, Stefan? Oh. It depends on when, doesn't it?" She laughed. "In the cabin, while you and Niall were still looking for us. No, he doesn't know."

"He'll do right by you and the baby," Stefan assured her, although his tone had a faint uncertainty, for all it was Melfallan. The lords had their habit of overlooking inconvenient children, Stefan knew, but Brierley had no such fears about Melfallan. Amused, she sensed Stefan's resolve that he'd see his friend behaved properly when he knew, High Lord or not. She touched his arm.

"I think he will be joyful," she said, assuring him.

"If he claims her, she'll be noble and his daughter heir. Ocean alive, what will Saray say?"

"She'll be a witch, whatever the other. And I don't know what Saray will say." She grimaced. "I hate to harm that gentle lady. This is not respectable, you know."

"Don't you dare give him up because of that!" Stefan was quite fierce. "Yes, Saray is sweet and beautiful, but she's not a good match for Melfallan. You are."

"So that justifies it?" she asked unhappily.

Stefan glowered. "Why not? Where's the rule that you can't be happy with each other? I was lucky, Brierley. I chose rightly the first time, and I bless my fortune in finding Christina, and that she would accept me." Stefan blinked. "And he never told me!" he said in outrage. "We rode down the mountain for a whole day, and dined with the countess in her lodge, and rode another whole day to Darhel, and he never told me once. And I'm his friend! That fine gentleman has some explaining to do."

"He's not comfortable with it, either. He worries for Saray, as do I."

Stefan shook his head firmly. "I'll see that he doesn't make the wrong decision, either, when we meet up again. Ocean, I feel like a grandnanny arranging a match, with both dragging their shoes and tsking at me how it's not right." He glared at her. "Don't be stupid about this, Brierley."

She shrugged at him. "I hear you."

"Good," he declared, and added another fierce look. "Now I won't insult you by treating you like spun crystal, delicate you, 'will you faint now, my dear?' But you should have told me earlier. Those storms might have been dangerous."

"And what would you have done about the storms?" she asked sensibly. "We reached Mionn, and I'm fine."

"Well, I suppose you're right," he conceded, if grudgingly. He eyed her for a long moment, although she truly looked no different than yesterday. "Here, let me help you to your feet. Is that allowed?" he added anxiously.

She chuckled as she sensed the reason for his caution. "Why do I guess that Christina's pregnancies were hard on you both?"

"She would not let me pamper her, just wouldn't," he muttered. "It was horrible." He helped her stand, then lifted Megan high in the air and settled her on his shoulders. "We're all packed. Let's see if we can get away without trouble."

Bart was already up, his common practice for early guests, and saw them off genially, wishing them safe journey to Arlenn. They rode into the crisp dawn air. As they crested the bluff above the town and regained the coast road, the Daystar spread its light suddenly on the watery horizon of the great bay, sparkling off every wave on the surf far below. Far out on the horizon, a mist hovered over the bay waters, and the sea larks spun over the turbulent waves, distant blue-and-silver crescents hurtling on the wind.

The coast road clung to the sea bluff for the next several miles, its turns and straight stretches mirroring the turns and small inlets of the rocky Mionn coast. A few everpine clung to the bluffsides by the sea, but grew into thick dark-green shadow as they ascended the gentle slopes inland, rising higher and higher toward the distant peaks of the coastal mountains. They passed no one on the road. Beneath the long bluff overlooking the beach, the waves crashed on black jagged stones, an ever-moving sound of rushing water within the sigh of the sea wind. Brierley took a deep breath and watched the water move far out on the bay.

By the time the Daystar neared its zenith and the Companion was well up in the morning sky, they had traveled nearly fifteen miles. They stopped then for a meal from their packs and let Megan run out her stiff muscles from the long morning ride. Stefan walked the several yards to the bluffside and looked down at the sea, the wind buffeting at his clothes, then looked up to watch the sea larks spin.

"Catching their lunch, too," he said. It was as much as he had said all the morning, and Brierley walked to join him. She slipped her hand into his, and they stood there in companionable silence. All morning Stefan had chosen to worry about Derek, measuring the ways to avoid him on their further journey, and worrying also about the consequences when Derek bore his message to the duke. He did not trust the earl of Mionn, as many did not, and worried that he was not as familiar with Earl Giles's lands as Niall had been. She had followed his thoughts, and agreed that Arlenn, the count's town next on the coast, would be dangerous. The Arlenn count had married his daughter to Count Robert, and that loyalty bound him firmly to Earl Giles. There was a second county north of Arlenn, with its capital in Skelleford, but Stefan knew little about its count. And Efe itself—

But could they expect a Mionn count to guard Brierley when Earl Giles willed otherwise, if he did? As they had ridden through the morning, Stefan's doubts had grown. If Duke Tejar bid Earl Giles to mount a search—

"You're right," he finally said, resigned to it. "I couldn't murder a helpless man. It increases our danger, but I couldn't."

"Maybe Derek won't tell the duke," she suggested.

"A duke's paid spy?" Stefan snorted. "I doubt that."

"A spy can have an honorable trade," she said comfortably. "All the High Lords need spies, just as they need trusted liegemen to do more open tasks. Your current task is conducting a witch hither and yon, at least until your countess bids you otherwise." She smiled at his baffled expression.

"You defend him?" he asked incredulously.

"Derek might have been a gentleman knight, had Duke Selwyn not died with he did. Would that have made his character better in your eyes?" She pressed his hand. "I hear the inner self, Stefan. That measure rarely matches how the Allemanii label themselves, noble this or commoner that. In other circumstances, I believe you and Derek would have been friends. Don't snort at me: it's true. After all, I *know* things," she teased, "just like Megan does. Derek did not murder Roger, and he does not seek to murder me, only to serve his liege lord." She wrinkled her nose reflectively. "He will have a hard choice now. Derek Lanvalle is a knight at heart, and a knight believes in justice, even when his liege does not. A knight also believes in loyalty, and the duty owed by a sworn man."

Stefan shook his head. "I don't understand you at all. How can you—"

"He regretted Roger's death," she said quietly. "He buried him with respect. And he could have been your friend. Perhaps he still might be." Stefan scowled, unconvinced.

"I wish I had warned the countess about Cullen," he fretted. "I had the chance in the letter, but I didn't."

"Convict a man merely on a witch's word? That's all you had as your proof."

"A witch's word is proof enough," Stefan said stubbornly.

"Dangerous proof," she said, shaking her head. "Both for the lord and the witch. I must remember that; so should you."

"How can you step outside yourself and think like that?" he asked, baffled. "A duke's spy isn't a danger—"

"I didn't say that."

He grumped. "We could argue all day about Derek, I suppose, but enough. Now you warn me against you?"

"Witches are dangerous, Stefan." She smiled as he scowled even more fiercely. "Truly. We are perilous." Stefan pointedly looked her up and down, vastly skeptical, and she chuckled. "It's true."

"You'll never convince me." They watched the bay for a time, and Stefan's worrying shifted to his other topic of the morning. "I don't know enough about Mionn," he muttered. "I don't know where would be safest."

"I'd prefer to live in a town," she said, "if we can find one that seems suitable."

"Maybe we should find the cave Megan wanted and hide away from towns altogether."

"And hunt all our food? I had enough of that in the cabin." She sighed. "I have hidden all my life, Stefan, and sometimes I tire of it. Sometimes I wish I could live in the suns' light, hiding nothing of myself. Sometimes I believe that I could trust that light, and not fear it." She shrugged. "As I told you, in Yarvannet I believed I would be killed by my friends, the people I loved. But most championed me, and a farmer named Harmon, a man that comes as close to brother as I could ever have, honestly didn't care that I was a witch. It didn't matter at all, once he knew and really believed. 'Well,' he said, 'I'll have to rethink things,' and went on just as before. We shari'a have feared the Allemanii for three hundred years, hiding ourselves away, denying our very nature. What a pity, but what else could we do?"

"Three centuries is enough time for change," he said slowly. "I've heard the Mionn folk are good folk, if you want to take the risk of living in a town. There's still the earl and what he might do, but we might find a place to stay a while and live comfortably. Where, I don't know, but we can look." He blew out a breath, then shook his head. Brierley pressed his hand, then released it and turned away from the sea.

She called Megan back from her run and lifted her onto Gallant, then mounted behind her. With so much practice lately, she'd acquired some skill in riding, she noted, and had the twinges in her legs and seat to prove it. Megan patted Gallant's neck and leaned forward to whisper something into his ear. Behind them, Friend shook her head and stamped, and Megan craned to look around Brierley at the mare, then giggled. Brierley wondered idly what the joke had been. Whatever it was, Megan's fascination with horses had not diminished a jot, nor theirs with her.

Stefan swung onto Destin, and they rode onward as the suns moved into late afternoon, changing the direction of the shadows across the road. The wind began to blow more lustily off the bay, bringing the scent of salt and the high piping of the sea larks. Several miles farther, they came to a fork in the road, the more traveled lane bending westward, the other descending slowly down a ridge to the beach below.

Stefan glanced back at her and she nodded, then led them onto the beach road, the horses stilting comfortably on the steep dirt as they descended. The road curved as it roughened, with some dirt-falls cascading onto the road in some places from rain and wind. For their night camp, Stefan found a tall depression in the cliff-side, with prospect of a fire that would be visible only from the bay. With a sigh for her twinges, Brierley dismounted and walked to the edge of the roadway, where a steep bluff fell sixty feet to the beach. She turned and looked at Megan.

"Do you see how far down this is?" she asked sternly, pointing over the ledge.

Megan nodded obediently. "And I shouldn't go near it, not for any reason."

"Good girl." Brierley walked back to the campside and sat down on a blanket that Stefan had spread for her. Megan tucked herself into Brierley's lap, and they watched the shadows deepen over the sea. Jain popped in for a few minutes to nuzzle Megan's face, and then popped out somewhere, to Megan's disappointment. She sighed mournfully, then waited to see if Jain had noticed and would return. Then with another sigh when he did not, she watched the sea again.

"Pretty," she decided, and then yawned. Brierley kissed her hair. After a time, Brierley helped Megan into the rough bed of blankets and tucked the warm coverlet around her. Megan was soon fast asleep. Stefan made up his own bed on the other side of the fire, yawning as hugely, then found his own slumber.

Brierley pulled her blanket closer around her shoulders, then closed her eyes and listened contentedly to the sounds of the sea. How she had missed the sea these many weeks away from Yarvannet, how she had missed it. The gentle sighing of the surf, the harder crash of waves on the rocks, the distant piping of sea larks surrounded her, and she took a deep shuddering breath.

Mother Ocean,
Daughter Sea,
When I wander,
Walk with me.

~)

Brierley—

Brierley awoke suddenly at dawn when someone called her name. She blinked drowsily, then turned toward Stefan.

"Did you say something?" she asked, but he was asleep.

On her other side, Megan lay curled under the blankets, also asleep. Taking care not to wake her, Brierley sat up and looked around, but saw no one, then carefully eased from under the blankets and stood up. The morning was chill with the cold breeze that flowed up from the beach below. Half-concealed by drifting curtains of mist, the dawnlight of the Daystar hovered far over the bay, and the sea sounds rose up to surround her. Waves crashed against rocks and ran quickly up the sands in ceaseless motion, filling the air with sound.

Brierley— Her senses tingled, as if the very dawn held its breath.

She looked upward toward the road, casting her witch-sense, but there were no travelers passing on the road, no one descending this side-road to the beach. They were alone. She walked to the edge of the bluff and looked down at the beach below, but saw nothing but the spread of dark sands and the curl of the waves, with a bobbing long shadow of seaweed just beyond the breakers. She hesitated, then began walking down the rough path toward the sea.

As she stepped onto the sand of the beach, the air suddenly hushed with a sense of great expectation, a leaping of the heart, a catch of the breath. She froze, motionless for a moment, then raised her hands in sudden longing. She suddenly remembered a day on another beach when a Voice had called to her, called her to living and led her to the Everlight's cave. The world had hushed like this, exactly like this, muting even the ceaseless sound of the waves. From that single day everything else in her life had begun: her healing, her understanding of herself, her longing for a witch-daughter, the hope against hope that had guided her life. Her books had described only a life of hiding and desperate peril, of darkness ending in the pyre, but that Voice had promised other-wise, a hope beyond reason, a purpose when her mother had denied all purpose—

"Where are you?" Brierley cried aloud to the wind and sea.

Then she heard the Voice again, and her breath stopped.

Brierley—

She looked up and down the beach, out at the surging sea, but saw no one. Where? Should she look behind that rock, or fall to her knees to plunge her hands into the sand? Should she dash into the waves, to hunt—"Where are you?" she whispered.

Beyond the breakers of the waves, a great dark shape moved through the water, long blue shadow beneath the weight of water. The Beast? she wondered, suddenly afraid. Here? But this is not its beach! she protested. I've never seen this beach before! And the Voice cannot be the Beast! The thought twisted in its anguish. It cannot—

A blue shimmering shape emerged from the water, rising through a cascade of sparkling foam. The dragon turned her mas-sive head toward Brierley, her gaze mild and gentle, then drifted toward her on the waves. It was not the Beast, terrible and loathsome, but the sea dragon from the panels in the library, blue-scaled, silver-finned, graceful and limber, not blank and absent like the image in the panel's stones, but magnificently alive. Brierley groaned and sank to her knees.

"Basoul," she whispered.

The dragon smiled at her, not with a curving of her mouth, although Brierley might imagine she saw that curve: instead, the smile resonated through her mind and being, as if she had stepped into the home of her cave, as if she walked Yarvannet's roads again, tending the people. Basoul sported idly on the waves, then let the surf bring her gently to shore. *My child,* crooned a deep resonant voice into her mind.

Brierley felt the love penetrating the voice, the same Voice that had called her as a girl, and she bowed her head with a sigh. In that Voice was a communion deeper than she had ever known, as if she met herself in this magnificent vision and felt suddenly larger than she was, finer, purer, perfect. She could hardly draw breath as Basoul's love washed over and into her, cooling her spirit as the sea waves might cool her body, bringing peace. She looked up again through a blur of tears.

All that Brierley aspired to be, all that she had hoped for in life, all the good she revered since her earliest memories seemed caught between them, as if an unbreakable bond, too long silent and hidden, had now became visible. "You are the Voice," she whispered. "You called me to the cave."

Yes, it was my voice, the dragon replied. Basoul lowered her huge head to rest comfortably on the beach, her jeweled eyes gleaming, and her strong claws dug deep into the sand, resisting the pull of the retreating waves. *As Jain shares spirit with Megan, so I share my spirit with you, my beloved Brierley. You would not have understood my shape in those younger days. You would have doubted your sanity, as your mother did, and perhaps despaired. And so I came to you first as a Voice, and later in the love of the Everlight, and still later as part of Thora in your dreams. But I have always been with you, Brierley. You are dayi, a healer of the shari'a, and you are mine.*

Am I dreaming? Brierley wondered, and raised a shaky hand

to her forehead, as if that might clear the vision from her eyes. She tried to rise to her feet and half-fell to the side, then tried again and found her feet. She staggered toward Basoul, and reached out her hands—

The scales were warm, patterned texture beneath her fingers that looped and whorled over strong muscles and bone. She felt the slipping moisture of seawater glistening on the hide, the subtle texture of bony scale beneath—yet warm, alive and as real as the sand on which she stood, as the waves which tugged at her shoes. She slowly traced the pattern with her hands, fascinated, and thrilled to their touch, healing and healed, bonded as if they were one by the contact. Brierley slowly moved her hands over Basoul's shoulder, marveling, then looked up into the dragon's brilliant eyes, and found new wonder.

"But how can you be—?" she asked. "You can't exist. Dragons aren't real."

I am real, Basoul assured her. She rearranged herself comfortably on the sand, then moved a foreleg to encircle Brierley, carefully lest she alarm, firmly as she now willed. Brierley sensed Basoul's own overarching joy at this meeting, as if it were long awaited, a yearning denied only with firm self-discipline, and again Brierley recognized much of herself.

Brierley abruptly sighed, overwhelmed, and her legs faltered. She might have fallen, but Basoul gently eased her to sit on her massive clawed foot, then smiled again—

"Oh, please don't smile," Brierley protested, and held her head. "You daze me." She laughed softly. "I don't believe this."

Well, you knew there are four of us. Why is this surprising?

"I didn't know you were the Voice."

You should have, Basoul objected mildly.

Brierley shook her head. "You know very well my books don't talk about you. The Yarvannet witches forgot the Four even existed, and certainly never wrote about meeting you. You're just a fancy tale, Basoul."

If you wish. Basoul sniffed with amusement, then laid her chin on the sand and regarded Brierley with one huge aquamarine eye.

"Do you answer questions?" Brierley asked eagerly, and felt she was a young girl again, when all the world was filled with questions bursting with their answers. "Do you?" She held her breath.

I do, Basoul allowed. *But some answers you should discover yourself, daughter, lest you bind yourself into old error. Each turning of the seasons builds its own pattern of wind and wave, and the past should not rule the present.* She paused. *What do you want to know?*

What, indeed? Brierley took a deep breath—perhaps that would help—only to have her thoughts scattered again by the dragon's smile. She tried to focus, and then remembered the first question, the first of many.

"Were the shari'a evil, Basoul?" Brierley asked softly. "Like the tales say?"

Evil? Basoul sighed. *No, my child, only unwise. Long ago the shari'a placed themselves under the governance of the air witches, whose gift is knowledge of the mind, not of the heart. That was not evil, daughter, only unwise, and not unwise until much later. The air witches defined the gift into four distinct forms, and then refused any change in their ideas. The error began there.* Basoul stirred restlessly. *Life cannot be confined with intellectual theory, my daughter, and Witchmere's fierce insistence on its ideas grew into quarrel and divided the adepts. The anshani'a withdrew into the villages, taking their wisdom with them. Later the forest witches withdrew into the hills, preferring their animal friends over the folk they should have tended. Only the dayi, the sea witches, sought to keep the bonds, and their efforts were misunderstood, and by some highly resented.*

It could not last, and Witchmere's arrogance only helped to compel change. At the time the Allemanii came to our shores, a new awakening had finally begun among the shari'a, with questioning among the younger generation of the answers supposedly settled centuries before. Thought moved in new directions, to new purposes and patterns. Thora Jodann had a part in that, as did others. The air witches disliked these new schools, for the new gifts we promised did not fit their choosing, but in time there might have been a new flowering, with great insight and new discoveries, and ultimately profound change.

Brierley laid her cheek against the dragon's warm hide, and heard a great heart beating its slow rhythm, timed to the cycling waves, the silent spreading ripples on a pond, the slow drip of water within deep caverns. "But it didn't happen."

No, Basoul said sadly. *In that change, we Four might have become Six, perhaps even Seven. The shari'a had undergone such change before, when Two became Four, making us what they were, and now great change impended again. But the air witches of Witchmere opposed that change, and then involved themselves in conflict with the Allemanii duke. By misusing their gift against Rahorsum and his son, in their blindness, in their arrogance, they brought down the Disasters on the shari'a, ending both themselves and, for a time, even the Four.*

Brierley felt the aching regret in the dragon's thoughts, a regret accepted but still wished otherwise. *We dragons are limited, dear heart. We can guide, but not compel; we can warn, but cannot open fixed minds. All was cut short. We Four offered our counsel, appearing to the adepts who would see us, but too few chose to see us in those hard days, and all was unmended by pride. Now, through you, Brierley, comes a chance for renewal, a new beginning for what has nearly disappeared from the world. It is a slender chance, and much might go wrong, but the hope still begins.*

"But how can I know what to choose, Basoul?" Brierley asked huskily. She shook her head. "How am I to know? The books don't always know, even when I can read them."

To question, my child, is part of the joy of living, Basoul said comfortably.

Brierley made a face. "Oh, really? You sound like Jain."

Yes, really. And of course I do. To become confused is the entry to understanding, its beginning and often its ending as new thought emerges to challenge the pattern. As the waves cycle, as the suns approach and fall away from Pass, as new life appears at the end of winter, the pattern is a circle without end. Life exists within that pattern, and prospers when it takes its essence.

"Now you sound like Thora," Brierley complained. She smiled up into the great faceted eye.

Of course. Basoul rumbled with soft laughter. *The Everlight's* purpose, my beloved daughter, is the same as mine: to confuse, to prompt, and thereby to teach. I did not bind Thora to her choices when I vexed her in this same way, to her same complaints. Although Thora's choices brought her pain and eventual disgrace, she never minded the cost of the doorways she entered, the future she envisioned. And in her trust in that future, in her hope of a matter unproven, she has left you a legacy to refound the craft.

Basoul raised her head and nodded past Brierley to the inland mountains. Brierley's senses prickled, and she found herself holding her breath, then turned to look also. *Go upward in Mionn, Basoul* told her solemnly, *to the Flinders Lakes. There look for a girl named Ashdla Toldane: she is daughter to Megan's "girl in green," and she will show you what Thora left here in Mionn as her last great work.*

"There *are* other shari'a?" Brierley whispered, and tears filled her eyes.

Yes, more than you know. Now is is the time of the Finding, a promise long awaited, a hope too long concealed. Through the Star Well, you can summon the Exiles who fled into the eastern lands beyond the bay. Among them the Change has already flowered, but Thora's promise has slipped into legend, and thus into forgetfulness, and they do not know their danger. For three centuries we Four have sought you, my daughter, you and the Allemanii High Lord who can pattern a new beginning for the shari'a and Allemanii, and in that alliance build the defense against the storm that is coming. It is not too late, not yet.

"Storm?" Brierley asked, caught up into Basoul's dread—and the dragon's fear that it might indeed be too late, that the Four had failed despite all hopes. "What storm?"

Basoul shook her head regretfully. *I cannot tell you—but not because I choose to vex you. I have good reason, beloved; we Four as you know us are still caught in Witchmere's pattern, and I doubt my own wisdom. We have not changed here, as we have changed in the East. Before you choose, you must have answers I cannot give you.*

"Hmm." Brierley leaned against Basoul's warm hide, then slowly caressed her, reaching wide over the broad shoulder. "Can I ask another question?"

If you wish, the dragon said indulgently.

"Megan's fire ghost. How do I heal her? Jain will not help."

The books have given you the beginning, Basoul said. *Leaving Witch-mere greatly reduced the power upon which the ghost draws—not entirely, but enough to win time. I will guide you when Megan's need is acute. And don't blame Jain in this, Brierley. Both Megan and the fire ghost are his, as you and your unborn daughter are mine, and he cannot choose between them.* She snorted irritably. *Or should not: he prompted Taxl to attack the cabin, and sneered at us when we reproved him.* Basoul snorted again. *Fire is always unpredictable, but there are rules.*

"Are there?" Brierley asked with amused sympathy. She had endured her own trials with Jain's annoying attitudes. "Even for you?"

Especially for us. Basoul rearranged her front legs, and laid her chin upon them, one great eye gleaming at her. *And I have another caution, my daughter, one that your mother should have told you but would not. In early pregnancy, while the child still dreams more of the stars than of this world, you can heal without serious risk to yourself or the child, but as the pregnancy advances, she will become more aware of what you do and try to help. Again, that is not necessarily mortal, but definitely not wise.*

"Why?"

Her gift develops first within your own mind, Basoul said, *just as her body develops within you. If it is stressed by the Beast, it may be distorted. I speak now only to warn you against your further temptations.* She gave Brierley a stern look.

"Yes, Basoul," Brierley said obediently, then smiled. "The sea lark in my dream about Rowena? Was that my baby?"

It is likely, Basoul allowed, although her tone was doubtful. *Not even the Four understand the starry void your daughter still sails in part.* Basoul paused. *Will you do me a favor?* she asked, oddly hesitant.

"A favor? For you?"

Basoul twitched her ears reprovingly. *My daughter, I am not a deity, and even I have wishes others control. But this is my wish: do not name her Jocater, as you thought to do. You were not responsible for your mother's denials. You need not spend your life mending her choices, and certainly should not burden your daughter with that same effort. This* child is also Melfallan's, after all, and will be a lady of Yarvannet, nobly born, and much loved by him.

"And what about Melfallan?" Brierley asked in anguish. "Can I have a third question, Basoul? I was thinking of hiding away from him, for his safety. I bring him great danger. Would it not be wiser—"

Do not, Basoul said firmly.

"But what right have I to put myself first?" Brierley protested. "To choose what I want, and not care for the consequences to others? Isn't that what Witchmere did? Isn't that the same form of arrogance, as if what I want is all that matters?" She spread her hands entreatingly. "Thora has bid me to refound the craft, and so do you, but I don't know what you mean. I can see only Megan, and now my baby, and how I might throw away their chance for a normal life, a happy life, by choosing my own selfish hopes. Isn't that what Mother did to me, Basoul? Choosing her denials instead of me? She abandoned Jonalyn, abandoned Lana, then abandoned me, choosing what *she* wanted. I can accept that I can never have Melfallan: he is not for me. Oh, but how can I accept that?" she asked herself in anguish.

Dear one, Basoul began, and then paused. *As Stefan has asked you, where is it written that you are not entitled to joy? Where is it said that such a bond with a man must be denied? The error in Witchmere lay in denying such bonds, of refusing to trust in a different future, and instead clinging to what is and refusing all that might be. The future is not set. Life will have its perils, but the bonding of the heart, when it is given, is precious. The sea witches understand this profoundly, and you yourself are an example, in the choice you made to heal despite its perils. You could have refused me as your mother did and lived her careful and narrow life, tormented by your own denials but safe. Why didn't you?*

"Because you called me that day on the beach," Brierley said. "You know it's so."

Indeed? As if you had no power to say no, as if life tumbles you like a shell onto the beach, or seaweed upon the wave? I have been denied many times, dearest one. I also could live my careful and narrow life by turning my face away from the shari'a, if I could even have life without them. *It is a choice I will never make. I choose the future of my hopes, as you have, and in that you are my true daughter.*

"But I put him in danger!"

He was already in danger, and for reasons other than you. A man must have purpose to live the fullest of life, and the just must see truth to give justice. Consider this: had he not found you, would Melfallan ever have understood his own role as lord, or found strength and his skills to defeat Tejar? He, too, chooses a future now, and who can say if that future is lesser than what might otherwise have been? Who can say that any of his other futures ended in victory? As you have found life in healing, cannot Melfallan find life in defending the good? Basoul stirred restlessly, and Brierley sensed her impatience with her. For a moment, they glared mildly at each other. *You are not a blight, my child. You are not your mother, destined for self-torment and poor choices because she denied her own hopes.* Basoul twitched her ears, and her tone changed to teasing. *If for no other reason, you could take my word for it. I am Basoul, the sea dragon, and I know things, just like Jain does.* She sniffed, then lifted her head slightly and glared past Brierley at the empty air. *Usually more.*

"But if you do the choosing for me," Brierley argued, "how can I be certain? I mean, um—" Brierley stopped short. "I realize you're a dragon, but—" She stopped again, and felt her cheeks heat with embarrassment. She looked around at the sea and the beach, the waves lapping at her shoes, and suddenly worried this might be a start to insanity, talking to a—

Basoul chuckled. *A man who hesitates to enter the surf, it is true, is often tumbled feet over bottom because he doubts. But you are right to doubt some things. I cannot give you guarantees, dear one. If I could, the Disasters would never have happened. I, too, have my limits. But don't assume that your mother's failure to make a life with Alarson dooms you with Melfallan. Many hidden witches have found love with the man of their choice, as did even Thora for a time. Love itself is not evil, and love forged in adversity becomes a stronger love, lighting the world. In her troubled times, Thora and her Peladius could not survive for long, but they still chose one another, finding in one fragile summer enough reason for the choice. Besides, why do you expect Melfallan will give you up?*

"I can make him give me up."

Really? Basoul snorted skeptically. *You don't know him as well as you think. He will follow his heart now.*

"I can disappear," Brierley said stubbornly.

Once visible, witches find it very hard to "disappear." I don't recommend you try.

"You are certain?" Brierley asked plaintively, looking up at the great faceted eye above her.

I am your mother, teacher, and friend, a guide for your heart and judgment. I am part of you, and you are part of me, and in that binding we are more than we were. Is hiding the only wise response to fear? Is denial? You know better. Look within yourself. Deep tenderness suffused Basoul's mental voice, and for a moment Brierley was again dazzled by the dragon's smile.

"Hmm." Brierley laughed and spread her arms, then leapt to her feet. "I asked you for answers," she teased, "and now you offer only more questions."

As I said, Thora complained, too. Basoul lifted her head and looked up at the bluff above the beach. *Megan is waking.*

The Daystar's dawn light struck suddenly through the morning mist. Brierley threw up a hand to shield her eyes; when she lowered it, Basoul was gone.

"Wait!" Brierley shouted and stumbled forward a step, for all it was useless. "But I had other questions—" she complained, then suddenly laughed at herself.

Brierley spread her arms and turned round and round, then stamped over the sand, exulting in her own movement. The sea wind blew strongly against her body, whipping her skirts and hair. She splashed into the surf, then ran from the waves that chased her, then danced again in triumph. The Voice had come to her again, and it was Basoul.

Out of breath, she faced the bay and again spread her arms wide. "I love you!" she called to the sea and sky, to the ascending Daystar and its Companion, to all that lived, all that loved.

I am with you, the Voice answered, shuddering from deep within the waters.

For a moment, Brierley thought she saw a blue-scaled body emerge from the waves beyond the breakers, heading out into the bay, then saw the flash of a silver-tipped tail. Then, still farther out on the bay, a gomphrey sported on the waves, and dived deep, booming its voice against the sandy bottom. She craned forward eagerly, hoping for another glimpse, but saw only the moving waves abroad on the bay.

She turned and looked up at the inland mountains. They rose in gentle ascending cascade, rounded shape upon shape, furred with dark everpine and blue shadow. In Mionn, at the Flinders Lakes, Basoul had said, she would find a girl in green. And answers—for the Finding and the refounding of the craft, against a storm that would come.

With a shout, Brierley ran toward the road ascending to the bluff, to where Megan and Stefan awaited her.